W9-BUN-551

Under the Moons of Mars

Edgar Rice Burroughs

INTRODUCTION TO THE BISON BOOKS EDITION BY

James P. Hogan

ILLUSTRATIONS BY SCOTT BEACHLER

University of Nebraska Press
Lincoln and London

Introduction © 2003 by James P. Hogan
Illustrations © 2003 by Scott Beachler
Manufactured in the United States of America

∞

First Nebraska paperback printing: 2003

Cataloging-in-Publication data available
Library of Congress Control Number: 2002043575
ISBN 0-8032-6208-6 (pbk.: alk. paper)

Contents

JAMES P. HOGAN

Introduction

Since I was not raised in the United States, I'm in what I would imagine is a comparatively unusual situation among readers in this country: in the early years of my life I never encountered Edgar Rice Burroughs as virtually a national institution. My sole exposure had been a few vaguely remembered Tarzan movies at the Saturday morning "flea pit" in London's Portobello Road, where I come from—and how many kids knew or cared who had written the original books?—or occasional depictions in comic books swapped over doorsteps on long winter's evenings when new reading material was always in demand. Genuine American comic books were especially prized. Thicker and all-color, culturally exotic, and filled with ads for BB guns, binoculars, walkie-talkies, practical joke kits, and other wonders from that awe-inspiring place of huge cars and skyscrapers across the ocean, American comics traded for two or even three British comics apiece. That was before television arrived in the UK to any marked degree, which it did in 1953, the year of Elizabeth II's coronation. Not having grown up with it, and seeing what had once been lively homes being turned into mausoleums of comatose adults, we hated the thing. But at least it got us out of the house, I suppose. I still don't own a TV. But the upshot was that I had never heard of John Carter, Gentleman from Virginia (also Prince of Helium), the red men's twin city on Mars, Carter's devoted Shetland-pony-size Martian hound, Woola, or Carter's ferocious-enemy-turned-staunch-ally, Tars Tarkas, Jeddak of Thark. So I'm writing an introduction in every sense of the word.

Arthur C. Clarke said, in *Greetings, Carbon-Based Bipeds* (1999): "I want to go along with Ray Bradbury's views on the importance of Edgar Rice Burroughs. It was Burroughs who turned me on, and I think he is a much underrated writer. The man who can create Tarzan, the best-known character in the whole fiction, should not be taken too lightly!" A powerful statement, indeed. The writer who created the character that Clarke offers as the best known in the whole of fiction and who produced sixty-eight titles that inspired the making of fifty-seven movies by my count—the Tarzan books alone have been translated into fifty languages and sold more than twenty million copies—was satisfying a need that went a lot deeper than being just "entertainment," or something to while away the hours of a wintry evening. In the worlds that Burroughs created we are able to glimpse and feel, if only for a moment, those sides of ourselves that we secretly know exist but that will never find expression in the safe and secure conformist reality of routines that we find ourselves existing in (some would say trapped in).

Historians tell us that the First World War of 1914–18 was started by an underused aristocracy that had been raised in a military and diplomatic tradition. These were people bored and stifled by forty-three years of peace and prosperity after the conclusion of the Franco-Prussian War, in the days when warfare with its meticulously applied code of chivalry and honor was looked on as a glamorous expression of the noble and manly virtues. Unfulfilled European aristocrats weren't the only ones who sought outlet at some psychic level of need that exists below the mere gratification of material wants and bodily comfort. Across the Westernized world untold millions, from the socially strait-jacketed leisured class to the workaday drones in servants' quarters, offices, and factories, yearned to escape from the blandness and complacent predictability that came with the age of elegance and belief in unquestioned Darwinian supremacy, a world that went down with the *Titanic*. Burroughs provided that escape. And in providing that escape and enjoyment eagerly grasped, it is difficult not to conclude that he was carrying them with him in forging his own means of escape from frustration, and perhaps, at the beginning, not a little bitterness. Until he turned to writing his first short stories for the pulp fiction magazines at the age of thirty-five, Burroughs had been a failure in just about everything he had attempted.

Edgar Rice Burroughs was born in Chicago, Illinois, in 1875. However, presumably to glamorize and enhance his image, he claimed at one point to have been born in Peking (now Beijing), where his father, he said, was military adviser to the Chinese empress. It seems that the inspirations for John Carter and Dejah Thoris, the Martian princess, were never far from his mind. His father, George Tyler Burroughs, was in fact a Civil War veteran and, by the time of his son's birth, a fairly well-to-do businessman. After attending several private schools Edgar, too, set out upon a military career, which is reflected in his early tales. From 1892 to 1895 he was a cadet at the Michigan Military Academy in Orchard Lake, where he became instructor and assistant commandant (1895–96). He then served in the army in the Seventh Cavalry in Arizona Territory (1896–97), and later with the Illinois Reserve Militia (1918–19). His storytelling inclination and a hint of his future direction may have been awakened while he lived in the American Southwest, for in this period Burroughs met and listened to tales of men who had fought in the Sioux and Apache wars. After leaving the military he dabbled in business, owning a stationery store in Pocatello, Idaho (1898), and being associated with the American Battery Company in Chicago (1899–1903), before marrying Emma Centennia Hulbert in 1900. Their marriage, which produced two sons and one daughter, lasted until their divorce in 1934. Things did not go well, and for the first ten years following Burroughs's marriage the family lived in near-poverty. Burroughs's attempts at finding a successful career during this period, or simply bringing in enough money to meet the bills, included an association with the Sweetser-Burroughs Mining Company in Idaho (1903–4), working as a railroad policeman in Salt Lake City, Utah (1904), managing a stenographic department at Sears, Roebuck, and Co. in Chicago (1906–8), partnering in an advertising agency (1908–9), once again managing an office (1909), and then partnering in the running of a sales firm (1910–11). From 1910 to 1911 he was engaged with the Champlain Yardley Company, and from 1912 to 1913 he was manager for the System Service Bureau.

By the age of thirty-five Burroughs had achieved nothing that was satisfying or even halfway rewarding to him. The pulp fiction magazines had drawn his attention, however, and, perhaps out of chagrin at the thought of others gaining success and recognition for producing what he had no hesitation in dismissing as rubbish, he resolved that he could do better. (It is interesting to note how many writers I know today whose initial motivation came from similar sentiments harbored at some time. Of course, such feelings aren't confined to writers alone. What sets all writers apart is the difference between those who do something about it and those who don't.) For Burroughs his resolve was the turning point.

Burroughs's first professional sale, a short story titled "Under the Moons of Mars," was serialized in 1912 in *All-Story Magazine* and later renamed as the first of the books that make up the present volume. Here we meet the invincible John Carter, Civil War veteran, mining prospector, and Apache fighter in Arizona, who finds himself mysteriously transported to Mars after undergoing a strange mystical experience in which his earthly body remains behind, apparently dead. It was science fiction a hundred years ago, free of today's customary impedimenta.

The essence of science fiction is being able to liberate the imagination to run free in "what if" worlds, unrestricted by the realities of such things as technology, history, geography, ethics, or political systems as we know them. (Science fiction does try to avoid violating the laws of physics as we believe them to be; when you throw away that restriction you're into the fantasy genre.) On a planet that today is mapped from pole to pole, is surveyed by satellites, and is traversed in a day by commercial airliners, the only directions left in which such worlds can exist are those of space and time. Hence, to get to them one ordinarily needs a space machine or a time machine; today's science fiction authors can spend half a book ponderously maneuvering the pieces of the stage into place. Not so with Burroughs. Within a few pages of the hero's introduction he is loose in a world of gigantic savages and monsters, hose-mouthed plant-men, underground labyrinths, subterranean oceans, five-thousand-foot cliffs of gold, four-mile-square fortresses, mysterious rivers from which no one returns, and a torrent of other ideas and visions that continue through every volume—exactly what readers back then wanted and what editors paid for. Witness the opening of *A Princess of Mars* (immediately following a foreword in which John Carter's nephew, Jack, relates how he came across his uncle's strange manuscript): "I am a very old man; how old I do not know. Possibly I am a hundred, possibly more; but I cannot tell because I have never aged as other men, nor do I remember any childhood." Three lines into the book and it has grabbed us! We want to know more. We're immersed in a story already.

The Gods of Mars, another of Burroughs's early works, was also first serialized in *All-Story Magazine* in 1912, and *The Warlord of Mars* followed in the magazine's issues from December 1913 to March 1914. The first book collection of Carter's adventures was published as *A Princess of Mars* in 1917. The "Martian" series, sometimes called the "Barsoom books" (after the native name for the planet) eventually numbered eleven books.

In 1912, just a few months after the first "Martian" sale, Burroughs produced *Tarzan of the Apes*, his real breakthrough and the creation for which he is universally recognized and acclaimed. John Clayton, Lord Greystoke, along with his aristocratic parents, John Clayton and Lady Alice, are abandoned on the west coast of Africa by mutinous sailors. Lady Alice dies insane, while the father of the boy (who becomes Tarzan) is killed by a great ape named Kerchak. Tarzan is raised by the ape Kala, and by virtue of his intelligence and fighting skills becomes leader of the tribe, learning to read from books found in the remnants of his parents' hut. Tarzan eventually finds his aristocratic roots, wins his wife, Jane Porter, from another party of marooned whites, and with the help of animals—mostly elephants and apes—gains status as the king of the jungle.

Here we see again the suppressed wild man, warrior, and alpha male that every harassed store clerk, browbeaten breadwinner doomed to a life of cost accounting, or spurned nerdy college date *knew* lurked somewhere within, imprisoned by the cages of a society whose greatest boast was its ability to tame the forces of nature. Tarzan is John Carter remade in a world for those unable to make the mental leap to Burroughs's boundless Martian horizons of imagination. The repressed souls responded, and no fewer than twenty-four further Tarzan adventures followed. Burroughs himself later said, "If I had striven for long years of privation and effort to fit myself to become a writer, I might be warranted in patting myself on the back, but God knows I did not work and still do not understand how I happened to succeed."

In a more modern context, suppression of the inner man results not just from the domesticating efforts of society but from the attempt to deny the realities of gender itself. The characters created by Burroughs provide a fitting escape, if only temporary and in fiction. John F. Kasson, in *The White Male Body and the Challenge of Modernity in America* (2001), stresses "the urge to recover a primitive freedom and wildness," and sees Tarzan as the ultimate self-made, self-taught man who challenges the restrictions of modern civilization and shows his own answer to the "new 'crisis' of masculinity." It brings a certain satisfied delight to ears tired by the fawnings of today's politically correct wimps to hear John Carter's self-observation, from *The Gods of Mars*: "The confession of love which the girl's fright had wrung from her touched me deeply; but it humiliated me as well, since I felt that in some thoughtless word or act I had given her reason to believe that I reciprocated her affection. . . . Never have I been much of a ladies' man, being more concerned with fighting and the kindred arts, which have ever seemed to me more befitting a man than mooning over a scented glove four sizes too small for him, or kissing a dead flower that has begun to smell like cabbage."

Other popular series produced by Burroughs were the *Pellucidar* tales, concerning adventures inside the Earth, the *Carson of Venus* books, and *The Land that Time Forgot* trilogy. The *Pellucidar* series began in 1922 with *At the Earth's Core*, a work reminiscent of Jules Verne's 1864 classic *A Journey to the Center of the Earth* in which scientists drill a shaft down into a hollow space that exists at the center of the planet. They find it lit by a miniature sun and populated by various strange life forms, some of which have survived for millions of years. (Tarzan also visited this subterranean world in *Tarzan at the Earth's Core* [1930].) *The Land that Time Forgot* trilogy, which followed in 1924, consists of three novelettes—"The Land that Time Forgot," "The People that Time Forgot," and "Out of Time's Abyss"—set on a mysterious island near the South Pole where dinosaurs and other primitive species have survived. The *Carson of Venus* books came later, blending romance and comedy to describe the exploits of spaceman Carson Napier. *Pirates of Venus* appeared in 1934, and the last in the series, *Escape on Venus*, in 1946. The story "Wizard of Venus" was published posthumously in 1964, and also as the title story of a collection released in 1970.

In addition to these four major series Burroughs also wrote several other adventure novels between 1912 and 1933. Among them were *The Cave Girl* (1925), in which an initially weak aristocrat develops into a warrior; two Western novels about a white Apache, *The War Chief* (1927) and *Apache Devil* (1933), both of which are sympathetic toward the American Indian; and another published posthumously, *Beyond the Farthest Star* (1964), a science fiction novel focusing on the brutality of war.

The first of the Tarzan movies was produced in 1918, but their mass popularity really began when Olympic swimming champion Johnny Weissmuller took the role in the 1930s. Burroughs-Tarzan Enterprises and Burroughs-Tarzan Pictures were founded in 1934. *At the Earth's Core* was made into a movie in 1976, directed by Kevin Connor and starring Doug McClure, Peter Cushing, and Caroline Munro, with the screenplay written by Milton Subotsky. "The Land that Time Forgot" was also a 1976 film production, again directed by Kevin Connor and starring Doug McClure, John McEnery, Susan Penhaligon, and Keith Barron, with the screenplay by James Cawthorne and Michael Moorcock; that film's sequel, "The People that Time Forgot," followed in 1977.

In 1913 Burroughs founded his own publishing house, Edgar Rice Burroughs Inc., and in 1919 purchased a large ranch in the San Fernando Valley of California, which he later developed into the suburb of Tarzana. He cultivated an expensive lifestyle and proved less astute at managing financial investments than at gauging the public's taste for adventure, which necessitated producing an average of three novels a year. Burroughs was elected mayor of California Beach in 1933. In 1935 he married his second wife, Florence Dearholt, but they too divorced, in 1942. Even while in his sixties Burroughs was a war correspondent in the South Pacific during World War II. Edgar Rice Burroughs died of a heart ailment on 19 March 1950, while reading a comic book in bed.

People sometimes remark to me that they wonder why the movie "Stagecoach" is constantly being praised as such as classic. "It's got every cliché out of every Western ever made," they tell me. Well, probably not *every* cliché, but that's not really the issue. The point they miss is that when this movie was made, these trappings weren't clichés yet. They only became so by being copied so often. But "Stagecoach" had them *first*. A similar comment could be made about the work of Edgar Rice Burroughs. After four generations' worth of pulp science fiction, space opera, the "Golden Years" of the fifties and sixties, and the media explosion in recent times, it is difficult to come up with anything today that can be considered genuinely innovative as a concept or original in imagination. To us, death rays, hyperdrives, time machines, uploaded consciousness, and the rest of the accepted fare are as hackneyed as magic swords and secret potions, and if you're going to use them there had better be at least a hint of a redeeming, fresh angle. But with Burroughs we're talking about a production line of ideas that began in 1912, when the airplane and radio had scarcely been invented, when radioactivity was the newest plaything of physics, and when the notion of interplanetary travel was still being scoffed at by experts forty years hence. Yet in Burroughs's works we see clashes of alien armies amid strange, other-worldly landscapes, air battles between flying machines that roam from pole to pole, telepathically controlled beasts, and young knights defying the might of sinister warlords to rescue imprisoned princesses— all of it appearing well over half a century before "Star Wars" came on the scene. Scattered among the props we find glimpses that anticipate such developments as ID scanning machines, television, fax transmissions, tabletop ordering in restaurants, hydroponic farms, and uranium bullets. Biological growth, athletic performance, and physical dynamics are about what you'd expect in reduced Martian gravity. There's even the notion that Mars, a dying planet, has been kept habitable artificially by a kind of terraforming.

What is it that I can almost hear someone say? That those are just incidental details? The fact remains that there *aren't* any deserted cities on Mars, no huge shafts to the interior, and no warrior races with gigantic beasts roaming the surface in tens of thousands. One is tempted to shrug and say, "So, what of it? You can't have *everything* right." And what kind of fun would there be without them?

But it's more than just some escapist fun laced with a dash of willing suspension of disbelief that perhaps sets Burroughs's stories apart and could maybe help explain their extraordinary lasting popularity, while their one-time rivals have long since waned and been forgotten. To use a simple word that many might sneer at these days as old-fashioned and no longer relevant, it's "principle." Through all the battles and betrayals, conquests and rivalries, alliances and revolutions, the message is always clear as to what the characters are fighting for and against, and why. There's no nonsense about morality being relative, or agonized hand-wringing over whether one person's idea of what is right or wrong is as good as any other's. Religions, ideologies, deciding which faction has the power, or playing the odds to optimize the personal payoff in some kind of obscure game—none of these matter. Whatever the imagined short-term benefits or pretexts to the contrary, cruelty, greed, treachery, dishonesty, and cowardice are "bad"; kindness, generosity, loyalty, integrity, and courage are "good," and that's the end of it. Those are the things you fight to uphold, whatever the odds and regardless of the consequences. True friends fight alongside you for the same reasons, irrespective of status, race, prospects of gain, or even world of origin.

How welcome and refreshing it might be if society were able to provide such clear and unambiguous models for the younger people of today, many of whom are struggling to make sense of a world in which lying is the typical order of business of highly rewarded professions and publicly acknowledged thieves are honored while taxpayers lose their homes; where good and bad have become indistinguishable in the nightly media deluge, all being equally callous, slovenly, rude, barely articulate (except for a proclivity for the same foul language), and bereft of all principle save that of expediency. The only discernible difference qualifying for admiration or envy is having the luck not to be hit by a bullet, run off the road, or get caught. How does one work at improving oneself or expect any reward commensurate with one's effort in the face of rules that work like that? Small wonder that too often the result is disillusionment and despair, the abandoning of all attempt to find meaning or purpose, and the incalculable loss of wasted lives that could have been. Maybe they could use a few John Carters in their lives to see the alternatives possible.

For those who would like to delve further, the following is a list of selected biographies and references for further reading: *Golden Anniversary Bibliography of Edgar Rice Burroughs* by H. H. Heins (1964); *Edgar Rice Burroughs: Master of Adventure* by Richard A. Lupoff (1965); *Tarzan Alive* by Philip José Farmer (1972); *Burroughs's Science Fiction* by Robert R. Kudlay and Joan Leiby (1973); *Tarzan and Tradition* by Erling B. Holtsmark (1981); *Edgar Rice Burroughs* by Irwin Porges (1975); *Edgar Rice Burroughs* by Erling B. Holtsmark (1986); *Burroughs Dictionary* by George T. McWhorter (1987); *King of the Jungle* by David Fury (1994); *The Burroughs Cyclopaedia*, edited by Clark A. Brady (1996); *Edgar Rice Burroughs* by Robert B. Zeuschner (1996); and *Tarzan Forever: The Life of Edgar Rice Burroughs, the Creator of*

Tarzan by John Taliaferro (1999). The interested reader can also find many references on the Web as a reward for an hour or two of surfing.

The work of Edgar Rice Burroughs is also recognized in the Darrell Awards, sponsored each year by the Memphis Science Fiction Association (MSFA) to promote literacy in the Mid-South by recognizing the best published works of science fiction, fantasy, and horror. The awards are named in honor of Dr. Darrell C. Richardson, author, member of First Fandom, bibliophile, world traveler, founding member of the Burroughs Bibliophiles, pulp collector, founding member of MSFA, and, from my meeting him when I was guest of honor at Memphen (the Memphis Science Fiction Convention), an all-round very interesting person. Further information on the Darrell Awards or the Memphis Science Fiction Association can be obtained from Michael Kingsley, Darrell Awards Committee Chairman, 1742 Lawrence Avenue, #2, Memphis TN 38112. Email: *mailto:mike@memphen.org.*

Under The Moons Of Mars

A Princess of Mars

Foreword

To the Reader of this Work:

In submitting Captain Carter's strange manuscript to you in book form, I
believe that a few words relative to this remarkable personality will be of
interest.

My first recollection of Captain Carter is of the few months he spent
at my father's home in Virginia, just prior to the opening of the civil war.
I was then a child of but five years, yet I well remember the tall, dark,
smooth-faced, athletic man whom I called Uncle Jack.

He seemed always to be laughing; and he entered into the sports of the
children with the same hearty good fellowship he displayed toward those
pastimes in which the men and women of his own age indulged; or he
would sit for an hour at a time entertaining my old grandmother with
stories of his strange, wild life in all parts of the world. We all loved him,
and our slaves fairly worshipped the ground he trod.

He was a splendid specimen of manhood, standing a good two inches
over six feet, broad of shoulder and narrow of hip, with the carriage of the
trained fighting man. His features were regular and clear cut, his hair black
and closely cropped, while his eyes were of a steel gray, reflecting a strong and
loyal character, filled with fire and initiative. His manners were perfect, and
his courtliness was that of a typical southern gentleman of the highest type.

His horsemanship, especially after hounds, was a marvel and delight
even in that country of magnificent horsemen. I have often heard my
father caution him against his wild recklessness, but he would only laugh,
and say that the tumble that killed him would be from the back of a horse
yet unfoaled.

When the war broke out he left us, nor did I see him again for some
fifteen or sixteen years. When he returned it was without warning, and I

was much surprised to note that he had not aged apparently a moment, nor had he changed in any other outward way. He was, when others were with him, the same genial, happy fellow we had known of old, but when he thought himself alone I have seen him sit for hours gazing off into space, his face set in a look of wistful longing and hopeless misery; and at night he would sit thus looking up into the heavens, at what I did not know until I read his manuscript years afterwards.

He told us that he had been prospecting and mining in Arizona part of the time since the war; and that he had been very successful was evidenced by the unlimited amount of money with which he was supplied. As to the details of his life during these years he was very reticent, in fact he would not talk of them at all.

He remained with us for about a year and then went to New York, where he purchased a little place on the Hudson, where I visited him once a year on the occasions of my trips to the New York market—my father and I owning and operating a string of general stores throughout Virginia at that time. Captain Carter had a small but beautiful cottage, situated on a bluff overlooking the river, and during one of my last visits, in the winter of 1885, I observed that he was much occupied in writing, I presume now, upon this manuscript.

He told me at this time that if anything should happen to him he wished me to take charge of his estate, and he gave me a key to a compartment in the safe which stood in his study, telling me I would find his will there and some personal instructions which he had me pledge myself to carry out with absolute fidelity.

After I had retired for the night I have seen him from my window standing in the moonlight on the brink of the bluff overlooking the Hudson with his arms stretched out to the heavens as though in appeal. I thought at the time that he was praying, although I never had understood that he was in the strict sense of the term a religious man.

Several months after I had returned home from my last visit, the first of March, 1886, I think, I received a telegram from him asking me to come to him at once. I had always been his favorite among the younger generation of Carters and so I hastened to comply with his demand.

I arrived at the little station, about a mile from his grounds, on the morning of March 4, 1886, and when I asked the livery man to drive me out to Captain Carter's he replied that if I was a friend of the Captain's he had some very bad news for me: the Captain had been found dead shortly after daylight that very morning by the watchman attached to an adjoining property.

For some reason this news did not surprise me, but I hurried out to his place as quickly as possible, so that I could take charge of the body and of his affairs.

I found the watchman who had discovered him, together with the local police chief and several townspeople, assembled in his little study. The watchman related the few details connected with the finding of the body, which he said had been still warm when he came upon it. It lay, he said, stretched full length in the snow with the arms outstretched above the head toward the edge of the bluff, and when he showed me the spot it flashed upon me that it was the identical one where I had seen him on those other nights, with his arms raised in supplication to the skies.

There were no marks of violence on the body, and with the aid of a local physician the coroner's jury quickly reached a decision of death from heart failure. Left alone in the study, I opened the safe and withdrew the contents of the drawer in which he had told me I would find my instructions. They were in part peculiar indeed, but I have followed them to each last detail as faithfully as I was able.

He directed that I remove his body to Virginia without embalming, and that he be laid in an open coffin within a tomb which he previously had had constructed and which, as I later learned, was well ventilated. The instructions impressed upon me that I must personally see that this was carried out just as he directed, even in secrecy if necessary.

His property was left in such a way that I was to receive the entire income for twenty-five years, when the principal was to become mine. His further instructions related to this manuscript, which I was to retain sealed and unread, just as I found it for eleven years; nor was I to divulge its contents until twenty-one years after his death.

A strange feature about the tomb, where his body still lies, is that the massive door is equipped with a single, huge gold-plated spring lock which can be opened *only from the inside*.

Yours very sincerely,

EDGAR RICE BURROUGHS.

To
My Son Jack

ONE

On the Arizona Hills

I am a very old man; how old I do not know. Possibly I am a hundred, possibly more; but I cannot tell because I have never aged as other men, nor do I remember any childhood. So far as I can recollect I have always been a man, a man of about thirty. I appear today as I did forty years and more ago, and yet I feel that I cannot go on living forever; that some day I shall die the real death from which there is no resurrection. I do not know why I should fear death, I who have died twice and am still alive; but yet I have the same horror of it as you who have never died, and it is because of this terror of death, I believe, that I am so convinced of my mortality.

And because of this conviction I have determined to write down the story of the interesting periods of my life and of my death. I cannot explain the phenomena; I can only set down here in the words of an ordinary soldier of fortune a chronicle of the strange events that befell me during the ten years that my dead body lay undiscovered in an Arizona cave.

I have never told this story, nor shall mortal man see this manuscript until after I have passed over for eternity. I know that the average human mind will not believe what it cannot grasp, and so I do not purpose being pilloried by the public, the pulpit, and the press, and held up as a colossal liar when I am but telling the simple truths which some day science will substantiate. Possibly the suggestions which I gained upon Mars, and the knowledge which I can set down in this chronicle, will aid in an earlier understanding of the mysteries of our sister planet; mysteries to you, but no longer mysteries to me.

My name is John Carter; I am better known as Captain Jack Carter of Virginia. At the close of the Civil War I found myself possessed of several hundred thousand dollars (Confederate) and a captain's commission in the cavalry arm of an army which no longer existed; the servant of a state which had vanished with the hopes of the South. Masterless, penniless, and with my only means of livelihood, fighting, gone, I determined to work my way to the southwest and attempt to retrieve my fallen fortunes in a search for gold.

I spent nearly a year prospecting in company with another Confederate officer, Captain James K. Powell of Richmond. We were extremely fortunate, for late in the winter of 1865, after many hardships and privations, we located the most remarkable gold-bearing quartz vein that our wildest dreams had ever pictured. Powell, who was a mining engineer by education, stated that we had uncovered over a million dollars worth of ore in a trifle over three months.

As our equipment was crude in the extreme we decided that one of us must return to civilization, purchase the necessary machinery and return with a sufficient force of men properly to work the mine.

As Powell was familiar with the country, as well as with the mechanical requirements of mining we determined that it would be best for him to make the trip. It was agreed that I was to hold down our claim against the remote possibility of its being jumped by some wandering prospector.

On March 3, 1866, Powell and I packed his provisions on two of our burros, and bidding me good-bye he mounted his horse, and started down the mountainside toward the valley, across which led the first stage of his journey.

The morning of Powell's departure was, like nearly all Arizona mornings, clear and beautiful; I could see him and his little pack animals picking their way down the mountainside toward the valley, and all during the morning I would catch occasional glimpses of them as they topped a hog back or came out upon a level plateau. My last sight of Powell was about three in the afternoon as he entered the shadows of the range on the opposite side of the valley.

Some half hour later I happened to glance casually across the valley and was much surprised to note three little dots in about the same place I had last seen my friend and his two pack animals. I am not given to needless worrying, but the more I tried to convince myself that all was well with Powell, and that the dots I had seen on his trail were antelope or wild horses, the less I was able to assure myself.

Since we had entered the territory we had not seen a hostile Indian, and we had, therefore, become careless in the extreme, and were wont to ridicule the stories we had heard of the great numbers of these vicious marauders that were supposed to haunt the trails, taking their toll in lives and torture of every white party which fell into their merciless clutches.

Powell, I knew, was well armed and, further, an experienced Indian fighter; but I too had lived and fought for years among the Sioux in the North, and I knew that his chances were small against a party of cunning trailing Apaches. Finally I could endure the suspense no longer, and, arming myself with my two Colt revolvers and a carbine, I strapped two belts of cartridges about me and catching my saddle horse, started down the trail taken by Powell in the morning.

As soon as I reached comparatively level ground I urged my mount into a canter and continued this, where the going permitted, until, close upon dusk, I discovered the point where other tracks joined those of Powell. They were the tracks of unshod ponies, three of them, and the ponies had been galloping.

I followed rapidly until, darkness shutting down, I was forced to await the rising of the moon, and given an opportunity to speculate on the question of the wisdom of my chase. Possibly I had conjured up impossible dangers, like some nervous old housewife, and when I should catch up with Powell would get a good laugh for my pains. However, I am not prone to sensitiveness, and the following of a sense of duty, wherever it may lead, has always been a kind of fetich with me throughout my life; which may account for the honors bestowed upon me by three republics and the decorations and friendships of an old and powerful emperor and several lesser kings, in whose service my sword has been red many a time.

About nine o'clock the moon was sufficiently bright for me to proceed on my way and I had no difficulty in following the trail at a fast walk, and in some places at a brisk trot until, about midnight, I reached the water hole where Powell had expected to camp. I came upon the spot unexpectedly, finding it entirely deserted, with no signs of having been recently occupied as a camp.

I was interested to note that the tracks of the pursuing horsemen, for such I was now convinced they must be, continued after Powell with only a brief stop at the hole for water; and always at the same rate of speed as his.

I was positive now that the trailers were Apaches and that they wished to capture Powell alive for the fiendish pleasure of the torture, so I urged my horse onward at a most dangerous pace, hoping against hope that I would catch up with the red rascals before they attacked him.

Further speculation was suddenly cut short by the faint report of two shots far ahead of me. I knew that Powell would need me now if ever, and I instantly urged my horse to his topmost speed up the narrow and difficult mountain trail.

I had forged ahead for perhaps a mile or more without hearing further sounds, when the trail suddenly debouched onto a small, open plateau near the summit of the pass. I had passed through a narrow, overhanging gorge just before entering suddenly upon this table land, and the sight which met my eyes filled me with consternation and dismay.

The little stretch of level land was white with Indian tepees, and there were probably half a thousand red warriors clustered around some object near the center of the camp. Their attention was so wholly riveted to this point of interest that they did not notice me, and I easily could have turned back into the dark recesses of the gorge and made my escape with perfect safety. The fact, however, that this thought did not occur to me until the following day removes any possible right to a claim to heroism to which the narration of this episode might possibly otherwise entitle me.

I do not believe that I am made of the stuff which constitutes heroes, because, in all of the hundreds of instances that my voluntary acts have placed me face to face with death, I cannot recall a single one where any alternative step to that I took occurred to me until many hours later. My mind is evidently so constituted that I am subconsciously forced into the path of duty without recourse to tiresome mental processes. However that may be, I have never regretted that cowardice is not optional with me.

In this instance I was, of course, positive that Powell was the center of attraction, but whether I thought or acted first I do not know, but within an instant from the moment the scene broke upon my view I had whipped out my revolvers and was charging down upon the entire army of warriors, shooting rapidly, and whooping at the top of my lungs. Singlehanded, I could not have pursued better tactics, for the red men, convinced by sudden surprise that not less than a regiment of regulars was upon them, turned and fled in every direction for their bows, arrows, and rifles.

The view which their hurried routing disclosed filled me with apprehension and with rage. Under the clear rays of the Arizona moon lay Powell, his body fairly bristling with the hostile arrows of the braves. That he was already dead I could not but be convinced, and yet I would have saved his body from mutilation at the hands of the Apaches as quickly as I would have saved the man himself from death.

Riding close to him I reached down from the saddle, and grasping his cartridge belt drew him up across the withers of my mount. A backward glance convinced me that to return by the way I had come would be more hazardous than to continue across the plateau, so, putting spurs to my poor beast, I made a dash for the opening to the pass which I could distinguish on the far side of the table land.

The Indians had by this time discovered that I was alone and I was pursued with imprecations, arrows, and rifle balls. The fact that it is difficult to aim anything but imprecations accurately by moonlight, that they were upset by the sudden and unexpected manner of my advent, and that I was a rather rapidly moving target saved me from the various deadly projectiles of the enemy and permitted me to reach the shadows of the surrounding peaks before an orderly pursuit could be organized.

My horse was traveling practically unguided as I knew that I had probably less knowledge of the exact location of the trail to the pass than he, and thus it happened that he entered a defile which led to the summit of the range and not to the pass which I had hoped would carry me to the valley and to safety. It is probable, however, that to this fact I owe my life and the remarkable experiences and adventures which befell me during the following ten years.

My first knowledge that I was on the wrong trail came when I heard the yells of the pursuing savages suddenly grow fainter and fainter far off to my left.

I knew then that they had passed to the left of the jagged rock formation at the edge of the plateau, to the right of which my horse had borne me and the body of Powell.

I drew rein on a little level promontory overlooking the trail below and to my left, and saw the party of pursuing savages disappearing around the point of a neighboring peak.

I knew the Indians would soon discover that they were on the wrong trail and that the search for me would be renewed in the right direction as soon as they located my tracks.

I had gone but a short distance further when what seemed to be an excellent trail opened up around the face of a high cliff. The trail was level and quite broad and led upward and in the general direction I wished to go. The cliff arose for several hundred feet on my right, and on my left was an equal and nearly perpendicular drop to the bottom of a rocky ravine.

I had followed this trail for perhaps a hundred yards when a sharp turn to the right brought me to the mouth of a large cave. The opening was about four feet in height and three to four feet wide, and at this opening the trail ended.

It was now morning, and, with the customary lack of dawn which is a startling characteristic of Arizona, it had become daylight almost without warning.

Dismounting, I laid Powell upon the ground, but the most painstaking examination failed to reveal the faintest spark of life. I forced water from my canteen between his dead lips, bathed his face and rubbed his hands, working over him continuously for the better part of an hour in the face of the fact that I knew him to be dead.

I was very fond of Powell; he was thoroughly a man in every respect; a polished southern gentleman; a staunch and true friend; and it was with a feeling of the deepest grief that I finally gave up my crude endeavors at resuscitation.

Leaving Powell's body where it lay on the ledge I crept into the cave to reconnoiter. I found a large chamber, possibly a hundred feet in diameter and thirty or forty feet in height; a smooth and well-worn floor, and many other evidences that the cave had, at some remote period, been inhabited. The back of the cave was so lost in dense shadow that I could not distinguish whether there were openings into other apartments or not.

As I was continuing my examination I commenced to feel a pleasant drowsiness creeping over me which I attributed to the fatigue of my long and strenuous ride, and the reaction from the excitement of the fight and the pursuit. I felt comparatively safe in my present location as I knew that one man could defend the trail to the cave against an army.

I soon became so drowsy that I could scarcely resist the strong desire to throw myself on the floor of the cave for a few moments' rest, but I knew that this would never do, as it would mean certain death at the hands of my red friends, who might be upon me at any moment. With an effort I started toward the opening of the cave only to reel drunkenly against a side wall, and from there slip prone upon the floor.

TWO

The Escape of the Dead

A sense of delicious dreaminess overcame me, my muscles relaxed, and I was on the point of giving way to my desire to sleep when the sound of approaching horses reached my ears. I attempted to spring to my feet but was horrified to discover that my muscles refused to respond to my will. I was now thoroughly awake, but as unable to move a muscle as though turned to stone. It was then, for the first time, that I noticed a slight vapor filling the cave. It was extremely tenuous and only noticeable against the opening which led to daylight. There also came to my nostrils a faintly pungent odor, and I could only assume that I had been overcome by some poisonous gas, but why I should retain my mental faculties and yet be unable to move I could not fathom.

I lay facing the opening of the cave and where I could see the short stretch of trail which lay between the cave and the turn of the cliff around which the trail led. The noise of the approaching horses had ceased, and I judged the Indians were creeping stealthily upon me along the little ledge which led to my living tomb. I remember that I hoped they would make short work of me as I did not particularly relish the thought of the innumerable things they might do to me if the spirit prompted them.

I had not long to wait before a stealthy sound apprised me of their nearness, and then a war-bonneted, paint-streaked face was thrust cautiously around the shoulder of the cliff, and savage eyes looked into mine. That he could see me in the dim light of the cave I was sure for the early morning sun was falling full upon me through the opening.

The fellow, instead of approaching, merely stood and stared; his eyes bulging and his jaw dropped. And then another savage face appeared, and a third and fourth and fifth, craning their necks over the shoulders of their fellows whom they could not pass upon the narrow ledge. Each face was the picture of awe and fear, but for what reason I did not know, nor did I learn until ten years later. That there were still other braves behind those who regarded me was apparent from the fact that the leaders passed back whispered word to those behind them.

Suddenly a low but distinct moaning sound issued from the recesses of the cave behind me, and, as it reached the ears of the Indians, they turned and fled in terror, panic-stricken. So frantic were their efforts to escape from the unseen thing behind me that one of the braves was hurled headlong from the cliff to the rocks below. Their wild cries echoed in the canyon for a short time, and then all was still once more.

The sound which had frightened them was not repeated, but it had been sufficient as it was to start me speculating on the possible horror which lurked in the shadows at my back. Fear is a relative term and so I can only measure my feelings at that time by what I had experienced in previous positions of danger and by those that I have passed through since; but I can say without shame that if the sensations I endured during the next few minutes were fear, then may God help the coward, for cowardice is of a surety its own punishment.

To be held paralyzed, with one's back toward some horrible and unknown danger from the very sound of which the ferocious Apache warriors turn in wild stampede, as a flock of sheep would madly flee from a pack of wolves, seems to me the last word in fearsome predicaments for a man who had ever been used to fighting for his life with all the energy of a powerful physique.

Several times I thought I heard faint sounds behind me as of somebody moving cautiously, but eventually even these ceased, and I was left to the contemplation of my position without interruption. I could but vaguely conjecture the cause of my paralysis, and my only hope lay in that it might pass off as suddenly as it had fallen upon me.

Late in the afternoon my horse, which had been standing with dragging rein before the cave, started slowly down the trail, evidently in search of food and water, and I was left alone with my mysterious unknown companion and the dead body of my friend, which lay just within my range of vision upon the ledge where I had placed it in the early morning.

From then until possibly midnight all was silence, the silence of the dead; then, suddenly, the awful moan of the morning broke upon my startled ears, and there came again from the black shadows the sound of a moving thing, and a faint rustling as of dead leaves. The shock to my already overstrained nervous system was terrible in the extreme, and with a superhuman effort I strove to break my awful bonds. It was an effort of the mind, of the will, of the nerves; not muscular, for I could not move even so much as my little finger, but none the less mighty for all that. And then something gave, there was a momentary feeling of nausea, a sharp click as of the snapping of a steel wire, and I stood with my back against the wall of the cave facing my unknown foe.

And then the moonlight flooded the cave, and there before me lay my own body as it had been lying all these hours, with the eyes staring toward the open ledge and the hands resting limply upon the ground. I looked first at my lifeless clay there upon the floor of the cave and then down at myself in utter bewilderment; for there I lay clothed, and yet here I stood but naked as at the minute of my birth.

The transition had been so sudden and so unexpected that it left me for a moment forgetful of aught else than my strange metamorphosis. My first thought was, is this then death! Have I indeed passed over forever into that other life! But I could not well believe this, as I could feel my heart pounding against my ribs from the exertion of my efforts to release myself from the anaesthesis which had held me. My breath was coming in quick, short gasps, cold sweat stood out from every pore of my body, and the ancient experiment of pinching revealed the fact that I was anything other than a wraith.

Again was I suddenly recalled to my immediate surroundings by a repetition of the weird moan from the depths of the cave. Naked and unarmed as I was, I had no desire to face the unseen thing which menaced me.

My revolvers were strapped to my lifeless body which, for some unfathomable reason, I could not bring myself to touch. My carbine was in its boot, strapped to my saddle, and as my horse had wandered off I was left without means of defense. My only alternative seemed to lie in flight and my decision was crystallized by a recurrence of the rustling sound from the thing which now seemed, in the darkness of the cave and to my distorted imagination, to be creeping stealthily upon me.

Unable longer to resist the temptation to escape this horrible place I leaped quickly through the opening into the starlight of a clear Arizona night. The crisp, fresh mountain air outside the cave acted as an immediate tonic and I felt new life and new courage coursing through me. Pausing upon the brink of the ledge I upbraided myself for what now seemed to me wholly unwarranted apprehension. I reasoned with myself that I had lain helpless for many hours within the cave, yet nothing had molested me, and my better judgment, when permitted the direction of clear and logical reasoning, convinced me that the noises I had heard must have resulted from purely natural and harmless causes; probably the conformation of the cave was such that a slight breeze had caused the sounds I heard.

I decided to investigate, but first I lifted my head to fill my lungs with the pure, invigorating night air of the mountains. As I did so I saw stretching far below me the beautiful vista of rocky gorge, and level, cacti-studded flat, wrought by the moonlight into a miracle of soft splendor and wondrous enchantment.

Few western wonders are more inspiring than the beauties of an Arizona moonlit landscape; the silvered mountains in the distance, the strange lights and shadows upon hog back and arroyo, and the grotesque details of the stiff, yet beautiful cacti form a picture at once enchanting and inspiring; as though one were catching for the first time a glimpse of some dead and forgotten world, so different is it from the aspect of any other spot upon our earth.

As I stood thus meditating, I turned my gaze from the landscape to the heavens where the myriad stars formed a gorgeous and fitting canopy for the wonders of the earthly scene. My attention was quickly riveted by a large red star close to the distant horizon. As I gazed upon it I felt a spell of overpowering fascination—it was Mars, the god of war, and for me, the fighting man, it had always held the power of irresistible enchantment. As I gazed at it on that far-gone night it seemed to call across the unthinkable void, to lure me to it, to draw me as the lodestone attracts a particle of iron.

My longing was beyond the power of opposition; I closed my eyes, stretched out my arms toward the god of my vocation and felt myself drawn with the suddenness of thought through the trackless immensity of space. There was an instant of extreme cold and utter darkness.

THREE

My Advent on Mars

I opened my eyes upon a strange and weird landscape. I knew that I was on Mars; not once did I question either my sanity or my wakefulness. I was not asleep, no need for pinching here; my inner consciousness told me as plainly that I was upon Mars as your conscious mind tells you that you are upon Earth. You do not question the fact; neither did I.

I found myself lying prone upon a bed of yellowish, mosslike vegetation which stretched around me in all directions for interminable miles. I seemed to be lying in a deep, circular basin, along the outer verge of which I could distinguish the irregularities of low hills.

It was midday, the sun was shining full upon me and the heat of it was rather intense upon my naked body, yet no greater than would have been true under similar conditions on an Arizona desert. Here and there were slight outcroppings of quartz-bearing rock which glistened in the sunlight; and a little to my left, perhaps a hundred yards, appeared a low, walled enclosure about four feet in height. No water, and no other vegetation than the moss was in evidence, and as I was somewhat thirsty I determined to do a little exploring.

Springing to my feet I received my first Martian surprise, for the effort, which on Earth would have brought me standing upright, carried me into the Martian air to the height of about three yards. I alighted softly upon the ground, however, without appreciable shock or jar. Now commenced a series of evolutions which even then seemed ludicrous in the extreme. I found that I must learn to walk all over again, as the muscular exertion which carried me easily and safely upon Earth played strange antics with me upon Mars.

Instead of progressing in a sane and dignified manner, my attempts to walk resulted in a variety of hops which took me clear of the ground a couple of feet at each step and landed me sprawling upon my face or back at the end of each second or third hop. My muscles, perfectly attuned and accustomed to the force of gravity on Earth, played the mischief with me in attempting for the first time to cope with the lesser gravitation and lower air pressure on Mars.

I was determined, however, to explore the low structure which was the only evidence of habitation in sight, and so I hit upon the unique plan of reverting to first principles in locomotion, creeping. I did fairly well at this and in a few moments had reached the low, encircling wall of the enclosure.

There appeared to be no doors or windows upon the side nearest me, but as the wall was but about four feet high I cautiously gained my feet and peered over the top upon the strangest sight it had ever been given me to see.

The roof of the enclosure was of solid glass about four or five inches in thickness, and beneath this were several hundred large eggs, perfectly round and snowy white. The eggs were nearly uniform in size being about two and one-half feet in diameter.

Five or six had already hatched and the grotesque caricatures which sat blinking in the sunlight were enough to cause me to doubt my sanity. They seemed mostly head, with little scrawny bodies, long necks and six legs, or, as I afterward learned, two legs and two arms, with an intermediary pair of limbs which could be used at will either as arms or legs. Their eyes were set at the extreme sides of their heads a trifle above the center and protruded in such a manner that they could be directed either forward or back and also independently of each other, thus permitting this queer animal to look in any direction, or in two directions at once, without the necessity of turning the head.

The ears, which were slightly above the eyes and closer together, were small, cup-shaped antennae, protruding not more than an inch on these young specimens. Their noses were but longitudinal slits in the center of their faces, midway between their mouths and ears.

There was no hair on their bodies, which were of a very light yellowish-green color. In the adults, as I was to learn quite soon, this color deepens to an olive green and is darker in the male than in the female. Further, the heads of the adults are not so out of proportion to their bodies as in the case of the young.

The iris of the eyes is blood red, as in Albinos, while the pupil is dark. The eyeball itself is very white, as are the teeth. These latter add a most ferocious appearance to an otherwise fearsome and terrible countenance, as the lower tusks curve upward to sharp points which end about where the eyes of earthly human beings are located. The whiteness of the teeth is not

The roof of the enclosure was of solid glass about four or five inches in thickness, and beneath this were several hundred large eggs, perfectly round and snowy white.

that of ivory, but of the snowiest and most gleaming of china. Against the
dark background of their olive skins their tusks stand out in a most striking
manner, making these weapons present a singularly formidable appearance.

Most of these details I noted later, for I was given but little time to
speculate on the wonders of my new discovery. I had seen that the eggs
were in the process of hatching, and as I stood watching the hideous little
monsters break from their shells I failed to note the approach of a score of
full-grown Martians from behind me.

Coming, as they did, over the soft and soundless moss, which covers
practically the entire surface of Mars with the exception of the frozen areas
at the poles and the scattered cultivated districts, they might have captured
me easily, but their intentions were far more sinister. It was the rattling of
the accouterments of the foremost warrior which warned me.

On such a little thing my life hung that I often marvel that I escaped so
easily. Had not the rifle of the leader of the party swung from its fastenings
beside his saddle in such a way as to strike against the butt of his great metal
shod spear I should have snuffed out without ever knowing that death was
near me. But the little sound caused me to turn, and there upon me, not
ten feet from my breast, was the point of that huge spear, a spear forty feet
long, tipped with gleaming metal, and held low at the side of a mounted
replica of the little devils I had been watching.

But how puny and harmless they now looked beside this huge and terrific
incarnation of hate, of vengeance and of death. The man himself, for such
I may call him, was fully fifteen feet in height and, on Earth, would have
weighed some four hundred pounds. He sat his mount as we sit a horse,
grasping the animal's barrel with his lower limbs, while the hands of his
two right arms held his immense spear low at the side of his mount; his two
left arms were outstretched laterally to help preserve his balance, the thing
he rode having neither bridle or reins of any description for guidance.

And his mount! How can earthly words describe it! It towered ten feet
at the shoulder; had four legs on either side; a broad flat tail, larger at the
tip than at the root, and which it held straight out behind while running; a
gaping mouth which split its head from its snout to its long, massive neck.

Like its master, it was entirely devoid of hair, but was of a dark slate
color and exceeding smooth and glossy. Its belly was white, and its legs
shaded from the slate of its shoulders and hips to a vivid yellow at the feet.
The feet themselves were heavily padded and nailless, which fact had also
contributed to the noiselessness of their approach, and, in common with
a multiplicity of legs, is a characteristic feature of the fauna of Mars. The
highest type of man and one other animal, the only mammal existing on

Mars, alone have well-formed nails, and there are absolutely no hoofed animals in existence there.

Behind this first charging demon trailed nineteen others, similar in all respects, but, as I learned later, bearing individual characteristics peculiar to themselves; precisely as no two of us are identical although we are all cast in a similar mold. This picture, or rather materialized nightmare, which I have described at length, made but one terrible and swift impression on me as I turned to meet it.

Unarmed and naked as I was, the first law of nature manifested itself in the only possible solution of my immediate problem, and that was to get out of the vicinity of the point of the charging spear. Consequently I gave a very earthly and at the same time superhuman leap to reach the top of the Martian incubator, for such I had determined it must be.

My effort was crowned with a success which appalled me no less than it seemed to surprise the Martian warriors, for it carried me fully thirty feet into the air and landed me a hundred feet from my pursuers and on the opposite side of the enclosure.

I alighted upon the soft moss easily and without mishap, and turning saw my enemies lined up along the further wall. Some were surveying me with expressions which I afterward discovered marked extreme astonishment, and the others were evidently satisfying themselves that I had not molested their young.

They were conversing together in low tones, and gesticulating and pointing toward me. Their discovery that I had not harmed the little Martians, and that I was unarmed, must have caused them to look upon me with less ferocity; but, as I was to learn later, the thing which weighed most in my favor was my exhibition of hurdling.

While the Martians are immense, their bones are very large and they are muscled only in proportion to the gravitation which they must overcome. The result is that they are infinitely less agile and less powerful, in proportion to their weight, than an Earth man, and I doubt that were one of them suddenly to be transported to Earth he could lift his own weight from the ground; in fact, I am convinced that he could not do so.

My feat then was as marvelous upon Mars as it would have been upon Earth, and from desiring to annihilate me they suddenly looked upon me as a wonderful discovery to be captured and exhibited among their fellows.

The respite my unexpected agility had given me permitted me to formulate plans for the immediate future and to note more closely the appearance of the warriors, for I could not disassociate these people in my mind from those other warriors who, only the day before, had been pursuing me.

I noted that each was armed with several other weapons in addition to the huge spear which I have described. The weapon which caused me to decide against an attempt at escape by flight was what was evidently a rifle of some description, and which I felt, for some reason, they were peculiarly efficient in handling.

These rifles were of a white metal stocked with wood, which I learned later was a very light and intensely hard growth much prized on Mars, and entirely unknown to us denizens of Earth. The metal of the barrel is an alloy composed principally of aluminum and steel which they have learned to temper to a hardness far exceeding that of the steel with which we are familiar. The weight of these rifles is comparatively little, and with the small caliber, explosive, radium projectiles which they use, and the great length of the barrel, they are deadly in the extreme and at ranges which would be unthinkable on Earth. The theoretic effective radius of this rifle is three hundred miles, but the best they can do in actual service when equipped with their wireless finders and sighters is but a trifle over two hundred miles.

This is quite far enough to imbue me with great respect for the Martian firearm, and some telepathic force must have warned me against an attempt to escape in broad daylight from under the muzzles of twenty of these death-dealing machines.

The Martians, after conversing for a short time, turned and rode away in the direction from which they had come, leaving one of their number alone by the enclosure. When they had covered perhaps two hundred yards they halted, and turning their mounts toward us sat watching the warrior by the enclosure.

He was the one whose spear had so nearly transfixed me, and was evidently the leader of the band, as I had noted that they seemed to have moved to their present position at his direction. When his force had come to a halt he dismounted, threw down his spear and small arms, and came around the end of the incubator toward me, entirely unarmed and as naked as I, except for the ornaments strapped upon his head, limbs, and breast.

When he was within about fifty feet of me he unclasped an enormous metal armlet, and holding it toward me in the open palm of his hand, addressed me in a clear, resonant voice, but in a language, it is needless to say, I could not understand. He then stopped as though waiting for my reply, pricking up his antennae-like ears and cocking his strange-looking eyes still further toward me.

As the silence became painful I concluded to hazard a little conversation on my own part, as I had guessed that he was making overtures of peace. The throwing down of his weapons and the withdrawing of his troop before his advance toward me would have signified a peaceful mission anywhere on Earth, so why not, then, on Mars!

Placing my hand over my heart I bowed low to the Martian and explained to him that while I did not understand his language, his actions spoke for the peace and friendship that at the present moment were most dear to my heart. Of course I might have been a babbling brook for all the intelligence my speech carried to him, but he understood the action with which I immediately followed my words.

Stretching my hand toward him, I advanced and took the armlet from his open palm, clasping it about my arm above the elbow; smiled at him and stood waiting. His wide mouth spread into an answering smile, and locking one of his intermediary arms in mine we turned and walked back toward his mount. At the same time he motioned his followers to advance. They started toward us on a wild run, but were checked by a signal from him. Evidently he feared that were I to be really frightened again I might jump entirely out of the landscape.

He exchanged a few words with his men, motioned to me that I would ride behind one of them, and then mounted his own animal. The fellow designated reached down two or three hands and lifted me up behind him on the glossy back of his mount, where I hung on as best I could by the belts and straps which held the Martian's weapons and ornaments.

The entire cavalcade then turned and galloped away toward the range of hills in the distance.

FOUR

A Prisoner

We had gone perhaps ten miles when the ground began to rise very rapidly. We were, as I was later to learn, nearing the edge of one of Mars' long-dead seas, in the bottom of which my encounter with the Martians had taken place.

In a short time we gained the foot of the mountains, and after traversing a narrow gorge came to an open valley, at the far extremity of which was a low table land upon which I beheld an enormous city. Toward this we galloped, entering it by what appeared to be a ruined roadway leading out from the city, but only to the edge of the table land, where it ended abruptly in a flight of broad steps.

Upon closer observation I saw as we passed them that the buildings were deserted, and while not greatly decayed had the appearance of not having been tenanted for years, possibly for ages. Toward the center of the city was a large plaza, and upon this and in the buildings immediately surrounding it were camped some nine or ten hundred creatures of the same breed as my captors, for such I now considered them despite the suave manner in which I had been trapped.

With the exception of their ornaments all were naked. The women varied in appearance but little from the men, except that their tusks were much larger in proportion to their height, in some instances curving nearly to their high-set ears. Their bodies were smaller and lighter in color, and their fingers and toes bore the rudiments of nails, which were entirely lacking among the males. The adult females ranged in height from ten to twelve feet.

The children were light in color, even lighter than the women, and all looked precisely alike to me, except that some were taller than others; older, I presumed.

I saw no signs of extreme age among them, nor is there any appreciable difference in their appearance from the age of maturity, about forty, until, at about the age of one thousand years, they go voluntarily upon their last strange pilgrimage down the river Iss, which leads no living Martian knows whither and from whose bosom no Martian has ever returned, or would be allowed to live did he return after once embarking upon its cold, dark waters.

Only about one Martian in a thousand dies of sickness or disease, and possibly about twenty take the voluntary pilgrimage. The other nine hundred and seventy-nine die violent deaths in duels, in hunting, in aviation and in war; but perhaps by far the greatest death loss comes during the age of childhood, when vast numbers of the little Martians fall victims to the great white apes of Mars.

The average life expectancy of a Martian after the age of maturity is about three hundred years, but would be nearer the one-thousand mark were it not for the various means leading to violent death. Owing to the waning resources of the planet it evidently became necessary to counteract the increasing longevity which their remarkable skill in therapeutics and surgery produced, and so human life has come to be considered but lightly on Mars, as is evidenced by their dangerous sports and the almost continual warfare between the various communities.

There are other and natural causes tending toward a diminution of population, but nothing contributes so greatly to this end as the fact that no male or female Martian is ever voluntarily without a weapon of destruction.

As we neared the plaza and my presence was discovered we were immediately surrounded by hundreds of the creatures who seemed anxious to pluck me from my seat behind my guard. A word from the leader of the party stilled their clamor, and we proceeded at a trot across the plaza to the entrance of as magnificent an edifice as mortal eye has rested upon.

The building was low, but covered an enormous area. It was constructed of gleaming white marble inlaid with gold and brilliant stones which sparkled and scintillated in the sunlight. The main entrance was some hundred feet in width and projected from the building proper to form a huge canopy above the entrance hall. There was no stairway, but a gentle incline to the first floor of the building opened into an enormous chamber encircled by galleries.

On the floor of this chamber, which was dotted with highly carved wooden desks and chairs, were assembled about forty or fifty male Martians around the steps of a rostrum. On the platform proper squatted an enormous warrior heavily loaded with metal ornaments, gay-colored feathers and beautifully wrought leather trappings ingeniously set with precious stones. From his shoulders depended a short cape of white fur lined with brilliant scarlet silk.

What struck me as most remarkable about this assemblage and the hall in which they were congregated was the fact that the creatures were entirely out of proportion to the desks, chairs, and other furnishings; these being of a size adapted to human beings such as I, whereas the great bulks of the Martians could scarcely have squeezed into the chairs, nor was there room beneath the desks for their long legs. Evidently, then, there were other denizens on Mars than the wild and grotesque creatures into whose hands I had fallen, but the evidences of extreme antiquity which showed all around me indicated that these buildings might have belonged to some long-extinct and forgotten race in the dim antiquity of Mars.

Our party had halted at the entrance to the building, and at a sign from the leader I had been lowered to the ground. Again locking his arm in mine, we had proceeded into the audience chamber. There were few formalities observed in approaching the Martian chieftain. My captor merely strode up to the rostrum, the others making way for him as he advanced. The chieftain rose to his feet and uttered the name of my escort who, in turn, halted and repeated the name of the ruler followed by his title.

At the time, this ceremony and the words they uttered meant nothing to me, but later I came to know that this was the customary greeting between green Martians. Had the men been strangers, and therefore unable to exchange names, they would have silently exchanged ornaments, had their missions been peaceful—otherwise they would have exchanged shots, or have fought out their introduction with some other of their various weapons.

My captor, whose name was Tars Tarkas, was virtually the vice-chieftain of the community, and a man of great ability as a statesman and warrior. He evidently explained briefly the incidents connected with his expedition, including my capture, and when he had concluded the chieftain addressed me at some length.

I replied in our good old English tongue merely to convince him that neither of us could understand the other; but I noticed that when I smiled slightly on concluding, he did likewise. This fact, and the similar occurrence during my first talk with Tars Tarkas, convinced me that we had at least something in common; the ability to smile, therefore to laugh; denoting a sense of humor. But I was to learn that the Martian smile is merely perfunctory, and that the Martian laugh is a thing to cause strong men to blanch in horror.

The ideas of humor among the green men of Mars are widely at variance with our conceptions of incitants to merriment. The death agonies of a fellow being are, to these strange creatures, provocative of the wildest hilarity, while their chief form of commonest amusement is to inflict death on their prisoners of war in various ingenious and horrible ways.

The assembled warriors and chieftains examined me closely, feeling my muscles and the texture of my skin. The principal chieftain then evidently signified a desire to see me perform, and, motioning me to follow, he started with Tars Tarkas for the open plaza.

Now, I had made no attempt to walk, since my first signal failure, except while tightly grasping Tars Tarkas' arm, and so now I went skipping and flitting about among the desks and chairs like some monstrous grasshopper. After bruising myself severely, much to the amusement of the Martians, I again had recourse to creeping, but this did not suit them and I was roughly jerked to my feet by a towering fellow who had laughed most heartily at my misfortunes.

As he banged me down upon my feet his face was bent close to mine and I did the only thing a gentleman might do under the circumstances of brutality, boorishness, and lack of consideration for a stranger's rights; I swung my fist squarely to his jaw and he went down like a felled ox. As he sunk to the floor I wheeled around with my back toward the nearest desk, expecting to be overwhelmed by the vengeance of his fellows, but determined to give them as good a battle as the unequal odds would permit before I gave up my life.

My fears were groundless, however, as the other Martians, at first struck dumb with wonderment, finally broke into wild peals of laughter and applause. I did not recognize the applause as such, but later, when I had become acquainted with their customs, I learned that I had won what they seldom accord, a manifestation of approbation.

The fellow whom I had struck lay where he had fallen, nor did any of his mates approach him. Tars Tarkas advanced toward me, holding out one of his arms, and we thus proceeded to the plaza without further mishap. I did not, of course, know the reason for which we had come to the open, but I was not long in being enlightened. They first repeated the word "sak" a number of times, and then Tars Tarkas made several jumps, repeating the same word before each leap; then, turning to me, he said, "sak!" I saw what they were after, and gathering myself together I "sakked" with such marvelous success that I cleared a good hundred and fifty feet; nor did I this time, lose my equilibrium, but landed squarely upon my feet without falling. I then returned by easy jumps of twenty-five or thirty feet to the little group of warriors.

My exhibition had been witnessed by several hundred lesser Martians, and they immediately broke into demands for a repetition, which the chieftain then ordered me to make; but I was both hungry and thirsty, and determined on the spot that my only method of salvation was to demand the consideration from these creatures which they evidently would not voluntarily accord. I therefore ignored the repeated commands to "sak," and each time they were made I motioned to my mouth and rubbed my stomach.

Tars Tarkas and the chief exchanged a few words, and the former, calling to a young female among the throng, gave her some instructions and motioned me to accompany her. I grasped her proffered arm and together we crossed the plaza toward a large building on the far side.

My fair companion was about eight feet tall, having just arrived at maturity, but not yet to her full height. She was of a light olive-green color, with a smooth, glossy hide. Her name, as I afterward learned, was Sola, and she belonged to the retinue of Tars Tarkas. She conducted me to a spacious chamber in one of the buildings fronting on the plaza, and which, from the litter of silks and furs upon the floor, I took to be the sleeping quarters of several of the natives.

The room was well lighted by a number of large windows and was beautifully decorated with mural paintings and mosaics, but upon all there seemed to rest that indefinable touch of the finger of antiquity which convinced me that the architects and builders of these wondrous creations had nothing in common with the crude half-brutes which now occupied them.

Sola motioned me to be seated upon a pile of silks near the center of the room, and, turning, made a peculiar hissing sound, as though signaling to someone in an adjoining room. In response to her call I obtained my first sight of a new Martian wonder. It waddled in on its ten short legs, and squatted down before the girl like an obedient puppy. The thing was about the size of a Shetland pony, but its head bore a slight resemblance to that of a frog, except that the jaws were equipped with three rows of long, sharp tusks.

FIVE

I Elude My Watch Dog

Sola stared into the brute's wicked-looking eyes, muttered a word or two of command, pointed to me, and left the chamber. I could not but wonder what this ferocious-looking monstrosity might do when left alone in such close proximity to such a relatively tender morsel of meat; but my fears were groundless, as the beast, after surveying me intently for a moment, crossed the room to the only exit which led to the street, and lay down full length across the threshold.

This was my first experience with a Martian watch dog, but it was destined not to be my last, for this fellow guarded me carefully during the time I remained a captive among these green men; twice saving my life, and never voluntarily being away from me a moment.

While Sola was away I took occasion to examine more minutely the room in which I found myself captive. The mural painting depicted scenes of rare and wonderful beauty; mountains, rivers, lake, ocean, meadow, trees and flowers, winding roadways, sun-kissed gardens—scenes which might have portrayed earthly views but for the different colorings of the vegetation. The work had evidently been wrought by a master hand, so subtle the atmosphere, so perfect the technique; yet nowhere was there a representation of a living animal, either human or brute, by which I could guess at the likeness of these other and perhaps extinct denizens of Mars.

While I was allowing my fancy to run riot in wild conjecture on the possible explanation of the strange anomalies which I had so far met with on Mars, Sola returned bearing both food and drink. These she placed on the floor beside me, and seating herself a short ways off regarded me intently. The food consisted of about a pound of some solid substance of the consistency of cheese and almost tasteless, while the liquid was apparently milk from some animal. It was not unpleasant to the taste, though slightly acid, and I learned in a short time to prize it very highly. It came, as I later

The beast, after surveying me intently for a moment, crossed the room to the only exit which led to the street, and lay down full length across the threshold.

discovered, not from an animal, as there is only one mammal on Mars and that one very rare indeed, but from a large plant which grows practically without water, but seems to distill its plentiful supply of milk from the products of the soil, the moisture of the air, and the rays of the sun. A single plant of this species will give eight or ten quarts of milk per day.

After I had eaten I was greatly invigorated, but feeling the need of rest I stretched out upon the silks and was soon asleep. I must have slept several hours, as it was dark when I awoke, and I was very cold. I noticed that someone had thrown a fur over me, but it had become partially dislodged and in the darkness I could not see to replace it. Suddenly a hand reached out and pulled the fur over me, shortly afterwards adding another to my covering.

I presumed that my watchful guardian was Sola, nor was I wrong. This girl alone, among all the green Martians with whom I came in contact, disclosed characteristics of sympathy, kindliness, and affection; her ministrations to my bodily wants were unfailing, and her solicitous care saved me from much suffering and many hardships.

As I was to learn, the Martian nights are extremely cold, and as there is practically no twilight or dawn, the changes in temperature are sudden and most uncomfortable, as are the transitions from brilliant daylight to darkness. The nights are either brilliantly illumined or very dark, for if neither of the two moons of Mars happen to be in the sky almost total darkness results, since the lack of atmosphere, or, rather, the very thin atmosphere, fails to diffuse the starlight to any great extent; on the other hand, if both of the moons are in the heavens at night the surface of the ground is brightly illuminated.

Both of Mars' moons are vastly nearer her than is our moon to Earth; the nearer moon being but about five thousand miles distant, while the further is but little more than fourteen thousand miles away, against the nearly one-quarter million miles which separate us from our moon. The nearer moon of Mars makes a complete revolution around the planet in a little over seven and one-half hours, so that she may be seen hurtling through the sky like some huge meteor two or three times each night, revealing all her phases during each transit of the heavens.

The further moon revolves about Mars in something over thirty and one-quarter hours, and with her sister satellite makes a nocturnal Martian scene one of splendid and weird grandeur. And it is well that nature has so graciously and abundantly lighted the Martian night, for the green men of Mars, being a nomadic race without high intellectual development, have but crude means for artificial lighting; depending principally upon torches, a kind of candle, and a peculiar oil lamp which generates a gas and burns without a wick.

This last device produces an intensely brilliant far-reaching white light, but as the natural oil which it requires can only be obtained by mining in one of several widely separated and remote localities it is seldom used by these creatures whose only thought is for today, and whose hatred for manual labor has kept them in a semi-barbaric state for countless ages.

After Sola had replenished my coverings I again slept, nor did I awaken until daylight. The other occupants of the room, five in number, were all females, and they were still sleeping, piled high with a motley array of silks and furs. Across the threshold lay stretched the sleepless guardian brute, just as I had last seen him on the preceding day; apparently he had not moved a muscle; his eyes were fairly glued upon me, and I fell to wondering just what might befall me should I endeavor to escape.

I have ever been prone to seek adventure and to investigate and exper- iment where wiser men would have left well enough alone. It therefore now occurred to me that the surest way of learning the exact attitude of this beast toward me would be to attempt to leave the room. I felt fairly secure in my belief that I could escape him should he pursue me once I was outside the building, for I had begun to take great pride in my ability as a jumper. Furthermore, I could see from the shortness of his legs that the brute himself was no jumper and probably no runner.

Slowly and carefully, therefore, I gained my feet, only to see that my watcher did the same; cautiously I advanced toward him, finding that by moving with a shuffling gait I could retain my balance as well as make reasonably rapid progress. As I neared the brute he backed cautiously away from me, and when I had reached the open he moved to one side to let me pass. He then fell in behind me and followed about ten paces in my rear as I made my way along the deserted street.

Evidently his mission was to protect me only, I thought, but when we reached the edge of the city he suddenly sprang before me, uttering strange sounds and baring his ugly and ferocious tusks. Thinking to have some amusement at his expense, I rushed toward him, and when almost upon him sprang into the air, alighting far beyond him and away from the city. He wheeled instantly and charged me with the most appalling speed I had ever beheld. I had thought his short legs a bar to swiftness, but had he been coursing with greyhounds the latter would have appeared as though asleep on a door mat. As I was to learn, this is the fleetest animal on Mars, and owing to its intelligence, loyalty, and ferocity is used in hunting, in war, and as the protector of the Martian man.

I quickly saw that I would have difficulty in escaping the fangs of the beast on a straightaway course, and so I met his charge by doubling in my tracks and leaping over him as he was almost upon me. This maneuver gave me a considerable advantage, and I was able to reach the city quite a bit ahead of him, and as he came tearing after me I jumped for a window about thirty feet from the ground in the face of one of the buildings overlooking the valley.

Grasping the sill I pulled myself up to a sitting posture without looking into the building, and gazed down at the baffled animal beneath me. My exultation was short-lived, however, for scarcely had I gained a secure seat upon the sill than a huge hand grasped me by the neck from behind and dragged me violently into the room. Here I was thrown upon my back, and beheld standing over me a colossal ape-like creature, white and hairless except for an enormous shock of bristly hair upon its head.

SIX

A Fight That Won Friends

The thing, which more nearly resembled our earthly men than it did the Martians I had seen, held me pinioned to the ground with one huge foot, while it jabbered and gesticulated at some answering creature behind me. This other, which was evidently its mate, soon came toward us, bearing a mighty stone cudgel with which it evidently intended to brain me.

The creatures were about ten or fifteen feet tall, standing erect, and had, like the green Martians, an intermediary set of arms or legs, midway between their upper and lower limbs. Their eyes were close together and non-protruding; their ears were high set, but more laterally located than those of the Martians, while their snouts and teeth were strikingly like those of our African gorilla. Altogether they were not unlovely when viewed in comparison with the green Martians.

The cudgel was swinging in the arc which ended upon my upturned face when a bolt of myriad-legged horror hurled itself through the doorway full upon the breast of my executioner. With a shriek of fear the ape which held me leaped through the open window, but its mate closed in a terrific death struggle with my preserver, which was nothing less than my faithful watch-thing; I cannot bring myself to call so hideous a creature a dog.

As quickly as possible I gained my feet and backing against the wall I witnessed such a battle as it is vouchsafed few beings to see. The strength, agility, and blind ferocity of these two creatures is approached by nothing known to earthly man. My beast had an advantage in his first hold, having sunk his mighty fangs far into the breast of his adversary; but the great arms and paws of the ape, backed by muscles far transcending those of the Martian men I had seen, had locked the throat of my guardian and slowly were choking out his life, and bending back his head and neck upon his body, where I momentarily expected the former to fall limp at the end of a broken neck.

In accomplishing this the ape was tearing away the entire front of its breast, which was held in the vise-like grip of the powerful jaws. Back and forth upon the floor they rolled, neither one emitting a sound of fear or pain. Presently I saw the great eyes of my beast bulging completely from their sockets and blood flowing from its nostrils. That he was weakening perceptibly was evident, but so also was the ape, whose struggles were growing momentarily less.

Suddenly I came to myself and, with that strange instinct which seems ever to prompt me to my duty, I seized the cudgel, which had fallen to the floor at the commencement of the battle, and swinging it with all the power of my earthly arms I crashed it full upon the head of the ape, crushing his skull as though it had been an eggshell.

Scarcely had the blow descended when I was confronted with a new danger. The ape's mate, recovered from its first shock of terror, had returned to the scene of the encounter by way of the interior of the building. I glimpsed him just before he reached the doorway and the sight of him, now roaring as he perceived his lifeless fellow stretched upon the floor, and frothing at the mouth, in the extremity of his rage, filled me, I must confess, with dire forebodings.

I am ever willing to stand and fight when the odds are not too over-whelmingly against me, but in this instance I perceived neither glory nor profit in pitting my relatively puny strength against the iron muscles and brutal ferocity of this enraged denizen of an unknown world; in fact, the only outcome of such an encounter, so far as I might be concerned, seemed sudden death.

I was standing near the window and I knew that once in the street I might gain the plaza and safety before the creature could overtake me; at least there was a chance for safety in flight, against almost certain death should I remain and fight however desperately.

It is true I held the cudgel, but what could I do with it against his four great arms? Even should I break one of them with my first blow, for I figured that he would attempt to ward off the cudgel, he could reach out and annihilate me with the others before I could recover for a second attack.

In the instant that these thoughts passed through my mind I had turned to make for the window, but my eyes alighting on the form of my erstwhile guardian threw all thoughts of flight to the four winds. He lay gasping upon the floor of the chamber, his great eyes fastened upon me in what seemed a pitiful appeal for protection. I could not withstand that look, nor could I, on second thought, have deserted my rescuer without giving as good an account of myself in his behalf as he had in mine.

Without more ado, therefore, I turned to meet the charge of the infuriated bull ape. He was now too close upon me for the cudgel to prove of any effective assistance, so I merely threw it as heavily as I could at his advancing bulk. It struck him just below the knees, eliciting a howl of pain and rage, and so throwing him off his balance that he lunged full upon me with arms wide stretched to ease his fall.

Again, as on the preceding day, I had recourse to earthly tactics, and swinging my right fist full upon the point of his chin I followed it with a smashing left to the pit of his stomach. The effect was marvelous, for, as I lightly sidestepped, after delivering the second blow, he reeled and fell upon the floor doubled up with pain and gasping for wind. Leaping over his prostrate body, I seized the cudgel and finished the monster before he could regain his feet.

As I delivered the blow a low laugh rang out behind me, and, turning, I beheld Tars Tarkas, Sola, and three or four warriors standing in the doorway of the chamber. As my eyes met theirs I was, for the second time, the recipient of their zealously guarded applause.

My absence had been noted by Sola on her awakening, and she had quickly informed Tars Tarkas, who had set out immediately with a handful of warriors to search for me. As they had approached the limits of the city they had witnessed the actions of the bull ape as he bolted into the building, frothing with rage.

They had followed immediately behind him, thinking it barely possible that his actions might prove a clew to my whereabouts and had witnessed my short but decisive battle with him. This encounter, together with my set-to with the Martian warrior on the previous day and my feats of jumping placed me upon a high pinnacle in their regard. Evidently devoid of all the finer sentiments of friendship, love, or affection, these people fairly worship physical prowess and bravery, and nothing is too good for the object of their adoration as long as he maintains his position by repeated examples of his skill, strength, and courage.

Sola, who had accompanied the searching party of her own volition, was the only one of the Martians whose face had not been twisted in laughter as I battled for my life. She, on the contrary, was sober with apparent solicitude and, as soon as I had finished the monster, rushed to me and carefully examined my body for possible wounds or injuries. Satisfying herself that I had come off unscathed she smiled quietly, and, taking my hand, started toward the door of the chamber.

Tars Tarkas and the other warriors had entered and were standing over the now rapidly reviving brute which had saved my life, and whose life I, in turn, had rescued. They seemed to be deep in argument, and finally one of them addressed me, but remembering my ignorance of his language turned back to Tars Tarkas, who, with a word and gesture, gave some command to the fellow and turned to follow us from the room.

There seemed something menacing in their attitude toward my beast, and I hesitated to leave until I had learned the outcome. It was well I did so, for the warrior drew an evil looking pistol from its holster and was on the point of putting an end to the creature when I sprang forward and struck up his arm. The bullet striking the wooden casing of the window exploded, blowing a hole completely through the wood and masonry.

I then knelt down beside the fearsome-looking thing, and raising it to its feet motioned for it to follow me. The looks of surprise which my actions elicited from the Martians were ludicrous; they could not understand, except in a feeble and childish way, such attributes as gratitude and compassion. The warrior whose gun I had struck up looked enquiringly at Tars Tarkas, but the latter signed that I be left to my own devices, and so we returned to the plaza with my great beast following close at heel, and Sola grasping me tightly by the arm.

I had at least two friends on Mars; a young woman who watched over me with motherly solicitude, and a dumb brute which, as I later came to know, held in its poor ugly carcass more love, more loyalty, more gratitude than could have been found in the entire five million green Martians who rove the deserted cities and dead sea bottoms of Mars.

SEVEN

Child-Raising on Mars

After a breakfast, which was an exact replica of the meal of the preceding day and an index of practically every meal which followed while I was with the green men of Mars, Sola escorted me to the plaza, where I found the entire community engaged in watching or helping at the harnessing of huge mastodonian animals to great three-wheeled chariots. There were about two hundred and fifty of these vehicles, each drawn by a single animal, any one of which, from their appearance, might easily have drawn the entire wagon train when fully loaded.

The chariots themselves were large, commodious, and gorgeously decorated. In each was seated a female Martian loaded with ornaments of metal, with jewels and silks and furs, and upon the back of each of the beasts which drew the chariots was perched a young Martian driver. Like the animals upon which the warriors were mounted, the heavier draft animals wore neither bit nor bridle, but were guided entirely by telepathic means.

This power is wonderfully developed in all Martians, and accounts largely for the simplicity of their language and the relatively few spoken words exchanged even in long conversations. It is the universal language of Mars, through the medium of which the higher and lower animals of this world of paradoxes are able to communicate to a greater or less extent, depending upon the intellectual sphere of the species and the development of the individual.

As the cavalcade took up the line of march in single file, Sola dragged me into an empty chariot and we proceeded with the procession toward the point by which I had entered the city the day before. At the head of the caravan rode some two hundred warriors, five abreast, and a like number brought up the rear, while twenty-five or thirty outriders flanked us on either side.

Every one but myself—men, women, and children—were heavily

armed, and at the tail of each chariot trotted a Martian hound, my own beast following closely behind ours; in fact, the faithful creature never left me voluntarily during the entire ten years I spent on Mars. Our way led out across the little valley before the city, through the hills, and down into the dead sea bottom which I had traversed on my journey from the incubator to the plaza. The incubator, as it proved, was the terminal point of our journey this day, and, as the entire cavalcade broke into a mad gallop as soon as we reached the level expanse of sea bottom, we were soon within sight of our goal.

On reaching it the chariots were parked with military precision on the four sides of the enclosure, and half a score of warriors, headed by the enormous chieftain, and including Tars Tarkas and several other lesser chiefs, dismounted and advanced toward it. I could see Tars Tarkas explaining something to the principal chieftain, whose name, by the way, was, as nearly as I can translate it into English, Lorquas Ptomel, Jed; jed being his title.

I was soon appraised of the subject of their conversation, as, calling to Sola, Tars Tarkas signed for her to send me to him. I had by this time mastered the intricacies of walking under Martian conditions, and quickly responding to his command I advanced to the side of the incubator where the warriors stood.

As I reached their side a glance showed me that all but a very few eggs had hatched, the incubator being fairly alive with the hideous little devils. They ranged in height from three to four feet, and were moving restlessly about the enclosure as though searching for food.

As I came to a halt before him, Tars Tarkas pointed over the incubator and said, "Sak." I saw that he wanted me to repeat my performance of yesterday for the edification of Lorquas Ptomel, and, as I must confess that my prowess gave me no little satisfaction, I responded quickly, leaping entirely over the parked chariots on the far side of the incubator. As I returned, Lorquas Ptomel grunted something at me, and turning to his warriors gave a few words of command relative to the incubator. They paid no further attention to me and I was thus permitted to remain close and watch their operations, which consisted in breaking an opening in the wall of the incubator large enough to permit of the exit of the young Martians.

On either side of this opening the women and the younger Martians, both male and female, formed two solid walls leading out through the chariots and quite away into the plain beyond. Between these walls the little Martians scampered, wild as deer; being permitted to run the full length of the aisle, where they were captured one at a time by the women

and older children; the last in the line capturing the first little one to reach
the end of the gauntlet, her opposite in the line capturing the second, and
so on until all the little fellows had left the enclosure and been appropriated
by some youth or female. As the women caught the young they fell out of
line and returned to their respective chariots, while those who fell into the
hands of the young men were later turned over to some of the women.

I saw that the ceremony, if it could be dignified by such a name, was
over, and seeking out Sola I found her in our chariot with a hideous little
creature held tightly in her arms.

The work of rearing young, green Martians consists solely in teaching
them to talk, and to use the weapons of warfare with which they are loaded
down from the very first year of their lives. Coming from eggs in which
they have lain for five years, the period of incubation, they step forth into
the world perfectly developed except in size. Entirely unknown to their
mothers, who, in turn, would have difficulty in pointing out the fathers with
any degree of accuracy, they are the common children of the community,
and their education devolves upon the females who chance to capture them
as they leave the incubator.

Their foster mothers may not even have had an egg in the incubator,
as was the case with Sola, who had not commenced to lay, until less than
a year before she became the mother of another woman's offspring. But
this counts for little among the green Martians, as parental and filial love
is as unknown to them as it is common among us. I believe this horrible
system which has been carried on for ages is the direct cause of the loss of
all the finer feelings and higher humanitarian instincts among these poor
creatures. From birth they know no father or mother love, they know not
the meaning of the word home; they are taught that they are only suffered
to live until they can demonstrate by their physique and ferocity that they
are fit to live. Should they prove deformed or defective in any way they are
promptly shot; nor do they see a tear shed for a single one of the many
cruel hardships they pass through from earliest infancy.

I do not mean that the adult Martians are unnecessarily or intentionally
cruel to the young, but theirs is a hard and pitiless struggle for existence
upon a dying planet, the natural resources of which have dwindled to a
point where the support of each additional life means an added tax upon
the community into which it is thrown.

By careful selection they rear only the hardiest specimens of each species,
and with almost supernatural foresight they regulate the birth rate to merely
offset the loss by death. Each adult Martian female brings forth about
thirteen eggs each year, and those which meet the size, weight, and specific

gravity tests are hidden in the recesses of some subterranean vault where the temperature is too low for incubation. Every year these eggs are carefully examined by a council of twenty chieftains, and all but about one hundred of the most perfect are destroyed out of each yearly supply. At the end of five years about five hundred almost perfect eggs have been chosen from the thousands brought forth. These are then placed in the almost air-tight incubators to be hatched by the sun's rays after a period of another five years. The hatching which we had witnessed today was a fairly representative event of its kind, all but about one per cent of the eggs hatching in two days. If the remaining eggs ever hatched we knew nothing of the fate of the little Martians. They were not wanted, as their offspring might inherit and transmit the tendency to prolonged incubation, and thus upset the system which has maintained for ages and which permits the adult Martians to figure the proper time for return to the incubators, almost to an hour.

The incubators are built in remote fastnesses, where there is little or no likelihood of their being discovered by other tribes. The result of such a catastrophe would mean no children in the community for another five years. I was later to witness the results of the discovery of an alien incubator.

The community of which the green Martians with whom my lot was cast formed a part was composed of some thirty thousand souls. They roamed an enormous tract of arid and semi-arid land between forty and eighty degrees south latitude, and bounded on the east and west by two large fertile tracts. Their headquarters lay in the southwest corner of this district, near the crossing of two of the so-called Martian canals.

As the incubator had been placed far north of their own territory in a supposedly uninhabited and unfrequented area, we had before us a tremendous journey, concerning which I, of course, knew nothing.

After our return to the dead city I passed several days in comparative idleness. On the day following our return all the warriors had ridden forth early in the morning and had not returned until just before darkness fell. As I later learned, they had been to the subterranean vaults in which the eggs were kept and had transported them to the incubator, which they had then walled up for another five years, and which, in all probability, would not be visited again during that period.

The vaults which hid the eggs until they were ready for the incubator were located many miles south of the incubator, and would be visited yearly by the council of twenty chieftains. Why they did not arrange to build their vaults and incubators nearer home has always been a mystery to me, and, like many other Martian mysteries, unsolved and unsolvable by earthly reasoning and customs.

Sola's duties were now doubled, as she was compelled to care for the young Martian as well as for me, but neither one of us required much attention, and as we were both about equally advanced in Martian education, Sola took it upon herself to train us together.

Her prize consisted in a male about four feet tall, very strong and physically perfect; also, he learned quickly, and we had considerable amusement, at least I did, over the keen rivalry we displayed. The Martian language, as I have said, is extremely simple, and in a week I could make all my wants known and understand nearly everything that was said to me. Likewise, under Sola's tutelage, I developed my telepathic powers so that I shortly could sense practically everything that went on around me.

What surprised Sola most in me was that while I could catch telepathic messages easily from others, and often when they were not intended for me, no one could read a jot from my mind under any circumstances. At first this vexed me, but later I was very glad of it, as it gave me an undoubted advantage over the Martians.

EIGHT

A Fair Captive from the Sky

The third day after the incubator ceremony we set forth toward home, but scarcely had the head of the procession debouched into the open ground before the city than orders were given for an immediate and hasty return. As though trained for years in this particular evolution, the green Martians melted like mist into the spacious doorways of the nearby buildings, until, in less than three minutes, the entire cavalcade of chariots, mastodons and mounted warriors was nowhere to be seen.

Sola and I had entered a building upon the front of the city, in fact, the same one in which I had had my encounter with the apes, and, wishing to see what had caused the sudden retreat, I mounted to an upper floor and peered from the window out over the valley and the hills beyond; and there I saw the cause of their sudden scurrying to cover. A huge craft, long, low, and gray-painted, swung slowly over the crest of the nearest hill. Following it came another, and another, and another, until twenty of them, swinging low above the ground, sailed slowly and majestically toward us.

Each carried a strange banner swung from stem to stern above the upper works, and upon the prow of each was painted some odd device that gleamed in the sunlight and showed plainly even at the distance at which we were from the vessels. I could see figures crowding the forward decks and upper works of the air craft. Whether they had discovered us or simply were looking at the deserted city I could not say, but in any event they received a rude reception, for suddenly and without warning the green Martian warriors fired a terrific volley from the windows of the buildings facing the little valley across which the great ships were so peacefully advancing.

Instantly the scene changed as by magic; the foremost vessel swung broadside toward us, and bringing her guns into play returned our fire, at the same time moving parallel to our front for a short distance and then turning back with the evident intention of completing a great circle which would bring her up to position once more opposite our firing line; the other vessels followed in her wake, each one opening upon us as she swung into position. Our own fire never diminished, and I doubt if twenty-five per cent of our shots went wild. It had never been given me to see such deadly accuracy of aim, and it seemed as though a little figure on one of the craft dropped at the explosion of each bullet, while the banners and upper works dissolved in spurts of flame as the irresistible projectiles of our warriors mowed through them.

The fire from the vessels was most ineffectual, owing, as I afterward learned, to the unexpected suddenness of the first volley, which caught the ship's crews entirely unprepared and the sighting apparatus of the guns unprotected from the deadly aim of our warriors.

It seems that each green warrior has certain objective points for his fire under relatively identical circumstances of warfare. For example, a proportion of them, always the best marksmen, direct their fire entirely upon the wireless finding and sighting apparatus of the big guns of an attacking naval force; another detail attends to the smaller guns in the same way; others pick off the gunners; still others the officers; while certain other quotas concentrate their attention upon the other members of the crew, upon the upper works, and upon the steering gear and propellers.

Twenty minutes after the first volley the great fleet swung trailing off in the direction from which it had first appeared. Several of the craft were limping perceptibly, and seemed but barely under the control of their depleted crews. Their fire had ceased entirely and all their energies seemed focused upon escape. Our warriors then rushed up to the roofs of the buildings which we occupied and followed the retreating armada with a continuous fusillade of deadly fire.

One by one, however, the ships managed to dip below the crests of the outlying hills until only one barely moving craft was in sight. This had received the brunt of our fire and seemed to be entirely unmanned, as not a moving figure was visible upon her decks. Slowly she swung from her course, circling back toward us in an erratic and pitiful manner. Instantly the warriors ceased firing, for it was quite apparent that the vessel was entirely helpless, and, far from being in a position to inflict harm upon us, she could not even control herself sufficiently to escape.

As she neared the city the warriors rushed out upon the plain to meet her, but it was evident that she still was too high for them to hope to reach her decks. From my vantage point in the window I could see the bodies of her crew strewn about, although I could not make out what manner of creatures they might be. Not a sign of life was manifest upon her as she drifted slowly with the light breeze in a southeasterly direction.

She was drifting some fifty feet above the ground, followed by all but some hundred of the warriors who had been ordered back to the roofs to cover the possibility of a return of the fleet, or of reinforcements. It soon became evident that she would strike the face of the buildings about a mile south of our position, and as I watched the progress of the chase I saw a number of warriors gallop ahead, dismount and enter the building she seemed destined to touch.

As the craft neared the building, and just before she struck, the Martian warriors swarmed upon her from the windows, and with their great spears eased the shock of the collision, and in a few moments they had thrown out grappling hooks and the big boat was being hauled to ground by their fellows below.

After making her fast, they swarmed the sides and searched the vessel from stem to stern. I could see them examining the dead sailors, evidently for signs of life, and presently a party of them appeared from below dragging a little figure among them. The creature was considerably less than half as tall as the green Martian warriors, and from my balcony I could see that it walked erect upon two legs and surmised that it was some new and strange Martian monstrosity with which I had not as yet become acquainted.

They removed their prisoner to the ground and then commenced a systematic rifling of the vessel. This operation required several hours, during which time a number of the chariots were requisitioned to transport the loot, which consisted in arms, ammunition, silks, furs, jewels, strangely carved stone vessels, and a quantity of solid foods and liquids, including many casks of water, the first I had seen since my advent upon Mars.

After the last load had been removed the warriors made lines fast to the craft and towed her far out into the valley in a southwesterly direction. A few of them then boarded her and were busily engaged in what appeared, from my distant position, as the emptying of the contents of various carboys upon the dead bodies of the sailors and over the decks and works of the vessel.

This operation concluded, they hastily clambered over her sides, sliding down the guy ropes to the ground. The last warrior to leave the deck turned and threw something back upon the vessel, waiting an instant to note the outcome of his act. As a faint spurt of flame rose from the point where the missile struck he swung over the side and was quickly upon the ground. Scarcely had he alighted than the guy ropes were simultaneous released, and the great warship, lightened by the removal of the loot, soared majestically into the air, her decks and upper works a mass of roaring flames.

Slowly she drifted to the southeast, rising higher and higher as the flames ate away her wooden parts and diminished the weight upon her. Ascending to the roof of the building I watched her for hours, until finally she was lost in the dim vistas of the distance. The sight was awe-inspiring in the extreme as one contemplated this mighty floating funeral pyre, drifting unguided and unmanned through the lonely wastes of the Martian heavens; a derelict of death and destruction, typifying the life story of these strange and ferocious creatures into whose unfriendly hands fate had carried it.

Much depressed, and, to me, unaccountably so, I slowly descended to the street. The scene I had witnessed seemed to mark the defeat and annihilation of the forces of a kindred people, rather than the routing by our green warriors of a horde of similar, though unfriendly, creatures. I could not fathom the seeming hallucination, nor could I free myself from it; but somewhere in the innermost recesses of my soul I felt a strange yearning toward these unknown foemen, and a mighty hope surged through me that the fleet would return and demand a reckoning from the green warriors who had so ruthlessly and wantonly attacked it.

Close at my heel, in his now accustomed place, followed Woola, the hound, and as I emerged upon the street Sola rushed up to me as though I had been the object of some search on her part. The cavalcade was returning to the plaza, the homeward march having been given up for that day; nor, in fact, was it recommenced for more than a week, owing to the fear of a return attack by the air craft.

Lorquas Ptomel was too astute an old warrior to be caught upon the open plains with a caravan of chariots and children, and so we remained at the deserted city until the danger seemed passed.

As Sola and I entered the plaza a sight met my eyes which filled my whole being with a great surge of mingled hope, fear, exultation, and depression, and yet most dominant was a subtle sense of relief and happiness; for just as we neared the throng of Martians I caught a glimpse of the prisoner from the battle craft who was being roughly dragged into a nearby building by a couple of green Martian females.

And the sight which met my eyes was that of a slender, girlish figure, similar in every detail to the earthly women of my past life. She did not see me at first, but just as she was disappearing through the portal of the building which was to be her prison she turned, and her eyes met mine. Her face was oval and beautiful in the extreme, her every feature was finely chiseled and exquisite, her eyes large and lustrous and her head surmounted by a mass of coal black, waving hair, caught loosely into a strange yet becoming coiffure. Her skin was of a light reddish copper color,

against which the crimson glow of her cheeks and the ruby of her beautifully
molded lips shone with a strangely enhancing effect.

She was as destitute of clothes as the green Martians who accompanied her; indeed, save for her highly wrought ornaments she was entirely
naked, nor could any apparel have enhanced the beauty of her perfect and
symmetrical figure.

As her gaze rested on me her eyes opened wide in astonishment, and
she made a little sign with her free hand; a sign which I did not, of
course, understand. Just a moment we gazed upon each other, and then
the look of hope and renewed courage which had glorified her face as she
discovered me, faded into one of utter dejection, mingled with loathing
and contempt. I realized I had not answered her signal, and ignorant as I
was of Martian customs, I intuitively felt that she had made an appeal for
succor and protection which my unfortunate ignorance had prevented me
from answering. And then she was dragged out of my sight into the depths
of the deserted edifice.

NINE

I Learn the Language

As I came back to myself I glanced at Sola, who had witnessed this encounter and I was surprised to note a strange expression upon her usually expressionless countenance. What her thoughts were I did not know, for as yet I had learned but little of the Martian tongue; enough only to suffice for my daily needs.

As I reached the doorway of our building a strange surprise awaited me. A warrior approached bearing the arms, ornaments, and full accouterments of his kind. These he presented to me with a few unintelligible words, and a bearing at once respectful and menacing.

Later, Sola, with the aid of several of the other women, remodeled the trappings to fit my lesser proportions, and after they completed the work I went about garbed in all the panoply of war.

From then on Sola instructed me in the mysteries of the various weapons, and with the Martian young I spent several hours each day practicing upon the plaza. I was not yet proficient with all the weapons, but my great familiarity with similar earthly weapons made me an unusually apt pupil, and I progressed in a very satisfactory manner.

The training of myself and the young Martians was conducted solely by the women, who not only attend to the education of the young in the arts of individual defense and offense, but are also the artisans who produce every manufactured article wrought by the green Martians. They make the powder, the cartridges, the firearms; in fact everything of value is produced by the females. In time of actual warfare they form a part of the reserves, and when the necessity arises fight with even greater intelligence and ferocity than the men.

The men are trained in the higher branches of the art of war; in strategy and the maneuvering of large bodies of troops. They make the laws as they are needed; a new law for each emergency. They are unfettered by precedent in the administration of justice. Customs have been handed down by ages of repetition, but the punishment for ignoring a custom is a matter for individual treatment by a jury of the culprit's peers, and I may say that justice seldom misses fire, but seems rather to rule in inverse ratio to the ascendency of law. In one respect at least the Martians are a happy people; they have no lawyers.

I did not see the prisoner again for several days subsequent to our first encounter, and then only to catch a fleeting glimpse of her as she was being conducted to the great audience chamber where I had had my first meeting with Lorquas Ptomel. I could not but note the unnecessary harshness and brutality with which her guards treated her; so different from the almost maternal kindliness which Sola manifested toward me, and the respectful attitude of the few green Martians who took the trouble to notice me at all.

I had observed on the two occasions when I had seen her that the prisoner exchanged words with her guards, and this convinced me that they spoke, or at least could make themselves understood by a common language. With this added incentive I nearly drove Sola distracted by my importunities to hasten on my education and within a few more days I had mastered the Martian tongue sufficiently well to enable me to carry on a passable conversation and to fully understand practically all that I heard.

At this time our sleeping quarters were occupied by three or four females and a couple of the recently hatched young, beside Sola and her youthful ward, myself, and Woola the hound. After they had retired for the night it was customary for the adults to carry on a desultory conversation for a short time before lapsing into sleep, and now that I could understand their language I was always a keen listener, although I never proffered any remarks myself.

On the night following the prisoner's visit to the audience chamber the conversation finally fell upon this subject, and I was all ears on the instant. I had feared to question Sola relative to the beautiful captive, as I could not but recall the strange expression I had noted upon her face after my first encounter with the prisoner. That it denoted jealousy I could not say, and yet, judging all things by mundane standards as I still did, I felt it safer to affect indifference in the matter until I learned more surely Sola's attitude toward the object of my solicitude.

Sarkoja, one of the older women who shared our domicile, had been present at the audience as one of the captive's guards, and it was toward her the questioners turned.

"When," asked one of the women, "will we enjoy the death throes of the red one? or does Lorquas Ptomel, Jed, intend holding her for ransom?"

"They have decided to carry her with us back to Thark, and exhibit her last agonies at the great games before Tal Hajus," replied Sarkoja.

"What will be the manner of her going out?" inquired Sola. "She is very small and very beautiful; I had hoped that they would hold her for ransom."

Sarkoja and the other women grunted angrily at this evidence of weakness on the part of Sola.

"It is sad, Sola, that you were not born a million years ago," snapped Sarkoja, "when all the hollows of the land were filled with water, and the peoples were as soft as the stuff they sailed upon. In our day we have progressed to a point where such sentiments mark weakness and atavism. It will not be well for you to permit Tars Tarkas to learn that you hold such degenerate sentiments, as I doubt that he would care to entrust such as you with the grave responsibilities of maternity."

"I see nothing wrong with my expression of interest in this red woman," retorted Sola. "She has never harmed us, nor would she should we have fallen into her hands. It is only the men of her kind who war upon us, and I have ever thought that their attitude toward us is but the reflection of ours toward them. They live at peace with all their fellows, except when duty calls upon them to make war, while we are at peace with none; forever warring among our own kind as well as upon the red men, and even in our own communities the individuals fight amongst themselves. Oh, it is one continual, awful period of bloodshed from the time we break the shell until we gladly embrace the bosom of the river of mystery, the dark and ancient Iss which carries us to an unknown, but at least no more frightful and terrible existence! Fortunate indeed is he who meets his end in an early death. Say what you please to Tars Tarkas, he can mete out no worse fate to me than a continuation of the horrible existence we are forced to lead in this life."

This wild outbreak on the part of Sola so greatly surprised and shocked the other women, that, after a few words of general reprimand, they all lapsed into silence and were soon asleep. One thing the episode had accomplished was to assure me of Sola's friendliness toward the poor girl, and also to convince me that I had been extremely fortunate in falling into her hands rather than those of some of the other females. I knew that she was fond of me, and now that I had discovered that she hated cruelty and barbarity I was confident that I could depend upon her to aid me and the girl captive to escape, provided of course that such a thing was within the range of possibilities.

I did not even know that there were any better conditions to escape to, but I was more than willing to take my chances among people fashioned after my own mold rather than to remain longer among the hideous and bloodthirsty green men of Mars. But where to go, and how, was as much of a puzzle to me as the age-old search for the spring of eternal life has been to earthly men since the beginning of time.

I decided that at the first opportunity I would take Sola into my confidence and openly ask her to aid me, and with this resolution strong upon me I turned among my silks and furs and slept the dreamless and refreshing sleep of Mars.

TEN

Champion and Chief

Early the next morning I was astir. Considerable freedom was allowed me, as Sola had informed me that so long as I did not attempt to leave the city I was free to go and come as I pleased. She had warned me, however, against venturing forth unarmed, as this city, like all other deserted metropolises of an ancient Martian civilization, was peopled by the great white apes of my second day's adventure.

In advising me that I must not leave the boundaries of the city Sola had explained that Woola would prevent this anyway should I attempt it, and she warned me most urgently not to arouse his fierce nature by ignoring his warnings should I venture too close to the forbidden territory. His nature was such, she said, that he would bring me back into the city dead or alive should I persist in opposing him; "preferably dead," she added.

On this morning I had chosen a new street to explore when suddenly I found myself at the limits of the city. Before me were low hills pierced by narrow and inviting ravines. I longed to explore the country before me, and, like the pioneer stock from which I sprang, to view what the landscape beyond the encircling hills might disclose from the summits which shut out my view.

It also occurred to me that this would prove an excellent opportunity to test the qualities of Woola. I was convinced that the brute loved me; I had seen more evidences of affection in him than in any other Martian animal, man or beast, and I was sure that gratitude for the acts that had twice saved his life would more than outweigh his loyalty to the duty imposed upon him by cruel and loveless masters.

As I approached the boundary line Woola ran anxiously before me, and thrust his body against my legs. His expression was pleading rather than ferocious, nor did he bare his great tusks or utter his fearful guttural warnings. Denied the friendship and companionship of my kind, I had developed considerable affection for Woola and Sola, for the normal earthly man must have some outlet for his natural affections, and so I decided upon an appeal to a like instinct in this great brute, sure that I would not be disappointed.

I had never petted nor fondled him, but now I sat upon the ground and putting my arms around his heavy neck I stroked and coaxed him, talking in my newly acquired Martian tongue as I would have to my hound at home, as I would have talked to any other friend among the lower animals. His response to my manifestation of affection was remarkable to a degree; he stretched his great mouth to its full width, baring the entire expanse of his upper rows of tusks and wrinkling his snout until his great eyes were almost hidden by the folds of flesh. If you have ever seen a collie smile you may have some idea of Woola's facial distortion.

He threw himself upon his back and fairly wallowed at my feet; jumped up and sprang upon me, rolling me upon the ground by his great weight; then wriggling and squirming around me like a playful puppy presenting its back for the petting it craves. I could not resist the ludicrousness of the spectacle, and holding my sides I rocked back and forth in the first laughter which had passed my lips in many days; the first, in fact, since the morning Powell had left camp when his horse, long unused, had precipitately and unexpectedly bucked him off headforemost into a pot of frijoles.

My laughter frightened Woola, his antics ceased and he crawled pitifully toward me, poking his ugly head far into my lap; and then I remembered what laughter signified on Mars—torture, suffering, death. Quieting myself, I rubbed the poor old fellow's head and back, talked to him for a few minutes, and then in an authoritative tone commanded him to follow me, and arising started for the hills.

There was no further question of authority between us; Woola was my devoted slave from that moment hence, and I his only and undisputed master. My walk to the hills occupied but a few minutes, and I found nothing of particular interest to reward me. Numerous brilliantly colored and strangely formed wild flowers dotted the ravines and from the summit of the first hill I saw still other hills stretching off toward the north, and rising, one range above another, until lost in mountains of quite respectable dimensions; though I afterward found that only a few peaks on all Mars exceed four thousand feet in height; the suggestion of magnitude was merely relative.

My morning's walk had been large with importance to me for it had resulted in a perfect understanding with Woola, upon whom Tars Tarkas relied for my safe keeping. I now knew that while theoretically a prisoner

I was virtually free, and I hastened to regain the city limits before the defection of Woola could be discovered by his erstwhile masters. The adventure decided me never again to leave the limits of my prescribed stamping grounds until I was ready to venture forth for good and all, as it would certainly result in a curtailment of my liberties, as well as the probable death of Woola, were we to be discovered.

On regaining the plaza I had my third glimpse of the captive girl. She was standing with her guards before the entrance to the audience chamber, and as I approached she gave me one haughty glance and turned her back full upon me. The act was so womanly, so earthly womanly, that though it stung my pride it also warmed my heart with a feeling of companionship; it was good to know that someone else on Mars beside myself had human instincts of a civilized order, even though the manifestation of them was so painful and mortifying.

Had a green Martian woman desired to show dislike or contempt she would, in all likelihood, have done it with a sword thrust or a movement of her trigger finger; but as their sentiments are mostly atrophied it would have required a serious injury to have aroused such passions in them. Sola, let me add, was an exception; I never saw her perform a cruel or uncouth act, or fail in uniform kindliness and good nature. She was indeed, as her fellow Martian had said of her, an atavism; a dear and precious reversion to a former type of loved and loving ancestor.

Seeing that the prisoner seemed the center of attraction I halted to view the proceedings. I had not long to wait for presently Lorquas Ptomel and his retinue of chieftains approached the building and, signing the guards to follow with the prisoner, entered the audience chamber. Realizing that I was a somewhat favored character, and also convinced that the warriors did not know of my proficiency in their language, as I had pleaded with Sola to keep this a secret on the grounds that I did not wish to be forced to talk with the men until I had perfectly mastered the Martian tongue, I chanced an attempt to enter the audience chamber and listen to the proceedings.

The council squatted upon the steps of the rostrum, while below them stood the prisoner and her two guards. I saw that one of the women was Sarkoja, and thus understood how she had been present at the hearing of the preceding day, the results of which she had reported to the occupants of our dormitory last night. Her attitude toward the captive was most harsh and brutal. When she held her, she sunk her rudimentary nails into the poor girl's flesh, or twisted her arm in a most painful manner. When it was necessary to move from one spot to another she either jerked her roughly, or pushed her headlong before her. She seemed to be venting upon this poor defenseless creature all the hatred, cruelty, ferocity, and spite of her nine hundred years, backed by unguessable ages of fierce and brutal ancestors.

The other woman was less cruel because she was entirely indifferent; if the prisoner had been left to her alone, and fortunately she was at night, she would have received no harsh treatment, nor, by the same token would she have received any attention at all.

As Lorquas Ptomel raised his eyes to address the prisoner they fell on me and he turned to Tars Tarkas with a word, and gesture of impatience. Tars Tarkas made some reply which I could not catch, but which caused Lorquas Ptomel to smile; after which they paid no further attention to me.

"What is your name?" asked Lorquas Ptomel, addressing the prisoner.

"Dejah Thoris, daughter of Mors Kajak of Helium."

"And the nature of your expedition?" he continued.

"It was a purely scientific research party sent out by my father's father, the Jeddak of Helium, to rechart the air currents, and to take atmospheric density tests," replied the fair prisoner, in a low, well-modulated voice.

"We were unprepared for battle," she continued, "as we were on a peaceful mission, as our banners and the colors of our craft denoted. The work we were doing was as much in your interests as in ours, for you know full well that were it not for our labors and the fruits of our scientific operations there would not be enough air or water on Mars to support a single human life. For ages we have maintained the air and water supply at practically the same point without an appreciable loss, and we have done this in the face of the brutal and ignorant interference of your green men.

"Why, oh, why will you not learn to live in amity with your fellows, must you ever go on down the ages to your final extinction but little above the plane of the dumb brutes that serve you! A people without written language, without art, without homes, without love; the victim of eons of the horrible community idea. Owning everything in common, even to your women and children, has resulted in your owning nothing in common. You hate each other as you hate all else except yourselves. Come back to the ways of our common ancestors, come back to the light of kindliness and fellowship. The way is open to you, you will find the hands of the red men stretched out to aid you. Together we may do still more to regenerate our dying planet. The granddaughter of the greatest and mightiest of the red jeddaks has asked you. Will you come?"

Lorquas Ptomel and the warriors sat looking silently and intently at the young woman for several moments after she had ceased speaking. What was passing in their minds no man may know, but that they were moved I truly believe, and if one man high among them had been strong enough to rise above custom, that moment would have marked a new and mighty era for Mars.

I saw Tars Tarkas rise to speak, and on his face was such an expression as I had never seen upon the countenance of a green Martian warrior. It bespoke an inward and mighty battle with self, with heredity, with age-old custom, and as he opened his mouth to speak, a look almost of benignity, of kindliness, momentarily lighted up his fierce and terrible countenance.

What words of moment were to have fallen from his lips were never spoken, as just then a young warrior, evidently sensing the trend of thought among the older men, leaped down from the steps of the rostrum, and striking the frail captive a powerful blow across the face, which felled her to the floor, placed his foot upon her prostrate form and turning toward the assembled council broke into peals of horrid, mirthless laughter.

For an instant I thought Tars Tarkas would strike him dead, nor did the aspect of Lorquas Ptomel augur any too favorably for the brute, but the mood passed, their old selves reasserted their ascendency, and they smiled. It was portentous however that they did not laugh aloud, for the brute's act constituted a side-splitting witticism according to the ethics which rule green Martian humor.

That I have taken moments to write down a part of what occurred as that blow fell does not signify that I remained inactive for any such length of time. I think I must have sensed something of what was coming, for I realize now that I was crouched as for a spring as I saw the blow aimed at her beautiful, upturned, pleading face, and ere the hand descended I was halfway across the hall.

Scarcely had his hideous laugh rang out but once, when I was upon him. The brute was twelve feet in height and armed to the teeth, but I believe that I could have accounted for the whole roomful in the terrific intensity of my rage. Springing upward, I struck him full in the face as he turned at my warning cry and then as he drew his short-sword I drew mine and sprang up again upon his breast, hooking one leg over the butt of his pistol and grasping one of his huge tusks with my left hand while I delivered blow after blow upon his enormous chest.

He could not use his short-sword to advantage because I was too close to him, nor could he draw his pistol, which he attempted to do in direct opposition to Martian custom which says that you may not fight a fellow warrior in private combat with any other than the weapon with which you are attacked. In fact he could do nothing but make a wild and futile attempt to dislodge me. With all his immense bulk he was little if any stronger than

I, and it was but the matter of a moment or two before he sank, bleeding and lifeless, to the floor.

Dejah Thoris had raised herself upon one elbow and was watching the battle with wide, staring eyes. When I had regained my feet I raised her in my arms and bore her to one of the benches at the side of the room.

Again no Martian interfered with me, and tearing a piece of silk from my cape I endeavored to staunch the flow of blood from her nostrils. I was soon successful as her injuries amounted to little more than an ordinary nosebleed, and when she could speak she placed her hand upon my arm and looking up into my eyes, said:

"Why did you do it? You who refused me even friendly recognition in the first hour of my peril! And now you risk your life and kill one of your companions for my sake. I cannot understand. What strange manner of man are you, that you consort with the green men, though your form is that of my race, while your color is little darker than that of the white ape? Tell me, are you human, or are you more than human?"

"It is a strange tale," I replied, "too long to attempt to tell you now, and one which I so much doubt the credibility of myself that I fear to hope that others will believe it. Suffice it, for the present, that I am your friend, and, so far as our captors will permit, your protector and your servant."

"Then you too are a prisoner? But why, then, those arms and the regalia of a Tharkian chieftain? What is your name? Where your country?"

"Yes, Dejah Thoris, I too am a prisoner; my name is John Carter, and I claim Virginia, one of the United States of America, Earth, as my home; but why I am permitted to wear arms I do not know, nor was I aware that my regalia was that of a chieftain."

We were interrupted at this juncture by the approach of one of the warriors, bearing arms, accouterments and ornaments, and in a flash one of her questions was answered and a puzzle cleared up for me. I saw that the body of my dead antagonist had been stripped, and I read in the menacing yet respectful attitude of the warrior who had brought me these trophies of the kill the same demeanor as that evinced by the other who had brought me my original equipment, and now for the first time I realized that my blow, on the occasion of my first battle in the audience chamber had resulted in the death of my adversary.

The reason for the whole attitude displayed toward me was now apparent; I had won my spurs, so to speak, and in the crude justice, which always marks Martian dealings, and which, among other things, has caused me to call her the planet of paradoxes, I was accorded the honors due a conqueror; the trappings and the position of the man I killed. In truth, I was a Martian chieftain, and this I learned later was the cause of my great freedom and my toleration in the audience chamber.

As I had turned to receive the dead warrior's chattels I had noticed that Tars Tarkas and several others had pushed forward toward us, and the eyes of the former rested upon me in a most quizzical manner. Finally he addressed me:

"You speak the tongue of Barsoom quite readily for one who was deaf and dumb to us a few short days ago. Where did you learn it, John Carter?"

"You, yourself, are responsible, Tars Tarkas," I replied, "in that you furnished me with an instructress of remarkable ability; I have to thank Sola for my learning."

"She has done well," he answered, "but your education in other respects needs considerable polish. Do you know what your unprecedented temerity would have cost you had you failed to kill either of the two chieftains whose metal you now wear?"

"I presume that that one whom I had failed to kill, would have killed me," I answered, smiling.

"No, you are wrong. Only in the last extremity of self-defense would a Martian warrior kill a prisoner; we like to save them for other purposes," and his face bespoke possibilities that were not pleasant to dwell upon.

"But one thing can save you now," he continued. "Should you, in recognition of your remarkable valor, ferocity, and prowess, be considered by Tal Hajus as worthy of his service you may be taken into the community and become a full-fledged Tharkian. Until we reach the headquarters of Tal Hajus it is the will of Lorquas Ptomel that you be accorded the respect your acts have earned you. You will be treated by us as a Tharkian chieftain, but you must not forget that every chief who ranks you is responsible for your safe delivery to our mighty and most ferocious ruler. I am done."

"I hear you, Tars Tarkas," I answered. "As you know I am not of Barsoom; your ways are not my ways, and I can only act in the future as I have in the past, in accordance with the dictates of my conscience and guided by the standards of mine own people. If you will leave me alone I will go in peace, but if not, let the individual Barsoomians with whom I must deal either respect my rights as a stranger among you, or take whatever consequences may befall. Of one thing let us be sure, whatever may be your ultimate intentions toward this unfortunate young woman, whoever would offer her injury or insult in the future must figure on making a full accounting to me. I understand that you belittle all sentiments of generosity and kindliness, but I do not, and I can convince your most doughty warrior that these characteristics are not incompatible with an ability to fight."

Ordinarily I am not given to long speeches, nor ever before had I descended to bombast, but I had guessed at the keynote which would strike an answering chord in the breasts of the green Martians, nor was I wrong, for my harangue evidently deeply impressed them, and their attitude toward me thereafter was still further respectful.

Tars Tarkas himself seemed pleased with my reply, but his only comment was more or less enigmatical—"And I think I know Tal Hajus, Jeddak of Thark."

I now turned my attention to Dejah Thoris, and assisting her to her feet I turned with her toward the exit, ignoring her hovering guardian harpies as well as the inquiring glances of the chieftains. Was I not now a chieftain also! Well, then, I would assume the responsibilities of one. They did not molest us, and so Dejah Thoris, Princess of Helium, and John Carter, gentleman of Virginia, followed by the faithful Woola, passed through utter silence from the audience chamber of Lorquas Ptomel, Jed among the Tharks of Barsoom.

ELEVEN

With Dejah Thoris

As we reached the open the two female guards who had been detailed to watch over Dejah Thoris hurried up and made as though to assume custody of her once more. The poor child shrank against me and I felt her two little hands fold tightly over my arm. Waving the women away, I informed them that Sola would attend the captive hereafter, and I further warned Sarkoja that any more of her cruel attentions bestowed upon Dejah Thoris would result in Sarkoja's sudden and painful demise.

My threat was unfortunate and resulted in more harm than good to Dejah Thoris, for, as I learned later, men do not kill women upon Mars, nor women, men. So Sarkoja merely gave us an ugly look and departed to hatch up deviltries against us.

I soon found Sola and explained to her that I wished her to guard Dejah Thoris as she had guarded me; that I wished her to find other quarters where they would not be molested by Sarkoja, and I finally informed her that I myself would take up my quarters among the men.

Sola glanced at the accouterments which were carried in my hand and slung across my shoulder.

"You are a great chieftain now, John Carter," she said, "and I must do your bidding, though indeed I am glad to do it under any circumstances. The man whose metal you carry was young, but he was a great warrior, and had by his promotions and kills won his way close to the rank of Tars Tarkas, who, as you know, is second to Lorquas Ptomel only. You are eleventh, there are but ten chieftains in this community who rank you in prowess."

"And if I should kill Lorquas Ptomel?" I asked.

"You would be first, John Carter; but you may only win that honor by the will of the entire council that Lorquas Ptomel meet you in combat, or should he attack you, you may kill him in self-defense, and thus win first place."

I laughed, and changed the subject. I had no particular desire to kill Lorquas Ptomel, and less to be a jed among the Tharks.

I accompanied Sola and Dejah Thoris in a search for new quarters, which we found in a building nearer the audience chamber and of far more pretentious architecture than our former habitation. We also found in this building real sleeping apartments with ancient beds of highly wrought metal swinging from enormous gold chains depending from the marble ceilings. The decoration of the walls was most elaborate, and, unlike the frescoes in the other buildings I had examined, portrayed many human figures in the compositions. These were of people like myself, and of a much lighter color than Dejah Thoris. They were clad in graceful, flowing robes, highly ornamented with metal and jewels, and their luxuriant hair was of a beautiful golden and reddish bronze. The men were beardless and only a few wore arms. The scenes depicted for the most part, a fair-skinned, fair-haired people at play.

Dejah Thoris clasped her hands with an exclamation of rapture as she gazed upon these magnificent works of art, wrought by a people long extinct; while Sola, on the other hand, apparently did not see them.

We decided to use this room, on the second floor and overlooking the plaza, for Dejah Thoris and Sola, and another room adjoining and in the rear for the cooking and supplies. I then dispatched Sola to bring the bedding and such food and utensils as she might need, telling her that I would guard Dejah Thoris until her return.

As Sola departed Dejah Thoris turned to me with a faint smile.

"And whereto, then, would your prisoner escape should you leave her, unless it was to follow you and crave your protection, and ask your pardon for the cruel thoughts she has harbored against you these past few days?"

"You are right," I answered, "there is no escape for either of us unless we go together."

"I heard your challenge to the creature you call Tars Tarkas, and I think I understand your position among these people, but what I cannot fathom is your statement that you are not of Barsoom."

"In the name of my first ancestor, then," she continued, "where may you be from? You are like unto my people, and yet so unlike. You speak my language, and yet I heard you tell Tars Tarkas that you had but learned it recently. All Barsoomians speak the same tongue from the ice-clad south to the ice-clad north, though their written languages differ. Only in the valley Dor, where the river Iss empties into the lost sea of Korus, is there supposed to be a different language spoken, and, except in the legends of our ancestors, there is no record of a Barsoomian returning up the river Iss, from the shores of Korus in the valley of Dor. Do not tell me that you have thus returned! They would kill you horribly anywhere upon the surface of Barsoom if that were true; tell me it is not!"

Her eyes were filled with a strange, weird light; her voice was pleading, and her little hands, reached up upon my breast, were pressed against me as though to wring a denial from my very heart.

"I do not know your customs, Dejah Thoris, but in my own Virginia a gentleman does not lie to save himself; I am not of Dor; I have never seen the mysterious Iss; the lost sea of Korus is still lost, so far as I am concerned. Do you believe me?"

And then it struck me suddenly that I was very anxious that she should believe me. It was not that I feared the results which would follow a general belief that I had returned from the Barsoomian heaven or hell, or whatever it was. Why was it, then! Why should I care what she thought? I looked down at her; her beautiful face upturned, and her wonderful eyes opening up the very depth of her soul; and as my eyes met hers I knew why, and—I shuddered.

A similar wave of feeling seemed to stir her; she drew away from me with a sigh, and with her earnest, beautiful face turned up to mine, she whispered: "I believe you, John Carter; I do not know what a 'gentleman' is, nor have I ever heard before of Virginia; but on Barsoom no *man* lies; if he does not wish to speak the truth he is silent. Where is this Virginia, your country, John Carter?" she asked, and it seemed that this fair name of my fair land had never sounded more beautiful than as it fell from those perfect lips on that far-gone day.

"I am of another world," I answered, "the great planet Earth, which revolves about our common sun and next within the orbit of your Barsoom, which we know as Mars. How I came here I cannot tell you, for I do not know; but here I am, and since my presence has permitted me to serve Dejah Thoris I am glad that I am here."

She gazed at me with troubled eyes, long and questioningly. That it was difficult to believe my statement I well knew, nor could I hope that she would do so however much I craved her confidence and respect. I would much rather not have told her anything of my antecedents, but no man could look into the depth of those eyes and refuse her slightest behest.

Finally she smiled, and, rising, said: "I shall have to believe even though I cannot understand. I can readily perceive that you are not of the Barsoom of today; you are like us, yet different—but why should I trouble my poor head with such a problem, when my heart tells me that I believe because I wish to believe!"

It was good logic, good, earthly, feminine logic, and if it satisfied her I certainly could pick no flaws in it. As a matter of fact it was about the only kind of logic that could be brought to bear upon my problem. We fell into a general conversation then, asking and answering many questions on each side. She was curious to learn of the customs of my people and displayed a remarkable knowledge of events on Earth. When I questioned her closely on this seeming familiarity with earthly things she laughed, and cried out:

"Why, every school boy on Barsoom knows the geography,and much concerning the fauna and flora, as well as the history of your planet fully as well as of his own. Can we not see everything which takes place upon Earth, as you call it; is it not hanging there in the heavens in plain sight?"

This baffled me, I must confess, fully as much as my statements had confounded her; and I told her so. She then explained in general the instruments her people had used and been perfecting for ages, which permit them to throw upon a screen a perfect image of what is transpiring upon any planet and upon many of the stars. These pictures are so perfect in detail that, when photographed and enlarged, objects no greater than a blade of grass may be distinctly recognized. I afterward, in Helium, saw many of these pictures, as well as the instruments which produced them.

"If, then, you are so familiar with earthly things," I asked, "why is it that you do not recognize me as identical with the inhabitants of that planet?"

She smiled again as one might in bored indulgence of a questioning child.

"Because, John Carter," she replied, "nearly every planet and star having atmospheric conditions at all approaching those of Barsoom, shows forms of animal life almost identical with you and me; and, further, Earth men, almost without exception, cover their bodies with strange, unsightly pieces of cloth, and their heads with hideous contraptions the purpose of which we have been unable to conceive; while you, when found by the Tharkian warriors, were entirely undisfigured and unadorned.

"The fact that you wore no ornaments is a strong proof of your un-Barsoomian origin, while the absence of grotesque coverings might cause a doubt as to your earthliness."

I then narrated the details of my departure from the Earth, explaining that my body there lay fully clothed in all the, to her, strange garments of mundane dwellers. At this point Sola returned with our meager belongings and her young Martian protege, who, of course, would have to share the quarters with them.

Sola asked us if we had had a visitor during her absence, and seemed much surprised when we answered in the negative. It seemed that as she had mounted the approach to the upper floors where our quarters were located, she had met Sarkoja descending. We decided that she must have been eavesdropping, but as we could recall nothing of importance that had passed between us we dismissed the matter as of little consequence, merely promising ourselves to be warned to the utmost caution in the future.

Dejah Thoris and I then fell to examining the architecture and decorations of the beautiful chambers of the building we were occupying. She told me that these people had presumably flourished over a hundred thousand years before. They were the early progenitors of her race, but had mixed with the other great race of early Martians, who were very dark, almost black, and also with the reddish yellow race which had flourished at the same time.

These three great divisions of the higher Martians had been forced into a mighty alliance as the drying up of the Martian seas had compelled them to seek the comparatively few and always diminishing fertile areas, and to defend themselves, under new conditions of life, against the wild hordes of green men.

Ages of close relationship and intermarrying had resulted in the race of red men, of which Dejah Thoris was a fair and beautiful daughter. During the ages of hardships and incessant warring between their own various races, as well as with the green men, and before they had fitted themselves to the changed conditions, much of the high civilization and many of the arts of the fair-haired Martians had become lost; but the red race of today has reached a point where it feels that it has made up in new discoveries and in a more practical civilization for all that lies irretrievably buried with the ancient Barsoomians, beneath the countless intervening ages.

These ancient Martians had been a highly cultivated and literary race, but during the vicissitudes of those trying centuries of readjustment to new conditions, not only did their advancement and production cease entirely, but practically all their archives, records, and literature were lost.

Dejah Thoris related many interesting facts and legends concerning this lost race of noble and kindly people. She said that the city in which we were camping was supposed to have been a center of commerce and culture known as Korad. It had been built upon a beautiful, natural harbor, landlocked by magnificent hills. The little valley on the west front of the city, she explained, was all that remained of the harbor, while the pass through the hills to the old sea bottom had been the channel through which the shipping passed up to the city's gates.

The shores of the ancient seas were dotted with just such cities, and lesser ones, in diminishing numbers, were to be found converging toward the center of the oceans, as the people had found it necessary to follow the receding waters until necessity had forced upon them their ultimate salvation, the so-called Martian canals.

We had been so engrossed in exploration of the building and in our conversation that it was late in the afternoon before we realized it. We were brought back to a realization of our present conditions by a messenger bearing a summons from Lorquas Ptomel directing me to appear before him forthwith. Bidding Dejah Thoris and Sola farewell, and commanding Woola to remain on guard, I hastened to the audience chamber, where I found Lorquas Ptomel and Tars Tarkas seated upon the rostrum.

TWELVE

A Prisoner with Power

As I entered and saluted, Lorquas Ptomel signaled me to advance, and, fixing his great, hideous eyes upon me, addressed me thus:

"You have been with us a few days, yet during that time you have by your prowess won a high position among us. Be that as it may, you are not one of us; you owe us no allegiance.

"Your position is a peculiar one," he continued; "you are a prisoner and yet you give commands which must be obeyed; you are an alien and yet you are a Tharkian chieftain; you are a midget and yet you can kill a mighty warrior with one blow of your fist. And now you are reported to have been plotting to escape with another prisoner of another race; a prisoner who, from her own admission, half believes you are returned from the valley of Dor. Either one of these accusations, if proved, would be sufficient grounds for your execution, but we are a just people and you shall have a trial on our return to Thark, if Tal Hajus so commands.

"But," he continued, in his fierce guttural tones, "if you run off with the red girl it is I who shall have to account to Tal Hajus; it is I who shall have to face Tars Tarkas, and either demonstrate my right to command, or the metal from my dead carcass will go to a better man, for such is the custom of the Tharks.

"I have no quarrel with Tars Tarkas; together we rule supreme the greatest of the lesser communities among the green men; we do not wish to fight between ourselves; and so if you were dead, John Carter, I should be glad. Under two conditions only, however, may you be killed by us without orders from Tal Hajus; in personal combat in self-defense, should you attack one of us, or were you apprehended in an attempt to escape.

"As a matter of justice I must warn you that we only await one of these two excuses for ridding ourselves of so great a responsibility. The safe delivery of the red girl to Tal Hajus is of the greatest importance. Not in a thousand years have the Tharks made such a capture; she is the granddaughter of the greatest of the red jeddaks, who is also our bitterest enemy. I have spoken. The red girl told us that we were without the softer sentiments of humanity, but we are a just and truthful race. You may go."

Turning, I left the audience chamber. So this was the beginning of Sarkoja's persecution! I knew that none other could be responsible for this report which had reached the ears of Lorquas Ptomel so quickly, and now I recalled those portions of our conversation which had touched upon escape and upon my origin.

Sarkoja was at this time Tars Tarkas' oldest and most trusted female. As such she was a mighty power behind the throne, for no warrior had the confidence of Lorquas Ptomel to such an extent as did his ablest lieutenant, Tars Tarkas.

However, instead of putting thoughts of possible escape from my mind, my audience with Lorquas Ptomel only served to center my every faculty on this subject. Now, more than before, the absolute necessity for escape, in so far as Dejah Thoris was concerned, was impressed upon me, for I was convinced that some horrible fate awaited her at the headquarters of Tal Hajus.

As described by Sola, this monster was the exaggerated personification of all the ages of cruelty, ferocity, and brutality from which he had descended. Cold, cunning, calculating; he was, also, in marked contrast to most of his fellows, a slave to that brute passion which the waning demands for procreation upon their dying planet has almost stilled in the Martian breast.

The thought that the divine Dejah Thoris might fall into the clutches of such an abysmal atavism started the cold sweat upon me. Far better that we save friendly bullets for ourselves at the last moment, as did those brave frontier women of my lost land, who took their own lives rather than fall into the hands of the Indian braves.

As I wandered about the plaza lost in my gloomy forebodings Tars Tarkas approached me on his way from the audience chamber. His demeanor toward me was unchanged, and he greeted me as though we had not just parted a few moments before.

"Where are your quarters, John Carter?" he asked.

"I have selected none," I replied. "It seemed best that I quartered either by myself or among the other warriors, and I was awaiting an opportunity to ask your advice. As you know," and I smiled, "I am not yet familiar with all the customs of the Tharks."

"Come with me," he directed, and together we moved off across the plaza to a building which I was glad to see adjoined that occupied by Sola and her charges.

"My quarters are on the first floor of this building," he said, "and the second floor also is fully occupied by warriors, but the third floor and the floors above are vacant; you may take your choice of these.

"I understand," he continued, "that you have given up your woman to the red prisoner. Well, as you have said, your ways are not our ways, but you can fight well enough to do about as you please, and so, if you wish to give your woman to a captive, it is your own affair; but as a chieftain you should have those to serve you, and in accordance with our customs you may select any or all the females from the retinues of the chieftains whose metal you now wear."

I thanked him, but assured him that I could get along very nicely without assistance except in the matter of preparing food, and so he promised to send women to me for this purpose and also for the care of my arms and the manufacture of my ammunition, which he said would be necessary. I suggested that they might also bring some of the sleeping silks and furs which belonged to me as spoils of combat, for the nights were cold and I had none of my own.

He promised to do so, and departed. Left alone, I ascended the winding corridor to the upper floors in search of suitable quarters. The beauties of the other buildings were repeated in this, and, as usual, I was soon lost in a tour of investigation and discovery.

I finally chose a front room on the third floor, because this brought me nearer to Dejah Thoris, whose apartment was on the second floor of the adjoining building, and it flashed upon me that I could rig up some means of communication whereby she might signal me in case she needed either my services or my protection.

Adjoining my sleeping apartment were baths, dressing rooms, and other sleeping and living apartments, in all some ten rooms on this floor. The windows of the back rooms overlooked an enormous court, which formed the center of the square made by the buildings which faced the four contiguous streets, and which was now given over to the quartering of the various animals belonging to the warriors occupying the adjoining buildings.

While the court was entirely overgrown with the yellow, moss-like vegetation which blankets practically the entire surface of Mars, yet numerous fountains, statuary, benches, and pergola-like contraptions bore witness to the beauty which the court must have presented in bygone times, when graced by the fair-haired, laughing people whom stern and unalterable cosmic laws had driven not only from their homes, but from all except the vague legends of their descendants.

One could easily picture the gorgeous foliage of the luxuriant Martian vegetation which once filled this scene with life and color; the graceful figures of the beautiful women, the straight and handsome men; the happy frolicking children—all sunlight, happiness and peace. It was difficult to realize that they had gone; down through ages of darkness, cruelty, and ignorance, until their hereditary instincts of culture and humanitarianism had risen ascendant once more in the final composite race which now is dominant upon Mars.

My thoughts were cut short by the advent of several young females bearing loads of weapons, silks, furs, jewels, cooking utensils, and casks of food and drink, including considerable loot from the air craft. All this, it seemed, had been the property of the two chieftains I had slain, and now, by the customs of the Tharks, it had become mine. At my direction they placed the stuff in one of the back rooms, and then departed, only to return with a second load, which they advised me constituted the balance of my goods. On the second trip they were accompanied by ten or fifteen other women and youths, who, it seemed, formed the retinues of the two chieftains.

They were not their families, nor their wives, nor their servants; the relationship was peculiar, and so unlike anything known to us that it is most difficult to describe. All property among the green Martians is owned in common by the community, except the personal weapons, ornaments and sleeping silks and furs of the individuals. These alone can one claim undisputed right to, nor may he accumulate more of these than are required for his actual needs. The surplus he holds merely as custodian, and it is passed on to the younger members of the community as necessity demands.

The women and children of a man's retinue may be likened to a military unit for which he is responsible in various ways, as in matters of instruction, discipline, sustenance, and the exigencies of their continual roamings and their unending strife with other communities and with the red Martians. His women are in no sense wives. The green Martians use no word corresponding in meaning with this earthly word. Their mating is a matter of community interest solely, and is directed without reference to natural selection. The council of chieftains of each community control the matter as surely as the owner of a Kentucky racing stud directs the scientific breeding of his stock for the improvement of the whole.

In theory it may sound well, as is often the case with theories, but the results of ages of this unnatural practice, coupled with the community in-terest in the offspring being held paramount to that of the mother, is shown in the cold, cruel creatures, and their gloomy, loveless, mirthless existence.

It is true that the green Martians are absolutely virtuous, both men and women, with the exception of such degenerates as Tal Hajus; but better far a finer balance of human characteristics even at the expense of a slight and occasional loss of chastity.

Finding that I must assume responsibility for these creatures, whether I would or not, I made the best of it and directed them to find quarters on the upper floors, leaving the third floor to me. One of the girls I charged with the duties of my simple cuisine, and directed the others to take up the various activities which had formerly constituted their vocations. Thereafter I saw little of them, nor did I care to.

THIRTEEN

Love-Making on Mars

Following the battle with the air ships, the community remained within the city for several days, abandoning the homeward march until they could feel reasonably assured that the ships would not return; for to be caught on the open plains with a cavalcade of chariots and children was far from the desire of even so warlike a people as the green Martians.

During our period of inactivity, Tars Tarkas had instructed me in many of the customs and arts of war familiar to the Tharks, including lessons in riding and guiding the great beasts which bore the warriors. These creatures, which are known as thoats, are as dangerous and vicious as their masters, but when once subdued are sufficiently tractable for the purposes of the green Martians.

Two of these animals had fallen to me from the warriors whose metal I wore, and in a short time I could handle them quite as well as the native warriors. The method was not at all complicated. If the thoats did not respond with sufficient celerity to the telepathic instructions of their riders they were dealt a terrific blow between the ears with the butt of a pistol, and if they showed fight this treatment was continued until the brutes either were subdued, or had unseated their riders.

In the latter case it became a life and death struggle between the man and the beast. If the former were quick enough with his pistol he might live to ride again, though upon some other beast; if not, his torn and mangled body was gathered up by his women and burned in accordance with Tharkian custom.

My experience with Woola determined me to attempt the experiment of kindness in my treatment of my thoats. First I taught them that they could not unseat me, and even rapped them sharply between the ears to impress upon them my authority and mastery. Then, by degrees, I won their confidence in much the same manner as I had adopted countless times with my many mundane mounts. I was ever a good hand with animals, and by inclination, as well as because it brought more lasting and satisfactory results, I was always kind and humane in my dealings with the lower orders. I could take a human life, if necessary, with far less compunction than that of a poor, unreasoning, irresponsible brute.

In the course of a few days my thoats were the wonder of the entire community. They would follow me like dogs, rubbing their great snouts against my body in awkward evidence of affection, and respond to my every command with an alacrity and docility which caused the Martian warriors to ascribe to me the possession of some earthly power unknown on Mars.

"How have you bewitched them?" asked Tars Tarkas one afternoon, when he had seen me run my arm far between the great jaws of one of my thoats which had wedged a piece of stone between two of his teeth while feeding upon the moss-like vegetation within our court yard.

"By kindness," I replied. "You see, Tars Tarkas, the softer sentiments have their value, even to a warrior. In the height of battle as well as upon the march I know that my thoats will obey my every command, and therefore my fighting efficiency is enhanced, and I am a better warrior for the reason that I am a kind master. Your other warriors would find it to the advantage of themselves as well as of the community to adopt my methods in this respect. Only a few days since you, yourself, told me that these great brutes, by the uncertainty of their tempers, often were the means of turning victory into defeat, since, at a crucial moment, they might elect to unseat and rend their riders."

"Show me how you accomplish these results," was Tars Tarkas' only rejoinder.

And so I explained as carefully as I could the entire method of training I had adopted with my beasts, and later he had me repeat it before Lorquas Ptomel and the assembled warriors. That moment marked the beginning of a new existence for the poor thoats, and before I left the community of Lorquas Ptomel I had the satisfaction of observing a regiment of as tractable and docile mounts as one might care to see. The effect on the precision and celerity of the military movements was so remarkable that Lorquas Ptomel presented me with a massive anklet of gold from his own leg, as a sign of his appreciation of my service to the horde.

On the seventh day following the battle with the air craft we again took up the march toward Thark, all probability of another attack being deemed remote by Lorquas Ptomel.

During the days just preceding our departure I had seen but little of Dejah Thoris, as I had been kept very busy by Tars Tarkas with my lessons in the art of Martian warfare, as well as in the training of my thoats. The few times I had visited her quarters she had been absent, walking upon the streets with Sola, or investigating the buildings in the near vicinity of the plaza. I had warned them against venturing far from the plaza for fear of the great white apes, whose ferocity I was only too well acquainted with. However, since Woola accompanied them on all their excursions, and as Sola was well armed, there was comparatively little cause for fear.

On the evening before our departure I saw them approaching along one of the great avenues which lead into the plaza from the east. I advanced to meet them, and telling Sola that I would take the responsibility for Dejah Thoris' safekeeping, I directed her to return to her quarters on some trivial errand. I liked and trusted Sola, but for some reason I desired to be alone with Dejah Thoris, who represented to me all that I had left behind upon Earth in agreeable and congenial companionship. There seemed bonds of mutual interest between us as powerful as though we had been born under the same roof rather than upon different planets, hurtling through space some forty-eight million miles apart.

That she shared my sentiments in this respect I was positive, for on my approach the look of pitiful hopelessness left her sweet countenance to be replaced by a smile of joyful welcome, as she placed her little right hand upon my left shoulder in true red Martian salute.

"Sarkoja told Sola that you had become a true Thark," she said, "and that I would now see no more of you than of any of the other warriors."

"Sarkoja is a liar of the first magnitude," I replied, "notwithstanding the proud claim of the Tharks to absolute verity."

Dejah Thoris laughed.

"I knew that even though you became a member of the community you would not cease to be my friend; 'A warrior may change his metal, but not his heart,' as the saying is upon Barsoom."

"I think they have been trying to keep us apart," she continued, "for whenever you have been off duty one of the older women of Tars Tarkas' retinue has always arranged to trump up some excuse to get Sola and me out of sight. They have had me down in the pits below the buildings helping them mix their awful radium powder, and make their terrible projectiles. You know that these have to be manufactured by artificial light, as exposure to sunlight always results in an explosion. You have noticed that their bullets explode when they strike an object? Well, the opaque, outer coating is broken by the impact, exposing a glass cylinder, almost solid, in the forward end of which is a minute particle of radium powder. The moment the sunlight, even though diffused, strikes this powder it explodes with a violence which nothing can withstand. If you ever witness a night battle you will note the absence of these explosions, while the morning following the battle will be filled at sunrise with the sharp detonations of exploding missiles fired the preceding night. As a rule, however, non-exploding projectiles are used at night."[1]

While I was much interested in Dejah Thoris' explanation of this wonderful adjunct to Martian warfare, I was more concerned by the immediate problem of their treatment of her. That they were keeping her away from me was not a matter for surprise, but that they should subject her to dangerous and arduous labor filled me with rage.

"Have they ever subjected you to cruelty and ignominy, Dejah Thoris?" I asked, feeling the hot blood of my fighting ancestors leap in my veins as I awaited her reply.

"Only in little ways, John Carter," she answered. "Nothing that can harm me outside my pride. They know that I am the daughter of ten thousand jeddaks, that I trace my ancestry straight back without a break to the builder of the first great waterway, and they, who do not even know their own mothers, are jealous of me. At heart they hate their horrid fates, and so wreak their poor spite on me who stand for everything they have not, and for all they most crave and never can attain. Let us pity them, my chieftain, for even though we die at their hands we can afford them pity, since we are greater than they and they know it."

Had I known the significance of those words "my chieftain," as applied by a red Martian woman to a man, I should have had the surprise of my life, but I did not know at that time, nor for many months thereafter. Yes, I still had much to learn upon Barsoom.

"I presume it is the better part of wisdom that we bow to our fate with as good grace as possible, Dejah Thoris; but I hope, nevertheless, that I may be present the next time that any Martian, green, red, pink, or violet, has the temerity to even so much as frown on you, my princess."

Dejah Thoris caught her breath at my last words, and gazed upon me with dilated eyes and quickening breath, and then, with an odd little laugh, which brought roguish dimples to the corners of her mouth, she shook her head and cried:

"What a child! A great warrior and yet a stumbling little child."

"What have I done now?" I asked, in sore perplexity.

"Some day you shall know, John Carter, if we live; but I may not tell

---

1. I have used the word radium in describing this powder because in the light of recent discoveries on Earth I believe it to be a mixture of which radium is the base. In Captain Carter's manuscript it is mentioned always by the name used in the written language of Helium and is spelled in hieroglyphics which it would be difficult and useless to reproduce.

you. And I, the daughter of Mors Kajak, son of Tardos Mors, have listened without anger," she soliloquized in conclusion.

Then she broke out again into one of her gay, happy, laughing moods; joking with me on my prowess as a Thark warrior as contrasted with my soft heart and natural kindliness.

"I presume that should you accidentally wound an enemy you would take him home and nurse him back to health," she laughed.

"That is precisely what we do on Earth," I answered. "At least among civilized men."

This made her laugh again. She could not understand it, for, with all her tenderness and womanly sweetness, she was still a Martian, and to a Martian the only good enemy is a dead enemy; for every dead foeman means so much more to divide between those who live.

I was very curious to know what I had said or done to cause her so much perturbation a moment before and so I continued to importune her to enlighten me.

"No," she exclaimed, "it is enough that you have said it and that I have listened. And when you learn, John Carter, and if I be dead, as likely I shall be ere the further moon has circled Barsoom another twelve times, remember that I listened and that I—smiled."

It was all Greek to me, but the more I begged her to explain the more positive became her denials of my request, and, so, in very hopelessness, I desisted.

Day had now given away to night and as we wandered along the great avenue lighted by the two moons of Barsoom, and with Earth looking down upon us out of her luminous green eye, it seemed that we were alone in the universe, and I, at least, was content that it should be so.

The chill of the Martian night was upon us, and removing my silks I threw them across the shoulders of Dejah Thoris. As my arm rested for an instant upon her I felt a thrill pass through every fiber of my being such as contact with no other mortal had even produced; and it seemed to me that she had leaned slightly toward me, but of that I was not sure. Only I knew that as my arm rested there across her shoulders longer than the act of adjusting the silk required she did not draw away, nor did she speak. And so, in silence, we walked the surface of a dying world, but in the breast of one of us at least had been born that which is ever oldest, yet ever new.

I loved Dejah Thoris. The touch of my arm upon her naked shoulder had spoken to me in words I would not mistake, and I knew that I had loved her since the first moment that my eyes had met hers that first time in the plaza of the dead city of Korad.

FOURTEEN

A Duel to the Death

My first impulse was to tell her of my love, and then I thought of the helplessness of her position wherein I alone could lighten the burdens of her captivity, and protect her in my poor way against the thousands of hereditary enemies she must face upon our arrival at Thark. I could not chance causing her additional pain or sorrow by declaring a love which, in all probability she did not return. Should I be so indiscreet, her position would be even more unbearable than now, and the thought that she might feel that I was taking advantage of her helplessness, to influence her decision was the final argument which sealed my lips.

"Why are you so quiet, Dejah Thoris?" I asked. "Possibly you would rather return to Sola and your quarters."

"No," she murmured, "I am happy here. I do not know why it is that I should always be happy and contented when you, John Carter, a stranger, are with me; yet at such times it seems that I am safe and that, with you, I shall soon return to my father's court and feel his strong arms about me and my mother's tears and kisses on my cheek."

"Do people kiss, then, upon Barsoom?" I asked, when she had explained the word she used, in answer to my inquiry as to its meaning.

"Parents, brothers, and sisters, yes; and," she added in a low, thoughtful tone, "lovers."

"And you, Dejah Thoris, have parents and brothers and sisters?"

"Yes."

"And a—lover?"

She was silent, nor could I venture to repeat the question.

"The man of Barsoom," she finally ventured, "does not ask personal questions of women, except his mother, and the woman he has fought for and won."

"But I have fought—" I started, and then I wished my tongue had been cut from my mouth; for she turned even as I caught myself and ceased, and drawing my silks from her shoulder she held them out to me, and without a word, and with head held high, she moved with the carriage of the queen she was toward the plaza and the doorway of her quarters.

I did not attempt to follow her, other than to see that she reached the building in safety, but, directing Woola to accompany her, I turned disconsolately and entered my own house. I sat for hours cross-legged, and cross-tempered, upon my silks meditating upon the queer freaks chance plays upon us poor devils of mortals.

So this was love! I had escaped it for all the years I had roamed the five continents and their encircling seas; in spite of beautiful women and urging opportunity; in spite of a half-desire for love and a constant search for my ideal, it had remained for me to fall furiously and hopelessly in love with a creature from another world, of a species similar possibly, yet not identical with mine. A woman who was hatched from an egg, and whose span of life might cover a thousand years; whose people had strange customs and ideas; a woman whose hopes, whose pleasures, whose standards of virtue and of right and wrong might vary as greatly from mine as did those of the green Martians.

Yes, I was a fool, but I was in love, and though I was suffering the greatest misery I had ever known I would not have had it otherwise for all the riches of Barsoom. Such is love, and such are lovers wherever love is known.

To me, Dejah Thoris was all that was perfect; all that was virtuous and beautiful and noble and good. I believed that from the bottom of my heart, from the depth of my soul on that night in Korad as I sat cross-legged upon my silks while the nearer moon of Barsoom raced through the western sky toward the horizon, and lighted up the gold and marble, and jeweled mosaics of my world-old chamber, and I believe it today as I sit at my desk in the little study overlooking the Hudson. Twenty years have intervened; for ten of them I lived and fought for Dejah Thoris and her people, and for ten I have lived upon her memory.

The morning of our departure for Thark dawned clear and hot, as do all Martian mornings except for the six weeks when the snow melts at the poles.

I sought out Dejah Thoris in the throng of departing chariots, but she turned her shoulder to me, and I could see the red blood mount to her cheek. With the foolish inconsistency of love I held my peace when I might have plead ignorance of the nature of my offense, or at least the gravity of it, and so have effected, at worst, a half conciliation.

My duty dictated that I must see that she was comfortable, and so I glanced into her chariot and rearranged her silks and furs. In doing so I noted with horror that she was heavily chained by one ankle to the side of the vehicle.

"What does this mean?" I cried, turning to Sola.

"Sarkoja thought it best," she answered, her face betokening her disapproval of the procedure.

Examining the manacles I saw that they fastened with a massive spring lock.

"Where is the key, Sola? Let me have it."

"Sarkoja wears it, John Carter," she answered.

I turned without further word and sought out Tars Tarkas, to whom I vehemently objected to the unnecessary humiliations and cruelties, as they seemed to my lover's eyes, that were being heaped upon Dejah Thoris.

"John Carter," he answered, "if ever you and Dejah Thoris escape the Tharks it will be upon this journey. We know that you will not go without her. You have shown yourself a mighty fighter, and we do not wish to manacle you, so we hold you both in the easiest way that will yet ensure security. I have spoken."

I saw the strength of his reasoning at a flash, and knew that it were futile to appeal from his decision, but I asked that the key be taken from Sarkoja and that she be directed to leave the prisoner alone in future.

"This much, Tars Tarkas, you may do for me in return for the friendship that, I must confess, I feel for you."

"Friendship?" he replied. "There is no such thing, John Carter; but have your will. I shall direct that Sarkoja cease to annoy the girl, and I myself will take the custody of the key."

"Unless you wish me to assume the responsibility," I said, smiling.

He looked at me long and earnestly before he spoke.

"Were you to give me your word that neither you nor Dejah Thoris would attempt to escape until after we have safely reached the court of Tal Hajus you might have the key and throw the chains into the river Iss."

"It were better that you held the key, Tars Tarkas," I replied.

He smiled, and said no more, but that night as we were making camp I saw him unfasten Dejah Thoris' fetters himself.

With all his cruel ferocity and coldness there was an undercurrent of something in Tars Tarkas which he seemed ever battling to subdue. Could it be a vestige of some human instinct come back from an ancient forbear to haunt him with the horror of his people's ways!

As I was approaching Dejah Thoris' chariot I passed Sarkoja, and the black, venomous look she accorded me was the sweetest balm I had felt for many hours. Lord, how she hated me! It bristled from her so palpably that one might almost have cut it with a sword.

A few moments later I saw her deep in conversation with a warrior named Zad; a big, hulking, powerful brute, but one who had never made a kill among his own chieftains, and so was still an *o mad*, or man with one name; he could win a second name only with the metal of some chieftain. It was this custom which entitled me to the names of either of the chieftains I had killed; in fact, some of the warriors addressed me as Dotar Sojat, a combination of the surnames of the two warrior chieftains whose metal I had taken, or, in other words, whom I had slain in fair fight.

As Sarkoja talked with Zad he cast occasional glances in my direction, while she seemed to be urging him very strongly to some action. I paid little attention to it at the time, but the next day I had good reason to recall the circumstances, and at the same time gain a slight insight into the depths of Sarkoja's hatred and the lengths to which she was capable of going to wreak her horrid vengeance on me.

Dejah Thoris would have none of me again on this evening, and though I spoke her name she neither replied, nor conceded by so much as the flutter of an eyelid that she realized my existence. In my extremity I did what most other lovers would have done; I sought word from her through an intimate. In this instance it was Sola whom I intercepted in another part of camp.

"What is the matter with Dejah Thoris?" I blurted out at her. "Why will she not speak to me?"

Sola seemed puzzled herself, as though such strange actions on the part of two humans were quite beyond her, as indeed they were, poor child.

"She says you have angered her, and that is all she will say, except that she is the daughter of a jed and the granddaughter of a jeddak and she has been humiliated by a creature who could not polish the teeth of her grandmother's sorak."

I pondered over this report for some time, finally asking, "What might a sorak be, Sola?"

"A little animal about as big as my hand, which the red Martian women keep to play with," explained Sola.

Not fit to polish the teeth of her grandmother's cat! I must rank pretty low in the consideration of Dejah Thoris, I thought; but I could not help laughing at the strange figure of speech, so homely and in this respect so earthly. It made me homesick, for it sounded very much like "not fit to polish her shoes." And then commenced a train of thought quite new to me. I began to wonder what my people at home were doing. I had not seen them for years. There was a family of Carters in Virginia who claimed close relationship with me; I was supposed to be a great uncle, or something of the kind equally foolish. I could pass anywhere for twenty-five to thirty years of age, and to be a great uncle always seemed the height of incongruity, for my thoughts and feelings were those of a boy. There was two little kiddies in the Carter family whom I had loved and who had thought there was no one on Earth like Uncle Jack; I could see them just as plainly, as I stood there under the moonlit skies of Barsoom, and I longed for them as I had never longed for any mortals before. By nature a wanderer, I had never known the true meaning of the word home, but the great hall of the Carters had always stood for all that the word did mean to me, and now my heart turned toward it from the cold and unfriendly peoples I had been thrown amongst. For did not even Dejah Thoris despise me! I was a low creature, so low in fact that I was not even fit to polish the teeth of her grandmother's cat; and then my saving sense of humor came to my rescue, and laughing I turned into my silks and furs and slept upon the moon-haunted ground the sleep of a tired and healthy fighting man.

We broke camp the next day at an early hour and marched with only a single halt until just before dark. Two incidents broke the tediousness of the march. About noon we espied far to our right what was evidently an incubator, and Lorquas Ptomel directed Tars Tarkas to investigate it. The latter took a dozen warriors, including myself, and we raced across the velvety carpeting of moss to the little enclosure.

It was indeed an incubator, but the eggs were very small in comparison with those I had seen hatching in ours at the time of my arrival on Mars.

Tars Tarkas dismounted and examined the enclosure minutely, finally announcing that it belonged to the green men of Warhoon and that the cement was scarcely dry where it had been walled up.

"They cannot be a day's march ahead of us," he exclaimed, the light of battle leaping to his fierce face.

The work at the incubator was short indeed. The warriors tore open the entrance and a couple of them, crawling in, soon demolished all the eggs with their short-swords. Then remounting we dashed back to join the cavalcade. During the ride I took occasion to ask Tars Tarkas if these Warhoons whose eggs we had destroyed were a smaller people than his Tharks.

"I noticed that their eggs were so much smaller than those I saw hatching in your incubator," I added.

He explained that the eggs had just been placed there; but, like all green Martian eggs, they would grow during the five-year period of incubation until they obtained the size of those I had seen hatching on the day of my arrival on Barsoom. This was indeed an interesting piece of information, for it had always seemed remarkable to me that the green Martian women, large as they were, could bring forth such enormous eggs as I had seen the four-foot infants emerging from. As a matter of fact, the new-laid egg is but little larger than an ordinary goose egg, and as it does not commence to grow until subjected to the light of the sun the chieftains have little difficulty in transporting several hundreds of them at one time from the storage vaults to the incubators.

Shortly after the incident of the Warhoon eggs we halted to rest the animals, and it was during this halt that the second of the day's interesting episodes occurred. I was engaged in changing my riding cloths from one of my thoats to the other, for I divided the day's work between them, when Zad approached me, and without a word struck my animal a terrific blow with his long-sword.

I did not need a manual of green Martian etiquette to know what reply to make, for, in fact, I was so wild with anger that I could scarcely refrain from drawing my pistol and shooting him down for the brute he was; but he stood waiting with drawn long-sword, and my only choice was to draw my own and meet him in fair fight with his choice of weapons or a lesser one.

This latter alternative is always permissible, therefore I could have used my short-sword, my dagger, my hatchet, or my fists had I wished, and been entirely within my rights, but I could not use firearms or a spear while he held only his long-sword.

I chose the same weapon he had drawn because I knew he prided himself upon his ability with it, and I wished, if I worsted him at all, to do it with his own weapon. The fight that followed was a long one and delayed the resumption of the march for an hour. The entire community surrounded us, leaving a clear space about one hundred feet in diameter for our battle.

Zad first attempted to rush me down as a bull might a wolf, but I was much too quick for him, and each time I side-stepped his rushes he would go lunging past me, only to receive a nick from my sword upon his arm or back. He was soon streaming blood from a half dozen minor wounds, but I could not obtain an opening to deliver an effective thrust. Then he changed his tactics, and fighting warily and with extreme dexterity, he tried to do by science what he was unable to do by brute strength. I must admit that he was a magnificent swordsman, and had it not been for my greater endurance and the remarkable agility the lesser gravitation of Mars lent me I might not have been able to put up the creditable fight I did against him.

We circled for some time without doing much damage on either side; the long, straight, needle-like swords flashing in the sunlight, and ringing out upon the stillness as they crashed together with each effective parry. Finally Zad, realizing that he was tiring more than I, evidently decided to close in and end the battle in a final blaze of glory for himself; just as he rushed me a blinding flash of light struck full in my eyes, so that I could not see his approach and could only leap blindly to one side in an effort to escape the mighty blade that it seemed I could already feel in my vitals. I was only partially successful, as a sharp pain in my left shoulder attested, but in the sweep of my glance as I sought to again locate my adversary, a sight met my astonished gaze which paid me well for the wound the temporary blindness had caused me. There, upon Dejah Thoris' chariot stood three figures, for the purpose evidently of witnessing the encounter above the heads of the intervening Tharks. There were Dejah Thoris, Sola, and Sarkoja, and as my fleeting glance swept over them a little tableau was presented which will stand graven in my memory to the day of my death.

As I looked, Dejah Thoris turned upon Sarkoja with the fury of a young tigress and struck something from her upraised hand; something which flashed in the sunlight as it spun to the ground. Then I knew what had blinded me at that crucial moment of the fight, and how Sarkoja had found a way to kill me without herself delivering the final thrust. Another thing I saw, too, which almost lost my life for me then and there, for it took my mind for the fraction of an instant entirely from my antagonist; for, as Dejah Thoris struck the tiny mirror from her hand, Sarkoja, her face livid with hatred and baffled rage, whipped out her dagger and aimed a terrific blow at Dejah Thoris; and then Sola, our dear and faithful Sola, sprang between them; the last I saw was the great knife descending upon her shielding breast.

My enemy had recovered from his thrust and was making it extremely interesting for me, so I reluctantly gave my attention to the work in hand, but my mind was not upon the battle.

We rushed each other furiously time after time, 'til suddenly, feeling the sharp point of his sword at my breast in a thrust I could neither parry nor escape, I threw myself upon him with outstretched sword and with all the weight of my body, determined that I would not die alone if I could prevent it. I felt the steel tear into my chest, all went black before me, my head whirled in dizziness, and I felt my knees giving beneath me.

FIFTEEN

Sola Tells Me Her Story

When consciousness returned, and, as I soon learned, I was down but a moment, I sprang quickly to my feet searching for my sword, and there I found it, buried to the hilt in the green breast of Zad, who lay stone dead upon the ochre moss of the ancient sea bottom. As I regained my full senses I found his weapon piercing my left breast, but only through the flesh and muscles which cover my ribs, entering near the center of my chest and coming out below the shoulder. As I had lunged I had turned so that his sword merely passed beneath the muscles, inflicting a painful but not dangerous wound.

Removing the blade from my body I also regained my own, and turning my back upon his ugly carcass, I moved, sick, sore, and disgusted, toward the chariots which bore my retinue and my belongings. A murmur of Martian applause greeted me, but I cared not for it.

Bleeding and weak I reached my women, who, accustomed to such happenings, dressed my wounds, applying the wonderful healing and remedial agents which make only the most instantaneous of death blows fatal. Give a Martian woman a chance and death must take a back seat. They soon had me patched up so that, except for weakness from loss of blood and a little soreness around the wound, I suffered no great distress from this thrust which, under earthly treatment, undoubtedly would have put me flat on my back for days.

As soon as they were through with me I hastened to the chariot of Dejah Thoris, where I found my poor Sola with her chest swathed in bandages, but apparently little the worse for her encounter with Sarkoja, whose dagger it seemed had struck the edge of one of Sola's metal breast ornaments and, thus deflected, had inflicted but a slight flesh wound.

As I approached I found Dejah Thoris lying prone upon her silks and furs, her lithe form wracked with sobs. She did not notice my presence, nor did she hear me speaking with Sola, who was standing a short distance from the vehicle.

"Is she injured?" I asked of Sola, indicating Dejah Thoris by an inclination of my head.

"No," she answered, "she thinks that you are dead."

"And that her grandmother's cat may now have no one to polish its teeth?" I queried, smiling.

"I think you wrong her, John Carter," said Sola. "I do not understand either her ways or yours, but I am sure the granddaughter of ten thousand jeddaks would never grieve like this over the death of one she considered beneath her, or indeed over any who held but the highest claim upon her affections. They are a proud race, but they are just, as are all Barsoomians, and you must have hurt or wronged her grievously that she will not admit your existence living, though she mourns you dead.

"Tears are a strange sight upon Barsoom," she continued, "and so it is difficult for me to interpret them. I have seen but two people weep in all my life, other than Dejah Thoris; one wept from sorrow, the other from baffled rage. The first was my mother, years ago before they killed her; the other was Sarkoja, when they dragged her from me today."

"Your mother!" I exclaimed, "but, Sola, you could not have known your mother, child."

"But I did. And my father also," she added. "If you would like to hear the strange and un-Barsoomian story come to the chariot tonight, John Carter, and I will tell you that of which I have never spoken in all my life before. And now the signal has been given to resume the march, you must go."

"I will come tonight, Sola," I promised. "Be sure to tell Dejah Thoris I am alive and well. I shall not force myself upon her, and be sure that you do not let her know I saw her tears. If she would speak with me I but await her command."

Sola mounted the chariot, which was swinging into its place in line, and I hastened to my waiting thoat and galloped to my station beside Tars Tarkas at the rear of the column.

We made a most imposing and awe-inspiring spectacle as we strung out across the yellow landscape; the two hundred and fifty ornate and brightly colored chariots, preceded by an advance guard of some two hundred mounted warriors and chieftains riding five abreast and one hundred yards apart, and followed by a like number in the same formation, with a score or more of flankers on either side; the fifty extra mastodons, or heavy draught animals, known as zitidars, and the five or six hundred extra thoats of the warriors running loose within the hollow square formed by the surrounding warriors. The gleaming metal and jewels of the gorgeous ornaments of the men and women, duplicated in the trappings of the zitidars and thoats, and interspersed with the flashing colors of magnificent silks and furs and feathers, lent a barbaric splendor to the caravan which would have turned an East Indian potentate green with envy.

The enormous broad tires of the chariots and the padded feet of the animals brought forth no sound from the moss-covered sea bottom; and so we moved in utter silence, like some huge phantasmagoria, except when the stillness was broken by the guttural growling of a goaded zitidar, or the squealing of fighting thoats. The green Martians converse but little, and then usually in monosyllables, low and like the faint rumbling of distant thunder.

We traversed a trackless waste of moss which, bending to the pressure of broad tire or padded foot, rose up again behind us, leaving no sign that we had passed. We might indeed have been the wraiths of the departed dead upon the dead sea of that dying planet for all the sound or sign we made in passing. It was the first march of a large body of men and animals I had ever witnessed which raised no dust and left no spoor; for there is no dust upon Mars except in the cultivated districts during the winter months, and even then the absence of high winds renders it almost unnoticeable.

We camped that night at the foot of the hills we had been approaching for two days and which marked the southern boundary of this particular sea. Our animals had been two days without drink, nor had they had water for nearly two months, not since shortly after leaving Thark; but, as Tars Tarkas explained to me, they require but little and can live almost indefinitely upon the moss which covers Barsoom, and which, he told me, holds in its tiny stems sufficient moisture to meet the limited demands of the animals.

After partaking of my evening meal of cheese-like food and vegetable milk I sought out Sola, whom I found working by the light of a torch upon some of Tars Tarkas' trappings. She looked up at my approach, her face lighting with pleasure and with welcome.

"I am glad you came," she said; "Dejah Thoris sleeps and I am lonely. Mine own people do not care for me, John Carter; I am too unlike them. It is a sad fate, since I must live my life amongst them, and I often wish that I were a true green Martian woman, without love and without hope; but I have known love and so I am lost.

"I promised to tell you my story, or rather the story of my parents. From what I have learned of you and the ways of your people I am sure that the tale will not seem strange to you, but among green Martians it has no parallel within the memory of the oldest living Thark, nor do our legends hold many similar tales.

"My mother was rather small, in fact too small to be allowed the responsibilities of maternity, as our chieftains breed principally for size. She was also less cold and cruel than most green Martian women, and caring little for their society, she often roamed the deserted avenues of Thark alone, or went and sat among the wild flowers that deck the nearby hills, thinking thoughts and wishing wishes which I believe I alone among Tharkian women today may understand, for am I not the child of my mother?

"And there among the hills she met a young warrior, whose duty it was to guard the feeding zitidars and thoats and see that they roamed not beyond the hills. They spoke at first only of such things as interest a community of Tharks, but gradually, as they came to meet more often, and, as was now quite evident to both, no longer by chance, they talked about themselves, their likes, their ambitions and their hopes. She trusted him and told him of the awful repugnance she felt for the cruelties of their kind, for the hideous, loveless lives they must ever lead, and then she waited for the storm of denunciation to break from his cold, hard lips; but instead he took her in his arms and kissed her.

"They kept their love a secret for six long years. She, my mother, was of the retinue of the great Tal Hajus, while her lover was a simple warrior, wearing only his own metal. Had their defection from the traditions of the Tharks been discovered both would have paid the penalty in the great arena before Tal Hajus and the assembled hordes.

"The egg from which I came was hidden beneath a great glass vessel upon the highest and most inaccessible of the partially ruined towers of ancient Thark. Once each year my mother visited it for the five long years it lay there in the process of incubation. She dared not come oftener, for in the mighty guilt of her conscience she feared that her every move was watched. During this period my father gained great distinction as a warrior and had taken the metal from several chieftains. His love for my mother had never diminished, and his one ambition in life was to reach a point where he might wrest the metal from Tal Hajus himself, and thus, as ruler of the Tharks, be free to claim her as his own, as well as, by the might of his power, protect the child which otherwise would be quickly dispatched should the truth become known.

"It was a wild dream, that of wresting the metal from Tal Hajus in five short years, but his advance was rapid, and he soon stood high in the councils of Thark. But one day the chance was lost forever, in so far as it could come in time to save his loved ones, for he was ordered away upon a long expedition to the ice-clad south, to make war upon the natives there and despoil them of their furs, for such is the manner of the green Barsoomian; he does not labor for what he can wrest in battle from others.

"He was gone for four years, and when he returned all had been over for three; for about a year after his departure, and shortly before the time for the return of an expedition which had gone forth to fetch the fruits of a community incubator, the egg had hatched. Thereafter my mother continued to keep me in the old tower, visiting me nightly and lavishing upon me the love the community life would have robbed us both of. She hoped, upon the return of the expedition from the incubator, to mix me with the other young assigned to the quarters of Tal Hajus, and thus escape the fate which would surely follow discovery of her sin against the ancient traditions of the green men.

"She taught me rapidly the language and customs of my kind, and one night she told me the story I have told to you up to this point, impressing upon me the necessity for absolute secrecy and the great caution I must exercise after she had placed me with the other young Tharks to permit no one to guess that I was further advanced in education than they, nor by any sign to divulge in the presence of others my affection for her, or my knowledge of my parentage; and then drawing me close to her she whispered in my ear the name of my father.

"And then a light flashed out upon the darkness of the tower chamber, and there stood Sarkoja, her gleaming, baleful eyes fixed in a frenzy of loathing and contempt upon my mother. The torrent of hatred and abuse she poured out upon her turned my young heart cold in terror. That she had heard the entire story was apparent, and that she had suspected something wrong from my mother's long nightly absences from her quarters accounted for her presence there on that fateful night.

"One thing she had not heard, nor did she know, the whispered name of my father. This was apparent from her repeated demands upon my mother to disclose the name of her partner in sin, but no amount of abuse or threats could wring this from her, and to save me from needless torture she lied, for she told Sarkoja that she alone knew nor would she even tell her child.

"With final imprecations, Sarkoja hastened away to Tal Hajus to report her discovery, and while she was gone my mother, wrapping me in the silks and furs of her night coverings, so that I was scarcely noticeable, descended to the streets and ran wildly away toward the outskirts of the city, in the direction which led to the far south, out toward the man whose protection she might not claim, but on whose face she wished to look once more before she died.

"As we neared the city's southern extremity a sound came to us from across the mossy flat, from the direction of the only pass through the hills which led to the gates, the pass by which caravans from either north or south or east or west would enter the city. The sounds we heard were the squealing of thoats and the grumbling of zitidars, with the occasional clank of arms which announced the approach of a body of warriors. The thought uppermost in her mind was that it was my father returned from his expedition, but the cunning of the Thark held her from headlong and precipitate flight to greet him.

"Retreating into the shadows of a doorway she awaited the coming of the cavalcade which shortly entered the avenue, breaking its formation and thronging the thoroughfare from wall to wall. As the head of the procession passed us the lesser moon swung clear of the overhanging roofs and lit up the scene with all the brilliancy of her wondrous light. My mother shrank further back into the friendly shadows, and from her hiding place saw that the expedition was not that of my father, but the returning caravan bearing the young Tharks. Instantly her plan was formed, and as a great chariot swung close to our hiding place she slipped stealthily in upon the trailing tailboard, crouching low in the shadow of the high side, straining me to her bosom in a frenzy of love.

"She knew, what I did not, that never again after that night would she hold me to her breast, nor was it likely we would ever look upon each other's face again. In the confusion of the plaza she mixed me with the other children, whose guardians during the journey were now free to relinquish their responsibility. We were herded together into a great room, fed by women who had not accompanied the expedition, and the next day we were parceled out among the retinues of the chieftains.

"I never saw my mother after that night. She was imprisoned by Tal Hajus, and every effort, including the most horrible and shameful torture, was brought to bear upon her to wring from her lips the name of my father; but she remained steadfast and loyal, dying at last amidst the laughter of Tal Hajus and his chieftains during some awful torture she was undergoing.

"I learned afterwards that she told them that she had killed me to save me from a like fate at their hands, and that she had thrown my body to the white apes. Sarkoja alone disbelieved her, and I feel to this day that she suspects my true origin, but does not dare expose me, at the present, at all events, because she also guesses, I am sure, the identity of my father.

"When he returned from his expedition and learned the story of my mother's fate I was present as Tal Hajus told him; but never by the quiver of a muscle did he betray the slightest emotion; only he did not laugh as Tal Hajus gleefully described her death struggles. From that moment on he was the cruelest of the cruel, and I am awaiting the day when he shall win the goal of his ambition, and feel the carcass of Tal Hajus beneath his foot, for I am as sure that he but waits the opportunity to wreak a terrible vengeance, and that his great love is as strong in his breast as when it first transfigured him nearly forty years ago, as I am that we sit here upon the edge of a world-old ocean while sensible people sleep, John Carter."

"And your father, Sola, is he with us now?" I asked.

"Yes," she replied, "but he does not know me for what I am, nor does he know who betrayed my mother to Tal Hajus. I alone know my father's name, and only I and Tal Hajus and Sarkoja know that it was she who carried the tale that brought death and torture upon her he loved."

We sat silent for a few moments, she wrapped in the gloomy thoughts of her terrible past, and I in pity for the poor creatures whom the heartless, senseless customs of their race had doomed to loveless lives of cruelty and of hate. Presently she spoke.

"John Carter, if ever a real man walked the cold, dead bosom of Barsoom you are one. I know that I can trust you, and because the knowledge may someday help you or him or Dejah Thoris or myself, I am going to tell you the name of my father, nor place any restrictions or conditions upon your tongue. When the time comes, speak the truth if it seems best to you. I trust you because I know that you are not cursed with the terrible trait of absolute and unswerving truthfulness, that you could lie like one of your own Virginia gentlemen if a lie would save others from sorrow or suffering. My father's name is Tars Tarkas."

SIXTEEN

We Plan Escape

The remainder of our journey to Thark was uneventful. We were twenty days upon the road, crossing two sea bottoms and passing through or around a number of ruined cities, mostly smaller than Korad. Twice we crossed the famous Martian waterways, or canals, so-called by our earthly astronomers. When we approached these points a warrior would be sent far ahead with a powerful field glass, and if no great body of red Martian troops was in sight we would advance as close as possible without chance of being seen and then camp until dark, when we would slowly approach the cultivated tract, and, locating one of the numerous, broad highways which cross these areas at regular intervals, creep silently and stealthily across to the arid lands upon the other side. It required five hours to make one of these crossings without a single halt, and the other consumed the entire night, so that we were just leaving the confines of the high-walled fields when the sun broke out upon us.

Crossing in the darkness, as we did, I was unable to see but little, except as the nearer moon, in her wild and ceaseless hurtling through the Barsoomian heavens, lit up little patches of the landscape from time to time, disclosing walled fields and low, rambling buildings, presenting much the appearance of earthly farms. There were many trees, methodically arranged, and some of them were of enormous height; there were animals in some of the enclosures, and they announced their presence by terrified squealings and snortings as they scented our queer, wild beasts and wilder human beings.

Only once did I perceive a human being, and that was at the intersection of our crossroad with the wide, white turnpike which cuts each cultivated district longitudinally at its exact center. The fellow must have been sleeping beside the road, for, as I came abreast of him, he raised upon one elbow and after a single glance at the approaching caravan leaped shrieking to his feet and fled madly down the road, scaling a nearby wall with the agility of a scared cat. The Tharks paid him not the slightest attention; they were not out upon the warpath, and the only sign that I had that they had seen him was a quickening of the pace of the caravan as we hastened toward the bordering desert which marked our entrance into the realm of Tal Hajus.

Not once did I have speech with Dejah Thoris, as she sent no word to me that I would be welcome at her chariot, and my foolish pride kept me from making any advances. I verily believe that a man's way with women is in inverse ratio to his prowess among men. The weakling and the saphead have often great ability to charm the fair sex, while the fighting man who can face a thousand real dangers unafraid, sits hiding in the shadows like some frightened child.

Just thirty days after my advent upon Barsoom we entered the ancient city of Thark, from whose long-forgotten people this horde of green men have stolen even their name. The hordes of Thark number some thirty thousand souls, and are divided into twenty-five communities. Each community has its own jed and lesser chieftains, but all are under the rule of Tal Hajus, Jeddak of Thark. Five communities make their headquarters at the city of Thark, and the balance are scattered among other deserted cities of ancient Mars throughout the district claimed by Tal Hajus.

We made our entry into the great central plaza early in the afternoon. There were no enthusiastic friendly greetings for the returned expedition. Those who chanced to be in sight spoke the names of warriors or women with whom they came in direct contact, in the formal greeting of their kind, but when it was discovered that they brought two captives a greater interest was aroused, and Dejah Thoris and I were the centers of inquiring groups.

We were soon assigned to new quarters, and the balance of the day was devoted to settling ourselves to the changed conditions. My home now was upon an avenue leading into the plaza from the south, the main artery down which we had marched from the gates of the city. I was at the far end of the square and had an entire building to myself. The same grandeur of architecture which was so noticeable a characteristic of Korad was in evidence here, only, if that were possible, on a larger and richer scale. My quarters would have been suitable for housing the greatest of earthly emperors, but to these queer creatures nothing about a building appealed to them but its size and the enormity of its chambers; the larger the building, the more desirable; and so Tal Hajus occupied what must have been an enormous public building, the largest in the city, but entirely unfitted for residence purposes; the next largest was reserved for Lorquas Ptomel, the next for the jed of a lesser rank, and so on to the bottom of the list of five jeds. The warriors occupied the buildings with the chieftains to whose retinues they belonged; or, if they preferred, sought shelter among any of the thousands of untenanted buildings in their own quarter of town; each community being assigned a certain section of the city. The selection of building had to be made in accordance with these divisions, except in so far as the jeds were concerned, they all occupying edifices which fronted upon the plaza.

When I had finally put my house in order, or rather seen that it had been done, it was nearing sunset, and I hastened out with the intention of locating Sola and her charges, as I had determined upon having speech with Dejah Thoris and trying to impress on her the necessity of our at least patching up a truce until I could find some way of aiding her to escape. I searched in vain until the upper rim of the great red sun was just disappearing behind the horizon and then I spied the ugly head of Woola peering from a second-story window on the opposite side of the very street where I was quartered, but nearer the plaza.

Without waiting for a further invitation I bolted up the winding runway which led to the second floor, and entering a great chamber at the front of the building was greeted by the frenzied Woola, who threw his great carcass upon me, nearly hurling me to the floor; the poor old fellow was so glad to see me that I thought he would devour me, his head split from ear to ear, showing his three rows of tusks in his hobgoblin smile.

Quieting him with a word of command and a caress, I looked hurriedly through the approaching gloom for a sign of Dejah Thoris, and then, not seeing her, I called her name. There was an answering murmur from the far corner of the apartment, and with a couple of quick strides I was standing beside her where she crouched among the furs and silks upon an ancient carved wooden seat. As I waited she rose to her full height and looking me straight in the eye said:

"What would Dotar Sojat, Thark, of Dejah Thoris his captive?"

"Dejah Thoris, I do not know how I have angered you. It was furtherest from my desire to hurt or offend you, whom I had hoped to protect and comfort. Have none of me if it is your will, but that you must aid me in effecting your escape, if such a thing be possible, is not my request, but my command. When you are safe once more at your father's court you may do with me as you please, but from now on until that day I am your master, and you must obey and aid me."

She looked at me long and earnestly and I thought that she was softening toward me.

"I understand your words, Dotar Sojat," she replied, "but you I do not understand. You are a queer mixture of child and man, of brute and noble. I only wish that I might read your heart."

"Look down at your feet, Dejah Thoris; it lies there now where it has lain since that other night at Korad, and where it will ever lie beating alone for you until death stills it forever."

She took a little step toward me, her beautiful hands outstretched in a strange, groping gesture.

"What do you mean, John Carter?" she whispered. "What are you saying to me?"

"I am saying what I had promised myself that I would not say to you, at least until you were no longer a captive among the green men; what from your attitude toward me for the past twenty days I had thought never to say to you; I am saying, Dejah Thoris, that I am yours, body and soul, to serve you, to fight for you, and to die for you. Only one thing I ask of you in return, and that is that you make no sign, either of condemnation or of approbation of my words until you are safe among your own people, and that whatever sentiments you harbor toward me they be not influenced or colored by gratitude; whatever I may do to serve you will be prompted solely from selfish motives, since it gives me more pleasure to serve you than not."

"I will respect your wishes, John Carter, because I understand the motives which prompt them, and I accept your service no more willingly than I bow to your authority; your word shall be my law. I have twice wronged you in my thoughts and again I ask your forgiveness."

Further conversation of a personal nature was prevented by the entrance of Sola, who was much agitated and wholly unlike her usual calm and possessed self.

"That horrible Sarkoja has been before Tal Hajus," she cried, "and from what I heard upon the plaza there is little hope for either of you."

"What do they say?" inquired Dejah Thoris.

"That you will be thrown to the wild calots [dogs] in the great arena as soon as the hordes have assembled for the yearly games."

"Sola," I said, "you are a Thark, but you hate and loathe the customs of your people as much as we do. Will you not accompany us in one supreme effort to escape? I am sure that Dejah Thoris can offer you a home and protection among her people, and your fate can be no worse among them than it must ever be here."

"Yes," cried Dejah Thoris, "come with us, Sola, you will be better off among the red men of Helium than you are here, and I can promise you not only a home with us, but the love and affection your nature craves and which must always be denied you by the customs of your own race. Come with us, Sola; we might go without you, but your fate would be terrible if they thought you had connived to aid us. I know that even that fear would not tempt you to interfere in our escape, but we want you with us, we want you to come to a land of sunshine and happiness, amongst a people who know the meaning of love, of sympathy, and of gratitude. Say that you will, Sola; tell me that you will."

"The great waterway which leads to Helium is but fifty miles to the south," murmured Sola, half to herself; "a swift thoat might make it in three hours; and then to Helium it is five hundred miles, most of the way through thinly settled districts. They would know and they would follow us. We might hide among the great trees for a time, but the chances are small indeed for escape. They would follow us to the very gates of Helium, and they would take toll of life at every step; you do not know them."

"Is there no other way we might reach Helium?" I asked. "Can you not draw me a rough map of the country we must traverse, Dejah Thoris?"

"Yes," she replied, and taking a great diamond from her hair she drew upon the marble floor the first map of Barsoomian territory I had ever seen. It was crisscrossed in every direction with long straight lines, sometimes running parallel and sometimes converging toward some great circle. The lines, she said, were waterways; the circles, cities; and one far to the northwest of us she pointed out as Helium. There were other cities closer, but she said she feared to enter many of them, as they were not all friendly toward Helium.

Finally, after studying the map carefully in the moonlight which now flooded the room, I pointed out a waterway far to the north of us which also seemed to lead to Helium.

"Does not this pierce your grandfather's territory?" I asked.

"Yes," she answered, "but it is two hundred miles north of us; it is one of the waterways we crossed on the trip to Thark."

"They would never suspect that we would try for that distant waterway," I answered, "and that is why I think that it is the best route for our escape."

Sola agreed with me, and it was decided that we should leave Thark this same night; just as quickly, in fact, as I could find and saddle my thoats. Sola was to ride one and Dejah Thoris and I the other; each of us carrying sufficient food and drink to last us for two days, since the animals could not be urged too rapidly for so long a distance.

I directed Sola to proceed with Dejah Thoris along one of the less frequented avenues to the southern boundary of the city, where I would overtake them with the thoats as quickly as possible; then, leaving them to gather what food, silks, and furs we were to need, I slipped quietly to the rear of the first floor, and entered the courtyard, where our animals were moving restlessly about, as was their habit, before settling down for the night.

In the shadows of the buildings and out beneath the radiance of the Martian moons moved the great herd of thoats and zitidars, the latter grunting their low gutturals and the former occasionally emitting the sharp squeal which denotes the almost habitual state of rage in which these creatures passed their existence. They were quieter now, owing to the absence of man, but as they scented me they became more restless and their hideous noise increased. It was risky business, this entering a paddock of thoats alone and at night; first, because their increasing noisiness might warn the nearby warriors that something was amiss, and also because for the slightest cause, or for no cause at all some great bull thoat might take it upon himself to lead a charge upon me.

Having no desire to awaken their nasty tempers upon such a night as this, where so much depended upon secrecy and dispatch, I hugged the shadows of the buildings, ready at an instant's warning to leap into the safety of a nearby door or window. Thus I moved silently to the great gates which opened upon the street at the back of the court, and as I neared the exit I called softly to my two animals. How I thanked the kind providence which had given me the foresight to win the love and confidence of these wild dumb brutes, for presently from the far side of the court I saw two huge bulks forcing their way toward me through the surging mountains of flesh.

They came quite close to me, rubbing their muzzles against my body and nosing for the bits of food it was always my practice to reward them with. Opening the gates I ordered the two great beasts to pass out, and then slipping quietly after them I closed the portals behind me.

I did not saddle or mount the animals there, but instead walked quietly in the shadows of the buildings toward an unfrequented avenue which led toward the point I had arranged to meet Dejah Thoris and Sola. With the noiselessness of disembodied spirits we moved stealthily along the deserted streets, but not until we were within sight of the plain beyond the city did I commence to breathe freely. I was sure that Sola and Dejah Thoris would find no difficulty in reaching our rendezvous undetected, but with my great thoats I was not so sure for myself, as it was quite unusual for warriors to leave the city after dark; in fact there was no place for them to go within any but a long ride.

I reached the appointed meeting place safely, but as Dejah Thoris and

Sola were not there I led my animals into the entrance hall of one of the large buildings. Presuming that one of the other women of the same household may have come in to speak to Sola, and so delayed their departure, I did not feel any undue apprehension until nearly an hour had passed without a sign of them, and by the time another half hour had crawled away I was becoming filled with grave anxiety. Then there broke upon the stillness of the night the sound of an approaching party, which, from the noise, I knew could be no fugitives creeping stealthily toward liberty. Soon the party was near me, and from the black shadows of my entranceway I perceived a score of mounted warriors, who, in passing, dropped a dozen words that fetched my heart clean into the top of my head.

"He would likely have arranged to meet them just without the city, and so—" I heard no more, they had passed on; but it was enough. Our plan had been discovered, and the chances for escape from now on to the fearful end would be small indeed. My one hope now was to return undetected to the quarters of Dejah Thoris and learn what fate had overtaken her, but how to do it with these great monstrous thoats upon my hands, now that the city probably was aroused by the knowledge of my escape was a problem of no mean proportions.

Suddenly an idea occurred to me, and acting on my knowledge of the construction of the buildings of these ancient Martian cities with a hollow court within the center of each square, I groped my way blindly through the dark chambers, calling the great thoats after me. They had difficulty in negotiating some of the doorways, but as the buildings fronting the city's principal exposures were all designed upon a magnificent scale, they were able to wriggle through without sticking fast; and thus we finally made the inner court where I found, as I had expected, the usual carpet of moss-like vegetation which would prove their food and drink until I could return them to their own enclosure. That they would be as quiet and contented here as elsewhere I was confident, nor was there but the remotest possibility that they would be discovered, as the green men had no great desire to enter these outlying buildings, which were frequented by the only thing, I believe, which caused them the sensation of fear—the great white apes of Barsoom.

Removing the saddle trappings, I hid them just within the rear doorway of the building through which we had entered the court, and, turning the beasts loose, quickly made my way across the court to the rear of the buildings upon the further side, and thence to the avenue beyond. Waiting in the doorway of the building until I was assured that no one was approaching, I hurried across to the opposite side and through the first doorway to the court beyond; thus, crossing through court after court

with only the slight chance of detection which the necessary crossing of the
avenues entailed, I made my way in safety to the courtyard in the rear of
Dejah Thoris' quarters.

Here, of course, I found the beasts of the warriors who quartered in
the adjacent buildings, and the warriors themselves I might expect to meet
within if I entered; but, fortunately for me, I had another and safer method
of reaching the upper story where Dejah Thoris should be found, and, after
first determining as nearly as possible which of the buildings she occupied,
for I had never observed them before from the court side, I took advantage
of my relatively great strength and agility and sprang upward until I grasped
the sill of a second-story window which I thought to be in the rear of her
apartment. Drawing myself inside the room I moved stealthily toward the
front of the building, and not until I had quite reached the doorway of her
room was I made aware by voices that it was occupied.

I did not rush headlong in, but listened without to assure myself that it
was Dejah Thoris and that it was safe to venture within. It was well indeed
that I took this precaution, for the conversation I heard was in the low
gutturals of men, and the words which finally came to me proved a most
timely warning. The speaker was a chieftain and he was giving orders to
four of his warriors.

"And when he returns to this chamber," he was saying, "as he surely will
when he finds she does not meet him at the city's edge, you four are to spring
upon him and disarm him. It will require the combined strength of all of
you to do it if the reports they bring back from Korad are correct. When you
have him fast bound bear him to the vaults beneath the jeddak's quarters
and chain him securely where he may be found when Tal Hajus wishes him.
Allow him to speak with none, nor permit any other to enter this apartment
before he comes. There will be no danger of the girl returning, for by this
time she is safe in the arms of Tal Hajus, and may all her ancestors have
pity upon her, for Tal Hajus will have none; the great Sarkoja has done a
noble night's work. I go, and if you fail to capture him when he comes, I
commend your carcasses to the cold bosom of Iss."

SEVENTEEN

A Costly Recapture

As the speaker ceased he turned to leave the apartment by the door where I was standing, but I needed to wait no longer; I had heard enough to fill my soul with dread, and stealing quietly away I returned to the courtyard by the way I had come. My plan of action was formed upon the instant, and crossing the square and the bordering avenue upon the opposite side I soon stood within the courtyard of Tal Hajus.

The brilliantly lighted apartments of the first floor told me where first to seek, and advancing to the windows I peered within. I soon discovered that my approach was not to be the easy thing I had hoped, for the rear rooms bordering the court were filled with warriors and women. I then glanced up at the stories above, discovering that the third was apparently unlighted, and so decided to make my entrance to the building from that point. It was the work of but a moment for me to reach the windows above, and soon I had drawn myself within the sheltering shadows of the unlighted third floor.

Fortunately the room I had selected was untenanted, and creeping noiselessly to the corridor beyond I discovered a light in the apartments ahead of me. Reaching what appeared to be a doorway I discovered that it was but an opening upon an immense inner chamber which towered from the first floor, two stories below me, to the dome-like roof of the building, high above my head. The floor of this great circular hall was thronged with chieftains, warriors and women, and at one end was a great raised platform upon which squatted the most hideous beast I had ever put my eyes upon. He had all the cold, hard, cruel, terrible features of the green warriors, but accentuated and debased by the animal passions to which he had given himself over for many years. There was not a mark of dignity or pride upon his bestial countenance, while his enormous bulk spread itself out upon the platform where he squatted like some huge devil fish, his six limbs accentuating the similarity in a horrible and startling manner.

But the sight that froze me with apprehension was that of Dejah Thoris and Sola standing there before him, and the fiendish leer of him as he let his great protruding eyes gloat upon the lines of her beautiful figure. She was speaking, but I could not hear what she said, nor could I make out the low grumbling of his reply. She stood there erect before him, her head high held, and even at the distance I was from them I could read the scorn and disgust upon her face as she let her haughty glance rest without sign of fear upon him. She was indeed the proud daughter of a thousand jeddaks, every inch of her dear, precious little body; so small, so frail beside the towering warriors around her, but in her majesty dwarfing them into insignificance; she was the mightiest figure among them and I verily believe that they felt it.

Presently Tal Hajus made a sign that the chamber be cleared, and that the prisoners be left alone before him. Slowly the chieftains, the warriors and the women melted away into the shadows of the surrounding chambers, and Dejah Thoris and Sola stood alone before the jeddak of the Tharks.

One chieftain alone had hesitated before departing; I saw him standing in the shadows of a mighty column, his fingers nervously toying with the hilt of his great-sword and his cruel eyes bent in implacable hatred upon Tal Hajus. It was Tars Tarkas, and I could read his thoughts as they were an open book for the undisguised loathing upon his face. He was thinking of that other woman who, forty years ago, had stood before this beast, and could I have spoken a word into his ear at that moment the reign of Tal Hajus would have been over; but finally he also strode from the room, not knowing that he left his own daughter at the mercy of the creature he most loathed.

Tal Hajus arose, and I, half fearing, half anticipating his intentions, hurried to the winding runway which led to the floors below. No one was near to intercept me, and I reached the main floor of the chamber unobserved, taking my station in the shadow of the same column that Tars Tarkas had but just deserted. As I reached the floor Tal Hajus was speaking.

"Princess of Helium, I might wring a mighty ransom from your people would I but return you to them unharmed, but a thousand times rather would I watch that beautiful face writhe in the agony of torture; it shall be long drawn out, that I promise you; ten days of pleasure were all too short to show the love I harbor for your race. The terrors of your death shall haunt the slumbers of the red men through all the ages to come; they will shudder in the shadows of the night as their fathers tell them of the awful vengeance of the green men; of the power and might and hate and cruelty of Tal Hajus. But before the torture you shall be mine for one short hour, and word of that too shall go forth to Tardos Mors, Jeddak of Helium, your grandfather, that he may grovel upon the ground in the agony of his sorrow. Tomorrow the torture will commence; tonight thou art Tal Hajus'; come!"

He sprang down from the platform and grasped her roughly by the arm, but scarcely had he touched her than I leaped between them. My short-sword, sharp and gleaming was in my right hand; I could have plunged it into his putrid heart before he realized that I was upon him; but as I raised my arm to strike I thought of Tars Tarkas, and, with all my rage, with all my hatred, I could not rob him of that sweet moment for which he had lived and hoped all these long, weary years, and so, instead, I swung my good right fist full upon the point of his jaw. Without a sound he slipped to the floor as one dead.

In the same deathly silence I grasped Dejah Thoris by the hand, and motioning Sola to follow we sped noiselessly from the chamber and to the floor above. Unseen we reached a rear window and with the straps and leather of my trappings I lowered, first Sola and then Dejah Thoris to the ground below. Dropping lightly after them I drew them rapidly around the court in the shadows of the buildings, and thus we returned over the same course I had so recently followed from the distant boundary of the city.

We finally came upon my thoats in the courtyard where I had left them, and placing the trappings upon them we hastened through the building to the avenue beyond. Mounting, Sola upon one beast, and Dejah Thoris behind me upon the other, we rode from the city of Thark through the hills to the south.

Instead of circling back around the city to the northwest and toward the nearest waterway which lay so short a distance from us, we turned to the northeast and struck out upon the mossy waste across which, for two hundred dangerous and weary miles, lay another main artery leading to Helium.

No word was spoken until we had left the city far behind, but I could hear the quiet sobbing of Dejah Thoris as she clung to me with her dear head resting against my shoulder.

"If we make it, my chieftain, the debt of Helium will be a mighty one; greater than she can ever pay you; and should we not make it," she continued, "the debt is no less, though Helium will never know, for you have saved the last of our line from worse than death."

I did not answer, but instead reached to my side and pressed the little fingers of her I loved where they clung to me for support, and then, in unbroken silence, we sped over the yellow, moonlit moss; each of us occupied with his own thoughts. For my part I could not be other than joyful had I tried, with Dejah Thoris' warm body pressed close to mine, and with all our unpassed danger my heart was singing as gaily as though we were already entering the gates of Helium.

Our earlier plans had been so sadly upset that we now found ourselves without food or drink, and I alone was armed. We therefore urged our beasts to a speed that must tell on them sorely before we could hope to sight the ending of the first stage of our journey.

We rode all night and all the following day with only a few short rests. On the second night both we and our animals were completely fagged, and so we lay down upon the moss and slept for some five or six hours, taking up the journey once more before daylight. All the following day we rode, and when, late in the afternoon we had sighted no distant trees, the mark of the great waterways throughout all Barsoom, the terrible truth flashed upon us—we were lost.

Evidently we had circled, but which way it was difficult to say, nor did it seem possible with the sun to guide us by day and the moons and stars by night. At any rate no waterway was in sight, and the entire party was almost ready to drop from hunger, thirst and fatigue. Far ahead of us and a trifle to the right we could distinguish the outlines of low mountains. These we decided to attempt to reach in the hope that from some ridge we might discern the missing waterway. Night fell upon us before we reached our goal, and, almost fainting from weariness and weakness, we lay down and slept.

I was awakened early in the morning by some huge body pressing close to mine, and opening my eyes with a start I beheld my blessed old Woola snuggling close to me; the faithful brute had followed us across that trackless waste to share our fate, whatever it might be. Putting my arms about his neck I pressed my cheek close to his, nor am I ashamed that I did it, nor of the tears that came to my eyes as I thought of his love for me. Shortly after this Dejah Thoris and Sola awakened, and it was decided that we push on at once in an effort to gain the hills.

We had gone scarcely a mile when I noticed that my thoat was commencing to stumble and stagger in a most pitiful manner, although we had not attempted to force them out of a walk since about noon of the preceding day. Suddenly he lurched wildly to one side and pitched violently to the ground. Dejah Thoris and I were thrown clear of him and fell upon the soft moss with scarcely a jar; but the poor beast was in a pitiable condition, not even being able to rise, although relieved of our weight. Sola told me that the coolness of the night, when it fell, together with the rest would doubtless revive him, and so I decided not to kill him, as was my first intention, as I had thought it cruel to leave him alone there to die of hunger and thirst. Relieving him of his trappings, which I flung down beside him, we left the poor fellow to his fate, and pushed on with the one thoat as best we could. Sola and I walked, making Dejah Thoris ride, much against her will. In this way we had progressed to within about a mile of the hills we were endeavoring to reach when Dejah Thoris, from her point of vantage upon the thoat, cried out that she saw a great party of mounted men filing down from a pass in the hills several miles away. Sola and I both looked in the direction she indicated, and there, plainly discernible, were several hundred mounted warriors. They seemed to be headed in a southwesterly direction, which would take them away from us.

They doubtless were Thark warriors who had been sent out to capture us, and we breathed a great sigh of relief that they were traveling in the opposite direction. Quickly lifting Dejah Thoris from the thoat, I commanded the animal to lie down and we three did the same, presenting as small an object as possible for fear of attracting the attention of the warriors toward us.

We could see them as they filed out of the pass, just for an instant, before they were lost to view behind a friendly ridge; to us a most providential ridge; since, had they been in view for any great length of time, they scarcely could have failed to discover us. As what proved to be the last warrior came into view from the pass, he halted and, to our consternation, threw his small but powerful fieldglass to his eye and scanned the sea bottom in all directions. Evidently he was a chieftain, for in certain marching formations among the green men a chieftain brings up the extreme rear of the column. As his glass swung toward us our hearts stopped in our breasts, and I could feel the cold sweat start from every pore in my body.

Presently it swung full upon us and—stopped. The tension on our nerves was near the breaking point, and I doubt if any of us breathed for the few moments he held us covered by his glass; and then he lowered it and we could see him shout a command to the warriors who had passed from our sight behind the ridge. He did not wait for them to join him, however, instead he wheeled his thoat and came tearing madly in our direction.

There was but one slight chance and that we must take quickly. Raising my strange Martian rifle to my shoulder I sighted and touched the button which controlled the trigger; there was a sharp explosion as the missile reached its goal, and the charging chieftain pitched backward from his flying mount.

Springing to my feet I urged the thoat to rise, and directed Sola to take Dejah Thoris with her upon him and make a mighty effort to reach the hills before the green warriors were upon us. I knew that in the ravines and gullies they might find a temporary hiding place, and even though they died there of hunger and thirst it would be better so than that they fell into the hands of the Tharks. Forcing my two revolvers upon them as a slight means of protection, and, as a last resort, as an escape for themselves from the horrid death which recapture would surely mean, I lifted Dejah Thoris in my arms and placed her upon the thoat behind Sola, who had already mounted at my command.

"Good-bye, my princess," I whispered, "we may meet in Helium yet. I have escaped from worse plights than this," and I tried to smile as I lied.

"What," she cried, "are you not coming with us?"

"How may I, Dejah Thoris? Someone must hold these fellows off for a while, and I can better escape them alone than could the three of us together."

She sprang quickly from the thoat and, throwing her dear arms about my neck, turned to Sola, saying with quiet dignity: "Fly, Sola! Dejah Thoris remains to die with the man she loves."

Those words are engraved upon my heart. Ah, gladly would I give up my life a thousand times could I only hear them once again; but I could not then give even a second to the rapture of her sweet embrace, and pressing my lips to hers for the first time, I picked her up bodily and tossed her to her seat behind Sola again, commanding the latter in peremptory tones to hold her there by force, and then, slapping the thoat upon the flank, I saw them borne away; Dejah Thoris struggling to the last to free herself from Sola's grasp.

Turning, I beheld the green warriors mounting the ridge and looking for their chieftain. In a moment they saw him, and then me; but scarcely had they discovered me than I commenced firing, lying flat upon my belly in the moss. I had an even hundred rounds in the magazine of my rifle, and another hundred in the belt at my back, and I kept up a continuous stream of fire until I saw all of the warriors who had been first to return from behind the ridge either dead or scurrying to cover.

My respite was short-lived however, for soon the entire party, numbering some thousand men, came charging into view, racing madly toward me. I fired until my rifle was empty and they were almost upon me, and then a glance showing me that Dejah Thoris and Sola had disappeared among the hills, I sprang up, throwing down my useless gun, and started away in the direction opposite to that taken by Sola and her charge.

If ever Martians had an exhibition of jumping, it was granted those astonished warriors on that day long years ago, but while it led them away from Dejah Thoris it did not distract their attention from endeavoring to capture me.

They raced wildly after me until, finally, my foot struck a projecting piece of quartz, and down I went sprawling upon the moss. As I looked up they were upon me, and although I drew my long-sword in an attempt to sell my life as dearly as possible, it was soon over. I reeled beneath their blows which fell upon me in perfect torrents; my head swam; all was black, and I went down beneath them to oblivion.

EIGHTEEN

Chained in Warhoon

It must have been several hours before I regained consciousness and I well remember the feeling of surprise which swept over me as I realized that I was not dead.

I was lying among a pile of sleeping silks and furs in the corner of a small room in which were several green warriors, and bending over me was an ancient and ugly female.

As I opened my eyes she turned to one of the warriors, saying,

"He will live, O Jed."

" 'Tis well," replied the one so addressed, rising and approaching my couch, "he should render rare sport for the great games."

And now as my eyes fell upon him, I saw that he was no Thark, for his ornaments and metal were not of that horde. He was a huge fellow, terribly scarred about the face and chest, and with one broken tusk and a missing ear. Strapped on either breast were human skulls and depending from these a number of dried human hands.

His reference to the great games of which I had heard so much while among the Tharks convinced me that I had but jumped from purgatory into gehenna.

After a few more words with the female, during which she assured him that I was now fully fit to travel, the jed ordered that we mount and ride after the main column.

I was strapped securely to as wild and unmanageable a thoat as I had ever seen, and, with a mounted warrior on either side to prevent the beast from bolting, we rode forth at a furious pace in pursuit of the column. My wounds gave me but little pain, so wonderfully and rapidly had the applications and injections of the female exercised their therapeutic powers, and so deftly had she bound and plastered the injuries.

Just before dark we reached the main body of troops shortly after they had made camp for the night. I was immediately taken before the leader, who proved to be the jeddak of the hordes of Warhoon.

Like the jed who had brought me, he was frightfully scarred, and also decorated with the breastplate of human skulls and dried dead hands which seemed to mark all the greater warriors among the Warhoons, as well as to indicate their awful ferocity, which greatly transcends even that of the Tharks.

The jeddak, Bar Comas, who was comparatively young, was the object of the fierce and jealous hatred of his old lieutenant, Dak Kova, the jed who had captured me, and I could not but note the almost studied efforts which the latter made to affront his superior.

He entirely omitted the usual formal salutation as we entered the presence of the jeddak, and as he pushed me roughly before the ruler he exclaimed in a loud and menacing voice.

"I have brought a strange creature wearing the metal of a Thark whom it is my pleasure to have battle with a wild thoat at the great games."

"He will die as Bar Comas, your jeddak, sees fit, if at all," replied the young ruler, with emphasis and dignity.

"If at all?" roared Dak Kova. "By the dead hands at my throat but he shall die, Bar Comas. No maudlin weakness on your part shall save him. O, would that Warhoon were ruled by a real jeddak rather than by a water-hearted weakling from whom even old Dak Kova could tear the metal with his bare hands!"

Bar Comas eyed the defiant and insubordinate chieftain for an instant, his expression one of haughty, fearless contempt and hate, and then without drawing a weapon and without uttering a word he hurled himself at the throat of his defamer.

I never before had seen two green Martian warriors battle with nature's weapons and the exhibition of animal ferocity which ensued was as fearful a thing as the most disordered imagination could picture. They tore at each others' eyes and ears with their hands and with their gleaming tusks repeatedly slashed and gored until both were cut fairly to ribbons from head to foot.

Bar Comas had much the better of the battle as he was stronger, quicker and more intelligent. It soon seemed that the encounter was done saving only the final death thrust when Bar Comas slipped in breaking away from a clinch. It was the one little opening that Dak Kova needed, and hurling himself at the body of his adversary he buried his single mighty tusk in Bar Comas' groin and with a last powerful effort ripped the young jeddak wide open the full length of his body, the great tusk finally wedging in the bones of Bar Comas' jaw. Victor and vanquished rolled limp and lifeless upon the moss, a huge mass of torn and bloody flesh.

Bar Comas was stone dead, and only the most herculean efforts on the part of Dak Kova's females saved him from the fate he deserved. Three days later he walked without assistance to the body of Bar Comas which, by custom, had not been moved from where it fell, and placing his foot upon the neck of his erstwhile ruler he assumed the title of Jeddak of Warhoon.

The dead jeddak's hands and head were removed to be added to the ornaments of his conqueror, and then his women cremated what remained, amid wild and terrible laughter.

The injuries to Dak Kova had delayed the march so greatly that it was decided to give up the expedition, which was a raid upon a small Thark community in retaliation for the destruction of the incubator, until after the great games, and the entire body of warriors, ten thousand in number, turned back toward Warhoon.

My introduction to these cruel and bloodthirsty people was but an index to the scenes I witnessed almost daily while with them. They are a smaller horde than the Tharks but much more ferocious. Not a day passed but that some members of the various Warhoon communities met in deadly combat. I have seen as high as eight mortal duels within a single day.

We reached the city of Warhoon after some three days march and I was immediately cast into a dungeon and heavily chained to the floor and walls. Food was brought me at intervals but owing to the utter darkness of the place I do not know whether I lay there days, or weeks, or months. It was the most horrible experience of all my life and that my mind did not give way to the terrors of that inky blackness has been a wonder to me ever since. The place was filled with creeping, crawling things; cold, sinuous bodies passed over me when I lay down, and in the darkness I occasionally caught glimpses of gleaming, fiery eyes, fixed in horrible intentness upon me. No sound reached me from the world above and no word would my jailer vouchsafe when my food was brought to me, although I at first bombarded him with questions.

Finally all the hatred and maniacal loathing for these awful creatures who had placed me in this horrible place was centered by my tottering reason upon this single emissary who represented to me the entire horde of Warhoons.

I had noticed that he always advanced with his dim torch to where he could place the food within my reach and as he stooped to place it upon the floor his head was about on a level with my breast. So, with the cunning of a madman, I backed into the far corner of my cell when next I heard

him approaching and gathering a little slack of the great chain which held
me in my hand I waited his coming, crouching like some beast of prey. As
he stooped to place my food upon the ground I swung the chain above my
head and crashed the links with all my strength upon his skull. Without a
sound he slipped to the floor, stone dead.

Laughing and chattering like the idiot I was fast becoming I fell upon his
prostrate form my fingers feeling for his dead throat. Presently they came
in contact with a small chain at the end of which dangled a number of
keys. The touch of my fingers on these keys brought back my reason with
the suddenness of thought. No longer was I a jibbering idiot, but a sane,
reasoning man with the means of escape within my very hands.

As I was groping to remove the chain from about my victim's neck
I glanced up into the darkness to see six pairs of gleaming eyes fixed,
unwinking, upon me. Slowly they approached and slowly I shrank back
from the awful horror of them. Back into my corner I crouched holding
my hands palms out, before me, and stealthily on came the awful eyes until
they reached the dead body at my feet. Then slowly they retreated but this
time with a strange grating sound and finally they disappeared in some
black and distant recess of my dungeon.

NINETEEN

Battling in the Arena

Slowly I regained my composure and finally essayed again to attempt to remove the keys from the dead body of my former jailer. But as I reached out into the darkness to locate it I found to my horror that it was gone. Then the truth flashed on me; the owners of those gleaming eyes had dragged my prize away from me to be devoured in their neighboring lair; as they had been waiting for days, for weeks, for months, through all this awful eternity of my imprisonment to drag my dead carcass to their feast.

For two days no food was brought me, but then a new messenger appeared and my incarceration went on as before, but not again did I allow my reason to be submerged by the horror of my position.

Shortly after this episode another prisoner was brought in and chained near me. By the dim torch light I saw that he was a red Martian and I could scarcely await the departure of his guards to address him. As their retreating footsteps died away in the distance, I called out softly the Martian word of greeting, kaor.

"Who are you who speaks out of the darkness?" he answered

"John Carter, a friend of the red men of Helium."

"I am of Helium," he said, "but I do not recall your name."

And then I told him my story as I have written it here, omitting only any reference to my love for Dejah Thoris. He was much excited by the news of Helium's princess and seemed quite positive that she and Sola could easily have reached a point of safety from where they left me. He said that he knew the place well because the defile through which the Warhoon warriors had passed when they discovered us was the only one ever used by them when marching to the south.

"Dejah Thoris and Sola entered the hills not five miles from a great waterway and are now probably quite safe," he assured me.

My fellow prisoner was Kantos Kan, a padwar (lieutenant) in the navy of Helium. He had been a member of the ill-fated expedition which had fallen into the hands of the Tharks at the time of Dejah Thoris' capture, and he briefly related the events which followed the defeat of the battleships.

Badly injured and only partially manned they had limped slowly toward Helium, but while passing near the city of Zodanga, the capital of Helium's hereditary enemies among the red men of Barsoom, they had been attacked by a great body of war vessels and all but the craft to which Kantos Kan belonged were either destroyed or captured. His vessel was chased for days by three of the Zodangan war ships but finally escaped during the darkness of a moonless night.

Thirty days after the capture of Dejah Thoris, or about the time of our coming to Thark, his vessel had reached Helium with about ten survivors of the original crew of seven hundred officers and men. Immediately seven great fleets, each of one hundred mighty war ships, had been dispatched to search for Dejah Thoris, and from these vessels two thousand smaller craft had been kept out continuously in futile search for the missing princess.

Two green Martian communities had been wiped off the face of Barsoom by the avenging fleets, but no trace of Dejah Thoris had been found. They had been searching among the northern hordes, and only within the past few days had they extended their quest to the south.

Kantos Kan had been detailed to one of the small one-man fliers and had had the misfortune to be discovered by the Warhoons while exploring their city. The bravery and daring of the man won my greatest respect and admiration. Alone he had landed at the city's boundary and on foot had penetrated to the buildings surrounding the plaza. For two days and nights he had explored their quarters and their dungeons in search of his beloved princess only to fall into the hands of a party of Warhoons as he was about to leave, after assuring himself that Dejah Thoris was not a captive there.

During the period of our incarceration Kantos Kan and I became well acquainted, and formed a warm personal friendship. A few days only elapsed, however, before we were dragged forth from our dungeon for the great games. We were conducted early one morning to an enormous amphitheater, which instead of having been built upon the surface of the ground was excavated below the surface. It had partially filled with debris so that how large it had originally been was difficult to say. In its present condition it held the entire twenty thousand Warhoons of the assembled hordes.

The arena was immense but extremely uneven and unkempt. Around it the Warhoons had piled building stone from some of the ruined edifices of the ancient city to prevent the animals and the captives from escaping into the audience, and at each end had been constructed cages to hold them until their turns came to meet some horrible death upon the arena.

Kantos Kan and I were confined together in one of the cages. In the others were wild calots, thoats, mad zitidars, green warriors, and women of other hordes, and many strange and ferocious wild beasts of Barsoom which I had never before seen. The din of their roaring, growling and squealing was deafening and the formidable appearance of any one of them was enough to make the stoutest heart feel grave forebodings.

Kantos Kan explained to me that at the end of the day one of these prisoners would gain freedom and the others would lie dead about the arena. The winners in the various contests of the day would be pitted against each other until only two remained alive; the victor in the last encounter being set free, whether animal or man. The following morning the cages would be filled with a new consignment of victims, and so on throughout the ten days of the games.

Shortly after we had been caged the amphitheater began to fill and within an hour every available part of the seating space was occupied. Dak Kova, with his jeds and chieftains, sat at the center of one side of the arena upon a large raised platform.

At a signal from Dak Kova the doors of two cages were thrown open and a dozen green Martian females were driven to the center of the arena. Each was given a dagger and then, at the far end, a pack of twelve calots, or wild dogs were loosed upon them.

As the brutes, growling and foaming, rushed upon the almost defenseless women I turned my head that I might not see the horrid sight. The yells and laughter of the green horde bore witness to the excellent quality of the sport and when I turned back to the arena, as Kantos Kan told me it was over, I saw three victorious calots, snarling and growling over the bodies of their prey. The women had given a good account of themselves.

Next a mad zitidar was loosed among the remaining dogs, and so it went throughout the long, hot, horrible day.

During the day I was pitted against first men and then beasts, but as I was armed with a long-sword and always outclassed my adversary in agility and generally in strength as well, it proved but child's play to me. Time and time again I won the applause of the bloodthirsty multitude, and toward the end there were cries that I be taken from the arena and be made a member of the hordes of Warhoon.

Finally there were but three of us left, a great green warrior of some far northern horde, Kantos Kan, and myself. The other two were to battle and then I to fight the conqueror for the liberty which was accorded the final winner.

Kantos Kan had fought several times during the day and like myself had always proven victorious, but occasionally by the smallest of margins, especially when pitted against the green warriors. I had little hope that he could best his giant adversary who had mowed down all before him during the day. The fellow towered nearly sixteen feet in height, while Kantos Kan was some inches under six feet. As they advanced to meet one another I saw for the first time a trick of Martian swordsmanship which centered Kantos Kan's every hope of victory and life on one cast of the dice, for, as he came to within about twenty feet of the huge fellow he threw his sword arm far behind him over his shoulder and with a mighty sweep hurled his weapon point foremost at the green warrior. It flew true as an arrow and piercing the poor devil's heart laid him dead upon the arena.

Kantos Kan and I were now pitted against each other but as we approached to the encounter I whispered to him to prolong the battle until nearly dark in the hope that we might find some means of escape. The horde evidently guessed that we had no hearts to fight each other and so they howled in rage as neither of us placed a fatal thrust. Just as I saw the sudden coming of dark I whispered to Kantos Kan to thrust his sword between my left arm and my body. As he did so I staggered back clasping the sword tightly with my arm and thus fell to the ground with his weapon apparently protruding from my chest. Kantos Kan perceived my coup and stepping quickly to my side he placed his foot upon my neck and withdrawing his sword from my body gave me the final death blow through the neck which is supposed to sever the jugular vein, but in this instance the cold blade slipped harmlessly into the sand of the arena. In the darkness which had now fallen none could tell but that he had really finished me. I whispered to him to go and claim his freedom and then look for me in the hills east of the city, and so he left me.

When the amphitheater had cleared I crept stealthily to the top and as the great excavation lay far from the plaza and in an untenanted portion of the great dead city I had little trouble in reaching the hills beyond.

TWENTY

In the Atmosphere Factory

For two days I waited there for Kantos Kan, but as he did not come I started off on foot in a northwesterly direction toward a point where he had told me lay the nearest waterway. My only food consisted of vegetable milk from the plants which gave so bounteously of this priceless fluid.

Through two long weeks I wandered, stumbling through the nights guided only by the stars and hiding during the days behind some protruding rock or among the occasional hills I traversed. Several times I was attacked by wild beasts; strange, uncouth monstrosities that leaped upon me in the dark, so that I had ever to grasp my long-sword in my hand that I might be ready for them. Usually my strange, newly acquired telepathic power warned me in ample time, but once I was down with vicious fangs at my jugular and a hairy face pressed close to mine before I knew that I was even threatened.

What manner of thing was upon me I did not know, but that it was large and heavy and many-legged I could feel. My hands were at its throat before the fangs had a chance to bury themselves in my neck, and slowly I forced the hairy face from me and closed my fingers, vise-like, upon its windpipe.

Without sound we lay there, the beast exerting every effort to reach me with those awful fangs, and I straining to maintain my grip and choke the life from it as I kept it from my throat. Slowly my arms gave to the unequal struggle, and inch by inch the burning eyes and gleaming tusks of my antagonist crept toward me, until, as the hairy face touched mine again, I realized that all was over. And then a living mass of destruction sprang from the surrounding darkness full upon the creature that held me pinioned to the ground. The two rolled growling upon the moss, tearing and rending one another in a frightful manner, but it was soon over and my preserver stood with lowered head above the throat of the dead thing which would have killed me.

The nearer moon, hurtling suddenly above the horizon and lighting up the Barsoomian scene, showed me that my preserver was Woola, but from whence he had come, or how found me, I was at a loss to know. That I was glad of his companionship it is needless to say, but my pleasure at seeing him was tempered by anxiety as to the reason of his leaving Dejah Thoris. Only her death I felt sure, could account for his absence from her, so faithful I knew him to be to my commands.

By the light of the now brilliant moons I saw that he was but a shadow of his former self, and as he turned from my caress and commenced greedily to devour the dead carcass at my feet I realized that the poor fellow was more than half starved. I, myself, was in but little better plight but I could not bring myself to eat the uncooked flesh and I had no means of making a fire. When Woola had finished his meal I again took up my weary and seemingly endless wandering in quest of the elusive waterway.

At daybreak of the fifteenth day of my search I was overjoyed to see the high trees that denoted the object of my search. About noon I dragged myself wearily to the portals of a huge building which covered perhaps four square miles and towered two hundred feet in the air. It showed no aperture in the mighty walls other than the tiny door at which I sank exhausted, nor was there any sign of life about it.

I could find no bell or other method of making my presence known to the inmates of the place, unless a small round hole in the wall near the door was for that purpose. It was of about the bigness of a lead pencil and thinking that it might be in the nature of a speaking tube I put my mouth to it and was about to call into it when a voice issued from it asking me whom I might be, where from, and the nature of my errand.

I explained that I had escaped from the Warhoons and was dying of starvation and exhaustion.

"You wear the metal of a green warrior and are followed by a calot, yet you are of the figure of a red man. In color you are neither green nor red. In the name of the ninth day, what manner of creature are you?"

"I am a friend of the red men of Barsoom and I am starving. In the name of humanity open to us," I replied.

Presently the door commenced to recede before me until it had sunk into the wall fifty feet, then it stopped and slid easily to the left, exposing a short, narrow corridor of concrete, at the further end of which was another door, similar in every respect to the one I had just passed. No one was in sight, yet immediately we passed the first door it slid gently into place behind us and receded rapidly to its original position in the front wall of the building. As the door had slipped aside I had noted its great thickness, fully twenty feet, and as it reached its place once more after closing behind us, great cylinders of steel had dropped from the ceiling behind it and fitted their lower ends into apertures countersunk in the floor.

A second and third door receded before me and slipped to one side as the first, before I reached a large inner chamber where I found food and drink set out upon a great stone table. A voice directed me to satisfy my hunger and to feed my calot, and while I was thus engaged my invisible host put me through a severe and searching cross-examination.

"Your statements are most remarkable," said the voice, on concluding its questioning, "but you are evidently speaking the truth, and it is equally evident that you are not of Barsoom. I can tell that by the conformation of your brain and the strange location of your internal organs and the shape and size of your heart."

"Can you see through me?" I exclaimed.

"Yes, I can see all but your thoughts, and were you a Barsoomian I could read those."

Then a door opened at the far side of the chamber and a strange, dried up, little mummy of a man came toward me. He wore but a single article of clothing or adornment, a small collar of gold from which depended upon his chest a great ornament as large as a dinner plate set solid with huge diamonds, except for the exact center which was occupied by a strange stone, an inch in diameter, that scintillated nine different and distinct rays; the seven colors of our earthly prism and two beautiful rays which, to me, were new and nameless. I cannot describe them any more than you could describe red to a blind man. I only know that they were beautiful in the extreme.

The old man sat and talked with me for hours, and the strangest part of our intercourse was that I could read his every thought while he could not fathom an iota from my mind unless I spoke.

I did not apprise him of my ability to sense his mental operations, and thus I learned a great deal which proved of immense value to me later and which I would never have known had he suspected my strange power, for the Martians have such perfect control of their mental machinery that they are able to direct their thoughts with absolute precision.

The building in which I found myself contained the machinery which produces that artificial atmosphere which sustains life on Mars. The secret of the entire process hinges on the use of the ninth ray, one of the beautiful scintillations which I had noted emanating from the great stone in my host's diadem.

This ray is separated from the other rays of the sun by means of finely adjusted instruments placed upon the roof of the huge building, three-quarters of which is used for reservoirs in which the ninth ray is stored.

This product is then treated electrically, or rather certain proportions of refined electric vibrations are incorporated with it, and the result is then pumped to the five principal air centers of the planet where, as it is released, contact with the ether of space transforms it into atmosphere.

There is always sufficient reserve of the ninth ray stored in the great building to maintain the present Martian atmosphere for a thousand years, and the only fear, as my new friend told me, was that some accident might befall the pumping apparatus.

He led me to an inner chamber where I beheld a battery of twenty radium pumps any one of which was equal to the task of furnishing all Mars with the atmosphere compound. For eight hundred years, he told me, he had watched these pumps which are used alternately a day each at a stretch, or a little over twenty-four and one-half Earth hours. He has one assistant who divides the watch with him. Half a Martian year, about three hundred and forty-four of our days, each of these men spend alone in this huge, isolated plant.

Every red Martian is taught during earliest childhood the principles of the manufacture of atmosphere, but only two at one time ever hold the secret of ingress to the great building, which, built as it is with walls a hundred and fifty feet thick, is absolutely unassailable, even the roof being guarded from assault by air craft by a glass covering five feet thick.

The only fear they entertain of attack is from the green Martians or some demented red man, as all Barsoomians realize that the very existence of every form of life of Mars is dependent upon the uninterrupted working of this plant.

One curious fact I discovered as I watched his thoughts was that the outer doors are manipulated by telepathic means. The locks are so finely adjusted that the doors are released by the action of a certain combination of thought waves. To experiment with my new-found toy I thought to surprise him into revealing this combination and so I asked him in a casual manner how he had managed to unlock the massive doors for me from the inner chambers of the building. As quick as a flash there leaped to his mind nine Martian sounds, but as quickly faded as he answered that this was a secret he must not divulge.

From then on his manner toward me changed as though he feared that he had been surprised into divulging his great secret, and I read suspicion and fear in his looks and thoughts, though his words were still fair.

Before I retired for the night he promised to give me a letter to a nearby agricultural officer who would help me on my way to Zodanga, which he said, was the nearest Martian city.

"But be sure that you do not let them know you are bound for Helium as they are at war with that country. My assistant and I are of no country, we belong to all Barsoom and this talisman which we wear protects us in all lands, even among the green men—though we do not trust ourselves to their hands if we can avoid it," he added.

"And so good-night, my friend," he continued, "may you have a long and restful sleep—yes, a long sleep."

And though he smiled pleasantly I saw in his thoughts the wish that he had never admitted me, and then a picture of him standing over me in the night, and the swift thrust of a long dagger and the half formed words, "I am sorry, but it is for the best good of Barsoom."

As he closed the door of my chamber behind him his thoughts were cut off from me as was the sight of him, which seemed strange to me in my little knowledge of thought transference.

What was I to do? How could I escape through these mighty walls? Easily could I kill him now that I was warned, but once he was dead I could no more escape, and with the stopping of the machinery of the great plant I should die with all the other inhabitants of the planet—all, even Dejah Thoris were she not already dead. For the others I did not give the snap of my finger, but the thought of Dejah Thoris drove from my mind all desire to kill my mistaken host.

Cautiously I opened the door of my apartment and, followed by Woola, sought the inner of the great doors. A wild scheme had come to me; I would attempt to force the great locks by the nine thought waves I had read in my host's mind.

Creeping stealthily through corridor after corridor and down winding runways which turned hither and thither I finally reached the great hall in which I had broken my long fast that morning. Nowhere had I seen my host, nor did I know where he kept himself by night.

I was on the point of stepping boldly out into the room when a slight noise behind me warned me back into the shadows of a recess in the corridor. Dragging Woola after me I crouched low in the darkness.

Presently the old man passed close by me, and as he entered the dimly lighted chamber which I had been about to pass through I saw that he held a long thin dagger in his hand and that he was sharpening it upon a stone. In his mind was the decision to inspect the radium pumps, which would take about thirty minutes, and then return to my bed chamber and finish me.

As he passed through the great hall and disappeared down the runway which led to the pump-room, I stole stealthily from my hiding place and crossed to the great door, the inner of the three which stood between me and liberty.

Concentrating my mind upon the massive lock I hurled the nine thought waves against it. In breathless expectancy I waited, when finally the great door moved softly toward me and slid quietly to one side. One after the other the remaining mighty portals opened at my command and Woola and I stepped forth into the darkness, free, but little better off than we had been before, other than that we had full stomachs.

Hastening away from the shadows of the formidable pile I made for the first crossroad, intending to strike the central turnpike as quickly as possible. This I reached about morning and entering the first enclosure I came to I searched for some evidences of a habitation.

There were low rambling buildings of concrete barred with heavy impassable doors, and no amount of hammering and hallooing brought any response. Weary and exhausted from sleeplessness I threw myself upon the ground commanding Woola to stand guard.

Some time later I was awakened by his frightful growlings and opened my eyes to see three red Martians standing a short distance from us and covering me with their rifles.

"I am unarmed and no enemy," I hastened to explain. "I have been a prisoner among the green men and am on my way to Zodanga. All I ask is food and rest for myself and my calot and the proper directions for reaching my destination."

They lowered their rifles and advanced pleasantly toward me placing their right hands upon my left shoulder, after the manner of their custom of salute, and asking me many questions about myself and my wanderings. They then took me to the house of one of them which was only a short distance away.

The buildings I had been hammering at in the early morning were occupied only by stock and farm produce, the house proper standing among a grove of enormous trees, and, like all red-Martian homes, had been raised at night some forty or fifty feet from the ground on a large round metal shaft which slid up or down within a sleeve sunk in the ground, and was operated by a tiny radium engine in the entrance hall of the building. Instead of bothering with bolts and bars for their dwellings, the red Martians simply run them up out of harm's way during the night. They also have private means for lowering or raising them from the ground without if they wish to go away and leave them.

These brothers, with their wives and children, occupied three similar houses on this farm. They did no work themselves, being government officers in charge. The labor was performed by convicts, prisoners of war, delinquent debtors and confirmed bachelors who were too poor to pay the high celibate tax which all red-Martian governments impose.

They were the personification of cordiality and hospitality and I spent several days with them, resting and recuperating from my long and arduous experiences.

When they had heard my story—I omitted all reference to Dejah Thoris and the old man of the atmosphere plant—they advised me to color my body to more nearly resemble their own race and then attempt to find employment in Zodanga, either in the army or the navy.

"The chances are small that your tale will be believed until after you have proven your trustworthiness and won friends among the higher nobles of the court. This you can most easily do through military service, as we are a warlike people on Barsoom," explained one of them, "and save our richest favors for the fighting man."

When I was ready to depart they furnished me with a small domestic bull thoat, such as is used for saddle purposes by all red Martians. The animal is about the size of a horse and quite gentle, but in color and shape an exact replica of his huge and fierce cousin of the wilds.

The brothers had supplied me with a reddish oil with which I anointed my entire body and one of them cut my hair, which had grown quite long, in the prevailing fashion of the time, square at the back and banged in front, so that I could have passed anywhere upon Barsoom as a full-fledged red Martian. My metal and ornaments were also renewed in the style of a Zodangan gentleman, attached to the house of Ptor, which was the family name of my benefactors.

They filled a little sack at my side with Zodangan money. The medium of exchange upon Mars is not dissimilar from our own except that the coins are oval. Paper money is issued by individuals as they require it and redeemed twice yearly. If a man issues more than he can redeem, the government pays his creditors in full and the debtor works out the amount upon the farms or in mines, which are all owned by the government. This suits everybody except the debtor as it has been a difficult thing to obtain sufficient voluntary labor to work the great isolated farm lands of Mars, stretching as they do like narrow ribbons from pole to pole, through wild stretches peopled by wild animals and wilder men.

When I mentioned my inability to repay them for their kindness to me they assured me that I would have ample opportunity if I lived long upon Barsoom, and bidding me farewell they watched me until I was out of sight upon the broad white turnpike.

TWENTY-ONE

An Air Scout for Zodanga

As I proceeded on my journey toward Zodanga many strange and interesting sights arrested my attention, and at the several farm houses where I stopped I learned a number of new and instructive things concerning the methods and manners of Barsoom.

The water which supplies the farms of Mars is collected in immense underground reservoirs at either pole from the melting ice caps, and pumped through long conduits to the various populated centers. Along either side of these conduits, and extending their entire length, lie the cultivated districts. These are divided into tracts of about the same size, each tract being under the supervision of one or more government officers.

Instead of flooding the surface of the fields, and thus wasting immense quantities of water by evaporation, the precious liquid is carried underground through a vast network of small pipes directly to the roots of the vegetation. The crops upon Mars are always uniform, for there are no droughts, no rains, no high winds, and no insects, or destroying birds.

On this trip I tasted the first meat I had eaten since leaving Earth—large, juicy steaks and chops from the well-fed domestic animals of the farms. Also I enjoyed luscious fruits and vegetables, but not a single article of food which was exactly similar to anything on Earth. Every plant and flower and vegetable and animal has been so refined by ages of careful, scientific cultivation and breeding that the like of them on Earth dwindled into pale, gray, characterless nothingness by comparison.

At a second stop I met some highly cultivated people of the noble class and while in conversation we chanced to speak of Helium. One of the older men had been there on a diplomatic mission several years before and spoke with regret of the conditions which seemed destined ever to keep these two countries at war.

"Helium," he said, "rightly boasts the most beautiful women of Barsoom, and of all her treasures the wondrous daughter of Mors Kajak, Dejah Thoris, is the most exquisite flower.

"Why," he added, "the people really worship the ground she walks upon and since her loss on that ill-starred expedition all Helium has been draped in mourning.

"That our ruler should have attacked the disabled fleet as it was returning to Helium was but another of his awful blunders which I fear will sooner or later compel Zodanga to elevate a wiser man to his place."

"Even now, though our victorious armies are surrounding Helium, the people of Zodanga are voicing their displeasure, for the war is not a popular one, since it is not based on right or justice. Our forces took advantage of the absence of the principal fleet of Helium on their search for the princess, and so we have been able easily to reduce the city to a sorry plight. It is said she will fall within the next few passages of the further moon."

"And what, think you, may have been the fate of the princess, Dejah Thoris?" I asked as casually as possible.

"She is dead," he answered. "This much was learned from a green warrior recently captured by our forces in the south. She escaped from the hordes of Thark with a strange creature of another world, only to fall into the hands of the Warhoons. Their thoats were found wandering upon the sea bottom and evidences of a bloody conflict were discovered nearby."

While this information was in no way reassuring, neither was it at all conclusive proof of the death of Dejah Thoris, and so I determined to make every effort possible to reach Helium as quickly as I could and carry to Tardos Mors such news of his granddaughter's possible whereabouts as lay in my power.

Ten days after leaving the three Ptor brothers I arrived at Zodanga. From the moment that I had come in contact with the red inhabitants of Mars I had noticed that Woola drew a great amount of unwelcome attention to me, since the huge brute belonged to a species which is never domesticated by the red men. Were one to stroll down Broadway with a Numidian lion at his heels the effect would be somewhat similar to that which I should have produced had I entered Zodanga with Woola.

The very thought of parting with the faithful fellow caused me so great regret and genuine sorrow that I put it off until just before we arrived at the city's gates; but then, finally, it became imperative that we separate. Had nothing further than my own safety or pleasure been at stake no argument could have prevailed upon me to turn away the one creature upon Barsoom that had never failed in a demonstration of affection and loyalty; but as I would willingly have offered my life in the service of her in search of whom

I was about to challenge the unknown dangers of this, to me, mysterious city, I could not permit even Woola's life to threaten the success of my venture, much less his momentary happiness, for I doubted not he soon would forget me. And so I bade the poor beast an affectionate farewell, promising him, however, that if I came through my adventure in safety that in some way I should find the means to search him out.

He seemed to understand me fully, and when I pointed back in the direction of Thark he turned sorrowfully away, nor could I bear to watch him go; but resolutely set my face toward Zodanga and with a touch of heartsickness approached her frowning walls.

The letter I bore from them gained me immediate entrance to the vast, walled city. It was still very early in the morning and the streets were practically deserted. The residences, raised high upon their metal columns, resembled huge rookeries, while the uprights themselves presented the appearance of steel tree trunks. The shops as a rule were not raised from the ground nor were their doors bolted or barred, since thievery is practically unknown upon Barsoom. Assassination is the ever-present fear of all Barsoomians, and for this reason alone their homes are raised high above the ground at night, or in times of danger.

The Ptor brothers had given me explicit directions for reaching the point of the city where I could find living accommodations and be near the offices of the government agents to whom they had given me letters. My way led to the central square or plaza, which is a characteristic of all Martian cities.

The plaza of Zodanga covers a square mile and is bounded by the palaces of the jeddak, the jeds, and other members of the royalty and nobility of Zodanga, as well as by the principal public buildings, cafés, and shops.

As I was crossing the great square lost in wonder and admiration of the magnificent architecture and the gorgeous scarlet vegetation which carpeted the broad lawns I discovered a red Martian walking briskly toward me from one of the avenues. He paid not the slightest attention to me, but as he came abreast I recognized him, and turning I placed my hand upon his shoulder, calling out:

"Kaor, Kantos Kan!"

Like lightning he wheeled and before I could so much as lower my hand the point of his long-sword was at my breast.

"Who are you?" he growled, and then as a backward leap carried me fifty feet from his sword he dropped the point to the ground and exclaimed, laughing,

"I do not need a better reply, there is but one man upon all Barsoom who can bounce about like a rubber ball. By the mother of the further moon,

John Carter, how came you here, and have you become a Darseen that you can change your color at will?"

"You gave me a bad half minute my friend," he continued, after I had briefly outlined my adventures since parting with him in the arena at Warhoon. "Were my name and city known to the Zodangans I would shortly be sitting on the banks of the lost sea of Korus with my revered and departed ancestors. I am here in the interest of Tardos Mors, Jeddak of Helium, to discover the whereabouts of Dejah Thoris, our princess. Sab Than, prince of Zodanga, has her hidden in the city and has fallen madly in love with her. His father, Than Kosis, Jeddak of Zodanga, has made her voluntary marriage to his son the price of peace between our countries, but Tardos Mors will not accede to the demands and has sent word that he and his people would rather look upon the dead face of their princess than see her wed to any than her own choice, and that personally he would prefer being engulfed in the ashes of a lost and burning Helium to joining the metal of his house with that of Than Kosis. His reply was the deadliest affront he could have put upon Than Kosis and the Zodangans, but his people love him the more for it and his strength in Helium is greater today than ever.

"I have been here three days," continued Kantos Kan, "but I have not yet found where Dejah Thoris is imprisoned. Today I join the Zodangan navy as an air scout and I hope in this way to win the confidence of Sab Than, the prince, who is commander of this division of the navy, and thus learn the whereabouts of Dejah Thoris. I am glad that you are here, John Carter, for I know your loyalty to my princess and two of us working together should be able to accomplish much."

The plaza was now commencing to fill with people going and coming upon the daily activities of their duties. The shops were opening and the cafés filling with early morning patrons. Kantos Kan led me to one of these gorgeous eating places where we were served entirely by mechanical apparatus. No hand touched the food from the time it entered the building in its raw state until it emerged hot and delicious upon the tables before the guests, in response to the touching of tiny buttons to indicate their desires.

After our meal, Kantos Kan took me with him to the headquarters of the air-scout squadron and introducing me to his superior asked that I be enrolled as a member of the corps. In accordance with custom an examination was necessary, but Kantos Kan had told me to have no fear on this score as he would attend to that part of the matter. He accomplished this by taking my order for examination to the examining officer and representing himself as John Carter.

"This ruse will be discovered later," he cheerfully explained, "when they check up my weights, measurements, and other personal identification data, but it will be several months before this is done and our mission should be accomplished or have failed long before that time."

The next few days were spent by Kantos Kan in teaching me the intricacies of flying and of repairing the dainty little contrivances which the Martians use for this purpose. The body of the one-man air craft is about sixteen feet long, two feet wide and three inches thick, tapering to a point at each end. The driver sits on top of this plane upon a seat constructed over the small, noiseless radium engine which propels it. The medium of buoyancy is contained within the thin metal walls of the body and consists of the eighth Barsoomian ray, or ray of propulsion, as it may be termed in view of its properties.

This ray, like the ninth ray, is unknown on Earth, but the Martians have discovered that it is an inherent property of all light no matter from what source it emanates. They have learned that it is the solar eighth ray which propels the light of the sun to the various planets, and that it is the individual eighth ray of each planet which "reflects," or propels the light thus obtained out into space once more. The solar eighth ray would be absorbed by the surface of Barsoom, but the Barsoomian eighth ray, which tends to propel light from Mars into space, is constantly streaming out from the planet constituting a force of repulsion of gravity which when confined is able to lift enormous weights from the surface of the ground.

It is this ray which has enabled them to so perfect aviation that battle ships far outweighing anything known upon Earth sail as gracefully and lightly through the thin air of Barsoom as a toy balloon in the heavy atmosphere of Earth.

During the early years of the discovery of this ray many strange accidents occurred before the Martians learned to measure and control the wonderful power they had found. In one instance, some nine hundred years before, the first great battle ship to be built with eighth ray reservoirs was stored with too great a quantity of the rays and she had sailed up from Helium with five hundred officers and men, never to return.

Her power of repulsion for the planet was so great that it had carried her far into space, where she can be seen today, by the aid of powerful telescopes, hurtling through the heavens ten thousand miles from Mars; a tiny satellite that will thus encircle Barsoom to the end of time.

The fourth day after my arrival at Zodanga I made my first flight, and as a result of it I won a promotion which included quarters in the palace of Than Kosis.

As I rose above the city I circled several times, as I had seen Kantos Kan do, and then throwing my engine into top speed I raced at terrific velocity toward the south, following one of the great waterways which enter Zodanga from that direction.

I had traversed perhaps two hundred miles in a little less than an hour when I descried far below me a party of three green warriors racing madly toward a small figure on foot which seemed to be trying to reach the confines of one of the walled fields.

Dropping my machine rapidly toward them, and circling to the rear of the warriors, I soon saw that the object of their pursuit was a red Martian wearing the metal of the scout squadron to which I was attached. A short distance away lay his tiny flier, surrounded by the tools with which he had evidently been occupied in repairing some damage when surprised by the green warriors.

They were now almost upon him; their flying mounts charging down on the relatively puny figure at terrific speed, while the warriors leaned low to the right, with their great metal-shod spears. Each seemed striving to be the first to impale the poor Zodangan and in another moment his fate would have been sealed had it not been for my timely arrival.

Driving my fleet air craft at high speed directly behind the warriors I soon overtook them and without diminishing my speed I rammed the prow of my little flier between the shoulders of the nearest. The impact sufficient to have torn through inches of solid steel, hurled the fellow's headless body into the air over the head of his thoat, where it fell sprawling upon the moss. The mounts of the other two warriors turned squealing in terror, and bolted in opposite directions.

Reducing my speed I circled and came to the ground at the feet of the astonished Zodangan. He was warm in his thanks for my timely aid and promised that my day's work would bring the reward it merited, for it was none other than a cousin of the jeddak of Zodanga whose life I had saved.

We wasted no time in talk as we knew that the warriors would surely return as soon as they had gained control of their mounts. Hastening to his damaged machine we were bending every effort to finish the needed repairs and had almost completed them when we saw the two green monsters returning at top speed from opposite sides of us. When they had approached within a hundred yards their thoats again became unmanageable and absolutely refused to advance further toward the air craft which had frightened them.

The warriors finally dismounted and hobbling their animals advanced toward us on foot with drawn long-swords.

I advanced to meet the larger, telling the Zodangan to do the best he could with the other. Finishing my man with almost no effort, as had now from much practice become habitual with me, I hastened to return to my new acquaintance whom I found indeed in desperate straits.

He was wounded and down with the huge foot of his antagonist upon his throat and the great long-sword raised to deal the final thrust. With a bound I cleared the fifty feet intervening between us, and with outstretched point drove my sword completely through the body of the green warrior. His sword fell, harmless, to the ground and he sank limply upon the prostrate form of the Zodangan.

A cursory examination of the latter revealed no mortal injuries and after a brief rest he asserted that he felt fit to attempt the return voyage. He would have to pilot his own craft, however, as these frail vessels are not intended to convey but a single person.

Quickly completing the repairs we rose together into the still, cloudless Martian sky, and at great speed and without further mishap returned to Zodanga.

As we neared the city we discovered a mighty concourse of civilians and troops assembled upon the plain before the city. The sky was black with naval vessels and private and public pleasure craft, flying long streamers of gay-colored silks, and banners and flags of odd and picturesque design.

My companion signaled that I slow down, and running his machine close beside mine suggested that we approach and watch the ceremony, which, he said, was for the purpose of conferring honors on individual officers and men for bravery and other distinguished service. He then unfurled a little ensign which denoted that his craft bore a member of the royal family of Zodanga, and together we made our way through the maze of low-lying air vessels until we hung directly over the jeddak of Zodanga and his staff. All were mounted upon the small domestic bull thoats of the red Martians, and their trappings and ornamentation bore such a quantity of gorgeously colored feathers that I could not but be struck with the startling resemblance the concourse bore to a band of the red Indians of my own Earth.

One of the staff called the attention of Than Kosis to the presence of my companion above them and the ruler motioned for him to descend. As they waited for the troops to move into position facing the jeddak the two talked earnestly together, the jeddak and his staff occasionally glancing up at me. I could not hear their conversation and presently it ceased and all dismounted, as the last body of troops had wheeled into position before their emperor. A member of the staff advanced toward the troops, and calling the name of a soldier commanded him to advance. The officer then recited the nature of the heroic act which had won the approval of the jeddak, and the latter advanced and placed a metal ornament upon the left arm of the lucky man.

Ten men had been so decorated when the aide called out,

"John Carter, air scout!"

Never in my life had I been so surprised, but the habit of military discipline is strong within me, and I dropped my little machine lightly to the ground and advanced on foot as I had seen the others do. As I halted before the officer, he addressed me in a voice audible to the entire assemblage of troops and spectators.

"In recognition, John Carter," he said, "of your remarkable courage and skill in defending the person of the cousin of the jeddak Than Kosis and, singlehanded, vanquishing three green warriors, it is the pleasure of our jeddak to confer on you the mark of his esteem."

Than Kosis then advanced toward me and placing an ornament upon me, said:

"My cousin has narrated the details of your wonderful achievement, which seems little short of miraculous, and if you can so well defend a cousin of the jeddak how much better could you defend the person of the jeddak himself. You are therefore appointed a padwar of The Guards and will be quartered in my palace hereafter."

I thanked him, and at his direction joined the members of his staff. After the ceremony I returned my machine to its quarters on the roof of the barracks of the air-scout squadron, and with an orderly from the palace to guide me I reported to the officer in charge of the palace.

TWENTY-TWO

I Find Dejah

The major-domo to whom I reported had been given instructions to station me near the person of the jeddak, who, in time of war, is always in great danger of assassination, as the rule that all is fair in war seems to constitute the entire ethics of Martian conflict.

He therefore escorted me immediately to the apartment in which Than Kosis then was. The ruler was engaged in conversation with his son, Sab Than, and several courtiers of his household, and did not perceive my entrance.

The walls of the apartment were completely hung with splendid tapestries which hid any windows or doors which may have pierced them. The room was lighted by imprisoned rays of sunshine held between the ceiling proper and what appeared to be a ground-glass false ceiling a few inches below.

My guide drew aside one of the tapestries, disclosing a passage which encircled the room, between the hangings and the walls of the chamber. Within this passage I was to remain, he said, so long as Than Kosis was in the apartment. When he left I was to follow. My only duty was to guard the ruler and keep out of sight as much as possible. I would be relieved after a period of four hours. The major-domo then left me.

The tapestries were of a strange weaving which gave the appearance of heavy solidity from one side, but from my hiding place I could perceive all that took place within the room as readily as though there had been no curtain intervening.

Scarcely had I gained my post than the tapestry at the opposite end of the chamber separated and four soldiers of The Guard entered, surrounding a female figure. As they approached Than Kosis the soldiers fell to either side and there standing before the jeddak and not ten feet from me, her beautiful face radiant with smiles, was Dejah Thoris.

Sab Than, Prince of Zodanga, advanced to meet her, and hand in hand they approached close to the jeddak. Than Kosis looked up in surprise, and, rising, saluted her.

"To what strange freak do I owe this visit from the Princess of Helium, who, two days ago, with rare consideration for my pride, assured me that she would prefer Tal Hajus, the green Thark, to my son?"

Dejah Thoris only smiled the more and with the roguish dimples playing at the corners of her mouth she made answer:

"From the beginning of time upon Barsoom it has been the prerogative of woman to change her mind as she listed and to dissemble in matters concerning her heart. That you will forgive, Than Kosis, as has your son. Two days ago I was not sure of his love for me, but now I am, and I have come to beg of you to forget my rash words and to accept the assurance of the Princess of Helium that when the time comes she will wed Sab Than, Prince of Zodanga."

"I am glad that you have so decided," replied Than Kosis. "It is far from my desire to push war further against the people of Helium, and, your promise shall be recorded and a proclamation to my people issued forthwith."

"It were better, Than Kosis," interrupted Dejah Thoris, "that the procla-mation wait the ending of this war. It would look strange indeed to my people and to yours were the Princess of Helium to give herself to her country's enemy in the midst of hostilities."

"Cannot the war be ended at once?" spoke Sab Than. "It requires but the word of Than Kosis to bring peace. Say it, my father, say the word that will hasten my happiness, and end this unpopular strife."

"We shall see," replied Than Kosis, "how the people of Helium take to peace. I shall at least offer it to them."

Dejah Thoris, after a few words, turned and left the apartment, still followed by her guards.

Thus was the edifice of my brief dream of happiness dashed, broken, to the ground of reality. The woman for whom I had offered my life, and from whose lips I had so recently heard a declaration of love for me, had lightly forgotten my very existence and smilingly given herself to the son of her people's most hated enemy.

Although I had heard it with my own ears I could not believe it. I must search out her apartments and force her to repeat the cruel truth to me alone before I would be convinced, and so I deserted my post and hastened through the passage behind the tapestries toward the door by which she had left the chamber. Slipping quietly through this opening I discovered a maze of winding corridors, branching and turning in every direction.

Running rapidly down first one and then another of them I soon became hopelessly lost and was standing panting against a side wall when I heard voices near me. Apparently they were coming from the opposite side of the partition against which I leaned and presently I made out the tones of Dejah Thoris. I could not hear the words but I knew that I could not possibly be mistaken in the voice.

Moving on a few steps I discovered another passageway at the end of which lay a door. Walking boldly forward I pushed into the room only to find myself in a small ante-chamber in which were the four guards who had accompanied her. One of them instantly arose and accosted me, asking the nature of my business.

"I am from Than Kosis," I replied, "and wish to speak privately with Dejah Thoris, Princess of Helium."

"And your order?" asked the fellow.

I did not know what he meant, but replied that I was a member of The Guard, and without waiting for a reply from him I strode toward the opposite door of the ante-chamber, behind which I could hear Dejah Thoris conversing.

But my entrance was not to be so easily accomplished. The guardsman stepped before me, saying,

"No one comes from Than Kosis without carrying an order or the password. You must give me one or the other before you may pass."

"The only order I require, my friend, to enter where I will, hangs at my side," I answered, tapping my long-sword; "will you let me pass in peace or no?"

For reply he whipped out his own sword, calling to the others to join him, and thus the four stood, with drawn weapons, barring my further progress.

"You are not here by the order of Than Kosis," cried the one who had first addressed me, "and not only shall you not enter the apartments of the Princess of Helium but you shall go back to Than Kosis under guard to explain this unwarranted temerity. Throw down your sword; you cannot hope to overcome four of us," he added with a grim smile.

My reply was a quick thrust which left me but three antagonists and I can assure you that they were worthy of my metal. They had me backed against the wall in no time, fighting for my life. Slowly I worked my way to a corner of the room where I could force them to come at me only one at a time, and thus we fought upward of twenty minutes; the clanging of steel on steel producing a veritable bedlam in the little room.

The noise had brought Dejah Thoris to the door of her apartment, and there she stood throughout the conflict with Sola at her back peering over her shoulder. Her face was set and emotionless and I knew that she did not recognize me, nor did Sola.

Finally a lucky cut brought down a second guardsman and then, with only two opposing me, I changed my tactics and rushed them down after the fashion of my fighting that had won me many a victory. The third fell within ten seconds after the second, and the last lay dead upon the bloody floor a few moments later. They were brave men and noble fighters, and it grieved me that I had been forced to kill them, but I would have willingly depopulated all Barsoom could I have reached the side of my Dejah Thoris in no other way.

Sheathing my bloody blade I advanced toward my Martian Princess, who still stood mutely gazing at me without sign of recognition.

"Who are you, Zodangan?" she whispered. "Another enemy to harass me in my misery?"

"I am a friend," I answered, "a once cherished friend."

"No friend of Helium's princess wears that metal," she replied, "and yet the voice! I have heard it before; it is not—it cannot be—no, for he is dead."

"It is, though, my Princess, none other than John Carter," I said. "Do you not recognize, even through paint and strange metal, the heart of your chieftain?"

As I came close to her she swayed toward me with outstretched hands, but as I reached to take her in my arms she drew back with a shudder and a little moan of misery.

"Too late, too late," she grieved. "O my chieftain that was, and whom I thought dead, had you but returned one little hour before—but now it is too late, too late."

"What do you mean, Dejah Thoris?" I cried. "That you would not have promised yourself to the Zodangan prince had you known that I lived?"

"Think you, John Carter, that I would give my heart to you yesterday and today to another? I thought that it lay buried with your ashes in the pits of Warhoon, and so today I have promised my body to another to save my people from the curse of a victorious Zodangan army."

"But I am not dead, my princess. I have come to claim you, and all Zodanga cannot prevent it."

"It is too late, John Carter, my promise is given, and on Barsoom that is final. The ceremonies which follow later are but meaningless formalities. They make the fact of marriage no more certain than does the funeral cortege of a jeddak again place the seal of death upon him. I am as good as married, John Carter. No longer may you call me your princess. No longer are you my chieftain."

"I know but little of your customs here upon Barsoom, Dejah Thoris, but I do know that I love you, and if you meant the last words you spoke to me that day as the hordes of Warhoon were charging down upon us, no other man shall ever claim you as his bride. You meant them then, my princess, and you mean them still! Say that it is true."

"I meant them, John Carter," she whispered. "I cannot repeat them now for I have given myself to another. Ah, if you had only known our ways, my friend," she continued, half to herself, "the promise would have been yours long months ago, and you could have claimed me before all others. It might have meant the fall of Helium, but I would have given my empire for my Tharkian chief."

Then aloud she said: "Do you remember the night when you offended me? You called me your princess without having asked my hand of me, and then you boasted that you had fought for me. You did not know, and I should not have been offended; I see that now. But there was no one to tell you what I could not, that upon Barsoom there are two kinds of women in the cities of the red men. The one they fight for that they may ask them in marriage; the other kind they fight for also, but never ask their hands. When a man has won a woman he may address her as his princess, or in any of the several terms which signify possession. You had fought for me, but had never asked me in marriage, and so when you called me your princess, you see," she faltered, "I was hurt, but even then, John Carter, I did not repulse you, as I should have done, until you made it doubly worse by taunting me with having won me through combat."

"I do not need ask your forgiveness now, Dejah Thoris," I cried. "You must know that my fault was of ignorance of your Barsoomian customs. What I failed to do, through implicit belief that my petition would be presumptuous and unwelcome, I do now, Dejah Thoris; I ask you to be my wife, and by all the Virginian fighting blood that flows in my veins you shall be."

"No, John Carter, it is useless," she cried, hopelessly, "I may never be yours while Sab Than lives."

"You have sealed his death warrant, my princess—Sab Than dies."

"Nor that either," she hastened to explain. "I may not wed the man who slays my husband, even in self-defense. It is custom. We are ruled by custom upon Barsoom. It is useless, my friend. You must bear the sorrow with me. That at least we may share in common. That, and the memory of the brief days among the Tharks. You must go now, nor ever see me again. Good-bye, my chieftain that was."

Disheartened and dejected, I withdrew from the room, but I was not entirely discouraged, nor would I admit that Dejah Thoris was lost to me until the ceremony had actually been performed.

As I wandered along the corridors, I was as absolutely lost in the mazes of winding passageways as I had been before I discovered Dejah Thoris' apartments.

I knew that my only hope lay in escape from the city of Zodanga, for the matter of the four dead guardsmen would have to be explained, and as I could never reach my original post without a guide, suspicion would surely rest on me so soon as I was discovered wandering aimlessly through the palace.

Presently I came upon a spiral runway leading to a lower floor, and this I followed downward for several stories until I reached the doorway of a large apartment in which were a number of guardsmen. The walls of this room were hung with transparent tapestries behind which I secreted myself without being apprehended.

The conversation of the guardsmen was general, and awakened no interest in me until an officer entered the room and ordered four of the men to relieve the detail who were guarding the Princess of Helium. Now, I knew, my troubles would commence in earnest and indeed they were upon me all too soon, for it seemed that the squad had scarcely left the guardroom before one of their number burst in again breathlessly, crying that they had found their four comrades butchered in the antechamber.

In a moment the entire palace was alive with people. Guardsmen, officers, courtiers, servants, and slaves ran helter-skelter through the corridors and apartments carrying messages and orders, and searching for signs of the assassin.

This was my opportunity and slim as it appeared I grasped it, for as a number of soldiers came hurrying past my hiding place I fell in behind them and followed through the mazes of the palace until, in passing through a great hall, I saw the blessed light of day coming in through a series of larger windows.

Here I left my guides, and, slipping to the nearest window, sought for an avenue of escape. The windows opened upon a great balcony which overlooked one of the broad avenues of Zodanga. The ground was about thirty feet below, and at a like distance from the building was a wall fully twenty feet high, constructed of polished glass about a foot in thickness. To a red Martian escape by this path would have appeared impossible, but to me, with my earthly strength and agility, it seemed already accomplished. My only fear was in being detected before darkness fell, for I could not make the leap in broad daylight while the court below and the avenue beyond were crowded with Zodangans.

Accordingly I searched for a hiding place and finally found one by accident, inside a huge hanging ornament which swung from the ceiling of the hall, and about ten feet from the floor. Into the capacious bowl-like vase I sprang with ease, and scarcely had I settled down within it than I heard a number of people enter the apartment. The group stopped beneath my hiding place and I could plainly overhear their every word.

"It is the work of Heliumites," said one of the men.

"Yes, O Jeddak, but how had they access to the palace? I could believe that even with the diligent care of your guardsmen a single enemy might reach the inner chambers, but how a force of six or eight fighting men could have done so unobserved is beyond me. We shall soon know, however, for here comes the royal psychologist."

Another man now joined the group, and, after making his formal greetings to his ruler, said:

"O mighty Jeddak, it is a strange tale I read in the dead minds of your faithful guardsmen. They were felled not by a number of fighting men, but by a single opponent."

He paused to let the full weight of this announcement impress his hearers, and that his statement was scarcely credited was evidenced by the impatient exclamation of incredulity which escaped the lips of Than Kosis.

"What manner of weird tale are you bringing me, Notan?" he cried.

"It is the truth, my Jeddak," replied the psychologist. "In fact the impressions were strongly marked on the brain of each of the four guardsmen. Their antagonist was a very tall man, wearing the metal of one of your own guardsmen, and his fighting ability was little short of marvelous for he fought fair against the entire four and vanquished them by his surpassing skill and superhuman strength and endurance. Though he wore the metal of Zodanga, my Jeddak, such a man was never seen before in this or any other country upon Barsoom.

"The mind of the Princess of Helium whom I have examined and questioned was a blank to me, she has perfect control, and I could not read one iota of it. She said that she witnessed a portion of the encounter, and that when she looked there was but one man engaged with the guardsmen; a man whom she did not recognize as ever having seen."

"Where is my erstwhile savior?" spoke another of the party, and I recognized the voice of the cousin of Than Kosis, whom I had rescued from the green warriors. "By the metal of my first ancestor," he went on, "but the description fits him to perfection, especially as to his fighting ability."

"Where is this man?" cried Than Kosis. "Have him brought to me at once. What know you of him, cousin? It seemed strange to me now that I think upon it that there should have been such a fighting man in Zodanga, of whose name, even, we were ignorant before today. And his name too, John Carter, who ever heard of such a name upon Barsoom!"

Word was soon brought that I was nowhere to be found, either in the palace or at my former quarters in the barracks of the air-scout squadron. Kantos Kan, they had found and questioned, but he knew nothing of my whereabouts, and as to my past, he had told them he knew as little, since he had but recently met me during our captivity among the Warhoons.

"Keep your eyes on this other one," commanded Than Kosis. "He also is a stranger and likely as not they both hail from Helium, and where one is we shall sooner or later find the other. Quadruple the air patrol, and let every man who leaves the city by air or ground be subjected to the closest scrutiny."

Another messenger now entered with word that I was still within the palace walls.

"The likeness of every person who has entered or left the palace grounds today has been carefully examined," concluded the fellow, "and not one approaches the likeness of this new padwar of the guards, other than that which was recorded of him at the time he entered."

"Then we will have him shortly," commented Than Kosis contentedly, "and in the meanwhile we will repair to the apartments of the Princess of Helium and question her in regard to the affair. She may know more than she cared to divulge to you, Notan. Come."

They left the hall, and, as darkness had fallen without, I slipped lightly from my hiding place and hastened to the balcony. Few were in sight, and choosing a moment when none seemed near I sprang quickly to the top of the glass wall and from there to the avenue beyond the palace grounds.

TWENTY-THREE

Lost in the Sky

Without effort at concealment I hastened to the vicinity of our quarters, where I felt sure I should find Kantos Kan. As I neared the building I became more careful, as I judged, and rightly, that the place would be guarded. Several men in civilian metal loitered near the front entrance and in the rear were others. My only means of reaching, unseen, the upper story where our apartments were situated was through an adjoining building, and after considerable maneuvering I managed to attain the roof of a shop several doors away.

Leaping from roof to roof, I soon reached an open window in the building where I hoped to find the Heliumite, and in another moment I stood in the room before him. He was alone and showed no surprise at my coming, saying he had expected me much earlier, as my tour of duty must have ended some time since.

I saw that he knew nothing of the events of the day at the palace, and when I had enlightened him he was all excitement. The news that Dejah Thoris had promised her hand to Sab Than filled him with dismay.

"It cannot be," he exclaimed. "It is impossible! Why no man in all Helium but would prefer death to the selling of our loved princess to the ruling house of Zodanga. She must have lost her mind to have assented to such an atrocious bargain. You, who do not know how we of Helium love the members of our ruling house, cannot appreciate the horror with which I contemplate such an unholy alliance."

"What can be done, John Carter?" he continued. "You are a resourceful man. Can you not think of some way to save Helium from this disgrace?"

"If I can come within sword's reach of Sab Than," I answered, "I can solve the difficulty in so far as Helium is concerned, but for personal reasons I would prefer that another struck the blow that frees Dejah Thoris."

Kantos Kan eyed me narrowly before he spoke.

"You love her!" he said. "Does she know it?"

"She knows it, Kantos Kan, and repulses me only because she is promised to Sab Than."

The splendid fellow sprang to his feet, and grasping me by the shoulder raised his sword on high, exclaiming:

"And had the choice been left to me I could not have chosen a more fitting mate for the first princess of Barsoom. Here is my hand upon your shoulder, John Carter, and my word that Sab Than shall go out at the point of my sword for the sake of my love for Helium, for Dejah Thoris, and for you. This very night I shall try to reach his quarters in the palace."

"How?" I asked. "You are strongly guarded and a quadruple force patrols the sky."

He bent his head in thought a moment, then raised it with an air of confidence.

"I only need to pass these guards and I can do it," he said at last. "I know a secret entrance to the palace through the pinnacle of the highest tower. I fell upon it by chance one day as I was passing above the palace on patrol duty. In this work it is required that we investigate any unusual occurrence we may witness, and a face peering from the pinnacle of the high tower of the palace was, to me, most unusual. I therefore drew near and discovered that the possessor of the peering face was none other than Sab Than. He was slightly put out at being detected and commanded me to keep the matter to myself, explaining that the passage from the tower led directly to his apartments, and was known only to him. If I can reach the roof of the barracks and get my machine I can be in Sab Than's quarters in five minutes; but how am I to escape from this building, guarded as you say it is?"

"How well are the machine sheds at the barracks guarded?" I asked.

"There is usually but one man on duty there at night upon the roof."

"Go to the roof of this building, Kantos Kan, and wait me there."

Without stopping to explain my plans I retraced my way to the street and hastened to the barracks. I did not dare to enter the building, filled as it was with members of the air-scout squadron, who, in common with all Zodanga, were on the lookout for me.

The building was an enormous one, rearing its lofty head fully a thousand feet into the air. But few buildings in Zodanga were higher than these barracks, though several topped it by a few hundred feet; the docks of the great battleships of the line standing some fifteen hundred feet from the ground, while the freight and passenger stations of the merchant squadrons rose nearly as high.

It was a long climb up the face of the building, and one fraught with much danger, but there was no other way, and so I essayed the task. The fact that Barsoomian architecture is extremely ornate made the feat much simpler than I had anticipated, since I found ornamental ledges and projections which fairly formed a perfect ladder for me all the way to the eaves of the building. Here I met my first real obstacle. The eaves projected nearly twenty feet from the wall to which I clung, and though I encircled the great building I could find no opening through them.

The top floor was alight, and filled with soldiers engaged in the pastimes of their kind; I could not, therefore, reach the roof through the building.

There was one slight, desperate chance, and that I decided I must take—it was for Dejah Thoris, and no man has lived who would not risk a thousand deaths for such as she.

Clinging to the wall with my feet and one hand, I unloosened one of the long leather straps of my trappings at the end of which dangled a great hook by which air sailors are hung to the sides and bottoms of their craft for various purposes of repair, and by means of which landing parties are lowered to the ground from the battleships.

I swung this hook cautiously to the roof several times before it finally found lodgment; gently I pulled on it to strengthen its hold, but whether it would bear the weight of my body I did not know. It might be barely caught upon the very outer verge of the roof, so that as my body swung out at the end of the strap it would slip off and launch me to the pavement a thousand feet below.

An instant I hesitated, and then, releasing my grasp upon the supporting ornament, I swung out into space at the end of the strap. Far below me lay the brilliantly lighted streets, the hard pavements, and death. There was a little jerk at the top of the supporting eaves, and a nasty slipping, grating sound which turned me cold with apprehension; then the hook caught and I was safe.

Clambering quickly aloft I grasped the edge of the eaves and drew myself to the surface of the roof above. As I gained my feet I was confronted by the sentry on duty, into the muzzle of whose revolver I found myself looking.

"Who are you and whence came you?" he cried.

"I am an air scout, friend, and very near a dead one, for just by the merest chance I escaped falling to the avenue below," I replied.

"But how came you upon the roof, man? No one has landed or come up from the building for the past hour. Quick, explain yourself, or I call the guard."

"Look you here, sentry, and you shall see how I came and how close a shave I had to not coming at all," I answered, turning toward the edge of the roof, where, twenty feet below, at the end of my strap, hung all my weapons.

The fellow, acting on impulse of curiosity, stepped to my side and to his undoing, for as he leaned to peer over the eaves I grasped him by his throat and his pistol arm and threw him heavily to the roof. The weapon dropped from his grasp, and my fingers choked off his attempted cry for assistance. I gagged and bound him and then hung him over the edge of the roof as I myself had hung a few moments before. I knew it would be morning before he would be discovered, and I needed all the time that I could gain.

Donning my trappings and weapons I hastened to the sheds, and soon had out both my machine and Kantos Kan's. Making his fast behind mine I started my engine, and skimming over the edge of the roof I dove down into the streets of the city far below the plane usually occupied by the air patrol. In less than a minute I was settling safely upon the roof of our apartment beside the astonished Kantos Kan.

I lost no time in explanations, but plunged immediately into a discussion of our plans for the immediate future. It was decided that I was to try to make Helium while Kantos Kan was to enter the palace and dispatch Sab Than. If successful he was then to follow me. He set my compass for me, a clever little device which will remain steadfastly fixed upon any given point on the surface of Barsoom, and bidding each other farewell we rose together and sped in the direction of the palace which lay in the route which I must take to reach Helium.

As we neared the high tower a patrol shot down from above, throwing its piercing searchlight full upon my craft, and a voice roared out a command to halt, following with a shot as I paid no attention to his hail. Kantos Kan dropped quickly into the darkness, while I rose steadily and at terrific speed raced through the Martian sky followed by a dozen of the air-scout craft which had joined the pursuit, and later by a swift cruiser carrying a hundred men and a battery of rapid-fire guns. By twisting and turning my little machine, now rising and now falling, I managed to elude their search-lights most of the time, but I was also losing ground by these tactics, and so I decided to hazard everything on a straight-away course and leave the result to fate and the speed of my machine.

Kantos Kan had shown me a trick of gearing, which is known only to the navy of Helium, that greatly increased the speed of our machines, so that I felt sure I could distance my pursuers if I could dodge their projectiles for a few moments.

As I sped through the air the screeching of the bullets around me convinced me that only by a miracle could I escape, but the die was cast, and throwing on full speed I raced a straight course toward Helium. Gradually I left my pursuers further and further behind, and I was just congratulating myself on my lucky escape, when a well-directed shot from the cruiser exploded at the prow of my little craft. The concussion nearly capsized her, and with a sickening plunge she hurtled downward through the dark night.

How far I fell before I regained control of the plane I do not know, but I must have been very close to the ground when I started to rise again, as I plainly heard the squealing of animals below me. Rising again I scanned the heavens for my pursuers, and finally making out their lights far behind me, saw that they were landing, evidently in search of me.

Not until their lights were no longer discernible did I venture to flash my little lamp upon my compass, and then I found to my consternation that a fragment of the projectile had utterly destroyed my only guide, as well as my speedometer. It was true I could follow the stars in the general direction of Helium, but without knowing the exact location of the city or the speed at which I was traveling my chances for finding it were slim.

Helium lies a thousand miles southwest of Zodanga, and with my compass intact I should have made the trip, barring accidents, in between four and five hours. As it turned out, however, morning found me speeding over a vast expanse of dead sea bottom after nearly six hours of continuous flight at high speed. Presently a great city showed below me, but it was not Helium, as that alone of all Barsoomian metropolises consists in two immense circular walled cities about seventy-five miles apart and would have been easily distinguishable from the altitude at which I was flying.

Believing that I had come too far to the north and west, I turned back in a southeasterly direction, passing during the forenoon several other large cities, but none resembling the description which Kantos Kan had given me of Helium. In addition to the twin-city formation of Helium, another distinguishing feature is the two immense towers, one of vivid scarlet rising nearly a mile into the air from the center of one of the cities, while the other, of bright yellow and of the same height, marks her sister.

TWENTY-FOUR

Tars Tarkas Finds a Friend

About noon I passed low over a great dead city of ancient Mars, and as I skimmed out across the plain beyond I came full upon several thousand green warriors engaged in a terrific battle. Scarcely had I seen them than a volley of shots was directed at me, and with the almost unfailing accuracy of their aim my little craft was instantly a ruined wreck, sinking erratically to the ground.

I fell almost directly in the center of the fierce combat, among warriors who had not seen my approach so busily were they engaged in life and death struggles. The men were fighting on foot with long-swords, while an occasional shot from a sharpshooter on the outskirts of the conflict would bring down a warrior who might for an instant separate himself from the entangled mass.

As my machine sank among them I realized that it was fight or die, with good chances of dying in any event, and so I struck the ground with drawn long-sword ready to defend myself as I could.

I fell beside a huge monster who was engaged with three antagonists, and as I glanced at his fierce face, filled with the light of battle, I recognized Tars Tarkas the Thark. He did not see me, as I was a trifle behind him, and just then the three warriors opposing him, and whom I recognized as Warhoons, charged simultaneously. The mighty fellow made quick work of one of them, but in stepping back for another thrust he fell over a dead body behind him and was down and at the mercy of his foes in an instant. Quick as lightning they were upon him, and Tars Tarkas would have been gathered to his fathers in short order had I not sprung before his prostrate form and engaged his adversaries. I had accounted for one of them when the mighty Thark regained his feet and quickly settled the other.

He gave me one look, and a slight smile touched his grim lip as, touching my shoulder, he said,

"I would scarcely recognize you, John Carter, but there is no other mortal upon Barsoom who would have done what you have for me. I think I have learned that there is such a thing as friendship, my friend."

He said no more, nor was there opportunity, for the Warhoons were closing in about us, and together we fought, shoulder to shoulder, during all that long, hot afternoon, until the tide of battle turned and the remnant of the fierce Warhoon horde fell back upon their thoats, and fled into the gathering darkness.

Ten thousand men had been engaged in that titanic struggle, and upon the field of battle lay three thousand dead. Neither side asked or gave quarter, nor did they attempt to take prisoners.

On our return to the city after the battle we had gone directly to Tars Tarkas' quarters, where I was left alone while the chieftain attended the customary council which immediately follows an engagement.

As I sat awaiting the return of the green warrior I heard something move in an adjoining apartment, and as I glanced up there rushed suddenly upon me a huge and hideous creature which bore me backward upon the pile of silks and furs upon which I had been reclining. It was Woola—faithful, loving Woola. He had found his way back to Thark and, as Tars Tarkas later told me, had gone immediately to my former quarters where he had taken up his pathetic and seemingly hopeless watch for my return.

"Tal Hajus knows that you are here, John Carter," said Tars Tarkas, on his return from the jeddak's quarters; "Sarkoja saw and recognized you as we were returning. Tal Hajus has ordered me to bring you before him tonight. I have ten thoats, John Carter; you may take your choice from among them, and I will accompany you to the nearest waterway that leads to Helium. Tars Tarkas may be a cruel green warrior, but he can be a friend as well. Come, we must start."

"And when you return, Tars Tarkas?" I asked.

"The wild calots, possibly, or worse," he replied. "Unless I should chance to have the opportunity I have so long waited of battling with Tal Hajus."

"We will stay, Tars Tarkas, and see Tal Hajus tonight. You shall not sacrifice yourself, and it may be that tonight you can have the chance you wait."

He objected strenuously, saying that Tal Hajus often flew into wild fits of passion at the mere thought of the blow I had dealt him, and that if ever he laid his hands upon me I would be subjected to the most horrible tortures.

While we were eating I repeated to Tars Tarkas the story which Sola had told me that night upon the sea bottom during the march to Thark.

He said but little, but the great muscles of his face worked in passion and in agony at recollection of the horrors which had been heaped upon the only thing he had ever loved in all his cold, cruel, terrible existence.

He no longer demurred when I suggested that we go before Tal Hajus, only saying that he would like to speak to Sarkoja first. At his request I accompanied him to her quarters, and the look of venomous hatred she cast upon me was almost adequate recompense for any future misfortunes this accidental return to Thark might bring me.

"Sarkoja," said Tars Tarkas, "forty years ago you were instrumental in bringing about the torture and death of a woman named Gozava. I have just discovered that the warrior who loved that woman has learned of your part in the transaction. He may not kill you, Sarkoja, it is not our custom, but there is nothing to prevent him tying one end of a strap about your neck and the other end to a wild thoat, merely to test your fitness to survive and help perpetuate our race. Having heard that he would do this on the morrow, I thought it only right to warn you, for I am a just man. The river Iss is but a short pilgrimage, Sarkoja. Come, John Carter."

The next morning Sarkoja was gone, nor was she ever seen after.

In silence we hastened to the jeddak's palace, where we were immediately admitted to his presence; in fact, he could scarcely wait to see me and was standing erect upon his platform glowering at the entrance as I came in.

"Strap him to that pillar," he shrieked. "We shall see who it is dares strike the mighty Tal Hajus. Heat the irons; with my own hands I shall burn the eyes from his head that he may not pollute my person with his vile gaze."

"Chieftains of Thark," I cried, turning to the assembled council and ignoring Tal Hajus, "I have been a chief among you, and today I have fought for Thark shoulder to shoulder with her greatest warrior. You owe me, at least, a hearing. I have won that much today. You claim to be just people—"

"Silence," roared Tal Hajus. "Gag the creature and bind him as I command."

"Justice, Tal Hajus," exclaimed Lorquas Ptomel. "Who are you to set aside the customs of ages among the Tharks."

"Yes, justice!" echoed a dozen voices, and so, while Tal Hajus fumed and frothed, I continued.

"You are a brave people and you love bravery, but where was your mighty jeddak during the fighting today? I did not see him in the thick of battle; he was not there. He rends defenseless women and little children in his lair, but how recently has one of you seen him fight with men? Why, even I, a midget beside him, felled him with a single blow of my fist. Is it of such

that the Tharks fashion their jeddaks? There stands beside me now a great
Thark, a mighty warrior and a noble man. Chieftains, how sounds, Tars
Tarkas, Jeddak of Thark?"

A roar of deep-toned applause greeted this suggestion.

"It but remains for this council to command, and Tal Hajus must prove
his fitness to rule. Were he a brave man he would invite Tars Tarkas to
combat, for he does not love him, but Tal Hajus is afraid; Tal Hajus, your
jeddak, is a coward. With my bare hands I could kill him, and he knows it."

After I ceased there was tense silence, as all eyes were riveted upon Tal
Hajus. He did not speak or move, but the blotchy green of his countenance
turned livid, and the froth froze upon his lips.

"Tal Hajus," said Lorquas Ptomel in a cold, hard voice, "never in my
long life have I seen a jeddak of the Tharks so humiliated. There could be
but one answer to this arraignment. We wait it." And still Tal Hajus stood
as though petrified.

"Chieftains," continued Lorquas Ptomel, "shall the jeddak, Tal Hajus,
prove his fitness to rule over Tars Tarkas?"

There were twenty chieftains about the rostrum, and twenty swords
flashed high in assent.

There was no alternative. That decree was final, and so Tal Hajus drew
his long-sword and advanced to meet Tars Tarkas.

The combat was soon over, and, with his foot upon the neck of the dead
monster, Tars Tarkas became jeddak among the Tharks.

His first act was to make me a full-fledged chieftain with the rank I had
won by my combats the first few weeks of my captivity among them.

Seeing the favorable disposition of the warriors toward Tars Tarkas, as
well as toward me, I grasped the opportunity to enlist them in my cause
against Zodanga. I told Tars Tarkas the story of my adventures, and in a
few words had explained to him the thought I had in mind.

"John Carter has made a proposal," he said, addressing the council,
"which meets with my sanction. I shall put it to you briefly. Dejah Thoris,
the Princess of Helium, who was our prisoner, is now held by the jeddak
of Zodanga, whose son she must wed to save her country from devastation
at the hands of the Zodangan forces.

"John Carter suggests that we rescue her and return her to Helium.
The loot of Zodanga would be magnificent, and I have often thought that
had we an alliance with the people of Helium we could obtain sufficient
assurance of sustenance to permit us to increase the size and frequency of
our hatchings, and thus become unquestionably supreme among the green
men of all Barsoom. What say you?"

It was a chance to fight, an opportunity to loot, and they rose to the bait as a speckled trout to a fly.

For Tharks they were wildly enthusiastic, and before another half hour had passed twenty mounted messengers were speeding across dead sea bottoms to call the hordes together for the expedition.

In three days we were on the march toward Zodanga, one hundred thousand strong, as Tars Tarkas had been able to enlist the services of three smaller hordes on the promise of the great loot of Zodanga.

At the head of the column I rode beside the great Thark while at the heels of my mount trotted my beloved Woola.

We traveled entirely by night, timing our marches so that we camped during the day at deserted cities where, even to the beasts, we were all kept indoors during the daylight hours. On the march Tars Tarkas, through his remarkable ability and statesmanship, enlisted fifty thousand more warriors from various hordes, so that, ten days after we set out we halted at midnight outside the great walled city of Zodanga, one hundred and fifty thousand strong.

The fighting strength and efficiency of this horde of ferocious green monsters was equivalent to ten times their number of red men. Never in the history of Barsoom, Tars Tarkas told me, had such a force of green warriors marched to battle together. It was a monstrous task to keep even a semblance of harmony among them, and it was a marvel to me that he got them to the city without a mighty battle among themselves.

But as we neared Zodanga their personal quarrels were submerged by their greater hatred for the red men, and especially for the Zodangans, who had for years waged a ruthless campaign of extermination against the green men, directing special attention toward despoiling their incubators.

Now that we were before Zodanga the task of obtaining entry to the city devolved upon me, and directing Tars Tarkas to hold his forces in two divisions out of earshot of the city, with each division opposite a large gateway, I took twenty dismounted warriors and approached one of the small gates that pierced the walls at short intervals. These gates have no regular guard, but are covered by sentries, who patrol the avenue that encircles the city just within the walls as our metropolitan police patrol their beats.

The walls of Zodanga are seventy-five feet in height and fifty feet thick. They are built of enormous blocks of carborundum, and the task of entering the city seemed, to my escort of green warriors, an impossibility. The fellows who had been detailed to accompany me were of one of the smaller hordes, and therefore did not know me.

Placing three of them with their faces to the wall and arms locked, I commanded two more to mount to their shoulders, and a sixth I ordered to climb upon the shoulders of the upper two. The head of the topmost warrior towered over forty feet from the ground.

In this way, with ten warriors, I built a series of three steps from the ground to the shoulders of the topmost man. Then starting from a short distance behind them I ran swiftly up from one tier to the next, and with a final bound from the broad shoulders of the highest I clutched the top of the great wall and quietly drew myself to its broad expanse. After me I dragged six lengths of leather from an equal number of my warriors. These lengths we had previously fastened together, and passing one end to the topmost warrior I lowered the other end cautiously over the opposite side of the wall toward the avenue below. No one was in sight, so, lowering myself to the end of my leather strap, I dropped the remaining thirty feet to the pavement below.

I had learned from Kantos Kan the secret of opening these gates, and in another moment my twenty great fighting men stood within the doomed city of Zodanga.

I found to my delight that I had entered at the lower boundary of the enormous palace grounds. The building itself showed in the distance a blaze of glorious light, and on the instant I determined to lead a detachment of warriors directly within the palace itself, while the balance of the great horde was attacking the barracks of the soldiery.

Dispatching one of my men to Tars Tarkas for a detail of fifty Tharks, with word of my intentions, I ordered ten warriors to capture and open one of the great gates while with the nine remaining I took the other. We were to do our work quietly, no shots were to be fired and no general advance made until I had reached the palace with my fifty Tharks. Our plans worked to perfection. The two sentries we met were dispatched to their fathers upon the banks of the lost sea of Korus, and the guards at both gates followed them in silence.

TWENTY-FIVE

The Looting of Zodanga

As the great gate where I stood swung open my fifty Tharks, headed by Tars Tarkas himself, rode in upon their mighty thoats. I led them to the palace walls, which I negotiated easily without assistance. Once inside, however, the gate gave me considerable trouble, but I finally was rewarded by seeing it swing upon its huge hinges, and soon my fierce escort was riding across the gardens of the jeddak of Zodanga.

As we approached the palace I could see through the great windows of the first floor into the brilliantly illuminated audience chamber of Than Kosis. The immense hall was crowded with nobles and their women, as though some important function was in progress. There was not a guard in sight without the palace, due, I presume, to the fact that the city and palace walls were considered impregnable, and so I came close and peered within.

At one end of the chamber, upon massive golden thrones encrusted with diamonds, sat Than Kosis and his consort, surrounded by officers and dignitaries of state. Before them stretched a broad aisle lined on either side with soldiery, and as I looked there entered this aisle at the far end of the hall, the head of a procession which advanced to the foot of the throne.

First there marched four officers of the jeddak's Guard bearing a huge salver on which reposed, upon a cushion of scarlet silk, a great golden chain with a collar and padlock at each end. Directly behind these officers came four others carrying a similar salver which supported the magnificent ornaments of a prince and princess of the reigning house of Zodanga.

At the foot of the throne these two parties separated and halted, facing each other at opposite sides of the aisle. Then came more dignitaries, and the officers of the palace and of the army, and finally two figures entirely muffled in scarlet silk, so that not a feature of either was discernible. These two stopped at the foot of the throne, facing Than Kosis. When the balance of the procession had entered and assumed their stations Than Kosis addressed the couple standing before him. I could not hear his words, but presently two officers advanced and removed the scarlet robe from one of the figures, and I saw that Kantos Kan had failed in his mission, for it was Sab Than, Prince of Zodanga, who stood revealed before me.

Than Kosis now took a set of the ornaments from one of the salvers and placed one of the collars of gold about his son's neck, springing the padlock fast. After a few more words addressed to Sab Than he turned to the other figure, from which the officers now removed the enshrouding silks, disclosing to my now comprehending view Dejah Thoris, Princess of Helium.

The object of the ceremony was clear to me; in another moment Dejah Thoris would be joined forever to the Prince of Zodanga. It was an impressive and beautiful ceremony, I presume, but to me it seemed the most fiendish sight I had ever witnessed, and as the ornaments were adjusted upon her beautiful figure and her collar of gold swung open in the hands of Than Kosis I raised my long-sword above my head, and, with the heavy hilt, I shattered the glass of the great window and sprang into the midst of the astonished assemblage. With a bound I was on the steps of the platform beside Than Kosis, and as he stood riveted with surprise I brought my long-sword down upon the golden chain that would have bound Dejah Thoris to another.

In an instant all was confusion; a thousand drawn swords menaced me from every quarter, and Sab Than sprang upon me with a jeweled dagger he had drawn from his nuptial ornaments. I could have killed him as easily as I might a fly, but the age-old custom of Barsoom stayed my hand, and grasping his wrist as the dagger flew toward my heart I held him as though in a vise and with my long-sword pointed to the far end of the hall.

"Zodanga has fallen," I cried. "Look!"

All eyes turned in the direction I had indicated, and there, forging through the portals of the entranceway rode Tars Tarkas and his fifty warriors on their great thoats.

A cry of alarm and amazement broke from the assemblage, but no word of fear, and in a moment the soldiers and nobles of Zodanga were hurling themselves upon the advancing Tharks.

Thrusting Sab Than headlong from the platform, I drew Dejah Thoris to my side. Behind the throne was a narrow doorway and in this Than Kosis now stood facing me, with drawn long-sword. In an instant we were engaged, and I found no mean antagonist.

As we circled upon the broad platform I saw Sab Than rushing up the steps to aid his father, but, as he raised his hand to strike, Dejah Thoris sprang before him and then my sword found the spot that made Sab Than jeddak of Zodanga. As his father rolled dead upon the floor the new jeddak tore himself free from Dejah Thoris' grasp, and again we faced each other. He was soon joined by a quartet of officers, and, with my back against a golden throne, I fought once again for Dejah Thoris. I was hard pressed to defend myself and yet not strike down Sab Than and, with him, my last chance to win the woman I loved. My blade was swinging with the rapidity of lightning as I sought to parry the thrusts and cuts of my opponents. Two I had disarmed, and one was down, when several more rushed to the aid of their new ruler, and to avenge the death of the old.

As they advanced there were cries of "The woman! The woman! Strike her down; it is her plot. Kill her! Kill her!"

Calling to Dejah Thoris to get behind me I worked my way toward the little doorway back of the throne, but the officers realized my intentions, and three of them sprang in behind me and blocked my chances for gaining a position where I could have defended Dejah Thoris against any army of swordsmen.

The Tharks were having their hands full in the center of the room, and I began to realize that nothing short of a miracle could save Dejah Thoris and myself, when I saw Tars Tarkas surging through the crowd of pygmies that swarmed about him. With one swing of his mighty long-sword he laid a dozen corpses at his feet, and so he hewed a pathway before him until in another moment he stood upon the platform beside me, dealing death and destruction right and left.

The bravery of the Zodangans was awe-inspiring, not one attempted to escape, and when the fighting ceased it was because only Tharks remained alive in the great hall, other than Dejah Thoris and myself.

Sab Than lay dead beside his father, and the corpses of the flower of Zodangan nobility and chivalry covered the floor of the bloody shambles.

My first thought when the battle was over was for Kantos Kan, and leaving Dejah Thoris in charge of Tars Tarkas I took a dozen warriors and hastened to the dungeons beneath the palace. The jailers had all left to join the fighters in the throne room, so we searched the labyrinthine prison without opposition.

I called Kantos Kan's name aloud in each new corridor and compartment, and finally I was rewarded by hearing a faint response. Guided by the sound, we soon found him helpless in a dark recess.

He was overjoyed at seeing me, and to know the meaning of the fight, faint echoes of which had reached his prison cell. He told me that the air patrol had captured him before he reached the high tower of the palace, so that he had not even seen Sab Than.

We discovered that it would be futile to attempt to cut away the bars and chains which held him prisoner, so, at his suggestion I returned to search the bodies on the floor above for keys to open the padlocks of his cell and of his chains.

Fortunately among the first I examined I found his jailer, and soon we had Kantos Kan with us in the throne room.

The sounds of heavy firing, mingled with shouts and cries, came to us from the city's streets, and Tars Tarkas hastened away to direct the fighting without. Kantos Kan accompanied him to act as guide, the green warriors commencing a thorough search of the palace for other Zodangans and for loot, and Dejah Thoris and I were left alone.

She had sunk into one of the golden thrones, and as I turned to her she greeted me with a wan smile.

"Was there ever such a man!" she exclaimed. "I know that Barsoom has never before seen your like. Can it be that all Earth men are as you? Alone, a stranger, hunted, threatened, persecuted, you have done in a few short months what in all the past ages of Barsoom no man has ever done: joined together the wild hordes of the sea bottoms and brought them to fight as allies of a red Martian people."

"The answer is easy, Dejah Thoris," I replied smiling. "It was not I who did it, it was love, love for Dejah Thoris, a power that would work greater miracles than this you have seen."

A pretty flush overspread her face and she answered,

"You may say that now, John Carter, and I may listen, for I am free."

"And more still I have to say, ere it is again too late," I returned. "I have done many strange things in my life, many things that wiser men would not have dared, but never in my wildest fancies have I dreamed of winning a Dejah Thoris for myself—for never had I dreamed that in all the universe dwelt such a woman as the Princess of Helium. That you are a princess does not abash me, but that you are you is enough to make me doubt my sanity as I ask you, my princess, to be mine."

"He does not need to be abashed who so well knew the answer to his plea before the plea were made," she replied, rising and placing her dear hands upon my shoulders, and so I took her in my arms and kissed her.

And thus in the midst of a city of wild conflict, filled with the alarms of war; with death and destruction reaping their terrible harvest around her, did Dejah Thoris, Princess of Helium, true daughter of Mars, the God of War, promise herself in marriage to John Carter, Gentleman of Virginia.

TWENTY-SIX

Through Carnage to Joy

Sometime later Tars Tarkas and Kantos Kan returned to report that Zodanga had been completely reduced. Her forces were entirely destroyed or captured, and no further resistance was to be expected from within. Several battleships had escaped, but there were thousands of war and merchant vessels under guard of Thark warriors.

The lesser hordes had commenced looting and quarreling among themselves, so it was decided that we collect what warriors we could, man as many vessels as possible with Zodangan prisoners and make for Helium without further loss of time.

Five hours later we sailed from the roofs of the dock buildings with a fleet of two hundred and fifty battleships, carrying nearly one hundred thousand green warriors, followed by a fleet of transports with our thoats.

Behind us we left the stricken city in the fierce and brutal clutches of some forty thousand green warriors of the lesser hordes. They were looting, murdering, and fighting amongst themselves. In a hundred places they had applied the torch, and columns of dense smoke were rising above the city as though to blot out from the eye of heaven the horrid sights beneath.

In the middle of the afternoon we sighted the scarlet and yellow towers of Helium, and a short time later a great fleet of Zodangan battleships rose from the camps of the besiegers without the city, and advanced to meet us.

The banners of Helium had been strung from stem to stern of each of our mighty craft, but the Zodangans did not need this sign to realize that we were enemies, for our green Martian warriors had opened fire upon them almost as they left the ground. With their uncanny marksmanship they raked the on-coming fleet with volley after volley.

The twin cities of Helium, perceiving that we were friends, sent out hundreds of vessels to aid us, and then began the first real air battle I had ever witnessed.

The vessels carrying our green warriors were kept circling above the contending fleets of Helium and Zodanga, since their batteries were useless in the hands of the Tharks who, having no navy, have no skill in naval gunnery. Their small-arm fire, however, was most effective, and the final outcome of the engagement was strongly influenced, if not wholly determined, by their presence.

At first the two forces circled at the same altitude, pouring broadside after broadside into each other. Presently a great hole was torn in the hull of one of the immense battle craft from the Zodangan camp; with a lurch she turned completely over, the little figures of her crew plunging, turning and twisting toward the ground a thousand feet below; then with sickening velocity she tore after them, almost completely burying herself in the soft loam of the ancient sea bottom.

A wild cry of exultation arose from the Heliumite squadron, and with redoubled ferocity they fell upon the Zodangan fleet. By a pretty maneuver two of the vessels of Helium gained a position above their adversaries, from which they poured upon them from their keel bomb batteries a perfect torrent of exploding bombs.

Then, one by one, the battleships of Helium succeeded in rising above the Zodangans, and in a short time a number of the beleaguering battleships were drifting hopeless wrecks toward the high scarlet tower of greater Helium. Several others attempted to escape, but they were soon surrounded by thousands of tiny individual fliers, and above each hung a monster battleship of Helium ready to drop boarding parties upon their decks.

Within but little more than an hour from the moment the victorious Zodangan squadron had risen to meet us from the camp of the besiegers the battle was over, and the remaining vessels of the conquered Zodangans were headed toward the cities of Helium under prize crews.

There was an extremely pathetic side to the surrender of these mighty fliers, the result of an age-old custom which demanded that surrender should be signalized by the voluntary plunging to earth of the commander of the vanquished vessel. One after another the brave fellows, holding their colors high above their heads, leaped from the towering bows of their mighty craft to an awful death.

Not until the commander of the entire fleet took the fearful plunge, thus indicating the surrender of the remaining vessels, did the fighting cease, and the useless sacrifice of brave men come to an end.

We now signaled the flagship of Helium's navy to approach, and when she was within hailing distance I called out that we had the Princess Dejah

Thoris on board, and that we wished to transfer her to the flagship that she might be taken immediately to the city.

As the full import of my announcement bore in upon them a great cry arose from the decks of the flagship, and a moment later the colors of the Princess of Helium broke from a hundred points upon her upper works. When the other vessels of the squadron caught the meaning of the signals flashed them they took up the wild acclaim and unfurled her colors in the gleaming sunlight.

The flagship bore down upon us, and as she swung gracefully to and touched our side a dozen officers sprang upon our decks. As their astonished gaze fell upon the hundreds of green warriors, who now came forth from the fighting shelters, they stopped aghast, but at sight of Kantos Kan, who advanced to meet them, they came forward, crowding about him.

Dejah Thoris and I then advanced, and they had no eyes for other than her. She received them gracefully, calling each by name, for they were men high in the esteem and service of her grandfather, and she knew them well.

"Lay your hands upon the shoulder of John Carter," she said to them, turning toward me, "the man to whom Helium owes her princess as well as her victory today."

They were very courteous to me and said many kind and complimentary things, but what seemed to impress them most was that I had won the aid of the fierce Tharks in my campaign for the liberation of Dejah Thoris, and the relief of Helium.

"You owe your thanks more to another man than to me," I said, "and here he is; meet one of Barsoom's greatest soldiers and statesmen, Tars Tarkas, Jeddak of Thark."

With the same polished courtesy that had marked their manner toward me they extended their greetings to the great Thark, nor, to my surprise, was he much behind them in ease of bearing or in courtly speech. Though not a garrulous race, the Tharks are extremely formal, and their ways lend themselves amazingly well to dignified and courtly manners.

Dejah Thoris went aboard the flagship, and was much put out that I would not follow, but, as I explained to her, the battle was but partly won; we still had the land forces of the besieging Zodangans to account for, and I would not leave Tars Tarkas until that had been accomplished.

The commander of the naval forces of Helium promised to arrange to have the armies of Helium attack from the city in conjunction with our land attack, and so the vessels separated and Dejah Thoris was borne in triumph back to the court of her grandfather, Tardos Mors, Jeddak of Helium.

In the distance lay our fleet of transports, with the thoats of the green warriors, where they had remained during the battle. Without landing stages it was to be a difficult matter to unload these beasts upon the open plain, but there was nothing else for it, and so we put out for a point about ten miles from the city and began the task.

It was necessary to lower the animals to the ground in slings and this work occupied the remainder of the day and half the night. Twice we were attacked by parties of Zodangan cavalry, but with little loss, however, and after darkness shut down they withdrew.

As soon as the last thoat was unloaded Tars Tarkas gave the command to advance, and in three parties we crept upon the Zodangan camp from the north, the south and the east.

About a mile from the main camp we encountered their outposts and, as had been prearranged, accepted this as the signal to charge. With wild, ferocious cries and amidst the nasty squealing of battle-enraged thoats we bore down upon the Zodangans.

We did not catch them napping, but found a well-entrenched battle line confronting us. Time after time we were repulsed until, toward noon, I began to fear for the result of the battle.

The Zodangans numbered nearly a million fighting men, gathered from pole to pole, wherever stretched their ribbon-like waterways, while pitted against them were less than a hundred thousand green warriors. The forces from Helium had not arrived, nor could we receive any word from them.

Just at noon we heard heavy firing all along the line between the Zodangans and the cities, and we knew then that our much-needed reinforcements had come.

Again Tars Tarkas ordered the charge, and once more the mighty thoats bore their terrible riders against the ramparts of the enemy. At the same moment the battle line of Helium surged over the opposite breastworks of the Zodangans and in another moment they were being crushed as between two millstones. Nobly they fought, but in vain.

The plain before the city became a veritable shambles ere the last Zodangan surrendered, but finally the carnage ceased, the prisoners were marched back to Helium, and we entered the greater city's gates, a huge triumphal procession of conquering heroes.

The broad avenues were lined with women and children, among which were the few men whose duties necessitated that they remain within the city during the battle. We were greeted with an endless round of applause and showered with ornaments of gold, platinum, silver, and precious jewels. The city had gone mad with joy.

My fierce Tharks caused the wildest excitement and enthusiasm. Never before had an armed body of green warriors entered the gates of Helium, and that they came now as friends and allies filled the red men with rejoicing.

That my poor services to Dejah Thoris had become known to the Heliumites was evidenced by the loud crying of my name, and by the loads of ornaments that were fastened upon me and my huge thoat as we passed up the avenues to the palace, for even in the face of the ferocious appearance of Woola the populace pressed close about me.

As we approached this magnificent pile we were met by a party of officers who greeted us warmly and requested that Tars Tarkas and his jeds with the jeddaks and jeds of his wild allies, together with myself, dismount and accompany them to receive from Tardos Mors an expression of his gratitude for our services.

At the top of the great steps leading up to the main portals of the palace stood the royal party, and as we reached the lower steps one of their number descended to meet us. He was an almost perfect specimen of manhood; tall, straight as an arrow, superbly muscled and with the carriage and bearing of a ruler of men. I did not need to be told that he was Tardos Mors, Jeddak of Helium.

The first member of our party he met was Tars Tarkas and his first words sealed forever the new friendship between the races.

"That Tardos Mors," he said, earnestly, "may meet the greatest living warrior of Barsoom is a priceless honor, but that he may lay his hand on the shoulder of a friend and ally is a far greater boon."

"Jeddak of Helium," returned Tars Tarkas, "it has remained for a man of another world to teach the green warriors of Barsoom the meaning of friendship; to him we owe the fact that the hordes of Thark can understand you; that they can appreciate and reciprocate the sentiments so graciously expressed."

Tardos Mors then greeted each of the green jeddaks and jeds, and to each spoke words of friendship and appreciation.

As he approached me he laid both hands upon my shoulders.

"Welcome, my son," he said; "that you are granted, gladly, and without one word of opposition, the most precious jewel in all Helium, yes, on all Barsoom, is sufficient earnest of my esteem."

We were then presented to Mors Kajak, Jed of lesser Helium, and father of Dejah Thoris. He had followed close behind Tardos Mors and seemed even more affected by the meeting than had his father.

He tried a dozen times to express his gratitude to me, but his voice choked with emotion and he could not speak, and yet he had, as I was to later learn, a reputation for ferocity and fearlessness as a fighter that was remarkable even upon warlike Barsoom. In common with all Helium he worshiped his daughter, nor could he think of what she had escaped without deep emotion.

TWENTY-SEVEN

From Joy to Death

For ten days the hordes of Thark and their wild allies were feasted and entertained, and, then, loaded with costly presents and escorted by ten thousand soldiers of Helium commanded by Mors Kajak, they started on the return journey to their own lands. The jed of lesser Helium with a small party of nobles accompanied them all the way to Thark to cement more closely the new bonds of peace and friendship.

Sola also accompanied Tars Tarkas, her father, who before all his chieftains had acknowledged her as his daughter.

Three weeks later, Mors Kajak and his officers, accompanied by Tars Tarkas and Sola, returned upon a battleship that had been dispatched to Thark to fetch them in time for the ceremony which made Dejah Thoris and John Carter one.

For nine years I served in the councils and fought in the armies of Helium as a prince of the house of Tardos Mors. The people seemed never to tire of heaping honors upon me, and no day passed that did not bring some new proof of their love for my princess, the incomparable Dejah Thoris.

In a golden incubator upon the roof of our palace lay a snow-white egg. For nearly five years ten soldiers of the jeddak's Guard had constantly stood over it, and not a day passed when I was in the city that Dejah Thoris and I did not stand hand in hand before our little shrine planning for the future, when the delicate shell should break.

Vivid in my memory is the picture of the last night as we sat there talking in low tones of the strange romance which had woven our lives together and of this wonder which was coming to augment our happiness and fulfill our hopes.

In the distance we saw the bright-white light of an approaching airship, but we attached no special significance to so common a sight. Like a bolt of lightning it raced toward Helium until its very speed bespoke the unusual.

Flashing the signals which proclaimed it a dispatch bearer for the jeddak, it circled impatiently awaiting the tardy patrol boat which must convoy it to the palace docks.

Ten minutes after it touched at the palace a message called me to the council chamber, which I found filling with the members of that body.

On the raised platform of the throne was Tardos Mors, pacing back and forth with tense-drawn face. When all were in their seats he turned toward us.

"This morning," he said, "word reached the several governments of Barsoom that the keeper of the atmosphere plant had made no wireless report for two days, nor had almost ceaseless calls upon him from a score of capitals elicited a sign of response.

"The ambassadors of the other nations asked us to take the matter in hand and hasten the assistant keeper to the plant. All day a thousand cruisers have been searching for him until, just now one of them returns bearing his dead body, which was found in the pits beneath his house horribly mutilated by some assassin.

"I do not need to tell you what this means to Barsoom. It would take months to penetrate those mighty walls, in fact the work has already commenced, and there would be little to fear were the engine of the pumping plant to run as it should and as they all have for hundreds of years; but the worst, we fear, has happened. The instruments show a rapidly decreasing air pressure on all parts of Barsoom—the engine has stopped."

"My gentlemen," he concluded, "we have at best three days to live."

There was absolute silence for several minutes, and then a young noble arose, and with his drawn sword held high above his head addressed Tardos Mors.

"The men of Helium have prided themselves that they have ever shown Barsoom how a nation of red men should live, now is our opportunity to show them how they should die. Let us go about our duties as though a thousand useful years still lay before us."

The chamber rang with applause and as there was nothing better to do than to allay the fears of the people by our example we went our ways with smiles upon our faces and sorrow gnawing at our hearts.

When I returned to my palace I found that the rumor already had reached Dejah Thoris, so I told her all that I had heard.

"We have been very happy, John Carter," she said, "and I thank whatever fate overtakes us that it permits us to die together."

The next two days brought no noticeable change in the supply of air, but on the morning of the third day breathing became difficult at the higher altitudes of the rooftops. The avenues and plazas of Helium were filled with people. All business had ceased. For the most part the people looked bravely into the face of their unalterable doom. Here and there, however, men and women gave way to quiet grief.

Toward the middle of the day many of the weaker commenced to succumb and within an hour the people of Barsoom were sinking by thousands into the unconsciousness which precedes death by asphyxiation.

Dejah Thoris and I with the other members of the royal family had collected in a sunken garden within an inner courtyard of the palace. We conversed in low tones, when we conversed at all, as the awe of the grim shadow of death crept over us. Even Woola seemed to feel the weight of the impending calamity, for he pressed close to Dejah Thoris and to me, whining pitifully.

The little incubator had been brought from the roof of our palace at request of Dejah Thoris and now she sat gazing longingly upon the unknown little life that now she would never know.

As it was becoming perceptibly difficult to breathe Tardos Mors arose, saying,

"Let us bid each other farewell. The days of the greatness of Barsoom are over. Tomorrow's sun will look down upon a dead world which through all eternity must go swinging through the heavens peopled not even by memories. It is the end."

He stooped and kissed the women of his family, and laid his strong hand upon the shoulders of the men.

As I turned sadly from him my eyes fell upon Dejah Thoris. Her head was drooping upon her breast, to all appearances she was lifeless. With a cry I sprang to her and raised her in my arms.

Her eyes opened and looked into mine.

"Kiss me, John Carter," she murmured. "I love you! I love you! It is cruel that we must be torn apart who were just starting upon a life of love and happiness."

As I pressed her dear lips to mine the old feeling of unconquerable power and authority rose in me. The fighting blood of Virginia sprang to life in my veins.

"It shall not be, my princess," I cried. "There is, there must be some way, and John Carter, who has fought his way through a strange world for love of you, will find it."

And with my words there crept above the threshold of my conscious mind a series of nine long forgotten sounds. Like a flash of lightning in the darkness their full purport dawned upon me—the key to the three great doors of the atmosphere plant!

Turning suddenly toward Tardos Mors as I still clasped my dying love to my breast I cried.

"A flier, Jeddak! Quick! Order your swiftest flier to the palace top. I can save Barsoom yet."

He did not wait to question, but in an instant a guard was racing to the nearest dock and though the air was thin and almost gone at the rooftop they managed to launch the fastest one-man, air-scout machine that the skill of Barsoom had ever produced.

Kissing Dejah Thoris a dozen times and commanding Woola, who would have followed me, to remain and guard her, I bounded with my old agility and strength to the high ramparts of the palace, and in another moment I was headed toward the goal of the hopes of all Barsoom.

I had to fly low to get sufficient air to breathe, but I took a straight course across an old sea bottom and so had to rise only a few feet above the ground.

I traveled with awful velocity for my errand was a race against time with death. The face of Dejah Thoris hung always before me. As I turned for a last look as I left the palace garden I had seen her stagger and sink upon the ground beside the little incubator. That she had dropped into the last coma which would end in death, if the air supply remained unreplenished, I well knew, and so, throwing caution to the winds, I flung overboard everything but the engine and compass, even to my ornaments, and lying on my belly along the deck with one hand on the steering wheel and the other pushing the speed lever to its last notch I split the thin air of dying Mars with the speed of a meteor.

An hour before dark the great walls of the atmosphere plant loomed suddenly before me, and with a sickening thud I plunged to the ground before the small door which was withholding the spark of life from the inhabitants of an entire planet.

Beside the door a great crew of men had been laboring to pierce the wall, but they had scarcely scratched the flint-like surface, and now most of them lay in the last sleep from which not even air would awaken them.

Conditions seemed much worse here than at Helium, and it was with difficulty that I breathed at all. There were a few men still conscious, and to one of these I spoke.

"If I can open these doors is there a man who can start the engines?" I asked.

"I can," he replied, "if you open quickly. I can last but a few moments

But, with a final effort, as I sank weakly to my knees I hurled the nine thought waves at that awful thing before me.

more. But it is useless, they are both dead and no one else upon Barsoom knew the secret of these awful locks. For three days men crazed with fear have surged about this portal in vain attempts to solve its mystery."

I had no time to talk, I was becoming very weak and it was with difficulty that I controlled my mind at all.

But, with a final effort, as I sank weakly to my knees I hurled the nine thought waves at that awful thing before me. The Martian had crawled to my side and with staring eyes fixed on the single panel before us we waited in the silence of death.

Slowly the mighty door receded before us. I attempted to rise and follow it but I was too weak.

"After it," I cried to my companion, "and if you reach the pump room turn loose all the pumps. It is the only chance Barsoom has to exist tomorrow!"

From where I lay I opened the second door, and then the third, and as I saw the hope of Barsoom crawling weakly on hands and knees through the last doorway I sank unconscious upon the ground.

TWENTY-EIGHT

At the Arizona Cave

It was dark when I opened my eyes again. Strange, stiff garments were upon my body; garments that cracked and powdered away from me as I rose to a sitting posture.

I felt myself over from head to foot and from head to foot I was clothed, though when I fell unconscious at the little doorway I had been naked. Before me was a small patch of moonlit sky which showed through a ragged aperture.

As my hands passed over my body they came in contact with pockets and in one of these a small parcel of matches wrapped in oiled paper. One of these matches I struck, and its dim flame lighted up what appeared to be a huge cave, toward the back of which I discovered a strange, still figure huddled over a tiny bench. As I approached it I saw that it was the dead and mummified remains of a little old woman with long black hair, and the thing it leaned over was a small charcoal burner upon which rested a round copper vessel containing a small quantity of greenish powder.

Behind her, depending from the roof upon rawhide thongs, and stretching entirely across the cave, was a row of human skeletons. From the thong which held them stretched another to the dead hand of the little old woman; as I touched the cord the skeletons swung to the motion with a noise as of the rustling of dry leaves.

It was a most grotesque and horrid tableau and I hastened out into the fresh air; glad to escape from so gruesome a place.

The sight that met my eyes as I stepped out upon a small ledge which ran before the entrance of the cave filled me with consternation.

A new heaven and a new landscape met my gaze. The silvered mountains in the distance, the almost stationary moon hanging in the sky, the cacti-studded valley below me were not of Mars. I could scarcely believe my eyes, but the truth slowly forced itself upon me—I was looking upon Arizona from the same ledge from which ten years before I had gazed with longing upon Mars.

Burying my head in my arms I turned, broken, and sorrowful, down the trail from the cave.

Above me shone the red eye of Mars holding her awful secret, forty-eight million miles away.

Did the Martian reach the pump room? Did the vitalizing air reach the people of that distant planet in time to save them? Was my Dejah Thoris alive, or did her beautiful body lie cold in death beside the tiny golden incubator in the sunken garden of the inner courtyard of the palace of Tardos Mors, the jeddak of Helium?

For ten years I have waited and prayed for an answer to my questions. For ten years I have waited and prayed to be taken back to the world of my lost love. I would rather lie dead beside her there than live on Earth all those millions of terrible miles from her.

The old mine, which I found untouched, has made me fabulously wealthy; but what care I for wealth!

As I sit here tonight in my little study overlooking the Hudson, just twenty years have elapsed since I first opened my eyes upon Mars.

I can see her shining in the sky through the little window by my desk, and tonight she seems calling to me again as she has not called before since that long dead night, and I think I can see, across that awful abyss of space, a beautiful black-haired woman standing in the garden of a palace, and at her side is a little boy who puts his arm around her as she points into the sky toward the planet Earth, while at their feet is a huge and hideous creature with a heart of gold.

I believe that they are waiting there for me, and something tells me that I shall soon know.

THE GODS OF MARS

Foreword

Twelve years had passed since I had laid the body of my great-uncle, Captain John Carter, of Virginia, away from the sight of men in that strange mausoleum in the old cemetery at Richmond.

Often had I pondered on the odd instructions he had left me governing the construction of his mighty tomb, and especially those parts which directed that he be laid in an *open* casket and that the ponderous mechanism which controlled the bolts of the vault's huge door be accessible *only from the inside.*

Twelve years had passed since I had read the remarkable manuscript of this remarkable man; this man who remembered no childhood and who could not even offer a vague guess as to his age; who was always young and yet who had dandled my grandfather's great-grandfather upon his knee; this man who had spent ten years upon the planet Mars; who had fought for the green men of Barsoom and fought against them; who had fought for and against the red men and who had won the ever beautiful Dejah Thoris, Princess of Helium, for his wife, and for nearly ten years had been a prince of the house of Tardos Mors, Jeddak of Helium.

Twelve years had passed since his body had been found upon the bluff before his cottage overlooking the Hudson, and ofttimes during these long years I had wondered if John Carter were really dead, or if he again roamed the dead sea bottoms of that dying planet; if he had returned to Barsoom to find that he had opened the frowning portals of the mighty atmosphere plant in time to save the countless millions who were dying of asphyxiation on that far-gone day that had seen him hurtled ruthlessly through forty-eight million miles of space back to Earth once more. I had wondered if he had found his black-haired Princess and the slender son he had dreamed was with her in the royal gardens of Tardos Mors, awaiting his return.

Or, had he found that he had been too late, and thus gone back to a living death upon a dead world? Or was he really dead after all, never to return either to his mother Earth or his beloved Mars?

Thus was I lost in useless speculation one sultry August evening when old Ben, my body servant, handed me a telegram. Tearing it open I read:

'Meet me to-morrow hotel Raleigh Richmond.

'JOHN CARTER'

Early the next morning I took the first train for Richmond and within two hours was being ushered into the room occupied by John Carter.

As I entered he rose to greet me, his old-time cordial smile of welcome lighting his handsome face. Apparently he had not aged a minute, but was still the straight, clean-limbed fighting-man of thirty. His keen grey eyes were undimmed, and the only lines upon his face were the lines of iron character and determination that always had been there since first I remembered him nearly thirty-five years before.

'Well, nephew,' he greeted me, 'do you feel as though you were seeing a ghost, or suffering from the effects of too many of Uncle Ben's juleps?'

'Juleps, I reckon,' I replied, 'for I certainly feel mighty good; but maybe it's just the sight of you again that affects me. You have been back to Mars? Tell me. And Dejah Thoris? You found her well and awaiting you?'

'Yes, I have been to Barsoom again, and—but it's a long story, too long to tell in the limited time I have before I must return. I have learned the secret, nephew, and I may traverse the trackless void at my will, coming and going between the countless planets as I list; but my heart is always in Barsoom, and while it is there in the keeping of my Martian Princess, I doubt that I shall ever again leave the dying world that is my life.

'I have come now because my affection for you prompted me to see you once more before you pass over for ever into that other life that I shall never know, and which though I have died thrice and shall die again to-night, as you know death, I am as unable to fathom as are you.

'Even the wise and mysterious therns of Barsoom, that ancient cult which for countless ages has been credited with holding the secret of life and death in their impregnable fastnesses upon the hither slopes of the Mountains of Otz, are as ignorant as we. I have proved it, though I near lost my life in the doing of it; but you shall read it all in the notes I have been making during the last three months that I have been back upon Earth.'

He patted a swelling portfolio that lay on the table at his elbow.

'I know that you are interested and that you believe, and I know that the world, too, is interested, though they will not believe for many years; yes, for many ages, since they cannot understand. Earth men have not yet progressed to a point where they can comprehend the things that I have written in those notes.

'Give them what you wish of it, what you think will not harm them, but do not feel aggrieved if they laugh at you.'

That night I walked down to the cemetery with him. At the door of his vault he turned and pressed my hand.

'Good-bye, nephew,' he said. 'I may never see you again, for I doubt that I can ever bring myself to leave my wife and boy while they live, and the span of life upon Barsoom is often more than a thousand years.'

He entered the vault. The great door swung slowly to. The ponderous bolts grated into place. The lock clicked. I have never seen Captain John Carter, of Virginia, since.

But here is the story of his return to Mars on that other occasion, as I have gleaned it from the great mass of notes which he left for me upon the table of his room in the hotel at Richmond.

There is much which I have left out; much which I have not dared to tell; but you will find the story of his second search for Dejah Thoris, Princess of Helium, even more remarkable than was his first manuscript which I gave to an unbelieving world a short time since and through which we followed the fighting Virginian across dead sea bottoms under the moons of Mars.

E. R. B.

ONE

The Plant Men

As I stood upon the bluff before my cottage on that clear cold night in the early part of March, 1886, the noble Hudson flowing like the grey and silent spectre of a dead river below me, I felt again the strange, compelling influence of the mighty god of war, my beloved Mars, which for ten long and lonesome years I had implored with outstretched arms to carry me back to my lost love.

Not since that other March night in 1866, when I had stood without that Arizona cave in which my still and lifeless body lay wrapped in the similitude of earthly death had I felt the irresistible attraction of the god of my profession.

With arms outstretched toward the red eye of the great star I stood praying for a return of that strange power which twice had drawn me through the immensity of space, praying as I had prayed on a thousand nights before during the long ten years that I had waited and hoped.

Suddenly a qualm of nausea swept over me, my senses swam, my knees gave beneath me and I pitched headlong to the ground upon the very verge of the dizzy bluff.

Instantly my brain cleared and there swept back across the threshold of my memory the vivid picture of the horrors of that ghostly Arizona cave; again, as on that far-gone night, my muscles refused to respond to my will and again, as though even here upon the banks of the placid Hudson, I could hear the awful moans and rustling of the fearsome thing which had lurked and threatened me from the dark recesses of the cave, I made the same mighty and superhuman effort to break the bonds of the strange anæsthesia which held me, and again came the sharp click as of the sudden parting of a taut wire, and I stood naked and free beside the staring, lifeless thing that had so recently pulsed with the warm, red life-blood of John Carter.

With scarcely a parting glance I turned my eyes again toward Mars, lifted my hands toward his lurid rays, and waited.

Nor did I have long to wait; for scarce had I turned ere I shot with the rapidity of thought into the awful void before me. There was the same instant of unthinkable cold and utter darkness that I had experienced twenty years before, and then I opened my eyes in another world, beneath the burning rays of a hot sun, which beat through a tiny opening in the dome of the mighty forest in which I lay.

The scene that met my eyes was so un-Martian that my heart sprang to my throat as the sudden fear swept through me that I had been aimlessly tossed upon some strange planet by a cruel fate.

Why not? What guide had I through the trackless waste of interplanetary space? What assurance that I might not as well be hurtled to some far-distant star of another solar system, as to Mars?

I lay upon a close-cropped sward of red grasslike vegetation, and about me stretched a grove of strange and beautiful trees, covered with huge and gorgeous blossoms and filled with brilliant, voiceless birds. I call them birds since they were winged, but mortal eye ne'er rested on such odd, unearthly shapes.

The vegetation was similar to that which covers the lawns of the red Martians of the great waterways, but the trees and birds were unlike anything that I had ever seen upon Mars, and then through the further trees I could see that most un-Martian of all sights—an open sea, its blue waters shimmering beneath the brazen sun.

As I rose to investigate further I experienced the same ridiculous catastrophe that had met my first attempt to walk under Martian conditions. The lesser attraction of this smaller planet and the reduced air pressure of its greatly rarefied atmosphere, afforded so little resistance to my earthly muscles that the ordinary exertion of the mere act of rising sent me several feet into the air and precipitated me upon my face in the soft and brilliant grass of this strange world.

This experience, however, gave me some slightly increased assurance that, after all, I might indeed be in some, to me, unknown corner of Mars, and this was very possible since during my ten years' residence upon the planet I had explored but a comparatively tiny area of its vast expanse.

I arose again, laughing at my forgetfulness, and soon had mastered once more the art of attuning my earthly sinews to these changed conditions.

As I walked slowly down the imperceptible slope toward the sea I could not help but note the park-like appearance of the sward and trees. The grass was as close-cropped and carpet-like as some old English lawn and

the trees themselves showed evidence of careful pruning to a uniform height
of about fifteen feet from the ground, so that as one turned his glance in
any direction the forest had the appearance at a little distance of a vast,
high-ceiled chamber.

All these evidences of careful and systematic cultivation convinced me
that I had been fortunate enough to make my entry into Mars on this
second occasion through the domain of a civilized people and that when
I should find them I would be accorded the courtesy and protection that
my rank as a Prince of the house of Tardos Mors entitled me to.

The trees of the forest attracted my deep admiration as I proceeded
toward the sea. Their great stems, some of them fully a hundred feet in
diameter, attested their prodigious height, which I could only guess at,
since at no point could I penetrate their dense foliage above me to more
than sixty or eighty feet.

As far aloft as I could see the stems and branches and twigs were as
smooth and as highly polished as the newest of American-made pianos.
The wood of some of the trees was as black as ebony, while their nearest
neighbours might perhaps gleam in the subdued light of the forest as clear
and white as the finest china, or, again, they were azure, scarlet, yellow, or
deepest purple.

And in the same way was the foliage as gay and variegated as the stems,
while the blooms that clustered thick upon them may not be described in
any earthly tongue, and indeed might challenge the language of the gods.

As I neared the confines of the forest I beheld before me, and between
the grove and the open sea, a broad expanse of meadow land, and as I was
about to emerge from the shadows of the trees a sight met my eyes that
banished all romantic and poetic reflection upon the beauties of the strange
landscape.

To my left the sea extended as far as the eye could reach, before me only
a vague, dim line indicated its further shore, while at my right a mighty
river, broad, placid, and majestic, flowed between scarlet banks to empty
into the quiet sea before me.

At a little distance up the river rose mighty perpendicular bluffs, from
the very base of which the great river seemed to rise.

But it was not these inspiring and magnificent evidences of Nature's
grandeur that took my immediate attention from the beauties of the forest.
It was the sight of a score of figures moving slowly about the meadow near
the bank of the mighty river.

Odd, grotesque shapes they were; unlike anything that I had ever seen
upon Mars, and yet, at a distance, most manlike in appearance. The larger

specimens appeared to be about ten or twelve feet in height when they stood erect, and to be proportioned as to torso and lower extremities precisely as is earthly man.

Their arms, however, were very short, and from where I stood seemed as though fashioned much after the manner of an elephant's trunk, in that they moved in sinuous and snakelike undulations, as though entirely without bony structure, or if there were bones it seemed that they must be vertebral in nature.

As I watched them from behind the stem of a huge tree, one of the creatures moved slowly in my direction, engaged in the occupation that seemed to be the principal business of each of them, and which consisted in running their oddly shaped hands over the surface of the sward, for what purpose I could not determine.

As he approached quite close to me I obtained an excellent view of him, and though I was later to become better acquainted with his kind, I may say that that single cursory examination of this awful travesty on Nature would have proved quite sufficient to my desires had I been a free agent. The fastest flier of the Heliumetic Navy could not quickly enough have carried me far from this hideous creature.

Its hairless body was a strange and ghoulish blue, except for a broad band of white which encircled its protruding, single eye: an eye that was all dead white—pupil, iris, and ball.

Its nose was a ragged, inflamed, circular hole in the centre of its blank face; a hole that resembled more closely nothing that I could think of other than a fresh bullet wound which has not yet commenced to bleed.

Below this repulsive orifice the face was quite blank to the chin, for the thing had no mouth that I could discover.

The head, with the exception of the face, was covered by a tangled mass of jet-black hair some eight or ten inches in length. Each hair was about the bigness of a large angleworm, and as the thing moved the muscles of its scalp this awful head-covering seemed to writhe and wriggle and crawl about the fearsome face as though indeed each separate hair was endowed with independent life.

The body and the legs were as symmetrically human as Nature could have fashioned them, and the feet, too, were human in shape, but of monstrous proportions. From heel to toe they were fully three feet long, and very flat and very broad.

As it came quite close to me I discovered that its strange movements, running its odd hands over the surface of the turf, were the result of its peculiar method of feeding, which consists in cropping off the tender vegetation with its razorlike talons and sucking it up from its two mouths, which lie one in the palm of each hand, through its arm-like throats.

In addition to the features which I have already described, the beast was equipped with a massive tail about six feet in length, quite round where it joined the body, but tapering to a flat, thin blade toward the end, which trailed at right angles to the ground.

By far the most remarkable feature of this most remarkable creature, however, were the two tiny replicas of it, each about six inches in length, which dangled, one on either side, from its armpits. They were suspended by a small stem which seemed to grow from the exact tops of their heads to where it connected them with the body of the adult.

Whether they were the young, or merely portions of a composite creature, I did not know.

As I had been scrutinizing this weird monstrosity the balance of the herd had fed quite close to me and I now saw that while many had the smaller specimens dangling from them, not all were thus equipped, and I further noted that the little ones varied in size from what appeared to be but tiny unopened buds an inch in diameter through various stages of development to the full-fledged and perfectly formed creature of ten to twelve inches in length.

Feeding with the herd were many of the little fellows not much larger than those which remained attached to their parents, and from the young of that size the herd graded up to the immense adults.

Fearsome-looking as they were, I did not know whether to fear them or not, for they did not seem to be particularly well equipped for fighting, and I was on the point of stepping from my hiding-place and revealing myself to them to note the effect upon them of the sight of a man when my rash resolve was, fortunately for me, nipped in the bud by a strange shrieking wail, which seemed to come from the direction of the bluffs at my right.

Naked and unarmed, as I was, my end would have been both speedy and horrible at the hands of these cruel creatures had I had time to put my resolve into execution, but at the moment of the shriek each member of the herd turned in the direction from which the sound seemed to come, and at the same instant every particular snake-like hair upon their heads rose stiffly perpendicular as if each had been a sentient organism looking or listening for the source or meaning of the wail. And indeed the latter proved to be the truth, for this strange growth upon the craniums of the plant men of Barsoom represents the thousand ears of these hideous creatures, the last remnant of the strange race which sprang from the original Tree of Life.

Instantly every eye turned toward one member of the herd, a large fellow who evidently was the leader. A strange purring sound issued from the mouth in the palm of one of his hands, and at the same time he started rapidly toward the bluff, followed by the entire herd. Their speed and method of locomotion were both remarkable, springing as they did in great leaps of twenty or thirty feet, much after the manner of a kangaroo.

They were rapidly disappearing when it occurred to me to follow them, and so, hurling caution to the winds, I sprang across the meadow in their wake with leaps and bounds even more prodigious than their own, for the muscles of an athletic Earth man produce remarkable results when pitted against the lesser gravity and air pressure of Mars.

Their way led directly towards the apparent source of the river at the base of the cliffs, and as I neared this point I found the meadow dotted with huge boulders that the ravages of time had evidently dislodged from the towering crags above.

For this reason I came quite close to the cause of the disturbance before the scene broke upon my horrified gaze. As I topped a great boulder I saw the herd of plant men surrounding a little group of perhaps five or six green men and women of Barsoom.

That I was indeed upon Mars I now had no doubt, for here were members of the wild hordes that people the dead sea bottoms and deserted cities of that dying planet.

Here were the great males towering in all the majesty of their imposing height; here were the gleaming white tusks protruding from their massive lower jaws to a point near the centre of their foreheads, the laterally placed, protruding eyes with which they could look forward or backward, or to either side without turning their heads, here the strange antennæ-like ears rising from the tops of their foreheads; and the additional pair of arms extending from midway between the shoulders and the hips.

Even without the glossy green hide and the metal ornaments which denoted the tribes to which they belonged, I would have known them on the instant for what they were, for where else in all the universe is their like duplicated?

There were two men and four females in the party and their ornaments denoted them as members of different hordes, a fact which tended to puzzle me infinitely, since the various hordes of green men of Barsoom are eternally at deadly war with one another, and never, except on that single historic instance when the great Tars Tarkas of Thark gathered a hundred and fifty thousand green warriors from several hordes to march upon the doomed city of Zodanga to rescue Dejah Thoris, Princess of Helium, from the clutches of Than Kosis, had I seen green Martians of different hordes associated in other than mortal combat.

But now they stood back to back, facing, in wide-eyed amazement, the very evidently hostile demonstrations of a common enemy.

Both men and women were armed with long-swords and daggers, but no firearms were in evidence, else it had been short shrift for the gruesome plant men of Barsoom.

Presently the leader of the plant men charged the little party, and his method of attack was as remarkable as it was effective, and by its very strangeness was the more potent, since in the science of the green warriors there was no defence for this singular manner of attack, the like of which it soon was evident to me they were as unfamiliar with as they were with the monstrosities which confronted them.

The plant man charged to within a dozen feet of the party and then, with a bound, rose as though to pass directly above their heads. His powerful tail was raised high to one side, and as he passed close above them he brought it down in one terrific sweep that crushed a green warrior's skull as though it had been an eggshell.

The balance of the frightful herd was now circling rapidly and with bewildering speed about the little knot of victims. Their prodigious bounds and the shrill, screeching purr of their uncanny mouths were well calculated to confuse and terrorize their prey, so that as two of them leaped simultaneously from either side, the mighty sweep of those awful tails met with no resistance and two more green Martians went down to an ignoble death.

There were now but one warrior and two females left, and it seemed that it could be but a matter of seconds ere these, also, lay dead upon the scarlet sward.

But as two more of the plant men charged, the warrior, who was now prepared by the experiences of the past few minutes, swung his mighty long-sword aloft and met the hurtling bulk with a clean cut that clove one of the plant men from chin to groin.

The other, however, dealt a single blow with his cruel tail that laid both of the females crushed corpses upon the ground.

As the green warrior saw the last of his companions go down and at the same time perceived that the entire herd was charging him in a body, he rushed boldly to meet them, swinging his long-sword in the terrific manner that I had so often seen the men of his kind wield it in their ferocious and almost continual warfare among their own race.

Cutting and hewing to right and left, he laid an open path straight through the advancing plant men, and then commenced a mad race for the forest, in the shelter of which he evidently hoped that he might find a haven of refuge.

He had turned for that portion of the forest which abutted on the cliffs, and thus the mad race was taking the entire party farther and farther from the boulder where I lay concealed.

As I had watched the noble fight which the great warrior had put up against such enormous odds my heart had swelled in admiration for him, and acting as I am wont to do, more upon impulse than after mature deliberation, I instantly sprang from my sheltering rock and bounded quickly toward the bodies of the dead green Martians, a well-defined plan of action already formed.

Half a dozen great leaps brought me to the spot, and another instant saw me again in my stride in quick pursuit of the hideous monsters that were rapidly gaining on the fleeing warrior, but this time I grasped a mighty long-sword in my hand and in my heart was the old blood lust of the fighting-man, and a red mist swam before my eyes and I felt my lips respond to my heart in the old smile that has ever marked me in the midst of the joy of battle.

Swift as I was I was none too soon, for the green warrior had been overtaken ere he had made half the distance to the forest, and now he stood with his back to a boulder, while the herd, temporarily balked, hissed and screeched about him.

With their single eyes in the centre of their heads and every eye turned upon their prey, they did not note my soundless approach, so that I was upon them with my great long-sword and four of them lay dead ere they knew that I was among them.

For an instant they recoiled before my terrific onslaught, and in that instant the green warrior rose to the occasion and, springing to my side, laid to the right and left of him as I had never seen but one other warrior do, with great circling strokes that formed a figure eight about him and that never stopped until none stood living to oppose him, his keen blade passing through flesh and bone and metal as though each had been alike thin air.

As we bent to the slaughter, far above us rose that shrill, weird cry which I had heard once before, and which had called the herd to the attack upon their victims. Again and again it rose, but we were too much engaged with the fierce and powerful creatures about us to attempt to search out even with our eyes the author of the horrid notes.

Great tails lashed in frenzied anger about us, razor-like talons cut our

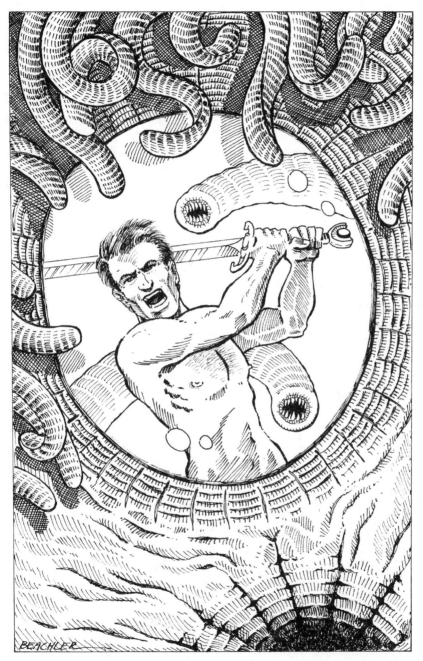

With their single eyes in the centre of their heads and every eye turned upon their prey, they did not note my soundless approach, so that I was upon them with my great long-sword and four of them lay dead ere they knew that I was among them.

limbs and bodies, and a green and sticky syrup, such as oozes from a crushed caterpillar, smeared us from head to foot, for every cut and thrust of our longswords brought spurts of this stuff upon us from the severed arteries of the plant men, through which it courses in its sluggish viscidity in lieu of blood.

Once I felt the great weight of one of the monsters upon my back and as keen talons sank into my flesh I experienced the frightful sensation of moist lips sucking the lifeblood from the wounds to which the claws still clung.

I was very much engaged with a ferocious fellow who was endeavouring to reach my throat from in front, while two more, one on either side, were lashing viciously at me with their tails.

The green warrior was much put to it to hold his own, and I felt that the unequal struggle could last but a moment longer when the huge fellow discovered my plight, and tearing himself from those that surrounded him, he raked the assailant from my back with a single sweep of his blade, and thus relieved I had little difficulty with the others.

Once together, we stood almost back to back against the great boulder, and thus the creatures were prevented from soaring above us to deliver their deadly blows, and as we were easily their match while they remained upon the ground, we were making great headway in dispatching what remained of them when our attention was again attracted by the shrill wail of the caller above our heads.

This time I glanced up, and far above us upon a little natural balcony on the face of the cliff stood a strange figure of a man shrieking out his shrill signal, the while he waved one hand in the direction of the river's mouth as though beckoning to some one there, and with the other pointed and gesticulated toward us.

A glance in the direction toward which he was looking was sufficient to apprise me of his aims and at the same time to fill me with the dread of dire apprehension, for, streaming in from all directions across the meadow, from out of the forest, and from the far distance of the flat land across the river, I could see converging upon us a hundred different lines of wildly leaping creatures such as we were now engaged with, and with them some strange new monsters which ran with great swiftness, now erect and now upon all fours.

"It will be a great death," I said to my companion. "Look!"

As he shot a quick glance in the direction I indicated he smiled.

"We may at least die fighting and as great warriors should, John Carter," he replied.

We had just finished the last of our immediate antagonists as he spoke, and I turned in surprised wonderment at the sound of my name.

And there before my astonished eyes I beheld the greatest of the green men of Barsoom; their shrewdest statesman, their mightiest general, my great and good friend, Tars Tarkas, Jeddak of Thark.

TWO

A Forest Battle

Tars Tarkas and I found no time for an exchange of experiences as we stood there before the great boulder surrounded by the corpses of our grotesque assailants, for from all directions down the broad valley was streaming a perfect torrent of terrifying creatures in response to the weird call of the strange figure far above us.

"Come," cried Tars Tarkas, "we must make for the cliffs. There lies our only hope of even temporary escape; there we may find a cave or a narrow ledge which two may defend for ever against this motley, unarmed horde."

Together we raced across the scarlet sward, I timing my speed that I might not outdistance my slower companion. We had, perhaps, three hundred yards to cover between our boulder and the cliffs, and then to search out a suitable shelter for our stand against the terrifying things that were pursuing us.

They were rapidly overhauling us when Tars Tarkas cried to me to hasten ahead and discover, if possible, the sanctuary we sought. The suggestion was a good one, for thus many valuable minutes might be saved to us, and, throwing every ounce of my earthly muscles into the effort, I cleared the remaining distance between myself and the cliffs in great leaps and bounds that put me at their base in a moment.

The cliffs rose perpendicular directly from the almost level sward of the valley. There was no accumulation of fallen debris, forming a more or less rough ascent to them, as is the case with nearly all other cliffs I have ever seen. The scattered boulders that had fallen from above and lay upon or partly buried in the turf, were the only indication that any disintegration of the massive, towering pile of rocks ever had taken place.

My first cursory inspection of the face of the cliffs filled my heart with forebodings, since nowhere could I discern, except where the weird herald stood still shrieking his shrill summons, the faintest indication of even a bare foothold upon the lofty escarpment.

To my right the bottom of the cliff was lost in the dense foliage of the forest, which terminated at its very foot, rearing its gorgeous foliage fully a thousand feet against its stern and forbidding neighbour.

To the left the cliff ran, apparently unbroken, across the head of the broad valley, to be lost in the outlines of what appeared to be a range of mighty mountains that skirted and confined the valley in every direction.

Perhaps a thousand feet from me the river broke, as it seemed, directly from the base of the cliffs, and as there seemed not the remotest chance for escape in that direction I turned my attention again toward the forest.

The cliffs towered above me a good five thousand feet. The sun was not quite upon them and they loomed a dull yellow in their own shade. Here and there they were broken with streaks and patches of dusky red, green, and occasional areas of white quartz.

Altogether they were very beautiful, but I fear that I did not regard them with a particularly appreciative eye on this, my first inspection of them.

Just then I was absorbed in them only as a medium of escape, and so, as my gaze ran quickly, time and again, over their vast expanse in search of some cranny or crevice, I came suddenly to loathe them as the prisoner must loathe the cruel and impregnable walls of his dungeon.

Tars Tarkas was approaching me rapidly, and still more rapidly came the awful horde at his heels.

It seemed the forest now or nothing, and I was just on the point of motioning Tars Tarkas to follow me in that direction when the sun passed the cliff's zenith, and as the bright rays touched the dull surface it burst out into a million scintillant lights of burnished gold, of flaming red, of soft greens, and gleaming whites—a more gorgeous and inspiring spectacle human eye has never rested upon.

The face of the entire cliff was, as later inspection conclusively proved, so shot with veins and patches of solid gold as to quite present the appearance of a solid wall of that precious metal except where it was broken by outcroppings of ruby, emerald, and diamond boulders—a faint and alluring indication of the vast and unguessable riches which lay deeply buried behind the magnificent surface.

But what caught my most interested attention at the moment that the sun's rays set the cliff's face a-shimmer, was the several black spots which now appeared quite plainly in evidence high across the gorgeous wall close to the forest's top, and extending apparently below and behind the branches.

Almost immediately I recognised them for what they were, the dark openings of caves entering the solid walls—possible avenues of escape or temporary shelter, could we but reach them.

There was but a single way, and that led through the mighty, towering trees upon our right. That I could scale them I knew full well, but Tars Tarkas, with his mighty bulk and enormous weight, would find it a task possibly quite beyond his prowess or his skill, for Martians are at best but poor climbers. Upon the entire surface of that ancient planet I never before had seen a hill or mountain that exceeded four thousand feet in height above the dead sea bottoms, and as the ascent was usually gradual, nearly to their summits they presented but few opportunities for the practice of climbing. Nor would the Martians have embraced even such opportunities as might present themselves, for they could always find a circuitous route about the base of any eminence, and these roads they preferred and followed in preference to the shorter but more arduous ways.

However, there was nothing else to consider than an attempt to scale the trees contiguous to the cliff in an effort to reach the caves above.

The Thark grasped the possibilities and the difficulties of the plan at once, but there was no alternative, and so we set out rapidly for the trees nearest the cliff.

Our relentless pursuers were now close to us, so close that it seemed that it would be an utter impossibility for the Jeddak of Thark to reach the forest in advance of them, nor was there any considerable will in the efforts that Tars Tarkas made, for the green men of Barsoom do not relish flight, nor ever before had I seen one fleeing from death in whatsoever form it might have confronted him. But that Tars Tarkas was the bravest of the brave he had proven thousands of times; yes, tens of thousands in countless mortal combats with men and beasts. And so I knew that there was another reason than fear of death behind his flight, as he knew that a greater power than pride or honour spurred me to escape these fierce destroyers. In my case it was love—love of the divine Dejah Thoris; and the cause of the Thark's great and sudden love of life I could not fathom, for it is oftener that they seek death than life—these strange, cruel, loveless, unhappy people.

At length, however, we reached the shadows of the forest, while right behind us sprang the swiftest of our pursuers—a giant plant man with claws outreaching to fasten his bloodsucking mouths upon us.

He was, I should say, a hundred yards in advance of his closest companion, and so I called to Tars Tarkas to ascend a great tree that brushed the cliff's face while I dispatched the fellow, thus giving the less agile Thark an opportunity to reach the higher branches before the entire horde should be upon us and every vestige of escape cut off.

But I had reckoned without a just appreciation either of the cunning of my immediate antagonist or the swiftness with which his fellows were covering the distance which had separated them from me.

As I raised my long-sword to deal the creature its death thrust it halted in its charge and, as my sword cut harmlessly through the empty air, the great tail of the thing swept with the power of a grizzly's arm across the sward and carried me bodily from my feet to the ground. In an instant the brute was upon me, but ere it could fasten its hideous mouths into my breast and throat I grasped a writhing tentacle in either hand.

The plant man was well muscled, heavy, and powerful but my earthly sinews and greater agility, in conjunction with the deathly strangle hold I had upon him, would have given me, I think, an eventual victory had we had time to discuss the merits of our relative prowess uninterrupted. But as we strained and struggled about the tree into which Tars Tarkas was clambering with infinite difficulty, I suddenly caught a glimpse over the shoulder of my antagonist of the great swarm of pursuers that now were fairly upon me.

Now, at last, I saw the nature of the other monsters who had come with the plant men in response to the weird calling of the man upon the cliff's face. They were that most dreaded of Martian creatures—great white apes of Barsoom.

My former experiences upon Mars had familiarized me thoroughly with them and their methods, and I may say that of all the fearsome and terrible, weird and grotesque inhabitants of that strange world, it is the white apes that come nearest to familiarizing me with the sensation of fear.

I think that the cause of this feeling which these apes engender within me is due to their remarkable resemblance in form to our Earth men, which gives them a human appearance that is most uncanny when coupled with their enormous size.

They stand fifteen feet in height and walk erect upon their hind feet. Like the green Martians, they have an intermediary set of arms midway between their upper and lower limbs. Their eyes are very close set, but do not protrude as do those of the green men of Mars; their ears are high set, but more laterally located than are the green men's, while their snouts and teeth are much like those of our African gorilla. Upon their heads grows an enormous shock of bristly hair.

It was into the eyes of such as these and the terrible plant men that I gazed above the shoulder of my foe, and then, in a mighty wave of snarling, snapping, screaming, purring rage, they swept over me—and of all the sounds that assailed my ears as I went down beneath them, to me the most hideous was the horrid purring of the plant men.

Instantly a score of cruel fangs and keen talons were sunk into my flesh; cold, sucking lips fastened themselves upon my arteries. I struggled to free myself, and even though weighed down by these immense bodies, I succeeded in struggling to my feet, where, still grasping my long-sword, and shortening my grip upon it until I could use it as a dagger, I wrought such havoc among them that at one time I stood for an instant free.

What it has taken minutes to write occurred in but a few seconds, but during that time Tars Tarkas had seen my plight and had dropped from the lower branches, which he had reached with such infinite labour, and as I flung the last of my immediate antagonists from me the great Thark leaped to my side, and again we fought, back to back, as we had done a hundred times before.

Time and again the ferocious apes sprang in to close with us, and time and again we beat them back with our swords. The great tails of the plant men lashed with tremendous power about us as they charged from various directions or sprang with the agility of greyhounds above our heads; but every attack met a gleaming blade in sword hands that had been reputed for twenty years the best that Mars ever had known; for Tars Tarkas and John Carter were names that the fighting men of the world of warriors loved best to speak.

But even the two best swords in a world of fighters can avail not for ever against overwhelming numbers of fierce and savage brutes that know not what defeat means until cold steel teaches their hearts no longer to beat, and so, step by step, we were forced back. At length we stood against the giant tree that we had chosen for our ascent, and then, as charge after charge hurled its weight upon us, we gave back again and again, until we had been forced half-way around the huge base of the colossal trunk.

Tars Tarkas was in the lead, and suddenly I heard a little cry of exultation from him.

"Here is shelter for one at least, John Carter," he said, and, glancing down, I saw an opening in the base of the tree about three feet in diameter.

"In with you, Tars Tarkas," I cried, but he would not go; saying that his bulk was too great for the little aperture, while I might slip in easily.

"We shall both die if we remain without, John Carter; here is a slight chance for one of us. Take it and you may live to avenge me, it is useless for me to attempt to worm my way into so small an opening with this horde of demons besetting us on all sides."

"Then we shall die together, Tars Tarkas," I replied, "for I shall not go first. Let me defend the opening while you get in, then my smaller stature will permit me to slip in with you before they can prevent."

We still were fighting furiously as we talked in broken sentences, punctured with vicious cuts and thrusts at our swarming enemy.

At length he yielded, for it seemed the only way in which either of us might be saved from the ever-increasing numbers of our assailants, who were still swarming upon us from all directions across the broad valley.

"It was ever your way, John Carter, to think last of your own life," he said; "but still more your way to command the lives and actions of others, even to the greatest of Jeddaks who rule upon Barsoom."

There was a grim smile upon his cruel, hard face, as he, the greatest Jeddak of them all, turned to obey the dictates of a creature of another world—of a man whose stature was less than half his own.

"If you fail, John Carter," he said, "know that the cruel and heartless Thark, to whom you taught the meaning of friendship, will come out to die beside you."

"As you will, my friend," I replied; "but quickly now, head first, while I cover your retreat."

He hesitated a little at that word, for never before in his whole life of continual strife had he turned his back upon aught than a dead or defeated enemy.

"Haste, Tars Tarkas," I urged, "or we shall both go down to profitless defeat; I cannot hold them for ever alone."

As he dropped to the ground to force his way into the tree, the whole howling pack of hideous devils hurled themselves upon me. To right and left flew my shimmering blade, now green with the sticky juice of a plant man, now red with the crimson blood of a great white ape; but always flying from one opponent to another, hesitating but the barest fraction of a second to drink the lifeblood in the centre of some savage heart.

And thus I fought as I never had fought before, against such frightful odds that I cannot realize even now that human muscles could have withstood that awful onslaught, that terrific weight of hurtling tons of ferocious, battling flesh.

With the fear that we would escape them, the creatures redoubled their efforts to pull me down, and though the ground about me was piled high with their dead and dying comrades, they succeeded at last in overwhelming me, and I went down beneath them for the second time that day, and once again felt those awful sucking lips against my flesh.

But scarce had I fallen ere I felt powerful hands grip my ankles, and in another second I was being drawn within the shelter of the tree's interior.

For a moment it was a tug of war between Tars Tarkas and a great plant man, who clung tenaciously to my breast, but presently I got the point of my long-sword beneath him and with a mighty thrust pierced his vitals.

Torn and bleeding from many cruel wounds, I lay panting upon the ground within the hollow of the tree, while Tars Tarkas defended the opening from the furious mob without.

For an hour they howled about the tree, but after a few attempts to reach us they confined their efforts to terrorizing shrieks and screams, to horrid growling on the part of the great white apes, and the fearsome and indescribable purring by the plant men.

At length, all but a score, who had apparently been left to prevent our escape, had left us, and our adventure seemed destined to result in a siege, the only outcome of which could be our death by starvation; for even should we be able to slip out after dark, whither in this unknown and hostile valley could we hope to turn our steps toward possible escape?

As the attacks of our enemies ceased and our eyes became accustomed to the semi-darkness of the interior of our strange retreat, I took the opportunity to explore our shelter.

The tree was hollow to an extent of about fifty feet in diameter, and from its flat, hard floor I judged that it had often been used to domicile others before our occupancy. As I raised my eyes toward its roof to note the height I saw far above me a faint glow of light.

There was an opening above. If we could but reach it we might still hope to make the shelter of the cliff caves. My eyes had now become quite used to the subdued light of the interior, and as I pursued my investigation I presently came upon a rough ladder at the far side of the cave.

Quickly I mounted it, only to find that it connected at the top with the lower of a series of horizontal wooden bars that spanned the now narrow and shaft-like interior of the tree's stem. These bars were set one above another about three feet apart, and formed a perfect ladder as far above me as I could see.

Dropping to the floor once more, I detailed my discovery to Tars Tarkas, who suggested that I explore aloft as far as I could go in safety while he guarded the entrance against a possible attack.

As I hastened above to explore the strange shaft I found that the ladder of horizontal bars mounted always as far above me as my eyes could reach, and as I ascended, the light from above grew brighter and brighter.

For fully five hundred feet I continued to climb, until at length I reached the opening in the stem which admitted the light. It was of about the same diameter as the entrance at the foot of the tree, and opened directly upon a large flat limb, the well worn surface of which testified to its long continued use as an avenue for some creature to and from this remarkable shaft.

I did not venture out upon the limb for fear that I might be discovered and our retreat in this direction cut off; but instead hurried to retrace my steps to Tars Tarkas.

I soon reached him and presently we were both ascending the long ladder toward the opening above.

Tars Tarkas went in advance and as I reached the first of the horizontal bars I drew the ladder up after me and, handing it to him, he carried it a hundred feet further aloft, where he wedged it safely between one of the bars and the side of the shaft. In like manner I dislodged the lower bars as I passed them, so that we soon had the interior of the tree denuded of all possible means of ascent for a distance of a hundred feet from the base; thus precluding possible pursuit and attack from the rear.

As we were to learn later, this precaution saved us from dire predicament, and was eventually the means of our salvation.

When we reached the opening at the top Tars Tarkas drew to one side that I might pass out and investigate, as, owing to my lesser weight and greater agility, I was better fitted for the perilous threading of this dizzy, hanging pathway.

The limb upon which I found myself ascended at a slight angle toward the cliff, and as I followed it I found that it terminated a few feet above a narrow ledge which protruded from the cliff's face at the entrance to a narrow cave.

As I approached the slightly more slender extremity of the branch it bent beneath my weight until, as I balanced perilously upon its outer tip, it swayed gently on a level with the ledge at a distance of a couple of feet.

Five hundred feet below me lay the vivid scarlet carpet of the valley; nearly five thousand feet above towered the mighty, gleaming face of the gorgeous cliffs.

The cave that I faced was not one of those that I had seen from the ground, and which lay much higher, possibly a thousand feet. But so far as I might know it was as good for our purpose as another, and so I returned to the tree for Tars Tarkas.

Together we wormed our way along the waving pathway, but when we reached the end of the branch we found that our combined weight so depressed the limb that the cave's mouth was now too far above us to be reached.

We finally agreed that Tars Tarkas should return along the branch, leaving his longest leather harness strap with me, and that when the limb had risen

to a height that would permit me to enter the cave I was to do so, and on
Tars Tarkas' return I could then lower the strap and haul him up to the
safety of the ledge.

This we did without mishap and soon found ourselves together upon
the verge of a dizzy little balcony, with a magnificent view of the valley
spreading out below us.

As far as the eye could reach gorgeous forest and crimson sward skirted a
silent sea, and about all towered the brilliant monster guardian cliffs. Once
we thought we discerned a gilded minaret gleaming in the sun amidst the
waving tops of far-distant trees, but we soon abandoned the idea in the
belief that it was but an hallucination born of our great desire to discover
the haunts of civilized men in this beautiful, yet forbidding, spot.

Below us upon the river's bank the great white apes were devouring the
last remnants of Tars Tarkas' former companions, while great herds of plant
men grazed in ever-widening circles about the sward which they kept as
close clipped as the smoothest of lawns.

Knowing that attack from the tree was now improbable, we determined
to explore the cave, which we had every reason to believe was but a
continuation of the path we had already traversed, leading the gods alone
knew where, but quite evidently away from this valley of grim ferocity.

As we advanced we found a well-proportioned tunnel cut from the solid
cliff. Its walls rose some twenty feet above the floor, which was about five
feet in width. The roof was arched. We had no means of making a light,
and so groped our way slowly into the ever-increasing darkness, Tars Tarkas
keeping in touch with one wall while I felt along the other, while, to prevent
our wandering into diverging branches and becoming separated or lost in
some intricate and labyrinthine maze, we clasped hands.

How far we traversed the tunnel in this manner I do not know, but
presently we came to an obstruction which blocked our further progress.
It seemed more like a partition than a sudden ending of the cave, for it was
constructed not of the material of the cliff, but of something which felt like
very hard wood.

Silently I groped over its surface with my hands, and presently was
rewarded by the feel of the button which as commonly denotes a door on
Mars as does a door knob on Earth.

Gently pressing it, I had the satisfaction of feeling the door slowly give
before me, and in another instant we were looking into a dimly lighted
apartment, which, so far as we could see, was unoccupied.

Without more ado I swung the door wide open and, followed by the huge
Thark, stepped into the chamber. As we stood for a moment in silence gazing

about the room a slight noise behind caused me to turn quickly, when, to my astonishment, I saw the door close with a sharp click as though by an unseen hand.

Instantly I sprang toward it to wrench it open again, for something in the uncanny movement of the thing and the tense and almost palpable silence of the chamber seemed to portend a lurking evil lying hidden in this rock-bound chamber within the bowels of the Golden Cliffs.

My fingers clawed futilely at the unyielding portal, while my eyes sought in vain for a duplicate of the button which had given us ingress.

And then, from unseen lips, a cruel and mocking peal of laughter rang through the desolate place.

THREE

The Chamber of Mystery

For moments after that awful laugh had ceased reverberating through the rocky room, Tars Tarkas and I stood in tense and expectant silence. But no further sound broke the stillness, nor within the range of our vision did aught move.

At length Tars Tarkas laughed softly, after the manner of his strange kind when in the presence of the horrible or terrifying. It is not an hysterical laugh, but rather the genuine expression of the pleasure they derive from the things that move Earth men to loathing or to tears.

Often and again have I seen them roll upon the ground in mad fits of uncontrollable mirth when witnessing the death agonies of women and little children beneath the torture of that hellish green Martian fête—the Great Games.

I looked up at the Thark, a smile upon my own lips, for here in truth was greater need for a smiling face than a trembling chin.

"What do you make of it all?" I asked. "Where in the deuce are we?"

He looked at me in surprise.

"Where are we?" he repeated. "Do you tell me, John Carter, that you know not where you be?"

"That I am upon Barsoom is all that I can guess, and but for you and the great white apes I should not even guess that, for the sights I have seen this day are as unlike the things of my beloved Barsoom as I knew it ten long years ago as they are unlike the world of my birth.

"No, Tars Tarkas, I know not where we be."

"Where have you been since you opened the mighty portals of the atmosphere plant years ago, after the keeper had died and the engines stopped and all Barsoom was dying, that had not already died, of asphyxiation? Your body even was never found, though the men of a whole world sought after it for years, though the Jeddak of Helium and his granddaughter, your princess, offered such fabulous rewards that even princes of royal blood joined in the search.

"There was but one conclusion to reach when all efforts to locate you had failed, and that, that you had taken the long, last pilgrimage down the mysterious River Iss, to await in the Valley Dor upon the shores of the Lost Sea of Korus the beautiful Dejah Thoris, your princess.

"Why you had gone none could guess, for your princess still lived—"

"Thank God," I interrupted him. "I did not dare to ask you, for I feared I might have been too late to save her—she was very low when I left her in the royal gardens of Tardos Mors that long-gone night; so very low that I scarcely hoped even then to reach the atmosphere plant ere her dear spirit had fled from me for ever. And she lives yet?"

"She lives, John Carter."

"You have not told me where we are," I reminded him.

"We are where I expected to find you, John Carter—and another. Many years ago you heard the story of the woman who taught me the thing that green Martians are reared to hate, the woman who taught me to love. You know the cruel tortures and the awful death her love won for her at the hands of the beast, Tal Hajus.

"She, I thought, awaited me by the Lost Sea of Korus.

"You know that it was left for a man from another world, for yourself, John Carter, to teach this cruel Thark what friendship is; and you, I thought, also roamed the care-free Valley Dor.

"Thus were the two I most longed for at the end of the long pilgrimage I must take some day, and so as the time had elapsed which Dejah Thoris had hoped might bring you once more to her side, for she has always tried to believe that you had but temporarily returned to your own planet, I at last gave way to my great yearning and a month since I started upon the journey, the end of which you have this day witnessed. Do you understand now where you be, John Carter?"

"And that was the River Iss, emptying into the Lost Sea of Korus in the Valley Dor?" I asked.

"This is the valley of love and peace and rest to which every Barsoomian since time immemorial has longed to pilgrimage at the end of a life of hate and strife and bloodshed," he replied. "This, John Carter, is Heaven."

His tone was cold and ironical; its bitterness but reflecting the terrible disappointment he had suffered. Such a fearful disillusionment, such a blasting of life-long hopes and aspirations, such an uprooting of age-old tradition might have excused a vastly greater demonstration on the part of the Thark.

I laid my hand upon his shoulder.

"I am sorry," I said, nor did there seem aught else to say.

"Think, John Carter, of the countless billions of Barsoomians who have taken the voluntary pilgrimage down this cruel river since the beginning of time, only to fall into the ferocious clutches of the terrible creatures that to-day assailed us.

"There is an ancient legend that once a red man returned from the banks of the Lost Sea of Korus, returned from the Valley Dor, back through the mysterious River Iss, and the legend has it that he narrated a fearful blasphemy of horrid brutes that inhabited a valley of wondrous loveliness, brutes that pounced upon each Barsoomian as he terminated his pilgrimage and devoured him upon the banks of the Lost Sea where he had looked to find love and peace and happiness; but the ancients killed the blasphemer, as tradition has ordained that any shall be killed who return from the bosom of the River of Mystery.

"But now we know that it was no blasphemy, that the legend is a true one, and that the man told only of what he saw; but what does it profit us, John Carter, since even should we escape, we also would be treated as blasphemers? We are between the wild thoat of certainty and the mad zitidar of fact—we can escape neither."

"As Earth men say, we are between the devil and the deep sea, Tars Tarkas," I replied, nor could I help but smile at our dilemma.

"There is naught that we can do but take things as they come, and at least have the satisfaction of knowing that whoever slays us eventually will have far greater numbers of their own dead to count than they will get in return. White ape or plant man, green Barsoomian or red man, whosoever it shall be that takes the last toll from us will know that it is costly in lives to wipe out John Carter, Prince of the House of Tardos Mors, and Tars Tarkas, Jeddak of Thark, at the same time."

I could not help but laugh at him grim humour, and he joined in with me in one of those rare laughs of real enjoyment which was one of the attributes of this fierce Tharkian chief which marked him from the others of his kind.

"But about yourself, John Carter," he cried at last. "If you have not been here all these years where indeed have you been, and how is it that I find you here to-day?"

"I have been back to Earth," I replied. "For ten long Earth years I have been praying and hoping for the day that would carry me once more to this grim old planet of yours, for which, with all its cruel and terrible customs, I feel a bond of sympathy and love even greater than for the world that gave me birth.

"For ten years have I been enduring a living death of uncertainty and doubt as to whether Dejah Thoris lived, and now that for the first time in all these years my prayers have been answered and my doubt relieved I find myself, through a cruel whim of fate, hurled into the one tiny spot of all Barsoom from which there is apparently no escape, and if there were, at a price which would put out for ever the last flickering hope which I may cling to of seeing my princess again in this life—and you have seen to-day with what pitiful futility man yearns toward a material hereafter.

"Only a bare half-hour before I saw you battling with the plant men I was standing in the moonlight upon the banks of a broad river that taps the eastern shore of Earth's most blessed land. I have answered you, my friend. Do you believe?"

"I believe," replied Tars Tarkas, "though I cannot understand."

As we talked I had been searching the interior of the chamber with my eyes. It was, perhaps, two hundred feet in length and half as broad, with what appeared to be a doorway in the centre of the wall directly opposite that through which we had entered.

The apartment was hewn from the material of the cliff, showing mostly dull gold in the dim light which a single minute radium illuminator in the centre of the roof diffused throughout its great dimensions. Here and there polished surfaces of ruby, emerald, and diamond patched the golden walls and ceiling. The floor was of another material, very hard, and worn by much use to the smoothness of glass. Aside from the two doors I could discern no sign of other aperture, and as one we knew to be locked against us I approached the other.

As I extended my hand to search for the controlling button, that cruel and mocking laugh rang out once more, so close to me this time that I involuntarily shrank back, tightening my grip upon the hilt of my great sword.

And then from the far corner of the great chamber a hollow voice chanted: "There is no hope, there is no hope; the dead return not, the dead return not; nor is there any resurrection. Hope not, for there is no hope."

Though our eyes instantly turned toward the spot from which the voice seemed to emanate, there was no one in sight, and I must admit that cold shivers played along my spine and the short hairs at the base of my head stiffened and rose up, as do those upon a hound's neck when in the night his eyes see those uncanny things which are hidden from the sight of man.

Quickly I walked toward the mournful voice, but it had ceased ere I reached the further wall, and then from the other end of the chamber came another voice, shrill and piercing:

"Fools! Fools!" it shrieked. "Thinkest thou to defeat the eternal laws of life and death? Wouldst cheat the mysterious Issus, Goddess of Death, of her just dues? Did not her mighty messenger, the ancient Iss, bear you upon her leaden bosom at your own behest to the Valley Dor?

"Thinkest thou, O fools, that Issus wilt give up her own? Thinkest thou to escape from whence in all the countless ages but a single soul has fled?

"Go back the way thou camest, to the merciful maws of the children of the Tree of Life or the gleaming fangs of the great white apes, for there lies speedy surcease from suffering; but insist in your rash purpose to thread the mazes of the Golden Cliffs of the Mountains of Otz, past the ramparts of the impregnable fortresses of the Holy Therns, and upon your way Death in its most frightful form will overtake you—a death so horrible that even the Holy Therns themselves, who conceived both Life and Death, avert their eyes from its fiendishness and close their ears against the hideous shrieks of its victims.

"Go back, O fools, the way thou camest."

And then the awful laugh broke out from another part of the chamber.

"Most uncanny," I remarked, turning to Tars Tarkas.

"What shall we do?" he asked. "We cannot fight empty air; I would almost sooner return and face foes into whose flesh I may feel my blade bite and know that I am selling my carcass dearly before I go down to that eternal oblivion which is evidently the fairest and most desirable eternity that mortal man has the right to hope for."

"If, as you say, we cannot fight empty air, Tars Tarkas," I replied, "neither, on the other hand, can empty air fight us. I, who have faced and conquered in my time thousands of sinewy warriors and tempered blades, shall not be turned back by wind; nor no more shall you, Thark."

"But unseen voices may emanate from unseen and unseeable creatures who wield invisible blades," answered the green warrior.

"Rot, Tars Tarkas," I cried, "those voices come from beings as real as you or as I. In their veins flows lifeblood that may be let as easily as ours, and the fact that they remain invisible to us is the best proof to my mind that they are mortal; nor overly courageous mortals at that. Think you, Tars Tarkas, that John Carter will fly at the first shriek of a cowardly foe who dare not come out into the open and face a good blade?"

I had spoken in a loud voice that there might be no question that our would-be terrorizers should hear me, for I was tiring of this nerve-racking fiasco. It had occurred to me, too, that the whole business was but a plan to frighten us back into the valley of death from which we had escaped, that we might be quickly disposed of by the savage creatures there.

For a long period there was silence, then of a sudden a soft, stealthy sound behind me caused me to turn suddenly to behold a great many-legged banth creeping sinuously upon me.

The banth is a fierce beast of prey that roams the low hills surrounding the dead seas of ancient Mars. Like nearly all Martian animals it is almost hairless, having only a great bristly mane about its thick neck.

Its long, lithe body is supported by ten powerful legs, its enormous jaws are equipped, like those of the calot, or Martian hound, with several rows of long needle-like fangs; its mouth reaches to a point far back of its tiny ears, while its enormous, protruding eyes of green add the last touch of terror to its awful aspect.

As it crept toward me it lashed its powerful tail against its yellow sides, and when it saw that it was discovered it emitted the terrifying roar which often freezes its prey into momentary paralysis in the instant that it makes its spring.

And so it launched its great bulk toward me, but its mighty voice had held no paralysing terrors for me, and it met cold steel instead of the tender flesh its cruel jaws gaped so widely to engulf.

An instant later I drew my blade from the still heart of this great Barsoomian lion, and turning toward Tars Tarkas was surprised to see him facing a similar monster.

No sooner had he dispatched his than I, turning, as though drawn by the instinct of my guardian subconscious mind, beheld another of the savage denizens of the Martian wilds leaping across the chamber toward me.

From then on for the better part of an hour one hideous creature after another was launched upon us, springing apparently from the empty air about us.

Tars Tarkas was satisfied; here was something tangible that he could cut and slash with his great blade, while I, for my part, may say that the diversion was a marked improvement over the uncanny voices from unseen lips.

That there was nothing supernatural about our new foes was well evidenced by their howls of rage and pain as they felt the sharp steel at their vitals, and the very real blood which flowed from their severed arteries as they died the real death.

I noticed during the period of this new persecution that the beasts appeared only when our backs were turned; we never saw one really materialize from thin air, nor did I for an instant sufficiently lose my excellent reasoning faculties to be once deluded into the belief that the beasts came into the room other than through some concealed and well-contrived doorway.

Among the ornaments of Tars Tarkas' leather harness, which is the only manner of clothing worn by Martians other than silk capes and robes of silk and fur for protection from the cold after dark, was a small mirror, about the bigness of a lady's hand glass, which hung midway between his shoulders and his waist against his broad back.

Once as he stood looking down at a newly fallen antagonist my eyes happened to fall upon this mirror and in its shiny surface I saw pictured a sight that caused me to whisper:

"Move not, Tars Tarkas! Move not a muscle!"

He did not ask why, but stood like a graven image while my eyes watched the strange thing that meant so much to us.

What I saw was the quick movement of a section of the wall behind me. It was turning upon pivots, and with it a section of the floor directly in front of it was turning. It was as though you placed a visiting-card upon end on a silver dollar that you had laid flat upon a table, so that the edge of the card perfectly bisected the surface of the coin.

The card might represent the section of the wall that turned and the silver dollar the section of the floor. Both were so nicely fitted into the adjacent portions of the floor and wall that no crack had been noticeable in the dim light of the chamber.

As the turn was half completed a great beast was revealed sitting upon its haunches upon that part of the revolving floor that had been on the opposite side before the wall commenced to move; when the section stopped, the beast was facing toward me on our side of the partition—it was very simple.

But what had interested me most was the sight that the half-turned section had presented through the opening that it had made. A great chamber, well lighted, in which were several men and women chained to the wall, and in front of them, evidently directing and operating the movement of the secret doorway, a wicked-faced man, neither red as are the red men of Mars, nor green as are the green men, but white, like myself, with a great mass of flowing yellow hair.

The prisoners behind him were red Martians. Chained with them were a number of fierce beasts, such as had been turned upon us, and others equally as ferocious.

As I turned to meet my new foe it was with a heart considerably lightened.

"Watch the wall at your end of the chamber, Tars Tarkas," I cautioned, "it is through secret doorways in the wall that the brutes are loosed upon us." I was very close to him and spoke in a low whisper that my knowledge of their secret might not be disclosed to our tormentors.

As long as we remained each facing an opposite end of the apartment no further attacks were made upon us, so it was quite clear to me that the partitions were in some way pierced that our actions might be observed from without.

At length a plan of action occurred to me, and backing quite close to Tars Tarkas I unfolded my scheme in a low whisper, keeping my eyes still glued upon my end of the room.

The great Thark grunted his assent to my proposition when I had done, and in accordance with my plan commenced backing toward the wall which I faced while I advanced slowly ahead of him.

When we had reached a point some ten feet from the secret doorway I halted my companion, and cautioning him to remain absolutely motionless until I gave the prearranged signal I quickly turned my back to the door through which I could almost feel the burning and baleful eyes of our would be executioner.

Instantly my own eyes sought the mirror upon Tars Tarkas' back and in another second I was closely watching the section of the wall which had been disgorging its savage terrors upon us.

I had not long to wait, for presently the golden surface commenced to move rapidly. Scarcely had it started than I gave the signal to Tars Tarkas, simultaneously springing for the receding half of the pivoting door. In like manner the Thark wheeled and leaped for the opening being made by the inswinging section.

A single bound carried me completely through into the adjoining room and brought me face to face with the fellow whose cruel face I had seen before. He was about my own height and well muscled and in every outward detail moulded precisely as are Earth men.

At his side hung a long-sword, a short-sword, a dagger, and one of the destructive radium revolvers that are common upon Mars.

The fact that I was armed only with a long-sword, and so according to the laws and ethics of battle everywhere upon Barsoom should only have been met with a similar or lesser weapon, seemed to have no effect upon the moral sense of my enemy, for he whipped out his revolver ere I scarce had touched the floor by his side, but an uppercut from my long-sword sent it flying from his grasp before he could discharge it.

Instantly he drew his long-sword, and thus evenly armed we set to in earnest for one of the closest battles I ever have fought.

The fellow was a marvellous swordsman and evidently in practice, while I had not gripped the hilt of a sword for ten long years before that morning.

But it did not take me long to fall easily into my fighting stride, so that in a few minutes the man began to realize that he had at last met his match.

His face became livid with rage as he found my guard impregnable, while blood flowed from a dozen minor wounds upon his face and body.

"Who are you, white man?" he hissed. "That you are no Barsoomian from the outer world is evident from your colour. And you are not of us."

His last statement was almost a question.

"What if I were from the Temple of Issus?" I hazarded on a wild guess.

"Fate forfend!" he exclaimed, his face going white under the blood that now nearly covered it.

I did not know how to follow up my lead, but I carefully laid the idea away for future use should circumstances require it. His answer indicated that for all he *knew* I might be from the Temple of Issus and in it were men like unto myself, and either this man feared the inmates of the temple or else he held their persons or their power in such reverence that he trembled to think of the harm and indignities he had heaped upon one of them.

But my present business with him was of a different nature than that which requires any considerable abstract reasoning; it was to get my sword between his ribs, and this I succeeded in doing within the next few seconds, nor was I an instant too soon.

The chained prisoners had been watching the combat in tense silence; not a sound had fallen in the room other than the clashing of our contending blades, the soft shuffling of our naked feet and the few whispered words we had hissed at each other through clenched teeth the while we continued our mortal duel.

But as the body of my antagonist sank an inert mass to the floor a cry of warning broke from one of the female prisoners.

"Turn! Turn! Behind you!" she shrieked, and as I wheeled at the first note of her shrill cry I found myself facing a second man of the same race as he who lay at my feet.

The fellow had crept stealthily from a dark corridor and was almost upon me with raised sword ere I saw him. Tars Tarkas was nowhere in sight and the secret panel in the wall, through which I had come, was closed.

How I wished that he were by my side now! I had fought almost continuously for many hours; I had passed through such experiences and adventures as must sap the vitality of man, and with all this I had not eaten for nearly twenty-four hours, nor slept.

I was fagged out, and for the first time in years felt a question as to my ability to cope with an antagonist; but there was naught else for it than to engage my man, and that as quickly and ferociously as lay in me, for my only salvation was to rush him off his feet by the impetuosity of my attack—I could not hope to win a long-drawn-out battle.

But the fellow was evidently of another mind, for he backed and parried and parried and sidestepped until I was almost completely fagged from the exertion of attempting to finish him.

He was a more adroit swordsman, if possible, than my previous foe, and I must admit that he led me a pretty chase and in the end came near to making a sorry fool of me—and a dead one into the bargain.

I could feel myself growing weaker and weaker, until at length objects commenced to blur before my eyes and I staggered and blundered about more asleep than awake, and then it was that he worked his pretty little coup that came near to losing me my life.

He had backed me around so that I stood in front of the corpse of his fellow, and then he rushed me suddenly so that I was forced back upon it, and as my heel struck it the impetus of my body flung me backward across the dead man.

My head struck the hard pavement with a resounding whack, and to that alone I owe my life, for it cleared my brain and the pain roused my temper, so that I was equal for the moment to tearing my enemy to pieces with my bare hands, and I verily believe that I should have attempted it had not my right hand, in the act of raising my body from the ground, come in contact with a bit of cold metal.

As the eyes of the layman so is the hand of the fighting man when it comes in contact with an implement of his vocation, and thus I did not need to look or reason to know that the dead man's revolver, lying where it had fallen when I struck it from his grasp, was at my disposal.

The fellow whose ruse had put me down was springing toward me, the point of his gleaming blade directed straight at my heart, and as he came there rang from his lips the cruel and mocking peal of laughter that I had heard within the Chamber of Mystery.

And so he died, his thin lips curled in the snarl of his hateful laugh, and a bullet from the revolver of his dead companion bursting in his heart.

His body, borne by the impetus of his headlong rush, plunged upon me. The hilt of his sword must have struck my head, for with the impact of the corpse I lost consciousness.

FOUR

Thuvia

It was the sound of conflict that aroused me once more to the realities of life. For a moment I could neither place my surroundings nor locate the sounds which had aroused me. And then from beyond the blank wall beside which I lay I heard the shuffling of feet, the snarling of grim beasts, the clank of metal accoutrements, and the heavy breathing of a man.

As I rose to my feet I glanced hurriedly about the chamber in which I had just encountered such a warm reception. The prisoners and the savage brutes rested in their chains by the opposite wall eyeing me with varying expressions of curiosity, sullen rage, surprise, and hope.

The latter emotion seemed plainly evident upon the handsome and intelligent face of the young red Martian woman whose cry of warning had been instrumental in saving my life.

She was the perfect type of that remarkably beautiful race whose outward appearance is identical with the more god-like races of Earth men, except that this higher race of Martians is of a light reddish copper colour. As she was entirely unadorned I could not even guess her station in life, though it was evident that she was either a prisoner or slave in her present environment.

It was several seconds before the sounds upon the opposite side of the partition jolted my slowly returning faculties into a realization of their probable import, and then of a sudden I grasped the fact that they were caused by Tars Tarkas in what was evidently a desperate struggle with wild beasts or savage men.

With a cry of encouragement I threw my weight against the secret door, but as well have assayed the down-hurling of the cliffs themselves. Then I sought feverishly for the secret of the revolving panel, but my search was fruitless, and I was about to raise my longsword against the sullen gold when the young woman prisoner called out to me.

"Save thy sword, O Mighty Warrior, for thou shalt need it more where it will avail to some purpose—shatter it not against senseless metal which yields better to the lightest finger touch of one who knows its secret."

"Know you the secret of it then?" I asked.

"Yes; release me and I will give you entrance to the other horror chamber, if you wish. The keys to my fetters are upon the first dead of thy foemen. But why would you return to face again the fierce banth, or whatever other form of destruction they have loosed within that awful trap?"

"Because my friend fights there alone," I answered, as I hastily sought and found the keys upon the carcass of the dead custodian of this grim chamber of horrors.

There were many keys upon the oval ring, but the fair Martian maid quickly selected that which sprung the great lock at her waist, and freed she hurried toward the secret panel.

Again she sought out a key upon the ring. This time a slender, needle-like affair which she inserted in an almost invisible hole in the wall. Instantly the door swung upon its pivot, and the contiguous section of the floor upon which I was standing carried me with it into the chamber where Tars Tarkas fought.

The great Thark stood with his back against an angle of the walls, while facing him in a semi-circle a half-dozen huge monsters crouched waiting for an opening. Their blood-streaked heads and shoulders testified to the cause of their wariness as well as to the swordsmanship of the green warrior whose glossy hide bore the same mute but eloquent witness to the ferocity of the attacks that he had so far withstood.

Sharp talons and cruel fangs had torn leg, arm, and breast literally to ribbons. So weak was he from continued exertion and loss of blood that but for the supporting wall I doubt that he even could have stood erect. But with the tenacity and indomitable courage of his kind he still faced his cruel and relentless foes—the personification of that ancient proverb of his tribe: "Leave to a Thark his head and one hand and he may yet conquer."

As he saw me enter, a grim smile touched those grim lips of his, but whether the smile signified relief or merely amusement at the sight of my own bloody and dishevelled condition I do not know.

As I was about to spring into the conflict with my sharp long-sword I felt a gentle hand upon my shoulder and turning found, to my surprise, that the young woman had followed me into the chamber.

"Wait," she whispered, "leave them to me," and pushing me advanced, all defenceless and unarmed, upon the snarling banths.

When quite close to them she spoke a single Martian word in low but peremptory tones. Like lightning the great beasts wheeled upon her, and I looked to see her torn to pieces before I could reach her side, but instead the creatures slunk to her feet like puppies that expect a merited whipping.

Again she spoke to them, but in tones so low I could not catch the words, and then she started toward the opposite side of the chamber with the six mighty monsters trailing at heel. One by one she sent them through the secret panel into the room beyond, and when the last had passed from the chamber where we stood in wide-eyed amazement she turned and smiled at us and then herself passed through, leaving us alone.

For a moment neither of us spoke. Then Tars Tarkas said:

"I heard the fighting beyond the partition through which you passed, but I did not fear for you, John Carter, until I heard the report of a revolver shot. I knew that there lived no man upon all Barsoom who could face you with naked steel and live, but the shot stripped the last vestige of hope from me, since you I knew to be without firearms. Tell me of it."

I did as he bade, and then together we sought the secret panel through which I had just entered the apartment—the one at the opposite end of the room from that through which the girl had led her savage companions.

To our disappointment the panel eluded our every effort to negotiate its secret lock. We felt that once beyond it we might look with some little hope of success for a passage to the outside world.

The fact that the prisoners within were securely chained led us to believe that surely there must be an avenue of escape from the terrible creatures which inhabited this unspeakable place.

Again and again we turned from one door to another, from the baffling golden panel at one end of the chamber to its mate at the other—equally baffling.

When we had about given up all hope one of the panels turned silently toward us, and the young woman who had led away the banths stood once more beside us.

"Who are you?" she asked, "and what your mission, that you have the temerity to attempt to escape from the Valley Dor and the death you have chosen?"

"I have chosen no death, maiden," I replied. "I am not of Barsoom, nor have I taken yet the voluntary pilgrimage upon the River Iss. My friend here is Jeddak of all the Tharks, and though he has not yet expressed a desire to return to the living world, I am taking him with me from the living lie that hath lured him to this frightful place.

"I am of another world. I am John Carter, Prince of the House of Tardos

Mors, Jeddak of Helium. Perchance some faint rumour of me may have leaked within the confines of your hellish abode."

She smiled.

"Yes," she replied, "naught that passes in the world we have left is unknown here. I have heard of you, many years ago. The therns have ofttimes wondered whither you had flown, since you had neither taken the pilgrimage, nor could be found upon the face of Barsoom."

"Tell me," I said, "and who be you, and why a prisoner, yet with power over the ferocious beasts of the place that denotes familiarity and authority far beyond that which might be expected of a prisoner or a slave?"

"Slave I am," she answered. "For fifteen years a slave in this terrible place, and now that they have tired of me and become fearful of the power which my knowledge of their ways has given me I am but recently condemned to die the death."

She shuddered.

"What death?" I asked.

"The Holy Therns eat human flesh," she answered me; "but only that which has died beneath the sucking lips of a plant man—flesh from which the defiling blood of life has been drawn. And to this cruel end I have been condemned. It was to be within a few hours, had your advent not caused an interruption of their plans."

"Was it then Holy Therns who felt the weight of John Carter's hand?" I asked.

"Oh, no; those whom you laid low are lesser therns; but of the same cruel and hateful race. The Holy Therns abide upon the outer slopes of these grim hills, facing the broad world from which they harvest their victims and their spoils.

"Labyrinthine passages connect these caves with the luxurious palaces of the Holy Therns, and through them pass upon their many duties the lesser therns, and hordes of slaves, and prisoners, and fierce beasts; the grim inhabitants of this sunless world.

"There be within this vast network of winding passages and countless chambers men, women, and beasts who, born within its dim and gruesome underworld, have never seen the light of day—nor ever shall.

"They are kept to do the bidding of the race of therns; to furnish at once their sport and their sustenance.

"Now and again some hapless pilgrim, drifting out upon the silent sea from the cold Iss, escapes the plant men and the great white apes that guard the Temple of Issus and falls into the remorseless clutches of the therns; or, as was my misfortune, is coveted by the Holy Thern who chances to be upon watch in the balcony above the river where it issues from the bowels of the mountains through the cliffs of gold to empty into the Lost Sea of Korus.

"All who reach the Valley Dor are, by custom, the rightful prey of the plant men and the apes, while their arms and ornaments become the portion of the therns; but if one escapes the terrible denizens of the valley for even a few hours the therns may claim such a one as their own. And again the Holy Thern on watch, should he see a victim he covets, often tramples upon the rights of the unreasoning brutes of the valley and takes his prize by foul means if he cannot gain it by fair.

"It is said that occasionally some deluded victim of Barsoomian superstition will so far escape the clutches of the countless enemies that beset his path from the moment that he emerges from the subterranean passage through which the Iss flows for a thousand miles before it enters the Valley Dor as to reach the very walls of the Temple of Issus; but what fate awaits one there not even the Holy Therns may guess, for who has passed within those gilded walls never has returned to unfold the mysteries they have held since the beginning of time.

"The Temple of Issus is to the therns what the Valley Dor is imagined by the peoples of the outer world to be to them; it is the ultimate haven of peace, refuge, and happiness to which they pass after this life and wherein an eternity of eternities is spent amidst the delights of the flesh which appeal most strongly to this race of mental giants and moral pygmies."

"The Temple of Issus is, I take it, a heaven within a heaven," I said. "Let us hope that there it will be meted to the therns as they have meted it here unto others."

"Who knows?" the girl murmured.

"The therns, I judge from what you have said, are no less mortal than we; and yet have I always heard them spoken of with the utmost awe and reverence by the people of Barsoom, as one might speak of the gods themselves."

"The therns are mortal," she replied. "They die from the same causes as you or I might: those who do not live their allotted span of life, one thousand years, when by the authority of custom they may take their way in happiness through the long tunnel that leads to Issus.

"Those who die before are supposed to spend the balance of their allotted time in the image of a plant man, and it is for this reason that the plant men are held sacred by the therns, since they believe that each of these hideous creatures was formerly a thern." "And should a plant man die?" I asked.

"Should he die before the expiration of the thousand years from the birth of the thern whose immortality abides within him then the soul passes into a great white ape, but should the ape die short of the exact hour that terminates the thousand years the soul is for ever lost and passes for all eternity into the carcass of the slimy and fearsome silian whose wriggling thousands seethe the silent sea beneath the hurtling moons when the sun has gone and strange shapes walk through the Valley Dor."

"We sent several Holy Therns to the silians to-day, then," said Tars Tarkas, laughing.

"And so will your death be the more terrible when it comes," said the maiden. "And come it will—you cannot escape."

"One has escaped, centuries ago," I reminded her, "and what has been done may be done again."

"It is useless even to try," she answered hopelessly.

"But try we shall," I cried, and you shall go with us, if you wish."

"To be put to death by mine own people, and render my memory a disgrace to my family and my nation? A Prince of the House of Tardos Mors should know better than to suggest such a thing."

Tars Tarkas listened in silence, but I could feel his eyes riveted upon me and I knew that he awaited my answer as one might listen to the reading of his sentence by the foreman of a jury.

What I advised the girl to do would seal our fate as well, since if I bowed to the inevitable decree of age-old superstition we must all remain and meet our fate in some horrible form within this awful abode of horror and cruelty.

"We have the right to escape if we can," I answered. "Our own moral senses will not be offended if we succeed, for we know that the fabled life of love and peace in the blessed Valley of Dor is a rank and wicked deception. We know that the valley is not sacred; we know that the Holy Therns are not holy; that they are a race of cruel and heartless mortals, knowing no more of the real life to come than we do.

"Not only is it our right to bend every effort to escape—it is a solemn duty from which we should not shrink even though we know that we should be reviled and tortured by our own peoples when we returned to them.

"Only thus may we carry the truth to those without, and though the likelihood of our narrative being given credence is, I grant you, remote, so wedded are mortals to their stupid infatuation for impossible superstitions, we should be craven cowards indeed were we to shirk the plain duty which confronts us.

"Again there is a chance that with the weight of the testimony of several of us the truth of our statements may be accepted, and at least a compromise effected which will result in the dispatching of an expedition of investigation to this hideous mockery of heaven."

Both the girl and the green warrior stood silent in thought for some moments. The former it was who eventually broke the silence.

"Never had I considered the matter in that light before," she said. "Indeed would I give my life a thousand times if I could but save a single soul from the awful life that I have led in this cruel place. Yes, you are right, and I will go with you as far as we can go; but I doubt that we ever shall escape."

I turned an inquiring glance toward the Thark.

"To the gates of Issus, or to the bottom of Korus," spoke the green warrior; "to the snows to the north or to the snows to the south, Tars Tarkas follows where John Carter leads. I have spoken."

"Come, then," I cried, "we must make the start, for we could not be further from escape than we now are in the heart of this mountain and within the four walls of this chamber of death."

"Come, then," said the girl, "but do not flatter yourself that you can find no worse place than this within the territory of the therns."

So saying she swung the secret panel that separated us from the apartment in which I had found her, and we stepped through once more into the presence of the other prisoners.

There were in all ten red Martians, men and women, and when we had briefly explained our plan they decided to join forces with us, though it was evident that it was with some considerable misgivings that they thus tempted fate by opposing an ancient superstition, even though each knew through cruel experience the fallacy of its entire fabric.

Thuvia, the girl whom I had first freed, soon had the others at liberty. Tars Tarkas and I stripped the bodies of the two therns of their weapons, which included swords, daggers, and two revolvers of the curious and deadly type manufactured by the red Martians.

We distributed the weapons as far as they would go among our followers, giving the firearms to two of the women; Thuvia being one so armed.

With the latter as our guide we set off rapidly but cautiously through a maze of passages, crossing great chambers hewn from the solid metal of the cliff, following winding corridors, ascending steep inclines, and now and again concealing ourselves in dark recesses at the sound of approaching footsteps.

Our destination, Thuvia said, was a distant storeroom where arms and ammunition in plenty might be found. From there she was to lead us to the summit of the cliffs, from where it would require both wondrous wit and

mighty fighting to win our way through the very heart of the stronghold
of the Holy Therns to the world without.

"And even then, O Prince," she cried, "the arm of the Holy Thern is
long. It reaches to every nation of Barsoom. His secret temples are hidden
in the heart of every community. Wherever we go should we escape we shall
find that word of our coming has preceded us, and death awaits us before
we may pollute the air with our blasphemies."

We had proceeded for possibly an hour without serious interruption,
and Thuvia had just whispered to me that we were approaching our first
destination, when on entering a great chamber we came upon a man,
evidently a thern.

He wore in addition to his leathern trappings and jewelled ornaments
a great circlet of gold about his brow in the exact centre of which was set
an immense stone, the exact counterpart of that which I had seen upon
the breast of the little old man at the atmosphere plant nearly twenty years
before.

It is the one priceless jewel of Barsoom. Only two are known to exist, and
these were worn as the insignia of their rank and position by the two old men
in whose charge was placed the operation of the great engines which pump
the artificial atmosphere to all parts of Mars from the huge atmosphere
plant, the secret to whose mighty portals placed in my possession the ability
to save from immediate extinction the life of a whole world.

The stone worn by the thern who confronted us was of about the same
size as that which I had seen before; an inch in diameter I should say. It
scintillated nine different and distinct rays; the seven primary colours of
our earthly prism and the two rays which are unknown upon Earth, but
whose wondrous beauty is indescribable.

As the thern saw us his eyes narrowed to two nasty slits. "Stop!" he cried.
"What means this, Thuvia?"

For answer the girl raised her revolver and fired point-blank at him.
Without a sound he sank to the earth, dead.

"Beast!" she hissed. "After all these years I am at last revenged."

Then as she turned toward me, evidently with a word of explanation
on her lips, her eyes suddenly widened as they rested upon me, and with a
little exclamation she started toward me.

"O Prince," she cried, "Fate is indeed kind to us. The way is still difficult,
but through this vile thing upon the floor we may yet win to the outer world.
Notest thou not the remarkable resemblance between this Holy Thern and
thyself?"

The man was indeed of my precise stature, nor were his eyes and features unlike mine; but his hair was a mass of flowing yellow locks, like those of the two I had killed, while mine is black and close cropped.

"What of the resemblance?" I asked the girl Thuvia. "Do you wish me with my black, short hair to pose as a yellow- haired priest of this infernal cult?"

She smiled, and for answer approached the body of the man she had slain, and kneeling beside it removed the circlet of gold from the forehead, and then to my utter amazement lifted the entire scalp bodily from the corpse's head.

Rising, she advanced to my side and placing the yellow wig over my black hair, crowned me with the golden circlet set with the magnificent gem.

"Now don his harness, Prince," she said, "and you may pass where you will in the realms of the therns, for Sator Throg was a Holy Thern of the Tenth Cycle, and mighty among his kind."

As I stooped to the dead man to do her bidding I noted that not a hair grew upon his head, which was quite as bald as an egg.

"They are all thus from birth," explained Thuvia noting my surprise. "The race from which they sprang were crowned with a luxuriant growth of golden hair, but for many ages the present race has been entirely bald. The wig, however, has come to be a part of their apparel, and so important a part do they consider it that it is cause for the deepest disgrace were a thern to appear in public without it."

In another moment I stood garbed in the habiliments of a Holy Thern.

At Thuvia's suggestion two of the released prisoners bore the body of the dead thern upon their shoulders with us as we continued our journey toward the storeroom, which we reached without further mishap.

Here the keys which Thuvia bore from the dead thern of the prison vault were the means of giving us immediate entrance to the chamber, and very quickly we were thoroughly outfitted with arms and ammunition.

By this time I was so thoroughly fagged out that I could go no further, so I threw myself upon the floor, bidding Tars Tarkas to do likewise, and cautioning two of the released prisoners to keep careful watch.

In an instant I was asleep.

FIVE

Corridors of Peril

How long I slept upon the floor of the storeroom I do not know, but it must have been many hours.

I was awakened with a start by cries of alarm, and scarce were my eyes opened, nor had I yet sufficiently collected my wits to quite realize where I was, when a fusillade of shots rang out, reverberating through the subterranean corridors in a series of deafening echoes.

In an instant I was upon my feet. A dozen lesser therns confronted us from a large doorway at the opposite end of the storeroom from which we had entered. About me lay the bodies of my companions, with the exception of Thuvia and Tars Tarkas, who, like myself, had been asleep upon the floor and thus escaped the first raking fire.

As I gained my feet the therns lowered their wicked rifles, their faces distorted in mingled chagrin, consternation, and alarm.

Instantly I rose to the occasion.

"What means this?" I cried in tones of fierce anger. "Is Sator Throg to be murdered by his own vassals?"

"Have mercy, O Master of the Tenth Cycle!" cried one of the fellows, while the others edged toward the doorway as though to attempt a surreptitious escape from the presence of the mighty one.

"Ask them their mission here," whispered Thuvia at my elbow.

"What do you here, fellows?" I cried.

"Two from the outer world are at large within the dominions of the therns. We sought them at the command of the Father of Therns. One was white with black hair, the other a huge green warrior," and here the fellow cast a suspicious glance toward Tars Tarkas.

"Here, then, is one of them," spoke Thuvia, indicating the Thark, "and if you will look upon this dead man by the door perhaps you will recognize the other. It was left for Sator Throg and his poor slaves to accomplish what the lesser therns of the guard were unable to do—we have killed one and captured the other; for this had Sator Throg given us our liberty. And now in your stupidity have you come and killed all but myself, and like to have killed the mighty Sator Throg himself."

The men looked very sheepish and very scared.

"Had they not better throw these bodies to the plant men and then return to their quarters, O Mighty One?" asked Thuvia of me.

"Yes; do as Thuvia bids you," I said.

As the men picked up the bodies I noticed that the one who stooped to gather up the late Sator Throg started as his closer scrutiny fell upon the upturned face, and then the fellow stole a furtive, sneaking glance in my direction from the corner of his eye.

That he suspicioned something of the truth I could have sworn; but that it was only a suspicion which he did not dare voice was evidenced by his silence.

Again, as he bore the body from the room, he shot a quick but searching glance toward me, and then his eyes fell once more upon the bald and shiny dome of the dead man in his arms. The last fleeting glimpse that I obtained of his profile as he passed from my sight without the chamber revealed a cunning smile of triumph upon his lips.

Only Tars Tarkas, Thuvia, and I were left. The fatal marksmanship of the therns had snatched from our companions whatever slender chance they had of gaining the perilous freedom of the world without.

So soon as the last of the gruesome procession had disappeared the girl urged us to take up our flight once more.

She, too, had noted the questioning attitude of the thern who had borne Sator Throg away.

"It bodes no good for us, O Prince," she said. "For even though this fellow dared not chance accusing you in error, there be those above with power sufficient to demand a closer scrutiny, and that, Prince would indeed prove fatal."

I shrugged my shoulders. It seemed that in any event the outcome of our plight must end in death. I was refreshed from my sleep, but still weak from loss of blood. My wounds were painful. No medicinal aid seemed possible. How I longed for the almost miraculous healing power of the strange salves and lotions of the green Martian women. In an hour they would have had me as new.

I was discouraged. Never had a feeling of such utter hopelessness come over me in the face of danger. Then the long flowing, yellow locks of the Holy Thern, caught by some vagrant draught, blew about my face.

Might they not still open the way of freedom? If we acted in time, might we not even yet escape before the general alarm was sounded? We could at least try.

"What will the fellow do first, Thuvia?" I asked. "How long will it be before they may return for us?"

"He will go directly to the Father of Therns, old Matai Shang. He may have to wait for an audience, but since he is very high among the lesser therns, in fact as a thorian among them, it will not be long that Matai Shang will keep him waiting.

"Then if the Father of Therns puts credence in his story, another hour will see the galleries and chambers, the courts and gardens, filled with searchers."

"What we do then must be done within an hour. What is the best way, Thuvia, the shortest way out of this celestial Hades?"

"Straight to the top of the cliffs, Prince," she replied, "and then through the gardens to the inner courts. From there our way will lie within the temples of the therns and across them to the outer court. Then the ramparts—O Prince, it is hopeless. Ten thousand warriors could not hew a way to liberty from out this awful place.

"Since the beginning of time, little by little, stone by stone, have the therns been ever adding to the defences of their stronghold. A continuous line of impregnable fortifications circles the outer slopes of the Mountains of Otz.

"Within the temples that lie behind the ramparts a million fighting-men are ever ready. The courts and gardens are filled with slaves, with women and with children.

"None could go a stone's throw without detection."

"If there is no other way, Thuvia, why dwell upon the difficulties of this. We must face them."

"Can we not better make the attempt after dark?" asked Tars Tarkas. "There would seem to be no chance by day."

"There would be a little better chance by night, but even then the ramparts are well guarded; possibly better than by day. There are fewer abroad in the courts and gardens, though," said Thuvia.

"What is the hour?" I asked.

"It was midnight when you released me from my chains," said Thuvia. "Two hours later we reached the storeroom. There you slept for fourteen hours. It must now be nearly sundown again. Come, we will go to some nearby window in the cliff and make sure."

So saying, she led the way through winding corridors until at a sudden turn we came upon an opening which overlooked the Valley Dor.

At our right the sun was setting, a huge red orb, below the western range of Otz. A little below us stood the Holy Thern on watch upon his balcony. His scarlet robe of office was pulled tightly about him in anticipation of the cold that comes so suddenly with darkness as the sun sets. So rare is the atmosphere of Mars that it absorbs very little heat from the sun. During the daylight hours it is always extremely hot; at night it is intensely cold. Nor does the thin atmosphere refract the sun's rays or diffuse its light as upon Earth. There is no twilight on Mars. When the great orb of day disappears beneath the horizon the effect is precisely as that of the extinguishing of a single lamp within a chamber. From brilliant light you are plunged without warning into utter darkness. Then the moons come; the mysterious, magic moons of Mars, hurtling like monster meteors low across the face of the planet.

The declining sun lighted brilliantly the eastern banks of Korus, the crimson sward, the gorgeous forest. Beneath the trees we saw feeding many herds of plant men. The adults stood aloft upon their toes and their mighty tails, their talons pruning every available leaf and twig. It was then that I understood the careful trimming of the trees which had led me to form the mistaken idea when first I opened my eyes upon the grove that it was the playground of a civilized people.

As we watched, our eyes wandered to the rolling Iss, which issued from the base of the cliffs beneath us. Presently there emerged from the mountain a canoe laden with lost souls from the outer world. There were a dozen of them. All were of the highly civilized and cultured race of red men who are dominant on Mars.

The eyes of the herald upon the balcony beneath us fell upon the doomed party as soon as did ours. He raised his head and leaning far out over the low rail that rimmed his dizzy perch, voiced the shrill, weird wail that called the demons of this hellish place to the attack.

For an instant the brutes stood with stiffly erected ears, then they poured from the grove toward the river's bank, covering the distance with great, ungainly leaps.

The party had landed and was standing on the sward as the awful horde came in sight. There was a brief and futile effort of defence. Then silence as the huge, repulsive shapes covered the bodies of their victims and scores of sucking mouths fastened themselves to the flesh of their prey.

I turned away in disgust.

"Their part is soon over," said Thuvia. "The great white apes get the flesh when the plant men have drained the arteries. Look, they are coming now."

As I turned my eyes in the direction the girl indicated, I saw a dozen of the great white monsters running across the valley toward the river bank. Then the sun went down and darkness that could almost be felt engulfed us.

Thuvia lost no time in leading us toward the corridor which winds back and forth up through the cliffs toward the surface thousands of feet above the level on which we had been.

Twice great banths, wandering loose through the galleries, blocked our progress, but in each instance Thuvia spoke a low word of command and the snarling beasts slunk sullenly away.

"If you can dissolve all our obstacles as easily as you master these fierce brutes I can see no difficulties in our way," I said to the girl, smiling. "How do you do it?"

She laughed, and then shuddered.

"I do not quite know," she said. "When first I came here I angered Sator Throg, because I repulsed him. He ordered me to be thrown into one of the great pits in the inner gardens. It was filled with banths. In my own country I had been accustomed to command. Something in my voice, I do not know what, cowed the beasts as they sprang to attack me.

"Instead of tearing me to pieces, as Sator Throg had desired, they fawned at my feet. So greatly were Sator Throg and his friends amused by the sight that they kept me to train and handle the terrible creatures. I know them all by name. There are many of them wandering through these lower regions. They are the scavengers. Many prisoners die here in their chains. The banths solve the problem of sanitation, at least in this respect.

"In the gardens and temples above they are kept in pits. The therns fear them. It is because of the banths that they seldom venture below ground except as their duties call them."

An idea occurred to me, suggested by what Thuvia had just said.

"Why not take a number of banths and set them loose before us above ground?" I asked.

Thuvia laughed.

"It would distract attention from us, I am sure," she said.

She commenced calling in a low singsong voice that was half purr. She continued this as we wound our tedious way through the maze of subterranean passages and chambers.

Presently soft, padded feet sounded close behind us, and as I turned I saw a pair of great, green eyes shining in the dark shadows at our rear. From a diverging tunnel a sinuous, tawny form crept stealthily toward us.

Low growls and angry snarls assailed our ears on every side as we hastened on and one by one the ferocious creatures answered the call of their mistress.

She spoke a word to each as it joined us. Like well-schooled terriers, they paced the corridors with us, but I could not help but note the lathering jowls, nor the hungry expressions with which they eyed Tars Tarkas and myself.

Soon we were entirely surrounded by some fifty of the brutes. Two walked close on either side of Thuvia, as guards might walk. The sleek sides of others now and then touched my own naked limbs. It was a strange experience; the almost noiseless passage of naked human feet and padded paws; the golden walls splashed with precious stones; the dim light cast by the tiny radium bulbs set at considerable distances along the roof; the huge, maned beasts of prey crowding with low growls about us; the mighty green warrior towering high above us all; myself crowned with the priceless diadem of a Holy Thern; and leading the procession the beautiful girl, Thuvia.

I shall not soon forget it.

Presently we approached a great chamber more brightly lighted than the corridors. Thuvia halted us. Quietly she stole toward the entrance and glanced within. Then she motioned us to follow her.

The room was filled with specimens of the strange beings that inhabit this underworld; a heterogeneous collection of hybrids—the offspring of the prisoners from the outside world; red and green Martians and the white race of therns.

Constant confinement below ground had wrought odd freaks upon their skins. They more resemble corpses than living beings. Many are deformed, others maimed, while the majority, Thuvia explained, are sightless.

As they lay sprawled about the floor, sometimes overlapping one another, again in heaps of several bodies, they suggested instantly to me the grotesque illustrations that I had seen in copies of Dante's *Inferno*, and what more fitting comparison? Was this not indeed a veritable hell, peopled by lost souls, dead and damned beyond all hope?

Picking our way carefully we threaded a winding path across the chamber, the great banths sniffing hungrily at the tempting prey spread before them in such tantalizing and defenceless profusion.

Several times we passed the entrances to other chambers similarly peopled, and twice again we were compelled to cross directly through them. In others were chained prisoners and beasts.

"Why is it that we see no therns?" I asked of Thuvia.

"They seldom traverse the underworld at night, for then it is that the great banths prowl the dim corridors seeking their prey. The therns fear the awful denizens of this cruel and hopeless world that they have fostered and allowed to grow beneath their feet. The prisoners even sometimes turn upon them and rend them. The thern can never tell from what dark shadow an assassin may spring upon his back.

"By day it is different. Then the corridors and chambers are filled with guards passing to and fro; slaves from the temples above come by hundreds to the granaries and storerooms. All is life then. You did not see it because I led you not in the beaten tracks, but through roundabout passages seldom used. Yet it is possible that we may meet a thern even yet. They do occasionally find it necessary to come here after the sun has set. Because of this I have moved with such great caution."

But we reached the upper galleries without detection and presently Thuvia halted us at the foot of a short, steep ascent.

"Above us," she said, "is a doorway which opens on to the inner gardens. I have brought you thus far. From here on for four miles to the outer ramparts our way will be beset by countless dangers. Guards patrol the courts, the temples, the gardens. Every inch of the ramparts themselves is beneath the eye of a sentry."

I could not understand the necessity for such an enormous force of armed men about a spot so surrounded by mystery and superstition that not a soul upon Barsoom would have dared to approach it even had they known its exact location. I questioned Thuvia, asking her what enemies the therns could fear in their impregnable fortress.

We had reached the doorway now and Thuvia was opening it.

"They fear the black pirates of Barsoom, O Prince," she said, "from whom may our first ancestors preserve us."

The door swung open; the smell of growing things greeted my nostrils; the cool night air blew against my cheek. The great banths sniffed the unfamiliar odours, and then with a rush they broke past us with low growls, swarming across the gardens beneath the lurid light of the nearer moon.

Suddenly a great cry arose from the roofs of the temples; a cry of alarm and warning that, taken up from point to point, ran off to the east and to the west, from temple, court, and rampart, until it sounded as a dim echo in the distance.

The great Thark's long-sword leaped from its scabbard; Thuvia shrank shuddering to my side.

SIX

The Black Pirates of Barsoom

"What is it?" I asked of the girl.

For answer she pointed to the sky.

I looked, and there, above us, I saw shadowy bodies flitting hither and thither high over temple, court, and garden.

Almost immediately flashes of light broke from these strange objects. There was a roar of musketry, and then answering flashes and roars from temple and rampart.

"The black pirates of Barsoom, O Prince," said Thuvia.

In great circles the air craft of the marauders swept lower and lower toward the defending forces of the therns.

Volley after volley they vomited upon the temple guards; volley on volley crashed through the thin air toward the fleeting and illusive fliers.

As the pirates swooped closer toward the ground, thern soldiery poured from the temples into the gardens and courts. The sight of them in the open brought a score of fliers darting toward us from all directions.

The therns fired upon them through shields affixed to their rifles, but on, steadily on, came the grim, black craft. They were small fliers for the most part, built for two to three men. A few larger ones there were, but these kept high aloft dropping bombs upon the temples from their keel batteries.

At length, with a concerted rush, evidently in response to a signal of command, the pirates in our immediate vicinity dashed recklessly to the ground in the very midst of the thern soldiery.

Scarcely waiting for their craft to touch, the creatures manning them leaped among the therns with the fury of demons. Such fighting! Never had I witnessed its like before. I had thought the green Martians the most ferocious warriors in the universe, but the awful abandon with which the black pirates threw themselves upon their foes transcended everything I ever before had seen.

Beneath the brilliant light of Mars' two glorious moons the whole scene presented itself in vivid distinctness. The golden-haired, white-skinned therns battling with desperate courage in hand-to-hand conflict with their ebony-skinned foemen.

Here a little knot of struggling warriors trampled a bed of gorgeous pimalia; there the curved sword of a black man found the heart of a thern and left its dead foeman at the foot of a wondrous statue carved from a living ruby; yonder a dozen therns pressed a single pirate back upon a bench of emerald, upon whose iridescent surface a strangely beautiful Barsoomian design was traced out in inlaid diamonds.

A little to one side stood Thuvia, the Thark, and I. The tide of battle had not reached us, but the fighters from time to time swung close enough that we might distinctly note them.

The black pirates interested me immensely. I had heard vague rumours, little more than legends they were, during my former life on Mars; but never had I seen them, nor talked with one who had.

They were popularly supposed to inhabit the lesser moon, from which they descended upon Barsoom at long intervals. Where they visited they wrought the most horrible atrocities, and when they left carried away with them firearms and ammunition, and young girls as prisoners. These latter, the rumour had it, they sacrificed to some terrible god in an orgy which ended in the eating of their victims.

I had an excellent opportunity to examine them, as the strife occasionally brought now one and now another close to where I stood. They were large men, possibly six feet and over in height. Their features were clear cut and handsome in the extreme; their eyes were well set and large, though a slight narrowness lent them a crafty appearance; the iris, as well as I could determine by moonlight, was of extreme blackness, while the eyeball itself was quite white and clear. The physical structure of their bodies seemed identical with those of the therns, the red men, and my own. Only in the colour of their skin did they differ materially from us; that is of the appearance of polished ebony, and odd as it may seem for a Southerner to say it, adds to rather than detracts from their marvellous beauty.

But if their bodies are divine, their hearts, apparently, are quite the reverse. Never did I witness such a malign lust for blood as these demons of the outer air evinced in their mad battle with the therns.

All about us in the garden lay their sinister craft, which the therns for some reason, then unaccountable to me, made no effort to injure. Now and again a black warrior would rush from a near by temple bearing a young woman in his arms. Straight for his flier he would leap while those of his comrades who fought near by would rush to cover his escape.

The therns on their side would hasten to rescue the girl, and in an instant the two would be swallowed in the vortex of a maelstrom of yelling devils, hacking and hewing at one another, like fiends incarnate.

But always, it seemed, were the black pirates of Barsoom victorious, and the girl, brought miraculously unharmed through the conflict, borne away into the outer darkness upon the deck of a swift flier.

Fighting similar to that which surrounded us could be heard in both directions as far as sound carried, and Thuvia told me that the attacks of the black pirates were usually made simultaneously along the entire ribbon-like domain of the therns, which circles the Valley Dor on the outer slopes of the Mountains of Otz.

As the fighting receded from our position for a moment, Thuvia turned toward me with a question.

"Do you understand now, O Prince," she said, "why a million warriors guard the domains of the Holy Therns by day and by night?"

"The scene you are witnessing now is but a repetition of what I have seen enacted a score of times during the fifteen years I have been a prisoner here. From time immemorial the black pirates of Barsoom have preyed upon the Holy Therns.

"Yet they never carry their expeditions to a point, as one might readily believe it was in their power to do, where the extermination of the race of therns is threatened. It is as though they but utilized the race as playthings, with which they satisfy their ferocious lust for fighting; and from whom they collect toll in arms and ammunition and in prisoners."

"Why don't they jump in and destroy these fliers?" I asked. "That would soon put a stop to the attacks, or at least the blacks would scarce be so bold. Why, see how perfectly unguarded they leave their craft, as though they were lying safe in their own hangars at home."

"The therns do not dare. They tried it once, ages ago, but the next night and for a whole moon thereafter a thousand great black battleships circled the Mountains of Otz, pouring tons of projectiles upon the temples, the gardens, and the courts, until every thern who was not killed was driven for safety into the subterranean galleries.

"The therns know that they live at all only by the sufferance of the black men. They were near to extermination that once and they will not venture risking it again."

As she ceased talking a new element was instilled into the conflict. It came from a source equally unlooked for by either thern or pirate. The great banths which we had liberated in the garden had evidently been awed at first by the sound of the battle, the yelling of the warriors and the loud report of rifle and bomb.

But now they must have become angered by the continuous noise and excited by the smell of new blood, for all of a sudden a great form shot from a clump of low shrubbery into the midst of a struggling mass of humanity. A horrid scream of bestial rage broke from the banth as he felt warm flesh beneath his powerful talons.

As though his cry was but a signal to the others, the entire great pack hurled themselves among the fighters. Panic reigned in an instant. Thern and black man turned alike against the common enemy, for the banths showed no partiality toward either.

The awful beasts bore down a hundred men by the mere weight of their great bodies as they hurled themselves into the thick of the fight. Leaping and clawing, they mowed down the warriors with their powerful paws, turning for an instant to rend their victims with frightful fangs.

The scene was fascinating in its terribleness, but suddenly it came to me that we were wasting valuable time watching this conflict, which in itself might prove a means of our escape.

The therns were so engaged with their terrible assailants that now, if ever, escape should be comparatively easy. I turned to search for an opening through the contending hordes. If we could but reach the ramparts we might find that the pirates somewhere had thinned the guarding forces and left a way open to us to the world without.

As my eyes wandered about the garden, the sight of the hundreds of air craft lying unguarded around us suggested the simplest avenue to freedom. Why it had not occurred to me before! I was thoroughly familiar with the mechanism of every known make of flier on Barsoom. For nine years I had sailed and fought with the navy of Helium. I had raced through space on the tiny one-man air scout and I had commanded the greatest battleship that ever had floated in the thin air of dying Mars.

To think, with me, is to act. Grasping Thuvia by the arm, I whispered to Tars Tarkas to follow me. Quickly we glided toward a small flier which lay furthest from the battling warriors. Another instant found us huddled on the tiny deck. My hand was on the starting lever. I pressed my thumb upon the button which controls the ray of repulsion, that splendid discovery of the Martians which permits them to navigate the thin atmosphere of their planet in huge ships that dwarf the dreadnoughts of our earthly navies into pitiful significance.

The craft swayed slightly but she did not move. Then a new cry of warning broke upon our ears. Turning, I saw a dozen black pirates dashing toward us from the mêlée. We had been discovered. With shrieks of rage the demons sprang for us. With frenzied insistence I continued to press the little button which should have sent us racing out into space, but still the vessel refused to budge. Then it came to me—the reason that she would not rise.

We had stumbled upon a two-man flier. Its ray tanks were charged only with sufficient repulsive energy to lift two ordinary men. The Thark's great weight was anchoring us to our doom.

The blacks were nearly upon us. There was not an instant to be lost in hesitation or doubt.

I pressed the button far in and locked it. Then I set the lever at high speed and as the blacks came yelling upon us I slipped from the craft's deck and with drawn long-sword met the attack.

At the same moment a girl's shriek rang out behind me and an instant later, as the blacks fell upon me. I heard far above my head, and faintly, in Thuvia's voice: "My Prince, O my Prince; I would rather remain and die with—" But the rest was lost in the noise of my assailants.

I knew though that my ruse had worked and that temporarily at least Thuvia and Tars Tarkas were safe, and the means of escape was theirs.

For a moment it seemed that I could not withstand the weight of numbers that confronted me, but again, as on so many other occasions when I had been called upon to face fearful odds upon this planet of warriors and fierce beasts, I found that my earthly strength so far transcended that of my opponents that the odds were not so greatly against me as they appeared.

My seething blade wove a net of death about me. For an instant the blacks pressed close to reach me with their shorter swords, but presently they gave back, and the esteem in which they suddenly had learned to hold my sword arm was writ large upon each countenance.

I knew though that it was but a question of minutes before their greater numbers would wear me down, or get around my guard. I must go down eventually to certain death before them. I shuddered at the thought of it, dying thus in this terrible place where no word of my end ever could reach my Dejah Thoris. Dying at the hands of nameless black men in the gardens of the cruel therns.

Then my old-time spirit reasserted itself. The fighting blood of my Virginian sires coursed hot through my veins. The fierce blood lust and the joy of battle surged over me. The fighting smile that has brought consternation to a thousand foemen touched my lips. I put the thought of death out of my mind, and fell upon my antagonists with fury that those who escaped will remember to their dying day.

That others would press to the support of those who faced me I knew, so even as I fought I kept my wits at work, searching for an avenue of escape.

It came from an unexpected quarter out of the black night behind me. I had just disarmed a huge fellow who had given me a desperate struggle, and for a moment the blacks stood back for a breathing spell.

They eyed me with malignant fury, yet withal there was a touch of respect in their demeanour.

"Thern," said one, "you fight like a Dator. But for your detestable yellow hair and your white skin you would be an honour to the First Born of Barsoom."

"I am no thern," I said, and was about to explain that I was from another world, thinking that by patching a truce with these fellows and fighting with them against the therns I might enlist their aid in regaining my liberty. But just at that moment a heavy object smote me a resounding whack between my shoulders that nearly felled me to the ground.

As I turned to meet this new enemy an object passed over my shoulder, striking one of my assailants squarely in the face and knocking him senseless to the sward. At the same instant I saw that the thing that had struck us was the trailing anchor of a rather fair-sized air vessel; possibly a ten man cruiser.

The ship was floating slowly above us, not more than fifty feet over our heads. Instantly the one chance for escape that it offered presented itself to me. The vessel was slowly rising and now the anchor was beyond the blacks who faced me and several feet above their heads.

With a bound that left them gaping in wide-eyed astonishment I sprang completely over them. A second leap carried me just high enough to grasp the now rapidly receding anchor.

But I was successful, and there I hung by one hand, dragging through the branches of the higher vegetation of the gardens, while my late foemen shrieked and howled beneath me.

Presently the vessel veered toward the west and then swung gracefully to the south. In another instant I was carried beyond the crest of the Golden Cliffs, out over the Valley Dor, where, six thousand feet below me, the Lost Sea of Korus lay shimmering in the moonlight.

Carefully I climbed to a sitting posture across the anchor's arms. I wondered if by chance the vessel might be deserted. I hoped so. Or possibly it might belong to a friendly people, and have wandered by accident almost within the clutches of the pirates and the therns. The fact that it was retreating from the scene of battle lent colour to this hypothesis.

But I decided to know positively, and at once, so, with the greatest caution, I commenced to climb slowly up the anchor chain toward the deck above me.

One hand had just reached for the vessel's rail and found it when a fierce black face was thrust over the side and eyes filled with triumphant hate looked into mine.

SEVEN

A Fair Goddess

For an instant the black pirate and I remained motionless, glaring into each other's eyes. Then a grim smile curled the handsome lips above me, as an ebony hand came slowly in sight from above the edge of the deck and the cold, hollow eye of a revolver sought the centre of my forehead.

Simultaneously my free hand shot out for the black throat, just within reach, and the ebony finger tightened on the trigger. The pirate's hissing, "Die, cursed thern," was half choked in his windpipe by my clutching fingers. The hammer fell with a futile click upon an empty chamber.

Before he could fire again I had pulled him so far over the edge of the deck that he was forced to drop his firearm and clutch the rail with both hands.

My grasp upon his throat effectually prevented any outcry, and so we struggled in grim silence; he to tear away from my hold, I to drag him over to his death.

His face was taking on a livid hue, his eyes were bulging from their sockets. It was evident to him that he soon must die unless he tore loose from the steel fingers that were choking the life from him. With a final effort he threw himself further back upon the deck, at the same instant releasing his hold upon the rail to tear frantically with both hands at my fingers in an effort to drag them from his throat.

That little second was all that I awaited. With one mighty downward surge I swept him clear of the deck. His falling body came near to tearing me from the frail hold that my single free hand had upon the anchor chain and plunging me with him to the waters of the sea below.

I did not relinquish my grasp upon him, however, for I knew that a single shriek from those lips as he hurtled to his death in the silent waters of the sea would bring his comrades from above to avenge him.

Instead I held grimly to him, choking, ever choking, while his frantic struggles dragged me lower and lower toward the end of the chain.

Gradually his contortions became spasmodic, lessening by degrees until they ceased entirely. Then I released my hold upon him and in an instant he was swallowed by the black shadows far below.

Again I climbed to the ship's rail. This time I succeeded in raising my eyes to the level of the deck, where I could take a careful survey of the conditions immediately confronting me.

The nearer moon had passed below the horizon, but the clear effulgence of the further satellite bathed the deck of the cruiser, bringing into sharp relief the bodies of six or eight black men sprawled about in sleep.

Huddled close to the base of a rapid fire gun was a young white girl, securely bound. Her eyes were widespread in an expression of horrified anticipation and fixed directly upon me as I came in sight above the edge of the deck.

Unutterable relief instantly filled them as they fell upon the mystic jewel which sparkled in the centre of my stolen headpiece. She did not speak. Instead her eyes warned me to beware the sleeping figures that surrounded her.

Noiselessly I gained the deck. The girl nodded to me to approach her. As I bent low she whispered to me to release her.

"I can aid you," she said, "and you will need all the aid available when they awaken."

"Some of them will awake in Korus," I replied smiling.

She caught the meaning of my words, and the cruelty of her answering smile horrified me. One is not astonished by cruelty in a hideous face, but when it touches the features of a goddess whose fine-chiselled lineaments might more fittingly portray love and beauty, the contrast is appalling.

Quickly I released her.

"Give me a revolver," she whispered. "I can use that upon those your sword does not silence in time."

I did as she bid. Then I turned toward the distasteful work that lay before me. This was no time for fine compunctions, nor for a chivalry that these cruel demons would neither appreciate nor reciprocate.

Stealthily I approached the nearest sleeper. When he awoke he was well on his journey to the bosom of Korus. His piercing shriek as consciousness returned to him came faintly up to us from the black depths beneath.

The second awoke as I touched him, and, though I succeeded in hurling him from the cruiser's deck, his wild cry of alarm brought the remaining pirates to their feet. There were five of them.

As they arose the girl's revolver spoke in sharp staccato and one sank back to the deck again to rise no more.

The others rushed madly upon me with drawn swords. The girl evidently dared not fire for fear of wounding me, but I saw her sneak stealthily and cat-like toward the flank of the attackers. Then they were on me.

For a few minutes I experienced some of the hottest fighting I had ever passed through. The quarters were too small for foot work. It was stand your ground and give and take. At first I took considerably more than I gave, but presently I got beneath one fellow's guard and had the satisfaction of seeing him collapse upon the deck.

The others redoubled their efforts. The crashing of their blades upon mine raised a terrific din that might have been heard for miles through the silent night. Sparks flew as steel smote steel, and then there was the dull and sickening sound of a shoulder bone parting beneath the keen edge of my Martian sword.

Three now faced me, but the girl was working her way to a point that would soon permit her to reduce the number by one at least. Then things happened with such amazing rapidity that I can scarce comprehend even now all that took place in that brief instant.

The three rushed me with the evident purpose of forcing me back the few steps that would carry my body over the rail into the void below. At the same instant the girl fired and my sword arm made two moves. One man dropped with a bullet in his brain; a sword flew clattering across the deck and dropped over the edge beyond as I disarmed one of my opponents and the third went down with my blade buried to the hilt in his breast and three feet of it protruding from his back, and falling wrenched the sword from my grasp.

Disarmed myself, I now faced my remaining foeman, whose own sword lay somewhere thousands of feet below us, lost in the Lost Sea.

The new conditions seemed to please my adversary, for a smile of satisfaction bared his gleaming teeth as he rushed at me bare-handed. The great muscles which rolled beneath his glossy black hide evidently assured him that here was easy prey, not worth the trouble of drawing the dagger from his harness.

I let him come almost upon me. Then I ducked beneath his outstretched arms, at the same time sidestepping to the right. Pivoting on my left toe, I swung a terrific right to his jaw, and, like a felled ox, he dropped in his tracks.

A low, silvery laugh rang out behind me.

"You are no thern," said the sweet voice of my companion, "for all your golden locks or the harness of Sator Throg. Never lived there upon all Barsoom before one who could fight as you have fought this night. Who are you?"

"I am John Carter, Prince of the House of Tardos Mors, Jeddak of Helium," I replied. "And whom," I added, "has the honour of serving been accorded me?"

She hesitated a moment before speaking. Then she asked:

"You are no thern. Are you an enemy of the therns?"

"I have been in the territory of the therns for a day and a half. During that entire time my life has been in constant danger. I have been harassed and persecuted. Armed men and fierce beasts have been set upon me. I had no quarrel with the therns before, but can you wonder that I feel no great love for them now? I have spoken."

She looked at me intently for several minutes before she replied. It was as though she were attempting to read my inmost soul, to judge my character and my standards of chivalry in that long-drawn, searching gaze.

Apparently the inventory satisfied her.

"I am Phaidor, daughter of Matai Shang, Holy Hekkador of the Holy Therns, Father of Therns, Master of Life and Death upon Barsoom, Brother of Issus, Prince of Life Eternal."

At that moment I noticed that the black I had dropped with my fist was commencing to show signs of returning consciousness. I sprang to his side. Stripping his harness from him I securely bound his hands behind his back, and after similarly fastening his feet tied him to a heavy gun carriage.

"Why not the simpler way?" asked Phaidor.

"I do not understand. What 'simpler way'?" I replied.

With a slight shrug of her lovely shoulders she made a gesture with her hands personating the casting of something over the craft's side.

"I am no murderer," I said. "I kill in self-defence only."

She looked at me narrowly. Then she puckered those divine brows of hers, and shook her head. She could not comprehend.

Well, neither had my own Dejah Thoris been able to understand what to her had seemed a foolish and dangerous policy toward enemies. Upon Barsoom, quarter is neither asked nor given, and each dead man means so much more of the waning resources of this dying planet to be divided amongst those who survive.

But there seemed a subtle difference here between the manner in which this girl contemplated the dispatching of an enemy and the tender-hearted regret of my own princess for the stern necessity which demanded it.

I think that Phaidor regretted the thrill that the spectacle would have afforded her rather than the fact that my decision left another enemy alive to threaten us.

The man had now regained full possession of his faculties, and was regarding us intently from where he lay bound upon the deck. He was a handsome fellow, clean limbed and powerful, with an intelligent face and features of such exquisite chiselling that Adonis himself might have envied him.

The vessel, unguided, had been moving slowly across the valley; but now I thought it time to take the helm and direct her course. Only in a very general way could I guess the location of the Valley Dor. That it was far south of the equator was evident from the constellations, but I was not sufficiently a Martian astronomer to come much closer than a rough guess without the splendid charts and delicate instruments with which, as an officer in the Heliumite Navy, I had formerly reckoned the positions of the vessels on which I sailed.

That a northerly course would quickest lead me toward the more settled portions of the planet immediately decided the direction that I should steer. Beneath my hand the cruiser swung gracefully about. Then the button which controlled the repulsive rays sent us soaring far out into space. With speed lever pulled to the last notch, we raced toward the north as we rose ever farther and farther above that terrible valley of death.

As we passed at a dizzy height over the narrow domains of the therns the flash of powder far below bore mute witness to the ferocity of the battle that still raged along that cruel frontier. No sound of conflict reached our ears, for in the rarefied atmosphere of our great altitude no sound wave could penetrate; they were dissipated in thin air far below us.

It became intensely cold. Breathing was difficult. The girl, Phaidor, and the black pirate kept their eyes glued upon me. At length the girl spoke.

"Unconsciousness comes quickly at this altitude," she said quietly. "Unless you are inviting death for us all you had best drop, and that quickly."

There was no fear in her voice. It was as one might say: "You had better carry an umbrella. It is going to rain."

I dropped the vessel quickly to a lower level. Nor was I a moment too soon. The girl had swooned.

The black, too, was unconscious, while I, myself, retained my senses, I think, only by sheer will. The one on whom all responsibility rests is apt to endure the most.

We were swinging along low above the foothills of the Otz. It was comparatively warm and there was plenty of air for our starved lungs, so I was not surprised to see the black open his eyes, and a moment later the girl also.

"It was a close call," she said.

"It has taught me two things though," I replied.

"What?"

"That even Phaidor, daughter of the Master of Life and Death, is mortal," I said smiling.

"There is immortality only in Issus," she replied. "And Issus is for the race of therns alone. Thus am I immortal."

I caught a fleeting grin passing across the features of the black as he heard her words. I did not then understand why he smiled. Later I was to learn, and she, too, in a most horrible manner.

"If the other thing you have just learned," she continued, "has led to as erroneous deductions as the first you are little richer in knowledge than you were before."

"The other," I replied, "is that our dusky friend here does not hail from the nearer moon—he was like to have died at a few thousand feet above Barsoom. Had we continued the five thousand miles that lie between Thuria and the planet he would have been but the frozen memory of a man."

Phaidor looked at the black in evident astonishment.

"If you are not of Thuria, then where?" she asked.

He shrugged his shoulders and turned his eyes elsewhere, but did not reply.

The girl stamped her little foot in a peremptory manner.

"The daughter of Matai Shang is not accustomed to having her queries remain unanswered," she said. "One of the lesser breed should feel honoured that a member of the holy race that was born to inherit life eternal should deign even to notice him."

Again the black smiled that wicked, knowing smile.

"Xodar, Dator of the First Born of Barsoom, is accustomed to give commands, not to receive them," replied the black pirate. Then, turning to me, "What are your intentions concerning me?"

"I intend taking you both back to Helium," I said. "No harm will come to you. You will find the red men of Helium a kindly and magnanimous race, but if they listen to me there will be no more voluntary pilgrimages down the river Iss, and the impossible belief that they have cherished for ages will be shattered into a thousand pieces."

"Are you of Helium?" he asked.

"I am a Prince of the House of Tardos Mors, Jeddak of Helium," I replied, "but I am not of Barsoom. I am of another world."

Xodar looked at me intently for a few moments.

"I can well believe that you are not of Barsoom," he said at length. "None of this world could have bested eight of the First Born single-handed. But how is it that you wear the golden hair and the jewelled circlet of a Holy Thern?" He emphasized the word holy with a touch of irony.

"I had forgotten them," I said. "They are the spoils of conquest," and with a sweep of my hand I removed the disguise from my head.

When the black's eyes fell on my close-cropped black hair they opened in astonishment. Evidently he had looked for the bald pate of a thern.

"You are indeed of another world," he said, a touch of awe in his voice. "With the skin of a thern, the black hair of a First Born and the muscles of a dozen Dators it was no disgrace even for Xodar to acknowledge your supremacy. A thing he could never do were you a Barsoomian," he added.

"You are travelling several laps ahead of me, my friend," I interrupted. "I glean that your name is Xodar, but whom, pray, are the First Born, and what a Dator, and why, if you were conquered by a Barsoomian, could you not acknowledge it?"

"The First Born of Barsoom," he explained, "are the race of black men of which I am a Dator, or, as the lesser Barsoomians would say, Prince. My race is the oldest on the planet. We trace our lineage, unbroken, direct to the Tree of Life which flourished in the centre of the Valley Dor twenty-three million years ago.

"For countless ages the fruit of this tree underwent the gradual changes of evolution, passing by degrees from true plant life to a combination of plant and animal. In the first stages the fruit of the tree possessed only the power of independent muscular action, while the stem remained attached to the parent plant; later a brain developed in the fruit, so that hanging there by their long stems they thought and moved as individuals.

"Then, with the development of perceptions came a comparison of them; judgments were reached and compared, and thus reason and the power to reason were born upon Barsoom.

"Ages passed. Many forms of life came and went upon the Tree of Life, but still all were attached to the parent plant by stems of varying lengths. At length the fruit tree consisted in tiny plant men, such as we now see reproduced in such huge dimensions in the Valley Dor, but still hanging to the limbs and branches of the tree by the stems which grew from the tops of their heads.

"The buds from which the plant men blossomed resembled large nuts about a foot in diameter, divided by double partition walls into four sections. In one section grew the plant man, in another a sixteen-legged worm, in the third the progenitor of the white ape and in the fourth the primæval black man of Barsoom.

"When the bud burst the plant man remained dangling at the end of his stem, but the three other sections fell to the ground, where the efforts of their imprisoned occupants to escape sent them hopping about in all directions.

"Thus as time went on, all Barsoom was covered with these imprisoned creatures. For countless ages they lived their long lives within their hard shells, hopping and skipping about the broad planet; falling into rivers, lakes, and seas, to be still further spread about the surface of the new world.

"Countless billions died before the first black man broke through his prison walls into the light of day. Prompted by curiosity, he broke open other shells and the peopling of Barsoom commenced.

"The pure strain of the blood of this first black man has remained untainted by admixture with other creatures in the race of which I am a member; but from the sixteen-legged worm, the first ape and renegade black man has sprung every other form of animal life upon Barsoom.

"The therns," and he smiled maliciously as he spoke, "are but the result of ages of evolution from the pure white ape of antiquity. They are a lower order still. There is but one race of true and immortal humans on Barsoom. It is the race of black men.

"The Tree of Life is dead, but before it died the plant men learned to detach themselves from it and roam the face of Barsoom with the other children of the First Parent.

"Now their bisexuality permits them to reproduce themselves after the manner of true plants, but otherwise they have progressed but little in all the ages of their existence. Their actions and movements are largely matters of instinct and not guided to any great extent by reason, since the brain of a plant man is but a trifle larger than the end of your smallest finger. They live upon vegetation and the blood of animals, and their brain is just large enough to direct their movements in the direction of food, and to translate the food sensations which are carried to it from their eyes and ears. They have no sense of self-preservation and so are entirely without fear in the face of danger. That is why they are such terrible antagonists in combat."

I wondered why the black man took such pains to discourse thus at length to enemies upon the genesis of life Barsoomian. It seemed a strangely inopportune moment for a proud member of a proud race to unbend in casual conversation with a captor. Especially in view of the fact that the black still lay securely bound upon the deck.

It was the faintest straying of his eye beyond me for the barest fraction of a second that explained his motive for thus dragging out my interest in his truly absorbing story.

He lay a little forward of where I stood at the levers, and thus he faced the stern of the vessel as he addressed me. It was at the end of his description of the plant men that I caught his eye fixed momentarily upon something behind me.

Nor could I be mistaken in the swift gleam of triumph that brightened those dark orbs for an instant.

Some time before I had reduced our speed, for we had left the Valley Dor many miles astern, and I felt comparatively safe.

I turned an apprehensive glance behind me, and the sight that I saw froze the new-born hope of freedom that had been springing up within me.

A great battleship, forging silent and unlighted through the dark night, loomed close astern.

EIGHT

The Depths of Omean

Now I realized why the black pirate had kept me engrossed with his strange tale. For miles he had sensed the approach of succour, and but for that single tell-tale glance the battleship would have been directly above us in another moment, and the boarding party which was doubtless even now swinging in their harness from the ship's keel, would have swarmed our deck, placing my rising hope of escape in sudden and total eclipse.

I was too old a hand in aerial warfare to be at a loss now for the right manœuvre. Simultaneously I reversed the engines and dropped the little vessel a sheer hundred feet.

Above my head I could see the dangling forms of the boarding party as the battleship raced over us. Then I rose at a sharp angle, throwing my speed lever to its last notch.

Like a bolt from a crossbow my splendid craft shot its steel prow straight at the whirring propellers of the giant above us. If I could but touch them the huge bulk would be disabled for hours and escape once more possible.

At the same instant the sun shot above the horizon, disclosing a hundred grim, black faces peering over the stern of the battleship upon us.

At sight of us a shout of rage went up from a hundred throats. Orders were shouted, but it was too late to save the giant propellers, and with a crash we rammed them.

Instantly with the shock of impact I reversed my engine, but my prow was wedged in the hole it had made in the battleship's stern. Only a second I hung there before tearing away, but that second was amply long to swarm my deck with black devils.

There was no fight. In the first place there was no room to fight. We were simply submerged by numbers. Then as swords menaced me a command from Xodar stayed the hands of his fellows.

"Secure them," he said, "but do not injure them."

Several of the pirates already had released Xodar. He now personally attended to my disarming and saw that I was properly bound. At least he thought that the binding was secure. It would have been had I been a Martian, but I had to smile at the puny strands that confined my wrists. When the time came I could snap them as they had been cotton string.

The girl they bound also, and then they fastened us together. In the meantime they had brought our craft alongside the disabled battleship, and soon we were transported to the latter's deck.

Fully a thousand black men manned the great engine of destruction. Her decks were crowded with them as they pressed forward as far as discipline would permit to get a glimpse of their captives. The girl's beauty elicited many brutal comments and vulgar jests. It was evident that these self-thought supermen were far inferior to the red men of Barsoom in refinement and in chivalry.

My close-cropped black hair and thern complexion were the subjects of much comment. When Xodar told his fellow nobles of my fighting ability and strange origin they crowded about me with numerous questions.

The fact that I wore the harness and metal of a thern who had been killed by a member of my party convinced them that I was an enemy of their hereditary foes, and placed me on a better footing in their estimation.

Without exception the blacks were handsome men, and well built. The officers were conspicuous through the wondrous magnificence of their resplendent trappings. Many harnesses were so encrusted with gold, platinum, silver and precious stones as to entirely hide the leather beneath.

The harness of the commanding officer was a solid mass of diamonds. Against the ebony background of his skin they blazed out with a peculiarly accentuated effulgence. The whole scene was enchanting. The handsome men; the barbaric splendour of the accoutrements; the polished skeel wood of the deck; the gloriously grained sorapus of the cabins, inlaid with priceless jewels and precious metals in intricate and beautiful design; the burnished gold of hand rails; the shining metal of the guns.

Phaidor and I were taken below decks, where, still fast bound, we were thrown into a small compartment which contained a single port-hole. As our escort left us they barred the door behind them.

We could hear the men working on the broken propellers, and from the port-hole we could see that the vessel was drifting lazily toward the south.

For some time neither of us spoke. Each was occupied with his own thoughts. For my part I was wondering as to the fate of Tars Tarkas and the girl, Thuvia.

Even if they succeeded in eluding pursuit they must eventually fall into the hands of either red men or green, and as fugitives from the Valley Dor they could look for but little else than a swift and terrible death.

How I wished that I might have accompanied them. It seemed to me that I could not fail to impress upon the intelligent red men of Barsoom the wicked deception that a cruel and senseless superstition had foisted upon them.

Tardos Mors would believe me. Of that I was positive. And that he would have the courage of his convictions my knowledge of his character assured me. Dejah Thoris would believe me. Not a doubt as to that entered my head. Then there were a thousand of my red and green warrior friends whom I knew would face eternal damnation gladly for my sake. Like Tars Tarkas, where I led they would follow.

My only danger lay in that should I ever escape the black pirates it might be to fall into the hands of unfriendly red or green men. Then it would mean short shrift for me.

Well, there seemed little to worry about on that score, for the likelihood of my ever escaping the blacks was extremely remote.

The girl and I were linked together by a rope which permitted us to move only about three or four feet from each other. When we had entered the compartment we had seated ourselves upon a low bench beneath the port-hole. The bench was the only furniture of the room. It was of sorapus wood. The floor, ceiling and walls were of carborundum aluminum, a light, impenetrable composition extensively utilized in the construction of Martian fighting ships.

As I had sat meditating upon the future my eyes had been riveted upon the port-hole which was just level with them as I sat. Suddenly I looked toward Phaidor. She was regarding me with a strange expression I had not before seen upon her face. She was very beautiful then.

Instantly her white lids veiled her eyes, and I thought I discovered a delicate flush tinging her cheek. Evidently she was embarrassed at having been detected in the act of staring at a lesser creature, I thought.

"Do you find the study of the lower orders interesting?" I asked, laughing.

She looked up again with a nervous but relieved little laugh.

"Oh very," she said, "especially when they have such excellent profiles."

It was my turn to flush, but I did not. I felt that she was poking fun at me, and I admired a brave heart that could look for humour on the road to death, and so I laughed with her.

"Do you know where we are going?" she said.

"To solve the mystery of the eternal hereafter, I imagine," I replied.

"I am going to a worse fate than that," she said, with a little shudder.

"What do you mean?"

"I can only guess," she replied, "since no thern damsel of all the millions that have been stolen away by black pirates during the ages they have raided our domains has ever returned to narrate her experiences among them. That they never take a man prisoner lends strength to the belief that the fate of the girls they steal is worse than death."

"Is it not a just retribution?" I could not help but ask.

"What do you mean?"

"Do not the therns themselves do likewise with the poor creatures who take the voluntary pilgrimage down the River of Mystery? Was not Thuvia for fifteen years a plaything and a slave? Is it less than just that you should suffer as you have caused others to suffer?"

"You do not understand," she replied. "We therns are a holy race. It is an honour to a lesser creature to be a slave among us. Did we not occasionally save a few of the lower orders that stupidly float down an unknown river to an unknown end all would become the prey of the plant men and the apes."

"But do you not by every means encourage the superstition among those of the outside world?" I argued. "That is the wickedest of your deeds. Can you tell me why you foster the cruel deception?"

"All life on Barsoom," she said, "is created solely for the support of the race of therns. How else could we live did the outer world not furnish our labour and our food? Think you that a thern would demean himself by labour?"

"It is true then that you eat human flesh?" I asked in horror.

She looked at me in pitying commiseration for my ignorance.

"Truly we eat the flesh of the lower orders. Do not you also?"

"The flesh of beasts, yes," I replied, "but not the flesh of man."

"As man may eat of the flesh of beasts, so may gods eat of the flesh of man. The Holy Therns are the gods of Barsoom."

I was disgusted and I imagine that I showed it.

"You are an unbeliever now," she continued gently, "but should we be fortunate enough to escape the clutches of the black pirates and come again to the court of Matai Shang I think that we shall find an argument to convince you of the error of your ways. And—," she hesitated, "perhaps we shall find a way to keep you as—as—one of us."

Again her eyes dropped to the floor, and a faint colour suffused her cheek. I could not understand her meaning; nor did I for a long time. Dejah Thoris was wont to say that in some things I was a veritable simpleton, and I guess that she was right.

"I fear that I would ill requite your father's hospitality," I answered, "since the first thing that I should do were I a thern would be to set an armed guard at the mouth of the River Iss to escort the poor deluded voyagers back to the outer world. Also should I devote my life to the extermination of the hideous plant men and their horrible companions, the great white apes."

She looked at me really horror struck.

"No, no," she cried, "you must not say such terribly sacrilegious things— you must not even think them. Should they ever guess that you entertained such frightful thoughts, should we chance to regain the temples of the therns, they would mete out a frightful death to you. Not even my—my— " Again she flushed, and started over. "Not even I could save you."

I said no more. Evidently it was useless. She was even more steeped in superstition than the Martians of the outer world. They only worshipped a beautiful hope for a life of love and peace and happiness in the hereafter. The therns worshipped the hideous plant men and the apes, or at least they reverenced them as the abodes of the departed spirits of their own dead.

At this point the door of our prison opened to admit Xodar.

He smiled pleasantly at me, and when he smiled his expression was kindly—anything but cruel or vindictive.

"Since you cannot escape under any circumstances," he said, "I cannot see the necessity for keeping you confined below. I will cut your bonds and you may come on deck. You will witness something very interesting, and as you never shall return to the outer world it will do no harm to permit you to see it. You will see what no other than the First Born and their slaves know the existence of—the subterranean entrance to the Holy Land, to the real heaven of Barsoom.

"It will be an excellent lesson for this daughter of the therns," he added, "for she shall see the Temple of Issus, and Issus, perchance, shall embrace her."

Phaidor's head went high.

"What blasphemy is this, dog of a pirate?" she cried. "Issus would wipe out your entire breed an' you ever came within sight of her temple."

"You have much to learn, thern," replied Xodar, with an ugly smile, "nor do I envy you the manner in which you will learn it."

As we came on deck I saw to my surprise that the vessel was passing over a great field of snow and ice. As far as the eye could reach in any direction naught else was visible.

There could be but one solution to the mystery. We were above the south polar ice cap. Only at the poles of Mars is there ice or snow upon the planet.

No sign of life appeared below us. Evidently we were too far south even for the great fur-bearing animals which the Martians so delight in hunting.

Xodar was at my side as I stood looking out over the ship's rail.

"What course?" I asked him.

"A little west of south," he replied. "You will see the Otz Valley directly. We shall skirt it for a few hundred miles."

"The Otz Valley!" I exclaimed; "but, man, is not there where lie the domains of the therns from which I but just escaped?"

"Yes," answered Xodar. "You crossed this ice field last night in the long chase that you led us. The Otz Valley lies in a mighty depression at the south pole. It is sunk thousands of feet below the level of the surrounding country, like a great round bowl. A hundred miles from its northern boundary rise the Otz Mountains which circle the inner Valley of Dor, in the exact centre of which lies the Lost Sea of Korus. On the shore of this sea stands the Golden Temple of Issus in the Land of the First Born. It is there that we are bound."

As I looked I commenced to realize why it was that in all the ages only one had escaped from the Valley Dor. My only wonder was that even the one had been successful. To cross this frozen, wind-swept waste of bleak ice alone and on foot would be impossible.

"Only by air boat could the journey be made," I finished aloud.

"It was thus that one did escape the therns in bygone times; but none has ever escaped the First Born," said Xodar, with a touch of pride in his voice.

We had now reached the southernmost extremity of the great ice barrier. It ended abruptly in a sheer wall thousands of feet high at the base of which stretched a level valley, broken here and there by low rolling hills and little clumps of forest, and with tiny rivers formed by the melting of the ice barrier at its base.

Once we passed far above what seemed to be a deep canyon-like rift stretching from the ice wall on the north across the valley as far as the eye could reach. "That is the bed of the River Iss," said Xodar. "It runs far beneath the ice field, and below the level of the Valley Otz, but its canyon is open here."

Presently I descried what I took to be a village, and pointing it out to Xodar asked him what it might be.

"It is a village of lost souls," he answered, laughing. "This strip between the ice barrier and the mountains is considered neutral ground. Some turn off from their voluntary pilgrimage down the Iss, and, scaling the awful walls of its canyon below us, stop in the valley. Also a slave now and then escapes from the therns and makes his way hither.

"They do not attempt to recapture such, since there is no escape from this outer valley, and as a matter of fact they fear the patrolling cruisers of the First Born too much to venture from their own domains.

"The poor creatures of this outer valley are not molested by us since they have nothing that we desire, nor are they numerically strong enough to give us an interesting fight—so we too leave them alone.

"There are several villages of them, but they have increased in numbers but little in many years since they are always warring among themselves."

Now we swung a little north of west, leaving the valley of lost souls, and shortly I discerned over our starboard bow what appeared to be a black mountain rising from the desolate waste of ice. It was not high and seemed to have a flat top.

Xodar had left us to attend to some duty on the vessel, and Phaidor and I stood alone beside the rail. The girl had not once spoken since we had been brought to the deck.

"Is what he has been telling me true?" I asked her.

"In part, yes," she answered. "That about the outer valley is true, but what he says of the location of the Temple of Issus in the centre of his country is false. If it is not false—" she hesitated. "Oh it cannot be true, it cannot be true. For if it were true then for countless ages have my people gone to torture and ignominious death at the hands of their cruel enemies, instead of to the beautiful Life Eternal that we have been taught to believe Issus holds for us."

"As the lesser Barsoomians of the outer world have been lured by you to the terrible Valley Dor, so may it be that the therns themselves have been lured by the First Born to an equally horrid fate," I suggested. "It would be a stern and awful retribution, Phaidor; but a just one."

"I cannot believe it," she said.

"We shall see," I answered, and then we fell silent again for we were rapidly approaching the black mountains, which in some indefinable way seemed linked with the answer to our problem.

As we neared the dark, truncated cone the vessel's speed was diminished until we barely moved. Then we topped the crest of the mountain and below us I saw yawning the mouth of a huge circular well, the bottom of which was lost in inky blackness.

The diameter of this enormous pit was fully a thousand feet. The walls were smooth and appeared to be composed of a black, basaltic rock.

For a moment the vessel hovered motionless directly above the centre of the gaping void, then slowly she began to settle into the black chasm. Lower and lower she sank until as darkness enveloped us her lights were thrown on and in the dim halo of her own radiance the monster battleship dropped on and on down into what seemed to me must be the very bowels of Barsoom.

For quite half an hour we descended and then the shaft terminated abruptly in the dome of a mighty subterranean world. Below us rose and fell the billows of a buried sea. A phosphorescent radiance illuminated the scene. Thousands of ships dotted the bosom of the ocean. Little islands rose here and there to support the strange and colourless vegetation of this strange world.

Slowly and with majestic grace the battleship dropped until she rested on the water. Her great propellers had been drawn and housed during our descent of the shaft and in their place had been run out the smaller but more powerful water propellers. As these commenced to revolve the ship took up its journey once more, riding the new element as buoyantly and as safely as she had the air.

Phaidor and I were dumbfounded. Neither had either heard or dreamed that such a world existed beneath the surface of Barsoom. Nearly all the vessels we saw were war craft. There were a few lighters and barges, but none of the great merchantmen such as ply the upper air between the cities of the outer world.

"Here is the harbour of the navy of the First Born," said a voice behind us, and turning we saw Xodar watching us with an amused smile on his lips.

"This sea," he continued, "is larger than Korus. It receives the waters of the lesser sea above it. To keep it from filling above a certain level we have four great pumping stations that force the oversupply back into the reservoirs far north from which the red men draw the water which irrigates their farm lands."

A new light burst on me with this explanation. The red men had always considered it a miracle that caused great columns of water to spurt from the solid rock of their reservoir sides to increase the supply of the precious liquid which is so scarce in the outer world of Mars.

Never had their learned men been able to fathom the secret of the source of this enormous volume of water. As ages passed they had simply come to accept it as a matter of course and ceased to question its origin.

We passed several islands on which were strangely shaped circular buildings, apparently roofless, and pierced midway between the ground and their tops with small, heavily barred windows. They bore the earmarks of prisons, which were further accentuated by the armed guards who squatted on low benches without, or patrolled the short beach lines.

Few of these islets contained over an acre of ground, but presently we sighted a much larger one directly ahead. This proved to be our destination, and the great ship was soon made fast against the steep shore.

Xodar signalled us to follow him and with a half-dozen officers and men we left the battleship and approached a large oval structure a couple of hundred yards from the shore.

"You shall soon see Issus," said Xodar to Phaidor. "The few prisoners we take are presented to her. Occasionally she selects slaves from among them to replenish the ranks of her handmaidens. None serves Issus above a single year," and there was a grim smile on the black's lips that lent a cruel and sinister meaning to his simple statement.

Phaidor, though loath to believe that Issus was allied to such as these, had commenced to entertain doubts and fears. She clung very closely to me, no longer the proud daughter of the Master of Life and Death upon Barsoom, but a young and frightened girl in the power of relentless enemies.

The building which we now entered was entirely roofless. In its centre was a long tank of water, set below the level of the floor like the swimming pool of a natatorium. Near one side of the pool floated an odd-looking black object. Whether it were some strange monster of these buried waters, or a queer raft, I could not at once perceive.

We were soon to know, however, for as we reached the edge of the pool directly above the thing, Xodar cried out a few words in a strange tongue. Immediately a hatch cover was raised from the surface of the object, and a black seaman sprang from the bowels of the strange craft.

Xodar addressed the seaman.

"Transmit to your officer," he said, "the commands of Dator Xodar. Say to him that Dator Xodar, with officers and men, escorting two prisoners, would be transported to the gardens of Issus beside the Golden Temple."

"Blessed be the shell of thy first ancestor, most noble Dator," replied the man. "It shall be done even as thou sayest," and raising both hands, palms backward, above his head after the manner of salute which is common to all races of Barsoom, he disappeared once more into the entrails of his ship.

A moment later an officer resplendent in the gorgeous trappings of his rank appeared on deck and welcomed Xodar to the vessel, and in the latter's wake we filed aboard and below.

The cabin in which we found ourselves extended entirely across the ship, having port-holes on either side below the water line. No sooner were all below than a number of commands were given, in accordance with which the hatch was closed and secured, and the vessel commenced to vibrate to the rhythmic purr of its machinery.

"Where can we be going in such a tiny pool of water?" asked Phaidor.

"Not up," I replied, "for I noticed particularly that while the building is roofless it is covered with a strong metal grating."

"Then where?" she asked again.

"From the appearance of the craft I judge we are going down," I replied.

Phaidor shuddered. For such long ages have the waters of Barsoom's seas been a thing of tradition only that even this daughter of the therns, born as she had been within sight of Mars' only remaining sea, had the same terror of deep water as is a common attribute of all Martians.

Presently the sensation of sinking became very apparent. We were going down swiftly. Now we could hear the water rushing past the port-holes, and in the dim light that filtered through them to the water beyond the swirling eddies were plainly visible.

Phaidor grasped my arm.

"Save me!" she whispered. "Save me and your every wish shall be granted. Anything within the power of the Holy Therns to give will be yours. Phaidor—" she stumbled a little here, and then in a very low voice, "Phaidor already is yours."

I felt very sorry for the poor child, and placed my hand over hers where it rested on my arm. I presume my motive was misunderstood, for with a swift glance about the apartment to assure herself that we were alone, she threw both her arms about my neck and dragged my face down to hers.

NINE

Issus, Goddess of Life Eternal

The confession of love which the girl's fright had wrung from her touched me deeply; but it humiliated me as well, since I felt that in some thoughtless word or act I had given her reason to believe that I reciprocated her affection.

Never have I been much of a ladies' man, being more concerned with fighting and kindred arts which have ever seemed to me more befitting a man than mooning over a scented glove four sizes too small for him, or kissing a dead flower that has begun to smell like a cabbage. So I was quite at a loss as to what to do or say. A thousand times rather face the wild hordes of the dead sea bottoms than meet the eyes of this beautiful young girl and tell her the thing that I must tell her.

But there was nothing else to be done, and so I did it. Very clumsily too, I fear.

Gently I unclasped her hands from about my neck, and still holding them in mine I told her the story of my love for Dejah Thoris. That of all the women of two worlds that I had known and admired during my long life she alone had I loved.

The tale did not seem to please her. Like a tigress she sprang, panting, to her feet. Her beautiful face was distorted in an expression of horrible malevolence. Her eyes fairly blazed into mine.

"Dog," she hissed. "Dog of a blasphemer! Think you that Phaidor, daughter of Matai Shang, supplicates? She commands. What to her is your puny outer world passion for the vile creature you chose in your other life?

"Phaidor has glorified you with her love, and you have spurned her. Ten thousand unthinkably atrocious deaths could not atone for the affront that you have put upon me. The thing that you call Dejah Thoris shall die the most horrible of them all. You have sealed the warrant for her doom.

"And you! You shall be the meanest slave in the service of the goddess you have attempted to humiliate. Tortures and ignominies shall be heaped upon you until you grovel at my feet asking the boon of death.

"In my gracious generosity I shall at length grant your prayer, and from the high balcony of the Golden Cliffs I shall watch the great white apes tear you asunder."

She had it all fixed up. The whole lovely programme from start to finish. It amazed me to think that one so divinely beautiful could at the same time be so fiendishly vindictive. It occurred to me, however, that she had overlooked one little factor in her revenge, and so, without any intent to add to her discomfiture, but rather to permit her to rearrange her plans along more practical lines, I pointed to the nearest port-hole.

Evidently she had entirely forgotten her surroundings and her present circumstances, for a single glance at the dark, swirling waters without sent her crumpled upon a low bench, where with her face buried in her arms she sobbed more like a very unhappy little girl than a proud and all-powerful goddess.

Down, down we continued to sink until the heavy glass of the port-holes became noticeably warm from the heat of the water without. Evidently we were very far beneath the surface crust of Mars.

Presently our downward motion ceased, and I could hear the propellers swirling through the water at our stern and forcing us ahead at high speed. It was very dark down there, but the light from our port-holes, and the reflection from what must have been a powerful searchlight on the submarine's nose showed that we were forging through a narrow passage, rock-lined, and tube-like.

After a few minutes the propellers ceased their whirring. We came to a full stop, and then commenced to rise swiftly toward the surface. Soon the light from without increased and we came to a stop.

Xodar entered the cabin with his men.

"Come," he said, and we followed him through the hatchway which had been opened by one of the seamen.

We found ourselves in a small subterranean vault, in the centre of which was the pool in which lay our submarine, floating as we had first seen her with only her black back showing.

Around the edge of the pool was a level platform, and then the walls of the cave rose perpendicularly for a few feet to arch toward the centre of the low roof. The walls about the ledge were pierced with a number of entrances to dimly lighted passageways.

Toward one of these our captors led us, and after a short walk halted before a steel cage which lay at the bottom of a shaft rising above us as far as one could see.

The cage proved to be one of the common types of elevator cars that I had seen in other parts of Barsoom. They are operated by means of enormous magnets which are suspended at the top of the shaft. By an electrical device the volume of magnetism generated is regulated and the speed of the car varied.

In long stretches they move at a sickening speed, especially on the upward trip, since the small force of gravity inherent to Mars results in very little opposition to the powerful force above.

Scarcely had the door of the car closed behind us than we were slowing up to stop at the landing above, so rapid was our ascent of the long shaft.

When we emerged from the little building which houses the upper terminus of the elevator, we found ourselves in the midst of a veritable fairyland of beauty. The combined languages of Earth men hold no words to convey to the mind the gorgeous beauties of the scene.

One may speak of scarlet sward and ivory-stemmed trees decked with brilliant purple blooms; of winding walks paved with crushed rubies, with emerald, with turquoise, even with diamonds themselves; of a magnificent temple of burnished gold, hand-wrought with marvellous designs; but where are the words to describe the glorious colours that are unknown to earthly eyes? where the mind or the imagination that can grasp the gorgeous scintillations of unheard-of rays as they emanate from the thousand nameless jewels of Barsoom?

Even my eyes, for long years accustomed to the barbaric splendours of a Martian Jeddak's court, were amazed at the glory of the scene.

Phaidor's eyes were wide in amazement.

"The Temple of Issus," she whispered, half to herself.

Xodar watched us with his grim smile, partly of amusement and partly of malicious gloating.

The gardens swarmed with brilliantly trapped black men and women. Among them moved red and white females serving their every want. The places of the outer world and the temples of the therns had been robbed of their princesses and goddesses that the blacks might have their slaves.

Through this scene we moved toward the temple. At the main entrance we were halted by a cordon of armed guards. Xodar spoke a few words to an officer who came forward to question us. Together they entered the temple, where they remained for some time.

When they returned it was to announce that Issus desired to look upon the daughter of Matai Shang, and the strange creature from another world who had been a Prince of Helium.

Slowly we moved through endless corridors of unthinkable beauty; through magnificent apartments, and noble halls. At length we were halted in a spacious chamber in the centre of the temple. One of the officers who had accompanied us advanced to a large door in the further end of the chamber. Here he must have made some sort of signal for immediately the door opened and another richly trapped courtier emerged.

We were then led up to the door, where we were directed to get down on our hands and knees with our backs toward the room we were to enter. The doors were swung open and after being cautioned not to turn our heads under penalty of instant death we were commanded to back into the presence of Issus.

Never have I been in so humiliating a position in my life, and only my love for Dejah Thoris and the hope which still clung to me that I might again see her kept me from rising to face the goddess of the First Born and go down to my death like a gentleman, facing my foes and with their blood mingling with mine.

After we had crawled in this disgusting fashion for a matter of a couple of hundred feet we were halted by our escort.

"Let them rise," said a voice behind us; a thin, wavering voice, yet one that had evidently been accustomed to command for many years.

"Rise," said our escort, "but do not face toward Issus."

"The woman pleases me," said the thin, wavering voice again after a few moments of silence. "She shall serve me the allotted time. The man you may return to the Isle of Shador which lies against the northern shore of the Sea of Omean. Let the woman turn and look upon Issus, knowing that those of the lower orders who gaze upon the holy vision of her radiant face survive the blinding glory but a single year."

I watched Phaidor from the corner of my eye. She paled to a ghastly hue. Slowly, very slowly she turned, as though drawn by some invisible yet irresistible force. She was standing quite close to me, so close that her bare arm touched mine as she finally faced Issus, Goddess of Life Eternal.

I could not see the girl's face as her eyes rested for the first time on the Supreme Deity of Mars, but felt the shudder that ran through her in the trembling flesh of the arm that touched mine.

"It must be dazzling loveliness indeed," thought I, "to cause such emotion in the breast of so radiant a beauty as Phaidor, daughter of Matai Shang."

"Let the woman remain. Remove the man. Go." Thus spoke Issus, and the heavy hand of the officer fell upon my shoulder. In accordance with his instructions I dropped to my hands and knees once more and crawled from the Presence. It had been my first audience with deity, but I am free to confess that I was not greatly impressed—other than with the ridiculous figure I cut scrambling about on my marrow bones.

Once without the chamber the doors closed behind us and I was bid to rise. Xodar joined me and together we slowly retraced our steps toward the gardens.

"You spared my life when you easily might have taken it," he said after we had proceeded some little way in silence, "and I would aid you if I might. I can help to make your life here more bearable, but your fate is inevitable. You may never hope to return to the outer world."

"What will be my fate?" I asked.

"That will depend largely upon Issus. So long as she does not send for you and reveal her face to you, you may live on for years in as mild a form of bondage as I can arrange for you."

"Why should she send for me?" I asked.

"The men of the lower orders she often uses for various purposes of amusement. Such a fighter as you, for example, would render fine sport in the monthly rites of the temple. There are men pitted against men, and against beasts for the edification of Issus and the replenishment of her larder."

"She eats human flesh?" I asked. Not in horror, however, for since my recently acquired knowledge of the Holy Therns I was prepared for anything in this still less accessible heaven, where all was evidently dictated by a single omnipotence; where ages of narrow fanaticism and self-worship had eradicated all the broader humanitarian instincts that the race might once have possessed.

They were a people drunk with power and success, looking upon the other inhabitants of Mars as we look upon the beasts of the field and the forest. Why then should they not eat of the flesh of the lower orders whose lives and characters they no more understood than do we the inmost thoughts and sensibilities of the cattle we slaughter for our earthly tables.

"She eats only the flesh of the best bred of the Holy Therns and the red Barsoomians. The flesh of the others goes to our boards. The animals are eaten by the slaves. She also eats other dainties."

I did not understand then that there lay any special significance in his reference to other dainties. I thought the limit of ghoulishness already had been reached in the recitation of Issus' menu. I still had much to learn as to the depths of cruelty and bestiality to which omnipotence may drag its possessor.

We had about reached the last of the many chambers and corridors which led to the gardens when an officer overtook us.

"Issus would look again upon this man," he said. "The girl has told her that he is of wondrous beauty and of such prowess that alone he slew seven of the First Born, and with his bare hands took Xodar captive, binding him with his own harness."

Xodar looked uncomfortable. Evidently he did not relish the thought that Issus had learned of his inglorious defeat.

Without a word he turned and we followed the officer once again to the closed doors before the audience chamber of Issus, Goddess of Life Eternal.

Here the ceremony of entrance was repeated. Again Issus bid me rise. For several minutes all was silent as the tomb. The eyes of deity were appraising me.

Presently the thin wavering voice broke the stillness, repeating in a singsong drone the words which for countless ages had sealed the doom of numberless victims.

"Let the man turn and look upon Issus, knowing that those of the lower orders who gaze upon the holy vision of her radiant face survive the blinding glory but a single year."

I turned as I had been bid, expecting such a treat as only the revealment of divine glory to mortal eyes might produce. What I saw was a solid phalanx of armed men between myself and a dais supporting a great bench of carved sorapus wood. On this bench, or throne, squatted a female black. She was evidently very old. Not a hair remained upon her wrinkled skull. With the exception of two yellow fangs she was entirely toothless. On either side of her thin, hawk-like nose her eyes burned from the depths of horribly sunken sockets. The skin of her face was seamed and creased with a million deepcut furrows. Her body was as wrinkled as her face, and as repulsive.

Emaciated arms and legs attached to a torso which seemed to be mostly distorted abdomen completed the "holy vision of her radiant beauty."

Surrounding her were a number of female slaves, among them Phaidor, white and trembling.

"This is the man who slew seven of the First Born and, bare-handed, bound Dator Xodar with his own harness?" asked Issus.

"Most glorious vision of divine loveliness, it is," replied the officer who stood at my side.

"Produce Dator Xodar," she commanded.

Xodar was brought from the adjoining room.

Issus glared at him, a baleful light in her hideous eyes.

"And such as you are a Dator of the First Born?" she squealed. "For the disgrace you have brought upon the Immortal Race you shall be degraded to a rank below the lowest. No longer be you a Dator, but for evermore a slave of slaves, to fetch and carry for the lower orders that serve in the gardens of Issus. Remove his harness. Cowards and slaves wear no trappings."

Xodar stood stiffly erect. Not a muscle twitched, nor a tremor shook his giant frame as a soldier of the guard roughly stripped his gorgeous trappings from him.

"Begone," screamed the infuriated little old woman. "Begone, but instead of the light of the gardens of Issus let you serve as a slave of this slave who conquered you in the prison on the Isle of Shador in the Sea of Omean. Take him away out of the sight of my divine eyes."

Slowly and with high held head the proud Xodar turned and stalked from the chamber. Issus rose and turned to leave the room by another exit.

Turning to me, she said: "You shall be returned to Shador for the present. Later Issus will see the manner of your fighting. Go." Then she disappeared, followed by her retinue. Only Phaidor lagged behind, and as I started to follow my guard toward the gardens, the girl came running after me.

"Oh, do not leave me in this terrible place," she begged. "Forgive the things I said to you, my Prince. I did not mean them. Only take me away with you. Let me share your imprisonment on Shador." Her words were an almost incoherent volley of thoughts, so rapidly she spoke. "You did not understand the honour that I did you. Among the therns there is no marriage or giving in marriage, as among the lower orders of the outer world. We might have lived together for ever in love and happiness. We have both looked upon Issus and in a year we die. Let us live that year at least together in what measure of joy remains for the doomed."

"If it was difficult for me to understand you, Phaidor," I replied, "can you not understand that possibly it is equally difficult for you to understand the motives, the customs and the social laws that guide me? I do not wish to hurt you, nor to seem to undervalue the honour which you have done me, but the thing you desire may not be. Regardless of the foolish belief of the peoples of the outer world, or of Holy Thern, or ebon First Born, I am not dead. While I live my heart beats for but one woman—the incomparable Dejah Thoris, Princess of Helium. When death overtakes me my heart shall have ceased to beat; but what comes after that I know not. And in that I am as wise as Matai Shang, Master of Life and Death upon Barsoom; or Issus, Goddess of Life Eternal."

Phaidor stood looking at me intently for a moment. No anger showed in her eyes this time, only a pathetic expression of hopeless sorrow.

"I do not understand," she said, and turning walked slowly in the direction of the door through which Issus and her retinue had passed. A moment later she had passed from my sight.

TEN

The Prison Isle of Shador

In the outer gardens to which the guard now escorted me, I found Xodar surrounded by a crowd of noble blacks. They were reviling and cursing him. The men slapped his face. The women spat upon him.

When I appeared they turned their attentions toward me.

"Ah," cried one, "so this is the creature who overcame the great Xodar bare-handed. Let us see how it was done."

"Let him bind Thurid," suggested a beautiful woman, laughing. "Thurid is a noble Dator. Let Thurid show the dog what it means to face a real man."

"Yes, Thurid! Thurid!" cried a dozen voices.

"Here he is now," exclaimed another, and turning in the direction indicated I saw a huge black weighed down with resplendent ornaments and arms advancing with noble and gallant bearing toward us.

"What now?" he cried. "What would you of Thurid?"

Quickly a dozen voices explained.

Thurid turned toward Xodar, his eyes narrowing to two nasty slits.

"Calot!" he hissed. "Ever did I think you carried the heart of a sorak in your putrid breast. Often have you bested me in the secret councils of Issus, but now in the field of war where men are truly gauged your scabby heart hath revealed its sores to all the world. Calot, I spurn you with my foot," and with the words he turned to kick Xodar.

My blood was up. For minutes it had been boiling at the cowardly treatment they had been according this once powerful comrade because he had fallen from the favour of Issus. I had no love for Xodar, but I cannot stand the sight of cowardly injustice and persecution without seeing red as through a haze of bloody mist, and doing things on the impulse of the moment that I presume I never should do after mature deliberation.

I was standing close beside Xodar as Thurid swung his foot for the cowardly kick. The degraded Dator stood erect and motionless as a carven image. He was prepared to take whatever his former comrades had to offer in the way of insults and reproaches, and take them in manly silence and stoicism.

But as Thurid's foot swung so did mine, and I caught him a painful blow upon the shin bone that saved Xodar from this added ignominy.

For a moment there was tense silence, then Thurid, with a roar of rage sprang for my throat; just as Xodar had upon the deck of the cruiser. The results were identical. I ducked beneath his outstretched arms, and as he lunged past me planted a terrific right on the side of his jaw.

The big fellow spun around like a top, his knees gave beneath him and he crumpled to the ground at my feet.

The blacks gazed in astonishment, first at the still form of the proud Dator lying there in the ruby dust of the pathway, then at me as though they could not believe that such a thing could be.

"You asked me to bind Thurid," I cried; "behold!" And then I stooped beside the prostrate form, tore the harness from it, and bound the fellow's arms and legs securely.

"As you have done to Xodar, now do you likewise to Thurid. Take him before Issus, bound in his own harness, that she may see with her own eyes that there be one among you now who is greater than the First Born."

"Who are you?" whispered the woman who had first suggested that I attempt to bind Thurid.

"I am a citizen of two worlds; Captain John Carter of Virginia, Prince of the House of Tardos Mors, Jeddak of Helium. Take this man to your goddess, as I have said, and tell her, too, that as I have done to Xodar and Thurid, so also can I do to the mightiest of her Dators. With naked hands, with long-sword or with short-sword, I challenge the flower of her fighting-men to combat."

"Come," said the officer who was guarding me back to Shador; "my orders are imperative; there is to be no delay. Xodar, come you also."

There was little of disrespect in the tone that the man used in addressing either Xodar or myself. It was evident that he felt less contempt for the former Dator since he had witnessed the ease with which I disposed of the powerful Thurid.

That his respect for me was greater than it should have been for a slave was quite apparent from the fact that during the balance of the return journey he walked or stood always behind me, a drawn short-sword in his hand.

The return to the Sea of Omean was uneventful. We dropped down

the awful shaft in the same car that had brought us to the surface. There
we entered the submarine, taking the long dive to the tunnel far beneath
the upper world. Then through the tunnel and up again to the pool from
which we had had our first introduction to the wonderful passageway from
Omean to the Temple of Issus.

From the island of the submarine we were transported on a small cruiser
to the distant Isle of Shador. Here we found a small stone prison and a guard
of half a dozen blacks. There was no ceremony wasted in completing our
incarceration. One of the blacks opened the door of the prison with a huge
key, we walked in, the door closed behind us, the lock grated, and with
the sound there swept over me again that terrible feeling of hopelessness
that I had felt in the Chamber of Mystery in the Golden Cliffs beneath the
gardens of the Holy Therns.

Then Tars Tarkas had been with me, but now I was utterly alone in so
far as friendly companionship was concerned. I fell to wondering about the
fate of the great Thark, and of his beautiful companion, the girl, Thuvia.
Even should they by some miracle have escaped and been received and
spared by a friendly nation, what hope had I of the succour which I knew
they would gladly extend if it lay in their power.

They could not guess my whereabouts or my fate, for none on all
Barsoom even dream of such a place as this. Nor would it have advantaged
me any had they known the exact location of my prison, for who could
hope to penetrate to this buried sea in the face of the mighty navy of the
First Born? No: my case was hopeless.

Well, I would make the best of it, and, rising, I swept aside the brooding
despair that had been endeavouring to claim me. With the idea of exploring
my prison, I started to look around.

Xodar sat, with bowed head, upon a low stone bench near the centre of
the room in which we were. He had not spoken since Issus had degraded
him.

The building was roofless, the walls rising to a height of about thirty feet.
Half-way up were a couple of small, heavily barred windows. The prison
was divided into several rooms by partitions twenty feet high. There was
no one in the room which we occupied, but two doors which led to other
rooms were opened. I entered one of these rooms, but found it vacant. Thus
I continued through several of the chambers until in the last one I found a
young red Martian boy sleeping upon the stone bench which constituted
the only furniture of any of the prison cells.

Evidently he was the only other prisoner. As he slept I leaned over and
looked at him. There was something strangely familiar about his face, and

yet I could not place him. His features were very regular and, like the proportions of his graceful limbs and body, beautiful in the extreme. He was very light in colour for a red man, but in other respects he seemed a typical specimen of this handsome race.

I did not awaken him, for sleep in prison is such a priceless boon that I have seen men transformed into raging brutes when robbed by one of their fellow-prisoners of a few precious moments of it.

Returning to my own cell, I found Xodar still sitting in the same position in which I had left him.

"Man," I cried, "it will profit you nothing to mope thus. It were no disgrace to be bested by John Carter. You have seen that in the ease with which I accounted for Thurid. You knew it before when on the cruiser's deck you saw me slay three of your comrades."

"I would that you had dispatched me at the same time," he said.

"Come, come!" I cried. "There is hope yet. Neither of us is dead. We are great fighters. Why not win to freedom?"

He looked at me in amazement.

"You know not of what you speak," he replied. "Issus is omnipotent. Issus is omniscient. She hears now the words you speak. She knows the thoughts you think. It is sacrilege even to dream of breaking her commands."

"Rot, Xodar," I ejaculated impatiently.

He sprang to his feet in horror.

"The curse of Issus will fall upon you," he cried. "In another instant you will be smitten down, writhing to your death in horrible agony."

"Do you believe that, Xodar?" I asked.

"Of course; who would dare doubt?"

"I doubt; yes, and further, I deny," I said. "Why, Xodar, you tell me that she even knows my thoughts. The red men have all had that power for ages. And another wonderful power. They can shut their minds so that none may read their thoughts. I learned the first secret years ago; the other I never had to learn, since upon all Barsoom is none who can read what passes in the secret chambers of my brain.

"Your goddess cannot read my thoughts; nor can she read yours when you are out of sight, unless you will it. Had she been able to read mine, I am afraid that her pride would have suffered a rather severe shock when I turned at her command to 'gaze upon the holy vision of her radiant face.'"

"What do you mean?" he whispered in an affrighted voice, so low that I could scarcely hear him.

"I mean that I thought her the most repulsive and vilely hideous creature my eyes ever had rested upon."

For a moment he eyed me in horror-stricken amazement, and then with a cry of "Blasphemer" he sprang upon me.

I did not wish to strike him again, nor was it necessary, since he was unarmed and therefore quite harmless to me.

As he came I grasped his left wrist with my left hand, and, swinging my right arm about his left shoulder, caught him beneath the chin with my elbow and bore him backward across my thigh.

There he hung helpless for a moment, glaring up at me in impotent rage.

"Xodar," I said, "let us be friends. For a year, possibly, we may be forced to live together in the narrow confines of this tiny room. I am sorry to have offended you, but I could not dream that one who had suffered from the cruel injustice of Issus still could believe her divine.

"I will say a few more words, Xodar, with no intent to wound your feelings further, but rather that you may give thought to the fact that while we live we are still more the arbiters of our own fate than is any god.

"Issus, you see, has not struck me dead, nor is she rescuing her faithful Xodar from the clutches of the unbeliever who defamed her fair beauty. No, Xodar, your Issus is a mortal old woman. Once out of her clutches and she cannot harm you.

"With your knowledge of this strange land, and my knowledge of the outer world, two such fighting-men as you and I should be able to win our way to freedom. Even though we died in the attempt, would not our memories be fairer than as though we remained in servile fear to be butchered by a cruel and unjust tyrant—call her goddess or mortal, as you will."

As I finished I raised Xodar to his feet and released him. He did not renew the attack upon me, nor did he speak. Instead, he walked toward the bench, and, sinking down upon it, remained lost in deep thought for hours.

A long time afterward I heard a soft sound at the doorway leading to one of the other apartments, and, looking up, beheld the red Martian youth gazing intently at us.

"Kaor," I cried, after the red Martian manner of greeting.

"Kaor," he replied. "What do you here?"

"I await my death, I presume," I replied with a wry smile.

He too smiled, a brave and winning smile.

"I also," he said. "Mine will come soon. I looked upon the radiant beauty of Issus nearly a year since. It has always been a source of keen wonder to me that I did not drop dead at the first sight of that hideous countenance. And her belly! By my first ancestor, but never was there so grotesque a figure in all the universe. That they should call such a one Goddess of Life Eternal, Goddess of Death, Mother of the Nearer Moon, and fifty other equally impossible titles, is quite beyond me."

"How came you here?" I asked.

"It is very simple. I was flying a one-man air scout far to the south when the brilliant idea occurred to me that I should like to search for the Lost Sea of Korus which tradition places near to the south pole. I must have inherited from my father a wild lust for adventure, as well as a hollow where my bump of reverence should be.

"I had reached the area of eternal ice when my port propeller jammed, and I dropped to the ground to make repairs. Before I knew it the air was black with fliers, and a hundred of these First Born devils were leaping to the ground all about me.

"With drawn swords they made for me, but before I went down beneath them they had tasted of the steel of my father's sword, and I had given such an account of myself as I know would have pleased my sire had he lived to witness it."

"Your father is dead?" I asked.

"He died before the shell broke to let me step out into a world that has been very good to me. But for the sorrow that I had never the honour to know my father, I have been very happy. My only sorrow now is that my mother must mourn me as she has for ten long years mourned my father."

"Who was your father?" I asked.

He was about to reply when the outer door of our prison opened and a burly guard entered and ordered him to his own quarters for the night, locking the door after him as he passed through into the further chamber.

"It is Issus' wish that you two be confined in the same room," said the guard when he had returned to our cell. "This cowardly slave of a slave is to serve you well," he said to me, indicating Xodar with a wave of his hand. "If he does not, you are to beat him into submission. It is Issus' wish that you heap upon him every indignity and degradation of which you can conceive."

With these words he left us.

Xodar still sat with his face buried in his hands. I walked to his side and placed my hand upon his shoulder.

"Xodar," I said, "you have heard the commands of Issus, but you need not fear that I shall attempt to put them into execution. You are a brave man, Xodar. It is your own affair if you wish to be persecuted and humiliated; but were I you I should assert my manhood and defy my enemies."

"I have been thinking very hard, John Carter," he said, "of all the new ideas you gave me a few hours since. Little by little I have been piecing together the things that you said which sounded blasphemous to me then with the things that I have seen in my past life and dared not even think about for fear of bringing down upon me the wrath of Issus.

"I believe now that she is a fraud; no more divine than you or I. More I am willing to concede—that the First Born are no holier than the Holy Therns, nor the Holy Therns more holy than the red men.

"The whole fabric of our religion is based on superstitious belief in lies that have been foisted upon us for ages by those directly above us, to whose personal profit and aggrandizement it was to have us continue to believe as they wished us to believe.

"I am ready to cast off the ties that have bound me. I am ready to defy Issus herself; but what will it avail us? Be the First Born gods or mortals, they are a powerful race, and we are as fast in their clutches as though we were already dead. There is no escape."

"I have escaped from bad plights in the past, my friend," I replied; "nor while life is in me shall I despair of escaping from the Isle of Shador and the Sea of Omean."

"But we cannot escape even from the four walls of our prison," urged Xodar. "Test this flint-like surface," he cried, smiting the solid rock that confined us. "And look upon this polished surface; none could cling to it to reach the top."

I smiled.

"That is the least of our troubles, Xodar," I replied. "I will guarantee to scale the wall and take you with me, if you will help with your knowledge of the customs here to appoint the best time for the attempt, and guide me to the shaft that lets from the dome of this abysmal sea to the light of God's pure air above."

"Night time is the best and offers the only slender chance we have, for then men sleep, and only a dozing watch nods in the tops of the battleships. No watch is kept upon the cruisers and smaller craft. The watchers upon the larger vessels see to all about them. It is night now."

"But," I exclaimed, "it is not dark! How can it be night, then?"

He smiled.

"You forget," he said, "that we are far below ground. The light of the sun never penetrates here. There are no moons and no stars reflected in the bosom of Omean. The phosphorescent light you now see pervading this great subterranean vault emanates from the rocks that form its dome; it is always thus upon Omean, just as the billows are always as you see them—rolling, ever rolling over a windless sea.

"At the appointed hour of night upon the world above, the men whose duties hold them here sleep, but the light is ever the same."

"It will make escape more difficult," I said, and then I shrugged my shoulders; for what, pray, is the pleasure of doing an easy thing?

"Let us sleep on it to-night," said Xodar. "A plan may come with our awakening."

So we threw ourselves upon the hard stone floor of our prison and slept the sleep of tired men.

ELEVEN

When Hell Broke Loose

Early the next morning Xodar and I commenced work upon our plans for escape. First I had him sketch upon the stone floor of our cell as accurate a map of the south polar regions as was possible with the crude instruments at our disposal—a buckle from my harness, and the sharp edge of the wondrous gem I had taken from Sator Throg.

From this I computed the general direction of Helium and the distance at which it lay from the opening which led to Omean.

Then I had him draw a map of Omean, indicating plainly the position of Shador and of the opening in the dome which led to the outer world.

These I studied until they were indelibly imprinted in my memory. From Xodar I learned the duties and customs of the guards who patrolled Shador. It seemed that during the hours set aside for sleep only one man was on duty at a time. He paced a beat that passed around the prison, at a distance of about a hundred feet from the building.

The pace of the sentries, Xodar said, was very slow, requiring nearly ten minutes to make a single round. This meant that for practically five minutes at a time each side of the prison was unguarded as the sentry pursued his snail like pace upon the opposite side.

"This information you ask," said Xodar, "will be all very valuable *after* we get out, but nothing that you have asked has any bearing on that first and most important consideration."

"We will get out all right," I replied, laughing. "Leave that to me."

"When shall we make the attempt?" he asked.

"The first night that finds a small craft moored near the shore of Shador," I replied.

"But how will you know that any craft is moored near Shador? The windows are far beyond our reach."

"Not so, friend Xodar; look!"

With a bound I sprang to the bars of the window opposite us, and took a quick survey of the scene without.

Several small craft and two large battleships lay within a hundred yards of Shador.

"To-night," I thought, and was just about to voice my decision to Xodar, when, without warning, the door of our prison opened and a guard stepped in.

If the fellow saw me there our chances of escape might quickly go glimmering, for I knew that they would put me in irons if they had the slightest conception of the wonderful agility which my earthly muscles gave me upon Mars.

The man had entered and was standing facing the centre of the room, so that his back was toward me. Five feet above me was the top of a partition wall separating our cell from the next.

There was my only chance to escape detection. If the fellow turned, I was lost; nor could I have dropped to the floor undetected, since he was no nearly below me that I would have struck him had I done so.

"Where is the white man?" cried the guard of Xodar. "Issus commands his presence." He started to turn to see if I were in another part of the cell.

I scrambled up the iron grating of the window until I could catch a good footing on the sill with one foot; then I let go my hold and sprang for the partition top.

"What was that?" I heard the deep voice of the black bellow as my metal grated against the stone wall as I slipped over. Then I dropped lightly to the floor of the cell beyond.

"Where is the white slave?" again cried the guard.

"I know not," replied Xodar. "He was here even as you entered. I am not his keeper—go find him."

The black grumbled something that I could not understand, and then I heard him unlocking the door into one of the other cells on the further side. Listening intently, I caught the sound as the door closed behind him. Then I sprang once more to the top of the partition and dropped into my own cell beside the astonished Xodar.

"Do you see now how we will escape?" I asked him in a whisper.

"I see how you may," he replied, "but I am no wiser than before as to how I am to pass these walls. Certain it is that I cannot bounce over them as you do."

We heard the guard moving about from cell to cell, and finally, his rounds completed, he again entered ours. When his eyes fell upon me they fairly bulged from his head.

"By the shell of my first ancestor!" he roared. "Where have you been?"

"I have been in prison since you put me here yesterday," I answered. "I was in this room when you entered. You had better look to your eyesight."

He glared at me in mingled rage and relief.

"Come," he said. "Issus commands your presence."

He conducted me outside the prison, leaving Xodar behind. There we found several other guards, and with them the red Martian youth who occupied another cell upon Shador.

The journey I had taken to the Temple of Issus on the preceding day was repeated. The guards kept the red boy and myself separated, so that we had no opportunity to continue the conversation that had been interrupted the previous night.

The youth's face had haunted me. Where had I seen him before. There was something strangely familiar in every line of him; in his carriage, his manner of speaking, his gestures. I could have sworn that I knew him, and yet I knew too that I had never seen him before.

When we reached the gardens of Issus we were led away from the temple instead of toward it. The way wound through enchanted parks to a mighty wall that towered a hundred feet in air.

Massive gates gave egress upon a small plain, surrounded by the same gorgeous forests that I had seen at the foot of the Golden Cliffs.

Crowds of blacks were strolling in the same direction that our guards were leading us, and with them mingled my old friends the plant men and great white apes.

The brutal beasts moved among the crowd as pet dogs might. If they were in the way the blacks pushed them roughly to one side, or whacked them with the flat of a sword, and the animals slunk away as in great fear.

Presently we came upon our destination, a great amphitheatre situated at the further edge of the plain, and about half a mile beyond the garden walls.

Through a massive arched gateway the blacks poured in to take their seats, while our guards led us to a smaller entrance near one end of the structure.

Through this we passed into an enclosure beneath the seats, where we found a number of other prisoners herded together under guard. Some of them were in irons, but for the most part they seemed sufficiently awed by the presence of their guards to preclude any possibility of attempted escape.

During the trip from Shador I had had no opportunity to talk with my fellow-prisoner, but now that we were safely within the barred paddock our guards abated their watchfulness, with the result that I found myself able to approach the red Martian youth for whom I felt such a strange attraction.

"What is the object of this assembly?" I asked him. "Are we to fight for the edification of the First Born, or is it something worse than that?"

"It is a part of the monthly rites of Issus," he replied, "in which black men wash the sins from their souls in the blood of men from the outer world. If, perchance, the black is killed, it is evidence of his disloyalty to Issus—the unpardonable sin. If he lives through the contest he is held acquitted of the charge that forced the sentence of the rites, as it is called, upon him.

"The forms of combat vary. A number of us may be pitted together against an equal number, or twice the number of blacks; or singly we may be sent forth to face wild beasts, or some famous black warrior."

"And if we are victorious," I asked, "what then—freedom?"

He laughed.

"Freedom, forsooth. The only freedom for us death. None who enters the domains of the First Born ever leave. If we prove able fighters we are permitted to fight often. If we are not mighty fighters—" He shrugged his shoulders. "Sooner or later we die in the arena."

"And you have fought often?" I asked.

"Very often," he replied. "It is my only pleasure. Some hundred black devils have I accounted for during nearly a year of the rites of Issus. My mother would be very proud could she only know how well I have maintained the traditions of my father's prowess."

"Your father must have been a mighty warrior!" I said. "I have known most of the warriors of Barsoom in my time; doubtless I knew him. Who was he?"

"My father was—"

"Come, calots!" cried the rough voice of a guard. "To the slaughter with you," and roughly we were hustled to the steep incline that led to the chambers far below which let out upon the arena.

The amphitheatre, like all I had ever seen upon Barsoom, was built in a large excavation. Only the highest seats, which formed the low wall surrounding the pit, were above the level of the ground. The arena itself was far below the surface.

Just beneath the lowest tier of seats was a series of barred cages on a level with the surface of the arena. Into these we were herded. But, unfortunately, my youthful friend was not of those who occupied a cage with me.

Directly opposite my cage was the throne of Issus. Here the horrid creature squatted, surrounded by a hundred slave maidens sparkling in jewelled trappings. Brilliant cloths of many hues and strange patterns formed the soft cushion covering of the dais upon which they reclined about her.

On four sides of the throne and several feet below it stood three solid ranks of heavily armed soldiery, elbow to elbow. In front of these were the high dignitaries of this mock heaven—gleaming blacks bedecked with precious stones, upon their foreheads the insignia of their rank set in circles of gold.

On both sides of the throne stretched a solid mass of humanity from top to bottom of the amphitheatre. There were as many women as men, and each was clothed in the wondrously wrought harness of his station and his house. With each black was from one to three slaves, drawn from the domains of the therns and from the outer world. The blacks are all "noble." There is no peasantry among the First Born. Even the lowest soldier is a god, and has his slaves to wait upon him.

The First Born do no work. The men fight—that is a sacred privilege and duty; to fight and die for Issus. The women do nothing, absolutely nothing. Slaves wash them, slaves dress them, slaves feed them. There are some, even, who have slaves that talk for them, and I saw one who sat during the rites with closed eyes while a slave narrated to her the events that were transpiring within the arena.

The first event of the day was the Tribute to Issus. It marked the end of those poor unfortunates who had looked upon the divine glory of the goddess a full year before. There were ten of them—splendid beauties from the proud courts of mighty Jeddaks and from the temples of the Holy Therns. For a year they had served in the retinue of Issus; to-day they were to pay the price of this divine preferment with their lives; tomorrow they would grace the tables of the court functionaries.

A huge black entered the arena with the young women. Carefully he inspected them, felt of their limbs and poked them in the ribs. Presently he selected one of their number whom he led before the throne of Issus. He addressed some words to the goddess which I could not hear. Issus nodded her head. The black raised his hands above his head in token of salute, grasped the girl by the wrist, and dragged her from the arena through a small doorway below the throne.

"Issus will dine well to-night," said a prisoner beside me.

"What do you mean?" I asked.

"That was her dinner that old Thabis is taking to the kitchens. Didst not note how carefully he selected the plumpest and tenderest of the lot?"

I growled out my curses on the monster sitting opposite us on the gorgeous throne.

"Fume not," admonished my companion; "you will see far worse than that if you live even a month among the First Born."

I turned again in time to see the gate of a nearby cage thrown open and three monstrous white apes spring into the arena. The girls shrank in a frightened group in the centre of the enclosure.

One was on her knees with imploring hands outstretched toward Issus; but the hideous deity only leaned further forward in keener anticipation of the entertainment to come. At length the apes spied the huddled knot of terror-stricken maidens and with demoniacal shrieks of bestial frenzy, charged upon them.

A wave of mad fury surged over me. The cruel cowardliness of the power-drunk creature whose malignant mind conceived such frightful forms of torture stirred to their uttermost depths my resentment and my manhood. The blood-red haze that presaged death to my foes swam before my eyes.

The guard lolled before the unbarred gate of the cage which confined me. What need of bars, indeed, to keep those poor victims from rushing into the arena which the edict of the gods had appointed as their death place!

A single blow sent the black unconscious to the ground. Snatching up his long-sword, I sprang into the arena. The apes were almost upon the maidens, but a couple of mighty bounds were all my earthly muscles required to carry me to the centre of the sand-strewn floor.

For an instant silence reigned in the great amphitheatre, then a wild shout arose from the cages of the doomed. My long-sword circled whirring through the air, and a great ape sprawled, headless, at the feet of the fainting girls.

The other apes turned now upon me, and as I stood facing them a sullen roar from the audience answered the wild cheers from the cages. From the tail of my eye I saw a score of guards rushing across the glistening sand toward me. Then a figure broke from one of the cages behind them. It was the youth whose personality so fascinated me.

He paused a moment before the cages, with upraised sword.

"Come, men of the outer world!" he shouted. "Let us make our deaths worth while, and at the back of this unknown warrior turn this day's Tribute to Issus into an orgy of revenge that will echo through the ages and cause black skins to blanch at each repetition of the rites of Issus. Come! The racks without your cages are filled with blades."

Without waiting to note the outcome of his plea, he turned and bounded toward me. From every cage that harboured red men a thunderous shout went up in answer to his exhortation. The inner guards went down beneath howling mobs, and the cages vomited forth their inmates hot with the lust to kill.

Snatching up his long-sword, I sprang into the arena. The apes were almost upon the maidens, but a couple of mighty bounds were all my earthly muscles required to carry me to the centre of the sand-strewn floor.

The racks that stood without were stripped of the swords with which the prisoners were to have been armed to enter their allotted combats, and a swarm of determined warriors sped to our support.

The great apes, towering in all their fifteen feet of height, had gone down before my sword while the charging guards were still some distance away. Close behind them pursued the youth. At my back were the young girls, and as it was in their service that I fought, I remained standing there to meet my inevitable death, but with the determination to give such an account of myself as would long be remembered in the land of the First Born.

I noted the marvellous speed of the young red man as he raced after the guards. Never had I seen such speed in any Martian. His leaps and bounds were little short of those which my earthly muscles had produced to create such awe and respect on the part of the green Martians into whose hands I had fallen on that long-gone day that had seen my first advent upon Mars.

The guards had not reached me when he fell upon them from the rear, and as they turned, thinking from the fierceness of his onslaught that a dozen were attacking them, I rushed them from my side.

In the rapid fighting that followed I had little chance to note aught else than the movements of my immediate adversaries, but now and again I caught a fleeting glimpse of a purring sword and a lightly springing figure of sinewy steel that filled my heart with a strange yearning and a mighty but unaccountable pride.

On the handsome face of the boy a grim smile played, and ever and anon he threw a taunting challenge to the foes that faced him. In this and other ways his manner of fighting was similar to that which had always marked me on the field of combat.

Perhaps it was this vague likeness which made me love the boy, while the awful havoc that his sword played amongst the blacks filled my soul with a tremendous respect for him.

For my part, I was fighting as I had fought a thousand times before— now sidestepping a wicked thrust, now stepping quickly in to let my sword's point drink deep in a foeman's heart, before it buried itself in the throat of his companion.

We were having a merry time of it, we two, when a great body of Issus' own guards were ordered into the arena. On they came with fierce cries, while from every side the armed prisoners swarmed upon them.

For half an hour it was as though all hell had broken loose. In the walled confines of the arena we fought in an inextricable mass—howling, cursing, blood-streaked demons; and ever the sword of the young red man flashed beside me.

Slowly and by repeated commands I had succeeded in drawing the prisoners into a rough formation about us, so that at last we fought formed into a rude circle in the centre of which were the doomed maids.

Many had gone down on both sides, but by far the greater havoc had been wrought in the ranks of the guards of Issus. I could see messengers running swiftly through the audience, and as they passed the nobles there unsheathed their swords and sprang into the arena. They were going to annihilate us by force of numbers—that was quite evidently their plan.

I caught a glimpse of Issus leaning far forward upon her throne, her hideous countenance distorted in a horrid grimace of hate and rage, in which I thought I could distinguish an expression of fear. It was that face that inspired me to the thing that followed.

Quickly I ordered fifty of the prisoners to drop back behind us and form a new circle about the maidens.

"Remain and protect them until I return," I commanded.

Then, turning to those who formed the outer line, I cried, "Down with Issus! Follow me to the throne; we will reap vengeance where vengeance is deserved."

The youth at my side was the first to take up the cry of "Down with Issus!" and then at my back and from all sides rose a hoarse shout, "To the throne! To the throne!"

As one man we moved, an irresistible fighting mass, over the bodies of dead and dying foes toward the gorgeous throne of the Martian deity. Hordes of the doughtiest fighting-men of the First Born poured from the audience to check our progress. We mowed them down before us as they had been paper men.

"To the seats, some of you!" I cried as we approached the arena's barrier wall. "Ten of us can take the throne," for I had seen that Issus' guards had for the most part entered the fray within the arena.

On both sides of me the prisoners broke to left and right for the seats, vaulting the low wall with dripping swords lusting for the crowded victims who awaited them.

In another moment the entire amphitheatre was filled with the shrieks of the dying and the wounded, mingled with the clash of arms and triumphant shouts of the victors.

Side by side the young red man and I, with perhaps a dozen others, fought our way to the foot of the throne. The remaining guards, reinforced by the high dignitaries and nobles of the First Born, closed in between us and Issus, who sat leaning far forward upon her carved sorapus bench, now screaming high-pitched commands to her following, now hurling blighting curses upon those who sought to desecrate her godhood.

The frightened slaves about her trembled in wide-eyed expectancy, knowing not whether to pray for our victory or our defeat. Several among them, proud daughters no doubt of some of Barsoom's noblest warriors, snatched swords from the hands of the fallen and fell upon the guards of Issus, but they were soon cut down; glorious martyrs to a hopeless cause.

The men with us fought well, but never since Tars Tarkas and I fought out that long, hot afternoon shoulder to shoulder against the hordes of Warhoon in the dead sea bottom before Thark, had I seen two men fight to such good purpose and with such unconquerable ferocity as the young red man and I fought that day before the throne of Issus, Goddess of Death, and of Life Eternal.

Man by man those who stood between us and the carven sorapus wood bench went down before our blades. Others swarmed in to fill the breach, but inch by inch, foot by foot we won nearer and nearer to our goal.

Presently a cry went up from a section of the stands near by—"Rise slaves!" "Rise slaves!" it rose and fell until it swelled to a mighty volume of sound that swept in great billows around the entire amphitheatre.

For an instant, as though by common assent, we ceased our fighting to look for the meaning of this new note nor did it take but a moment to translate its significance. In all parts of the structure the female slaves were falling upon their masters with whatever weapon came first to hand. A dagger snatched from the harness of her mistress was waved aloft by some fair slave, its shimmering blade crimson with the lifeblood of its owner; swords plucked from the bodies of the dead about them; heavy ornaments which could be turned into bludgeons—such were the implements with which these fair women wreaked the long-pent vengeance which at best could but partially recompense them for the unspeakable cruelties and indignities which their black masters had heaped upon them. And those who could find no other weapons used their strong fingers and their gleaming teeth.

It was at once a sight to make one shudder and to cheer; but in a brief second we were engaged once more in our own battle with only the unquenchable battle cry of the women to remind us that they still fought—"Rise slaves!" "Rise slaves!"

Only a single thin rank of men now stood between us and Issus. Her face was blue with terror. Foam flecked her lips. She seemed too paralysed with fear to move. Only the youth and I fought now. The others all had fallen, and I was like to have gone down too from a nasty long-sword cut had not a hand reached out from behind my adversary and clutched his elbow as the blade was falling upon me. The youth sprang to my side and ran his sword through the fellow before he could recover to deliver another blow.

I should have died even then but for that as my sword was tight wedged in the breastbone of a Dator of the First Born. As the fellow went down I snatched his sword from him and over his prostrate body looked into the eyes of the one whose quick hand had saved me from the first cut of his sword—it was Phaidor, daughter of Matai Shang.

"Fly, my Prince!" she cried. "It is useless to fight them longer. All within the arena are dead. All who charged the throne are dead but you and this youth. Only among the seats are there left any of your fighting-men, and they and the slave women are fast being cut down. Listen! You can scarce hear the battle-cry of the women now for nearly all are dead. For each one of you there are ten thousand blacks within the domains of the First Born. Break for the open and the sea of Korus. With your mighty sword arm you may yet win to the Golden Cliffs and the templed gardens of the Holy Therns. There tell your story to Matai Shang, my father. He will keep you, and together you may find a way to rescue me. Fly while there is yet a bare chance for flight."

But that was not my mission, nor could I see much to be preferred in the cruel hospitality of the Holy Therns to that of the First Born.

"Down with Issus!" I shouted, and together the boy and I took up the fight once more. Two blacks went down with our swords in their vitals, and we stood face to face with Issus. As my sword went up to end her horrid career her paralysis left her, and with an ear-piercing shriek she turned to flee. Directly behind her a black gulf suddenly yawned in the flooring of the dais. She sprang for the opening with the youth and I close at her heels. Her scattered guard rallied at her cry and rushed for us. A blow fell upon the head of the youth. He staggered and would have fallen, but I caught him in my left arm and turned to face an infuriated mob of religious fanatics crazed by the affront I had put upon their goddess, just as Issus disappeared into the black depths beneath me.

TWELVE

Doomed to Die

For an instant I stood there before they fell upon me, but the first rush of them forced me back a step or two. My foot felt for the floor but found only empty space. I had backed into the pit which had received Issus. For a second I toppled there upon the brink. Then I too with the boy still tightly clutched in my arms pitched backward into the black abyss.

We struck a polished chute, the opening above us closed as magically as it had opened, and we shot down, unharmed, into a dimly lighted apartment far below the arena.

As I rose to my feet the first thing I saw was the malignant countenance of Issus glaring at me through the heavy bars of a grated door at one side of the chamber.

"Rash mortal!" she shrilled. "You shall pay the awful penalty for your blasphemy in this secret cell. Here you shall lie alone and in darkness with the carcass of your accomplice festering in its rottenness by your side, until crazed by loneliness and hunger you feed upon the crawling maggots that were once a man."

That was all. In another instant she was gone, and the dim light which had filled the cell faded into Cimmerian blackness.

"Pleasant old lady," said a voice at my side.

"Who speaks?" I asked.

"'Tis I, your companion, who has had the honour this day of fighting shoulder to shoulder with the greatest warrior that ever wore metal upon Barsoom."

"I thank God that you are not dead," I said. "I feared for that nasty cut upon your head."

"It but stunned me," he replied. "A mere scratch."

"Maybe it were as well had it been final," I said. "We seem to be in a pretty fix here with a splendid chance of dying of starvation and thirst."

"Where are we?"

"Beneath the arena," I replied. "We tumbled down the shaft that swallowed Issus as she was almost at our mercy."

He laughed a low laugh of pleasure and relief, and then reaching out through the inky blackness he sought my shoulder and pulled my ear close to his mouth.

"Nothing could be better," he whispered. "There are secrets within the secrets of Issus of which Issus herself does not dream."

"What do you mean?"

"I laboured with the other slaves a year since in the remodelling of these subterranean galleries, and at that time we found below these an ancient system of corridors and chambers that had been sealed up for ages. The blacks in charge of the work explored them, taking several of us along to do whatever work there might be occasion for. I know the entire system perfectly.

"There are miles of corridors honeycombing the ground beneath the gardens and the temple itself, and there is one passage that leads down to and connects with the lower regions that open on the water shaft that gives passage to Omean.

"If we can reach the submarine undetected we may yet make the sea in which there are many islands where the blacks never go. There we may live for a time, and who knows what may transpire to aid us to escape?"

He had spoken all in a low whisper, evidently fearing spying ears even here, and so I answered him in the same subdued tone.

"Lead back to Shador, my friend," I whispered. "Xodar, the black, is there. We were to attempt our escape together, so I cannot desert him."

"No," said the boy, "one cannot desert a friend. It were better to be recaptured ourselves than that."

Then he commenced groping his way about the floor of the dark chamber searching for the trap that led to the corridors beneath. At length he summoned me by a low, "S-s-t," and I crept toward the sound of his voice to find him kneeling on the brink of an opening in the floor.

"There is a drop here of about ten feet," he whispered. "Hang by your hands and you will alight safely on a level floor of soft sand."

Very quietly I lowered myself from the inky cell above into the inky pit below. So utterly dark was it that we could not see our hands at an inch from our noses. Never, I think, have I known such complete absence of light as existed in the pits of Issus.

For an instant I hung in mid air. There is a strange sensation connected with an experience of that nature which is quite difficult to describe. When the feet tread empty air and the distance below is shrouded in darkness there is a feeling akin to panic at the thought of releasing the hold and taking the plunge into unknown depths.

Although the boy had told me that it was but ten feet to the floor below I experienced the same thrills as though I were hanging above a bottomless pit. Then I released my hold and dropped—four feet to a soft cushion of sand.

The boy followed me.

"Raise me to your shoulders," he said, "and I will replace the trap."

This done he took me by the hand, leading me very slowly, with much feeling about and frequent halts to assure himself that he did not stray into wrong passageways.

Presently we commenced the descent of a very steep incline.

"It will not be long," he said, "before we shall have light. At the lower levels we meet the same strata of phosphorescent rock that illuminates Omean."

Never shall I forget that trip through the pits of Issus. While it was devoid of important incidents yet it was filled for me with a strange charm of excitement and adventure which I think I must have hinged principally on the unguessable antiquity of these long-forgotten corridors. The things which the Stygian darkness hid from my objective eye could not have been half so wonderful as the pictures which my imagination wrought as it conjured to life again the ancient peoples of this dying world and set them once more to the labours, the intrigues, the mysteries and the cruelties which they had practised to make their last stand against the swarming hordes of the dead sea bottoms that had driven them step by step to the uttermost pinnacle of the world where they were now intrenched behind an impenetrable barrier of superstition.

In addition to the green men there had been three principal races upon Barsoom. The blacks, the whites, and a race of yellow men. As the waters of the planet dried and the seas receded, all other resources dwindled until life upon the planet became a constant battle for survival.

The various races had made war upon one another for ages, and the three higher types had easily bested the green savages of the water places of the world, but now that the receding seas necessitated constant abandonment of their fortified cities and forced upon them a more or less nomadic life in which they became separated into smaller communities they soon fell prey to the fierce hordes of green men. The result was a partial amalgamation of the blacks, whites and yellows, the result of which is shown in the present splendid race of red men.

I had always supposed that all traces of the original races had disappeared from the face of Mars, yet within the past four days I had found both whites and blacks in great multitudes. Could it be possible that in some far-off corner of the planet there still existed a remnant of the ancient race of yellow men?

My reveries were broken in upon by a low exclamation from the boy.

"At last, the lighted way," he cried, and looking up I beheld at a long distance before us a dim radiance.

As we advanced the light increased until presently we emerged into well-lighted passageways. From then on our progress was rapid until we came suddenly to the end of a corridor that let directly upon the ledge surrounding the pool of the submarine.

The craft lay at her moorings with uncovered hatch. Raising his finger to his lips and then tapping his sword in a significant manner, the youth crept noiselessly toward the vessel. I was close at his heels.

Silently we dropped to the deserted deck, and on hands and knees crawled toward the hatchway. A stealthy glance below revealed no guard in sight, and so with the quickness and the soundlessness of cats we dropped together into the main cabin of the submarine. Even here was no sign of life. Quickly we covered and secured the hatch.

Then the boy stepped into the pilot house, touched a button and the boat sank amid swirling waters toward the bottom of the shaft. Even then there was no scurrying of feet as we had expected, and while the boy remained to direct the boat I slid from cabin to cabin in futile search for some member of the crew. The craft was entirely deserted. Such good fortune seemed almost unbelievable.

When I returned to the pilot house to report the good news to my companion he handed me a paper.

"This may explain the absence of the crew," he said.

It was a radio-aerial message to the commander of the submarine:

"The slaves have risen. Come with what men you have and those that you can gather on the way. Too late to get aid from Omean. They are massacring all within the amphitheatre. Issus is threatened. Haste.

"ZITHAD"

"Zithad is Dator of the guards of Issus," explained the youth. "We gave them a bad scare—one that they will not soon forget."

"Let us hope that it is but the beginning of the end of Issus," I said.

"Only our first ancestor knows," he replied.

We reached the submarine pool in Omean without incident. Here we debated the wisdom of sinking the craft before leaving her, but finally

UNDER THE MOONS OF MARS

decided that it would add nothing to our chances for escape. There were plenty of blacks on Omean to thwart us were we apprehended; however many more might come from the temples and gardens of Issus would not in any way decrease our chances.

We were now in a quandary as to how to pass the guards who patrolled the island about the pool. At last I hit upon a plan.

"What is the name or title of the officer in charge of these guards?" I asked the boy.

"A fellow named Torith was on duty when we entered this morning," he replied.

"Good. And what is the name of the commander of the submarine?"

"Yersted."

I found a dispatch blank in the cabin and wrote the following order:

"Dator Torith: Return these two slaves at once to Shador.

"YERSTED"

That will be the simpler way to return," I said, smiling, as I handed the forged order to the boy. "Come, we shall see now how well it works."

"But our swords!" he exclaimed. "What shall we say to explain them?"

"Since we cannot explain them we shall have to leave them behind us," I replied.

"Is it not the extreme of rashness to thus put ourselves again, unarmed, in the power of the First Born?"

"It is the only way," I answered. "You may trust me to find a way out of the prison of Shador, and I think, once out, that we shall find no great difficulty in arming ourselves once more in a country which abounds so plentifully in armed men."

"As you say," he replied with a smile and shrug. "I could not follow another leader who inspired greater confidence than you. Come, let us put your ruse to the test."

Boldly we emerged from the hatchway of the craft, leaving our swords behind us, and strode to the main exit which led to the sentry's post and the office of the Dator of the guard.

At sight of us the members of the guard sprang forward in surprise, and with levelled rifles halted us. I held out the message to one of them. He took it and seeing to whom it was addressed turned and handed it to Torith who was emerging from his office to learn the cause of the commotion.

The black read the order, and for a moment eyed us with evident suspicion.

"Where is Dator Yersted?" he asked, and my heart sank within me, as I cursed myself for a stupid fool in not having sunk the submarine to make good the lie that I must tell.

"His orders were to return immediately to the temple landing," I replied.

Torith took a half step toward the entrance to the pool as though to corroborate my story. For that instant everything hung in the balance, for had he done so and found the empty submarine still lying at her wharf the whole weak fabric of my concoction would have tumbled about our heads; but evidently he decided the message must be genuine, nor indeed was there any good reason to doubt it since it would scarce have seemed credible to him that two slaves would voluntarily have given themselves into custody in any such manner as this. It was the very boldness of the plan which rendered it successful.

"Were you connected with the rising of the slaves?" asked Torith. "We have just had meagre reports of some such event."

"All were involved," I replied. "But it amounted to little. The guards quickly overcame and killed the majority of us."

He seemed satisfied with this reply. "Take them to Shador," he ordered, turning to one of his subordinates. We entered a small boat lying beside the island, and in a few minutes were disembarking upon Shador. Here we were returned to our respective cells; I with Xodar, the boy by himself; and behind locked doors we were again prisoners of the First Born.

THIRTEEN

A Break for Liberty

Xodar listened in incredulous astonishment to my narration of the events which had transpired within the arena at the rites of Issus. He could scarce conceive, even though he had already professed his doubt as to the deity of Issus, that one could threaten her with sword in hand and not be blasted into a thousand fragments by the mere fury of her divine wrath.

"It is the final proof," he said, at last. "No more is needed to completely shatter the last remnant of my superstitious belief in the divinity of Issus. She is only a wicked old woman, wielding a mighty power for evil through machinations that have kept her own people and all Barsoom in religious ignorance for ages."

"She is still all-powerful here, however," I replied. "So it behooves us to leave at the first moment that appears at all propitious."

"I hope that you may find a propitious moment," he said, with a laugh, "for it is certain that in all my life I have never seen one in which a prisoner of the First Born might escape."

"To-night will do as well as any," I replied.

"It will soon be night," said Xodar. "How may I aid in the adventure?"

"Can you swim?" I asked him.

"No slimy silian that haunts the depths of Korus is more at home in water than is Xodar," he replied.

"Good. The red one in all probability cannot swim," I said, "since there is scarce enough water in all their domains to float the tiniest craft. One of us therefore will have to support him through the sea to the craft we select. I had hoped that we might make the entire distance below the surface, but I fear that the red youth could not thus perform the trip. Even the bravest of the brave among them are terrorized at the mere thought of deep water, for it has been ages since their forebears saw a lake, a river or a sea."

"The red one is to accompany us?" asked Xodar.

"Yes."

"It is well. Three swords are better than two. Especially when the third is as mighty as this fellow's. I have seen him battle in the arena at the rites of Issus many times. Never, until I saw you fight, had I seen one who seemed unconquerable even in the face of great odds. One might think you two master and pupil, or father and son. Come to recall his face there is a resemblance between you. It is very marked when you fight—there is the same grim smile, the same maddening contempt for your adversary apparent in every movement of your bodies and in every changing expression of your faces."

"Be that as it may, Xodar, he is a great fighter. I think that we will make a trio difficult to overcome, and if my friend Tars Tarkas, Jeddak of Thark, were but one of us we could fight our way from one end of Barsoom to the other even though the whole world were pitted against us."

"It will be," said Xodar, "when they find from whence you have come. That is but one of the superstitions which Issus has foisted upon a credulous humanity. She works through the Holy Therns who are as ignorant of her real self as are the Barsoomians of the outer world. Her decrees are borne to the therns written in blood upon a strange parchment. The poor deluded fools think that they are receiving the revelations of a goddess through some supernatural agency, since they find these messages upon their guarded altars to which none could have access without detection. I myself have borne these messages for Issus for many years. There is a long tunnel from the temple of Issus to the principal temple of Matai Shang. It was dug ages ago by the slaves of the First Born in such utter secrecy that no thern ever guessed its existence.

"The therns for their part have temples dotted about the entire civilized world. Here priests whom the people never see communicate the doctrine of the Mysterious River Iss, the Valley Dor, and the Lost Sea of Korus to persuade the poor deluded creatures to take the voluntary pilgrimage that swells the wealth of the Holy Therns and adds to the numbers of their slaves.

"Thus the therns are used as the principal means for collecting the wealth and labour that the First Born wrest from them as they need it. Occasionally the First Born themselves make raids upon the outer world. It is then that they capture many females of the royal houses of the red men, and take the newest in battleships and the trained artisans who build them, that they may copy what they cannot create.

"We are a non-productive race, priding ourselves upon our non-productiveness. It is criminal for a First Born to labour or invent. That is the work of the lower orders, who live merely that the First Born may enjoy long lives of luxury and idleness. With us fighting is all that counts; were it not for that there would be more of the First Born than all the creatures of Barsoom could support, for in so far as I know none of us ever dies a natural death. Our females would live for ever but for the fact that we tire of them and remove them to make place for others. Issus alone of all is protected against death. She has lived for countless ages."

"Would not the other Barsoomians live for ever but for the doctrine of the voluntary pilgrimage which drags them to the bosom of Iss at or before their thousandth year?" I asked him.

"I feel now that there is no doubt but that they are precisely the same species of creature as the First Born, and I hope that I shall live to fight for them in atonement of the sins I have committed against them through the ignorance born of generations of false teaching."

As he ceased speaking a weird call rang out across the waters of Omean. I had heard it at the same time the previous evening and knew that it marked the ending of the day, when the men of Omean spread their silks upon the deck of battleship and cruiser and fall into the dreamless sleep of Mars.

Our guard entered to inspect us for the last time before the new day broke upon the world above. His duty was soon performed and the heavy door of our prison closed behind him —we were alone for the night.

I gave him time to return to his quarters, as Xodar said he probably would do, then I sprang to the grated window and surveyed the nearby waters. At a little distance from the island, a quarter of a mile perhaps, lay a monster battleship, while between her and the shore were a number of smaller cruisers and one-man scouts. Upon the battleship alone was there a watch. I could see him plainly in the upper works of the ship, and as I watched I saw him spread his sleeping silks upon the tiny platform in which he was stationed. Soon he threw himself at full length upon his couch. The discipline on Omean was lax indeed. But it is not to be wondered at since no enemy guessed the existence upon Barsoom of such a fleet, or even of the First Born, or the Sea of Omean. Why indeed should they maintain a watch?

Presently I dropped to the floor again and talked with Xodar, describing the various craft I had seen.

"There is one there," he said, "my personal property, built to carry five men, that is the swiftest of the swift. If we can board her we can at least make a memorable run for liberty," and then he went on to describe to me the equipment of the boat; her engines, and all that went to make her the flier that she was.

In his explanation I recognized a trick of gearing that Kantos Kan had taught me that time we sailed under false names in the navy of Zodanga beneath Sab Than, the Prince. And I knew then that the First Born had stolen it from the ships of Helium, for only they are thus geared. And I knew too that Xodar spoke the truth when he lauded the speed of his little craft, for nothing that cleaves the thin air of Mars can approximate the speed of the ships of Helium.

We decided to wait for an hour at least until all the stragglers had sought their silks. In the meantime I was to fetch the red youth to our cell so that we would be in readiness to make our rash break for freedom together.

I sprang to the top of our partition wall and pulled myself up on to it. There I found a flat surface about a foot in width and along this I walked until I came to the cell in which I saw the boy sitting upon his bench. He had been leaning back against the wall looking up at the glowing dome above Omean, and when he spied me balancing upon the partition wall above him his eyes opened wide in astonishment. Then a wide grin of appreciative understanding spread across his countenance.

As I stooped to drop to the floor beside him he motioned me to wait, and coming close below me whispered: "Catch my hand; I can almost leap to the top of that wall myself. I have tried it many times, and each day I come a little closer. Some day I should have been able to make it."

I lay upon my belly across the wall and reached my hand far down toward him. With a little run from the centre of the cell he sprang up until I grasped his outstretched hand, and thus I pulled him to the wall's top beside me.

"You are the first jumper I ever saw among the red men of Barsoom," I said.

He smiled. "It is not strange. I will tell you why when we have more time."

Together we returned to the cell in which Xodar sat; descending to talk with him until the hour had passed.

There we made our plans for the immediate future, binding ourselves by a solemn oath to fight to the death for one another against whatsoever enemies should confront us, for we knew that even should we succeed in escaping the First Born we might still have a whole world against us—the power of religious superstition is mighty.

It was agreed that I should navigate the craft after we had reached her, and that if we made the outer world in safety we should attempt to reach Helium without a stop.

"Why Helium?" asked the red youth.

"I am a prince of Helium," I replied.

He gave me a peculiar look, but said nothing further on the subject. I wondered at the time what the significance of his expression might be, but in the press of other matters it soon left my mind, nor did I have occasion to think of it again until later.

"Come," I said at length, "now is as good a time as any. Let us go."

Another moment found me at the top of the partition wall again with the boy beside me. Unbuckling my harness I snapped it together with a single long strap which I lowered to the waiting Xodar below. He grasped the end and was soon sitting beside us.

"How simple," he laughed.

"The balance should be even simpler," I replied. Then I raised myself to the top of the outer wall of the prison, just so that I could peer over and locate the passing sentry. For a matter of five minutes I waited and then he came in sight on his slow and snail-like beat about the structure.

I watched him until he had made the turn at the end of the building which carried him out of sight of the side of the prison that was to witness our dash for freedom. The moment his form disappeared I grasped Xodar and drew him to the top of the wall. Placing one end of my harness strap in his hands I lowered him quickly to the ground below. Then the boy grasped the strap and slid down to Xodar's side.

In accordance with our arrangement they did not wait for me, but walked slowly toward the water, a matter of a hundred yards, directly past the guard-house filled with sleeping soldiers.

They had taken scarce a dozen steps when I too dropped to the ground and followed them leisurely toward the shore. As I passed the guard-house the thought of all the good blades lying there gave me pause, for if ever men were to have need of swords it was my companions and I on the perilous trip upon which we were about to embark.

I glanced toward Xodar and the youth and saw that they had slipped over the edge of the dock into the water. In accordance with our plan they were to remain there clinging to the metal rings which studded the concrete-like substance of the dock at the water's level, with only their mouths and noses above the surface of the sea, until I should join them.

The lure of the swords within the guard-house was strong upon me, and I hesitated a moment, half inclined to risk the attempt to take the few we needed. That he who hesitates is lost proved itself a true aphorism in this instance, for another moment saw me creeping stealthily toward the door of the guard-house.

Gently I pressed it open a crack; enough to discover a dozen blacks stretched upon their silks in profound slumber. At the far side of the room a rack held the swords and firearms of the men. Warily I pushed the door a trifle wider to admit my body. A hinge gave out a resentful groan. One of the men stirred, and my heart stood still. I cursed myself for a fool to have thus jeopardized our chances for escape; but there was nothing for it now but to see the adventure through.

With a spring as swift and as noiseless as a tiger's I lit beside the guardsman who had moved. My hands hovered about his throat awaiting the moment that his eyes should open. For what seemed an eternity to my overwrought nerves I remained poised thus. Then the fellow turned again upon his side and resumed the even respiration of deep slumber.

Carefully I picked my way between and over the soldiers until I had gained the rack at the far side of the room. Here I turned to survey the sleeping men. All were quiet. Their regular breathing rose and fell in a soothing rhythm that seemed to me the sweetest music I ever had heard.

Gingerly I drew a long-sword from the rack. The scraping of the scabbard against its holder as I withdrew it sounded like the filing of cast iron with a great rasp, and I looked to see the room immediately filled with alarmed and attacking guardsmen. But none stirred.

The second sword I withdrew noiselessly, but the third clanked in its scabbard with a frightful din. I knew that it must awaken some of the men at least, and was on the point of forestalling their attack by a rapid charge for the doorway, when again, to my intense surprise, not a black moved. Either they were wondrous heavy sleepers or else the noises that I made were really much less than they seemed to me.

I was about to leave the rack when my attention was attracted by the revolvers. I knew that I could not carry more than one away with me, for I was already too heavily laden to move quietly with any degree of safety or speed. As I took one of them from its pin my eye fell for the first time on an open window beside the rack. Ah, here was a splendid means of escape, for it let directly upon the dock, not twenty feet from the water's edge.

And as I congratulated myself, I heard the door opposite me open, and there looking me full in the face stood the officer of the guard. He evidently took in the situation at a glance and appreciated the gravity of it as quickly as I, for our revolvers came up simultaneously and the sounds of the two reports were as one as we touched the buttons on the grips that exploded the cartridges.

I felt the wind of his bullet as it whizzed past my ear, and at the same instant I saw him crumple to the ground. Where I hit him I do not know, nor if I killed him, for scarce had he started to collapse when I was through the window at my rear. In another second the waters of Omean closed above my head, and the three of us were making for the little flier a hundred yards away.

Xodar was burdened with the boy, and I with the three long-swords. The revolver I had dropped, so that while we were both strong swimmers it seemed to me that we moved at a snail's pace through the water. I was swimming entirely beneath the surface, but Xodar was compelled to rise often to let the youth breathe, so it was a wonder that we were not discovered long before we were.

In fact we reached the boat's side and were all aboard before the watch upon the battleship, aroused by the shots, detected us. Then an alarm gun bellowed from a ship's bow, its deep boom reverberating in deafening tones beneath the rocky dome of Omean.

Instantly the sleeping thousands were awake. The decks of a thousand monster craft teemed with fighting-men, for an alarm on Omean was a thing of rare occurrence.

We cast away before the sound of the first gun had died, and another second saw us rising swiftly from the surface of the sea. I lay at full length along the deck with the levers and buttons of control before me. Xodar and the boy were stretched directly behind me, prone also that we might offer as little resistance to the air as possible.

"Rise high," whispered Xodar. "They dare not fire their heavy guns toward the dome—the fragments of the shells would drop back among their own craft. If we are high enough our keel plates will protect us from rifle fire."

I did as he bade. Below us we could see the men leaping into the water by hundreds, and striking out for the small cruisers and one-man fliers that lay moored about the big ships. The larger craft were getting under way, following us rapidly, but not rising from the water.

"A little to your right," cried Xodar, for there are no points of compass upon Omean where every direction is due north.

The pandemonium that had broken out below us was deafening. Rifles cracked, officers shouted orders, men yelled directions to one another from the water and from the decks of myriad boats, while through all ran the purr of countless propellers cutting water and air.

I had not dared pull my speed lever to the highest for fear of overrunning the mouth of the shaft that passed from Omean's dome to the world above, but even so we were hitting a clip that I doubt has ever been equalled on the windless sea.

The smaller fliers were commencing to rise toward us when Xodar shouted: "The shaft! The shaft! Dead ahead," and I saw the opening, black and yawning in the glowing dome of this underworld.

A ten-man cruiser was rising directly in front to cut off our escape. It was the only vessel that stood in our way, but at the rate that it was traveling it would come between us and the shaft in plenty of time to thwart our plans.

It was rising at an angle of about forty-five degrees dead ahead of us, with the evident intention of combing us with grappling hooks from above as it skimmed low over our deck. There was but one forlorn hope for us, and I took it.

It was useless to try to pass over her, for that would have allowed her to force us against the rocky dome above, and we were already too near that as it was. To have attempted to dive below her would have put us entirely at her mercy, and precisely where she wanted us. On either side a hundred other menacing craft were hastening toward us. The alternative was filled with risk—in fact it was all risk, with but a slender chance of success.

As we neared the cruiser I rose as though to pass above her, so that she would do just what she did do, rise at a steeper angle to force me still higher. Then as we were almost upon her I yelled to my companions to hold tight, and throwing the little vessel into her highest speed I deflected her bows at the same instant until we were running horizontally and at terrific velocity straight for the cruiser's keel.

Her commander may have seen my intentions then, but it was too late. Almost at the instant of impact I turned my bows upward, and then with a shattering jolt we were in collision. What I had hoped for happened. The cruiser, already tilted at a perilous angle, was carried completely over backward by the impact of my smaller vessel. Her crew fell twisting and screaming through the air to the water far below, while the cruiser, her propellers still madly churning, dived swiftly headforemost after them to the bottom of the Sea of Omean.

The collision crushed our steel bows, and notwithstanding every effort on our part came near to hurling us from the deck. As it was we landed in a wildly clutching heap at the very extremity of the flier, where Xodar and I succeeded in grasping the hand-rail, but the boy would have plunged overboard had I not fortunately grasped his ankle as he was already partially over.

Unguided, our vessel careened wildly in its mad flight, rising ever nearer the rocks above. It took but an instant, however, for me to regain the levers, and with the roof barely fifty feet above I turned her nose once more into the horizontal plane and headed her again for the black mouth of the shaft.

The collision had retarded our progress and now a hundred swift scouts were close upon us. Xodar had told me that ascending the shaft by virtue of our repulsive rays alone would give our enemies their best chance to overtake us, since our propellers would be idle and in rising we would be outclassed by many of our pursuers. The swifter craft are seldom equipped with large buoyancy tanks, since the added bulk of them tends to reduce a vessel's speed.

As many boats were now quite close to us it was inevitable that we would be quickly overhauled in the shaft, and captured or killed in short order.

To me there always seems a way to gain the opposite side of an obstacle. If one cannot pass over it, or below it, or around it, why then there is but a single alternative left, and that is to pass through it. I could not get around the fact that many of these other boats could rise faster than ours by the fact of their greater buoyancy, but I was none the less determined to reach the outer world far in advance of them or die a death of my own choosing in event of failure.

"Reverse!" screamed Xodar, behind me. "For the love of your first ancestor, reverse. We are at the shaft."

"Hold tight!" I screamed in reply. "Grasp the boy and hold tight—we are going straight up the shaft."

The words were scarce out of my mouth as we swept beneath the pitch-black opening. I threw the bow hard up, dragged the speed lever to its last notch, and clutching a stanchion with one hand and the steering-wheel with the other hung on like grim death and consigned my soul to its author.

I heard a little exclamation of surprise from Xodar, followed by a grim laugh. The boy laughed too and said something which I could not catch for the whistling of the wind of our awful speed.

I looked above my head, hoping to catch the gleam of stars by which I could direct our course and hold the hurtling thing that bore us true to the centre of the shaft. To have touched the side at the speed we were making would doubtless have resulted in instant death for us all. But not a star showed above—only utter and impenetrable darkness.

Then I glanced below me, and there I saw a rapidly diminishing circle of light—the mouth of the opening above the phosphorescent radiance of Omean. By this I steered, endeavouring to keep the circle of light below me ever perfect. At best it was but a slender cord that held us from destruction, and I think that I steered that night more by intuition and blind faith than by skill or reason.

We were not long in the shaft, and possibly the very fact of our enormous speed saved us, for evidently we started in the right direction and so quickly were we out again that we had no time to alter our course. Omean lies perhaps two miles below the surface crust of Mars. Our speed must have approximated two hundred miles an hour, for Martian fliers are swift, so that at most we were in the shaft not over forty seconds.

We must have been out of it for some seconds before I realised that we had accomplished the impossible. Black darkness enshrouded all about us. There were neither moons nor stars. Never before had I seen such a thing upon Mars, and for the moment I was nonplussed. Then the explanation came to me. It was summer at the south pole. The ice cap was melting and those meteoric phenomena, clouds, unknown upon the greater part of Barsoom, were shutting out the light of heaven from this portion of the planet.

Fortunate indeed it was for us, nor did it take me long to grasp the opportunity for escape which this happy condition offered us. Keeping the boat's nose at a stiff angle I raced her for the impenetrable curtain which Nature had hung above this dying world to shut us out from the sight of our pursuing enemies.

We plunged through the cold camp fog without diminishing our speed, and in a moment emerged into the glorious light of the two moons and the million stars. I dropped into a horizontal course and headed due north. Our enemies were a good half-hour behind us with no conception of our direction. We had performed the miraculous and come through a thousand dangers unscathed—we had escaped from the land of the First Born. No other prisoners in all the ages of Barsoom had done this thing, and now as I looked back upon it it did not seem to have been so difficult after all.

I said as much to Xodar, over my shoulder.

"It is very wonderful, nevertheless," he replied. "No one else could have accomplished it but John Carter."

At the sound of that name the boy jumped to his feet.

"John Carter!" he cried. "John Carter! Why, man, John Carter, Prince of Helium, has been dead for years. I am his son."

FOURTEEN

The Eyes in the Dark

My son! I could not believe my ears. Slowly I rose and faced the handsome youth. Now that I looked at him closely I commenced to see why his face and personality had attracted me so strongly. There was much of his mother's incomparable beauty in his clear-cut features, but it was strongly masculine beauty, and his grey eyes and the expression of them were mine.

The boy stood facing me, half hope and half uncertainty in his look.

"Tell me of your mother," I said. "Tell me all you can of the years that I have been robbed by a relentless fate of her dear companionship."

With a cry of pleasure he sprang toward me and threw his arms about my neck, and for a brief moment as I held my boy close to me the tears welled to my eyes and I was like to have choked after the manner of some maudlin fool—but I do not regret it, nor am I ashamed. A long life has taught me that a man may seem weak where women and children are concerned and yet be anything but a weakling in the sterner avenues of life.

"Your stature, your manner, the terrible ferocity of your swordsmanship," said the boy, "are as my mother has described them to me a thousand times—but even with such evidence I could scarce credit the truth of what seemed so improbable to me, however much I desired it to be true. Do you know what thing it was that convinced me more than all the others?"

"What, my boy?" I asked.

"Your first words to me—they were of my mother. None else but the man who loved her as she has told me my father did would have thought first of her."

"For long years, my son, I can scarce recall a moment that the radiant vision of your mother's face has not been ever before me. Tell me of her."

"Those who have known her longest say that she has not changed, unless it be to grow more beautiful—were that possible. Only, when she thinks I am not about to see her, her face grows very sad, and, oh, so wistful. She thinks ever of you, my father, and all Helium mourns with her and for her. Her grandfather's people love her. They loved you also, and fairly worship your memory as the saviour of Barsoom.

"Each year that brings its anniversary of the day that saw you racing across a near dead world to unlock the secret of that awful portal behind which lay the mighty power of life for countless millions a great festival is held in your honour; but there are tears mingled with the thanksgiving— tears of real regret that the author of the happiness is not with them to share the joy of living he died to give them. Upon all Barsoom there is no greater name than John Carter."

"And by what name has your mother called you, my boy?" I asked.

"The people of Helium asked that I be named with my father's name, but my mother said no, that you and she had chosen a name for me together, and that your wish must be honoured before all others, so the name that she called me is the one that you desired, a combination of hers and yours— Carthoris."

Xodar had been at the wheel as I talked with my son, and now he called me.

"She is dropping badly by the head, John Carter," he said. "So long as we were rising at a stiff angle it was not noticeable, but now that I am trying to keep a horizontal course it is different. The wound in her bow has opened one of her forward ray tanks."

It was true, and after I had examined the damage I found it a much graver matter than I had anticipated. Not only was the forced angle at which we were compelled to maintain the bow in order to keep a horizontal course greatly impeding our speed, but at the rate that we were losing our repulsive rays from the forward tanks it was but a question of an hour or more when we would be floating stern up and helpless.

We had slightly reduced our speed with the dawning of a sense of security, but now I took the helm once more and pulled the noble little engine wide open, so that again we raced north at terrific velocity. In the meantime Carthoris and Xodar with tools in hand were puttering with the great rent in the bow in a hopeless endeavour to stem the tide of escaping rays.

It was still dark when we passed the northern boundary of the ice cap and the area of clouds. Below us lay a typical Martian landscape. Rolling ochre sea bottom of long dead seas, low surrounding hills, with here and there the grim and silent cities of the dead past; great piles of mighty architecture tenanted only by age-old memories of a once powerful race, and by the great white apes of Barsoom.

It was becoming more and more difficult to maintain our little vessel in a horizontal position. Lower and lower sagged the bow until it became necessary to stop the engine to prevent our flight terminating in a swift dive to the ground.

As the sun rose and the light of a new day swept away the darkness of night our craft gave a final spasmodic plunge, turned half upon her side, and then with deck tilting at a sickening angle swung in a slow circle, her bow dropping further below her stern each moment.

To hand-rail and stanchion we clung, and finally as we saw the end approaching, snapped the buckles of our harness to the rings at her sides. In another moment the deck reared at an angle of ninety degrees and we hung in our leather with feet dangling a thousand yards above the ground.

I was swinging quite close to the controlling devices, so I reached out to the lever that directed the rays of repulsion. The boat responded to the touch, and very gently we began to sink toward the ground.

It was fully half an hour before we touched. Directly north of us rose a rather lofty range of hills, toward which we decided to make our way, since they afforded greater opportunity for concealment from the pursuers we were confident might stumble in this direction.

An hour later found us in the time-rounded gullies of the hills, amid the beautiful flowering plants that abound in the arid waste places of Barsoom. There we found numbers of huge milk-giving shrubs—that strange plant which serves in great part as food and drink for the wild hordes of green men. It was indeed a boon to us, for we all were nearly famished.

Beneath a cluster of these which afforded perfect concealment from wandering air scouts, we lay down to sleep—for me the first time in many hours. This was the beginning of my fifth day upon Barsoom since I had found myself suddenly translated from my cottage on the Hudson to Dor, the valley beautiful, the valley hideous. In all this time I had slept but twice, though once the clock around within the storehouse of the therns.

It was mid-afternoon when I was awakened by some one seizing my hand and covering it with kisses. With a start I opened my eyes to look into the beautiful face of Thuvia.

"My Prince! My Prince!" she cried, in an ecstasy of happiness. " 'Tis you whom I had mourned as dead. My ancestors have been good to me; I have not lived in vain."

The girl's voice awoke Xodar and Carthoris. The boy gazed upon the woman in surprise, but she did not seem to realize the presence of another than I. She would have thrown her arms about my neck and smothered me with caresses, had I not gently but firmly disengaged myself.

"Come, come, Thuvia," I said soothingly; "you are overwrought by the danger and hardships you have passed through. You forget yourself, as you forget that I am the husband of the Princess of Helium."

"I forget nothing, my Prince," she replied. "You have spoken no word of love to me, nor do I expect that you ever shall; but nothing can prevent me loving you. I would not take the place of Dejah Thoris. My greatest ambition is to serve you, my Prince, for ever as your slave. No greater boon could I ask, no greater honour could I crave, no greater happiness could I hope."

As I have before said, I am no ladies' man, and I must admit that I seldom have felt so uncomfortable and embarrassed as I did that moment. While I was quite familiar with the Martian custom which allows female slaves to Martian men, whose high and chivalrous honour is always ample protection for every woman in his household, yet I had never myself chosen other than men as my body servants.

"And I ever return to Helium, Thuvia," I said, "you shall go with me, but as an honoured equal, and not as a slave. There you shall find plenty of handsome young nobles who would face Issus herself to win a smile from you, and we shall have you married in short order to one of the best of them. Forget your foolish gratitude-begotten infatuation, which your innocence has mistaken for love. I like your friendship better, Thuvia."

"You are my master; it shall be as you say," she replied simply, but there was a note of sadness in her voice.

"How came you here, Thuvia?" I asked. "And where is Tars Tarkas?"

"The great Thark, I fear, is dead," she replied sadly. "He was a mighty fighter, but a multitude of green warriors of another horde than his over-whelmed him. The last that I saw of him they were bearing him, wounded and bleeding, to the deserted city from which they had sallied to attack us."

"You are not sure that he is dead, then?" I asked. "And where is this city of which you speak?"

"It is just beyond this range of hills. The vessel in which you so nobly resigned a place that we might find escape defied our small skill in naviga-tion, with the result that we drifted aimlessly about for two days. Then we decided to abandon the craft and attempt to make our way on foot to the nearest waterway. Yesterday we crossed these hills and came upon the dead city beyond. We had passed within its streets and were walking toward the central portion, when at an intersecting avenue we saw a body of green warriors approaching.

"Tars Tarkas was in advance, and they saw him, but me they did not see. The Thark sprang back to my side and forced me into an adjacent doorway, where he told me to remain in hiding until I could escape, making my way to Helium if possible.

" 'There will be no escape for me now,' he said, 'for these be the Warhoon of the South. When they have seen my metal it will be to the death.'

"Then he stepped out to meet them. Ah, my Prince, such fighting! For an hour they swarmed about him, until the Warhoon dead formed a hill where he had stood; but at last they overwhelmed him, those behind pushing the foremost upon him until there remained no space to swing his great sword. Then he stumbled and went down and they rolled over him like a huge wave. When they carried him away toward the heart of the city, he was dead, I think, for I did not see him move."

"Before we go farther we must be sure," I said. "I cannot leave Tars Tarkas alive among the Warhoons. To-night I shall enter the city and make sure."

"And I shall go with you," spoke Carthoris.

"And I," said Xodar.

"Neither one of you shall go," I replied. "It is work that requires stealth and strategy, not force. One man alone may succeed where more would invite disaster. I shall go alone. If I need your help, I will return for you."

They did not like it, but both were good soldiers, and it had been agreed that I should command. The sun already was low, so that I did not have long to wait before the sudden darkness of Barsoom engulfed us.

With a parting word of instructions to Carthoris and Xodar, in case I should not return, I bade them all farewell and set forth at a rapid dogtrot toward the city.

As I emerged from the hills the nearer moon was winging its wild flight through the heavens, its bright beams turning to burnished silver the barbaric splendour of the ancient metropolis. The city had been built upon the gently rolling foothills that in the dim and distant past had sloped down to meet the sea. It was due to this fact that I had no difficulty in entering the streets unobserved.

The green hordes that use these deserted cities seldom occupy more than a few squares about the central plaza, and as they come and go always across the dead sea bottoms that the cities face, it is usually a matter of comparative ease to enter from the hillside.

Once within the streets, I kept close in the dense shadows of the walls. At intersections I halted a moment to make sure that none was in sight before I sprang quickly to the shadows of the opposite side. Thus I made the journey to the vicinity of the plaza without detection. As I approached the purlieus of the inhabited portion of the city I was made aware of the proximity of the warriors' quarters by the squealing and grunting of the thoats and zitidars corralled within the hollow courtyards formed by the buildings surrounding each square.

These old familiar sounds that are so distinctive of green Martian life sent a thrill of pleasure surging through me. It was as one might feel on coming home after a long absence. It was amid such sounds that I had first courted the incomparable Dejah Thoris in the age-old marble halls of the dead city of Korad.

As I stood in the shadows at the far corner of the first square which housed members of the horde, I saw warriors emerging from several of the buildings. They all went in the same direction, toward a great building which stood in the centre of the plaza. My knowledge of green Martian customs convinced me that this was either the quarters of the principal chieftain or contained the audience chamber wherein the Jeddak met his jeds and lesser chieftains. In either event, it was evident that something was afoot which might have a bearing on the recent capture of Tars Tarkas.

To reach this building, which I now felt it imperative that I do, I must needs traverse the entire length of one square and cross a broad avenue and a portion of the plaza. From the noises of the animals which came from every courtyard about me, I knew that there were many people in the surrounding buildings—probably several communities of the great horde of the Warhoons of the South.

To pass undetected among all these people was in itself a difficult task, but if I was to find and rescue the great Thark I must expect even more formidable obstacles before success could be mine. I had entered the city from the south and now stood on the corner of the avenue through which I had passed and the first intersecting avenue south of the plaza. The buildings upon the south side of this square did not appear to be inhabited, as I could see no lights, and so I decided to gain the inner courtyard through one of them.

Nothing occurred to interrupt my progress through the deserted pile I chose, and I came into the inner court close to the rear walls of the east buildings without detection. Within the court a great herd of thoats and zitidars moved restlessly about, cropping the moss-like ochre vegetation which overgrows practically the entire uncultivated area of Mars. What breeze there was came from the north-west, so there was little danger that the beasts would scent me. Had they, their squealing and grunting would have grown to such a volume as to attract the attention of the warriors within the buildings.

Close to the east wall, beneath the overhanging balconies of the second floors, I crept in dense shadows the full length of the courtyard, until I came to the buildings at the north end. These were lighted for about three floors up, but above the third floor all was dark.

To pass through the lighted rooms was, of course, out of the question, since they swarmed with green Martian men and women. My only path lay through the upper floors, and to gain these it was necessary to scale the face of the wall. The reaching of the balcony of the second floor was a matter of easy accomplishment—an agile leap gave my hands a grasp upon the stone hand-rail above. In another instant I had drawn myself upon the balcony.

Here through the open windows I saw the green folk squatting upon their sleeping silks and furs, grunting an occasional monosyllable, which, in connection with their wondrous telepathic powers, is ample for their conversational requirements. As I drew closer to listen to their words a warrior entered the room from the hall beyond.

"Come, Tan Gama," he cried, "we are to take the Thark before Kab Kadja. Bring another with you."

The warrior addressed arose and, beckoning to a fellow squatting near, the three turned and left the apartment.

If I could but follow them the chance might come to free Tars Tarkas at once. At least I would learn the location of his prison.

At my right was a door leading from the balcony into the building. It was at the end of an unlighted hall, and on the impulse of the moment I stepped within. The hall was broad and led straight through to the front of the building. On either side were the doorways of the various apartments which lined it.

I had no more than entered the corridor than I saw the three warriors at the other end—those whom I had just seen leaving the apartment. Then a turn to the right took them from my sight again. Quickly I hastened along the hallway in pursuit. My gait was reckless, but I felt that Fate had been kind indeed to throw such an opportunity within my grasp, and I could not afford to allow it to elude me now.

At the far end of the corridor I found a spiral stairway leading to the floors above and below. The three had evidently left the floor by this avenue. That they had gone down and not up I was sure from my knowledge of these ancient buildings and the methods of the Warhoons.

I myself had once been a prisoner of the cruel hordes of northern Warhoon, and the memory of the underground dungeon in which I lay still is vivid in my memory. And so I felt certain that Tars Tarkas lay in the dark pits beneath some nearby building, and that in that direction I should find the trail of the three warriors leading to his cell.

Nor was I wrong. At the bottom of the runway, or rather at the landing on the floor below, I saw that the shaft descended into the pits beneath, and as I glanced down the flickering light of a torch revealed the presence of the three I was trailing.

Down they went toward the pits beneath the structure, and at a safe distance behind I followed the flicker of their torch. The way led through a maze of tortuous corridors, unlighted save for the wavering light they carried. We had gone perhaps a hundred yards when the party turned abruptly through a doorway at their right. I hastened on as rapidly as I dared through the darkness until I reached the point at which they had left the corridor. There, through an open door, I saw them removing the chains that secured the great Thark, Tars Tarkas, to the wall.

Hustling him roughly between them, they came immediately from the chamber, so quickly in fact that I was near to being apprehended. But I managed to run along the corridor in the direction I had been going in my pursuit of them far enough to be without the radius of their meagre light as they emerged from the cell.

I had naturally assumed that they would return with Tars Tarkas the same way that they had come, which would have carried them away from me; but, to my chagrin, they wheeled directly in my direction as they left the room. There was nothing for me but to hasten on in advance and keep out of the light of their torch. I dared not attempt to halt in the darkness of any of the many intersecting corridors, for I knew nothing of the direction they might take. Chance was as likely as not to carry me into the very corridor they might choose to enter.

The sensation of moving rapidly through these dark passages was far from reassuring. I knew not at what moment I might plunge headlong into some terrible pit or meet with some of the ghoulish creatures that inhabit these lower worlds beneath the dead cities of dying Mars. There filtered to me a faint radiance from the torch of the men behind—just enough to permit me to trace the direction of the winding passageways directly before me, and so keep me from dashing myself against the walls at the turns.

Presently I came to a place where five corridors diverged from a common point. I had hastened along one of them for some little distance when suddenly the faint light of the torch disappeared from about me. I paused to listen for sounds of the party behind me, but the silence was as utter as the silence of the tomb.

Quickly I realized that the warriors had taken one of the other corridors with their prisoner, and so I hastened back with a feeling of considerable relief to take up a much safer and more desirable position behind them. It was much slower work returning, however, than it had been coming, for now the darkness was as utter as the silence.

It was necessary to feel every foot of the way back with my hand against the side wall, that I might not pass the spot where the five roads radiated. After what seemed an eternity to me, I reached the place and recognized it by groping across the entrances to the several corridors until I had counted five of them. In not one, however, showed the faintest sign of light.

I listened intently, but the naked feet of the green men sent back no guiding echoes, though presently I thought I detected the clank of side arms in the far distance of the middle corridor. Up this, then, I hastened, searching for the light, and stopping to listen occasionally for a repetition of the sound; but soon I was forced to admit that I must have been following a blind lead, as only darkness and silence rewarded my efforts.

Again I retraced my steps toward the parting of the ways, when to my surprise I came upon the entrance to three diverging corridors, any one of which I might have traversed in my hasty dash after the false clue I had been following. Here was a pretty fix, indeed! Once back at the point where the five passageways met, I might wait with some assurance for the return of the warriors with Tars Tarkas. My knowledge of their customs lent colour to the belief that he was but being escorted to the audience chamber to have sentence passed upon him. I had not the slightest doubt but that they would preserve so doughty a warrior as the great Thark for the rare sport he would furnish at the Great Games.

But unless I could find my way back to that point the chances were most excellent that I would wander for days through the awful blackness, until, overcome by thirst and hunger, I lay down to die, or—What was that!

A faint shuffling sounded behind me, and as I cast a hasty glance over my shoulder my blood froze in my veins for the thing I saw there. It was not so much fear of the present danger as it was the horrifying memories it recalled of that time I near went mad over the corpse of the man I had killed in the dungeons of the Warhoons, when blazing eyes came out of the dark recesses and dragged the thing that had been a man from my clutches and I heard it scraping over the stone of my prison as they bore it away to their terrible feast.

And now in these black pits of the other Warhoons I looked into those same fiery eyes, blazing at me through the terrible darkness, revealing no sign of the beast behind them. I think that the most fearsome attribute of these awesome creatures is their silence and the fact that one never sees them—nothing but those baleful eyes glaring unblinkingly out of the dark void behind.

Grasping my long-sword tightly in my hand, I backed slowly along the corridor away from the thing that watched me, but ever as I retreated the eyes advanced, nor was there any sound, not even the sound of breathing, except the occasional shuffling sound as of the dragging of a dead limb, that had first attracted my attention.

On and on I went, but I could not escape my sinister pursuer. Suddenly I heard the shuffling noise at my right, and, looking, saw another pair of eyes, evidently approaching from an intersecting corridor. As I started to renew my slow retreat I heard the noise repeated behind me, and then before I could turn I heard it again at my left.

The things were all about me. They had me surrounded at the intersection of two corridors. Retreat was cut off in all directions, unless I chose to charge one of the beasts. Even then I had no doubt but that the others would hurl themselves upon my back. I could not even guess the size or nature of the weird creatures. That they were of goodly proportions I guessed from the fact that the eyes were on a level with my own.

Why is it that darkness so magnifies our dangers? By day I would have charged the great banth itself, had I thought it necessary, but hemmed in by the darkness of these silent pits I hesitated before a pair of eyes.

Soon I saw that the matter shortly would be taken entirely from my hands, for the eyes at my right were moving slowly nearer me, as were those at my left and those behind and before me. Gradually they were closing in upon me—but still that awful stealthy silence!

For what seemed hours the eyes approached gradually closer and closer, until I felt that I should go mad for the horror of it. I had been constantly turning this way and that to prevent any sudden rush from behind, until I was fairly worn out. At length I could endure it no longer, and, taking a fresh grasp upon my long-sword, I turned suddenly and charged down upon one of my tormentors.

As I was almost upon it the thing retreated before me, but a sound from behind caused me to wheel in time to see three pairs of eyes rushing at me from the rear. With a cry of rage I turned to meet the cowardly beasts, but as I advanced they retreated as had their fellow. Another glance over my shoulder discovered the first eyes sneaking on me again. And again I charged, only to see the eyes retreat before me and hear the muffled rush of the three at my back.

Thus we continued, the eyes always a little closer in the end than they had been before, until I thought that I should go mad with the terrible strain of the ordeal. That they were waiting to spring upon my back seemed evident, and that it would not be long before they succeeded was equally apparent, for I could not endure the wear of this repeated charge and countercharge indefinitely. In fact, I could feel myself weakening from the mental and physical strain I had been undergoing.

At that moment I caught another glimpse from the corner of my eye of the single pair of eyes at my back making a sudden rush upon me. I turned to meet the charge; there was a quick rush of the three from the other direction; but I determined to pursue the single pair until I should have at least settled my account with one of the beasts and thus be relieved of the strain of meeting attacks from both directions.

There was no sound in the corridor, only that of my own breathing, yet I knew that those three uncanny creatures were almost upon me. The eyes in front were not retreating so rapidly now; I was almost within sword reach of them. I raised my sword arm to deal the blow that should free me, and then I felt a heavy body upon my back. A cold, moist, slimy something fastened itself upon my throat. I stumbled and went down.

FIFTEEN

Flight and Pursuit

I could not have been unconscious more than a few seconds, and yet I know that I was unconscious, for the next thing I realized was that a growing radiance was illuminating the corridor about me and the eyes were gone.

I was unharmed except for a slight bruise upon my forehead where it had struck the stone flagging as I fell.

I sprang to my feet to ascertain the cause of the light. It came from a torch in the hand of one of a party of four green warriors, who were coming rapidly down the corridor toward me. They had not yet seen me, and so I lost no time in slipping into the first intersecting corridor that I could find. This time, however, I did not advance so far away from the main corridor as on the other occasion that had resulted in my losing Tars Tarkas and his guards.

The party came rapidly toward the opening of the passageway in which I crouched against the wall. As they passed by I breathed a sigh of relief. I had not been discovered, and, best of all, the party was the same that I had followed into the pits. It consisted of Tars Tarkas and his three guards.

I fell in behind them and soon we were at the cell in which the great Thark had been chained. Two of the warriors remained without while the man with the keys entered with the Thark to fasten his irons upon him once more. The two outside started to stroll slowly in the direction of the spiral runway which led to the floors above, and in a moment were lost to view beyond a turn in the corridor.

The torch had been stuck in a socket beside the door, so that its rays illuminated both the corridor and the cell at the same time. As I saw the two warriors disappear I approached the entrance to the cell, with a well-defined plan already formulated.

While I disliked the thought of carrying out the thing that I had decided upon, there seemed no alternative if Tars Tarkas and I were to go back together to my little camp in the hills.

Keeping near the wall, I came quite close to the door to Tars Tarkas' cell, and there I stood with my longsword above my head, grasped with both hands, that I might bring it down in one quick cut upon the skull of the jailer as he emerged.

I dislike to dwell upon what followed after I heard the footsteps of the man as he approached the doorway. It is enough that within another minute or two, Tars Tarkas, wearing the metal of a Warhoon chief, was hurrying down the corridor toward the spiral runway, bearing the Warhoon's torch to light his way. A dozen paces behind him followed John Carter, Prince of Helium.

The two companions of the man who lay now beside the door of the cell that had been Tars Tarkas' had just started to ascend the runway as the Thark came in view.

"Why so long, Tan Gama?" cried one of the men.

"I had trouble with a lock," replied Tars Tarkas. "And now I find that I have left my short-sword in the Thark's cell. Go you on, I'll return and fetch it."

"As you will, Tan Gama," replied he who had before spoken. "We shall see you above directly."

"Yes," replied Tars Tarkas, and turned as though to retrace his steps to the cell, but he only waited until the two had disappeared at the floor above. Then I joined him, we extinguished the torch, and together we crept toward the spiral incline that led to the upper floors of the building.

At the first floor we found that the hallway ran but halfway through, necessitating the crossing of a rear room full of green folk, ere we could reach the inner courtyard, so there was but one thing left for us to do, and that was to gain the second floor and the hallway through which I had traversed the length of the building.

Cautiously we ascended. We could hear the sounds of conversation coming from the room above, but the hall still was unlighted, nor was any one in sight as we gained the top of the runway. Together we threaded the long hall and reached the balcony overlooking the courtyard, without being detected.

At our right was the window letting into the room in which I had seen Tan Gama and the other warriors as they started to Tars Tarkas' cell earlier in the evening. His companions had returned here, and we now overheard a portion of their conversation.

"What can be detaining Tan Gama?" asked one.

"He certainly could not be all this time fetching his short-sword from the Thark's cell," spoke another.

"His short-sword?" asked a woman. "What mean you?"

"Tan Gama left his short-sword in the Thark's cell," explained the first speaker, "and left us at the runway, to return and get it."

"Tan Gama wore no short-sword this night," said the woman. "It was broken in to-day's battle with the Thark, and Tan Gama gave it to me to repair. See, I have it here," and as she spoke she drew Tan Gama's short-sword from beneath her sleeping silks and furs.

The warriors sprang to their feet.

"There is something amiss here," cried one.

" 'Tis even what I myself thought when Tan Gama left us at the runway," said another. "Methought then that his voice sounded strangely."

"Come! let us hasten to the pits."

We waited to hear no more. Slinging my harness into a long single strap, I lowered Tars Tarkas to the courtyard beneath, and an instant later dropped to his side.

We had spoken scarcely a dozen words since I had felled Tan Gama at the cell door and seen in the torch's light the expression of utter bewilderment upon the great Thark's face.

"By this time," he had said, "I should have learned to wonder at nothing which John Carter accomplishes." That was all. He did not need to tell me that he appreciated the friendship which had prompted me to risk my life to rescue him, nor did he need to say that he was glad to see me.

This fierce green warrior had been the first to greet me that day, now twenty years gone, which had witnessed my first advent upon Mars. He had met me with levelled spear and cruel hatred in his heart as he charged down upon me, bending low at the side of his mighty thoat as I stood beside the incubator of his horde upon the dead sea bottom beyond Korad. And now among the inhabitants of two worlds I counted none a better friend than Tars Tarkas, Jeddak of the Tharks.

As we reached the courtyard we stood in the shadows beneath the balcony for a moment to discuss our plans.

"There be five now in the party, Tars Tarkas," I said; "Thuvia, Xodar, Carthoris, and ourselves. We shall need five thoats to bear us."

"Carthoris!" he cried. "Your son?"

"Yes. I found him in the prison of Shador, on the Sea of Omean, in the land of the First Born."

"I know not any of these places, John Carter. Be they upon Barsoom?"

"Upon and below, my friend; but wait until we shall have made good our escape, and you shall hear the strangest narrative that ever a Barsoomian of the outer world gave ear to. Now we must steal our thoats and be well away to the north before these fellows discover how we have tricked them."

In safety we reached the great gates at the far end of the courtyard, through which it was necessary to take our thoats to the avenue beyond. It is no easy matter to handle five of these great, fierce beasts, which by nature are as wild and ferocious as their masters and held in subjection by cruelty and brute force alone.

As we approached them they sniffed our unfamiliar scent and with squeals of rage circled about us. Their long, massive necks upreared raised their great, gaping mouths high above our heads. They are fearsome appearing brutes at best, but when they are aroused they are fully as dangerous as they look. The thoat stands a good ten feet at the shoulder. His hide is sleek and hairless, and of a dark slate colour on back and sides, shading down his eight legs to a vivid yellow at the huge, padded, nailless feet; the belly is pure white. A broad, flat tail, larger at the tip than at the root, completes the picture of this ferocious green Martian mount—a fit war steed for these warlike people.

As the thoats are guided by telepathic means alone, there is no need for rein or bridle, and so our object now was to find two that would obey our unspoken commands. As they charged about us we succeeded in mastering them sufficiently to prevent any concerted attack upon us, but the din of their squealing was certain to bring investigating warriors into the courtyard were it to continue much longer.

At length I was successful in reaching the side of one great brute, and ere he knew what I was about I was firmly seated astride his glossy back. A moment later Tars Tarkas had caught and mounted another, and then between us we herded three or four more toward the great gates.

Tars Tarkas rode ahead and, leaning down to the latch, threw the barriers open, while I held the loose thoats from breaking back to the herd. Then together we rode through into the avenue with our stolen mounts and, without waiting to close the gates, hurried off toward the southern boundary of the city.

Thus far our escape had been little short of marvellous, nor did our good fortune desert us, for we passed the outer purlieus of the dead city and came to our camp without hearing even the faintest sound of pursuit.

Here a low whistle, the prearranged signal, apprised the balance of our party that I was returning, and we were met by the three with every manifestation of enthusiastic rejoicing.

But little time was wasted in narration of our adventure. Tars Tarkas and Carthoris exchanged the dignified and formal greetings common upon

Barsoom, but I could tell intuitively that the Thark loved my boy and that Carthoris reciprocated his affection.

Xodar and the green Jeddak were formally presented to each other. Then Thuvia was lifted to the least fractious thoat, Xodar and Carthoris mounted two others, and we set out at a rapid pace toward the east. At the far extremity of the city we circled toward the north, and under the glorious rays of the two moons we sped noiselessly across the dead sea bottom, away from the Warhoons and the First Born, but to what new dangers and adventures we knew not.

Toward noon of the following day we halted to rest our mounts and ourselves. The beasts we hobbled, that they might move slowly about cropping the ochre moss-like vegetation which constitutes both food and drink for them on the march. Thuvia volunteered to remain on watch while the balance of the party slept for an hour.

It seemed to me that I had but closed my eyes when I felt her hand upon my shoulder and heard her soft voice warning me of a new danger.

"Arise, O Prince," she whispered. "There be that behind us which has the appearance of a great body of pursuers."

The girl stood pointing in the direction from whence we had come, and as I arose and looked, I, too, thought that I could detect a thin dark line on the far horizon. I awoke the others. Tars Tarkas, whose giant stature towered high above the rest of us, could see the farthest.

"It is a great body of mounted men," he said, "and they are travelling at high speed."

There was no time to be lost. We sprang to our hobbled thoats, freed them, and mounted. Then we turned our faces once more toward the north and took our flight again at the highest speed of our slowest beast.

For the balance of the day and all the following night we raced across that ochre wilderness with the pursuers at our back ever gaining upon us. Slowly but surely they were lessening the distance between us. Just before dark they had been close enough for us to plainly distinguish that they were green Martians, and all during the long night we distinctly heard the clanking of their accoutrements behind us.

As the sun rose on the second day of our flight it disclosed the pursuing horde not a half-mile in our rear. As they saw us a fiendish shout of triumph rose from their ranks.

Several miles in advance lay a range of hills—the farther shore of the dead sea we had been crossing. Could we but reach these hills our chances of escape would be greatly enhanced, but Thuvia's mount, although carrying the lightest burden, already was showing signs of exhaustion. I was riding beside her when suddenly her animal staggered and lurched against mine. I saw that he was going down, but ere he fell I snatched the girl from his back and swung her to a place upon my own thoat, behind me, where she clung with her arms about me.

This double burden soon proved too much for my already overtaxed beast, and thus our speed was terribly diminished, for the others would proceed no faster than the slowest of us could go. In that little party there was not one who would desert another; yet we were of different countries, different colours, different races, different religions—and one of us was of a different world.

We were quite close to the hills, but the Warhoons were gaining so rapidly that we had given up all hope of reaching them in time. Thuvia and I were in the rear, for our beast was lagging more and more. Suddenly I felt the girl's warm lips press a kiss upon my shoulder. "For thy sake, O my Prince," she murmured. Then her arms slipped from about my waist and she was gone.

I turned and saw that she had deliberately slipped to the ground in the very path of the cruel demons who pursued us, thinking that by lightening the burden of my mount it might thus be enabled to bear me to the safety of the hills. Poor child! She should have known John Carter better than that.

Turning my thoat, I urged him after her, hoping to reach her side and bear her on again in our hopeless flight. Carthoris must have glanced behind him at about the same time and taken in the situation, for by the time I had reached Thuvia's side he was there also, and, springing from his mount, he threw her upon its back and, turning the animal's head toward the hills, gave the beast a sharp crack across the rump with the flat of his sword. Then he attempted to do the same with mine.

The brave boy's act of chivalrous self-sacrifice filled me with pride, nor did I care that it had wrested from us our last frail chance for escape. The Warhoons were now close upon us. Tars Tarkas and Xodar had discovered our absence and were charging rapidly to our support. Everything pointed toward a splendid ending of my second journey to Barsoom. I hated to go out without having seen my divine Princess, and held her in my arms once again; but if it were not writ upon the book of Fate that such was to be, then would I take the most that was coming to me, and in these last few moments that were to be vouchsafed me before I passed over into that unguessed future I could at least give such an account of myself in my chosen vocation as would leave the Warhoons of the South food for discourse for the next twenty generations.

As Carthoris was not mounted, I slipped from the back of my own mount and took my place at his side to meet the charge of the howling devils bearing down upon us. A moment later Tars Tarkas and Xodar ranged themselves on either hand, turning their thoats loose that we might all be on an equal footing.

The Warhoons were perhaps a hundred yards from us when a loud explosion sounded from above and behind us, and almost at the same instant a shell burst in their advancing ranks. At once all was confusion. A hundred warriors toppled to the ground. Riderless thoats plunged hither and thither among the dead and dying. Dismounted warriors were trampled underfoot in the stampede which followed. All semblance of order had left the ranks of the green men, and as they looked far above our heads to trace the origin of this unexpected attack, disorder turned to retreat and retreat to a wild panic. In another moment they were racing as madly away from us as they had before been charging down upon us.

We turned to look in the direction from whence the first report had come, and there we saw, just clearing the tops of the nearer hills, a great battleship swinging majestically through the air. Her bow gun spoke again even as we looked, and another shell burst among the fleeing Warhoons.

As she drew nearer I could not repress a wild cry of elation, for upon her bows I saw the device of Helium.

SIXTEEN

Under Arrest

As Carthoris, Xodar, Tars Tarkas, and I stood gazing at the magnificent vessel which meant so much to all of us, we saw a second and then a third top the summit of the hills and glide gracefully after their sister.

Now a score of one-man air scouts were launching from the upper decks of the nearer vessel, and in a moment more were speeding in long, swift dives to the ground about us.

In another instant we were surrounded by armed sailors, and an officer had stepped forward to address us, when his eyes fell upon Carthoris. With an exclamation of surprised pleasure he sprang forward, and, placing his hands upon the boy's shoulder, called him by name.

"Carthoris, my Prince," he cried, "Kaor! Kaor! Hor Vastus greets the son of Dejah Thoris, Princess of Helium, and of her husband, John Carter. Where have you been, O my Prince? All Helium has been plunged in sorrow. Terrible have been the calamities that have befallen your great-grandsire's mighty nation since the fatal day that saw you leave our midst."

"Grieve not, my good Hor Vastus," cried Carthoris, "since I bring not back myself alone to cheer my mother's heart and the hearts of my beloved people, but also one whom all Barsoom loved best—her greatest warrior and her saviour—John Carter, Prince of Helium!"

Hor Vastus turned in the direction indicated by Carthoris, and as his eyes fell upon me he was like to have collapsed from sheer surprise.

"John Carter!" he exclaimed, and then a sudden troubled look came into his eyes. "My Prince," he started, "where hast thou—" and then he stopped, but I knew the question that his lips dared not frame. The loyal fellow would not be the one to force from mine a confession of the terrible truth that I had returned from the bosom of the Iss, the River of Mystery, back from the shore of the Lost Sea of Korus, and the Valley Dor.

"Ah, my Prince," he continued, as though no thought had interrupted his greeting, "that you are back is sufficient, and let Hor Vastus' sword have the high honour of being first at thy feet." With these words the noble fellow unbuckled his scabbard and flung his sword upon the ground before me.

Could you know the customs and the character of red Martians you would appreciate the depth of meaning that that simple act conveyed to me and to all about us who witnessed it. The thing was equivalent to saying, "My sword, my body, my life, my soul are yours to do with as you wish. Until death and after death I look to you alone for authority for my every act. Be you right or wrong, your word shall be my only truth. Whoso raises his hand against you must answer to my sword."

It is the oath of fealty that men occasionally pay to a Jeddak whose high character and chivalrous acts have inspired the enthusiastic love of his followers. Never had I known this high tribute paid to a lesser mortal. There was but one response possible. I stooped and lifted the sword from the ground, raised the hilt to my lips, and then, stepping to Hor Vastus, I buckled the weapon upon him with my own hands.

"Hor Vastus," I said, placing my hand upon his shoulder, "you know best the promptings of your own heart. That I shall need your sword I have little doubt, but accept from John Carter upon his sacred honour the assurance that he will never call upon you to draw this sword other than in the cause of truth, justice, and righteousness."

"That I knew, my Prince," he replied, "ere ever I threw my beloved blade at thy feet."

As we spoke other fliers came and went between the ground and the battleship, and presently a larger boat was launched from above, one capable of carrying a dozen persons, perhaps, and dropped lightly near us. As she touched, an officer sprang from her deck to the ground, and, advancing to Hor Vastus, saluted.

"Kantos Kan desires that this party whom we have rescued be brought immediately to the deck of the *Xavarian*," he said.

As we approached the little craft I looked about for the members of my party and for the first time noticed that Thuvia was not among them. Questioning elicited the fact that none had seen her since Carthoris had sent her thoat galloping madly toward the hills, in the hope of carrying her out of harm's way.

Immediately Hor Vastus dispatched a dozen air scouts in as many directions to search for her. It could not be possible that she had gone far since we had last seen her. We others stepped to the deck of the craft that had been sent to fetch us, and a moment later were upon the *Xavarian*.

The first man to greet me was Kantos Kan himself. My old friend had won to the highest place in the navy of Helium, but he was still to me the same brave comrade who had shared with me the privations of a Warhoon dungeon, the terrible atrocities of the Great Games, and later the dangers of our search for Dejah Thoris within the hostile city of Zodanga.

Then I had been an unknown wanderer upon a strange planet, and he a simple padwar in the navy of Helium. To-day he commanded all Helium's great terrors of the skies, and I was a Prince of the House of Tardos Mors, Jeddak of Helium.

He did not ask me where I had been. Like Hor Vastus, he too dreaded the truth and would not be the one to wrest a statement from me. That it must come some time he well knew, but until it came he seemed satisfied to but know that I was with him once more. He greeted Carthoris and Tars Tarkas with the keenest delight, but he asked neither where he had been. He could scarcely keep his hands off the boy.

"You do not know, John Carter," he said to me, "how we of Helium love this son of yours. It is as though all the great love we bore his noble father and his poor mother had been centred in him. When it became known that he was lost, ten million people wept."

"What mean you, Kantos Kan," I whispered, "by 'his poor mother'?" for the words had seemed to carry a sinister meaning which I could not fathom.

He drew me to one side.

"For a year," he said, "Ever since Carthoris disappeared, Dejah Thoris has grieved and mourned for her lost boy. The blow of years ago, when you did not return from the atmosphere plant, was lessened to some extent by the duties of motherhood, for your son broke his white shell that very night."

"That she suffered terribly then, all Helium knew, for did not all Helium suffer with her the loss of her lord! But with the boy gone there was nothing left, and after expedition upon expedition returned with the same hopeless tale of no clue as to his whereabouts, our beloved Princess drooped lower and lower, until all who saw her felt that it could be but a matter of days ere she went to join her loved ones within the precincts of the Valley Dor.

"As a last resort, Mors Kajak, her father, and Tardos Mors, her grandfather, took command of two mighty expeditions, and a month ago sailed away to explore every inch of ground in the northern hemisphere of Barsoom. For two weeks no word has come back from them, but rumours were rife that they had met with a terrible disaster and that all were dead.

"About this time Zat Arras renewed his importunities for her hand in marriage. He has been for ever after her since you disappeared. She hated him and feared him, but with both her father and grandfather gone, Zat Arras was very powerful, for he is still Jed of Zodanga, to which position, you will remember, Tardos Mors appointed him after you had refused the honour.

"He had a secret audience with her six days ago. What took place none knows, but the next day Dejah Thoris had disappeared, and with her had gone a dozen of her household guard and body servants, including Sola the green woman—Tars Tarkas' daughter, you recall. No word left they of their intentions, but it is always thus with those who go upon the voluntary pilgrimage from which none returns. We cannot think aught than that Dejah Thoris has sought the icy bosom of Iss, and that her devoted servants have chosen to accompany her.

"Zat Arras was at Helium when she disappeared. He commands this fleet which has been searching for her since. No trace of her have we found, and I fear that it be a futile quest."

While we talked, Hor Vastus' fliers were returning to the *Xavarian*. Not one, however, had discovered a trace of Thuvia. I was much depressed over the news of Dejah Thoris' disappearance, and now there was added the further burden of apprehension concerning the fate of Thuvia. I felt keen responsibility for the welfare of this girl whom I believed to be the daughter of some proud Barsoomian house, and it had been my intention to make every effort to return her to her people.

I was about to ask Kantos Kan to prosecute a further search for her when a flier from the flagship of the fleet arrived at the *Xavarian* with an officer bearing a message to Kantos Kan from Arras.

My friend read the dispatch and then turned to me.

"Zat Arras commands me to bring our 'prisoners' before him. There is naught else to do. He is supreme in Helium, yet it would be far more in keeping with chivalry and good taste were he to come hither and greet the saviour of Barsoom with the honours that are his due."

"You know full well, my friend," I said, smiling, "that Zat Arras has good cause to hate me. Nothing would please him better than to humiliate me and then to kill me. Now that he has so excellent an excuse, let us go and see if he has the courage to take advantage of it."

Summoning Carthoris, Tars Tarkas, and Xodar, we entered the small flier with Kantos Kan and Zat Arras' officer, and in a moment were stepping to the deck of Zat Arras' flagship. As we approached the Jed of Zodanga no sign of greeting or recognition crossed his face; not even to Carthoris did he vouchsafe a friendly word. His attitude was cold, haughty, and uncompromising.

"Kaor, Zat Arras," I said in greeting, but he did not respond.

"Why were these prisoners not disarmed?" he asked to Kantos Kan.

"They are not prisoners, Zat Arras," replied the officer.

"Two of them are of Helium's noblest family. Tars Tarkas, Jeddak of Thark, is Tardos Mors' best beloved ally. The other is a friend and companion of the Prince of Helium—that is enough for me to know."

"It is not enough for me, however," retorted Zat Arras. "More must I hear from those who have taken the pilgrimage than their names. Where have you been, John Carter?"

"I have just come from the Valley Dor and the Land of the First Born, Zat Arras," I replied.

"Ah!" he exclaimed in evident pleasure, "you do not deny it, then? You have returned from the bosom of Iss?"

"I have come back from a land of false hope, from a valley of torture and death; with my companions I have escaped from the hideous clutches of lying fiends. I have come back to the Barsoom that I saved from a painless death to again save her, but this time from death in its most frightful form."

"Cease, blasphemer!" cried Zat Arras. "Hope not to save thy cowardly carcass by inventing horrid lies to—" But he got no further. One does not call John Carter "coward" and "liar" thus lightly, and Zat Arras should have known it. Before a hand could be raised to stop me, I was at his side and one hand grasped his throat.

"Come I from heaven or hell, Zat Arras, you will find me still the same John Carter that I have always been; nor did ever man call me such names and live—without apologizing." And with that I commenced to bend him back across my knee and tighten my grip upon his throat.

"Seize him!" cried Zat Arras, and a dozen officers sprang forward to assist him.

Kantos Kan came close and whispered to me.

"Desist, I beg of you. It will but involve us all, for I cannot see these men lay hands upon you without aiding you. My officers and men will join me and we shall have a mutiny then that may lead to the revolution. For the sake of Tardos Mors and Helium, desist."

At his words I released Zat Arras and, turning my back upon him, walked toward the ship's rail.

"Come, Kantos Kan," I said, "the Prince of Helium would return to the *Xavarian*."

None interfered. Zat Arras stood white and trembling amidst his officers. Some there were who looked upon him with scorn and drew toward me, while one, a man long in the service and confidence of Tardos Mors, spoke to me in a low tone as I passed him.

"You may count my metal among your fighting-men, John Carter," he said.

I thanked him and passed on. In silence we embarked, and shortly after stepped once more upon the deck of the *Xavarian*. Fifteen minutes later we received orders from the flagship to proceed toward Helium.

Our journey thither was uneventful. Carthoris and I were wrapped in the gloomiest of thoughts. Kantos Kan was sombre in contemplation of the further calamity that might fall upon Helium should Zat Arras attempt to follow the age-old precedent that allotted a terrible death to fugitives from the Valley Dor. Tars Tarkas grieved for the loss of his daughter. Xodar alone was care-free—a fugitive and outlaw, he could be no worse off in Helium than elsewhere.

"Let us hope that we may at least go out with good red blood upon our blades," he said. It was a simple wish and one most likely to be gratified.

Among the officers of the *Xavarian* I thought I could discern division into factions ere we had reached Helium. There were those who gathered about Carthoris and myself whenever the opportunity presented, while about an equal number held aloof from us. They offered us only the most courteous treatment, but were evidently bound by their superstitious belief in the doctrine of Dor and Iss and Korus. I could not blame them, for I knew how strong a hold a creed, however ridiculous it may be, may gain upon an otherwise intelligent people.

By returning from Dor we had committed a sacrilege; by recounting our adventures there, and stating the facts as they existed we had outraged the religion of their fathers. We were blasphemers—lying heretics. Even those who still clung to us from personal love and loyalty I think did so in the face of the fact that at heart they questioned our veracity—it is very hard to accept a new religion for an old, no matter how alluring the promises of the new may be; but to reject the old as a tissue of falsehoods without being offered anything in its stead is indeed a most difficult thing to ask of any people.

Kantos Kan would not talk of our experiences among the therns and the First Born.

"It is enough," he said, "that I jeopardize my life here and hereafter by countenancing you at all—do not ask me to add still further to my sins by listening to what I have always been taught was the rankest heresy."

I knew that sooner or later the time must come when our friends and enemies would be forced to declare themselves openly. When we reached

Helium there must be an accounting, and if Tardos Mors had not returned I feared that the enmity of Zat Arras might weigh heavily against us, for he represented the government of Helium. To take sides against him were equivalent to treason. The majority of the troops would doubtless follow the lead of their officers, and I knew that many of the highest and most powerful men of both land and air forces would cleave to John Carter in the face of god, man, or devil.

On the other hand, the majority of the populace unquestionably would demand that we pay the penalty of our sacrilege. The outlook seemed dark from whatever angle I viewed it, but my mind was so torn with anguish at the thought of Dejah Thoris that I realize now that I gave the terrible question of Helium's plight but scant attention at that time.

There was always before me, day and night, a horrible nightmare of the frightful scenes through which I knew my Princess might even then be passing—the horrid plant men—the ferocious white apes. At times I would cover my face with my hands in a vain effort to shut out the fearful thing from my mind.

It was in the forenoon that we arrived above the mile-high scarlet tower which marks greater Helium from her twin city. As we descended in great circles toward the navy docks a mighty multitude could be seen surging in the streets beneath. Helium had been notified by radio-aerogram of our approach.

From the deck of the *Xavarian* we four, Carthoris, Tars Tarkas, Xodar, and I, were transferred to a lesser flier to be transported to quarters within the Temple of Reward. It is here that Martian justice is meted to benefactor and malefactor. Here the hero is decorated. Here the felon is condemned. We were taken into the temple from the landing stage upon the roof, so that we did not pass among the people at all, as is customary. Always before I had seen prisoners of note, or returned wanderers of eminence, paraded from the Gate of Jeddaks to the Temple of Reward up the broad Avenue of Ancestors through dense crowds of jeering or cheering citizens.

I knew that Zat Arras dared not trust the people near to us, for he feared that their love for Carthoris and myself might break into a demonstration which would wipe out their superstitious horror of the crime we were to be charged with. What his plans were I could only guess, but that they were sinister was evidenced by the fact that only his most trusted servitors accompanied us upon the flier to the Temple of Reward.

We were lodged in a room upon the south side of the temple, overlooking the Avenue of Ancestors down which we could see the full length to the Gate of Jeddaks, five miles away. The people in the temple plaza and in the streets for a distance of a full mile were standing as close packed as it was possible for them to get. They were very orderly—there were neither scoffs nor plaudits, and when they saw us at the window above them there were many who buried their faces in their arms and wept.

Late in the afternoon a messenger arrived from Zat Arras to inform us that we would be tried by an impartial body of nobles in the great hall of the temple at the 1st zode[1] on the following day, or about 8:40 A.M. Earth time.

---

1. Wherever Captain Carter has used Martian measurements of time, distance, weight, and the like I have translated them into as nearly their equivalent in earthly values as is possible. His notes contain many Martian tables, and a great volume of scientific data, but since the International Astronomic Society is at present engaged in classifying, investigating, and verifying this vast fund of remarkable and valuable information, I have felt that it will add nothing to the interest of Captain Carter's story or to the sum total of human knowledge to maintain a strict adherence to the original manuscript in these matters, while it might readily confuse the reader and detract from the interest of the history. For those who may be interested, however, I will explain that the Martian day is a trifle over 24 hours 37 minutes duration (Earth time). This the Martians divide into ten equal parts, commencing the day at about 6 A.M. Earth time. The zodes are divided into fifty shorter periods, each of which in turn is composed of 200 brief periods of time, about equivalent to the earthly second. The Barsoomian Table of Time as here given is but a part of the full table appearing in Captain Carter's notes.

TABLE

200 tals . . . . 1 xat
50 xats . . . . 1 zode
10 zodes . . . . 1 revolution of Mars upon its axis.

SEVENTEEN

The Death Sentence

A few moments before the appointed time on the following morning a strong guard of Zat Arras' officers appeared at our quarters to conduct us to the great hall of the temple.

In twos we entered the chamber and marched down the broad Aisle of Hope, as it is called, to the platform in the centre of the hall. Before and behind us marched armed guards, while three solid ranks of Zodangan soldiery lined either side of the aisle from the entrance to the rostrum.

As we reached the raised enclosure I saw our judges. As is the custom upon Barsoom there were thirty-one, supposedly selected by lot from men of the noble class, for nobles were on trial. But to my amazement I saw no single friendly face among them. Practically all were Zodangans, and it was I to whom Zodanga owed her defeat at the hands of the green hordes and her subsequent vassalage to Helium. There could be little justice here for John Carter, or his son, or for the great Thark who had commanded the savage tribesmen who overran Zodanga's broad avenues, looting, burning, and murdering.

About us the vast circular coliseum was packed to its full capacity. All classes were represented—all ages, and both sexes. As we entered the hall the hum of subdued conversation ceased until as we halted upon the platform, or Throne of Righteousness, the silence of death enveloped the ten thousand spectators.

The judges were seated in a great circle about the periphery of the circular platform. We were assigned seats with our backs toward a small platform in the exact centre of the larger one. This placed us facing the judges and the audience. Upon the smaller platform each would take his place while his case was being heard.

Zat Arras himself sat in the golden chair of the presiding magistrate. As we were seated and our guards retired to the foot of the stairway leading to the platform, he arose and called my name.

"John Carter," he cried, "take your place upon the Pedestal of Truth to be judged impartially according to your acts and here to know the reward you have earned thereby." Then turning to and fro toward the audience he narrated the acts upon the value of which my reward was to be determined.

"Know you, O judges and people of Helium," he said, "that John Carter, one time Prince of Helium, has returned by his own statement from the Valley Dor and even from the Temple of Issus itself. That, in the presence of many men of Helium he has blasphemed against the Sacred Iss, and against the Valley Dor, and the Lost Sea of Korus, and the Holy Therns themselves, and even against Issus, Goddess of Death, and of Life Eternal. And know you further by witness of thine own eyes that see him here now upon the Pedestal of Truth that he has indeed returned from these sacred precincts in the face of our ancient customs, and in violation of the sanctity of our ancient religion.

"He who be once dead may not live again. He who attempts it must be made dead for ever. Judges, your duty lies plain before you—here can be no testimony in contravention of truth. What reward shall be meted to John Carter in accordance with the acts he has committed?"

"Death!" shouted one of the judges.

And then a man sprang to his feet in the audience, and raising his hand on high, cried: "Justice! Justice! Justice!" It was Kantos Kan, and as all eyes turned toward him he leaped past the Zodangan soldiery and sprang upon the platform.

"What manner of justice be this?" he cried to Zat Arras. "The defendant has not been heard, nor has he had an opportunity to call others in his behalf. In the name of the people of Helium I demand fair and impartial treatment for the Prince of Helium."

A great cry arose from the audience then: "Justice! Justice! Justice!" and Zat Arras dared not deny them.

"Speak, then," he snarled, turning to me; "but blaspheme not against the things that are sacred upon Barsoom."

"Men of Helium," I cried, turning to the spectators, and speaking over the heads of my judges, "how can John Carter expect justice from the men of Zodanga? He cannot nor does he ask it. It is to the men of Helium that he states his case; nor does he appeal for mercy to any. It is not in his own cause that he speaks now—it is in thine. In the cause of your wives and daughters, and of wives and daughters yet unborn. It is to save them from the unthinkably atrocious indignities that I have seen heaped upon the fair women of Barsoom in the place men call the Temple of Issus. It is to save them from the sucking embrace of the plant men, from the fangs of the great white apes of Dor, from the cruel lust of the Holy Therns, from all that the cold, dead Iss carries them to from homes of love and life and happiness.

"Sits there no man here who does not know the history of John Carter. How he came among you from another world and rose from a prisoner among the green men, through torture and persecution, to a place high among the highest of Barsoom. Nor ever did you know John Carter to lie in his own behalf, or to say aught that might harm the people of Barsoom, or to speak lightly of the strange religion which he respected without understanding.

"There be no man here, or elsewhere upon Barsoom to-day who does not owe his life directly to a single act of mine, in which I sacrificed myself and the happiness of my Princess that you might live. And so, men of Helium, I think that I have the right to demand that I be heard, that I be believed, and that you let me serve you and save you from the false hereafter of Dor and Issus as I saved you from the real death that other day.

"It is to you of Helium that I speak now. When I am done let the men of Zodanga have their will with me. Zat Arras has taken my sword from me, so the men of Zodanga no longer fear me. Will you listen?"

"Speak, John Carter, Prince of Helium," cried a great noble from the audience, and the multitude echoed his permission, until the building rocked with the noise of their demonstration. Zat Arras knew better than to interfere with such a sentiment as was expressed that day in the Temple of Reward, and so for two hours I talked with the people of Helium.

But when I had finished, Zat Arras arose and, turning to the judges, said in a low tone: "My nobles, you have heard John Carter's plea; every opportunity has been given him to prove his innocence if he be not guilty; but instead he has but utilized the time in further blasphemy. What, gentlemen, is your verdict?"

"Death to the blasphemer!" cried one, springing to his feet, and in an instant the entire thirty-one judges were on their feet with upraised swords in token of the unanimity of their verdict.

If the people did not hear Zat Arras' charge, they certainly did hear the verdict of the tribunal. A sullen murmur rose louder and louder about the packed coliseum, and then Kantos Kan, who had not left the platform since first he had taken his place near me, raised his hand for silence. When he could be heard he spoke to the people in a cool and level voice.

"You have heard the fate that the men of Zodanga would mete to

Helium's noblest hero. It may be the duty of the men of Helium to accept the verdict as final. Let each man act according to his own heart. Here is the answer of Kantos Kan, head of the navy of Helium, to Zat Arras and his judges," and with that he unbuckled his scabbard and threw his sword at my feet.

In an instant soldiers and citizens, officers and nobles were crowding past the soldiers of Zodanga and forcing their way to the Throne of Righteousness. A hundred men surged upon the platform, and a hundred blades rattled and clanked to the floor at my feet. Zat Arras and his officers were furious, but they were helpless. One by one I raised the swords to my lips and buckled them again upon their owners.

"Come," sand Kantos Kan, "we will escort John Carter and his party to his own palace," and they formed about us and started toward the stairs leading to the Aisle of Hope.

"Stop!" cried Zat Arras. "Soldiers of Helium, let no prisoner leave the Throne of Righteousness."

The soldiery from Zodanga were the only organized body of Heliumetic troops within the temple, so Zat Arras was confident that his orders would be obeyed, but I do not think that he looked for the opposition that was raised the moment the soldiers advanced toward the throne.

From every quarter of the coliseum swords flashed and men rushed threateningly upon the Zodangans. Some one raised a cry: "Tardos Mors is dead—a thousand years to John Carter, Jeddak of Helium." As I heard that and saw the ugly attitude of the men of Helium toward the soldiers of Zat Arras, I knew that only a miracle could avert a clash that would end in civil war.

"Hold!" I cried, leaping to the Pedestal of Truth once more. "Let no man move till I am done. A single sword thrust here to-day may plunge Helium into a bitter and bloody war the results of which none can foresee. It will turn brother against brother and father against son. No man's life is worth that sacrifice. Rather would I submit to the biased judgment of Zat Arras than be the cause of civil strife in Helium.

"Let us each give in a point to the other, and let this entire matter rest until Tardos Mors returns, or Mors Kajak, his son. If neither be back at the end of a year a second trial may be held—the thing has a precedent." And then turning to Zat Arras, I said in a low voice: "Unless you be a bigger fool than I take you to be, you will grasp the chance I am offering you ere it is too late. Once that multitude of swords below is drawn against your soldiery no man upon Barsoom—not even Tardos Mors himself—can avert the consequences. What say you? Speak quickly."

The Jed of Zodangan Helium raised his voice to the angry sea beneath us.

"Stay your hands, men of Helium," he shouted, his voice trembling with rage. "The sentence of the court is passed, but the day of retribution has not been set. I, Zat Arras, Jed of Zodanga, appreciating the royal connections of the prisoner and his past services to Helium and Barsoom, grant a respite of one year, or until the return of Mors Kajak, or Tardos Mors to Helium. Disperse quietly to your houses. Go."

No one moved. Instead, they stood in tense silence with their eyes fastened upon me, as though waiting for a signal to attack.

"Clear the temple," commanded Zat Arras, in a low tone to one of his officers.

Fearing the result of an attempt to carry out this order by force, I stepped to the edge of the platform and, pointing toward the main entrance, bid them pass out. As one man they turned at my request and filed, silent and threatening, past the soldiers of Zat Arras, Jed of Zodanga, who stood scowling in impotent rage.

Kantos Kan with the others who had sworn allegiance to me still stood upon the Throne of Righteousness with me.

"Come," said Kantos Kan to me, "we will escort you to your palace, my Prince. Come, Carthoris and Xodar. Come, Tars Tarkas." And with a haughty sneer for Zat Arras upon his handsome lips, he turned and strode to the throne steps and up the Aisle of Hope. We four and the hundred loyal ones followed behind him, nor was a hand raised to stay us, though glowering eyes followed our triumphal march through the temple.

In the avenues we found a press of people, but they opened a pathway for us, and many were the swords that were flung at my feet as I passed through the city of Helium toward my palace upon the outskirts. Here my old slaves fell upon their knees and kissed my hands as I greeted them. They cared not where I had been. It was enough that I had returned to them.

"Ah, master," cried one, "if our divine Princess were but here this would be a day indeed."

Tears came to my eyes, so that I was forced to turn away that I might hide my emotions. Carthoris wept openly as the slaves pressed about him with expressions of affection, and words of sorrow for our common loss. It was now that Tars Tarkas for the first time learned that his daughter, Sola, had accompanied Dejah Thoris upon the last long pilgrimage. I had not had the heart to tell him what Kantos Kan had told me. With the stoicism of the green Martian he showed no sign of suffering, yet I knew that his grief was as poignant as my own. In marked contrast to his kind, he had in well-developed form the kindlier human characteristics of love, friendship, and charity.

It was a sad and sombre party that sat at the feast of welcome in the great dining hall of the palace of the Prince of Helium that day. We were over a hundred strong, not counting the members of my little court, for Dejah Thoris and I had maintained a household consistent with our royal rank.

The board, according to red Martian custom, was triangular, for there were three in our family. Carthoris and I presided in the centre of our sides of the table—midway of the third side Dejah Thoris' high-backed, carven chair stood vacant except for her gorgeous wedding trappings and jewels which were draped upon it. Behind stood a slave as in the days when his mistress had occupied her place at the board, ready to do her bidding. It was the way upon Barsoom, so I endured the anguish of it, though it wrung my heart to see that silent chair where should have been my laughing and vivacious Princess keeping the great hall ringing with her merry gaiety.

At my right sat Kantos Kan, while to the right of Dejah Thoris' empty place Tars Tarkas sat in a huge chair before a raised section of the board which years ago I had had constructed to meet the requirements of his mighty bulk. The place of honour at a Martian hoard is always at the hostess's right, and this place was ever reserved by Dejah Thoris for the great Thark upon the occasions that he was in Helium.

Hor Vastus sat in the seat of honour upon Carthoris' side of the table. There was little general conversation. It was a quiet and saddened party. The loss of Dejah Thoris was still fresh in the minds of all, and to this was added fear for the safety of Tardos Mors and Mors Kajak, as well as doubt and uncertainty as to the fate of Helium, should it prove true that she was permanently deprived of her great Jeddak.

Suddenly our attention was attracted by the sound of distant shouting, as of many people raising their voices at once, but whether in anger or rejoicing, we could not tell. Nearer and nearer came the tumult. A slave rushed into the dining hall to cry that a great concourse of people was swarming through the palace gates. A second burst upon the heels of the first alternately laughing and shrieking as a madman.

"Dejah Thoris is found!" he cried. "A messenger from Dejah Thoris!"

I waited to hear no more. The great windows of the dining hall over-looked the avenue leading to the main gates —they were upon the opposite side of the hall from me with the table intervening. I did not waste time in circling the great board—with a single leap I cleared table and diners and sprang upon the balcony beyond. Thirty feet below lay the scarlet sward of the lawn and beyond were many people crowding about a great thoat which bore a rider headed toward the palace. I vaulted to the ground below and ran swiftly toward the advancing party.

As I came near to them I saw that the figure on the thoat was Sola.

"Where is the Princess of Helium?" I cried.

The green girl slid from her mighty mount and ran toward me.

"O my Prince! My Prince!" she cried. "She is gone for ever. Even now she may be a captive upon the lesser moon. The black pirates of Barsoom have stolen her."

EIGHTEEN

Sola's Story

Once within the palace, I drew Sola to the dining hall, and, when she had greeted her father after the formal manner of the green men, she told the story of the pilgrimage and capture of Dejah Thoris.

"Seven days ago, after her audience with Zat Arras, Dejah Thoris attempted to slip from the palace in the dead of night. Although I had not heard the outcome of her interview with Zat Arras I knew that something had occurred then to cause her the keenest mental agony, and when I discovered her creeping from the palace I did not need to be told her destination.

"Hastily arousing a dozen of her most faithful guards, I explained my fears to them, and as one they enlisted with me to follow our beloved Princess in her wanderings, even to the Sacred Iss and the Valley Dor. We came upon her but a short distance from the palace. With her was faithful Woola the hound, but none other. When we overtook her she feigned anger, and ordered us back to the palace, but for once we disobeyed her, and when she found that we would not let her go upon the last long pilgrimage alone, she wept and embraced us, and together we went out into the night toward the south.

"The following day we came upon a herd of small thoats, and thereafter we were mounted and made good time. We travelled very fast and very far due south until the morning of the fifth day we sighted a great fleet of battleships sailing north. They saw us before we could seek shelter, and soon we were surrounded by a horde of black men. The Princess's guard fought nobly to the end, but they were soon overcome and slain. Only Dejah Thoris and I were spared.

When she realized that she was in the clutches of the black pirates, she attempted to take her own life, but one of the blacks tore her dagger from her, and then they bound us both so that we could not use our hands.

"The fleet continued north after capturing us. There were about twenty large battleships in all, besides a number of small swift cruisers. That evening one of the smaller cruisers that had been far in advance of the fleet returned with a prisoner—a young red woman whom they had picked up in a range of hills under the very noses, they said, of a fleet of three red Martian battleships.

"From scraps of conversation which we overheard it was evident that the black pirates were searching for a party of fugitives that had escaped them several days prior. That they considered the capture of the young woman important was evident from the long and earnest interview the commander of the fleet held with her when she was brought to him. Later she was bound and placed in the compartment with Dejah Thoris and myself.

"The new captive was a very beautiful girl. She told Dejah Thoris that many years ago she had taken the voluntary pilgrimage from the court of her father, the Jeddak of Ptarth. She was Thuvia, the Princess of Ptarth. And then she asked Dejah Thoris who she might be, and when she heard she fell upon her knees and kissed Dejah Thoris' fettered hands, and told her that that very morning she had been with John Carter, Prince of Helium, and Carthoris, her son.

"Dejah Thoris could not believe her at first, but finally when the girl had narrated all the strange adventures that had befallen her since she had met John Carter, and told her of the things John Carter, and Carthoris, and Xodar had narrated of their adventures in the Land of the First Born, Dejah Thoris knew that it could be none other than the Prince of Helium; 'For who,' she said, 'upon all Barsoom other than John Carter could have done the deeds you tell of.' And when Thuvia told Dejah Thoris of her love for John Carter, and his loyalty and devotion to the Princess of his choice, Dejah Thoris broke down and wept—cursing Zat Arras and the cruel fate that had driven her from Helium but a few brief days before the return of her beloved lord.

" 'I do not blame you for loving him, Thuvia,' she said; 'and that your affection for him is pure and sincere I can well believe from the candour of your avowal of it to me.'

"The fleet continued north nearly to Helium, but last night they evidently realized that John Carter had indeed escaped them and so they turned toward the south once more. Shortly thereafter a guard entered our compartment and dragged me to the deck.

" 'There is no place in the Land of the First Born for a green one,' he said, and with that he gave me a terrific shove that carried me toppling from the deck of the battleship. Evidently this seemed to him the easiest way of ridding the vessel of my presence and killing me at the same time.

"But a kind fate intervened, and by a miracle I escaped with but slight bruises. The ship was moving slowly at the time, and as I lunged overboard into the darkness beneath I shuddered at the awful plunge I thought awaited me, for all day the fleet had sailed thousands of feet above the ground; but to my utter surprise I struck upon a soft mass of vegetation not twenty feet from the deck of the ship. In fact, the keel of the vessel must have been grazing the surface of the ground at the time.

"I lay all night where I had fallen and the next morning brought an explanation of the fortunate coincidence that had saved me from a terrible death. As the sun rose I saw a vast panorama of sea bottom and distant hills lying far below me. I was upon the highest peak of a lofty range. The fleet in the darkness of the preceding night had barely grazed the crest of the hills, and in the brief span that they hovered close to the surface the black guard had pitched me, as he supposed, to my death.

"A few miles west of me was a great waterway. When I reached it I found to my delight that it belonged to Helium. Here a thoat was procured for me—the rest you know."

For many minutes none spoke. Dejah Thoris in the clutches of the First Born! I shuddered at the thought, but of a sudden the old fire of unconquerable self-confidence surged through me. I sprang to my feet, and with back-thrown shoulders and upraised sword took a solemn vow to reach, rescue, and revenge my Princess.

A hundred swords leaped from a hundred scabbards, and a hundred fighting-men sprang to the table-top and pledged me their lives and fortunes to the expedition. Already my plans were formulated. I thanked each loyal friend, and leaving Carthoris to entertain them, withdrew to my own audience chamber with Kantos Kan, Tars Tarkas, Xodar, and Hor Vastus.

Here we discussed the details of our expedition until long after dark. Xodar was positive that Issus would choose both Dejah Thoris and Thuvia to serve her for a year.

"For that length of time at least they will be comparatively safe," he said, "and we will at least know where to look for them."

In the matter of equipping a fleet to enter Omean the details were left to Kantos Kan and Xodar. The former agreed to take such vessels as we required into dock as rapidly as possible, where Xodar would direct their equipment with water propellers.

For many years the black had been in charge of the refitting of captured battleships that they might navigate Omean, and so was familiar with the construction of the propellers, housings, and the auxiliary gearing required.

It was estimated that it would require six months to complete our preparations in view of the fact that the utmost secrecy must be maintained to keep the project from the ears of Zat Arras. Kantos Kan was confident now that the man's ambitions were fully aroused and that nothing short of the title of Jeddak of Helium would satisfy him.

"I doubt," he said, "if he would even welcome Dejah Thoris' return, for it would mean another nearer the throne than he. With you and Carthoris out of the way there would be little to prevent him from assuming the title of Jeddak, and you may rest assured that so long as he is supreme here there is no safety for either of you."

"There is a way," cried Hor Vastus, "to thwart him effectually and for ever."

"What?" I asked.

He smiled.

"I shall whisper it here, but some day I shall stand upon the dome of the Temple of Reward and shout it to cheering multitudes below."

"What do you mean?" asked Kantos Kan.

"John Carter, Jeddak of Helium," said Hor Vastus in a low voice.

The eyes of my companions lighted, and grim smiles of pleasure and anticipation overspread their faces, as each eye turned toward me questioningly. But I shook my head.

"No, my friends," I said, smiling, "I thank you, but it cannot be. Not yet, at least. When we know that Tardos Mors and Mors Kajak are gone to return no more; if I be here, then I shall join you all to see that the people of Helium are permitted to choose fairly their next Jeddak. Whom they choose may count upon the loyalty of my sword, nor shall I seek the honour for myself. Until then Tardos Mors is Jeddak of Helium, and Zat Arras is his representative."

"As you will, John Carter," said Hor Vastus, "but—What was that?" he whispered, pointing toward the window overlooking the gardens.

The words were scarce out of his mouth ere he had sprung to the balcony without.

"There he goes!" he cried excitedly. "The guards! Below there! The guards!"

We were close behind him, and all saw the figure of a man run quickly across a little piece of sward and disappear in the shrubbery beyond.

"He was on the balcony when I first saw him," cried Hor Vastus. "Quick! Let us follow him!"

Together we ran to the gardens, but even though we scoured the grounds with the entire guard for hours, no trace could we find of the night marauder.

"What do you make of it, Kantos Kan?" asked Tars Tarkas.

"A spy sent by Zat Arras," he replied. "It was ever his way."

"He will have something interesting to report to his master then," laughed Hor Vastus.

"I hope he heard only our references to a new Jeddak," I said. "If he overheard our plans to rescue Dejah Thoris, it will mean civil war, for he will attempt to thwart us, and in that I will not be thwarted. There would I turn against Tardos Mors himself, were it necessary. If it throws all Helium into a bloody conflict, I shall go on with these plans to save my Princess. Nothing shall stay me now short of death, and should I die, my friends, will you take oath to prosecute the search for her and bring her back in safety to her grandfather's court?"

Upon the hilt of his sword each of them swore to do as I had asked.

It was agreed that the battleships that were to be remodelled should be ordered to Hastor, another Heliumetic city, far to the south-west. Kantos Kan thought that the docks there, in addition to their regular work, would accommodate at least six battleships at a time. As he was commander-in-chief of the navy, it would be a simple matter for him to order the vessels there as they could be handled, and thereafter keep the remodelled fleet in remote parts of the empire until we should be ready to assemble it for the dash upon Omean.

It was late that night before our conference broke up, but each man there had his particular duties outlined, and the details of the entire plan had been mapped out.

Kantos Kan and Xodar were to attend to the remodelling of the ships. Tars Tarkas was to get into communication with Thark and learn the sentiments of his people toward his return from Dor. If favourable, he was to repair immediately to Thark and devote his time to the assembling of a great horde of green warriors whom it was our plan to send in transports directly to the Valley Dor and the Temple of Issus, while the fleet entered Omean and destroyed the vessels of the First Born.

Upon Hor Vastus devolved the delicate mission of organising a secret force of fighting-men sworn to follow John Carter wherever he might lead. As we estimated that it would require over a million men to man the thousand great battleships we intended to use on Omean and the transports for the green men as well as the ships that were to convoy the transports, it was no trifling job that Hor Vastus had before him.

After they had left I bid Carthoris good-night, for I was very tired, and going to my own apartments, bathed and lay down upon my sleeping silks and furs for the first good night's sleep I had had an opportunity to look forward to since I had returned to Barsoom. But even now I was to be disappointed.

How long I slept I do not know. When I awoke suddenly it was to find a half-dozen powerful men upon me, a gag already in my mouth, and a moment later my arms and legs securely bound. So quickly had they worked and to such good purpose, that I was utterly beyond the power to resist them by the time I was fully awake.

Never a word spoke they, and the gag effectually prevented me speaking. Silently they lifted me and bore me toward the door of my chamber. As they passed the window through which the farther moon was casting its brilliant beams, I saw that each of the party had his face swathed in layers of silk—I could not recognize one of them.

When they had come into the corridor with me, they turned toward a secret panel in the wall which led to the passage that terminated in the pits beneath the palace. That any knew of this panel outside my own household, I was doubtful. Yet the leader of the band did not hesitate a moment. He stepped directly to the panel, touched the concealed button, and as the door swung open he stood aside while his companions entered with me. Then he closed the panel behind him and followed us.

Down through the passageways to the pits we went. Along winding corridors that I myself had never explored. On and on until I felt confident that we were far beyond the confines of the palace grounds, and then the way led upward again toward the surface.

Presently the party halted before a blank wall. The leader rapped upon it with the hilt of his sword—three quick, sharp blows, a pause, then three more, another pause, and then two. A second later the wall swung in, and I was pushed within a brilliantly lighted chamber in which sat three richly trapped men.

One of them turned toward me with a sardonic smile upon his thin, cruel lips—it was Zat Arras.

NINETEEN

Black Despair

"Ah," said Zat Arras, "to what kindly circumstance am I indebted for the pleasure of this unexpected visit from the Prince of Helium?"

While he was speaking, one of my guards had removed the gag from my mouth, but I made no reply to Zat Arras: simply standing there in silence with level gaze fixed upon the Jed of Zodanga. And I doubt not that my expression was coloured by the contempt I felt for the man.

The eyes of those within the chamber were fixed first upon me and then upon Zat Arras, until finally a flush of anger crept slowly over his face.

"You may go," he said to those who had brought me, and when only his two companions and ourselves were left in the chamber, he spoke to me again in a voice of ice—very slowly and deliberately, with many pauses, as though he would choose his words cautiously.

"John Carter," he said, "by the edict of custom, by the law of our religion, and by the verdict of an impartial court, you are condemned to die. The people cannot save you—I alone may accomplish that. You are absolutely in my power to do with as I wish—I may kill you, or I may free you, and should I elect to kill you, none would be the wiser.

"Should you go free in Helium for a year, in accordance with the conditions of your reprieve, there is little fear that the people would ever insist upon the execution of the sentence imposed upon you.

"You may go free within two minutes, upon one condition. Tardos Mors will never return to Helium. Neither will Mors Kajak, nor Dejah Thoris. Helium must select a new Jeddak within the year. Zat Arras would be Jeddak of Helium. Say that you will espouse my cause. This is the price of your freedom. I am done."

I knew it was within the scope of Zat Arras' cruel heart to destroy me, and if I were dead I could see little reason to doubt that he might easily become Jeddak of Helium. Free, I could prosecute the search for Dejah

Thoris. Were I dead, my brave comrades might not be able to carry out our plans. So, by refusing to accede to his request, it was quite probable that not only would I not prevent him from becoming Jeddak of Helium, but that I would be the means of sealing Dejah Thoris' fate—of consigning her, through my refusal, to the horrors of the arena of Issus.

For a moment I was perplexed, but for a moment only. The proud daughter of a thousand Jeddaks would choose death to a dishonorable alliance such as this, nor could John Carter do less for Helium than his Princess would do.

Then I turned to Zat Arras.

"There can be no alliance," I said, "between a traitor to Helium and a prince of the House of Tardos Mors. I do not believe, Zat Arras, that the great Jeddak is dead."

Zat Arras shrugged his shoulders.

"It will not be long, John Carter," he said, "that your opinions will be of interest even to yourself, so make the best of them while you can. Zat Arras will permit you in due time to reflect further upon the magnanimous offer he has made you. Into the silence and darkness of the pits you will enter upon your reflection this night with the knowledge that should you fail within a reasonable time to agree to the alternative which has been offered you, never shall you emerge from the darkness and the silence again. Nor shall you know at what minute the hand will reach out through the darkness and the silence with the keen dagger that shall rob you of your last chance to win again the warmth and the freedom and joyousness of the outer world."

Zat Arras clapped his hands as he ceased speaking. The guards returned. Zat Arras waved his hand in my direction.

"To the pits," he said. That was all. Four men accompanied me from the chamber, and with a radium hand-light to illumine the way, escorted me through seemingly interminable tunnels, down, ever down beneath the city of Helium.

At length they halted within a fair-sized chamber. There were rings set in the rocky walls. To them chains were fastened, and at the ends of many of the chains were human skeletons. One of these they kicked aside, and, unlocking the huge padlock that had held a chain about what had once been a human ankle, they snapped the iron band about my own leg. Then they left me, taking the light with them.

Utter darkness prevailed. For a few minutes I could hear the clanking of accoutrements, but even this grew fainter and fainter, until at last the silence was as complete as the darkness. I was alone with my gruesome companions—with the bones of dead men whose fate was likely but the index of my own.

How long I stood listening in the darkness I do not know, but the silence was unbroken, and at last I sunk to the hard floor of my prison, where, leaning my head against the stony wall, I slept.

It must have been several hours later that I awakened to find a young man standing before me. In one hand he bore a light, in the other a receptacle containing a gruel-like mixture—the common prison fare of Barsoom.

"Zat Arras sends you greetings," said the young man, "and commands me to inform you that though he is fully advised of the plot to make you Jeddak of Helium, he is, however, not inclined to withdraw the offer which he has made you. To gain your freedom you have but to request me to advise Zat Arras that you accept the terms of his proposition."

I but shook my head. The youth said no more, and, after placing the food upon the floor at my side, returned up the corridor, taking the light with him.

Twice a day for many days this youth came to my cell with food, and ever the same greetings from Zat Arras. For a long time I tried to engage him in conversation upon other matters, but he would not talk, and so, at length, I desisted.

For months I sought to devise methods to inform Carthoris of my whereabouts. For months I scraped and scraped upon a single link of the massive chain which held me, hoping eventually to wear it through, that I might follow the youth back through the winding tunnels to a point where I could make a break for liberty.

I was beside myself with anxiety for knowledge of the progress of the expedition which was to rescue Dejah Thoris. I felt that Carthoris would not let the matter drop, were he free to act, but in so far as I knew, he also might be a prisoner in Zat Arras' pits.

That Zat Arras' spy had overheard our conversation relative to the selection of a new Jeddak, I knew, and scarcely a half-dozen minutes prior we had discussed the details of the plan to rescue Dejah Thoris. The chances were that that matter, too, was well known to him. Carthoris, Kantos Kan, Tars Tarkas, Hor Vastus, and Xodar might even now be the victims of Zat Arras' assassins, or else his prisoners.

I determined to make at least one more effort to learn something, and to this end I adopted strategy when next the youth came to my cell. I had noticed that he was a handsome fellow, about the size and age of Carthoris. And I had also noticed that his shabby trappings but illy comported with his dignified and noble bearing.

It was with these observations as a basis that I opened my negotiations with him upon his next subsequent visit.

"You have been very kind to me during my imprisonment here," I said to him, "and as I feel that I have at best but a very short time to live, I wish, ere it is too late, to furnish substantial testimony of my appreciation of all that you have done to render my imprisonment bearable.

"Promptly you have brought my food each day, seeing that it was pure and of sufficient quantity. Never by word or deed have you attempted to take advantage of my defenceless condition to insult or torture me. You have been uniformly courteous and considerate—it is this more than any other thing which prompts my feeling of gratitude and my desire to give you some slight token of it.

"In the guard-room of my palace are many fine trappings. Go thou there and select the harness which most pleases you—it shall be yours. All I ask is that you wear it, that I may know that my wish has been realized. Tell me that you will do it."

The boy's eyes had lighted with pleasure as I spoke, and I saw him glance from his rusty trappings to the magnificence of my own. For a moment he stood in thought before he spoke, and for that moment my heart fairly ceased beating—so much for me there was which hung upon the substance of his answer.

"And I went to the palace of the Prince of Helium with any such demand, they would laugh at me and, into the bargain, would more than likely throw me headforemost into the avenue. No, it cannot be, though I thank you for the offer. Why, if Zat Arras even dreamed that I contemplated such a thing he would have my heart cut out of me."

"There can be no harm in it, my boy," I urged. "By night you may go to my palace with a note from me to Carthoris, my son. You may read the note before you deliver it, that you may know that it contains nothing harmful to Zat Arras. My son will be discreet, and so none but us three need know. It is very simple, and such a harmless act that it could be condemned by no one."

Again he stood silently in deep thought.

"And there is a jewelled short-sword which I took from the body of a northern Jeddak. When you get the harness, see that Carthoris gives you that also. With it and the harness which you may select there will be no more handsomely accoutred warrior in all Zodanga.

"Bring writing materials when you come next to my cell, and within a few hours we shall see you garbed in a style befitting your birth and carriage."

Still in thought, and without speaking, he turned and left me. I could not guess what his decision might be, and for hours I sat fretting over the outcome of the matter.

If he accepted a message to Carthoris it would mean to me that Carthoris still lived and was free. If the youth returned wearing the harness and the sword, I would know that Carthoris had received my note and that he knew that I still lived. That the bearer of the note was a Zodangan would be sufficient to explain to Carthoris that I was a prisoner of Zat Arras.

It was with feelings of excited expectancy which I could scarce hide that I heard the youth's approach upon the occasion of his next regular visit. I did not speak beyond my accustomed greeting of him. As he placed the food upon the floor by my side he also deposited writing materials at the same time.

My heart fairly bounded for joy. I had won my point. For a moment I looked at the materials in feigned surprise, but soon I permitted an expression of dawning comprehension to come into my face, and then, picking them up, I penned a brief order to Carthoris to deliver to Parthak a harness of his selection and the short-sword which I described. That was all. But it meant everything to me and to Carthoris.

I laid the note open upon the floor. Parthak picked it up and, without a word, left me.

As nearly as I could estimate, I had at this time been in the pits for three hundred days. If anything was to be done to save Dejah Thoris it must be done quickly, for, were she not already dead, her end must soon come, since those whom Issus chose lived but a single year.

The next time I heard approaching footsteps I could scarce await to see if Parthak wore the harness and the sword, but judge, if you can, my chagrin and disappointment when I saw that he who bore my food was not Parthak.

"What has become of Parthak?" I asked, but the fellow would not answer, and as soon as he had deposited my food, turned and retraced his steps to the world above.

Days came and went, and still my new jailer continued his duties, nor would he ever speak a word to me, either in reply to the simplest question or of his own initiative.

I could only speculate on the cause of Parthak's removal, but that it was connected in some way directly with the note I had given him was most apparent to me. After all my rejoicing, I was no better off than before, for now I did not even know that Carthoris lived, for if Parthak had wished to raise himself in the estimation of Zat Arras he would have permitted me to go on precisely as I did, so that he could carry my note to his master, in proof of his own loyalty and devotion.

Thirty days had passed since I had given the youth the note. Three hundred and thirty days had passed since my incarceration. As closely as I could figure, there remained a bare thirty days ere Dejah Thoris would be ordered to the arena for the rites of Issus.

As the terrible picture forced itself vividly across my imagination, I buried my face in my arms, and only with the greatest difficulty was it that I repressed the tears that welled to my eyes despite my every effort. To think of that beautiful creature torn and rended by the cruel fangs of the hideous white apes! It was unthinkable. Such a horrid fact could not be; and yet my reason told me that within thirty days my incomparable Princess would be fought over in the arena of the First Born by those very wild beasts; that her bleeding corpse would be dragged through the dirt and the dust, until at last a part of it would be rescued to be served as food upon the tables of the black nobles.

I think that I should have gone crazy but for the sound of my approaching jailer. It distracted my attention from the terrible thoughts that had been occupying my entire mind. Now a new and grim determination came to me. I would make one super-human effort to escape. Kill my jailer by a ruse, and trust to fate to lead me to the outer world in safety.

With the thought came instant action. I threw myself upon the floor of my cell close by the wall, in a strained and distorted posture, as though I were dead after a struggle or convulsions. When he should stoop over me I had but to grasp his throat with one hand and strike him a terrific blow with the slack of my chain, which I gripped firmly in my right hand for the purpose.

Nearer and nearer came the doomed man. Now I heard him halt before me. There was a muttered exclamation, and then a step as he came to my side. I felt him kneel beside me. My grip tightened upon the chain. He leaned close to me. I must open my eyes to find his throat, grasp it, and strike one mighty final blow all at the same instant.

The thing worked just as I had planned. So brief was the interval between the opening of my eyes and the fall of the chain that I could not check it, though it that minute interval I recognized the face so close to mine as that of my son, Carthoris.

God! What cruel and malign fate had worked to such a frightful end! What devious chain of circumstances had led my boy to my side at this one particular minute of our lives when I could strike him down and kill him, in ignorance of his identity! A benign though tardy Providence blurred my vision and my mind as I sank into unconsciousness across the lifeless body of my only son.

When I regained consciousness it was to feel a cool, firm hand pressed upon my forehead. For an instant I did not open my eyes. I was endeavouring to gather the loose ends of many thoughts and memories which flitted elusively through my tired and overwrought brain.

At length came the cruel recollection of the thing that I had done in my last conscious act, and then I dared not to open my eyes for fear of what I should see lying beside me. I wondered who it could be who ministered to me. Carthoris must have had a companion whom I had not seen. Well, I must face the inevitable some time, so why not now, and with a sigh I opened my eyes.

Leaning over me was Carthoris, a great bruise upon his forehead where the chain had struck, but alive, thank God, alive! There was no one with him. Reaching out my arms, I took my boy within them, and if ever there arose from any planet a fervent prayer of gratitude, it was there beneath the crust of dying Mars as I thanked the Eternal Mystery for my son's life.

The brief instant in which I had seen and recognized Carthoris before the chain fell must have been ample to check the force of the blow. He told me that he had lain unconscious for a time—how long he did not know.

"How came you here at all?" I asked, mystified that he had found me without a guide.

"It was by your wit in apprising me of your existence and imprisonment through the youth, Parthak. Until he came for his harness and his sword, we had thought you dead. When I had read your note I did as you had bid, giving Parthak his choice of the harnesses in the guardroom, and later bringing the jewelled short-sword to him; but the minute that I had fulfilled the promise you evidently had made him, my obligation to him ceased. Then I commenced to question him, but he would give me no information as to your whereabouts. He was intensely loyal to Zat Arras.

"Finally I gave him a fair choice between freedom and the pits beneath the palace—the price of freedom to be full information as to where you were imprisoned and directions which would lead us to you; but still he maintained his stubborn partisanship. Despairing, I had him removed to the pits, where he still is.

"No threats of torture or death, no bribes, however fabulous, would move him. His only reply to all our importunities was that whenever Parthak died, were it to-morrow or a thousand years hence, no man could truly say, 'A traitor is gone to his deserts.'

"Finally, Xodar, who is a fiend for subtle craftiness, evolved a plan whereby we might worm the information from him. And so I caused Hor Vastus to be harnessed in the metal of a Zodangan soldier and chained in Parthak's cell beside him. For fifteen days the noble Hor Vastus has languished in the darkness of the pits, but not in vain. Little by little he won the confidence and friendship of the Zodangan, until only to-day Parthak, thinking that he was speaking not only to a countryman, but to a dear friend, revealed to Hor Vastus the exact cell in which you lay.

"It took me but a short time to locate the plans of the pits of Helium among thy official papers. To come to you, though, was a trifle more difficult matter. As you know, while all the pits beneath the city are connected, there are but single entrances from those beneath each section and its neighbour, and that at the upper level just underneath the ground.

"Of course, these openings which lead from contiguous pits to those beneath government buildings are always guarded, and so, while I easily came to the entrance to the pits beneath the palace which Zat Arras is occupying, I found there a Zodangan soldier on guard. There I left him when I had gone by, but his soul was no longer with him.

"And here I am, just in time to be nearly killed by you," he ended, laughing.

As he talked Carthoris had been working at the lock which held my fetters, and now, with an exclamation of pleasure, he dropped the end of the chain to the floor, and I stood up once more, freed from the galling irons I had chafed in for almost a year.

He had brought a long-sword and a dagger for me, and thus armed we set out upon the return journey to my palace.

At the point where we left the pits of Zat Arras we found the body of the guard Carthoris had slain. It had not yet been discovered, and, in order to still further delay search and mystify the jed's people, we carried the body with us for a short distance, hiding it in a tiny cell off the main corridor of the pits beneath an adjoining estate.

Some half-hour later we came to the pits beneath our own palace, and soon thereafter emerged into the audience chamber itself, where we found Kantos Kan, Tars Tarkas, Hor Vastus, and Xodar awaiting us most impatiently.

No time was lost in fruitless recounting of my imprisonment. What I desired to know was how well the plans we had laid nearly a year ago had been carried out.

"It has taken much longer than we had expected," replied Kantos Kan. "The fact that we were compelled to maintain utter secrecy has handicapped us terribly. Zat Arras' spies are everywhere. Yet, to the best of my knowledge, no word of our real plans has reached the villain's ear.

"To-night there lies about the great docks at Hastor a fleet of a thousand of the mightiest battleships that ever sailed above Barsoom, and each equipped to navigate the air of Omean and the waters of Omean itself. Upon each battleship there are five ten-man cruisers, and ten five-man scouts, and a hundred one-man scouts; in all, one hundred and sixteen thousand craft fitted with both air and water propellers.

"At Thark lie the transports for the green warriors of Tars Tarkas, nine hundred large troopships, and with them their convoys. Seven days ago all was in readiness, but we waited in the hope that by so doing your rescue might be encompassed in time for you to command the expedition. It is well we waited, my Prince."

"How is it, Tars Tarkas," I asked, "that the men of Thark take not the accustomed action against one who returns from the bosom of Iss?"

"They sent a council of fifty chieftains to talk with me here," replied the Thark. "We are a just people, and when I had told them the entire story they were as one man in agreeing that their action toward me would be guided by the action of Helium toward John Carter. In the meantime, at their request, I was to resume my throne as Jeddak of Thark, that I might negotiate with neighboring hordes for warriors to compose the land forces of the expedition. I have done that which I agreed. Two hundred and fifty thousand fighting men, gathered from the ice cap at the north to the ice cap at the south, and representing a thousand different communities, from a hundred wild and warlike hordes, fill the great city of Thark to-night. They are ready to sail for the Land of the First Born when I give the word and fight there until I bid them stop. All they ask is the loot they take and transportation to their own territories when the fighting and the looting are over. I am done."

"And thou, Hor Vastus," I asked, "what has been thy success?"

"A million veteran fighting-men from Helium's thin waterways man the battleships, the transports, and the convoys," he replied. "Each is sworn to loyalty and secrecy, nor were enough recruited from a single district to cause suspicion."

"Good!" I cried. "Each has done his duty, and now, Kantos Kan, may we not repair at once to Hastor and get under way before to-morrow's sun?"

"We should lose no time, Prince," replied Kantos Kan. "Already the people of Hastor are questioning the purpose of so great a fleet fully manned with fighting-men. I wonder much that word of it has not before reached Zat Arras. A cruiser awaits above at your own dock; let us leave at—" A fusillade of shots from the palace gardens just without cut short his further words.

Together we rushed to the balcony in time to see a dozen members of my palace guard disappear in the shadows of some distant shrubbery as in pursuit of one who fled. Directly beneath us upon the scarlet sward a handful of guardsmen were stooping above a still and prostrate form.

While we watched they lifted the figure in their arms and at my command bore it to the audience chamber where we had been in council. When they stretched the body at our feet we saw that it was that of a red man in the prime of life—his metal was plain, such as common soldiers wear, or those who wish to conceal their identity.

"Another of Zat Arras' spies," said Hor Vastus.

"So it would seem," I replied, and then to the guard: "You may remove the body."

"Wait!" said Xodar. "If you will, Prince, ask that a cloth and a little thoat oil be brought."

I nodded to one of the soldiers, who left the chamber, returning presently with the things that Xodar had requested. The black kneeled beside the body and, dipping a corner of the cloth in the thoat oil, rubbed for a moment on the dead face before him, Then he turned to me with a smile, pointing to his work. I looked and saw that where Xodar had applied the thoat oil the face was white, as white as mine, and then Xodar seized the black hair of the corpse and with a sudden wrench tore it all away, revealing a hairless pate beneath.

Guardsmen and nobles pressed close about the silent witness upon the marble floor. Many were the exclamations of astonishment and questioning wonder as Xodar's acts confirmed the suspicion which he had held.

"A thern!" whispered Tars Tarkas.

"Worse than that, I fear," replied Xodar. "But let us see."

With that he drew his dagger and cut open a locked pouch which had dangled from the thern's harness, and from it he brought forth a circlet of gold set with a large gem—it was the mate to that which I had taken from Sator Throg.

"He was a Holy Thern," said Xodar. "Fortunate indeed it is for us that he did not escape."

The officer of the guard entered the chamber at this juncture.

"My Prince," he said, "I have to report that this fellow's companion escaped us. I think that it was with the connivance of one or more of the men at the gate. I have ordered them all under arrest."

Xodar handed him the thoat oil and cloth.

"With this you may discover the spy among you," he said.

I at once ordered a secret search within the city, for every Martian noble maintains a secret service of his own.

A half-hour later the officer of the guard came again to report. This time it was to confirm our worst fears—half the guards at the gate that night had been therns disguised as red men.

"Come!" I cried. "We must lose no time. On to Hastor at once. Should the therns attempt to check us at the southern verge of the ice cap it may result in the wrecking of all our plans and the total destruction of the expedition."

Ten minutes later we were speeding through the night toward Hastor, prepared to strike the first blow for the preservation of Dejah Thoris.

TWENTY

The Air Battle

Two hours after leaving my palace at Helium, or about midnight, Kantos Kan, Xodar, and I arrived at Hastor. Carthoris, Tars Tarkas, and Hor Vastus had gone directly to Thark upon another cruiser.

The transports were to get under way immediately and move slowly south. The fleet of battleships would overtake them on the morning of the second day.

At Hastor we found all in readiness, and so perfectly had Kantos Kan planned every detail of the campaign that within ten minutes of our arrival the first of the fleet had soared aloft from its dock, and thereafter, at the rate of one a second, the great ships floated gracefully out into the night to form a long, thin line which stretched for miles toward the south.

It was not until after we had entered the cabin of Kantos Kan that I thought to ask the date, for up to now I was not positive how long I had lain in the pits of Zat Arras. When Kantos Kan told me, I realized with a pang of dismay that I had misreckoned the time while I lay in the utter darkness of my cell. Three hundred and sixty-five days had passed—it was too late to save Dejah Thoris.

The expedition was no longer one of rescue but of revenge. I did not remind Kantos Kan of the terrible fact that ere we could hope to enter the Temple of Issus, the Princess of Helium would be no more. In so far as I knew she might be already dead, for I did not know the exact date on which she first viewed Issus.

What now the value of burdening my friends with my added personal sorrows—they had shared quite enough of them with me in the past. Hereafter I would keep my grief to myself, and so I said nothing to any other of the fact that we were too late. The expedition could yet do much if it could but teach the people of Barsoom the facts of the cruel deception that had been worked upon them for countless ages, and thus save thousands each year from the horrid fate that awaited them at the conclusion of the voluntary pilgrimage.

If it could open to the red men the fair Valley Dor it would have accomplished much, and in the Land of Lost Souls between the Mountains of Otz and the ice barrier were many broad acres that needed no irrigation to bear rich harvests.

Here at the bottom of a dying world was the only naturally productive area upon its surface. Here alone were dews and rains, here alone was an open sea, here was water in plenty; and all this was but the stamping ground of fierce brutes and from its beauteous and fertile expanse the wicked remnants of two once mighty races barred all the other millions of Barsoom. Could I but succeed in once breaking down the barrier of religious superstition which had kept the red races from this El Dorado it would be a fitting memorial to the immortal virtues of my Princess—I should have again served Barsoom and Dejah Thoris' martyrdom would not have been in vain.

On the morning of the second day we raised the great fleet of transports and their consorts at the first flood of dawn, and soon were near enough to exchange signals. I may mention here that radio-aerograms are seldom if ever used in war time, or for the transmission of secret dispatches at any time, for as often as one nation discovers a new cipher, or invents a new instrument for wireless purposes its neighbours bend every effort until they are able to intercept and translate the messages. For so long a time has this gone on that practically every possibility of wireless communication has been exhausted and no nation dares transmit dispatches of importance in this way.

Tars Tarkas reported all well with the transports. The battleships passed through to take an advanced position, and the combined fleets moved slowly over the ice cap, hugging the surface closely to prevent detection by the therns whose land we were approaching.

Far in advance of all a thin line of one-man air scouts protected us from surprise, and on either side they flanked us, while a smaller number brought up the rear some twenty miles behind the transports. In this formation we had progressed toward the entrance to Omean for several hours when one of our scouts returned from the front to report that the cone-like summit of the entrance was in sight. At almost the same instant another scout from the left flank came racing toward the flagship.

His very speed bespoke the importance of his information. Kantos Kan and I awaited him upon the little forward deck which corresponds with the bridge of earthly battleships. Scarcely had his tiny flier come to rest upon the broad landing-deck of the flagship ere he was bounding up the stairway to the deck where we stood.

"A great fleet of battleships south-south-east, my Prince," he cried. "There must be several thousands and they are bearing down directly upon us."

"The thern spies were not in the palace of John Carter for nothing," said Kantos Kan to me. "Your orders, Prince."

"Dispatch ten battleships to guard the entrance to Omean, with orders to let no hostile enter or leave the shaft. That will bottle up the great fleet of the First Born.

"Form the balance of the battleships into a great V with the apex pointing directly south-south-east. Order the transports, surrounded by their convoys, to follow closely in the wake of the battleships until the point of the V has entered the enemies' line, then the V must open outward at the apex, the battleships of each leg engage the enemy fiercely and drive him back to form a lane through his line into which the transports with their convoys must race at top speed that they may gain a position above the temples and gardens of the therns.

"Here let them land and teach the Holy Therns such a lesson in ferocious warfare as they will not forget for countless ages. It had not been my intention to be distracted from the main issue of the campaign, but we must settle this attack with the therns once and for all, or there will be no peace for us while our fleet remains near Dor, and our chances of ever returning to the outer world will be greatly minimized."

Kantos Kan saluted and turned to deliver my instructions to his waiting aides. In an incredibly short space of time the formation of the battleships changed in accordance with my commands, the ten that were to guard the way to Omean were speeding toward their destination, and the troopships and convoys were closing up in preparation for the spurt through the lane.

The order of full speed ahead was given, the fleet sprang through the air like coursing greyhounds, and in another moment the ships of the enemy were in full view. They formed a ragged line as far as the eye could reach in either direction and about three ships deep. So sudden was our onslaught that they had no time to prepare for it. It was as unexpected as lightning from a clear sky.

Every phase of my plan worked splendidly. Our huge ships mowed their way entirely through the line of thern battlecraft; then the V opened up and a broad lane appeared through which the transports leaped toward the temples of the therns which could now be plainly seen glistening in the sunlight. By the time the therns had rallied from the attack a hundred thousand green warriors were already pouring through their courts and gardens, while a hundred and fifty thousand others leaned from low swinging transports to direct their almost uncanny marksmanship upon the thern soldiery that manned the ramparts, or attempted to defend the temples.

Now the two great fleets closed in a titanic struggle far above the fiendish din of battle in the gorgeous gardens of the therns. Slowly the two lines of Helium's battleships joined their ends, and then commenced the circling within the line of the enemy which is so marked a characteristic of Barsoomian naval warfare.

Around and around in each other's tracks moved the ships under Kantos Kan, until at length they formed nearly a perfect circle. By this time they were moving at high speed so that they presented a difficult target for the enemy. Broadside after broadside they delivered as each vessel came in line with the ships of the therns. The latter attempted to rush in and break up the formation, but it was like stopping a buzz saw with the bare hand.

From my position on the deck beside Kantos Kan I saw ship after ship of the enemy take the awful, sickening dive which proclaims its total destruction. Slowly we manœuvered our circle of death until we hung above the gardens where our green warriors were engaged. The order was passed down for them to embark. Then they rose slowly to a position within the centre of the circle.

In the meantime the therns' fire had practically ceased. They had had enough of us and were only too glad to let us go on our way in peace. But our escape was not to be encompassed with such ease, for scarcely had we gotten under way once more in the direction of the entrance to Omean than we saw far to the north a great black line topping the horizon. It could be nothing other than a fleet of war.

Whose or whither bound, we could not even conjecture. When they had come close enough to make us out at all, Kantos Kan's operator received a radio-aerogram, which he immediately handed to my companion. He read the thing and handed it to me.

"Kantos Kan:" it read. "Surrender, in the name of the Jeddak of Helium, for you cannot escape," and it was signed, "Zat Arras."

The therns must have caught and translated the message almost as soon as did we, for they immediately renewed hostilities when they realized that we were soon to be set upon by other enemies.

Before Zat Arras had approached near enough to fire a shot we were again hotly engaged with the thern fleet, and as soon as he drew near he too commenced to pour a terrific fusillade of heavy shot into us. Ship after ship reeled and staggered into uselessness beneath the pitiless fire that we were undergoing.

The thing could not last much longer. I ordered the transports to descend again into the gardens of the therns.

"Wreak your vengeance to the utmost," was my message to the green allies, "for by night there will be none left to avenge your wrongs."

Presently I saw the ten battleships that had been ordered to hold the shaft of Omean. They were returning at full speed, firing their stern batteries almost continuously. There could be but one explanation. They were being pursued by another hostile fleet. Well, the situation could be no worse. The expedition already was doomed. No man that had embarked upon it would return across that dreary ice cap. How I wished that I fight face Zat Arras with my longsword for just an instant before I died! It was he who had caused our failure.

As I watched the oncoming ten I saw their pursuers race swiftly into sight. It was another great fleet; for a moment I could not believe my eyes, but finally I was forced to admit that the most fatal calamity had overtaken the expedition, for the fleet I saw was none other than the fleet of the First Born, that should have been safely bottled up in Omean. What a series of misfortunes and disasters! What awful fate hovered over me, that I should have been so terribly thwarted at every angle of my search for my lost love! Could it be possible that the curse of Issus was upon me! That there was, indeed, some malign divinity in that hideous carcass! I would not believe it, and, throwing back my shoulders, I ran to the deck below to join my men in repelling boarders from one of the thern craft that had grappled us broadside. In the wild lust of hand-to-hand combat my old dauntless hopefulness returned. And as thern after thern went down beneath my blade, I could almost feel that we should win success in the end, even from apparent failure.

My presence among the men so greatly inspirited them that they fell upon the luckless whites with such terrible ferocity that within a few moments we had turned the tables upon them and a second later as we swarmed their own decks I had the satisfaction of seeing their commander take the long leap from the bows of his vessel in token of surrender and defeat.

Then I joined Kantos Kan. He had been watching what had taken place on the deck below, and it seemed to have given him a new thought. Immediately he passed an order to one of his officers, and presently the colours of the Prince of Helium broke from every point of the flagship. A great cheer arose from the men of our own ship, a cheer that was taken up by every other vessel of our expedition as they in turn broke my colours from their upper works.

Then Kantos Kan sprang his coup. A signal legible to every sailor of all the fleets engaged in that fierce struggle was strung aloft upon the flagship.

"Men of Helium for the Prince of Helium against all his enemies," it read. Presently my colours broke from one of Zat Arras' ships. Then from another and another. On some we could see fierce battles waging between the Zodangan soldiery and the Heliumetic crews, but eventually the colours of the Prince of Helium floated above every ship that had followed Zat Arras upon our trail—only his flagship flew them not.

Zat Arras had brought five thousand ships. The sky was black with the three enormous fleets. It was Helium against the field now, and the fight had settled to countless individual duels. There could be little or no manoeuvering of fleets in that crowded, fire-split sky.

Zat Arras' flagship was close to my own. I could see the thin features of the man from where I stood. His Zodangan crew was pouring broadside after broadside into us and we were returning their fire with equal ferocity. Closer and closer came the two vessels until but a few yards intervened. Grapplers and boarders lined the contiguous rails of each. We were preparing for the death struggle with our hated enemy.

There was but a yard between the two mighty ships as the first grappling irons were hurled. I rushed to the deck to be with my men as they boarded. Just as the vessels came together with a slight shock, I forced my way through the lines and was the first to spring to the deck of Zat Arras' ship. After me poured a yelling, cheering, cursing throng of Helium's best fighting-men. Nothing could withstand them in the fever of battle lust which enthralled them.

Down went the Zodangans before that surging tide of war, and as my men cleared the lower decks I sprang to the forward deck where stood Zat Arras.

"You are my prisoner, Zat Arras," I cried. "Yield and you shall have quarter."

For a moment I could not tell whether he contemplated acceding to my demand or facing me with drawn sword. For an instant he stood hesitating, and then throwing down his arms he turned and rushed to the opposite side of the deck. Before I could overtake him he had sprung to the rail and hurled himself headforemost into the awful depths below.

And thus came Zat Arras, Jed of Zodanga, to his end.

On and on went that strange battle. The therns and blacks had not combined against us. Wherever thern ship met ship of the First Born was a battle royal, and in this I thought I saw our salvation. Wherever messages could be passed between us that could not be intercepted by our enemies I passed the word that all our vessels were to withdraw from the fight as rapidly as possible, taking a position to the west and south of the combatants. I also sent an air scout to the fighting green men in the gardens below to re-embark, and to the transports to join us.

My commanders were further instructed than when engaged with an enemy to draw him as rapidly as possible toward a ship of his hereditary foeman, and by careful manœuvring to force the two to engage, thus leaving him- self free to withdraw. This stratagem worked to perfection, and just before the sun went down I had the satisfaction of seeing all that was left of my once mighty fleet gathered nearly twenty miles southwest of the still terrific battle between the blacks and whites.

I now transferred Xodar to another battleship and sent him with all the transports and five thousand battleships directly overhead to the Temple of Issus. Carthoris and I, with Kantos Kan, took the remaining ships and headed for the entrance to Omean.

Our plan now was to attempt to make a combined assault upon Issus at dawn of the following day. Tars Tarkas with his green warriors and Hor Vastus with the red men, guided by Xodar, were to land within the garden of Issus or the surrounding plains; while Carthoris, Kantos Kan, and I were to lead our smaller force from the sea of Omean through the pits beneath the temple, which Carthoris knew so well.

I now learned for the first time the cause of my ten ships' retreat from the mouth of the shaft. It seemed that when they had come upon the shaft the navy of the First Born were already issuing from its mouth. Fully twenty vessels had emerged, and though they gave battle immediately in an effort to stem the tide that rolled from the black pit, the odds against them were too great and they were forced to flee.

With great caution we approached the shaft, under cover of darkness. At a distance of several miles I caused the fleet to be halted, and from there Carthoris went ahead alone upon a one-man flier to reconnoitre. In perhaps half an hour he returned to report that there was no sign of a patrol boat or of the enemy in any form, and so we moved swiftly and noiselessly forward once more toward Omean.

At the mouth of the shaft we stopped again for a moment for all the vessels to reach their previously appointed stations, then with the flagship I dropped quickly into the black depths, while one by one the other vessels followed me in quick succession.

We had decided to stake all on the chance that we would be able to reach the temple by the subterranean way and so we left no guard of vessels at the shaft's mouth. Nor would it have profited us any to have done so, for we did not have sufficient force all told to have withstood the vast navy of the First Born had they returned to engage us.

For the safety of our entrance upon Omean we depended largely upon the very boldness of it, believing that it would be some little time before the First Born on guard there would realize that it was an enemy and not their own returning fleet that was entering the vault of the buried sea.

And such proved to be the case. In fact, four hundred of my fleet of five hundred rested safely upon the bosom of Omean before the first shot was fired. The battle was short and hot, but there could have been but one outcome, for the First Born in the carelessness of fancied security had left but a handful of ancient and obsolete hulks to guard their mighty harbour.

It was at Carthoris' suggestion that we landed our prisoners under guard upon a couple of the larger islands, and then towed the ships of the First Born to the shaft, where we managed to wedge a number of them securely in the interior of the great well. Then we turned on the buoyancy rays in the balance of them and let them rise by themselves to further block the passage to Omean as they came into contact with the vessels already lodged there.

We now felt that it would be some time at least before the returning First Born could reach the surface of Omean, and that we would have ample opportunity to make for the subterranean passages which lead to Issus. One of the first steps I took was to hasten personally with a good-sized force to the island of the submarine, which I took without resistance on the part of the small guard there.

I found the submarine in its pool, and at once placed a strong guard upon it and the island, where I remained to wait the coming of Carthoris and the others.

Among the prisoners was Yersted, commander of the submarine. He recognized me from the three trips that I had taken with him during my captivity among the First Born.

"How does it seem," I asked him, "to have the tables turned? To be prisoner of your erstwhile captive?"

He smiled, a very grim smile pregnant with hidden meaning.

"It will not be for long, John Carter," he replied. "We have been expecting you and we are prepared."

"So it would appear," I answered, "for you were all ready to become my prisoners with scarce a blow struck on either side."

"The fleet must have missed you," he said, "but it will return to Omean, and then that will be a very different matter—for John Carter."

"I do not know that the fleet has missed me as yet," I said, but of course he did not grasp my meaning, and only looked puzzled.

"Many prisoners travel to Issus in your grim craft, Yersted?" I asked.

"Very many," he assented.

Might you remember one whom men called Dejah Thoris?"

"Well, indeed, for her great beauty, and then, too, for the fact that she was wife to the first mortal that ever escaped from Issus through all the countless ages of her godhood. And they say that Issus remembers her best as the wife of one and the mother of another who raised their hands against the Goddess of Life Eternal."

I shuddered for fear of the cowardly revenge that I knew Issus might have taken upon the innocent Dejah Thoris for the sacrilege of her son and her husband.

"And where is Dejah Thoris now?" I asked, knowing that he would say the words I most dreaded, but yet I loved her so that I could not refrain from hearing even the worst about her fate so that it fell from the lips of one who had seen her but recently. It was to me as though it brought her closer to me.

"Yesterday the monthly rites of Issus were held," replied Yersted, "and I saw her then sitting in her accustomed place at the foot of Issus."

"What," I cried, "she is not dead, then?"

"Why, no," replied the black, "it has been no year since she gazed upon the divine glory of the radiant face of—"

"No year?" I interrupted.

"Why, no," insisted Yersted. "It cannot have been upward of three hundred and seventy or eighty days."

A great light burst upon me. How stupid I had been! I could scarcely retain an outward exhibition of my great joy. Why had I forgotten the great difference in the length of Martian and Earthly years! The ten Earth years I had spent upon Barsoom had encompassed but five years and ninety-six days of Martian time, whose days are forty-one minutes longer than ours, and whose years number six hundred and eighty-seven days.

I am in time! I am in time! The words surged through my brain again and again, until at last I must have voiced them audibly, for Yersted shook his head.

"In time to save your Princess?" he asked, and then without waiting for my reply, "No, John Carter, Issus will not give up her own. She knows that you are coming, and ere ever a vandal foot is set within the precincts of the Temple of Issus, if such a calamity should befall, Dejah Thoris will be put away for ever from the last faint hope of rescue."

"You mean that she will be killed merely to thwart me?" I asked.

"Not that, other than as a last resort," he replied. "Hast ever heard of the Temple of the Sun? It is there that they will put her. It lies far within the inner court of the Temple of Issus, a little temple that raises a thin spire far above the spires and minarets of the great temple that surrounds it. Beneath it, in the ground, there lies the main body of the temple consisting in six hundred and eighty-seven circular chambers, one below another. To each chamber a single corridor leads through solid rock from the pits of Issus.

"As the entire Temple of the Sun revolves once with each revolution of Barsoom about the sun, but once each year does the entrance to each separate chamber come opposite the mouth of the corridor which forms its only link to the world without.

"Here Issus puts those who displease her, but whom she does not care to execute forthwith. Or to punish a noble of the First Born she may cause him to be placed within a chamber of the Temple of the Sun for a year. Ofttimes she imprisons an executioner with the condemned, that death may come in a certain horrible form upon a given day, or again but enough food is deposited in the chamber to sustain life but the number of days that Issus has allotted for mental anguish.

"Thus will Dejah Thoris die, and her fate will be sealed by the first alien foot that crosses the threshold of Issus."

So I was to be thwarted in the end, although I had performed the miraculous and come within a few short moments of my divine Princess, yet was I as far from her as when I stood upon the banks of the Hudson forty-eight million miles away.

TWENTY-ONE

Through Flood and Flame

Yersted's information convinced me that there was no time to be lost. I must reach the Temple of Issus secretly before the forces under Tars Tarkas assaulted at dawn. Once within its hated walls I was positive that I could overcome the guards of Issus and bear away my Princess, for at my back I would have a force ample for the occasion.

No sooner had Carthoris and the others joined me than we commenced the transportation of our men through the submerged passage to the mouth of the gangways which lead from the submarine pool at the temple end of the watery tunnel to the pits of Issus.

Many trips were required, but at last all stood safely together again at the beginning of the end of our quest. Five thousand strong we were, all seasoned fighting-men of the most warlike race of the red men of Barsoom.

As Carthoris alone knew the hidden ways of the tunnels we could not divide the party and attack the temple at several points at once as would have been most desirable, and so it was decided that he lead us all as quickly as possible to a point near the temple's centre.

As we were about to leave the pool and enter the corridor, an officer called my attention to the waters upon which the submarine floated. At first they seemed to be merely agitated as from the movement of some great body beneath the surface, and I at once conjectured that another submarine was rising to the surface in pursuit of us; but presently it became apparent that the level of the waters was rising, not with extreme rapidity, but very surely, and that soon they would overflow the sides of the pool and submerge the floor of the chamber.

For a moment I did not fully grasp the terrible import of the slowly rising water. It was Carthoris who realized the full meaning of the thing—its cause and the reason for it.

"Haste!" he cried. "If we delay, we all are lost. The pumps of Omean have been stopped. They would drown us like rats in a trap. We must reach the upper levels of the pits in advance of the flood or we shall never reach them. Come."

"Lead the way, Carthoris," I cried. "We will follow."

At my command, the youth leaped into one of the corridors, and in columns of twos the soldiers followed him in good order, each company entering the corridor only at the command of its dwar, or captain.

Before the last company filed from the chamber the water was ankle deep, and that the men were nervous was quite evident. Entirely unaccustomed to water except in quantities sufficient for drinking and bathing purposes the red Martians instinctively shrank from it in such formidable depths and menacing activity. That they were undaunted while it swirled and eddied about their ankles, spoke well for their bravery and their discipline.

I was the last to leave the chamber of the submarine, and as I followed the rear of the column toward the corridor, I moved through water to my knees. The corridor, too, was flooded to the same depth, for its floor was on a level with the floor of the chamber from which it led, nor was there any perceptible rise for many yards.

The march of the troops through the corridor was as rapid as was consistent with the number of men that moved through so narrow a passage, but it was not ample to permit us to gain appreciably on the pursuing tide. As the level of the passage rose, so, too, did the waters rise until it soon became apparent to me, who brought up the rear, that they were gaining rapidly upon us. I could understand the reason for this, as with the narrowing expanse of Omean as the waters rose toward the apex of its dome, the rapidity of its rise would increase in inverse ratio to the ever-lessening space to be filled.

Long ere the last of the column could hope to reach the upper pits which lay above the danger point I was convinced that the waters would surge after us in overwhelming volume, and that fully half the expedition would be snuffed out.

As I cast about for some means of saving as many as possible of the doomed men, I saw a diverging corridor which seemed to rise at a steep angle at my right. The waters were now swirling about my waist. The men directly before me were quickly becoming panic-stricken. Something must be done at once or they would rush forward upon their fellows in a mad stampede that would result in trampling down hundreds beneath the flood and eventually clogging the passage beyond any hope of retreat for those in advance.

Raising my voice to its utmost, I shouted my command to the dwars ahead of me.

"Call back the last twenty-five utans," I shouted. "Here seems a way of escape. Turn back and follow me."

My orders were obeyed by nearer thirty utans, so that some three thousand men came about and hastened into the teeth of the flood to reach the corridor up which I directed them.

As the first dwar passed in with his utan I cautioned him to listen closely for my commands, and under no circumstances to venture into the open, or leave the pits for the temple proper until I should have come up with him, "or you know that I died before I could reach you."

The officer saluted and left me. The men filed rapidly past me and entered the diverging corridor which I hoped would lead to safety. The water rose breast high. Men stumbled, floundered, and went down. Many I grasped and set upon their feet again, but alone the work was greater than I could cope with. Soldiers were being swept beneath the boiling torrent, never to rise. At length the dwar of the 10th utan took a stand beside me. He was a valorous soldier, Gur Tus by name, and together we kept the now thoroughly frightened troops in the semblance of order and rescued many that would have drowned otherwise.

Djor Kantos, son of Kantos Kan, and a padwar of the fifth utan joined us when his utan reached the opening through which the men were fleeing. Thereafter not a man was lost of all the hundreds that remained to pass from the main corridor to the branch.

As the last utan was filing past us the waters had risen until they surged about our necks, but we clasped hands and stood our ground until the last man had passed to the comparative safety of the new passageway. Here we found an immediate and steep ascent, so that within a hundred yards we had reached a point above the waters.

For a few minutes we continued rapidly up the steep grade, which I hoped would soon bring us quickly to the upper pits that let into the Temple of Issus. But I was to meet with a cruel disappointment.

Suddenly I heard a cry of "fire" far ahead, followed almost at once by cries of terror and the loud commands of dwars and padwars who were evidently attempting to direct their men away from some grave danger. At last the report came back to us. "They have fired the pits ahead." "We are hemmed in by flames in front and flood behind." "Help, John Carter; we are suffocating," and then there swept back upon us at the rear a wave of dense smoke that sent us, stumbling and blinded, into a choking retreat.

There was naught to do other than seek a new avenue of escape. The fire and smoke were to be feared a thousand times over the water, and so I seized upon the first gallery which led out of and up from the suffocating smoke that was engulfing us.

Again I stood to one side while the soldiers hastened through on the new way. Some two thousand must have passed at a rapid run, when the stream ceased, but I was not sure that all had been rescued who had not passed the point of origin of the flames, and so to assure myself that no poor devil was left behind to die a horrible death, unsuccoured, I ran quickly up the gallery in the direction of the flames which I could now see burning with a dull glow far ahead.

It was hot and stifling work, but at last I reached a point where the fire lit up the corridor sufficiently for me to see that no soldier of Helium lay between me and the conflagration—what was in it or upon the far side I could not know, nor could any man have passed through that seething hell of chemicals and lived to learn.

Having satisfied my sense of duty, I turned and ran rapidly back to the corridor through which my men had passed. To my horror, however, I found that my retreat in this direction had been blocked—across the mouth of the corridor stood a massive steel grating that had evidently been lowered from its resting-place above for the purpose of effectually cutting off my escape.

That our principal movements were known to the First Born I could not have doubted, in view of the attack of the fleet upon us the day before, nor could the stopping of the pumps of Omean at the psychological moment have been due to chance, nor the starting of a chemical combustion within the one corridor through which we were advancing upon the Temple of Issus been due to aught than well-calculated design.

And now the dropping of the steel gate to pen me effectually between fire and flood seemed to indicate that invisible eyes were upon us at every moment. What chance had I, then, to rescue Dejah Thoris were I to be compelled to fight foes who never showed themselves. A thousand times I berated myself for being drawn into such a trap as I might have known these pits easily could be. Now I saw that it would have been much better to have kept our force intact and made a concerted attack upon the temple from the valley side, trusting to chance and our great fighting ability to have overwhelmed the First Born and compelled the safe delivery of Dejah Thoris to me.

The smoke from the fire was forcing me further and further back down the corridor toward the waters which I could hear surging through the darkness. With my men had gone the last torch, nor was this corridor lighted by the radiance of phosphorescent rock as were those of the lower levels. It was this fact that assured me that I was not far from the upper pits which lie directly beneath the temple.

Finally I felt the lapping waters about my feet. The smoke was thick behind me. My suffering was intense. There seemed but one thing to do, and that to choose the easier death which confronted me, and so I moved on down the corridor until the cold waters of Omean closed about me, and I swam on through utter blackness toward—what?

The instinct of self-preservation is strong even when one, unafraid and in the possession of his highest reasoning faculties, knows that death—positive and unalterable—lies just ahead. And so I swam slowly on, waiting for my head to touch the top of the corridor, which would mean that I had reached the limit of my flight and the point where I must sink for ever to an unmarked grave.

But to my surprise I ran against a blank wall before I reached a point where the waters came to the roof of the corridor. Could I be mistaken? I felt around. No, I had come to the main corridor, and still there was a breathing space between the surface of the water and the rocky ceiling above. And then I turned up the main corridor in the direction that Carthoris and the head of the column had passed a half-hour before. On and on I swam, my heart growing lighter at every stroke, for I knew that I was approaching closer and closer to the point where there would be no chance that the waters ahead could be deeper than they were about me. I was positive that I must soon feel the solid floor beneath my feet again and that once more my chance would come to reach the Temple of Issus and the side of the fair prisoner who languished there.

But even as hope was at its highest I felt the sudden shock of contact as my head struck the rocks above. The worst, then, had come to me. I had reached one of those rare places where a Martian tunnel dips suddenly to a lower level. Somewhere beyond I knew that it rose again, but of what value was that to me, since I did not know how great the distance that it maintained a level entirely beneath the surface of the water!

There was but a single forlorn hope, and I took it. Filling my lungs with air, I dived beneath the surface and swam through the inky, icy blackness on and on along the submerged gallery. Time and time again I rose with upstretched hand, only to feel the disappointing rocks close above me.

Not for much longer would my lungs withstand the strain upon them. I felt that I must soon succumb, nor was there any retreating now that I had gone this far. I knew positively that I could never endure to retrace my path now to the point from which I had felt the waters close above my head.

Death stared me in the face, nor ever can I recall a time that I so distinctly felt the icy breath from his dead lips upon my brow.

One more frantic effort I made with my fast ebbing strength. Weakly I rose for the last time—my tortured lungs gasped for the breath that would fill them with a strange and numbing element, but instead I felt the revivifying breath of life-giving air surge through my starving nostrils into my dying lungs. I was saved.

A few more strokes brought me to a point where my feet touched the floor, and soon thereafter I was above the water level entirely, and racing like mad along the corridor searching for the first doorway that would lead me to Issus. If I could not have Dejah Thoris again I was at least determined to avenge her death, nor would any life satisfy me other than that of the fiend incarnate who was the cause of such immeasurable suffering upon Barsoom.

Sooner than I had expected I came to what appeared to me to be a sudden exit into the temple above. It was at the right side of the corridor, which ran on, probably, to other entrances to the pile above.

To me one point was as good as another. What knew I where any of them led! And so without waiting to be again discovered and thwarted, I ran quickly up the short, steep incline and pushed open the doorway at its end.

The portal swung slowly in, and before it could be slammed against me I sprang into the chamber beyond. Although not yet dawn, the room was brilliantly lighted. Its sole occupant lay prone upon a low couch at the further side, apparently in sleep. From the hangings and sumptuous furniture of the room I judged it to be a living-room of some priestess, possibly of Issus herself.

At the thought the blood tingled through my veins. What, indeed, if fortune had been kind enough to place the hideous creature alone and unguarded in my hands. With her as hostage I could force acquiescence to my every demand. Cautiously I approached the recumbent figure, on noiseless feet. Closer and closer I came to it, but I had crossed but little more than half the chamber when the figure stirred, and, as I sprang, rose and faced me.

At first an expression of terror overspread the features of the woman who confronted me—then startled incredulity—hope—thanksgiving.

My heart pounded within my breast as I advanced toward her—tears came to my eyes—and the words that would have poured forth in a perfect torrent choked in my throat as I opened my arms and took into them once more the woman I loved—Dejah Thoris, Princess of Helium.

TWENTY-TWO

Victory and Defeat

"John Carter, John Carter," she sobbed, with her dear head upon my shoulder; "even now I can scarce believe the witness of my own eyes. When the girl, Thuvia, told me that you had returned to Barsoom, I listened, but I could not understand, for it seemed that such happiness would be impossible for one who had suffered so in silent loneliness for all these long years. At last, when I realized that it was truth, and then came to know the awful place in which I was held prisoner, I learned to doubt that even you could reach me here.

"As the days passed, and moon after moon went by without bringing even the faintest rumour of you, I resigned myself to my fate. And now that you have come, scarce can I believe it. For an hour I have heard the sounds of conflict within the palace. I knew not what they meant, but I have hoped against hope that it might be the men of Helium headed by my Prince.

"And tell me, what of Carthoris, our son?"

"He was with me less than an hour since, Dejah Thoris," I replied. "It must have been he whose men you have heard battling within the precincts of the temple.

"Where is Issus?" I asked suddenly.

Dejah Thoris shrugged her shoulders.

"She sent me under guard to this room just before the fighting began within the temple halls. She said that she would send for me later. She seemed very angry and somewhat fearful. Never have I seen her act in so uncertain and almost terrified a manner. Now I know that it must have been because she had learned that John Carter, Prince of Helium, was approaching to demand an accounting of her for the imprisonment of his Princess."

The sounds of conflict, the clash of arms, the shouting and the hurrying of many feet came to us from various parts of the temple. I knew that I was needed there, but I dared not leave Dejah Thoris, nor dared I take her with me into the turmoil and danger of battle.

At last I bethought me of the pits from which I had just emerged. Why not secrete her there until I could return and fetch her away in safety and for ever from this awful place. I explained my plan to her.

For a moment she clung more closely to me.

"I cannot bear to be parted from you now, even for a moment, John Carter," she said. "I shudder at the thought of being alone again where that terrible creature might discover me. You do not know her. None can imagine her ferocious cruelty who has not witnessed her daily acts for over half a year. It has taken me nearly all this time to realize even the things that I have seen with my own eyes."

"I shall not leave you, then, my Princess," I replied.

She was silent for a moment, then she drew my face to hers and kissed me.

"Go, John Carter," she said. "Our son is there, and the soldiers of Helium, fighting for the Princess of Helium. Where they are you should be. I must not think of myself now, but of them and of my husband's duty. I may not stand in the way of that. Hide me in the pits, and go."

I led her to the door through which I had entered the chamber from below. There I pressed her dear form to me, and then, though it tore my heart to do it, and filled me only with the blackest shadows of terrible foreboding, I guided her across the threshold, kissed her once again, and closed the door upon her.

Without hesitating longer, I hurried from the chamber in the direction of the greatest tumult. Scarce half a dozen chambers had I traversed before I came upon the theatre of a fierce struggle. The blacks were massed at the entrance to a great chamber where they were attempting to block the further progress of a body of red men toward the inner sacred precincts of the temple.

Coming from within as I did, I found myself behind the blacks, and, without waiting to even calculate their numbers or the foolhardiness of my venture, I charged swiftly across the chamber and fell upon them from the rear with my keen long-sword.

As I struck the first blow I cried aloud, "For Helium!" And then I rained cut after cut upon the surprised warriors, while the reds without took heart at the sound of my voice, and with shouts of "John Carter! John Carter!" redoubled their efforts so effectually that before the blacks could recover from their temporary demoralization their ranks were broken and the red men had burst into the chamber.

The fight within that room, had it had but a competent chronicler, would go down in the annals of Barsoom as a historic memorial to the grim ferocity of her warlike people. Five hundred men fought there that day, the black men against the red. No man asked quarter or gave it. As though by common assent they fought, as though to determine once and for all their right to live, in accordance with the law of the survival of the fittest.

I think we all knew that upon the outcome of this battle would hinge for ever the relative positions of these two races upon Barsoom. It was a battle between the old and the new, but not for once did I question the outcome of it. With Carthoris at my side I fought for the red men of Barsoom and for their total emancipation from the throttling bondage of a hideous superstition.

Back and forth across the room we surged, until the floor was ankle deep in blood, and dead men lay so thickly there that half the time we stood upon their bodies as we fought. As we swung toward the great windows which overlooked the gardens of Issus a sight met my gaze which sent a wave of exultation over me.

"Look!" I cried. "Men of the First Born, look!"

For an instant the fighting ceased, and with one accord every eye turned in the direction I had indicated, and the sight they saw was one no man of the First Born had ever imagined could be.

Across the gardens, from side to side, stood a wavering line of black warriors, while beyond them and forcing them ever back was a great horde of green warriors astride their mighty thoats. And as we watched, one, fiercer and more grimly terrible than his fellows, rode forward from the rear, and as he came he shouted some fierce command to his terrible legion.

It was Tars Tarkas, Jeddak of Thark, and as he couched his great forty-foot metal-shod lance we saw his warriors do likewise. Then it was that we interpreted his command. Twenty yards now separated the green men from the black line. Another word from the great Thark, and with a wild and terrifying battle-cry the green warriors charged. For a moment the black line held, but only for a moment—then the fearsome beasts that bore equally terrible riders passed completely through it.

After them came utan upon utan of red men. The green horde broke to surround the temple. The red men charged for the interior, and then we turned to continue our interrupted battle; but our foes had vanished.

My first thought was of Dejah Thoris. Calling to Carthoris that I had found his mother, I started on a run toward the chamber where I had left her, with my boy close beside me. After us came those of our little force who had survived the bloody conflict.

The moment I entered the room I saw that some one had been there since I had left. A silk lay upon the floor. It had not been there before. There were also a dagger and several metal ornaments strewn about as though torn from their wearer in a struggle. But worst of all, the door leading to the pits where I had hidden my Princess was ajar.

With a bound I was before it, and, thrusting it open, rushed within. Dejah Thoris had vanished. I called her name aloud again and again, but there was no response. I think in that instant I hovered upon the verge of insanity. I do not recall what I said or did, but I know that for an instant I was seized with the rage of a maniac.

"Issus!" I cried. "Issus! Where is Issus? Search the temple for her, but let no man harm her but John Carter. Carthoris, where are the apartments of Issus?"

"This way," cried the boy, and, without waiting to know that I had heard him, he dashed off at breakneck speed, further into the bowels of the temple. As fast as he went, however, I was still beside him, urging him on to greater speed.

At last we came to a great carved door, and through this Carthoris dashed, a foot ahead of me. Within, we came upon such a scene as I had witnessed within the temple once before—the throne of Issus, with the reclining slaves, and about it the ranks of soldiery.

We did not even give the men a chance to draw, so quickly were we upon them. With a single cut I struck down two in the front rank. And then by the mere weight and momentum of my body, I rushed completely through the two remaining ranks and sprang upon the dais beside the carved sorapus throne.

The repulsive creature, squatting there in terror, attempted to escape me and leap into a trap behind her. But this time I was not to be outwitted by any such petty subterfuge. Before she had half arisen I had grasped her by the arm, and then, as I saw the guard starting to make a concerted rush upon me from all sides, I whipped out my dagger and, holding it close to that vile breast, ordered them to halt.

"Back!" I cried to them. "Back! The first black foot that is planted upon this platform sends my dagger into Issus' heart."

For an instant they hesitated. Then an officer ordered them back, while from the outer corridor there swept into the throne room at the heels of my little party of survivors a full thousand red men under Kantos Kan, Hor Vastus, and Xodar.

"Where is Dejah Thoris?" I cried to the thing within my hands.

For a moment her eyes roved wildly about the scene beneath her. I think that it took a moment for the true condition to make any impression upon her—she could not at first realize that the temple had fallen before the assault of men of the outer world. When she did, there must have come, too, a terrible realization of what it meant to her—the loss of power—humiliation—the exposure of the fraud and imposture which she had for so long played upon her own people.

There was just one thing needed to complete the reality of the picture she was seeing, and that was added by the highest noble of her realm—the high priest of her religion—the prime minister of her government.

"Issus, Goddess of Death, and of Life Eternal," he cried, "arise in the might of thy righteous wrath and with one single wave of thy omnipotent hand strike dead thy blasphemers! Let not one escape. Issus, thy people depend upon thee. Daughter of the Lesser Moon, thou only art all-powerful. Thou only canst save thy people. I am done. We await thy will. Strike!"

And then it was that she went mad. A screaming, gibbering maniac writhed in my grasp. It bit and clawed and scratched in impotent fury. And then it laughed a weird and terrible laughter that froze the blood. The slave girls upon the dais shrieked and cowered away. And the thing jumped at them and gnashed its teeth and then spat upon them from frothing lips. God, but it was a horrid sight.

Finally, I shook the thing, hoping to recall it for a moment to rationality.

"Where is Dejah Thoris?" I cried again.

The awful creature in my grasp mumbled inarticulately for a moment, then a sudden gleam of cunning shot into those hideous, close-set eyes.

"Dejah Thoris? Dejah Thoris?" and then that shrill, unearthly laugh pierced our ears once more.

"Yes, Dejah Thoris—I know. And Thuvia, and Phaidor, daughter of Matai Shang. They each love John Carter. Ha-ah! but it is droll. Together for a year they will meditate within the Temple of the Sun, but ere the year is quite gone there will be no more food for them. Ho-oh! what divine entertainment," and she licked the froth from her cruel lips. "There will be no more food—except each other. Ha-ah! Ha-ah!"

The horror of the suggestion nearly paralysed me. To this awful fate the creature within my power had condemned my Princess. I trembled in the ferocity of my rage. As a terrier shakes a rat I shook Issus, Goddess of Life Eternal.

"Countermand your orders!" I cried. "Recall the condemned. Haste, or you die!"

"It is too late. Ha-ah! Ha-ah!" and then she commenced her gibbering and shrieking again.

Almost of its own volition, my dagger flew up above that putrid heart. But something stayed my hand, and I am now glad that it did. It were a terrible thing to have struck down a woman with one's own hand. But a fitter fate occurred to me for this false deity.

"First Born," I cried, turning to those who stood within the chamber, "you have seen to-day the impotency of Issus—the gods are impotent. Issus is no god. She is a cruel and wicked old woman, who has deceived and played upon you for ages. Take her. John Carter, Prince of Helium, would not contaminate his hand with her blood," and with that I pushed the raving beast, whom a short half-hour before a whole world had worshipped as divine, from the platform of her throne into the waiting clutches of her betrayed and vengeful people.

Spying Xodar among the officers of the red men, I called him to lead me quickly to the Temple of the Sun, and, without waiting to learn what fate the First Born would wreak upon their goddess, I rushed from the chamber with Xodar, Carthoris, Hor Vastus, Kantos Kan, and a score of other red nobles.

The black led us rapidly through the inner chambers of the temple, until we stood within the central court—a great circular space paved with a transparent marble of exquisite whiteness. Before us rose a golden temple wrought in the most wondrous and fanciful designs, inlaid with diamond, ruby, sapphire, turquoise, emerald, and the thousand nameless gems of Mars, which far transcend in loveliness and purity of ray the most priceless stones of Earth.

"This way," cried Xodar, leading us toward the entrance to a tunnel which opened in the courtyard beside the temple. Just as we were on the point of descending we heard a deep-toned roar burst from the Temple of Issus, which we had but just quitted, and then a red man, Djor Kantos, padwar of the fifth utan, broke from a nearby gate, crying to us to return.

"The blacks have fired the temple," he cried. "In a thousand places it is burning now. Haste to the outer gardens, or you are lost."

As he spoke we saw smoke pouring from a dozen windows looking out upon the courtyard of the Temple of the Sun, and far above the highest minaret of Issus hung an ever-growing pall of smoke.

"Go back! Go back!" I cried to those who had accompanied me. "The way! Xodar; point the way and leave me. I shall reach my Princess yet."

"Follow me, John Carter," replied Xodar, and without waiting for my reply he dashed down into the tunnel at our feet. At his heels I ran down through a half-dozen tiers of galleries, until at last he led me along a level floor at the end of which I discerned a lighted chamber.

Massive bars blocked our further progress, but beyond I saw her—my incomparable Princess, and with her were Thuvia and Phaidor. When she saw me she rushed toward the bars that separated us. Already the chamber had turned upon its slow way so far that but a portion of the opening in the temple wall was opposite the barred end of the corridor. Slowly the interval was closing. In a short time there would be but a tiny crack, and then even that would be closed, and for a long Barsoomian year the chamber would slowly revolve until once more for a brief day the aperture in its wall would pass the corridor's end.

But in the meantime what horrible things would go on within that chamber!

"Xodar!" I cried. "Can no power stop this awful revolving thing? Is there none who holds the secret of these terrible bars?"

"None, I fear, whom we could fetch in time, though I shall go and make the attempt. Wait for me here."

After he had left I stood and talked with Dejah Thoris, and she stretched her dear hand through those cruel bars that I might hold it until the last moment.

Thuvia and Phaidor came close also, but when Thuvia saw that we would be alone she withdrew to the further side of the chamber. Not so the daughter of Matai Shang.

"John Carter," she said, "this be the last time that you shall see any of us. Tell me that you love me, that I may die happy."

"I love only the Princess of Helium," I replied quietly. "I am sorry, Phaidor, but it is as I have told you from the beginning."

She bit her lip and turned away, but not before I saw the black and ugly scowl she turned upon Dejah Thoris. Thereafter she stood a little way apart, but not so far as I should have desired, for I had many little confidences to impart to my long-lost love.

For a few minutes we stood thus talking in low tones. Ever smaller and smaller grew the opening. In a short time now it would be too small even to permit the slender form of my Princess to pass. Oh, why did not Xodar haste. Above we could hear the faint echoes of a great tumult. It was the multitude of black and red and green men fighting their way through the fire from the burning Temple of Issus.

A draught from above brought the fumes of smoke to our nostrils. As we stood waiting for Xodar the smoke became thicker and thicker. Presently we heard shouting at the far end of the corridor, and hurrying feet.

"Come back, John Carter, come back!" cried a voice, "even the pits are burning."

In a moment a dozen men broke through the now blinding smoke to my side. There was Carthoris, and Kantos Kan, and Hor Vastus, and Xodar, with a few more who had followed me to the temple court.

"There is no hope, John Carter," cried Xodar. "The keeper of the keys is dead and his keys are not upon his carcass. Our only hope is to quench this conflagration and trust to fate that a year will find your Princess alive and well. I have brought sufficient food to last them. When this crack closes no smoke can reach them, and if we hasten to extinguish the flames I believe they will be safe."

"Go, then, yourself and take these others with you," I replied. "I shall remain here beside my Princess until a merciful death releases me from my anguish. I care not to live."

As I spoke Xodar had been tossing a great number of tiny cans within the prison cell. The remaining crack was not over an inch in width a moment later. Dejah Thoris stood as close to it as she could, whispering words of hope and courage to me, and urging me to save myself.

Suddenly beyond her I saw the beautiful face of Phaidor contorted into an expression of malign hatred. As my eyes met hers she spoke.

"Think not, John Carter, that you may so lightly cast aside the love of Phaidor, daughter of Matai Shang. Nor ever hope to hold thy Dejah Thoris in thy arms again. Wait you the long, long year; but know that when the waiting is over it shall be Phaidor's arms which shall welcome you—not those of the Princess of Helium. Behold, she dies!"

And as she finished speaking I saw her raise a dagger on high, and then I saw another figure. It was Thuvia's. As the dagger fell toward the unprotected breast of my love, Thuvia was almost between them. A blinding gust of smoke blotted out the tragedy within that fearsome cell—a shriek rang out, a single shriek, as the dagger fell.

The smoke cleared away, but we stood gazing upon a blank wall. The last crevice had closed, and for a long year that hideous chamber would retain its secret from the eyes of men.

They urged me to leave.

"In a moment it will be too late," cried Xodar. "There is, in fact, but a bare chance that we can come through to the outer garden alive even now. I have ordered the pumps started, and in five minutes the pits will be flooded. If we would not drown like rats in a trap we must hasten above and make a dash for safety through the burning temple."

"Go," I urged them. "Let me die here beside my Princess—there is no hope or happiness elsewhere for me. When they carry her dear body from

Suddenly beyond her I saw the beautiful face of Phaidor contorted into an expression of malign hatred.

that terrible place a year hence let them find the body of her lord awaiting her."

Of what happened after that I have only a confused recollection. It seems as though I struggled with many men, and then that I was picked bodily from the ground and borne away. I do not know. I have never asked, nor has any other who was there that day intruded on my sorrow or recalled to my mind the occurrences which they know could but at best reopen the terrible wound within my heart.

Ah! If I could but know one thing, what a burden of suspense would be lifted from my shoulders! But whether the assassin's dagger reached one fair bosom or another, only time will divulge.

The Warlord of Mars

ONE

On the River Iss

In the shadows of the forest that flanks the crimson plain by the side of the Lost Sea of Korus in the Valley Dor, beneath the hurtling moons of Mars, speeding their meteoric way close above the bosom of the dying planet, I crept stealthily along the trail of a shadowy form that hugged the darker places with a persistency that proclaimed the sinister nature of its errand.

For six long Martian months I had haunted the vicinity of the hateful Temple of the Sun, within whose slow-revolving shaft, far beneath the surface of Mars, my princess lay entombed—but whether alive or dead I knew not. Had Phaidor's slim blade found that beloved heart? Time only would reveal the truth.

Six hundred and eighty-seven Martian days must come and go before the cell's door would again come opposite the tunnel's end where last I had seen my ever-beautiful Dejah Thoris.

Half of them had passed, or would on the morrow, yet vivid in my memory, obliterating every event that had come before or after, there remained the last scene before the gust of smoke blinded my eyes and the narrow slit that had given me sight of the interior of her cell closed between me and the Princess of Helium for a long Martian year.

As if it were yesterday, I still saw the beautiful face of Phaidor, daughter of Matai Shang, distorted with jealous rage and hatred as she sprang forward with raised dagger upon the woman I loved.

I saw the red girl, Thuvia of Ptarth, leap forward to prevent the hideous deed.

The smoke from the burning temple had come then to blot out the tragedy, but in my ears rang the single shriek as the knife fell. Then silence, and when the smoke had cleared, the revolving temple had shut off all sight or sound from the chamber in which the three beautiful women were imprisoned.

Much there had been to occupy my attention since that terrible moment; but never for an instant had the memory of the thing faded, and all the time that I could spare from the numerous duties that had devolved upon me in the reconstruction of the government of the First Born since our victorious fleet and land forces had overwhelmed them, had been spent close to the grim shaft that held the mother of my boy, Carthoris of Helium.

The race of blacks that for ages had worshiped Issus, the false deity of Mars, had been left in a state of chaos by my revealment of her as naught more than a wicked old woman. In their rage they had torn her to pieces.

From the high pinnacle of their egotism the First Born had been plunged to the depths of humiliation. Their deity was gone, and with her the whole false fabric of their religion. Their vaunted navy had fallen in defeat before the superior ships and fighting men of the red men of Helium.

Fierce green warriors from the ocher sea bottoms of outer Mars had ridden their wild thoats across the sacred gardens of the Temple of Issus, and Tars Tarkas, Jeddak of Thark, fiercest of them all, had sat upon the throne of Issus and ruled the First Born while the allies were deciding the conquered nation's fate.

Almost unanimous was the request that I ascend the ancient throne of the black men, even the First Born themselves concurring in it; but I would have none of it. My heart could never be with the race that had heaped indignities upon my princess and my son.

At my suggestion Xodar became Jeddak of the First Born. He had been a dator, or prince, until Issus had degraded him, so that his fitness for the high office bestowed was unquestioned.

The peace of the Valley Dor thus assured, the green warriors dispersed to their desolate sea bottoms, while we of Helium returned to our own country. Here again was a throne offered me, since no word had been received from the missing Jeddak of Helium, Tardos Mors, grandfather of Dejah Thoris, or his son, Mors Kajak, Jed of Helium, her father.

Over a year had elapsed since they had set out to explore the northern hemisphere in search of Carthoris, and at last their disheartened people had accepted as truth the vague rumors of their death that had filtered in from the frozen region of the pole.

Once again I refused a throne, for I would not believe that the mighty Tardos Mors, or his no less redoubtable son, was dead.

"Let one of their own blood rule you until they return," I said to the assembled nobles of Helium, as I addressed them from the Pedestal of Truth beside the Throne of Righteousness in the Temple of Reward, from the very spot where I had stood a year before when Zat Arras pronounced the sentence of death upon me.

As I spoke I stepped forward and laid my hand upon the shoulder of Carthoris where he stood in the front rank of the circle of nobles about me.

As one, the nobles and the people lifted their voices in a long cheer of approbation. Ten thousand swords sprang on high from as many scabbards, and the glorious fighting men of ancient Helium hailed Carthoris Jeddak of Helium.

His tenure of office was to be for life or until his great-grandfather, or grandfather, should return. Having thus satisfactorily arranged this important duty for Helium, I started the following day for the Valley Dor that I might remain close to the Temple of the Sun until the fateful day that should see the opening of the prison cell where my lost love lay buried.

Hor Vastus and Kantos Kan, with my other noble lieutenants, I left with Carthoris at Helium, that he might have the benefit of their wisdom, bravery, and loyalty in the performance of the arduous duties which had devolved upon him. Only Woola, my Martian hound, accompanied me.

At my heels tonight the faithful beast moved softly in my tracks. As large as a Shetland pony, with hideous head and frightful fangs, he was indeed an awesome spectacle, as he crept after me on his ten short, muscular legs; but to me he was the embodiment of love and loyalty.

The figure ahead was that of the black dator of the First Born, Thurid, whose undying enmity I had earned that time I laid him low with my bare hands in the courtyard of the Temple of Issus, and bound him with his own harness before the noble men and women who had but a moment before been extolling his prowess.

Like many of his fellows, he had apparently accepted the new order of things with good grace, and had sworn fealty to Xodar, his new ruler; but I knew that he hated me, and I was sure that in his heart he envied and hated Xodar, so I had kept a watch upon his comings and goings, to the end that of late I had become convinced that he was occupied with some manner of intrigue.

Several times I had observed him leaving the walled city of the First Born after dark, taking his way out into the cruel and horrible Valley Dor, where no honest business could lead any man.

Tonight he moved quickly along the edge of the forest until well beyond sight or sound of the city, then he turned across the crimson sward toward the shore of the Lost Sea of Korus.

The rays of the nearer moon, swinging low across the valley, touched his jewel-incrusted harness with a thousand changing lights and glanced from the glossy ebony of his smooth hide. Twice he turned his head back toward the forest, after the manner of one who is upon an evil errand, though he must have felt quite safe from pursuit.

I did not dare follow him there beneath the moonlight, since it best suited my plans not to interrupt his—I wished him to reach his destination unsuspecting, that I might learn just where that destination lay and the business that awaited the night prowler there.

So it was that I remained hidden until after Thurid had disappeared over the edge of the steep bank beside the sea a quarter of a mile away. Then, with Woola following, I hastened across the open after the black dator.

The quiet of the tomb lay upon the mysterious valley of death, crouching deep in its warm nest within the sunken area at the south pole of the dying planet. In the far distance the Golden Cliffs raised their mighty barrier faces far into the starlit heavens, the precious metals and scintillating jewels that composed them sparkling in the brilliant light of Mars's two gorgeous moons.

At my back was the forest, pruned and trimmed like the sward to parklike symmetry by the browsing of the ghoulish plant men.

Before me lay the Lost Sea of Korus, while farther on I caught the shimmering ribbon of Iss, the River of Mystery, where it wound out from beneath the Golden Cliffs to empty into Korus, to which for countless ages had been borne the deluded and unhappy Martians of the outer world upon the voluntary pilgrimage to this false heaven.

The plant men, with their blood-sucking hands, and the monstrous white apes that make Dor hideous by day, were hidden in their lairs for the night.

There was no longer a Holy Thern upon the balcony in the Golden Cliffs above the Iss to summon them with weird cry to the victims floating down to their maws upon the cold, broad bosom of ancient Iss.

The navies of Helium and the First Born had cleared the fortresses and the temples of the therns when they had refused to surrender and accept the new order of things that had swept their false religion from long-suffering Mars.

In a few isolated countries they still retained their age-old power; but Matai Shang, their hekkador, Father of Therns, had been driven from his temple. Strenuous had been our endeavors to capture him; but with a few of the faithful he had escaped, and was in hiding—where we knew not.

As I came cautiously to the edge of the low cliff overlooking the Lost Sea of Korus I saw Thurid pushing out upon the bosom of the shimmering water in a small skiff—one of those strangely wrought craft of unthinkable age which the Holy Therns, with their organization of priests and lesser therns, were wont to distribute along the banks of the Iss, that the long journey of their victims might be facilitated.

Drawn up on the beach below me were a score of similar boats, each with its long pole, at one end of which was a pike, at the other a paddle. Thurid was hugging the shore, and as he passed out of sight round a near-by promontory I shoved one of the boats into the water and, calling Woola into it, pushed out from shore.

The pursuit of Thurid carried me along the edge of the sea toward the mouth of the Iss. The farther moon lay close to the horizon, casting a dense shadow beneath the cliffs that fringed the water. Thuria, the nearer moon, had set, nor would it rise again for near four hours, so that I was ensured concealing darkness for that length of time at least.

On and on went the black warrior. Now he was opposite the mouth of the Iss. Without an instant's hesitation he turned up the grim river, paddling hard against the strong current.

After him came Woola and I, closer now, for the man was too intent upon forcing his craft up the river to have any eyes for what might be transpiring behind him. He hugged the shore where the current was less strong.

Presently he came to the dark cavernous portal in the face of the Golden Cliffs, through which the river poured. On into the Stygian darkness beyond he urged his craft.

It seemed hopeless to attempt to follow him here where I could not see my hand before my face, and I was almost on the point of giving up the pursuit and drifting back to the mouth of the river, there to await his return, when a sudden bend showed a faint luminosity ahead.

My quarry was plainly visible again, and in the increasing light from the phosphorescent rock that lay embedded in great patches in the roughly arched roof of the cavern I had no difficulty in following him.

It was my first trip upon the bosom of Iss, and the things I saw there will live forever in my memory.

Terrible as they were, they could not have commenced to approximate the horrible conditions which must have obtained before Tars Tarkas, the great green warrior, Xodar, the black dator, and I brought the light of truth to the outer world and stopped the mad rush of millions upon the voluntary pilgrimage to what they believed would end in a beautiful valley of peace and happiness and love.

Even now the low islands which dotted the broad stream were choked with the skeletons and half devoured carcasses of those who, through fear or a sudden awakening to the truth, had halted almost at the completion of their journey.

In the awful stench of these frightful charnel isles haggard maniacs screamed and gibbered and fought among the torn remnants of their grisly feasts; while on those which contained but clean-picked bones they battled with one another, the weaker furnishing sustenance for the stronger; or with clawlike hands clutched at the bloated bodies that drifted down with the current.

Thurid paid not the slightest attention to the screaming things that either menaced or pleaded with him as the mood directed them—evidently he was familiar with the horrid sights that surrounded him. He continued up the river for perhaps a mile; and then, crossing over to the left bank, drew his craft up on a low ledge that lay almost on a level with the water.

I dared not follow across the stream, for he most surely would have seen me. Instead I stopped close to the opposite wall beneath an overhanging mass of rock that cast a dense shadow beneath it. Here I could watch Thurid without danger of discovery.

The black was standing upon the ledge beside his boat, looking up the river, as though he were awaiting one whom he expected from that direction.

As I lay there beneath the dark rocks I noticed that a strong current seemed to flow directly toward the center of the river, so that it was difficult to hold my craft in its position. I edged farther into the shadow that I might find a hold upon the bank; but, though I proceeded several yards, I touched nothing; and then, finding that I would soon reach a point from where I could no longer see the black man, I was compelled to remain where I was, holding my position as best I could by paddling strongly against the current which flowed from beneath the rocky mass behind me.

I could not imagine what might cause this strong lateral flow, for the main channel of the river was plainly visible to me from where I sat, and I could see the rippling junction of it and the mysterious current which had aroused my curiosity.

While I was still speculating upon the phenomenon, my attention was suddenly riveted upon Thurid, who had raised both palms forward above his head in the universal salute of Martians, and a moment later his "Kaor!" the Barsoomian word of greeting, came in low but distinct tones.

I turned my eyes up the river in the direction that his were bent, and presently there came within my limited range of vision a long boat, in which were six men. Five were at the paddles, while the sixth sat in the seat of honor.

The white skins, the flowing yellow wigs which covered their bald pates,

The black was standing upon the ledge beside his boat, looking up the river, as though he were awaiting one whom he expected from that direction.

and the gorgeous diadems set in circlets of gold about their heads marked them as Holy Therns.

As they drew up beside the ledge upon which Thurid awaited them, he in the bow of the boat arose to step ashore, and then I saw that it was none other than Matai Shang, Father of Therns.

The evident cordiality with which the two men exchanged greetings filled me with wonder, for the black and white men of Barsoom were hereditary enemies—nor ever before had I known of two meeting other than in battle.

Evidently the reverses that had recently overtaken both peoples had resulted in an alliance between these two individuals—at least against the common enemy—and now I saw why Thurid had come so often out into the Valley Dor by night, and that the nature of his conspiring might be such as to strike very close to me or to my friends.

I wished that I might have found a point closer to the two men from which to have heard their conversation; but it was out of the question now to attempt to cross the river, and so I lay quietly watching them, who would have given so much to have known how close I lay to them, and how easily they might have overcome and killed me with their superior force.

Several times Thurid pointed across the river in my direction, but that his gestures had any reference to me I did not for a moment believe. Presently he and Matai Shang entered the latter's boat, which turned out into the river and, swinging round, forged steadily across in my direction.

As they advanced I moved my boat farther and farther in beneath the overhanging wall, but at last it became evident that their craft was holding the same course. The five paddlers sent the larger boat ahead at a speed that taxed my energies to equal.

Every instant I expected to feel my prow crash against solid rock. The light from the river was no longer visible, but ahead I saw the faint tinge of a distant radiance, and still the water before me was open.

At last the truth dawned upon me—I was following a subterranean river which emptied into the Iss at the very point where I had hidden.

The rowers were now quite close to me. The noise of their own paddles drowned the sound of mine, but in another instant the growing light ahead would reveal me to them.

There was no time to be lost. Whatever action I was to take must be taken at once. Swinging the prow of my boat toward the right, I sought the river's rocky side, and there I lay while Matai Shang and Thurid approached up the center of the stream, which was much narrower than the Iss.

As they came nearer I heard the voices of Thurid and the Father of Therns raised in argument.

"I tell you, Thern," the black dator was saying, "that I wish only vengeance upon John Carter, Prince of Helium. I am leading you into no trap. What could I gain by betraying you to those who have ruined my nation and my house?"

"Let us stop here a moment that I may hear your plans," replied the hekkador, "and then we may proceed with a better understanding of our duties and obligations."

To the rowers he issued the command that brought their boat in toward the bank not a dozen paces beyond the spot where I lay.

Had they pulled in below me they must surely have seen me against the faint glow of light ahead, but from where they finally came to rest I was as secure from detection as though miles separated us.

The few words I had already overheard whetted my curiosity, and I was anxious to learn what manner of vengeance Thurid was planning against me. Nor had I long to wait. I listened intently.

"There are no obligations, Father of Therns," continued the First Born. "Thurid, Dator of Issus, has no price. When the thing has been accomplished I shall be glad if you will see to it that I am well received, as is befitting my ancient lineage and noble rank, at some court that is yet loyal to thy ancient faith, for I cannot return to the Valley Dor or elsewhere within the power of the Prince of Helium; but even that I do not demand—it shall be as your own desire in the matter directs."

"It shall be as you wish, Dator," replied Matai Shang; "nor is that all—power and riches shall be yours if you restore my daughter, Phaidor, to me, and place within my power Dejah Thoris, Princess of Helium.

"Ah," he continued with a malicious snarl, "but the Earth man shall suffer for the indignities he has put upon the holy of holies, nor shall any vileness be too vile to inflict upon his princess. Would that it were in my power to force him to witness the humiliation and degradation of the red woman."

"You shall have your way with her before another day has passed, Matai Shang," said Thurid, "if you but say the word."

"I have heard of the Temple of the Sun, Dator," replied Matai Shang, "but never have I heard that its prisoners could be released before the allotted year of their incarceration had elapsed. How, then, may you accomplish the impossible?"

"Access may be had to any cell of the temple at any time," replied Thurid. "Only Issus knew this; nor was it ever Issus' way to divulge more of her secrets than were necessary. By chance, after her death, I came upon an ancient plan of the temple, and there I found, plainly writ, the most minute directions for reaching the cells at any time.

"And more I learned—that many men had gone thither for Issus in the past, always on errands of death and torture to the prisoners; but those who thus learned the secret way were wont to die mysteriously immediately they had returned and made their reports to cruel Issus."

"Let us proceed, then," said Matai Shang at last. "I must trust you, yet at the same time you must trust me, for we are six to your one."

"I do not fear," replied Thurid, "nor need you. Our hatred of the common enemy is sufficient bond to insure our loyalty to each other, and after we have defiled the Princess of Helium there will be still greater reason for the maintenance of our allegiance— unless I greatly mistake the temper of her lord."

Matai Shang spoke to the paddlers. The boat moved on up the tributary.

It was with difficulty that I restrained myself from rushing upon them and slaying the two vile plotters; but quickly I saw the mad rashness of such an act, which would cut down the only man who could lead the way to Dejah Thoris' prison before the long Martian year had swung its interminable circle.

If he should lead Matai Shang to that hollowed spot, then, too, should he lead John Carter, Prince of Helium.

With silent paddle I swung slowly into the wake of the larger craft.

TWO

Under the Mountains

As we advanced up the river which winds beneath the Golden Cliffs out of the bowels of the Mountains of Otz to mingle its dark waters with the grim and mysterious Iss the faint glow which had appeared before us grew gradually into an all-enveloping radiance.

The river widened until it presented the aspect of a large lake whose vaulted dome, lighted by glowing phosphorescent rock, was splashed with the vivid rays of the diamond, the sapphire, the ruby, and the countless, nameless jewels of Barsoom which lay incrusted in the virgin gold which forms the major portion of these magnificent cliffs.

Beyond the lighted chamber of the lake was darkness—what lay behind the darkness I could not even guess.

To have followed the thern boat across the gleaming water would have been to invite instant detection, and so, though I was loath to permit Thurid to pass even for an instant beyond my sight, I was forced to wait in the shadows until the other boat had passed from my sight at the far extremity of the lake.

Then I paddled out upon the brilliant surface in the direction they had taken.

When, after what seemed an eternity, I reached the shadows at the upper end of the lake I found that the river issued from a low aperture, to pass beneath which it was necessary that I compel Woola to lie flat in the boat, and I, myself, must need bend double before the low roof cleared my head.

Immediately the roof rose again upon the other side, but no longer was the way brilliantly lighted. Instead only a feeble glow emanated from small and scattered patches of phosphorescent rock in wall and roof.

Directly before me the river ran into this smaller chamber through three separate arched openings.

Thurid and the therns were nowhere to be seen—into which of the dark holes had they disappeared? There was no means by which I might know, and so I chose the center opening as being as likely to lead me in the right direction as another.

Here the way was through utter darkness. The stream was narrow—so narrow that in the blackness I was constantly bumping first one rock wall and then another as the river wound hither and thither along its flinty bed.

Far ahead I presently heard a deep and sullen roar which increased in volume as I advanced, and then broke upon my ears with all the intensity of its mad fury as I swung round a sharp curve into a dimly lighted stretch of water.

Directly before me the river thundered down from above in a mighty waterfall that filled the narrow gorge from side to side, rising far above me several hundred feet—as magnificent a spectacle as I ever had seen.

But the roar—the awful, deafening roar of those tumbling waters penned in the rocky, subterranean vault! Had the fall not entirely blocked my further passage and shown me that I had followed the wrong course I believe that I should have fled anyway before the maddening tumult.

Thurid and the therns could not have come this way. By stumbling upon the wrong course I had lost the trail, and they had gained so much ahead of me that now I might not be able to find them before it was too late, if, in fact, I could find them at all.

It had taken several hours to force my way up to the falls against the strong current, and other hours would be required for the descent, although the pace would be much swifter.

With a sigh I turned the prow of my craft down stream, and with mighty strokes hastened with reckless speed through the dark and tortuous channel until once again I came to the chamber into which flowed the three branches of the river.

Two unexplored channels still remained from which to choose; nor was there any means by which I could judge which was the more likely to lead me to the plotters.

Never in my life, that I can recall, have I suffered such an agony of indecision. So much depended upon a correct choice; so much depended upon haste.

The hours that I had already lost might seal the fate of the incomparable Dejah Thoris were she not already dead—to sacrifice other hours, and maybe days in a fruitless exploration of another blind lead would unquestionably prove fatal.

Several times I essayed the right-hand entrance only to turn back as though warned by some strange intuitive sense that this was not the way. At last, convinced by the oft-recurring phenomenon, I cast my all upon the left-hand archway; yet it was with a lingering doubt that I turned a parting look at the sullen waters which rolled, dark and forbidding, from beneath the grim, low archway on the right.

And as I looked there came bobbing out upon the current from the Stygian darkness of the interior the shell of one of the great, succulent fruits of the sorapus tree.

I could scarce restrain a shout of elation as this silent, insensate messenger floated past me, on toward the Iss and Korus, for it told me that journeying Martians were above me on that very stream.

They had eaten of this marvelous fruit which nature concentrates within the hard shell of the sorapus nut, and having eaten had cast the husk overboard. It could have come from no others than the party I sought.

Quickly I abandoned all thought of the left-hand passage, and a moment later had turned into the right. The stream soon widened, and recurring areas of phosphorescent rock lighted my way.

I made good time, but was convinced that I was nearly a day behind those I was tracking. Neither Woola nor I had eaten since the previous day, but in so far as he was concerned it mattered but little, since practically all the animals of the dead sea bottoms of Mars are able to go for incredible periods without nourishment.

Nor did I suffer. The water of the river was sweet and cold, for it was unpolluted by decaying bodies—like the Iss—and as for food, why the mere thought that I was nearing my beloved princess raised me above every material want.

As I proceeded, the river became narrower and the current swift and turbulent—so swift in fact that it was with difficulty that I forced my craft upward at all. I could not have been making to exceed a hundred yards an hour when, at a bend, I was confronted by a series of rapids through which the river foamed and boiled at a terrific rate.

My heart sank within me. The sorapus nutshell had proved a false prophet, and, after all, my intuition had been correct—it was the left-hand channel that I should have followed.

Had I been a woman I should have wept. At my right was a great, slow-moving eddy that circled far beneath the cliff's overhanging side, and to rest my tired muscles before turning back I let my boat drift into its embrace.

I was almost prostrated by disappointment. It would mean another half-day's loss of time to retrace my way and take the only passage that yet remained unexplored. What hellish fate had led me to select from three possible avenues the two that were wrong?

As the lazy current of the eddy carried me slowly about the periphery of the watery circle my boat twice touched the rocky side of the river in the dark recess beneath the cliff. A third time it struck, gently as it had before, but the contact resulted in a different sound—the sound of wood scraping upon wood.

In an instant I was on the alert, for there could be no wood within that buried river that had not been man brought. Almost coincidentally with my first apprehension of the noise, my hand shot out across the boat's side, and a second later I felt my fingers gripping the gunwale of another craft.

As though turned to stone I sat in tense and rigid silence, straining my eyes into the utter darkness before me in an effort to discover if the boat were occupied.

It was entirely possible that there might be men on board it who were still ignorant of my presence, for the boat was scraping gently against the rocks upon one side, so that the gentle touch of my boat upon the other easily could have gone unnoticed.

Peer as I would I could not penetrate the darkness, and then I listened intently for the sound of breathing near me; but except for the noise of the rapids, the soft scraping of the boats, and the lapping of the water at their sides I could distinguish no sound. As usual, I thought rapidly.

A rope lay coiled in the bottom of my own craft. Very softly I gathered it up, and making one end fast to the bronze ring in the prow I stepped gingerly into the boat beside me. In one hand I grasped the rope, in the other my keen long-sword.

For a full minute, perhaps, I stood motionless after entering the strange craft. It had rocked a trifle beneath my weight, but it had been the scraping of its side against the side of my own boat that had seemed most likely to alarm its occupants, if there were any.

But there was no answering sound, and a moment later I had felt from stem to stern and found the boat deserted.

Groping with my hands along the face of the rocks to which the craft was moored, I discovered a narrow ledge which I knew must be the avenue taken by those who had come before me. That they could be none other than Thurid and his party I was convinced by the size and build of the boat I had found.

Calling to Woola to follow me I stepped out upon the ledge. The great, savage brute, agile as a cat, crept after me.

As he passed through the boat that had been occupied by Thurid and the therns he emitted a single low growl, and when he came beside me upon the ledge and my hand rested upon his neck I felt his short mane bristling with anger. I think he sensed telepathically the recent presence of an enemy, for I had made no effort to impart to him the nature of our quest or the status of those we tracked.

This omission I now made haste to correct, and, after the manner of green Martians with their beasts, I let him know partially by the weird and uncanny telepathy of Barsoom and partly by word of mouth that we were upon the trail of those who had recently occupied the boat through which we had just passed.

A soft purr, like that of a great cat, indicated that Woola understood, and then, with a word to him to follow, I turned to the right along the ledge, but scarcely had I done so than I felt his mighty fangs tugging at my leathern harness.

As I turned to discover the cause of his act he continued to pull me steadily in the opposite direction, nor would he desist until I had turned about and indicated that I would follow him voluntarily.

Never had I known him to be in error in a matter of tracking, so it was with a feeling of entire security that I moved cautiously in the huge beast's wake. Through Cimmerian darkness he moved along the narrow ledge beside the boiling rapids.

As we advanced, the way led from beneath the overhanging cliffs out into a dim light, and then it was that I saw that the trail had been cut from the living rock, and that it ran up along the river's side beyond the rapids.

For hours we followed the dark and gloomy river farther and farther into the bowels of Mars. From the direction and distance I knew that we must be well beneath the Valley Dor, and possibly beneath the Sea of Omean as well—it could not be much farther now to the Temple of the Sun.

Even as my mind framed the thought, Woola halted suddenly before a narrow, arched doorway in the cliff by the trail's side. Quickly he crouched back away from the entrance, at the same time turning his eyes toward me.

Words could not have more plainly told me that danger of some sort lay near by, and so I pressed quietly forward to his side, and passing him looked into the aperture at our right.

Before me was a fair-sized chamber that, from its appointments, I knew must have at one time been a guardroom. There were racks for weapons, and slightly raised platforms for the sleeping silks and furs of the warriors, but now its only occupants were two of the therns who had been of the party with Thurid and Matai Shang.

The men were in earnest conversation, and from their tones it was apparent that they were entirely unaware that they had listeners.

"I tell you," one of them was saying, "I do not trust the black one. There was no necessity for leaving us here to guard the way. Against what, pray, should we guard this long-forgotten, abysmal path? It was but a ruse to divide our numbers.

"He will have Matai Shang leave others elsewhere on some pretext or other, and then at last he will fall upon us with his confederates and slay us all."

"I believe you, Lakor," replied the other, "there can never be aught else than deadly hatred between Thern and First Born. And what think you of the ridiculous matter of the light? 'Let the light shine with the intensity of three radium units for fifty tals, and for one xat let it shine with the intensity of one radium unit, and then for twenty-five tals with nine units.' Those were his very words, and to think that wise old Matai Shang should listen to such foolishness."

"Indeed, it is silly," replied Lakor. "It will open nothing other than the way to a quick death for us all. He had to make some answer when Matai Shang asked him flatly what he should do when he came to the Temple of the Sun, and so he made his answer quickly from his imagination— I would wager a hekkador's diadem that he could not now repeat it himself."

"Let us not remain here longer, Lakor," spoke the other thern. "Perchance if we hasten after them we may come in time to rescue Matai Shang, and wreak our own vengeance upon the black dator. What say you?"

"Never in a long life," answered Lakor, "have I disobeyed a single command of the Father of Therns. I shall stay here until I rot if he does not return to bid me elsewhere."

Lakor's companion shook his head.

"You are my superior," he said; "I cannot do other than you sanction, though I still believe that we are foolish to remain."

I, too, thought that they were foolish to remain, for I saw from Woola's actions that the trail led through the room where the two therns held guard. I had no reason to harbor any considerable love for this race of self-deified demons, yet I would have passed them by were it possible without molesting them.

It was worth trying anyway, for a fight might delay us considerably, or even put an end entirely to my search—better men than I have gone down before fighters of meaner ability than that possessed by the fierce thern warriors.

Signaling Woola to heel I stepped suddenly into the room before the two men. At sight of me their long-swords flashed from the harness at their sides, but I raised my hand in a gesture of restraint.

"I seek Thurid, the black dator," I said. "My quarrel is with him, not with you. Let me pass then in peace, for if I mistake not he is as much your enemy as mine, and you can have no cause to protect him."

They lowered their swords and Lakor spoke.

"I know not whom you may be, with the white skin of a thern and the black hair of a red man; but were it only Thurid whose safety were at stake you might pass, and welcome, in so far as we be concerned.

"Tell us who you be, and what mission calls you to this unknown world beneath the Valley Dor, then maybe we can see our way to let you pass upon the errand which we should like to undertake would our orders permit."

I was surprised that neither of them had recognized me, for I thought that I was quite sufficiently well known either by personal experience or reputation to every thern upon Barsoom as to make my identity immediately apparent in any part of the planet. In fact, I was the only white man upon Mars whose hair was black and whose eyes were gray, with the exception of my son, Carthoris.

To reveal my identity might be to precipitate an attack, for every thern upon Barsoom knew that to me they owed the fall of their age-old spiritual supremacy. On the other hand my reputation as a fighting man might be sufficient to pass me by these two were their livers not of the right complexion to welcome a battle to the death.

To be quite candid I did not attempt to delude myself with any such sophistry, since I knew well that upon war-like Mars there are few cowards, and that every man, whether prince, priest, or peasant, glories in deadly strife. And so I gripped my long-sword the tighter as I replied to Lakor.

"I believe that you will see the wisdom of permitting me to pass unmolested," I said, "for it would avail you nothing to die uselessly in the rocky bowels of Barsoom merely to protect a hereditary enemy, such as Thurid, Dator of the First Born.

"That you shall die should you elect to oppose me is evidenced by the moldering corpses of all the many great Barsoomian warriors who have gone down beneath this blade—I am John Carter, Prince of Helium."

For a moment that name seemed to paralyze the two men; but only for a moment, and then the younger of them, with a vile name upon his lips, rushed toward me with ready sword.

He had been standing a little behind his companion, Lakor, during our parley, and now, ere he could engage me, the older man grasped his harness and drew him back.

"Hold!" commanded Lakor. "There will be plenty of time to fight if we find it wise to fight at all. There be good reasons why every thern upon Barsoom should yearn to spill the blood of the blasphemer, the sacrilegist; but let us mix wisdom with our righteous hate. The Prince of Helium is bound upon an errand which we ourselves, but a moment since, were wishing that we might undertake.

"Let him go then and slay the black. When he returns we shall still be here to bar his way to the outer world, and thus we shall have rid ourselves of two enemies, nor have incurred the displeasure of the Father of Therns."

As he spoke I could not but note the crafty glint in his evil eyes, and while I saw the apparent logic of his reasoning I felt, subconsciously perhaps, that his words did but veil some sinister intent. The other thern turned toward him in evident surprise, but when Lakor had whispered a few brief words into his ear he, too, drew back and nodded acquiescence to his superior's suggestion.

"Proceed, John Carter," said Lakor; "but know that if Thurid does not lay you low there will be those awaiting your return who will see that you never pass again into the sunlight of the upper world. Go!"

During our conversation Woola had been growling and bristling close to my side. Occasionally he would look up into my face with a low, pleading whine, as though begging for the word that would send him headlong at the bare throats before him. He, too, sensed the villainy behind the smooth words.

Beyond the therns several doorways opened off the guardroom, and toward the one upon the extreme right Lakor motioned.

"That way leads to Thurid," he said.

But when I would have called Woola to follow me there the beast whined and held back, and at last ran quickly to the first opening at the left, where he stood emitting his coughing bark, as though urging me to follow him upon the right way.

I turned a questioning look upon Lakor.

"The brute is seldom wrong," I said, "and while I do not doubt your superior knowledge, Thern, I think that I shall do well to listen to the voice of instinct that is backed by love and loyalty."

As I spoke I smiled grimly that he might know without words that I distrusted him.

"As you will," the fellow replied with a shrug. "In the end it shall be all the same."

I turned and followed Woola into the left-hand passage, and though my back was toward my enemies, my ears were on the alert; yet I heard no sound of pursuit. The passageway was dimly lighted by occasional radium bulbs, the universal lighting medium of Barsoom.

These same lamps may have been doing continuous duty in these subterranean chambers for ages, since they require no attention and are so compounded that they give off but the minutest of their substance in the generation of years of luminosity.

We had proceeded for but a short distance when we commenced to pass the mouths of diverging corridors, but not once did Woola hesitate. It was at the opening to one of these corridors upon my right that I presently heard a sound that spoke more plainly to John Carter, fighting man, than could the words of my mother tongue—it was the clank of metal—the metal of a warrior's harness—and it came from a little distance up the corridor upon my right.

Woola heard it, too, and like a flash he had wheeled and stood facing the threatened danger, his mane all abristle and all his rows of glistening fangs bared by snarling, backdrawn lips. With a gesture I silenced him, and together we drew aside into another corridor a few paces farther on.

Here we waited; nor did we have long to wait, for presently we saw the shadows of two men fall upon the floor of the main corridor athwart the doorway of our hiding place. Very cautiously they were moving now—the accidental clank that had alarmed me was not repeated.

Presently they came opposite our station; nor was I surprised to see that the two were Lakor and his companion of the guardroom.

They walked very softly, and in the right hand of each gleamed a keen long-sword. They halted quite close to the entrance of our retreat, whispering to each other.

"Can it be that we have distanced them already?" said Lakor.

"Either that or the beast has led the man upon a wrong trail," replied the other, "for the way which we took is by far the shorter to this point—for him who knows it. John Carter would have found it a short road to death had he taken it as you suggested to him."

"Yes," said Lakor, "no amount of fighting ability would have saved him from the pivoted flagstone. He surely would have stepped upon it, and by now, if the pit beneath it has a bottom, which Thurid denies, he should have been rapidly approaching it. Curses on that calot of his that warned him toward the safer avenue!"

"There be other dangers ahead of him, though," spoke Lakor's fellow, "which he may not so easily escape—should he succeed in escaping our two good swords. Consider, for example, what chance he will have, coming unexpectedly into the chamber of——"

I would have given much to have heard the balance of that conversation that I might have been warned of the perils that lay ahead, but fate intervened, and just at the very instant of all other instants that I would not have elected to do it, I sneezed.

THREE

The Temple of the Sun

There was nothing for it now other than to fight; nor did I have any advantage as I sprang, sword in hand, into the corridor before the two therns, for my untimely sneeze had warned them of my presence and they were ready for me.

There were no words, for they would have been a waste of breath. The very presence of the two proclaimed their treachery. That they were following to fall upon me unawares was all too plain, and they, of course, must have known that I understood their plan.

In an instant I was engaged with both, and though I loathe the very name of thern, I must in all fairness admit that they are mighty swordsmen; and these two were no exception, unless it were that they were even more skilled and fearless than the average among their race.

While it lasted it was indeed as joyous a conflict as I ever had experienced. Twice at least I saved my breast from the mortal thrust of piercing steel only by the wondrous agility with which my earthly muscles endow me under the conditions of lesser gravity and air pressure upon Mars.

Yet even so I came near to tasting death that day in the gloomy corridor beneath Mars's southern pole, for Lakor played a trick upon me that in all my experience of fighting upon two planets I never before had witnessed the like of.

The other thern was engaging me at the time, and I was forcing him back—touching him here and there with my point until he was bleeding from a dozen wounds, yet not being able to penetrate his marvelous guard to reach a vulnerable spot for the brief instant that would have been sufficient to send him to his ancestors.

It was then that Lakor quickly unslung a belt from his harness, and as I stepped back to parry a wicked thrust he lashed one end of it about my left ankle so that it wound there for an instant, while he jerked suddenly upon the other end, throwing me heavily upon my back.

Then, like leaping panthers, they were upon me; but they had reckoned without Woola, and before ever a blade touched me, a roaring embodiment of a thousand demons hurtled above my prostrate form and my loyal Martian calot was upon them.

Imagine, if you can, a huge grizzly with ten legs armed with mighty talons and an enormous froglike mouth splitting his head from ear to ear, exposing three rows of long, white tusks. Then endow this creature of your imagination with the agility and ferocity of a half-starved Bengal tiger and the strength of a span of bulls, and you will have some faint conception of Woola in action.

Before I could call him off he had crushed Lakor into a jelly with a single blow of one mighty paw, and had literally torn the other thern to ribbons; yet when I spoke to him sharply he cowed sheepishly as though he had done a thing to deserve censure and chastisement.

Never had I had the heart to punish Woola during the long years that had passed since that first day upon Mars when the green jed of the Tharks had placed him on guard over me, and I had won his love and loyalty from the cruel and loveless masters of his former life, yet I believe he would have submitted to any cruelty that I might have inflicted upon him, so wondrous was his affection for me.

The diadem in the center of the circlet of gold upon the brow of Lakor proclaimed him a Holy Thern, while his companion, not thus adorned, was a lesser thern, though from his harness I gleaned that he had reached the Ninth Cycle, which is but one below that of the Holy Therns.

As I stood for a moment looking at the gruesome havoc Woola had wrought, there recurred to me the memory of that other occasion upon which I had masqueraded in the wig, diadem, and harness of Sator Throg, the Holy Thern whom Thuvia of Ptarth had slain, and now it occurred to me that it might prove of worth to utilize Lakor's trappings for the same purpose.

A moment later I had torn his yellow wig from his bald pate and transferred it and the circlet, as well as all his harness, to my own person.

Woola did not approve of the metamorphosis. He sniffed at me and growled ominously, but when I spoke to him and patted his huge head he at length became reconciled to the change, and at my command trotted off along the corridor in the direction we had been going when our progress had been interrupted by the therns.

We moved cautiously now, warned by the fragment of conversation I had overheard. I kept abreast of Woola that we might have the benefit of all our eyes for what might appear suddenly ahead to menace us, and well it was that we were forewarned.

At the bottom of a flight of narrow steps the corridor turned sharply back upon itself, immediately making another turn in the original direction, so that at that point it formed a perfect letter S, the top leg of which debouched suddenly into a large chamber, illy lighted, and the floor of which was completely covered by venomous snakes and loathsome reptiles.

To have attempted to cross that floor would have been to court instant death, and for a moment I was almost completely discouraged. Then it occurred to me that Thurid and Matai Shang with their party must have crossed it, and so there was a way.

Had it not been for the fortunate accident by which I overheard even so small a portion of the therns' conversation we should have blundered at least a step or two into that wriggling mass of destruction, and a single step would have been all-sufficient to have sealed our doom.

These were the only reptiles I had ever seen upon Barsoom, but I knew from their similarity to the fossilized remains of supposedly extinct species I had seen in the museums of Helium that they comprised many of the known prehistoric reptilian genera, as well as others undiscovered.

A more hideous aggregation of monsters had never before assailed my vision. It would be futile to attempt to describe them to Earth men, since substance is the only thing which they possess in common with any creature of the past or present with which you are familiar—even their venom is of an unearthly virulence that, by comparison, would make the cobra de capello seem quite as harmless as an angleworm.

As they spied me there was a concerted rush by those nearest the entrance where we stood, but a line of radium bulbs inset along the threshold of their chamber brought them to a sudden halt—evidently they dared not cross that line of light.

I had been quite sure that they would not venture beyond the room in which I had discovered them, though I had not guessed at what deterred them. The simple fact that we had found no reptiles in the corridor through which we had just come was sufficient assurance that they did not venture there.

I drew Woola out of harm's way, and then began a careful survey of as much of the Chamber of Reptiles as I could see from where I stood. As my eyes became accustomed to the dim light of its interior I gradually made out a low gallery at the far end of the apartment from which opened several exits.

Coming as close to the threshold as I dared, I followed this gallery with my eyes, discovering that it circled the room as far as I could see. Then I glanced above me along the upper edge of the entrance to which we had come, and there, to my delight, I saw an end of the gallery not a foot above my head. In an instant I had leaped to it and called Woola after me.

Here there were no reptiles—the way was clear to the opposite side of the hideous chamber—and a moment later Woola and I dropped down to safety in the corridor beyond.

Not ten minutes later we came into a vast circular apartment of white marble, the walls of which were inlaid with gold in the strange hieroglyphics of the First Born.

From the high dome of this mighty apartment a huge circular column extended to the floor, and as I watched I saw that it slowly revolved.

I had reached the base of the Temple of the Sun!

Somewhere above me lay Dejah Thoris, and with her were Phaidor, daughter of Matai Shang, and Thuvia of Ptarth. But how to reach them, now that I had found the only vulnerable spot in their mighty prison, was still a baffling riddle.

Slowly I circled the great shaft, looking for a means of ingress. Part way around I found a tiny radium flash torch, and as I examined it in mild curiosity as to its presence there in this almost inaccessible and unknown spot, I came suddenly upon the insignia of the house of Thurid jewel-inset in its metal case.

I am upon the right trail, I thought, as I slipped the bauble into the pocket-pouch which hung from my harness. Then I continued my search for the entrance, which I knew must be somewhere about; nor had I long to search, for almost immediately thereafter I came upon a small door so cunningly inlaid in the shaft's base that it might have passed unnoticed by a less keen or careful observer.

There was the door that would lead me within the prison, but where was the means to open it? No button or lock were visible. Again and again I went carefully over every square inch of its surface, but the most that I could find was a tiny pinhole a little above and to the right of the door's center—a pinhole that seemed only an accident of manufacture or an imperfection of material.

Into this minute aperture I attempted to peer, but whether it was but a fraction of an inch deep or passed completely through the door I could not tell—at least no light showed beyond it. I put my ear to it next and listened, but again my efforts brought negligible results.

During these experiments Woola had been standing at my side gazing intently at the door, and as my glance fell upon him it occurred to me to test the correctness of my hypothesis, that this portal had been the means of ingress to the temple used by Thurid, the black dator, and Matai Shang, Father of Therns.

Turning away abruptly, I called to him to follow me. For a moment he hesitated, and then leaped after me, whining and tugging at my harness to draw me back. I walked on, however, some distance from the door before I let him have his way, that I might see precisely what he would do. Then I permitted him to lead me wherever he would.

Straight back to that baffling portal he dragged me, again taking up his position facing the blank stone, gazing straight at its shining surface. For an hour I worked to solve the mystery of the combination that would open the way before me.

Carefully I recalled every circumstance of my pursuit of Thurid, and my conclusion was identical with my original belief—that Thurid had come this way without other assistance than his own knowledge and passed through the door that barred my progress, unaided from within. But how had he accomplished it?

I recalled the incident of the Chamber of Mystery in the Golden Cliffs that time I had freed Thuvia of Ptarth from the dungeon of the therns, and she had taken a slender, needle-like key from the keyring of her dead jailer to open the door leading back into the Chamber of Mystery where Tars Tarkas fought for his life with the great banths. Such a tiny keyhole as now defied me had opened the way to the intricate lock in that other door.

Hastily I dumped the contents of my pocket-pouch upon the ground before me. Could I but find a slender bit of steel I might yet fashion a key that would give me ingress to the temple prison.

As I examined the heterogeneous collection of odds and ends that is always to be found in the pocket-pouch of a Martian warrior my hand fell upon the emblazoned radium flash torch of the black dator.

As I was about to lay the thing aside as of no value in my present predicament my eyes chanced upon a few strange characters roughly and freshly scratched upon the soft gold of the case.

Casual curiosity prompted me to decipher them, but what I read carried no immediate meaning to my mind. There were three sets of characters, one below another:

$$3 \vdash\dashv 50\ T$$
$$1 \vdash\dashv 1\ X$$
$$9 \vdash\dashv 25\ T$$

For only an instant my curiosity was piqued, and then I replaced the torch in my pocket-pouch, but my fingers had not unclasped from it when there rushed to my memory the recollection of the conversation between Lakor and his companion when the lesser thern had quoted the words of Thurid and scoffed at them: "And what think you of the ridiculous matter of the light? Let the light shine with the intensity of three radium units for fifty tals"—ah, there was the first line of characters upon the torch's metal case—3—50 T; "and for one xat let it shine with the intensity of one radium unit"—there was the second line; "and then for twenty-five tals with nine units."

The formula was complete; but—what did it mean?

I thought I knew, and, seizing a powerful magnifying glass from the litter of my pocket-pouch, I applied myself to a careful examination of the marble immediately about the pinhole in the door. I could have cried aloud in exultation when my scrutiny disclosed the almost invisible incrustation of particles of carbonized electrons which are thrown off by these Martian torches.

It was evident that for countless ages radium torches had been applied to this pinhole, and for what purpose there could be but a single answer—the mechanism of the lock was actuated by light rays; and I, John Carter, Prince of Helium, held the combination in my hand—scratched by the hand of my enemy upon his own torch case.

In a cylindrical bracelet of gold about my wrist was my Barsoomian chronometer—a delicate instrument that records the tals and xats and zodes of Martian time, presenting them to view beneath a strong crystal much after the manner of an earthly odometer.

Timing my operations carefully, I held the torch to the small aperture in the door, regulating the intensity of the light by means of the thumb-lever upon the side of the case.

For fifty tals I let three units of light shine full in the pinhole, then one unit for one xat, and for twenty-five tals nine units. Those last twenty-five tals were the longest twenty-five seconds of my life. Would the lock click at the end of those seemingly interminable intervals of time?

Twenty-three! Twenty-four! Twenty-five!

I shut off the light with a snap. For seven tals I waited—there had been no appreciable effect upon the lock's mechanism. Could it be that my theory was entirely wrong?

Hold! Had the nervous strain resulted in a hallucination, or did the door really move? Slowly the solid stone sank noiselessly back into the wall—there was no hallucination here.

Back and back it slid for ten feet until it had disclosed at its right a narrow doorway leading into a dark and narrow corridor that paralleled the outer wall. Scarcely was the entrance uncovered than Woola and I had leaped through—then the door slipped quietly back into place.

Down the corridor at some distance I saw the faint reflection of a light, and toward this we made our way. At the point where the light shone was a sharp turn, and a little distance beyond this a brilliantly lighted chamber.

Here we discovered a spiral stairway leading up from the center of the circular room.

Immediately I knew that we had reached the center of the base of the Temple of the Sun—the spiral runway led upward past the inner walls of the prison cells. Somewhere above me was Dejah Thoris, unless Thurid and Matai Shang had already succeeded in stealing her.

We had scarcely started up the runway when Woola suddenly displayed the wildest excitement. He leaped back and forth, snapping at my legs and harness, until I thought that he was mad, and finally when I pushed him from me and started once more to ascend he grasped my sword arm between his jaws and dragged me back.

No amount of scolding or cuffing would suffice to make him release me, and I was entirely at the mercy of his brute strength unless I cared to use my dagger upon him with my left hand; but, mad or no, I had not the heart to run the sharp blade into that faithful body.

Down into the chamber he dragged me, and across it to the side opposite that at which we had entered. Here was another doorway leading into a corridor which ran directly down a steep incline. Without a moment's hesitation Woola jerked me along this rocky passage.

Presently he stopped and released me, standing between me and the way we had come, looking up into my face as though to ask if I would now follow him voluntarily or if he must still resort to force.

Looking ruefully at the marks of his great teeth upon my bare arm I decided to do as he seemed to wish me to do. After all, his strange instinct might be more dependable than my faulty human judgment.

And well it was that I had been forced to follow him. But a short distance from the circular chamber we came suddenly into a brilliantly lighted labyrinth of crystal glass partitioned passages.

At first I thought it was one vast, unbroken chamber, so clear and transparent were the walls of the winding corridors, but after I had nearly brained myself a couple of times by attempting to pass through solid vitreous walls I went more carefully.

We had proceeded but a few yards along the corridor that had given us entrance to this strange maze when Woola gave mouth to a most frightful roar, at the same time dashing against the clear partition at our left.

The resounding echoes of that fearsome cry were still reverberating through the subterranean chambers when I saw the thing that had startled it from the faithful beast.

Far in the distance, dimly through the many thicknesses of intervening crystal, as in a haze that made them seem unreal and ghostly, I discerned the figures of eight people—three females and five men.

At the same instant, evidently startled by Woola's fierce cry, they halted and looked about. Then, of a sudden, one of them, a woman, held her arms out toward me, and even at that great distance I could see that her lips moved—it was Dejah Thoris, my ever beautiful and ever youthful Princess of Helium.

With her were Thuvia of Ptarth, Phaidor, daughter of Matai Shang, and Thurid, and the Father of Therns, and the three lesser therns that had accompanied them.

Thurid shook his fist at me, and then two of the therns grasped Dejah Thoris and Thuvia roughly by their arms and hurried them on. A moment later they had disappeared into a stone corridor beyond the labyrinth of glass.

They say that love is blind; but so great a love as that of Dejah Thoris that knew me even beneath the thern disguise I wore and across the misty vista of that crystal maze must indeed be far from blind.

FOUR

The Secret Tower

I have no stomach to narrate the monotonous events of the tedious days that Woola and I spent ferreting our way across the labyrinth of glass, through the dark and devious ways beyond that led beneath the Valley Dor and Golden Cliffs to emerge at last upon the flank of the Otz Mountains just above the Valley of Lost Souls—that pitiful purgatory peopled by the poor unfortunates who dare not continue their abandoned pilgrimage to Dor, or return to the various lands of the outer world from whence they came.

Here the trail of Dejah Thoris' abductors led along the mountains' base, across steep and rugged ravines, by the side of appalling precipices, and sometimes out into the valley, where we found fighting aplenty with the members of the various tribes that make up the population of this vale of hopelessness.

But through it all we came at last to where the way led up a narrow gorge that grew steeper and more impracticable at every step until before us loomed a mighty fortress buried beneath the side of an overhanging cliff.

Here was the secret hiding place of Matai Shang, Father of Therns. Here, surrounded by a handful of the faithful, the hekkador of the ancient faith, who had once been served by millions of vassals and dependents, dispensed the spiritual words among the half dozen nations of Barsoom that still clung tenaciously to their false and discredited religion.

Darkness was just falling as we came in sight of the seemingly impregnable walls of this mountain stronghold, and lest we be seen I drew back with Woola behind a jutting granite promontory, into a clump of the hardy, purple scrub that thrives upon the barren sides of Otz.

Here we lay until the quick transition from daylight to darkness had passed. Then I crept out to approach the fortress walls in search of a way within.

Either through carelessness or over-confidence in the supposed inaccessibility of their hiding place, the triple-barred gate stood ajar. Beyond were a handful of guards, laughing and talking over one of their incomprehensible Barsoomian games.

I saw that none of the guardsmen had been of the party that accompanied Thurid and Matai Shang; and so, relying entirely upon my disguise, I walked boldly through the gateway and up to the thern guard.

The men stopped their game and looked up at me, but there was no sign of suspicion. Similarly they looked at Woola, growling at my heel.

"Kaor!" I said in true Martian greeting, and the warriors arose and saluted me. "I have but just found my way hither from the Golden Cliffs," I continued, "and seek audience with the hekkador, Matai Shang, Father of Therns. Where may he be found?"

"Follow me," said one of the guard, and, turning, led me across the outer courtyard toward a second buttressed wall.

Why the apparent ease with which I seemingly deceived them did not rouse my suspicions I know not, unless it was that my mind was still so full of that fleeting glimpse of my beloved princess that there was room in it for naught else. Be that as it may, the fact is that I marched buoyantly behind my guide straight into the jaws of death.

Afterward I learned that thern spies had been aware of my coming for hours before I reached the hidden fortress.

The gate had been purposely left ajar to tempt me on. The guards had been schooled well in their part of the conspiracy; and I, more like a schoolboy than a seasoned warrior, ran headlong into the trap.

At the far side of the outer court a narrow door let into the angle made by one of the buttresses with the wall. Here my guide produced a key and opened the way within; then, stepping back, he motioned me to enter.

"Matai Shang is in the temple court beyond," he said; and as Woola and I passed through, the fellow closed the door quickly upon us.

The nasty laugh that came to my ears through the heavy planking of the door after the lock clicked was my first intimation that all was not as it should be.

I found myself in a small, circular chamber within the buttress. Before me a door opened, presumably, upon the inner court beyond. For a moment I hesitated, all my suspicions now suddenly, though tardily, aroused; then, with a shrug of my shoulders, I opened the door and stepped out into the glare of torches that lighted the inner court.

Directly opposite me a massive tower rose to a height of three hundred feet. It was of the strangely beautiful modern Barsoomian style of architecture, its entire surface hand carved in bold relief with intricate and fanciful designs. Thirty feet above the courtyard and overlooking it was a broad balcony, and there, indeed, was Matai Shang, and with him were Thurid and Phaidor, Thuvia, and Dejah Thoris—the last two heavily ironed. A handful of thern warriors stood just behind the little party.

As I entered the enclosure the eyes of those in the balcony were full upon me.

An ugly smile distorted the cruel lips of Matai Shang. Thurid hurled a taunt at me and placed a familiar hand upon the shoulder of my princess. Like a tigress she turned upon him, striking the beast a heavy blow with the manacles upon her wrist.

He would have struck back had not Matai Shang interfered, and then I saw that the two men were not over-friendly; for the manner of the thern was arrogant and domineering as he made it plain to the First Born that the Princess of Helium was the personal property of the Father of Therns. And Thurid's bearing toward the ancient hekkador savored not at all of liking or respect.

When the altercation in the balcony had subsided Matai Shang turned again to me.

"Earth man," he cried, "you have earned a more ignoble death than now lies within our weakened power to inflict upon you; but that the death you die tonight may be doubly bitter, know you that when you have passed, your widow becomes the wife of Matai Shang, Hekkador of the Holy Therns, for a Martian year.

"At the end of that time, as you know, she shall be discarded, as is the law among us, but not, as is usual, to lead a quiet and honored life as high priestess of some hallowed shrine. Instead, Dejah Thoris, Princess of Helium, shall become the plaything of my lieutenants—perhaps of thy most hated enemy, Thurid, the black dator."

As he ceased speaking he awaited in silence evidently for some outbreak of rage upon my part—something that would have added to the spice of his revenge. But I did not give him the satisfaction that he craved.

Instead, I did the one thing of all others that might rouse his anger and increase his hatred of me; for I knew that if I died Dejah Thoris, too, would find a way to die before they could heap further tortures or indignities upon her.

Of all the holy of holies which the thern venerates and worships none is more revered than the yellow wig which covers his bald pate, and next thereto comes the circlet of gold and the great diadem, whose scintillant rays mark the attainment of the Tenth Cycle.

And, knowing this, I removed the wig and circlet from my head, tossing them carelessly upon the flagging of the court. Then I wiped my feet upon the yellow tresses; and as a groan of rage arose from the balcony I spat full upon the holy diadem.

Matai Shang went livid with anger, but upon the lips of Thurid I could see a grim smile of amusement, for to him these things were not holy; so, lest he should derive too much amusement from my act, I cried: "And thus did I with the holies of Issus, Goddess of Life Eternal, ere I threw Issus herself to the mob that once had worshiped her, to be torn to pieces in her own temple."

That put an end to Thurid's grinning, for he had been high in the favor of Issus.

"Let us have an end to this blaspheming!" he cried, turning to the Father of Therns.

Matai Shang rose and, leaning over the edge of the balcony, gave voice to the weird call that I had heard from the lips of the priests upon the tiny balcony upon the face of the Golden Cliffs overlooking the Valley Dor, when, in times past, they called the fearsome white apes and the hideous plant men to the feast of victims floating down the broad bosom of the mysterious Iss toward the silian-infested waters of the Lost Sea of Korus.

"Let loose the death!" he cried, and immediately a dozen doors in the base of the tower swung open, and a dozen grim and terrible banths sprang into the arena.

This was not the first time that I had faced the ferocious Barsoomian lion, but never had I been pitted, single-handed, against a full dozen of them. Even with the assistance of the fierce Woola, there could be but a single outcome to so unequal a struggle.

For a moment the beasts hesitated beneath the brilliant glare of the torches; but presently their eyes, becoming accustomed to the light, fell upon Woola and me, and with bristling manes and deep-throated roars they advanced, lashing their tawny sides with their powerful tails.

In the brief interval of life that was left me I shot a last, parting glance toward my Dejah Thoris. Her beautiful face was set in an expression of horror; and as my eyes met hers she extended both arms toward me as, struggling with the guards who now held her, she endeavored to cast herself from the balcony into the pit beneath, that she might share my death with me. Then, as the banths were about to close upon me, she turned and buried her dear face in her arms.

Suddenly my attention was drawn toward Thuvia of Ptarth. The beautiful girl was leaning far over the edge of the balcony, her eyes bright with excitement.

In another instant the banths would be upon me, but I could not force my gaze from the features of the red girl, for I knew that her expression meant anything but the enjoyment of the grim tragedy that would so soon be enacted below her; there was some deeper, hidden meaning which I sought to solve.

For an instant I thought of relying on my earthly muscles and agility to escape the banths and reach the balcony, which I could easily have done, but I could not bring myself to desert the faithful Woola and leave him to die alone beneath the cruel fangs of the hungry banths; that is not the way upon Barsoom, nor was it ever the way of John Carter.

Then the secret of Thuvia's excitement became apparent as from her lips there issued the purring sound I had heard once before; that time that, within the Golden Cliffs, she called the fierce banths about her and led them as a shepherdess might lead her flock of meek and harmless sheep.

At the first note of that soothing sound the banths halted in their tracks, and every fierce head went high as the beasts sought the origin of the familiar call. Presently they discovered the red girl in the balcony above them, and, turning, roared out their recognition and their greeting.

Guards sprang to drag Thuvia away, but ere they had succeeded she had hurled a volley of commands at the listening brutes, and as one they turned and marched back into their dens.

"You need not fear them now, John Carter!" cried Thuvia, before they could silence her. "Those banths will never harm you now, nor Woola, either."

It was all I cared to know. There was naught to keep me from that balcony now, and with a long, running leap I sprang far aloft until my hands grasped its lowest sill.

In an instant all was wild confusion. Matai Shang shrank back. Thurid sprang forward with drawn sword to cut me down.

Again Dejah Thoris wielded her heavy irons and fought him back. Then Matai Shang grasped her about the waist and dragged her away through a door leading within the tower.

For an instant Thurid hesitated, and then, as though fearing that the Father of Therns would escape him with the Princess of Helium, he, too, dashed from the balcony in their wake.

Phaidor alone retained her presence of mind. Two of the guards she ordered to bear away Thuvia of Ptarth; the others she commanded to remain and prevent me from following. Then she turned toward me.

"John Carter," she cried, "for the last time I offer you the love of Phaidor, daughter of the Holy Hekkador. Accept and your princess shall be returned to the court of her grandfather, and you shall live in peace and happiness. Refuse and the fate that my father has threatened shall fall upon Dejah Thoris.

"You cannot save her now, for by this time they have reached a place where even you may not follow. Refuse and naught can save you; for, though the way to the last stronghold of the Holy Therns was made easy for you, the way hence hath been made impossible. What say you?"

"You knew my answer, Phaidor," I replied, "before ever you spoke. Make way," I cried to the guards, "for John Carter, Prince of Helium, would pass!"

With that I leaped over the low baluster that surrounded the balcony, and with drawn long-sword faced my enemies.

There were three of them; but Phaidor must have guessed what the outcome of the battle would be, for she turned and fled from the balcony the moment she saw that I would have none of her proposition.

The three guardsmen did not wait for my attack. Instead, they rushed me—the three of them simultaneously; and it was that which gave me an advantage, for they fouled one another in the narrow precincts of the balcony, so that the foremost of them stumbled full upon my blade at the first onslaught.

The red stain upon my point roused to its full the old blood-lust of the fighting man that has ever been so strong within my breast, so that my blade flew through the air with a swiftness and deadly accuracy that threw the two remaining therns into wild despair.

When at last the sharp steel found the heart of one of them the other turned to flee, and, guessing that his steps would lead him along the way taken by those I sought, I let him keep ever far enough ahead to think that he was safely escaping my sword.

Through several inner chambers he raced until he came to a spiral runway. Up this he dashed, I in close pursuit. At the upper end we came out into a small chamber, the walls of which were blank except for a single window overlooking the slopes of Otz and the Valley of Lost Souls beyond.

Here the fellow tore frantically at what appeared to be but a piece of the blank wall opposite the single window. In an instant I guessed that it was a secret exit from the room, and so I paused that he might have an opportunity to negotiate it, for I cared nothing to take the life of this poor servitor—all I craved was a clear road in pursuit of Dejah Thoris, my long-lost princess.

But, try as he would, the panel would yield neither to cunning nor force, so that eventually he gave it up and turned to face me.

"Go thy way, Thern," I said to him, pointing toward the entrance to the runway up which we had but just come. "I have no quarrel with you, nor do I crave your life. Go!"

For answer he sprang upon me with his sword, and so suddenly, at that, that I was like to have gone down before his first rush. So there was nothing for it but to give him what he sought, and that as quickly as might be, that I might not be delayed too long in this chamber while Matai Shang and Thurid made way with Dejah Thoris and Thuvia of Ptarth.

The fellow was a clever swordsman—resourceful and extremely tricky. In fact, he seemed never to have heard that there existed such a thing as a code of honor, for he repeatedly outraged a dozen Barsoomian fighting customs that an honorable man would rather die than ignore.

He even went so far as to snatch his holy wig from his head and throw it in my face, so as to blind me for a moment while he thrust at my unprotected breast.

When he thrust, however, I was not there, for I had fought with therns before; and while none had ever resorted to precisely that same expedient, I knew them to be the least honorable and most treacherous fighters upon Mars, and so was ever on the alert for some new and devilish subterfuge when I was engaged with one of their race.

But at length he overdid the thing; for, drawing his shortsword, he hurled it, javelinwise, at my body, at the same instant rushing upon me with his long-sword. A single sweeping circle of my own blade caught the flying weapon and hurled it clattering against the far wall, and then, as I sidestepped my antagonist's impetuous rush, I let him have my point full in the stomach as he hurtled by.

Clear to the hilt my weapon passed through his body, and with a frightful shriek he sank to the floor, dead.

Halting only for the brief instant that was required to wrench my sword from the carcass of my late antagonist, I sprang across the chamber to the blank wall beyond, through which the thern had attempted to pass. Here I sought for the secret of its lock, but all to no avail.

In despair I tried to force the thing, but the cold, unyielding stone might well have laughed at my futile, puny endeavors. In fact, I could have sworn that I caught the faint suggestion of taunting laughter from beyond the baffling panel.

In disgust I desisted from my useless efforts and stepped to the chamber's single window.

The slopes of Otz and the distant Valley of Lost Souls held nothing to compel my interest then; but, towering far above me, the tower's carved wall riveted my keenest attention.

Somewhere within that massive pile was Dejah Thoris. Above me I could see windows. There, possibly, lay the only way by which I could reach her. The risk was great, but not too great when the fate of a world's most wondrous woman was at stake.

I glanced below. A hundred feet beneath lay jagged granite boulders at the brink of a frightful chasm upon which the tower abutted; and if not upon the boulders, then at the chasm's bottom, lay death, should a foot slip but once, or clutching fingers loose their hold for the fraction of an instant.

But there was no other way and with a shrug, which I must admit was half shudder, I stepped to the window's outer sill and began my perilous ascent.

To my dismay I found that, unlike the ornamentation upon most Heli-umetic structures, the edges of the carvings were quite generally rounded, so that at best my every hold was most precarious.

Fifty feet above me commenced a series of projecting cylindrical stones some six inches in diameter. These apparently circled the tower at six-foot intervals, in bands six feet apart; and as each stone cylinder protruded some four or five inches beyond the surface of the other ornamentation, they presented a comparatively easy mode of ascent could I but reach them.

Laboriously I climbed toward them by way of some windows which lay below them, for I hoped that I might find ingress to the tower through one of these, and thence an easier avenue along which to prosecute my search.

At times so slight was my hold upon the rounded surfaces of the carving's edges that a sneeze, a cough, or even a slight gust of wind would have dislodged me and sent me hurtling to the depths below.

But finally I reached a point where my fingers could just clutch the sill of the lowest window, and I was on the point of breathing a sigh of relief when the sound of voices came to me from above through the open window.

"He can never solve the secret of that lock." The voice was Matai Shang's. "Let us proceed to the hangar above that we may be far to the south before he finds another way—should that be possible."

"All things seem possible to that vile calot," replied another voice, which I recognized as Thurid's.

"Then let us haste," said Matai Shang. "But to be doubly sure, I will leave two who shall patrol this runway. Later they may follow us upon another flier—overtaking us at Kaol."

My upstretched fingers never reached the window's sill. At the first sound of the voices I drew back my hand and clung there to my perilous perch, flattened against the perpendicular wall, scarce daring to breathe.

What a horrible position, indeed, in which to be discovered by Thurid! He had but to lean from the window to push me with his sword's point into eternity.

Presently the sound of the voices became fainter, and once again I took up my hazardous ascent, now more difficult, since more circuitous, for I must climb so as to avoid the windows.

Matai Shang's reference to the hangar and the fliers indicated that my destination lay nothing short of the roof of the tower, and toward this seemingly distant goal I set my face.

The most difficult and dangerous part of the journey was accomplished at last, and it was with relief that I felt my fingers close about the lowest of the stone cylinders.

It is true that these projections were too far apart to make the balance of the ascent anything of a sinecure, but I at least had always within my reach a point of safety to which I might cling in case of accident.

Some ten feet below the roof, the wall inclined slightly inward possibly a foot in the last ten feet, and here the climbing was indeed immeasurably easier, so that my fingers soon clutched the eaves.

As I drew my eyes above the level of the tower's top I saw a flier all but ready to rise.

Upon her deck were Matai Shang, Phaidor, Dejah Thoris, Thuvia of Ptarth, and a few thern warriors, while near her was Thurid in the act of clambering aboard.

He was not ten paces from me, facing in the opposite direction; and what cruel freak of fate should have caused him to turn about just as my eyes topped the roof's edge I may not even guess.

But turn he did; and when his eyes met mine his wicked face lighted with a malignant smile as he leaped toward me, where I was hastening to scramble to the secure footing of the roof.

Dejah Thoris must have seen me at the same instant, for she screamed a useless warning just as Thurid's foot, swinging in a mighty kick, landed full in my face.

Like a felled ox, I reeled and tumbled backward over the tower's side.

FIVE

On the Kaolian Road

If there be a fate that is sometimes cruel to me, there surely is a kind and merciful Providence which watches over me.

As I toppled from the tower into the horrid abyss below I counted myself already dead; and Thurid must have done likewise, for he evidently did not even trouble himself to look after me, but must have turned and mounted the waiting flier at once.

Ten feet only I fell, and then a loop of my tough, leathern harness caught upon one of the cylindrical stone projections in the tower's surface—and held. Even when I had ceased to fall I could not believe the miracle that had preserved me from instant death, and for a moment I hung there, cold sweat exuding from every pore of my body.

But when at last I had worked myself back to a firm position I hesitated to ascend, since I could not know that Thurid was not still awaiting me above.

Presently, however, there came to my ears the whirring of the propellers of a flier, and as each moment the sound grew fainter I realized that the party had proceeded toward the south without assuring themselves as to my fate.

Cautiously I retraced my way to the roof, and I must admit that it was with no pleasant sensation that I raised my eyes once more above its edge; but, to my relief, there was no one in sight, and a moment later I stood safely upon its broad surface.

To reach the hangar and drag forth the only other flier which it contained was the work of but an instant; and just as the two thern warriors whom Matai Shang had left to prevent this very contingency emerged upon the roof from the tower's interior, I rose above them with a taunting laugh.

Then I dived rapidly to the inner court where I had last seen Woola, and to my immense relief found the faithful beast still there.

The twelve great banths lay in the doorways of their lairs, eyeing him and growling ominously, but they had not disobeyed Thuvia's injunction; and I thanked the fate that had made her their keeper within the Golden Cliffs, and endowed her with the kind and sympathetic nature that had won the loyalty and affection of these fierce beasts for her.

Woola leaped in frantic joy when he discovered me; and as the flier touched the pavement of the court for a brief instant he bounded to the deck beside me, and in the bearlike manifestation of his exuberant happiness all but caused me to wreck the vessel against the courtyard's rocky wall.

Amid the angry shouting of thern guardsmen we rose high above the last fortress of the Holy Therns, and then raced straight toward the northeast and Kaol, the destination which I had heard from the lips of Matai Shang.

Far ahead, a tiny speck in the distance, I made out another flier late in the afternoon. It could be none other than that which bore my lost love and my enemies.

I had gained considerably on the craft by night; and then, knowing that they must have sighted me and would show no lights after dark, I set my destination compass upon her—that wonderful little Martian mechanism which, once attuned to the object of destination, points away toward it, irrespective of every change in its location.

All that night we raced through the Barsoomian void, passing over low hills and dead sea bottoms; above long-deserted cities and populous centers of red Martian habitation upon the ribbon-like lines of cultivated land which border the globe-encircling waterways, which Earth men call the canals of Mars.

Dawn showed that I had gained appreciably upon the flier ahead of me. It was a larger craft than mine, and not so swift; but even so, it had covered an immense distance since the flight began.

The change in vegetation below showed me that we were rapidly nearing the equator. I was now near enough to my quarry to have used my bow gun; but, though I could see that Dejah Thoris was not on deck, I feared to fire upon the craft which bore her.

Thurid was deterred by no such scruples; and though it must have been difficult for him to believe that it was really I who followed them, he could not very well doubt the witness of his own eyes; and so he trained their stern gun upon me with his own hands, and an instant later an explosive radium projectile whizzed perilously close above my deck.

The black's next shot was more accurate, striking my flier full upon the prow and exploding with the instant of contact, ripping wide open the bow buoyancy tanks and disabling the engine.

So quickly did my bow drop after the shot that I scarce had time to lash Woola to the deck and buckle my own harness to a gunwale ring before the craft was hanging stern up and making her last long drop to ground.

Her stern buoyancy tanks prevented her dropping with great rapidity; but Thurid was firing rapidly now in an attempt to burst these also, that I might be dashed to death in the swift fall that would instantly follow a successful shot.

Shot after shot tore past or into us, but by a miracle neither Woola nor I was hit, nor were the after tanks punctured. This good fortune could not last indefinitely, and, assured that Thurid would not again leave me alive, I awaited the bursting of the next shell that hit; and then, throwing my hands above my head, I let go my hold and crumpled, limp and inert, dangling in my harness like a corpse.

The ruse worked, and Thurid fired no more at us. Presently I heard the diminishing sound of whirring propellers and realized that again I was safe.

Slowly the stricken flier sank to the ground, and when I had freed myself and Woola from the entangling wreckage I found that we were upon the verge of a natural forest—so rare a thing upon the bosom of dying Mars that, outside of the forest in the Valley Dor beside the Lost Sea of Korus, I never before had seen its like upon the planet.

From books and travelers I had learned something of the little-known land of Kaol, which lies along the equator almost halfway round the planet to the east of Helium.

It comprises a sunken area of extreme tropical heat, and is inhabited by a nation of red men varying but little in manners, customs, and appearance from the balance of the red men of Barsoom.

I knew that they were among those of the outer world who still clung tenaciously to the discredited religion of the Holy Therns, and that Matai Shang would find a ready welcome and safe refuge among them; while John Carter could look for nothing better than an ignoble death at their hands.

The isolation of the Kaolians is rendered almost complete by the fact that no waterway connects their land with that of any other nation, nor have they any need of a waterway since the low, swampy land which comprises the entire area of their domain self-waters their abundant tropical crops.

For great distances in all directions rugged hills and arid stretches of dead sea bottom discourage intercourse with them, and since there is practically no such thing as foreign commerce upon warlike Barsoom, where each nation is sufficient to itself, really little has been known relative to the court of the Jeddak of Kaol and the numerous strange, but interesting, people over whom he rules.

Occasional hunting parties have traveled to this out-of-the-way corner of the globe, but the hostility of the natives has usually brought disaster upon them, so that even the sport of hunting the strange and savage creatures which haunt the jungle fastnesses of Kaol has of later years proved insufficient lure even to the most intrepid warriors.

It was upon the verge of the land of the Kaols that I now knew myself to be, but in what direction to search for Dejah Thoris, or how far into the heart of the great forest I might have to penetrate I had not the faintest idea.

But not so Woola.

Scarcely had I disentangled him than he raised his head high in air and commenced circling about at the edge of the forest. Presently he halted, and, turning to see if I were following, set off straight into the maze of trees in the direction we had been going before Thurid's shot had put an end to our flier.

As best I could, I stumbled after him down a steep declivity beginning at the forest's edge.

Immense trees reared their mighty heads far above us, their broad fronds completely shutting off the slightest glimpse of the sky. It was easy to see why the Kaolians needed no navy; their cities, hidden in the midst of this towering forest, must be entirely invisible from above, nor could a landing be made by any but the smallest fliers, and then only with the greatest risk of accident.

How Thurid and Matai Shang were to land I could not imagine, though later I was to learn that to the level of the forest top there rises in each city of Kaol a slender watchtower which guards the Kaolians by day and by night against the secret approach of a hostile fleet. To one of these the hekkador of the Holy Therns had no difficulty in approaching, and by its means the party was safely lowered to the ground.

As Woola and I approached the bottom of the declivity the ground became soft and mushy, so that it was with the greatest difficulty that we made any headway whatever.

Slender purple grasses topped with red and yellow fern-like fronds grew rankly all about us to the height of several feet above my head.

Myriad creepers hung festooned in graceful loops from tree to tree, and among them were several varieties of the Martian "man-flower," whose blooms have eyes and hands with which to see and seize the insects which form their diet.

The repulsive calot tree was, too, much in evidence. It is a carnivorous plant of about the bigness of a large sage-brush such as dots our western plains. Each branch ends in a set of strong jaws, which have been known to drag down and devour large and formidable beasts of prey.

Both Woola and I had several narrow escapes from these greedy, arboreous monsters.

Occasional areas of firm sod gave us intervals of rest from the arduous labor of traversing this gorgeous, twilight swamp, and it was upon one of these that I finally decided to make camp for the night which my chronometer warned me would soon be upon us.

Many varieties of fruit grew in abundance about us; and as Martian calots are omnivorous, Woola had no difficulty in making a square meal after I had brought down the viands for him. Then, having eaten, too, I lay down with my back to that of my faithful hound, and dropped into a deep and dreamless sleep.

The forest was shrouded in impenetrable darkness when a low growl from Woola awakened me. All about us I could hear the stealthy movement of great, padded feet, and now and then the wicked gleam of green eyes upon us. Arising, I drew my long-sword and waited.

Suddenly a deep-toned, horrid roar burst from some savage throat almost at my side. What a fool I had been not to have found safer lodgings for myself and Woola among the branches of one of the countless trees that surrounded us!

By daylight it would have been comparatively easy to have hoisted Woola aloft in one manner or another, but now it was too late. There was nothing for it but to stand our ground and take our medicine, though, from the hideous racket which now assailed our ears, and for which that first roar had seemed to be the signal, I judged that we must be in the midst of hundreds, perhaps thousands, of the fierce, man-eating denizens of the Kaolian jungle.

All the balance of the night they kept up their infernal din, but why they did not attack us I could not guess, nor am I sure to this day, unless it is that none of them ever venture upon the patches of scarlet sward which dot the swamp.

When morning broke they were still there, walking about as in a circle, but always just beyond the edge of the sward. A more terrifying aggregation of fierce and blood-thirsty monsters it would be difficult to imagine.

Singly and in pairs they commenced wandering off into the jungle shortly after sunrise, and when the last of them had departed Woola and I resumed our journey.

Occasionally we caught glimpses of horrid beasts all during the day; but, fortunately, we were never far from a sward island, and when they saw us their pursuit always ended at the verge of the solid sod.

Toward noon we stumbled upon a well-constructed road running in the general direction we had been pursuing. Everything about this highway marked it as the work of skilled engineers, and I was confident, from the indications of antiquity which it bore, as well as from the very evident signs of its being still in everyday use, that it must lead to one of the principal cities of Kaol.

Just as we entered it from one side a huge monster emerged from the jungle upon the other, and at sight of us charged madly in our direction.

Imagine, if you can, a bald-faced hornet of your earthly experience grown to the size of a prize Hereford bull, and you will have some faint conception of the ferocious appearance and awesome formidability of the winged monster that bore down upon me.

Frightful jaws in front and mighty, poisoned sting behind made my relatively puny long-sword seem a pitiful weapon of defense indeed. Nor could I hope to escape the lightning-like movements or hide from those myriad facet eyes which covered three-fourths of the hideous head, permitting the creature to see in all directions at one and the same time.

Even my powerful and ferocious Woola was as helpless as a kitten before that frightful thing. But to flee were useless, even had it ever been to my liking to turn my back upon a danger; so I stood my ground, Woola snarling at my side, my only hope to die as I had always lived—fighting.

The creature was upon us now, and at the instant there seemed to me a single slight chance for victory. If I could but remove the terrible menace of certain death hidden in the poison sacs that fed the sting the struggle would be less unequal.

At the thought I called to Woola to leap upon the creature's head and hang there, and as his mighty jaws closed upon that fiendish face, and glistening fangs buried themselves in the bone and cartilage and lower part of one of the huge eyes, I dived beneath the great body as the creature rose, dragging Woola from the ground, that it might bring its sting beneath and pierce the body of the thing hanging to its head.

To put myself in the path of that poison-laden lance was to court instant death, but it was the only way; and as the thing shot lightning-like toward me I swung my long-sword in a terrific cut that severed the deadly member close to the gorgeously marked body.

Then, like a battering-ram, one of the powerful hind legs caught me full in the chest and hurled me, half stunned and wholly winded, clear across the broad highway and into the underbrush of the jungle that fringes it.

Fortunately, I passed between the boles of trees; had I struck one of

Frightful jaws in front and mighty, poisoned sting behind made my relatively puny long-sword seem a pitiful weapon of defense indeed. Nor could I hope to escape the lightning-like movements or hide from those myriad facet eyes which covered three-fourths of the hideous head, permitting the creature to see in all directions at one and the same time.

them I should have been badly injured, if not killed, so swiftly had I been catapulted by that enormous hind leg.

Dazed though I was, I stumbled to my feet and staggered back to Woola's assistance, to find his savage antagonist circling ten feet above the ground, beating madly at the clinging calot with all six powerful legs.

Even during my sudden flight through the air I had not once released my grip upon my long-sword, and now I ran beneath the two battling monsters, jabbing the winged terror repeatedly with its sharp point.

The thing might easily have risen out of my reach, but evidently it knew as little concerning retreat in the face of danger as either Woola or I, for it dropped quickly toward me, and before I could escape had grasped my shoulder between its powerful jaws.

Time and again the now useless stub of its giant sting struck futilely against my body, but the blows alone were almost as effective as the kick of a horse; so that when I say futilely, I refer only to the natural function of the disabled member—eventually the thing would have hammered me to a pulp.

Nor was it far from accomplishing this when an interruption occurred that put an end forever to its hostilities.

From where I hung a few feet above the road I could see along the highway a few hundred yards to where it turned toward the east, and just as I had about given up all hope of escaping the perilous position in which I now was I saw a red warrior come into view from around the bend.

He was mounted on a splendid thoat, one of the smaller species used by red men, and in his hand was a wondrous long, light lance.

His mount was walking sedately when I first perceived them, but the instant that the red man's eyes fell upon us a word to the thoat brought the animal at full charge down upon us. The long lance of the warrior dipped toward us, and as thoat and rider hurtled beneath, the point passed through the body of our antagonist.

With a convulsive shudder the thing stiffened, the jaws relaxed, dropping me to the ground, and then, careening once in mid air, the creature plunged headforemost to the road, full upon Woola, who still clung tenaciously to its gory head.

By the time I had regained my feet the red man had turned and ridden back to us. Woola, finding his enemy inert and lifeless, released his hold at my command and wriggled from beneath the body that had covered him, and together we faced the warrior looking down upon us.

I started to thank the stranger for his timely assistance, but he cut me off peremptorily.

"Who are you," he asked, "who dare enter the land of Kaol and hunt in the royal forest of the jeddak?"

Then, as he noted my white skin through the coating of grime and blood that covered me, his eyes went wide and in an altered tone he whispered: "Can it be that you are a Holy Thern?"

I might have deceived the fellow for a time, as I had deceived others, but I had cast away the yellow wig and the holy diadem in the presence of Matai Shang, and I knew that it would not be long ere my new acquaintance discovered that I was no thern at all.

"I am not a thern," I replied, and then, flinging caution to the winds, I said: "I am John Carter, Prince of Helium, whose name may not be entirely unknown to you."

If his eyes had gone wide when he thought that I was a Holy Thern, they fairly popped now that he knew that I was John Carter. I grasped my long-sword more firmly as I spoke the words which I was sure would precipitate an attack, but to my surprise they precipitated nothing of the kind.

"John Carter, Prince of Helium," he repeated slowly, as though he could not quite grasp the truth of the statement. "John Carter, the mightiest warrior of Barsoom!"

And then he dismounted and placed his hand upon my shoulder after the manner of most friendly greeting upon Mars.

"It is my duty, and it should be my pleasure, to kill you, John Carter," he said, "but always in my heart of hearts have I admired your prowess and believed in your sincerity the while I have questioned and disbelieved the therns and their religion.

"It would mean my instant death were my heresy to be suspected in the court of Kulan Tith, but if I may serve you, Prince, you have but to command Torkar Bar, Dwar of the Kaolian Road."

Truth and honesty were writ large upon the warrior's noble countenance, so that I could not but have trusted him, enemy though he should have been. His title of Captain of the Kaolian Road explained his timely presence in the heart of the savage forest, for every highway upon Barsoom is patrolled by doughty warriors of the noble class, nor is there any service more honorable than this lonely and dangerous duty in the less frequented sections of the domains of the red men of Barsoom.

"Torkar Bar has already placed a great debt of gratitude upon my shoulders," I replied, pointing to the carcass of the creature from whose heart he was dragging his long spear.

The red man smiled.

"It was fortunate that I came when I did," he said. "Only this poisoned spear pricking the very heart of a sith can kill it quickly enough to save its prey. In this section of Kaol we are all armed with a long sith spear, whose point is smeared with the poison of the creature it is intended to kill; no other virus acts so quickly upon the beast as its own.

"Look," he continued, drawing his dagger and making an incision in the carcass a foot above the root of the sting, from which he presently drew forth two sacs, each of which held fully a gallon of the deadly liquid.

"Thus we maintain our supply, though were it not for certain commercial uses to which the virus is put, it would scarcely be necessary to add to our present store, since the sith is almost extinct.

"Only occasionally do we now run upon one. Of old, however, Kaol was overrun with the frightful monsters that often came in herds of twenty or thirty, darting down from above into our cities and carrying away women, children, and even warriors."

As he spoke I had been wondering just how much I might safely tell this man of the mission which brought me to his land, but his next words anticipated the broaching of the subject on my part, and rendered me thankful that I had not spoken too soon.

"And now as to yourself, John Carter," he said, "I shall not ask your business here, nor do I wish to hear it. I have eyes and ears and ordinary intelligence, and yesterday morning I saw the party that came to the city of Kaol from the north in a small flier. But one thing I ask of you, and that is: the word of John Carter that he contemplates no overt act against either the nation of Kaol or its jeddak."

"You may have my word as to that, Torkar Bar," I replied.

"My way leads along the Kaolian road, away from the city of Kaol," he continued. "I have seen no one—John Carter least of all. Nor have you seen Torkar Bar, nor ever heard of him. You understand?"

"Perfectly," I replied.

He laid his hand upon my shoulder.

"This road leads directly into the city of Kaol," he said. "I wish you fortune," and vaulting to the back of his thoat he trotted away without even a backward glance.

It was after dark when Woola and I spied through the mighty forest the great wall which surrounds the city of Kaol.

We had traversed the entire way without mishap or adventure, and though the few we had met had eyed the great calot wonderingly, none had pierced the red pigment with which I had smoothly smeared every square inch of my body.

But to traverse the surrounding country, and to enter the guarded city of Kulan Tith, Jeddak of Kaol, were two very different things. No man enters a Martian city without giving a very detailed and satisfactory account of himself, nor did I delude myself with the belief that I could for a moment impose upon the acumen of the officers of the guard to whom I should be taken the moment I applied at any one of the gates.

My only hope seemed to lie in entering the city surreptitiously under cover of the darkness, and once in, trust to my own wits to hide myself in some crowded quarter where detection would be less liable to occur.

With this idea in view I circled the great wall, keeping within the fringe of the forest, which is cut away for a short distance from the wall all about the city, that no enemy may utilize the trees as a means of ingress.

Several times I attempted to scale the barrier at different points, but not even my earthly muscles could overcome that cleverly constructed rampart. To a height of thirty feet the face of the wall slanted outward, and then for almost an equal distance it was perpendicular, above which it slanted in again for some fifteen feet to the crest.

And smooth! Polished glass could not be more so. Finally I had to admit that at last I had discovered a Barsoomian fortification which I could not negotiate.

Discouraged, I withdrew into the forest beside a broad highway which entered the city from the east, and with Woola beside me lay down to sleep.

SIX

A Hero in Kaol

It was daylight when I was awakened by the sound of stealthy movement near by.

As I opened my eyes Woola, too, moved and, coming up to his haunches, stared through the intervening brush toward the road, each hair upon his neck stiffly erect.

At first I could see nothing, but presently I caught a glimpse of a bit of smooth and glossy green moving among the scarlet and purple and yellow of the vegetation.

Motioning Woola to remain quietly where he was, I crept forward to investigate, and from behind the bole of a great tree I saw a long line of the hideous green warriors of the dead sea bottoms hiding in the dense jungle beside the road.

As far as I could see, the silent line of destruction and death stretched away from the city of Kaol. There could be but one explanation. The green men were expecting an exodus of a body of red troops from the nearest city gate, and they were lying there in ambush to leap upon them.

I owed no fealty to the Jeddak of Kaol, but he was of the same race of noble red men as my own princess, and I would not stand supinely by and see his warriors butchered by the cruel and heartless demons of the waste places of Barsoom.

Cautiously I retraced my steps to where I had left Woola, and warning him to silence, signaled him to follow me. Making a considerable detour to avoid the chance of falling into the hands of the green men, I came at last to the great wall.

A hundred yards to my right was the gate from which the troops were evidently expected to issue, but to reach it I must pass the flank of the green warriors within easy sight of them, and, fearing that my plan to warn the

Kaolians might thus be thwarted, I decided upon hastening toward the left, where another gate a mile away would give me ingress to the city.

I knew that the word I brought would prove a splendid passport to Kaol, and I must admit that my caution was due more to my ardent desire to make my way into the city than to avoid a brush with the green men. As much as I enjoy a fight, I cannot always indulge myself, and just now I had more weighty matters to occupy my time than spilling the blood of strange warriors.

Could I but win beyond the city's wall, there might be opportunity in the confusion and excitement which were sure to follow my announcement of an invading force of green warriors to find my way within the palace of the jeddak, where I was sure Matai Shang and his party would be quartered.

But scarcely had I taken a hundred steps in the direction of the farther gate when the sound of marching troops, the clank of metal, and the squealing of thoats just within the city apprised me of the fact that the Kaolians were already moving toward the other gate.

There was no time to be lost. In another moment the gate would be opened and the head of the column pass out upon the death-bordered highway.

Turning back toward the fateful gate, I ran rapidly along the edge of the clearing, taking the ground in the mighty leaps that had first made me famous upon Barsoom. Thirty, fifty, a hundred feet at a bound are nothing for the muscles of an athletic Earth man upon Mars.

As I passed the flank of the waiting green men they saw my eyes turned upon them, and in an instant, knowing that all secrecy was at an end, those nearest me sprang to their feet in an effort to cut me off before I could reach the gate.

At the same instant the mighty portal swung wide and the head of the Kaolian column emerged. A dozen green warriors had succeeded in reaching a point between me and the gate, but they had but little idea who it was they had elected to detain.

I did not slacken my speed an iota as I dashed among them, and as they fell before my blade I could not but recall the happy memory of those other battles when Tars Tarkas, Jeddak of Thark, mightiest of Martian green men, had stood shoulder to shoulder with me through long, hot Martian days, as together we hewed down our enemies until the pile of corpses about us rose higher than a tall man's head.

When several pressed me too closely, there before the carved gateway of Kaol, I leaped above their heads, and fashioning my tactics after those of the hideous plant men of Dor, struck down upon my enemies' heads as I passed above them.

From the city the red warriors were rushing toward us, and from the jungle the savage horde of green men were coming to meet them. In a moment I was in the very center of as fierce and bloody a battle as I had ever passed through.

These Kaolians are most noble fighters, nor are the green men of the equator one whit less warlike than their cold, cruel cousins of the temperate zone. There were many times when either side might have withdrawn without dishonor and thus ended hostilities, but from the mad abandon with which each invariably renewed hostilities I soon came to believe that what need not have been more than a trifling skirmish would end only with the complete extermination of one force or the other.

With the joy of battle once roused within me, I took keen delight in the fray, and that my fighting was noted by the Kaolians was often evidenced by the shouts of applause directed at me.

If I sometimes seem to take too great pride in my fighting ability, it must be remembered that fighting is my vocation. If your vocation be shoeing horses, or painting pictures, and you can do one or the other better than your fellows, then you are a fool if you are not proud of your ability. And so I am very proud that upon two planets no greater fighter has ever lived than John Carter, Prince of Helium.

And I outdid myself that day to impress the fact upon the natives of Kaol, for I wished to win a way into their hearts—and their city. Nor was I to be disappointed in my desire.

All day we fought, until the road was red with blood and clogged with corpses. Back and forth along the slippery highway the tide of battle surged, but never once was the gateway to Kaol really in danger.

There were breathing spells when I had a chance to converse with the red men beside whom I fought, and once the jeddak, Kulan Tith himself, laid his hand upon my shoulder and asked my name.

"I am Dotar Sojat," I replied, recalling a name given me by the Tharks many years before, from the surnames of the first two of their warriors I had killed, which is the custom among them.

"You are a mighty warrior, Dotar Sojat," he replied, "and when this day is done I shall speak with you again in the great audience chamber."

And then the fight surged upon us once more and we were separated, but my heart's desire was attained, and it was with renewed vigor and a joyous soul that I laid about me with my long-sword until the last of the green men had had enough and had withdrawn toward their distant sea bottom.

Not until the battle was over did I learn why the red troops had sallied forth that day. It seemed that Kulan Tith was expecting a visit from a mighty jeddak of the north—a powerful and the only ally of the Kaolians, and it had been his wish to meet his guest a full day's journey from Kaol.

But now the march of the welcoming host was delayed until the following morning, when the troops again set out from Kaol. I had not been bidden to the presence of Kulan Tith after the battle, but he had sent an officer to find me and escort me to comfortable quarters in that part of the palace set aside for the officers of the royal guard.

There, with Woola, I had spent a comfortable night, and rose much refreshed after the arduous labors of the past few days. Woola had fought with me through the battle of the previous day, true to the instincts and training of a Martian war dog, great numbers of which are often to be found with the savage green hordes of the dead sea bottoms.

Neither of us had come through the conflict unscathed, but the marvelous, healing salves of Barsoom had sufficed, overnight, to make us as good as new.

I breakfasted with a number of the Kaolian officers, whom I found as courteous and delightful hosts as even the nobles of Helium, who are renowned for their ease of manners and excellence of breeding. The meal was scarcely concluded when a messenger arrived from Kulan Tith summoning me before him.

As I entered the royal presence the jeddak rose, and stepping from the dais which supported his magnificent throne, came forward to meet me—a mark of distinction that is seldom accorded to other than a visiting ruler.

"Kaor, Dotar Sojat!" he greeted me. "I have summoned you to receive the grateful thanks of the people of Kaol, for had it not been for your heroic bravery in daring fate to warn us of the ambuscade we must surely have fallen into the well-laid trap. Tell me more of yourself—from what country you come, and what errand brings you to the court of Kulan Tith."

"I am from Hastor," I said, for in truth I had a small palace in that southern city which lies within the far-flung dominions of the Heliumetic nation.

"My presence in the land of Kaol is partly due to accident, my flier being wrecked upon the southern fringe of your great forest. It was while seeking entrance to the city of Kaol that I discovered the green horde lying in wait for your troops."

If Kulan Tith wondered what business brought me in a flier to the very edge of his domain he was good enough not to press me further for an explanation, which I should indeed have had difficulty in rendering.

During my audience with the jeddak another party entered the chamber from behind me, so that I did not see their faces until Kulan Tith stepped past me to greet them, commanding me to follow and be presented.

As I turned toward them it was with difficulty that I controlled my features, for there, listening to Kulan Tith's eulogistic words concerning me, stood my arch-enemies, Matai Shang and Thurid.

"Holy Hekkador of the Holy Therns," the jeddak was saying, "shower thy blessings upon Dotar Sojat, the valorous stranger from distant Hastor, whose wondrous heroism and marvelous ferocity saved the day for Kaol yesterday."

Matai Shang stepped forward and laid his hand upon my shoulder. No slightest indication that he recognized me showed upon his countenance— my disguise was evidently complete.

He spoke kindly to me and then presented me to Thurid. The black, too, was evidently entirely deceived. Then Kulan Tith regaled them, much to my amusement, with details of my achievements upon the field of battle.

The thing that seemed to have impressed him most was my remarkable agility, and time and again he described the wondrous way in which I had leaped completely over an antagonist, cleaving his skull wide open with my long-sword as I passed above him.

I thought that I saw Thurid's eyes widen a bit during the narrative, and several times I surprised him gazing intently into my face through narrowed lids. Was he commencing to suspect? And then Kulan Tith told of the savage calot that fought beside me, and after that I saw suspicion in the eyes of Matai Shang—or did I but imagine it?

At the close of the audience Kulan Tith announced that he would have me accompany him upon the way to meet his royal guest, and as I departed with an officer who was to procure proper trappings and a suitable mount for me, both Matai Shang and Thurid seemed most sincere in professing their pleasure at having had an opportunity to know me. It was with a sigh of relief that I quitted the chamber, convinced that nothing more than a guilty conscience had prompted my belief that either of my enemies suspected my true identity.

A half-hour later I rode out of the city gate with the column that accompanied Kulan Tith upon the way to meet his friend and ally. Though my eyes and ears had been wide open during my audience with the jeddak and my various passages through the palace, I had seen or heard nothing of Dejah Thoris or Thuvia of Ptarth. That they must be somewhere within the great rambling edifice I was positive, and I should have given much to have found a way to remain behind during Kulan Tith's absence, that I might search for them.

Toward noon we came in touch with the head of the column we had set out to meet.

It was a gorgeous train that accompanied the visiting jeddak, and for miles it stretched along the wide, white road to Kaol. Mounted troops, their trappings of jewel and metal-incrusted leather glistening in the sunlight, formed the vanguard of the body, and then came a thousand gorgeous chariots drawn by huge zitidars.

These low, commodious wagons moved two abreast, and on either side of them marched solid ranks of mounted warriors, for in the chariots were the women and children of the royal court. Upon the back of each monster zitidar rode a Martian youth, and the whole scene carried me back to my first days upon Barsoom, now twenty-two years in the past, when I had first beheld the gorgeous spectacle of a caravan of the green horde of Tharks.

Never before today had I seen zitidars in the service of red men. These brutes are huge mastodonian animals that tower to an immense height even beside the giant green men and their giant thoats; but when compared to the relatively small red man and his breed of thoats they assume Brobdingnagian proportions that are truly appalling.

The beasts were hung with jeweled trappings and saddlepads of gay silk, embroidered in fanciful designs with strings of diamonds, pearls, rubies, emeralds, and the countless unnamed jewels of Mars, while from each chariot rose a dozen standards from which streamers, flags, and pennons fluttered in the breeze.

Just in front of the chariots the visiting jeddak rode alone upon a pure white thoat—another unusual sight upon Barsoom—and after them came interminable ranks of mounted spearmen, riflemen, and swordsmen. It was indeed a most imposing sight.

Except for the clanking of accouterments and the occasional squeal of an angry thoat or the low guttural of a zitidar, the passage of the cavalcade was almost noiseless, for neither thoat nor zitidar is a hoofed animal, and the broad tires of the chariots are of an elastic composition, which gives forth no sound.

Now and then the gay laughter of a woman or the chatter of children could be heard, for the red Martians are a social, pleasure-loving people—in direct antithesis to the cold and morbid race of green men.

The forms and ceremonials connected with the meeting of the two jeddaks consumed an hour, and then we turned and retraced our way toward the city of Kaol, which the head of the column reached just before dark, though it must have been nearly morning before the rear guard passed through the gateway.

Fortunately, I was well up toward the head of the column, and after the great banquet, which I attended with the officers of the royal guard, I was free to seek repose. There was so much activity and bustle about the palace all during the night with the constant arrival of the noble officers of the visiting jeddak's retinue that I dared not attempt to prosecute a search for Dejah Thoris, and so, as soon as it was seemly for me to do so, I returned to my quarters.

As I passed along the corridors between the banquet hall and the apartments that had been allotted me, I had a sudden feeling that I was under surveillance, and, turning quickly in my tracks, caught a glimpse of a figure which darted into an open doorway the instant I wheeled about.

Though I ran quickly back to the spot where the shadower had disappeared I could find no trace of him, yet in the brief glimpse that I had caught I could have sworn that I had seen a white face surmounted by a mass of yellow hair.

The incident gave me considerable food for speculation, since if I were right in the conclusion induced by the cursory glimpse I had had of the spy, then Matai Shang and Thurid must suspect my identity, and if that were true not even the service I had rendered Kulan Tith could save me from his religious fanaticism.

But never did vague conjecture or fruitless fears for the future lie with sufficient weight upon my mind to keep me from my rest, and so tonight I threw myself upon my sleeping silks and furs and passed at once into dreamless slumber.

Calots are not permitted within the walls of the palace proper, and so I had had to relegate poor Woola to quarters in the stables where the royal thoats are kept. He had comfortable even luxurious apartments, but I would have given much to have had him with me; and if he had been, the thing which happened that night would not have come to pass.

I could not have slept over a quarter of an hour when I was suddenly awakened by the passing of some cold and clammy thing across my forehead. Instantly I sprang to my feet, clutching in the direction I thought the presence lay. For an instant my hand touched against human flesh, and then, as I lunged headforemost through the darkness to seize my nocturnal visitor, my foot became entangled in my sleeping silks and I fell sprawling to the floor.

By the time I had resumed my feet and found the button which controlled the light my caller had disappeared. Careful search of the room revealed nothing to explain either the identity or business of the person who had thus secretly sought me in the dead of night.

That the purpose might be theft I could not believe, since thieves are practically unknown upon Barsoom. Assassination, however, is rampant, but even this could not have been the motive of my stealthy friend, for he might easily have killed me had he desired.

I had about given up fruitless conjecture and was on the point of returning to sleep when a dozen Kaolian guardsmen entered my apartment. The officer in charge was one of my genial hosts of the morning, but now upon his face was no sign of friendship.

"Kulan Tith commands your presence before him," he said. "Come!"

SEVEN

New Allies

Surrounded by guardsmen I marched back along the corridors of the palace of Kulan Tith, Jeddak of Kaol, to the great audience chamber in the center of the massive structure.

As I entered the brilliantly lighted apartment, filled with the nobles of Kaol and the officers of the visiting jeddak, all eyes were turned upon me. Upon the great dais at the end of the chamber stood three thrones, upon which sat Kulan Tith and his two guests, Matai Shang, and the visiting jeddak.

Up the broad center aisle we marched beneath deadly silence, and at the foot of the thrones we halted.

"Prefer thy charge," said Kulan Tith, turning to one who stood among the nobles at his right; and then Thurid, the black dator of the First Born, stepped forward and faced me.

"Most noble Jeddak," he said, addressing Kulan Tith, "from the first I suspected this stranger within thy palace. Your description of his fiendish prowess tallied with that of the arch-enemy of truth upon Barsoom.

"But that there might be no mistake I despatched a priest of your own holy cult to make the test that should pierce his disguise and reveal the truth. Behold the result!" and Thurid pointed a rigid finger at my forehead.

All eyes followed the direction of that accusing digit—I alone seemed at a loss to guess what fatal sign rested upon my brow.

The officer beside me guessed my perplexity; and as the brows of Kulan Tith darkened in a menacing scowl as his eyes rested upon me, the noble drew a small mirror from his pocket-pouch and held it before my face.

One glance at the reflection it gave back to me was sufficient.

From my forehead the hand of the sneaking thern had reached out through the concealing darkness of my bed-chamber and wiped away a patch of the disguising red pigment as broad as my palm. Beneath showed the tanned texture of my own white skin.

For a moment Thurid ceased speaking, to enhance, I suspect, the dramatic effect of his disclosure. Then he resumed.

"Here, O Kulan Tith," he cried, "is he who has desecrated the temples of the Gods of Mars, who has violated the persons of the Holy Therns themselves and turned a world against its age-old religion. Before you, in your power, Jeddak of Kaol, Defender of the Holies, stands John Carter, Prince of Helium!"

Kulan Tith looked toward Matai Shang as though for corroboration of these charges. The Holy Thern nodded his head.

"It is indeed the arch-blasphemer," he said. "Even now he has followed me to the very heart of thy palace, Kulan Tith, for the sole purpose of assassinating me. He ———"

"He lies!" I cried. "Kulan Tith, listen that you may know the truth. Listen while I tell you why John Carter has followed Matai Shang to the heart of thy palace. Listen to me as well as to them, and then judge if my acts be not more in accord with true Barsoomian chivalry and honor than those of these revengeful devotees of the spurious creeds from whose cruel bonds I have freed your planet."

"Silence!" roared the jeddak, leaping to his feet and laying his hand upon the hilt of his sword. "Silence, blasphemer! Kulan Tith need not permit the air of his audience chamber to be defiled by the heresies that issue from your polluted throat to judge you.

"You stand already self-condemned. It but remains to determine the manner of your death. Even the service that you rendered the arms of Kaol shall avail you naught; it was but a base subterfuge whereby you might win your way into my favor and reach the side of this holy man whose life you craved. To the pits with him!" he concluded, addressing the officer of my guard.

Here was a pretty pass, indeed! What chance had I against a whole nation? What hope for me of mercy at the hands of the fanatical Kulan Tith with such advisers as Matai Shang and Thurid. The black grinned malevolently in my face.

"You shall not escape this time, Earth man," he taunted.

The guards closed toward me. A red haze blurred my vision. The fighting blood of my Virginian sires coursed hot through my veins. The lust of battle in all its mad fury was upon me.

With a leap I was beside Thurid, and ere the devilish smirk had faded from his handsome face I had caught him full upon the mouth with my clenched fist; and as the good, old American blow landed, the black dator shot back a dozen feet, to crumple in a heap at the foot of Kulan Tith's throne, spitting blood and teeth from his hurt mouth.

Then I drew my sword and swung round, on guard, to face a nation.

In an instant the guardsmen were upon me, but before a blow had been struck a mighty voice rose above the din of shouting warriors, and a giant figure leaped from the dais beside Kulan Tith and, with drawn long-sword, threw himself between me and my adversaries.

It was the visiting jeddak.

"Hold!" he cried. "If you value my friendship, Kulan Tith, and the age-old peace that has existed between our peoples, call off your swordsmen; for wherever or against whomsoever fights John Carter, Prince of Helium, there beside him and to the death fights Thuvan Dihn, Jeddak of Ptarth."

The shouting ceased and the menacing points were lowered as a thousand eyes turned first toward Thuvan Dihn in surprise and then toward Kulan Tith in question. At first the Jeddak of Kaol went white in rage, but before he spoke he had mastered himself, so that his tone was calm and even as befitted intercourse between two great jeddaks.

"Thuvan Dihn," he said slowly, "must have great provocation thus to desecrate the ancient customs which inspire the deportment of a guest within the palace of his host. Lest I, too, should forget myself as has my royal friend, I should prefer to remain silent until the Jeddak of Ptarth has won from me applause for his action by relating the causes which provoked it."

I could see that the Jeddak of Ptarth was of half a mind to throw his metal in Kulan Tith's face, but he controlled himself even as well as had his host.

"None knows better than Thuvan Dihn," he said, "the laws which govern the acts of men in the domains of their neighbors; but Thuvan Dihn owes allegiance to a higher law than these—the law of gratitude. Nor to any man upon Barsoom does he owe a greater debt of gratitude than to John Carter, Prince of Helium.

"Years ago, Kulan Tith," he continued, "upon the occasion of your last visit to me, you were greatly taken with the charms and graces of my only daughter, Thuvia. You saw how I adored her, and later you learned that, inspired by some unfathomable whim, she had taken the last, long, voluntary pilgrimage upon the cold bosom of the mysterious Iss, leaving me desolate.

"Some months ago I first heard of the expedition which John Carter had led against Issus and the Holy Therns. Faint rumors of the atrocities reported to have been committed by the therns upon those who for countless ages have floated down the mighty Iss came to my ears.

"I heard that thousands of prisoners had been released, few of whom dared to return to their own countries owing to the mandate of terrible death which rests against all who return from the Valley Dor.

"For a time I could not believe the heresies which I heard, and I prayed that my daughter Thuvia might have died before she ever committed the sacrilege of returning to the outer world. But then my father's love asserted itself, and I vowed that I would prefer eternal damnation to further separation from her if she could be found.

"So I sent emissaries to Helium, and to the court of Xodar, Jeddak of the First Born, and to him who now rules those of the thern nation that have renounced their religion; and from each and all I heard the same story of unspeakable cruelties and atrocities perpetrated upon the poor defenseless victims of their religion by the Holy Therns.

"Many there were who had seen or known my daughter, and from therns who had been close to Matai Shang I learned of the indignities that he personally heaped upon her; and I was glad when I came here to find that Matai Shang was also your guest, for I should have sought him out had it taken a lifetime.

"More, too, I heard, and that of the chivalrous kindness that John Carter had accorded my daughter. They told me how he fought for her and rescued her, and how he spurned escape from the savage Warhoons of the south, sending her to safety upon his own thoat and remaining upon foot to meet the green warriors.

"Can you wonder, Kulan Tith, that I am willing to jeopardize my life, the peace of my nation, or even your friendship, which I prize more than aught else, to champion the Prince of Helium?"

For a moment Kulan Tith was silent. I could see by the expression of his face that he was sore perplexed. Then he spoke.

"Thuvan Dihn," he said, and his tone was friendly though sad, "who am I to judge my fellow-man? In my eyes the Father of Therns is still holy, and the religion which he teaches the only true religion, but were I faced by the same problem that has vexed you I doubt not that I should feel and act precisely as you have.

"In so far as the Prince of Helium is concerned I may act, but between you and Matai Shang my only office can be one of conciliation. The Prince of Helium shall be escorted in safety to the boundary of my domain ere the sun has set again, where he shall be free to go whither he will; but upon pain of death must he never again enter the land of Kaol.

"If there be a quarrel between you and the Father of Therns, I need not ask that the settlement of it be deferred until both have passed beyond the limits of my power. Are you satisfied, Thuvan Dihn?"

The Jeddak of Ptarth nodded his assent, but the ugly scowl that he bent upon Matai Shang harbored ill for that pasty-faced godling.

"The Prince of Helium is far from satisfied," I cried, breaking rudely in upon the beginnings of peace, for I had no stomach for peace at the price that had been named.

"I have escaped death in a dozen forms to follow Matai Shang and overtake him, and I do not intend to be led, like a decrepit thoat to the slaughter, from the goal that I have won by the prowess of my sword arm and the might of my muscles.

"Nor will Thuvan Dihn, Jeddak of Ptarth, be satisfied when he has heard me through. Do you know why I have followed Matai Shang and Thurid, the black dator, from the forests of the Valley Dor across half a world through almost insurmountable difficulties?

"Think you that John Carter, Prince of Helium, would stoop to assassination? Can Kulan Tith be such a fool as to believe that lie, whispered in his ear by the Holy Thern or Dator Thurid?

"I do not follow Matai Shang to kill him, though the God of mine own planet knows that my hands itch to be at his throat. I follow him, Thuvan Dihn, because with him are two prisoners— my wife, Dejah Thoris, Princess of Helium, and your daughter, Thuvia of Ptarth.

"Now think you that I shall permit myself to be led beyond the walls of Kaol unless the mother of my son accompanies me, and thy daughter be restored?"

Thuvan Dihn turned upon Kulan Tith. Rage flamed in his keen eyes; but by the masterfulness of his self-control he kept his tones level as he spoke.

"Knew you this thing, Kulan Tith?" he asked. "Knew you that my daughter lay a prisoner in your palace?"

"He could not know it," interrupted Matai Shang, white with what I am sure was more fear than rage. "He could not know it, for it is a lie."

I would have had his life for that upon the spot, but even as I sprang toward him Thuvan Dihn laid a heavy hand upon my shoulder.

"Wait," he said to me, and then to Kulan Tith. "It is not a lie. This much have I learned of the Prince of Helium—he does not lie. Answer me, Kulan Tith—I have asked you a question."

"Three women came with the Father of Therns," replied Kulan Tith. "Phaidor, his daughter, and two who were reported to be her slaves. If these be Thuvia of Ptarth and Dejah Thoris of Helium I did not know it—I have seen neither. But if they be, then shall they be returned to you on the morrow."

As he spoke he looked straight at Matai Shang, not as a devotee should look at a high priest, but as a ruler of men looks at one to whom he issues a command.

It must have been plain to the Father of Therns, as it was to me, that the recent disclosures of his true character had done much already to weaken the faith of Kulan Tith, and that it would require but little more to turn the powerful jeddak into an avowed enemy; but so strong are the seeds of superstition that even the great Kaolian still hesitated to cut the final strand that bound him to his ancient religion.

Matai Shang was wise enough to seem to accept the mandate of his follower, and promised to bring the two slave women to the audience chamber on the morrow.

"It is almost morning now," he said, "and I should dislike to break in upon the slumber of my daughter, or I would have them fetched at once that you might see that the Prince of Helium is mistaken," and he emphasized the last word in an effort to affront me so subtlely that I could not take open offense.

I was about to object to any delay, and demand that the Princess of Helium be brought to me forthwith, when Thuvan Dihn made such insistence seem unnecessary.

"I should like to see my daughter at once," he said, "but if Kulan Tith will give me his assurance that none will be permitted to leave the palace this night, and that no harm shall befall either Dejah Thoris or Thuvia of Ptarth between now and the moment they are brought into our presence in this chamber at daylight I shall not insist."

"None shall leave the palace tonight," replied the Jeddak of Kaol, "and Matai Shang will give us assurance that no harm will come to the two women?"

The thern assented with a nod. A few moments later Kulan Tith indicated that the audience was at an end, and at Thuvan Dihn's invitation I accompanied the Jeddak of Ptarth to his own apartments, where we sat until daylight, while he listened to the account of my experiences upon his planet and to all that had befallen his daughter during the time that we had been together.

I found the father of Thuvia a man after my own heart, and that night saw the beginning of a friendship which has grown until it is second only to that which obtains between Tars Tarkas, the green Jeddak of Thark, and myself.

The first burst of Mars's sudden dawn brought messengers from Kulan Tith, summoning us to the audience chamber where Thuvan Dihn was to receive his daughter after years of separation, and I was to be reunited with the glorious daughter of Helium after an almost unbroken separation of twelve years.

My heart pounded within my bosom until I looked about me in embarrassment, so sure was I that all within the room must hear. My arms ached to enfold once more the divine form of her whose eternal youth and undying beauty were but outward manifestations of a perfect soul.

At last the messenger despatched to fetch Matai Shang returned. I craned my neck to catch the first glimpse of those who should be following, but the messenger was alone.

Halting before the throne he addressed his jeddak in a voice that was plainly audible to all within the chamber.

"O Kulan Tith, Mightiest of Jeddaks," he cried, after the fashion of the court, "your messenger returns alone, for when he reached the apartments of the Father of Therns he found them empty, as were those occupied by his suite."

Kulan Tith went white.

A low groan burst from the lips of Thuvan Dihn who stood next me, not having ascended the throne which awaited him beside his host. For a moment the silence of death reigned in the great audience chamber of Kulan Tith, Jeddak of Kaol. It was he who broke the spell.

Rising from his throne he stepped down from the dais to the side of Thuvan Dihn. Tears dimmed his eyes as he placed both his hands upon the shoulders of his friend.

"O Thuvan Dihn," he cried, "that this should have happened in the palace of thy best friend! With my own hands would I have wrung the neck of Matai Shang had I guessed what was in his foul heart. Last night my life-long faith was weakened—this morning it has been shattered; but too late, too late.

"To wrest your daughter and the wife of this royal warrior from the clutches of these archfiends you have but to command the resources of a mighty nation, for all Kaol is at your disposal. What may be done? Say the word!"

"First," I suggested, "let us find those of your people who be responsible for the escape of Matai Shang and his followers. Without assistance on the part of the palace guard this thing could not have come to pass. Seek the guilty, and from them force an explanation of the manner of their going and the direction they have taken."

Before Kulan Tith could issue the commands that would initiate the investigation a handsome young officer stepped forward and addressed his jeddak.

"O Kulan Tith, Mightiest of Jeddaks," he said, "I alone be responsible for this grievous error. Last night it was I who commanded the palace guard. I was on duty in other parts of the palace during the audience of the early morning, and knew nothing of what transpired then, so that when the Father of Therns summoned me and explained that it was your wish that his party be hastened from the city because of the presence here of a deadly enemy who sought the Holy Hekkador's life I did only what a lifetime of training has taught me was the proper thing to do—I obeyed him whom I believed to be the ruler of us all, mightier even than thou, mightiest of jeddaks.

"Let the consequences and the punishment fall on me alone, for I alone am guilty. Those others of the palace guard who assisted in the flight did so under my instructions."

Kulan Tith looked first at me and then at Thuvan Dihn, as though to ask our judgment upon the man, but the error was so evidently excusable that neither of us had any mind to see the young officer suffer for a mistake that any might readily have made.

"How left they," asked Thuvan Dihn, "and what direction did they take?"

"They left as they came," replied the officer, "upon their own flier. For some time after they had departed I watched the vessel's lights, which vanished finally due north."

"Where north could Matai Shang find an asylum?" asked Thuvan Dihn of Kulan Tith.

For some moments the Jeddak of Kaol stood with bowed head, apparently deep in thought. Then a sudden light brightened his countenance.

"I have it!" he cried. "Only yesterday Matai Shang let drop a hint of his destination, telling me of a race of people unlike ourselves who dwell far to the north. They, he said, had always been known to the Holy Therns and were devout and faithful followers of the ancient cult. Among them would he find a perpetual haven of refuge, where no 'lying heretics' might seek him out. It is there that Matai Shang has gone."

"And in all Kaol there be no flier wherein to follow," I cried.

"Nor nearer than Ptarth," replied Thuvan Dihn.

"Wait!" I exclaimed, "beyond the southern fringe of this great forest lies the wreck of the thern flier which brought me that far upon my way. If you will loan me men to fetch it, and artificers to assist me, I can repair it in two days, Kulan Tith."

I had been more than half suspicious of the seeming sincerity of the Kaolian jeddak's sudden apostasy, but the alacrity with which he embraced my suggestion, and the despatch with which a force of officers and men were placed at my disposal entirely removed the last vestige of my doubts.

Two days later the flier rested upon the top of the watchtower, ready to depart. Thuvan Dihn and Kulan Tith had offered me the entire resources of two nations—millions of fighting men were at my disposal; but my flier could hold but one other than myself and Woola.

As I stepped aboard her, Thuvan Dihn took his place beside me. I cast a look of questioning surprise upon him. He turned to the highest of his own officers who had accompanied him to Kaol.

"To you I entrust the return of my retinue to Ptarth," he said. "There my son rules ably in my absence. The Prince of Helium shall not go alone into the land of his enemies. I have spoken. Farewell!"

EIGHT

Through the Carrion Caves

Straight toward the north, day and night, our destination compass led us after the fleeing flier upon which it had remained set since I first attuned it after leaving the thern fortress.

Early in the second night we noticed the air becoming perceptibly colder, and from the distance we had come from the equator were assured that we were rapidly approaching the north arctic region.

My knowledge of the efforts that had been made by countless expeditions to explore that unknown land bade me to caution, for never had flier returned who had passed to any considerable distance beyond the mighty ice-barrier that fringes the southern hem of the frigid zone.

What became of them none knew—only that they passed forever out of the sight of man into that grim and mysterious country of the pole.

The distance from the barrier to the pole was no more than a swift flier should cover in a few hours, and so it was assumed that some frightful catastrophe awaited those who reached the "forbidden land," as it had come to be called by the Martians of the outer world.

Thus it was that I went more slowly as we approached the barrier, for it was my intention to move cautiously by day over the ice-pack that I might discover, before I had run into a trap, if there really lay an inhabited country at the north pole, for there only could I imagine a spot where Matai Shang might feel secure from John Carter, Prince of Helium.

We were flying at a snail's pace but a few feet above the ground—literally feeling our way along through the darkness, for both moons had set, and the night was black with the clouds that are to be found only at Mars's two extremities.

Suddenly a towering wall of white rose directly in our path, and though I threw the helm hard over, and reversed our engine, I was too late to avoid collision.

With a sickening crash we struck the high looming obstacle three-quarters on.

The flier reeled half over; the engine stopped; as one, the patched buoyancy tanks burst, and we plunged, headforemost, to the ground twenty feet beneath.

Fortunately none of us was injured, and when we had disentangled ourselves from the wreckage, and the lesser moon had burst again from below the horizon, we found that we were at the foot of a mighty ice-barrier, from which outcropped great patches of the granite hills which hold it from encroaching farther toward the south.

What fate! With the journey all but completed to be thus wrecked upon the wrong side of that precipitous and unscalable wall of rock and ice!

I looked at Thuvan Dihn. He but shook his head dejectedly.

The balance of the night we spent shivering in our inadequate sleeping silks and furs upon the snow that lies at the foot of the ice-barrier.

With daylight my battered spirits regained something of their accustomed hopefulness, though I must admit that there was little enough for them to feed upon.

"What shall we do?" asked Thuvan Dihn. "How may we pass that which is impassable?"

"First we must disprove its impassability," I replied. "Nor shall I admit that it is impassable before I have followed its entire circle and stand again upon this spot, defeated. The sooner we start, the better, for I see no other way, and it will take us more than a month to travel the weary, frigid miles that lie before us."

For five days of cold and suffering and privation we traversed the rough and frozen way which lies at the foot of the ice-barrier. Fierce, fur-bearing creatures attacked us by daylight and by dark. Never for a moment were we safe from the sudden charge of some huge demon of the north.

The apt was our most consistent and dangerous foe.

It is a huge, white-furred creature with six limbs, four of which, short and heavy, carry it swiftly over the snow and ice; while the other two, growing forward from its shoulders on either side of its long, powerful neck, terminate in white, hairless hands, with which it seizes and holds its prey.

Its head and mouth are more similar in appearance to those of a hippopotamus than to any other earthly animal, except that from the sides of the lower jawbone two mighty horns curve slightly downward toward the front.

Its two huge eyes inspired my greatest curiosity. They extend in two vast, oval patches from the center of the top of the cranium down either side of the head to below the roots of the horns, so that these weapons really grow out from the lower part of the eyes, which are composed of several thousand ocelli each.

This eye structure seemed remarkable in a beast whose haunts were upon a glaring field of ice and snow, and though I found upon minute examination of several that we killed that each ocellus is furnished with its own lid, and that the animal can at will close as many of the facets of his huge eyes as he chooses, yet I was positive that nature had thus equipped him because much of his life was to be spent in dark, subterranean recesses.

Shortly after this we came upon the hugest apt that we had seen. The creature stood fully eight feet at the shoulder, and was so sleek and clean and glossy that I could have sworn that he had but recently been groomed.

He stood head-on eyeing us as we approached him, for we had found it a waste of time to attempt to escape the perpetual bestial rage which seems to possess these demon creatures, who rove the dismal north attacking every living thing that comes within the scope of their far-seeing eyes.

Even when their bellies are full and they can eat no more, they kill purely for the pleasure which they derive from taking life, and so when this particular apt failed to charge us, and instead wheeled and trotted away as we neared him, I should have been greatly surprised had I not chanced to glimpse the sheen of a golden collar about its neck.

Thuvan Dihn saw it, too, and it carried the same message of hope to us both. Only man could have placed that collar there, and as no race of Martians of which we knew aught ever had attempted to domesticate the ferocious apt, he must belong to a people of the north of whose very existence we were ignorant—possibly to the fabled yellow men of Barsoom; that once powerful race which was supposed to be extinct, though sometimes, by theorists, thought still to exist in the frozen north.

Simultaneously we started upon the trail of the great beast. Woola was quickly made to understand our desires, so that it was unnecessary to attempt to keep in sight of the animal whose swift flight over the rough ground soon put him beyond our vision.

For the better part of two hours the trail paralleled the barrier, and then suddenly turned toward it through the roughest and seemingly most impassable country I ever had beheld.

Enormous granite boulders blocked the way on every hand; deep rifts in the ice threatened to engulf us at the least misstep; and from the north a slight breeze wafted to our nostrils an unspeakable stench that almost choked us.

For another two hours we were occupied in traversing a few hundred yards to the foot of the barrier.

Then, turning about the corner of a wall-like outcropping of granite, we came upon a smooth area of two or three acres before the base of the towering pile of ice and rock that had baffled us for days, and before us beheld the dark and cavernous mouth of a cave.

From this repelling portal the horrid stench was emanating, and as Thuvan Dihn espied the place he halted with an exclamation of profound astonishment.

"By all my ancestors!" he ejaculated. "That I should have lived to witness the reality of the fabled Carrion Caves! If these indeed be they we have found a way beyond the ice-barrier.

"The ancient chronicles of the first historians of Barsoom—so ancient that we have for ages considered them mythology—record the passing of the yellow men from the ravages of the green hordes that overran Barsoom as the drying up of the great oceans drove the dominant races from their strongholds.

"They tell of the wanderings of the remnants of this once powerful race, harassed at every step, until at last they found a way through the ice-barrier of the north to a fertile valley at the pole.

"At the opening to the subterranean passage that led to their haven of refuge a mighty battle was fought in which the yellow men were victorious, and within the caves that gave ingress to their new home they piled the bodies of the dead, both yellow and green, that the stench might warn away their enemies from further pursuit.

"And ever since that long-gone day have the dead of this fabled land been carried to the Carrion Caves, that in death and decay they might serve their country and warn away invading enemies. Here, too, is brought, so the fable runs, all the waste stuff of the nation—everything that is subject to rot, and that can add to the foul stench that assails our nostrils.

"And death lurks at every step among rotting dead, for here the fierce apts lair, adding to the putrid accumulation with the fragments of their own prey which they cannot devour. It is a horrid avenue to our goal, but it is the only one."

"You are sure, then, that we have found the way to the land of the yellow men?" I cried.

"As sure as may be," he replied; "having only ancient legend to support my belief. But see how closely, so far, each detail tallies with the world-old story of the hegira of the yellow race. Yes, I am sure that we have discovered the way to their ancient hiding place."

"If it be true, and let us pray that such may be the case," I said, "then here may we solve the mystery of the disappearance of Tardos Mors, Jeddak of Helium, and Mors Kajak, his son, for no other spot upon Barsoom has remained unexplored by the many expeditions and the countless spies that have been searching for them for nearly two years. The last word that came from them was that they sought Carthoris, my own brave son, beyond the ice-barrier."

As we talked we had been approaching the entrance to the cave, and as we crossed the threshold I ceased to wonder that the ancient green enemies of the yellow men had been halted by the horrors of that awful way.

The bones of dead men lay man high upon the broad floor of the first cave, and over all was a putrid mush of decaying flesh, through which the apts had beaten a hideous trail toward the entrance to the second cave beyond.

The roof of this first apartment was low, like all that we traversed subsequently, so that the foul odors were confined and condensed to such an extent that they seemed to possess tangible substance. One was almost tempted to draw his short-sword and hew his way through in search of pure air beyond.

"Can man breathe this polluted air and live?" asked Thuvan Dihn, choking.

"Not for long, I imagine," I replied; "so let us make haste. I will go first, and you bring up the rear, with Woola between. Come," and with the words I dashed forward, across the fetid mass of putrefaction.

It was not until we had passed through seven caves of different sizes and varying but little in the power and quality of their stenches that we met with any physical opposition. Then, within the eighth cave, we came upon a lair of apts.

A full score of the mighty beasts were disposed about the chamber. Some were sleeping, while others tore at the fresh-killed carcasses of new-brought prey, or fought among themselves in their love-making.

Here in the dim light of their subterranean home the value of their great eyes was apparent, for these inner caves are shrouded in perpetual gloom that is but little less than utter darkness.

To attempt to pass through the midst of that fierce herd seemed, even to me, the height of folly, and so I proposed to Thuvan Dihn that he return to the outer world with Woola, that the two might find their way to civilization and come again with a sufficient force to overcome not only the apts, but any further obstacles that might lie between us and our goal.

"In the meantime," I continued, "I may discover some means of winning my way alone to the land of the yellow men, but if I am unsuccessful one life only will have been sacrificed. Should we all go on and perish, there will be none to guide a succoring party to Dejah Thoris and your daughter."

"I shall not return and leave you here alone, John Carter," replied Thuvan Dihn. "Whether you go on to victory or death, the Jeddak of Ptarth remains at your side. I have spoken."

I knew from his tone that it were useless to attempt to argue the question, and so I compromised by sending Woola back with a hastily penned note enclosed in a small metal case and fastened about his neck. I commanded the faithful creature to seek Carthoris at Helium, and though half a world and countless dangers lay between I knew that if the thing could be done Woola would do it.

Equipped as he was by nature with marvelous speed and endurance, and with frightful ferocity that made him a match for any single enemy of the way, his keen intelligence and wondrous instinct should easily furnish all else that was needed for the successful accomplishment of his mission.

It was with evident reluctance that the great beast turned to leave me in compliance with my command, and ere he had gone I could not resist the inclination to throw my arms about his great neck in a parting hug. He rubbed his cheek against mine in a final caress, and a moment later was speeding through the Carrion Caves toward the outer world.

In my note to Carthoris I had given explicit directions for locating the Carrion Caves, impressing upon him the necessity for making entrance to the country beyond through this avenue, and not to attempt under any circumstances to cross the ice-barrier with a fleet. I told him that what lay beyond the eighth cave I could not even guess; but I was sure that somewhere upon the other side of the ice-barrier his mother lay in the power of Matai Shang, and that possibly his grandfather and great-grandfather as well, if they lived.

Further, I advised him to call upon Kulan Tith and the son of Thuvan Dihn for warriors and ships that the expedition might be sufficiently strong to insure success at the first blow.

"And," I concluded, "if there be time bring Tars Tarkas with you, for if I live until you reach me I can think of few greater pleasures than to fight once more, shoulder to shoulder, with my old friend."

When Woola had left us Thuvan Dihn and I, hiding in the seventh cave, discussed and discarded many plans for crossing the eighth chamber. From where we stood we saw that the fighting among the apts was growing less, and that many that had been feeding had ceased and lain down to sleep.

Presently it became apparent that in a short time all the ferocious monsters might be peacefully slumbering, and thus a hazardous opportunity be presented to us to cross through their lair.

One by one the remaining brutes stretched themselves upon the bubbling decomposition that covered the mass of bones upon the floor of their den, until but a single apt remained awake. This huge fellow roamed restlessly about, nosing among his companion and the abhorrent litter of the cave.

Occasionally he would stop to peer intently toward first one of the exits from the chamber and then the other. His whole demeanor was as of one who acts as sentry.

We were at last forced to the belief that he would not sleep while the other occupants of the lair slept, and so cast about in our minds for some scheme whereby we might trick him. Finally I suggested a plan to Thuvan Dihn, and as it seemed as good as any that we had discussed we decided to put it to the test.

To this end Thuvan Dihn placed himself close against the cave's wall, beside the entrance to the eighth chamber, while I deliberately showed myself to the guardian apt as he looked toward our retreat. Then I sprang to the opposite side of the entrance, flattening my body close to the wall.

Without a sound the great beast moved rapidly toward the seventh cave to see what manner of intruder had thus rashly penetrated so far within the precincts of his habitation.

As he poked his head through the narrow aperture that connects the two caves a heavy long-sword was awaiting him upon either hand, and before he had an opportunity to emit even a single growl his severed head rolled at our feet.

Quickly we glanced into the eighth chamber—not an apt had moved. Crawling over the carcass of the huge beast that blocked the doorway Thuvan Dihn and I cautiously entered the forbidding and dangerous den.

Like snails we wound our silent and careful way among the huge, recumbent forms. The only sound above our breathing was the sucking noise of our feet as we lifted them from the ooze of decaying flesh through which we crept.

Halfway across the chamber and one of the mighty beasts directly before me moved restlessly at the very instant that my foot was poised above his head, over which I must step.

Breathlessly I waited, balancing upon one foot, for I did not dare move a muscle. In my right hand was my keen short-sword, the point hovering an inch above the thick fur beneath which beat the savage heart.

Finally the apt relaxed, sighing, as with the passing of a bad dream, and resumed the regular respiration of deep slumber. I planted my raised foot beyond the fierce head and an instant later had stepped over the beast.

Thuvan Dihn followed directly after me, and another moment found us at the further door, undetected.

The Carrion Caves consist of a series of twenty-seven connecting chambers, and present the appearance of having been eroded by running water in some far-gone age when a mighty river found its way to the south through this single breach in the barrier of rock and ice that hems the country of the pole.

Thuvan Dihn and I traversed the remaining nineteen caverns without adventure or mishap.

We were afterward to learn that but once a month is it possible to find all the apts of the Carrion Caves in a single chamber.

At other times they roam singly or in pairs in and out of the caves, so that it would have been practically impossible for two men to have passed through the entire twenty-seven chambers without encountering an apt in nearly every one of them. Once a month they sleep for a full day, and it was our good fortune to stumble by accident upon one of these occasions.

Beyond the last cave we emerged into a desolate country of snow and ice, but found a well-marked trail leading north. The way was boulder-strewn, as had been that south of the barrier, so that we could see but a short distance ahead of us at any time.

After a couple of hours we passed round a huge boulder to come to a steep declivity leading down into a valley.

Directly before us we saw a half dozen men—fierce, black-bearded fellows, with skins the color of a ripe lemon.

"The yellow men of Barsoom!" ejaculated Thuvan Dihn, as though even now that he saw them he found it scarce possible to believe that the very race we expected to find hidden in this remote and inaccessible land did really exist.

We withdrew behind an adjacent boulder to watch the actions of the little party, which stood huddled at the foot of another huge rock, their backs toward us.

One of them was peering round the edge of the granite mass as though watching one who approached from the opposite side.

Presently the object of his scrutiny came within the range of my vision and I saw that it was another yellow man. All were clothed in magnificent furs—the six in the black and yellow striped hide of the orluk, while he who approached alone was resplendent in the pure white skin of an apt.

The yellow men were armed with two swords, and a short javelin was slung across the back of each, while from their left arms hung cuplike shields no larger than a dinner plate, the concave sides of which turned outward toward an antagonist.

They seemed puny and futile implements of safety against an even ordinary swordsman, but I was later to see the purpose of them and with what wondrous dexterity the yellow men manipulate them.

One of the swords which each of the warriors carried caught my immediate attention. I call it a sword, but really it was a sharp-edged blade with a complete hook at the far end.

The other sword was of about the same length as the hooked instrument, and somewhere between that of my long-sword and my short-sword. It was straight and two-edged. In addition to the weapons I have ennumerated each man carried a dagger in his harness.

As the white-furred one approached, the six grasped their swords more firmly—the hooked instrument in the left hand, the straight sword in the right, while above the left wrist the small shield was held rigid upon a metal bracelet.

As the lone warrior came opposite them the six rushed out upon him with fiendish yells that resembled nothing more closely than the savage war cry of the Apaches of the South-west.

Instantly the attacked drew both his swords, and as the six fell upon him I witnessed as pretty fighting as one might care to see.

With their sharp hooks the combatants attempted to take hold of an adversary, but like lightning the cupshaped shield would spring before the darting weapon and into its hollow the hook would plunge.

Once the lone warrior caught an antagonist in the side with his hook, and drawing him close ran his sword through him.

But the odds were too unequal, and, though he who fought alone was by far the best and bravest of them all, I saw that it was but a question of time before the remaining five would find an opening through his marvelous guard and bring him down.

Now my sympathies have ever been with the weaker side of an argument, and though I knew nothing of the cause of the trouble I could not stand idly by and see a brave man butchered by superior numbers.

As a matter of fact I presume I gave little attention to seeking an excuse, for I love a good fight too well to need any other reason for joining in when one is afoot.

So it was that before Thuvan Dihn knew what I was about he saw me standing by the side of the white-clad yellow man, battling like mad with his five adversaries.

NINE

With the Yellow Men

Thuvan Dihn was not long in joining me; and, though we found the hooked weapon a strange and savage thing with which to deal, the three of us soon despatched the five black-bearded warriors who opposed us.

When the battle was over our new acquaintance turned to me, and removing the shield from his wrist, held it out. I did not know the significance of his act, but judged that it was but a form of expressing his gratitude to me.

I afterward learned that it symbolized the offering of a man's life in return for some great favor done him; and my act of refusing, which I had immediately done, was what was expected of me.

"Then accept from Talu, Prince of Marentina," said the yellow man, "this token of my gratitude," and reaching beneath one of his wide sleeves he withdrew a bracelet and placed it upon my arm. He then went through the same ceremony with Thuvan Dihn.

Next he asked our names, and from what land we hailed. He seemed quite familiar with the geography of the outerworld, and when I said I was from Helium he raised his brows.

"Ah," he said, "you seek your ruler and his company?"

"Know you of them?" I asked.

"But little more than that they were captured by my uncle, Salensus Oll, Jeddak of Jeddaks, Ruler of Okar, land of the yellow men of Barsoom. As to their fate I know nothing, for I am at war with my uncle, who would crush my power in the principality of Marentina.

"These from whom you have just saved me are warriors he has sent out to find and slay me, for they know that often I come alone to hunt and kill the sacred apt which Salensus Oll so much reveres. It is partly because I hate his religion that Salensus Oll hates me; but mostly does he fear my growing power and the great faction which has arisen throughout Okar that would be glad to see me ruler of Okar and Jeddak of Jeddaks in his place.

"He is a cruel and tyrannous master whom all hate, and were it not for the great fear they have of him I could raise an army overnight that would wipe out the few that might remain loyal to him. My own people are faithful to me, and the little valley of Marentina has paid no tribute to the court of Salensus Oll for a year.

"Nor can he force us, for a dozen men may hold the narrow way to Marentina against a million. But now, as to thine own affairs. How may I aid you? My palace is at your disposal, if you wish to honor me by coming to Marentina."

"When our work is done we shall be glad to accept your invitation," I replied. "But now you can assist us most by directing us to the court of Salensus Oll, and suggesting some means by which we may gain admission to the city and the palace, or whatever other place we find our friends to be confined."

Talu gazed ruefully at our smooth faces and at Thuvan Dihn's red skin and my white one.

"First you must come to Marentina," he said, "for a great change must be wrought in your appearance before you can hope to enter any city in Okar. You must have yellow faces and black beards, and your apparel and trappings must be those least likely to arouse suspicion. In my palace is one who can make you appear as truly yellow men as does Salensus Oll himself."

His counsel seemed wise; and as there was apparently no other way to insure a successful entry to Kadabra, the capital city of Okar, we set out with Talu, Prince of Marentina, for his little, rock-bound country.

The way was over some of the worst traveling I have ever seen, and I do not wonder that in this land where there are neither thoats nor fliers that Marentina is in little fear of invasion; but at last we reached our destination, the first view of which I had from a slight elevation a half-mile from the city.

Nestled in a deep valley lay a city of Martian concrete, whose every street and plaza and open space was roofed with glass. All about lay snow and ice, but there was none upon the rounded, domelike, crystal covering that enveloped the whole city.

Then I saw how these people combatted the rigors of the arctic, and lived in luxury and comfort in the midst of a land of perpetual ice. Their cities were veritable hothouses, and when I had come within this one my respect and admiration for the scientific and engineering skill of this buried nation was unbounded.

The moment we entered the city Talu threw off his outer garments of fur, as did we, and I saw that his apparel differed but little from that of the red races of Barsoom. Except for his leathern harness, covered thick with jewels and metal, he was naked, nor could one have comfortably worn apparel in that warm and humid atmosphere.

For three days we remained the guests of Prince Talu, and during that time he showered upon us every attention and courtesy within his power. He showed us all that was of interest in his great city.

The Marentina atmosphere plant will maintain life indefinitely in the cities of the north pole after all life upon the balance of dying Mars is extinct through the failure of the air supply, should the great central plant again cease functioning as it did upon that memorable occasion that gave me the opportunity of restoring life and happiness to the strange world that I had already learned to love so well.

He showed us the heating system that stores the sun's rays in great reservoirs beneath the city, and how little is necessary to maintain the perpetual summer heat of the glorious garden spot within this arctic paradise.

Broad avenues of sod sewn with the seed of the ocher vegetation of the dead sea bottoms carried the noiseless traffic of light and airy ground fliers that are the only form of artificial transportation used north of the gigantic ice-barrier.

The broad tires of these unique fliers are but rubber-like gas bags filled with the eighth Barsoomian ray, or ray of propulsion—that remarkable discovery of the Martians that has made possible the great fleets of mighty airships that render the red man of the outer world supreme. It is this ray which propels the inherent or reflected light of the planet off into space, and when confined gives to the Martian craft their airy buoyancy.

The ground fliers of Marentina contain just sufficient buoyancy in their automobile-like wheels to give the cars traction for steering purposes; and though the hind wheels are geared to the engine, and aid in driving the machine, the bulk of this work is carried by a small propeller at the stern.

I know of no more delightful sensation than that of riding in one of these luxuriously appointed cars which skim, light and airy as feathers, along the soft, mossy avenues of Marentina. They move with absolute noiselessness between borders of crimson sward and beneath arching trees gorgeous with the wondrous blooms that mark so many of the highly cultivated varieties of Barsoomian vegetation.

By the end of the third day the court barber—I can think of no other earthly appellation by which to describe him—had wrought so remarkable a transformation in both Thuvan Dihn and myself that our own wives would never have known us. Our skins were of the same lemon color as his own, and great, black beards and mustaches had been deftly affixed to our smooth faces. The trappings of warriors of Okar aided in the deception; and for wear beyond the hothouse cities we each had suits of the black- and yellow-striped orluk.

Talu gave us careful directions for the journey to Kadabra, the capital city of the Okar nation, which is the racial name of the yellow men. This good friend even accompanied us part way, and then, promising to aid us in any way that he found possible, bade us adieu.

On parting he slipped upon my finger a curiously wrought ring set with a dead-black, lusterless stone, which appeared more like a bit of bituminous coal than the priceless Barsoomian gem which in reality it is.

"There had been but three others cut from the mother stone," he said, "which is in my possession. These three are worn by nobles high in my confidence, all of whom have been sent on secret missions to the court of Salensus Oll.

"Should you come within fifty feet of any of these three you will feel a rapid, pricking sensation in the finger upon which you wear this ring. He who wears one of its mates will experience the same feeling; it is caused by an electrical action that takes place the moment two of these gems cut from the same mother stone come within the radius of each other's power. By it you will know that a friend is at hand upon whom you may depend for assistance in time of need.

"Should another wearer of one of these gems call upon you for aid do not deny him, and should death threaten you swallow the ring rather than let it fall into the hands of enemies. Guard it with your life, John Carter, for some day it may mean more than life to you."

With this parting admonition our good friend turned back toward Marentina, and we set our faces in the direction of the city of Kadabra and the court of Salensus Oll, Jeddak of Jeddaks.

That very evening we came within sight of the walled and glass-roofed city of Kadabra. It lies in a low depression near the pole, surrounded by rocky, snow-clad hills. From the pass through which we entered the valley we had a splendid view of this great city of the north. Its crystal domes sparkled in the brilliant sunlight gleaming above the frost-covered outer wall that circles the entire one hundred miles of its circumference.

At regular intervals great gates give entrance to the city; but even at the distance from which we looked upon the massive pile we could see that all were closed, and, in accordance with Talu's suggestion, we deferred attempting to enter the city until the following morning.

As he had said, we found numerous caves in the hillsides about us, and into one of these we crept for the night. Our warm orluk skins kept us perfectly comfortable, and it was only after a most refreshing sleep that we awoke shortly after daylight on the following morning.

Already the city was astir, and from several of the gates we saw parties of yellow men emerging. Following closely each detail of the instructions given us by our good friend of Marentina, we remained concealed for several hours until one party of some half dozen warriors had passed along the trail below our hiding place and entered the hills by way of the pass along which we had come the previous evening.

After giving them time to get well out of sight of our cave, Thuvan Dihn and I crept out and followed them, overtaking them when they were well into the hills.

When we had come almost to them I called aloud to their leader, when the whole party halted and turned toward us. The crucial test had come. Could we but deceive these men the rest would be comparatively easy.

"Kaor!" I cried as I came closer to them.

"Kaor!" responded the officer in charge of the party.

"We be from Illall," I continued, giving the name of the most remote city of Okar, which has little or no intercourse with Kadabra. "Only yesterday we arrived, and this morning the captain of the gate told us that you were setting out to hunt orluks, which is a sport we do not find in our own neighborhood. We have hastened after you to pray that you allow us to accompany you."

The officer was entirely deceived, and graciously permitted us to go with them for the day. The chance guess that they were bound upon an orluk hunt proved correct, and Talu had said that the chances were ten to one that such would be the mission of any party leaving Kadabra by the pass through which we entered the valley, since that way leads directly to the vast plains frequented by this elephantine beast of prey.

In so far as the hunt was concerned, the day was a failure, for we did not see a single orluk; but this proved more than fortunate for us, since the yellow men were so chagrined by their misfortune that they would not enter the city by the same gate by which they had left it in the morning, as it seemed that they had made great boasts to the captain of that gate about their skill at this dangerous sport.

We, therefore, approached Kadabra at a point several miles from that at which the party had quitted it in the morning, and so were relieved of the danger of embarrassing questions and explanations on the part of the gate captain, whom we had said had directed us to this particular hunting party.

We had come quite close to the city when my attention was attracted toward a tall, black shaft that reared its head several hundred feet into the air from what appeared to be a tangled mass of junk or wreckage, now partially snow-covered.

I did not dare venture an inquiry for fear of arousing suspicion by evident ignorance of something which as a yellow man I should have known; but before we reached the city gate I was to learn the purpose of that grim shaft and the meaning of the mighty accumulation beneath it.

We had come almost to the gate when one of the party called to his fellows, at the same time pointing toward the distant southern horizon. Following the direction he indicated, my eyes descried the hull of a large flier approaching rapidly from above the crest of the encircling hills.

"Still other fools who would solve the mysteries of the forbidden north," said the officer, half to himself. "Will they never cease their fatal curiosity?"

"Let us hope not," answered one of the warriors, "for then what should we do for slaves and sport?"

"True; but what stupid beasts they are to continue to come to a region from whence none of them ever has returned."

"Let us tarry and watch the end of this one," suggested one of the men.

The officer looked toward the city.

"The watch has seen him," he said; "we may remain, for we may be needed."

I looked toward the city and saw several hundred warriors issuing from the nearest gate. They moved leisurely, as though there were no need for haste—nor was there, as I was presently to learn.

Then I turned my eyes once more toward the flier. She was moving rapidly toward the city, and when she had come close enough I was surprised to see that her propellers were idle.

Straight for that grim shaft she bore. At the last minute I saw the great blades move to reverse her, yet on she came as though drawn by some mighty, irresistible power.

Intense excitement prevailed upon her deck, where men were running hither and thither, manning the guns and preparing to launch the small, one-man fliers, a fleet of which is part of the equipment of every Martian war vessel. Closer and closer to the black shaft the ship sped. In another instant she must strike, and then I saw the familiar signal flown that sends the lesser boats in a great flock from the deck of the mother ship.

Instantly a hundred tiny fliers rose from her deck, like a swarm of huge dragon flies; but scarcely were they clear of the battleship than the nose of each turned toward the shaft, and they, too, rushed on at frightful speed toward the same now seemingly inevitable end that menaced the larger vessel.

A moment later the collision came. Men were hurled in every direction from the ship's deck, while she, bent and crumpled, took the last, long plunge to the scrap-heap at the shaft's base.

With her fell a shower of her own tiny fliers, for each of them had come in violent collision with the solid shaft.

I noticed that the wrecked fliers scraped down the shaft's side, and that their fall was not as rapid as might have been expected; and then suddenly the secret of the shaft burst upon me, and with it an explanation of the cause that prevented a flier that passed too far across the ice-barrier ever returning.

The shaft was a mighty magnet, and when once a vessel came within the radius of its powerful attraction for the aluminum steel that enters so largely into the construction of all Barsoomian craft, no power on earth could prevent such an end as we had just witnessed.

I afterward learned that the shaft rests directly over the magnetic pole of Mars, but whether this adds in any way to its incalculable power of attraction I do not know. I am a fighting man, not a scientist.

Here, at last, was an explanation of the long absence of Tardos Mors and Mors Kajak. These valiant and intrepid warriors had dared the mysteries and dangers of the frozen north to search for Carthoris, whose long absence had bowed in grief the head of his beautiful mother, Dejah Thoris, Princess of Helium.

The moment that the last of the fliers came to rest at the base of the shaft the black-bearded, yellow warriors swarmed over the mass of wreckage upon which they lay, making prisoners of those who were uninjured and occasionally despatching with a sword-thrust one of the wounded who seemed prone to resent their taunts and insults.

A few of the uninjured red men battled bravely against their cruel foes, but for the most part they seemed too overwhelmed by the horror of the catastrophe that had befallen them to do more than submit supinely to the golden chains with which they were manacled.

When the last of the prisoners had been confined, the party returned to the city, at the gate of which we met a pack of fierce, gold-collared apts, each of which marched between two warriors, who held them with strong chains of the same metal as their collars.

Just beyond the gate the attendants loosened the whole terrible herd, and as they bounded off toward the grim, black shaft I did not need to ask to know their mission. Had there not been those within the cruel city

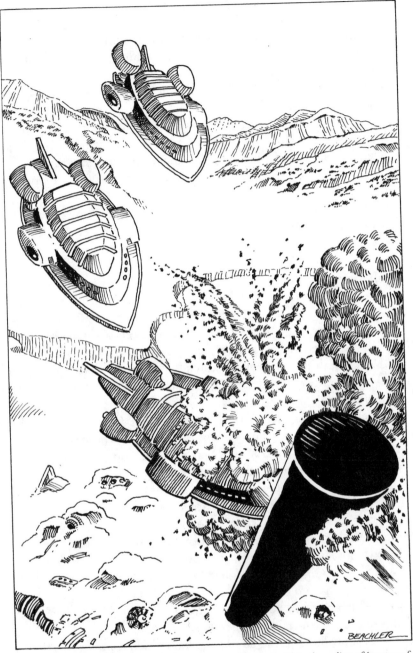

The shaft was a mighty magnet, and when once a vessel came within the radius of its powerful attraction for the aluminum steel that enters so largely into the construction of all Barsoomian craft, no power on earth could prevent such an end as we had just witnessed.

of Kadabra who needed succor far worse than the poor unfortunate dead and dying out there in the cold upon the bent and broken carcasses of a thousand fliers I could not have restrained my desire to hasten back and do battle with those horrid creatures that had been despatched to rend and devour them.

As it was I could but follow the yellow warriors, with bowed head, and give thanks for the chance that had given Thuvan Dihn and me such easy ingress to the capital of Salensus Oll.

Once within the gates, we had no difficulty in eluding our friends of the morning, and presently found ourselves in a Martian hostelry.

TEN

In Durance

The public houses of Barsoom, I have found, vary but little. There is no privacy for other than married couples.

Men without their wives are escorted to a large chamber, the floor of which is usually of white marble or heavy glass, kept scrupulously clean. Here are many small, raised platforms for the guest's sleeping silks and furs, and if he have none of his own clean, fresh ones are furnished at a nominal charge.

Once a man's belongings have been deposited upon one of these platforms he is a guest of the house, and that platform his own until he leaves. No one will disturb or molest his belongings, as there are no thieves upon Mars.

As assassination is the one thing to be feared, the proprietors of the hostelries furnish armed guards, who pace back and forth through the sleeping-rooms day and night. The number of guards and gorgeousness of their trappings quite usually denote the status of the hotel.

No meals are served in these houses, but generally a public eating place adjoins them. Baths are connected with the sleeping chambers, and each guest is required to bathe daily or depart from the hotel.

Usually on a second or third floor there is a large sleeping-room for single women guests, but its appointments do not vary materially from the chamber occupied by men. The guards who watch the women remain in the corridor outside the sleeping chamber, while female slaves pace back and forth among the sleepers within, ready to notify the warriors should their presence be required.

I was surprised to note that all the guards with the hotel at which we stopped were red men, and on inquiring of one of them I learned that they were slaves purchased by the proprietors of the hotels from the government. The man whose post was past my sleeping platform had been commander of the navy of a great Martian nation; but fate had carried his flagship across the ice-barrier within the radius of power of the magnetic shaft, and now for many tedious years he had been a slave of the yellow men.

He told me that princes, jeds, and even jeddaks of the outer world, were among the menials who served the yellow race; but when I asked him if he had heard of the fate of Mors Kajak or Tardos Mors he shook his head, saying that he never had heard of their being prisoners here, though he was very familiar with the reputations and fame they bore in the outer world.

Neither had he heard any rumor of the coming of the Father of Therns and the black dator of the First Born, but he hastened to explain that he knew little of what took place within the palace. I could see that he wondered not a little that a yellow man should be so inquisitive about certain red prisoners from beyond the ice-barrier, and that I should be so ignorant of customs and conditions among my own race.

In fact, I had forgotten my disguise upon discovering a red man pacing before my sleeping platform; but his growing expression of surprise warned me in time, for I had no mind to reveal my identity to any unless some good could come of it, and I did not see how this poor fellow could serve me yet, though I had it in my mind that later I might be the means of serving him and all the other thousands of prisoners who do the bidding of their stern masters in Kadabra.

Thuvan Dihn and I discussed our plans as we sat together among our sleeping silks and furs that night in the midst of the hundreds of yellow men who occupied the apartment with us. We spoke in low whispers, but, as that is only what courtesy demands in a public sleeping place, we roused no suspicion.

At last, determining that all must be but idle speculation until after we had had a chance to explore the city and attempt to put into execution the plan Talu had suggested, we bade each other good night and turned to sleep.

After breakfasting the following morning we set out to see Kadabra, and as, through the generosity of the prince of Marentina, we were well supplied with the funds current in Okar we purchased a handsome ground flier. Having learned to drive them while in Marentina, we spent a delightful and profitable day exploring the city, and late in the afternoon at the hour Talu told us we would find government officials in their offices, we stopped before a magnificent building on the plaza opposite the royal grounds and the palace.

Here we walked boldly in past the armed guard at the door, to be met by a red slave within who asked our wishes.

"Tell Sorav, your master, that two warriors from Illall wish to take service in the palace guard," I said.

Sorav, Talu had told us, was the commander of the forces of the palace, and as men from the further cities of Okar—and especially Illall—were less likely to be tainted with the germ of intrigue which had for years infected the household of Salensus Oll, he was sure that we would be welcomed and few questions asked us.

He had primed us with such general information as he thought would be necessary for us to pass muster before Sorav, after which we would have to undergo a further examination before Salensus Oll that he might determine our physical fitness and our ability as warriors.

The little experience we had had with the strange hooked sword of the yellow man and his cuplike shield made it seem rather unlikely that either of us could pass this final test, but there was the chance that we might be quartered in the palace of Salensus Oll for several days after being accepted by Sorav before the Jeddak of Jeddaks would find time to put us to the final test.

After a wait of several minutes in an ante-chamber we were summoned into the private office of Sorav, where we were courteously greeted by this ferocious-appearing, black-bearded officer. He asked us our names and stations in our own city, and having received replies that were evidently satisfactory to him, he put certain questions to us that Talu had foreseen and prepared us for.

The interview could not have lasted over ten minutes when Sorav summoned an aid whom he instructed to record us properly, and then escort us to the quarters in the palace which are set aside for aspirants to membership in the palace guard.

The aid took us to his own office first, where he measured and weighed and photographed us simultaneously with a machine ingeniously devised for that purpose, five copies being instantly reproduced in five different offices of the government, two of which are located in other cities miles distant. Then he led us through the palace grounds to the main guardroom of the palace, there turning us over to the officer in charge.

This individual again questioned us briefly, and finally despatched a soldier to guide us to our quarters. These we found located upon the second floor of the palace in a semi-detached tower at the rear of the edifice.

When we asked our guide why we were quartered so far from the guardroom he replied that the custom of the older members of the guard of picking quarrels with aspirants to try their metal had resulted in so many deaths that it was found difficult to maintain the guard at its full strength while this custom prevailed. Salensus Oll had, therefore, set apart these quarters for aspirants, and here they were securely locked against the danger of attack by members of the guard.

This unwelcome information put a sudden check to all our well-laid plans, for it meant that we should virtually be prisoners in the palace of Salensus Oll until the time that he should see fit to give us the final examination for efficiency.

As it was this interval upon which we had banked to accomplish so much in our search for Dejah Thoris and Thuvia of Ptarth, our chagrin was unbounded when we heard the great lock click behind our guide as he had quitted us after ushering us into the chambers we were to occupy.

With a wry face I turned to Thuvan Dihn. My companion but shook his head disconsolately and walked to one of the windows upon the far side of the apartment.

Scarcely had he gazed beyond them than he called to me in a tone of suppressed excitement and surprise. In an instant I was by his side.

"Look!" said Thuvan Dihn, pointing toward the courtyard below.

As my eyes followed the direction indicated I saw two women pacing back and forth in an enclosed garden.

At the same moment I recognized them—they were Dejah Thoris and Thuvia of Ptarth!

There were they whom I had trailed from one pole to another, the length of a world. Only ten feet of space and a few metal bars separated me from them.

With a cry I attracted their attention, and as Dejah Thoris looked up full into my eyes I made the sign of love that the men of Barsoom make to their women.

To my astonishment and horror her head went high, and as a look of utter contempt touched her finely chiseled features she turned her back full upon me. My body is covered with the scars of a thousand conflicts, but never in all my long life have I suffered such anguish from a wound, for this time the steel of a woman's look had entered my heart.

With a groan I turned away and buried my face in my arms. I heard Thuvan Dihn call aloud to Thuvia, but an instant later his exclamation of surprise betokened that he, too, had been repulsed by his own daughter.

"They will not even listen," he cried to me. "They have put their hands over their ears and walked to the farther end of the garden. Ever heard you of such mad work, John Carter? The two must be bewitched."

Presently I mustered the courage to return to the window, for even though she spurned me I loved her, and could not keep my eyes from feasting upon her divine face and figure, but when she saw me looking she again turned away.

I was at my wit's end to account for her strange actions, and that Thuvia, too, had turned against her father seemed incredible. Could it be that my incomparable princess still clung to the hideous faith from which I had rescued her world? Could it be that she looked upon me with loathing and contempt because I had returned from the Valley Dor, or because I had desecrated the temples and persons of the Holy Therns?

To naught else could I ascribe her strange deportment, yet it seemed far from possible that such could be the case, for the love of Dejah Thoris for John Carter had been a great and wondrous love—far above racial distinctions, creed, or religion.

As I gazed ruefully at the back of her haughty, royal head a gate at the opposite end of the garden opened and a man entered. As he did so he turned and slipped something into the hand of the yellow guardsman beyond the gate, nor was the distance too great that I might not see that money had passed between them.

Instantly I knew that this newcomer had bribed his way within the garden. Then he turned in the direction of the two women, and I saw that he was none other than Thurid, the black dator of the First Born.

He approached quite close to them before he spoke, and as they turned at the sound of his voice I saw Dejah Thoris shrink from him.

There was a nasty leer upon his face as he stepped close to her and spoke again. I could not hear his words, but her answer came clearly.

"The granddaughter of Tardos Mors can always die," she said, "but she could never live at the price you name."

Then I saw the black scoundrel go upon his knees beside her, fairly groveling in the dirt, pleading with her. Only part of what he said came to me, for though he was evidently laboring under the stress of passion and excitement, it was equally apparent that he did not dare raise his voice for fear of detection.

"I would save you from Matai Shang," I heard him say. "You know the fate that awaits you at his hands. Would you not choose me rather than the other?"

"I would choose neither," replied Dejah Thoris, "even were I free to choose, as you know well I am not."

"You *are* free!" he cried. "John Carter, Prince of Helium, is dead."

"I know better than that; but even were he dead, and I must needs choose another mate, it should be a plant man or a great white ape in preference to either Matai Shang or you, black calot," she answered with a sneer of contempt.

Of a sudden the vicious beast lost all control of himself, as with a vile oath he leaped at the slender woman, gripping her tender throat in his brute clutch. Thuvia screamed and sprang to aid her fellow-prisoner, and at the same instant I, too, went mad, and tearing at the bars that spanned my window I ripped them from their sockets as they had been but copper wire.

Hurling myself through the aperture I reached the garden, but a hundred feet from where the black was choking the life from my Dejah Thoris, and with a single great bound I was upon him. I spoke no word as I tore his defiling fingers from that beautiful throat, nor did I utter a sound as I hurled him twenty feet from me.

Foaming with rage, Thurid regained his feet and charged me like a mad bull.

"Yellow man," he shrieked, "you knew not upon whom you had laid your vile hands, but ere I am done with you, you will know well what it means to offend the person of a First Born."

Then he was upon me, reaching for my throat, and precisely as I had done that day in the courtyard of the Temple of Issus I did here in the garden of the palace of Salensus Oll. I ducked beneath his outstretched arms, and as he lunged past me I planted a terrific right upon the side of his jaw.

Just as he had done upon that other occasion he did now. Like a top he spun round, his knees gave beneath him, and he crumpled to the ground at my feet. Then I heard a voice behind me.

It was the deep voice of authority that marks the ruler of men, and when I turned to face the resplendent figure of a giant yellow man I did not need to ask to know that it was Salensus Oll. At his right stood Matai Shang, and behind them a score of guardsmen.

"Who are you," he cried, "and what means this intrusion within the precincts of the women's garden? I do not recall your face. How came you here?"

But for his last words I should have forgotten my disguise entirely and told him outright that I was John Carter, Prince of Helium; but his question recalled me to myself. I pointed to the dislodged bars of the window above.

"I am an aspirant to membership in the palace guard," I said, "and from yonder window in the tower where I was confined awaiting the final test for fitness I saw this brute attack the—this woman. I could not stand idly by, O Jeddak, and see this thing done within the very palace grounds, and yet feel that I was fit to serve and guard your royal person."

I had evidently made an impression upon the ruler of Okar by my fair words, and when he had turned to Dejah Thoris and Thuvia of Ptarth, and both had corroborated my statements it began to look pretty dark for Thurid.

I saw the ugly gleam in Matai Shang's evil eyes as Dejah Thoris narrated all that had passed between Thurid and herself, and when she came to that part which dealt with my interference with the dator of the First Born her gratitude was quite apparent, though I could see by her eyes that something puzzled her strangely.

I did not wonder at her attitude toward me while others were present; but that she should have denied me while she and Thuvia were the only occupants of the garden still cut me sorely.

As the examination proceeded I cast a glance at Thurid and startled him looking wide-eyed and wonderingly at me, and then of a sudden he laughed full in my face.

A moment later Salensus Oll turned toward the black.

"What have you to say in explanation of these charges?" he asked in a deep and terrible voice. "Dare you aspire to one whom the Father of Therns has chosen—one who might even be a fit mate for the Jeddak of Jeddaks himself?"

And then the black-bearded tyrant turned and cast a sudden greedy look upon Dejah Thoris, as though with the words a new thought and a new desire had sprung up within his mind and breast.

Thurid had been about to reply and, with a malicious grin upon his face, was pointing an accusing finger at me, when Salensus Oll's words and the expression of his face cut him short.

A cunning look crept into his eyes, and I knew from the expression of his face that his next words were not the ones he had intended to speak.

"O Mightiest of Jeddaks," he said, "the man and the women do not speak the truth. The fellow had come into the garden to assist them to escape. I was beyond and overheard their conversation, and when I entered, the woman screamed and the man sprang upon me and would have killed me.

"What know you of this man? He is a stranger to you, and I dare say that you will find him an enemy and a spy. Let him be put on trial, Salensus Oll, rather than your friend and guest, Thurid, Dator of the First Born."

Salensus Oll looked puzzled. He turned again and looked upon Dejah Thoris, and then Thurid stepped quite close to him and whispered something in his ear—what, I know not.

Presently the yellow ruler turned to one of his officers.

"See that this man be securely confined until we have time to go deeper into this affair," he commanded, "and as bars alone seem inadequate to restrain him, let chains be added."

Then he turned and left the garden, taking Dejah Thoris with him—his hand upon her shoulder. Thurid and Matai Shang went also, and as they reached the gateway the black turned and laughed again aloud in my face.

What could be the meaning of his sudden change toward me? Could he suspect my true identity? It must be that, and the thing that had betrayed me was the trick and blow that had laid him low for the second time.

As the guards dragged me away my heart was very sad and bitter indeed, for now to the two relentless enemies that had hounded her for so long another and a more powerful one had been added, for I would have been but a fool had I not recognized the sudden love for Dejah Thoris that had just been born in the terrible breast of Salensus Oll, Jeddak of Jeddaks, ruler of Okar.

ELEVEN

The Pit of Plenty

I did not languish long within the prison of Salensus Oll. During the short time that I lay there, fettered with chains of gold, I often wondered as to the fate of Thuvan Dihn, Jeddak of Ptarth.

My brave companion had followed me into the garden as I attacked Thurid, and when Salensus Oll had left with Dejah Thoris and the others, leaving Thuvia of Ptarth behind, he, too, had remained in the garden with his daughter, apparently unnoticed, for he was appareled similarly to the guards.

The last I had seen of him he stood waiting for the warriors who escorted me to close the gate behind them, that he might be alone with Thuvia. Could it be possible that they had escaped? I doubted it, and yet with all my heart I hoped that it might be true.

The third day of my incarceration brought a dozen warriors to escort me to the audience chamber, where Salensus Oll himself was to try me. A great number of nobles crowded the room, and among them I saw Thurid, but Matai Shang was not there.

Dejah Thoris, as radiantly beautiful as ever, sat upon a small throne beside Salensus Oll. The expression of sad hopelessness upon her dear face cut deep into my heart.

Her position beside the Jeddak of Jeddaks boded ill for her and me, and on the instant that I saw her there, there sprang to my mind the firm intention never to leave that chamber alive if I must leave her in the clutches of this powerful tyrant.

I had killed better men than Salensus Oll, and killed them with my bare hands, and now I swore to myself that I should kill him if I found that the only way to save the Princess of Helium. That it would mean almost instant death for me I cared not, except that it would remove me from further efforts in behalf of Dejah Thoris, and for this reason alone I would have chosen another way, for even though I should kill Salensus Oll that act would not restore my beloved wife to her own people. I determined to wait the final outcome of the trial, that I might learn all that I could of the Okarian ruler's intentions, and then act accordingly.

Scarcely had I come before him than Salensus Oll summoned Thurid also.

"Dator Thurid," he said, "you have made a strange request of me; but, in accordance with your wishes and your promise that it will result only to my interests, I have decided to accede.

"You tell me that a certain announcement will be the means of convicting this prisoner and, at the same time, open the way to the gratification of my dearest wish."

Thurid nodded.

"Then shall I make the announcement here before all my nobles," continued Salensus Oll. "For a year no queen has sat upon the throne beside me, and now it suits me to take to wife one who is reputed the most beautiful woman upon Barsoom. A statement which none may truthfully deny.

"Nobles of Okar, unsheathe your swords and do homage to Dejah Thoris, Princess of Helium and future Queen of Okar, for at the end of the allotted ten days she shall become the wife of Salensus Oll."

As the nobles drew their blades and lifted them on high, in accordance with the ancient custom of Okar when a jeddak announces his intention to wed, Dejah Thoris sprang to her feet and, raising her hand aloft, cried in a loud voice that they desist.

"I may not be the wife of Salensus Oll," she pleaded, "for already I be a wife and mother. John Carter, Prince of Helium, still lives. I know it to be true, for I overheard Matai Shang tell his daughter Phaidor that he had seen him in Kaor, at the court of Kulan Tith, Jeddak. A jeddak does not wed a married woman, nor will Salensus Oll thus violate the bonds of matrimony."

Salensus Oll turned upon Thurid with an ugly look.

"Is this the surprise you held in store for me?" he cried. "You assured me that no obstacle which might not be easily overcome stood between me and this woman, and now I find that the one insuperable obstacle intervenes. What mean you, man? What have you to say?"

"And should I deliver John Carter into your hands, Salensus Oll, would you not feel that I had more than satisfied the promise that I made you?" answered Thurid.

"Talk not like a fool," cried the enraged jeddak. "I am no child to be thus played with."

"I am talking only as a man who knows," replied Thurid. "Knows that he can do all that he claims."

"Then turn John Carter over to me within ten days or yourself suffer the end that I should mete out to him were he in my power!" snapped the Jeddak of Jeddaks, with an ugly scowl.

"You need not wait ten days, Salensus Oll," replied Thurid; and then, turning suddenly upon me as he extended a pointing finger, he cried: "There stands John Carter, Prince of Helium!"

"Fool!" shrieked Salensus Oll. "Fool! John Carter is a white man. This fellow be as yellow as myself. John Carter's face is smooth—Matai Shang has described him to me. This prisoner has a beard and mustache as large and black as any in Okar. Quick, guardsmen, to the pits with the black maniac who wishes to throw his life away for a poor joke upon your ruler!"

"Hold!" cried Thurid, and springing forward before I could guess his intention, he had grasped my beard and ripped the whole false fabric from my face and head, revealing my smooth, tanned skin beneath and my close-cropped black hair.

Instantly pandemonium reigned in the audience chamber of Salensus Oll. Warriors pressed forward with drawn blades, thinking that I might be contemplating the assassination of the Jeddak of Jeddaks; while others, out of curiosity to see one whose name was familiar from pole to pole, crowded behind their fellows.

As my identity was revealed I saw Dejah Thoris spring to her feet—amazement writ large upon her face—and then through that jam of armed men she forced her way before any could prevent. A moment only and she was before me with outstretched arms and eyes filled with the light of her great love.

"John Carter! John Carter!" she cried as I folded her to my breast, and then of a sudden I knew why she had denied me in the garden beneath the tower.

What a fool I had been! Expecting that she would penetrate the marvelous disguise that had been wrought for me by the barber of Marentina! She had not known me, that was all; and when she saw the sign of love from a stranger she was offended and righteously indignant. Indeed, but I had been a fool.

"And it was you," she cried, "who spoke to me from the tower! How could I dream that my beloved Virginian lay behind that fierce beard and that yellow skin?"

She had been wont to call me her Virginian as a term of endearment, for she knew that I loved the sound of that beautiful name, made a thousand times more beautiful and hallowed by her dear lips, and as I heard it again after all those long years my eyes became dimmed with tears and my voice choked with emotion.

But an instant did I crush that dear form to me ere Salensus Oll, trembling with rage and jealousy, shouldered his way to us.

"Seize the man," he cried to his warriors, and a hundred ruthless hands tore us apart.

Well it was for the nobles of the court of Okar that John Carter had been disarmed. As it was, a dozen of them felt the weight of my clenched fists, and I had fought my way half up the steps before the throne to which Salensus Oll had carried Dejah Thoris ere ever they could stop me.

Then I went down, fighting, beneath a half-hundred warriors; but before they had battered me into unconsciousness I heard that from the lips of Dejah Thoris that made all my suffering well worth while.

Standing there beside the great tyrant, who clutched her by the arm, she pointed to where I fought alone against such awful odds.

"Think you, Salensus Oll, that the wife of such as he is," she cried, "would ever dishonor his memory, were he a thousand times dead, by mating with a lesser mortal? Lives there upon any world such another as John Carter, Prince of Helium? Lives there another man who could fight his way back and forth across a warlike planet, facing savage beasts and hordes of savage men, for the love of a woman?

"I, Dejah Thoris, Princess of Helium, am his. He fought for me and won me. If you be a brave man you will honor the bravery that is his, and you will not kill him. Make him a slave if you will, Salensus Oll; but spare his life. I would rather be a slave with such as he than be Queen of Okar."

"Neither slave nor queen dictates to Salensus Oll," replied the Jeddak of Jeddaks. "John Carter shall die a natural death in the Pit of Plenty, and the day he dies Dejah Thoris shall become my queen."

I did not hear her reply, for it was then that a blow upon my head brought unconsciousness, and when I recovered my senses only a handful of guardsmen remained in the audience chamber with me. As I opened my eyes they goaded me with the points of their swords and bade me rise.

Then they led me through long corridors to a court far toward the center of the palace.

In the center of the court was a deep pit, near the edge of which stood half a dozen other guardsmen, awaiting me. One of them carried a long rope in his hands, which he commenced to make ready as we approached.

We had come to within fifty feet of these men when I felt a sudden strange and rapid pricking sensation in one of my fingers.

For a moment I was nonplused by the odd feeling, and then there came to me recollection of that which in the stress of my adventure I had entirely forgotten—the gift ring of Prince Talu of Marentina.

Instantly I looked toward the group we were nearing, at the same time raising my left hand to my forehead, that the ring might be visible to one who sought it. Simultaneously one of the waiting warriors raised his left hand, ostensibly to brush back his hair, and upon one of his fingers I saw the duplicate of my own ring.

A quick look of intelligence passed between us, after which I kept my eyes turned away from the warrior and did not look at him again, for fear that I might arouse the suspicion of the Okarians.

When we reached the edge of the pit I saw that it was very deep, and presently I realized I was soon to judge just how far it extended below the surface of the court, for he who held the rope passed it about my body in such a way that it could be released from above at any time; and then, as all the warriors grasped it, he pushed me forward, and I fell into the yawning abyss.

After the first jerk as I reached the end of the rope that had been paid out to let me fall below the pit's edge they lowered me quickly but smoothly. The moment before the plunge, while two or three of the men had been assisting in adjusting the rope about me, one of them had brought his mouth close to my cheek, and in the brief interval before I was cast into the forbidding hole he breathed a single word into my ear:

"Courage!"

The pit, which my imagination had pictured as bottomless, proved to be not more than a hundred feet in depth; but as its walls were smoothly polished it might as well have been a thousand feet, for I could never hope to escape without outside assistance.

For a day I was left in darkness; and then, quite suddenly, a brilliant light illumined my strange cell. I was reasonably hungry and thirsty by this time, not having tasted food or drink since the day prior to my incarceration.

To my amazement I found the sides of the pit, that I had thought smooth, lined with shelves, upon which were the most delicious viands and liquid refreshments that Okar afforded.

With an exclamation of delight I sprang forward to partake of some of the welcome food, but ere ever I reached it the light was extinguished, and, though I groped my way about the chamber, my hands came in contact with nothing beside the smooth, hard wall that I had felt on my first examination of my prison.

Immediately the pangs of hunger and thirst began to assail me. Where before I had had but a mild craving for food and drink, I now actually suffered for want of it, and all because of the tantalizing sight that I had had of food almost within my grasp.

Once more darkness and silence enveloped me, a silence that was broken only by a single mocking laugh.

For another day nothing occurred to break the monotony of my imprisonment or relieve the suffering superinduced by hunger and thirst. Slowly the pangs became less keen, as suffering deaded the activity of certain nerves; and then the light flashed on once again, and before me stood an array of new and tempting dishes, with great bottles of clear water and flagons of refreshing wine, upon the outside of which the cold sweat of condensation stood.

Again, with the hunger madness of a wild beast, I sprang forward to seize those tempting dishes; but, as before, the light went out and I came to a sudden stop against a hard wall.

Then the mocking laugh rang out for a second time.

The Pit of Plenty!

Ah, what a cruel mind must have devised this exquisite, hellish torture! Day after day was the thing repeated, until I was on the verge of madness; and then, as I had done in the pits of the Warhoons, I took a new, firm hold upon my reason and forced it back into the channels of sanity.

By sheer will-power I regained control over my tottering mentality, and so successful was I that the next time that the light came I sat quite still and looked indifferently at the fresh and tempting food almost within my reach. Glad I was that I had done so, for it gave me an opportunity to solve the seeming mystery of those vanishing banquets.

As I made no move to reach the food, the torturers left the light turned on in the hope that at last I could refrain no longer from giving them the delicious thrill of enjoyment that my former futile efforts to obtain it had caused.

And as I sat scrutinizing the laden shelves I presently saw how the thing was accomplished, and so simple was it that I wondered I had not guessed it before. The wall of my prison was of clearest glass—behind the glass were the tantalizing viands.

After nearly an hour the light went out, but this time there was no mocking laughter—at least not upon the part of my tormentors; but I, to be at quits with them, gave a low laugh that none might mistake for the cackle of a maniac.

Nine days passed, and I was weak from hunger and thirst, but no longer suffering—I was past that. Then, down through the darkness above, a little parcel fell to the floor at my side.

Indifferently I groped for it, thinking it but some new invention of my jailers to add to my sufferings.

At last I found it—a tiny package wrapped in paper, at the end of a strong and slender cord. As I opened it a few lozenges fell to the floor. As I gathered them up, feeling of them and smelling of them, I discovered that they were tablets of concentrated food such as are quite common in all parts of Barsoom.

Poison! I thought.

Well, what of it? Why not end my misery now rather than drag out a few more wretched days in this dark pit? Slowly I raised one of the little pellets to my lips.

"Good-bye, my Dejah Thoris!" I breathed. "I have lived for you and fought for you, and now my next dearest wish is to be realized, for I shall die for you," and, taking the morsel in my mouth, I devoured it.

One by one I ate them all, nor ever did anything taste better than those tiny bits of nourishment, within which I knew must lie the seeds of death—possibly of some hideous, torturing death.

As I sat quietly upon the floor of my prison, waiting for the end, my fingers by accident came in contact with the bit of paper in which the things had been wrapped; and as I idly played with it, my mind roaming far back into the past, that I might live again for a few brief moments before I died some of the many happy moments of a long and happy life, I became aware of strange protuberances upon the smooth surface of the parchment-like substance in my hands.

For a time they carried no special significance to my mind—I merely was mildly wondrous that they were there; but at last they seemed to take form, and then I realized that there was but a single line of them, like writing.

Now, more interestedly, my fingers traced and retraced them. There were four separate and distinct combinations of raised lines. Could it be that these were four words, and that they were intended to carry a message to me?

The more I thought of it the more excited I became, until my fingers raced madly back and forth over those bewildering little hills and valleys upon that bit of paper.

But I could make nothing of them, and at last I decided that my very haste was preventing me from solving the mystery. Then I took it more slowly. Again and again my forefinger traced the first of those four combinations.

Martian writing is rather difficult to explain to an Earth man—it is something of a cross between shorthand and picture-writing, and is an entirely different language from the spoken language of Mars.

Upon Barsoom there is but a single oral language.

It is spoken today by every race and nation, just as it was at the beginning of human life upon Barsoom. It has grown with the growth of the planet's learning and scientific achievements, but so ingenious a thing it is that new words to express new thoughts or describe new conditions or discoveries form themselves—no other word could explain the thing that a new word is required for other than the word that naturally falls to it, and so, no matter how far removed two nations or races, their spoken languages are identical.

Not so their written languages, however. No two nations have the same written language, and often cities of the same nation have a written language that differs greatly from that of the nation to which they belong.

Thus it was that the signs upon the paper, if in reality they were words, baffled me for some time; but at last I made out the first one.

It was "courage," and it was written in the letters of Marentina.

Courage!

That was the word the yellow guardsman had whispered in my ear as I stood upon the verge of the Pit of Plenty.

The message must be from him, and he I knew was a friend.

With renewed hope I bent my every energy to the deciphering of the balance of the message, and at last success rewarded my endeavor—I had read the four words:

"Courage! Follow the rope."

TWELVE

"Follow the Rope!"

What could it mean?

"Follow the rope." What rope?

Presently I recalled the cord that had been attached to the parcel when it fell at my side, and after a little groping my hand came in contact with it again. It depended from above, and when I pulled upon it I discovered that it was rigidly fastened, possibly at the pit's mouth.

Upon examination I found that the cord, though small, was amply able to sustain the weight of several men. Then I made another discovery—there was a second message knotted in the rope at about the height of my head. This I deciphered more easily, now that the key was mine.

"Bring the rope with you. Beyond the knots lies danger."

That was all there was to this message. It was evidently hastily formed—an afterthought.

I did not pause longer than to learn the contents of the second message, and, though I was none too sure of the meaning of the final admonition, "Beyond the knots lies danger," yet I was sure that here before me lay an avenue of escape, and that the sooner I took advantage of it the more likely was I to win to liberty.

At least, I could be but little worse off than I had been in the Pit of Plenty.

I was to find, however, ere I was well out of that damnable hole that I might have been very much worse off had I been compelled to remain there another two minutes.

It had taken me about that length of time to ascend some fifty feet above the bottom when a noise above attracted my attention. To my chagrin I saw that the covering of the pit was being removed far above me, and in the light of the courtyard beyond I saw a number of yellow warriors.

Could it be that I was laboriously working my way into some new trap?

Were the messages spurious, after all? And then, just as my hope and courage had ebbed to their lowest, I saw two things.

One was the body of a huge, struggling, snarling apt being lowered over the side of the pit toward me, and the other was an aperture in the side of the shaft—an aperture larger than a man's body, into which my rope led.

Just as I scrambled into the dark hole before me the apt passed me, reaching out with his mighty hands to clutch me, and snapping, growling, and roaring in a most frightful manner.

Plainly now I saw the end for which Salensus Oll had destined me. After first torturing me with starvation he had caused this fierce beast to be lowered into my prison to finish the work that the jeddak's hellish imagination had conceived.

And then another truth flashed upon me—I had lived nine days of the allotted ten which must intervene before Salensus Oll could make Dejah Thoris his queen. The purpose of the apt was to insure my death before the tenth day.

I almost laughed aloud as I thought how Salensus Oll's measure of safety was to aid in defeating the very end he sought, for when they discovered that the apt was alone in the Pit of Plenty they could not know but that he had completely devoured me, and so no suspicion of my escape would cause a search to be made for me.

Coiling the rope that had carried me thus far upon my strange journey, I sought for the other end, but found that as I followed it forward it extended always before me. So this was the meaning of the words: "Follow the rope."

The tunnel through which I crawled was low and dark. I had followed it for several hundred yards when I felt a knot beneath my fingers. "Beyond the knots lies danger."

Now I went with the utmost caution, and a moment later a sharp turn in the tunnel brought me to an opening into a large, brilliantly lighted chamber.

The trend of the tunnel I had been traversing had been slightly upward, and from this I judged that the chamber into which I now found myself looking must be either on the first floor of the palace or directly beneath the first floor.

Upon the opposite wall were many strange instruments and devices, and in the center of the room stood a long table, at which two men were seated in earnest conversation.

He who faced me was a yellow man—a little, wizened-up, pasty-faced old fellow with great eyes that showed the white round the entire circumference of the iris.

His companion was a black man, and I did not need to see his face to know that it was Thurid, for there was no other of the First Born north of the ice-barrier.

Thurid was speaking as I came within hearing of the men's voices.

"Solan," he was saying, "there is no risk and the reward is great. You know that you hate Salensus Oll and that nothing would please you more than to thwart him in some cherished plan. There be nothing that he more cherishes today than the idea of wedding the beautiful Princess of Helium; but I, too, want her, and with your help I may win her.

"You need not more than step from this room for an instant when I give you the signal. I will do the rest, and then, when I am gone, you may come and throw the great switch back into its place, and all will be as before. I need but an hour's start to be safe beyond the devilish power that you control in this hidden chamber beneath the palace of your master. See how easy," and with the words the black dator rose from his seat and, crossing the room, laid his hand upon a large, burnished lever that protruded from the opposite wall.

"No! No!" cried the little old man, springing after him, with a wild shriek. "Not that one! Not that one! That controls the sunray tanks, and should you pull it too far down, all Kadabra would be consumed by heat before I could replace it. Come away! Come away! You know not with what mighty powers you play. This is the lever that you seek. Note well the symbol inlaid in white upon its ebon surface."

Thurid approached and examined the handle of the lever.

"Ah, a magnet," he said. "I will remember. It is settled then I take it," he continued.

The old man hesitated. A look of combined greed and apprehension overspread his none too beautiful features.

"Double the figure," he said. "Even that were all too small an amount for the service you ask. Why, I risk my life by even entertaining you here within the forbidden precincts of my station. Should Salensus Oll learn of it he would have me thrown to the apts before the day was done."

"He dare not do that, and you know it full well, Solan," contradicted the black. "Too great a power of life and death you hold over the people of Kadabra for Salensus Oll ever to risk threatening you with death. Before ever his minions could lay their hands upon you, you might seize this very lever from which you have just warned me and wipe out the entire city."

"And myself into the bargain," said Solan, with a shudder.

"But if you were to die, anyway, you would find the nerve to do it," replied Thurid.

"Yes," muttered Solan, "I have often thought upon that very thing. Well, First Born, is your red princess worth the price I ask for my services, or will you go without her and see her in the arms of Salensus Oll tomorrow night?"

"Take your price, yellow man," replied Thurid, with an oath. "Half now and the balance when you have fulfilled your contract."

With that the dator threw a well-filled money-pouch upon the table.

Solan opened the pouch and with trembling fingers counted its contents. His weird eyes assumed a greedy expression, and his unkempt beard and mustache twitched with the muscles of his mouth and chin. It was quite evident from his very mannerism that Thurid had keenly guessed the man's weakness—even the clawlike, clutching movement of the fingers betokened the avariciousness of the miser.

Having satisfied himself that the amount was correct, Solan replaced the money in the pouch and rose from the table.

"Now," he said, "are you quite sure that you know the way to your destination? You must travel quickly to cover the ground to the cave and from thence beyond the Great Power, all within a brief hour, for no more dare I spare you."

"Let me repeat it to you," said Thurid, "that you may see if I be letter-perfect."

"Proceed," replied Solan.

"Through yonder door," he commenced, pointing to a door at the far end of the apartment, "I follow a corridor, passing three diverging corridors upon my right; then into the fourth right-hand corridor straight to where three corridors meet; here again I follow to the right, hugging the left wall closely to avoid the pit.

"At the end of this corridor I shall come to a spiral runway, which I must follow down instead of up; after that the way is along but a single branchless corridor. Am I right?"

"Quite right, Dator," answered Solan; "and now begone. Already have you tempted fate too long within this forbidden place."

"Tonight, or tomorrow, then, you may expect the signal," said Thurid, rising to go.

"Tonight, or tomorrow," repeated Solan, and as the door closed behind his guest the old man continued to mutter as he turned back to the table, where he again dumped the contents of the money-pouch, running his fingers through the heap of shining metal; piling the coins into little towers; counting, recounting, and fondling the wealth the while he muttered on and on in a crooning undertone.

Presently his fingers ceased their play; his eyes popped wider than ever as they fastened upon the door through which Thurid had disappeared. The croon changed to a querulous muttering, and finally to an ugly growl.

Then the old man rose from the table, shaking his fist at the closed door. Now he raised his voice, and his words came distinctly.

"Fool!" he muttered. "Think you that for your happiness Solan will give up his life? If you escaped, Salensus Oll would know that only through my connivance could you have succeeded. Then would he send for me. What would you have me do? Reduce the city and myself to ashes? No, fool, there is a better way—a better way for Solan to keep thy money and be revenged upon Salensus Oll."

He laughed in a nasty, cackling note.

"Poor fool! You may throw the great switch that will give you the freedom of the air of Okar, and then, in fatuous security, go on with thy red princess to the freedom of—death. When you have passed beyond this chamber in your flight, what can prevent Solan replacing the switch as it was before your vile hand touched it? Nothing; and then the Guardian of the North will claim you and your woman, and Salensus Oll, when he sees your dead bodies, will never dream that the hand of Solan had aught to do with the thing."

Then his voice dropped once more into mutterings that I could not translate, but I had heard enough to cause me to guess a great deal more, and I thanked the kind Providence that had led me to this chamber at a time so filled with importance to Dejah Thoris and myself as this.

But how to pass the old man now! The cord, almost invisible upon the floor, stretched straight across the apartment to a door upon the far side.

There was no other way of which I knew, nor could I afford to ignore the advice to "follow the rope." I must cross this room, but however I should accomplish it undetected with that old man in the very center of it baffled me.

Of course I might have sprung in upon him and with my bare hands silenced him forever, but I had heard enough to convince me that with him alive the knowledge that I had gained might serve me at some future moment, while should I kill him and another be stationed in his place Thurid would not come hither with Dejah Thoris, as was quite evidently his intention.

As I stood in the dark shadow of the tunnel's end racking my brain for a feasible plan the while I watched, catlike, the old man's every move, he took up the money-pouch and crossed to one end of the apartment, where, bending to his knees, he fumbled with a panel in the wall.

Instantly I guessed that here was the hiding place in which he hoarded his wealth, and while he bent there, his back toward me, I entered the chamber upon tiptoe, and with the utmost stealth essayed to reach the opposite side before he should complete his task and turn again toward the room's center.

Scarcely thirty steps, all told, must I take, and yet it seemed to my overwrought imagination that that farther wall was miles away; but at last I reached it, nor once had I taken my eyes from the back of the old miser's head.

He did not turn until my hand was upon the button that controlled the door through which my way led, and then he turned away from me as I passed through and gently closed the door.

For an instant I paused, my ear close to the panel, to learn if he had suspected aught, but as no sound of pursuit came from within I wheeled and made my way along the new corridor, following the rope, which I coiled and brought with me as I advanced.

But a short distance farther on I came to the rope's end at a point where five corridors met. What was I to do? Which way should I turn? I was nonplused.

A careful examination of the end of the rope revealed the fact that it had been cleanly cut with some sharp instrument. This fact and the words that had cautioned me that danger lay beyond the *knots* convinced me that the rope had been severed since my friend had placed it as my guide, for I had but passed a single knot, whereas there had evidently been two or more in the entire length of the cord.

Now, indeed, was I in a pretty fix, for neither did I know which avenue to follow nor when danger lay directly in my path; but there was nothing else to be done than follow one of the corridors, for I could gain nothing by remaining where I was.

So I chose the central opening, and passed on into its gloomy depths with a prayer upon my lips.

The floor of the tunnel rose rapidly as I advanced, and a moment later the way came to an abrupt end before a heavy door.

I could hear nothing beyond, and, with my accustomed rashness, pushed the portal wide to step into a room filled with yellow warriors.

The first to see me opened his eyes wide in astonishment, and at the same instant I felt the tingling sensation in my finger that denoted the presence of a friend of the ring.

Then others saw me, and there was a concerted rush to lay hands upon me, for these were all members of the palace guard—men familiar with my face.

The first to reach me was the wearer of the mate to my strange ring, and as he came close he whispered: "Surrender to me!" then in a loud voice shouted: "You are my prisoner, white man," and menaced me with his two weapons.

And so John Carter, Prince of Helium, meekly surrendered to a single antagonist. The others now swarmed about us, asking many questions, but I would not talk to them, and finally my captor announced that he would lead me back to my cell.

An officer ordered several other warriors to accompany him, and a moment later we were retracing the way I had just come. My friend walked close beside me, asking many silly questions about the country from which I had come, until finally his fellows paid no further attention to him or his gabbling.

Gradually, as he spoke, he lowered his voice, so that presently he was able to converse with me in a low tone without attracting attention. His ruse was a clever one, and showed that Talu had not misjudged the man's fitness for the dangerous duty upon which he was detailed.

When he had fully assured himself that the other guardsmen were not listening, he asked me why I had not followed the rope, and when I told him that it had ended at the five corridors he said that it must have been cut by someone in need of a piece of rope, for he was sure that "the stupid Kadabrans would never have guessed its purpose."

Before we had reached the spot from which the five corridors diverge my Marentinian friend had managed to drop to the rear of the little column with me, and when we came in sight of the branching ways he whispered:

"Run up the first upon the right. It leads to the watchtower upon the south wall. I will direct the pursuit up the next corridor," and with that he gave me a great shove into the dark mouth of the tunnel, at the same time crying out in simulated pain and alarm as he threw himself upon the floor as though I had felled him with a blow.

From behind the voices of the excited guardsmen came reverberating along the corridor, suddenly growing fainter as Talu's spy led them up the wrong passageway in fancied pursuit.

As I ran for my life through the dark galleries beneath the palace of Salensus Oll I must indeed have presented a remarkable appearance had there been any to note it, for though death loomed large about me, my face was split by a broad grin as I thought of the resourcefulness of the nameless hero of Marentina to whom I owed my life.

Of such stuff are the men of my beloved Helium, and when I meet another of their kind, of whatever race or color, my heart goes out to him as it did now to my new friend who had risked his life for me simply because I wore the mate to the ring his ruler had put upon his finger.

The corridor along which I ran led almost straight for a considerable distance, terminating at the foot of a spiral runway, up which I proceeded to emerge presently into a circular chamber upon the first floor of a tower.

In this apartment a dozen red slaves were employed polishing or repairing the weapons of the yellow men. The walls of the room were lined with racks in which were hundreds of straight and hooked swords, javelins, and daggers. It was evidently an armory. There were but three warriors guarding the workers.

My eyes took in the entire scene at a glance. Here were weapons in plenty! Here were sinewy red warriors to wield them!

And here now was John Carter, Prince of Helium, in need both of weapons and warriors!

As I stepped into the apartment, guards and prisoners saw me simultaneously.

Close to the entrance where I stood was a rack of straight swords, and as my hand closed upon the hilt of one of them my eyes fell upon the faces of two of the prisoners who worked side by side.

One of the guards started toward me. "Who are you?" he demanded. "What do you here?"

"I come for Tardos Mors, Jeddak of Helium, and his son, Mors Kajak," I cried, pointing to the two red prisoners, who had now sprung to their feet, wide-eyed in astonished recognition.

"Rise, red men! Before we die let us leave a memorial in the palace of Okar's tyrant that will stand forever in the annals of Kadabra to the honor and glory of Helium," for I had seen that all the prisoners there were men of Tardos Mors's navy.

Then the first guardsman was upon me and the fight was on, but scarce did we engage ere, to my horror, I saw that the red slaves were shackled to the floor.

THIRTEEN

The Magnet Switch

The guardsmen paid not the slightest attention to their wards, for the red men could not move over two feet from the great rings to which they were padlocked, though each had seized a weapon upon which he had been engaged when I entered the room, and stood ready to join me could they have but done so.

The yellow men devoted all their attention to me, nor were they long in discovering that the three of them were none too many to defend the armory against John Carter. Would that I had had my own good long-sword in my hand that day; but, as it was, I rendered a satisfactory account of myself with the unfamiliar weapon of the yellow man.

At first I had a time of it dodging their villainous hook-swords, but after a minute or two I had succeeded in wresting a second straight sword from one of the racks along the wall, and thereafter, using it to parry the hooks of my antagonists, I felt more evenly equipped.

The three of them were on me at once, and but for a lucky circumstance my end might have come quickly. The foremost guardsman made a vicious lunge for my side with his hook after the three of them had backed me against the wall, but as I sidestepped and raised my arm his weapon but grazed my side, passing into a rack of javelins, where it became entangled.

Before he could release it I had run him through, and then, falling back upon the tactics that have saved me a hundred times in tight pinches, I rushed the two remaining warriors, forcing them back with a perfect torrent of cuts and thrusts, weaving my sword in and out about their guards until I had the fear of death upon them.

Then one of them commenced calling for help, but it was too late to save them.

They were as putty in my hands now, and I backed them about the armory as I would until I had them where I wanted them—within reach of the swords of the shackled slaves. In an instant both lay dead upon the floor. But their cries had not been entirely fruitless, for now I heard answering shouts and the footfalls of many men running and the clank of accouterments and the commands of officers.

"The door! Quick, John Carter, bar the door!" cried Tardos Mors.

Already the guard was in sight, charging across the open court that was visible through the doorway.

A dozen seconds would bring them into the tower. A single leap carried me to the heavy portal. With a resounding bang I slammed it shut.

"The bar!" shouted Tardos Mors.

I tried to slip the huge fastening into place, but it defied my every attempt.

"Raise it a little to release the catch," cried one of the red men.

I could hear the yellow warriors leaping along the flagging just beyond the door. I raised the bar and shot it to the right just as the foremost of the guardsmen threw himself against the opposite side of the massive panels.

The barrier held—I had been in time, but by the fraction of a second only.

Now I turned my attention to the prisoners. To Tardos Mors I went first, asking where the keys might be which would unfasten their fetters.

"The officer of the guard has them," replied the Jeddak of Helium, "and he is among those without who seek entrance. You will have to force them."

Most of the prisoners were already hacking at their bonds with the swords in their hands. The yellow men were battering at the door with javelins and axes.

I turned my attention to the chains that held Tardos Mors. Again and again I cut deep into the metal with my sharp blade, but ever faster and faster fell the torrent of blows upon the portal.

At last a link parted beneath my efforts, and a moment later Tardos Mors was free, though a few inches of trailing chain still dangled from his ankle.

A splinter of wood falling inward from the door announced the headway that our enemies were making toward us.

The mighty panels trembled and bent beneath the furious onslaught of the enraged yellow men.

What with the battering upon the door and the hacking of the red men at their chains the din within the armory was appalling. No sooner was Tardos Mors free than he turned his attention to another of the prisoners, while I set to work to liberate Mors Kajak.

We must work fast if we would have all those fetters cut before the door gave way. Now a panel crashed inward upon the floor, and Mors Kajak sprang to the opening to defend the way until we should have time to release the others.

With javelins snatched from the wall he wrought havoc among the foremost of the Okarians while we battled with the insensate metal that stood between our fellows and freedom.

At length all but one of the prisoners were freed, and then the door fell with a mighty crash before a hastily improvised battering-ram, and the yellow horde was upon us.

"To the upper chambers!" shouted the red man who was still fettered to the floor. "To the upper chambers! There you may defend the tower against all Kadabra. Do not delay because of me, who could pray for no better death than in the service of Tardos Mors and the Prince of Helium."

But I would have sacrificed the life of every man of us rather than desert a single red man, much less the lion-hearted hero who begged us to leave him.

"Cut his chains," I cried to two of the red men, "while the balance of us hold off the foe."

There were ten of us now to do battle with the Okarian guard, and I warrant that that ancient watchtower never looked down upon a more hotly contested battle than took place that day within its own grim walls.

The first inrushing wave of yellow warriors recoiled from the slashing blades of ten of Helium's veteran fighting men. A dozen Okarian corpses blocked the doorway, but over the gruesome barrier a score more of their fellows dashed, shouting their hoarse and hideous war-cry.

Upon the bloody mound we met them, hand to hand, stabbing where the quarters were too close to cut, thrusting when we could push a foeman to arm's length; and mingled with the wild cry of the Okarian there rose and fell the glorious words: "For Helium! For Helium!" that for countless ages have spurred on the bravest of the brave to those deeds of valor that have sent the fame of Helium's heroes broadcast throughout the length and breadth of a world.

Now were the fetters struck from the last of the red men, and thirteen strong we met each new charge of the soldiers of Salensus Oll. Scarce one of us but bled from a score of wounds, yet none had fallen.

From without we saw hundreds of guardsmen pouring into the court-yard, and along the lower corridor from which I had found my way to the armory we could hear the clank of metal and the shouting of men.

In a moment we should be attacked from two sides, and with all our prowess we could not hope to withstand the unequal odds which would thus divide our attention and our small numbers.

"To the upper chambers!" cried Tardos Mors, and a moment later we fell back toward the runway that led to the floors above.

Here another bloody battle was waged with the force of yellow men who charged into the armory as we fell back from the doorway. Here we lost our first man, a noble fellow whom we could ill spare; but at length all had backed into the runway except myself, who remained to hold back the Okarians until the others were safe above.

In the mouth of the narrow spiral but a single warrior could attack me at a time, so that I had little difficulty in holding them all back for the brief moment that was necessary. Then, backing slowly before them, I commenced the ascent of the spiral.

All the long way to the tower's top the guardsmen pressed me closely. When one went down before my sword another scrambled over the dead man to take his place; and thus, taking an awful toll with each few feet gained, I came to the spacious glass-walled watchtower of Kadabra.

Here my companions clustered ready to take my place, and for a moment's respite I stepped to one side while they held the enemy off.

From the lofty perch a view could be had for miles in every direction. Toward the south stretched the rugged, ice-clad waste to the edge of the mighty barrier. Toward the east and west, and dimly toward the north I descried other Okarian cities, while in the immediate foreground, just beyond the walls of Kadabra, the grim guardian shaft reared its somber head.

Then I cast my eyes down into the streets of Kadabra, from which a sudden tumult had arisen, and there I saw a battle raging, and beyond the city's walls I saw armed men marching in great columns toward a near-by gate.

Eagerly I pressed forward against the glass wall of the observatory, scarce daring to credit the testimony of my own eyes. But at last I could doubt no longer, and with a shout of joy that rose strangely in the midst of the cursing and groaning of the battling men at the entrance to the chamber, I called to Tardos Mors.

As he joined me I pointed down into the streets of Kadabra and to the advancing columns beyond, above which floated bravely in the arctic air the flags and banners of Helium.

An instant later every red man in the lofty chamber had seen the inspiring sight, and such a shout of thanksgiving arose as I warrant never before echoed through that age-old pile of stone.

But still we must fight on, for though our troops had entered Kadabra, the city was yet far from capitulation, nor had the palace been even assaulted. Turn and turn about we held the top of the runway while the others feasted their eyes upon the sight of our valiant countrymen battling far beneath us.

Now they have rushed the palace gate! Great battering-rams are dashed against its formidable surface. Now they are repulsed by a deadly shower of javelins from the wall's top!

Once again they charge, but a sortie by a large force of Okarians from an intersecting avenue crumples the head of the column, and the men of Helium go down, fighting, beneath an overwhelming force.

The palace gate flies open and a force of the jeddak's own guard, picked men from the flower of the Okarian army, sallies forth to shatter the broken regiments. For a moment it looks as though nothing could avert defeat, and then I see a noble figure upon a mighty thoat—not the tiny thoat of the red man, but one of his huge cousins of the dead sea bottoms.

The warrior hews his way to the front, and behind him rally the disorganized soldiers of Helium. As he raises his head aloft to fling a challenge at the men upon the palace walls I see his face, and my heart swells in pride and happiness as the red warriors leap to the side of their leader and win back the ground that they had but just lost—the face of him upon the mighty thoat is the face of my son—Carthoris of Helium.

At his side fights a huge Martian war-hound, nor did I need a second look to know that it was Woola—my faithful Woola who had thus well performed his arduous task and brought the succoring legions in the nick of time.

"In the nick of time?"

Who yet might say that they were not too late to save, but surely they could avenge! And such retribution as that unconquered army would deal out to the hateful Okarians! I sighed to think that I might not be alive to witness it.

Again I turned to the windows. The red men had not yet forced the outer palace wall, but they were fighting nobly against the best that Okar afforded—valiant warriors who contested every inch of the way.

Now my attention was caught by a new element without the city wall—a great body of mounted warriors looming large above the red men. They were the huge green allies of Helium—the savage hordes from the dead sea bottoms of the far south.

In grim and terrible silence they sped on toward the gate, the padded hoofs of their frightful mounts giving forth no sound. Into the doomed city they charged, and as they wheeled across the wide plaza before the palace of the Jeddak of Jeddaks I saw, riding at their head, the mighty figure of their mighty leader—Tars Tarkas, Jeddak of Thark.

My wish, then, was to be gratified, for I was to see my old friend battling once again, and though not shoulder to shoulder with him, I, too, would be fighting in the same cause here in the high tower of Okar.

Nor did it seem that our foes would ever cease their stubborn attacks, for still they came, though the way to our chamber was often clogged with the bodies of their dead. At times they would pause long enough to drag back the impeding corpses, and then fresh warriors would forge upward to taste the cup of death.

I had been taking my turn with the others in defending the approach to our lofty retreat when Mors Kajak, who had been watching the battle in the street below, called aloud in sudden excitement. There was a note of apprehension in his voice that brought me to his side the instant that I could turn my place over to another, and as I reached him he pointed far out across the waste of snow and ice toward the southern horizon.

"Alas!" he cried, "that I should be forced to witness cruel fate betray them without power to warn or aid; but they be past either now."

As I looked in the direction he indicated I saw the cause of his perturbation. A mighty fleet of fliers was approaching majestically toward Kadabra from the direction of the ice-barrier. On and on they came with ever increasing velocity.

"The grim shaft that they call the Guardian of the North is beckoning to them," said Mors Kajak sadly, "just as it beckoned to Tardos Mors and his great fleet; see where they lie, crumpled and broken, a grim and terrible monument to the mighty force of destruction which naught can resist."

I, too, saw; but something else I saw that Mors Kajak did not; in my mind's eye I saw a buried chamber whose walls were lined with strange instruments and devices.

In the center of the chamber was a long table, and before it sat a little, pop-eyed old man counting his money; but, plainest of all, I saw upon the wall a great switch with a small magnet inlaid within the surface of its black handle.

Then I glanced out at the fast-approaching fleet. In five minutes that mighty armada of the skies would be bent and worthless scrap, lying at the base of the shaft beyond the city's wall, and yellow hordes would be loosed from another gate to rush out upon the few survivors stumbling blindly down through the mass of wreckage; then the apts would come. I shuddered at the thought, for I could vividly picture the whole horrible scene.

Quick have I always been to decide and act. The impulse that moves me and the doing of the thing seem simultaneous; for if my mind goes through the tedious formality of reasoning, it must be a subconscious act of which I am not objectively aware. Psychologists tell me that, as the subconscious does not reason, too close a scrutiny of my mental activities might prove anything but flattering; but be that as it may, I have often won success while the thinker would have been still at the endless task of comparing various judgments.

And now celerity of action was the prime essential to the success of the thing that I had decided upon.

Grasping my sword more firmly in my hand, I called to the red man at the opening to the runway to stand aside.

"Way for the Prince of Helium!" I shouted; and before the astonished yellow man whose misfortune it was to be at the fighting end of the line at that particular moment could gather his wits together my sword had decapitated him, and I was rushing like a mad bull down upon those behind him.

"Way for the Prince of Helium!" I shouted as I cut a path through the astonished guardsmen of Salensus Oll.

Hewing to right and left, I beat my way down that warrior-choked spiral until, near the bottom, those below, thinking that an army was descending upon them, turned and fled.

The armory at the first floor was vacant when I entered it, the last of the Okarians having fled into the courtyard, so none saw me continue down the spiral toward the corridor beneath.

Here I ran as rapidly as my legs would carry me toward the five corners, and there plunged into the passageway that led to the station of the old miser.

Without the formality of a knock, I burst into the room. There sat the old man at his table; but as he saw me he sprang to his feet, drawing his sword.

With scarce more than a glance toward him I leaped for the great switch; but, quick as I was, that wiry old fellow was there before me.

How he did it I shall never know, nor does it seem credible that any Martian-born creature could approximate the marvelous speed of my earthly muscles.

Like a tiger he turned upon me, and I was quick to see why Solan had been chosen for this important duty.

Never in all my life have I seen such wondrous swordsmanship and such uncanny agility as that ancient bag of bones displayed. He was in forty places at the same time, and before I had half a chance to awaken to my danger he was like to have made a monkey of me, and a dead monkey at that.

It is strange how new and unexpected conditions bring out unguessed ability to meet them.

That day in the buried chamber beneath the palace of Salensus Oll I learned what swordsmanship meant, and to what heights of sword mastery I could achieve when pitted against such a wizard of the blade as Solan.

For a time he liked to have bested me; but presently the latent possibilities that must have been lying dormant within me for a lifetime came to the fore, and I fought as I had never dreamed a human being could fight.

That that duel-royal should have taken place in the dark recesses of a cellar, without a single appreciative eye to witness it has always seemed to me almost a world calamity—at least from the viewpoint Barsoomian, where bloody strife is the first and greatest consideration of individuals, nations, and races.

I was fighting to reach the switch, Solan to prevent me; and, though we stood not three feet from it, I could not win an inch toward it, for he forced me back an inch for the first five minutes of our battle.

I knew that if I were to throw it in time to save the oncoming fleet it must be done in the next few seconds, and so I tried my old rushing tactics; but I might as well have rushed a brick wall for all that Solan gave way.

In fact, I came near to impaling myself upon his point for my pains; but right was on my side, and I think that that must give a man greater confidence than though he knew himself to be battling in a wicked cause.

At least, I did not want in confidence; and when I next rushed Solan it was to one side with implicit confidence that he must turn to meet my new line of attack, and turn he did, so that now we fought with our sides towards the coveted goal—the great switch stood within my reach upon my right hand.

To uncover my breast for an instant would have been to court sudden death, but I saw no other way than to chance it, if by so doing I might rescue that oncoming, succoring fleet; and so, in the face of a wicked sword-thrust, I reached out my point and caught the great switch a sudden blow that released it from its seating.

So surprised and horrified was Solan that he forgot to finish his thrust; instead, he wheeled toward the switch with a loud shriek—a shriek which was his last, for before his hand could touch the lever it sought, my sword's point had passed through his heart.

FOURTEEN

The Tide of Battle

But solan's last loud cry had not been without effect, for a moment later a dozen guardsmen burst into the chamber, though not before I had so bent and demolished the great switch that it could not be again used to turn the powerful current into the mighty magnet of destruction it controlled.

The result of the sudden coming of the guardsmen had been to compel me to seek seclusion in the first passageway that I could find, and that to my disappointment proved to be not the one with which I was familiar, but another upon its left.

They must have either heard or guessed which way I went, for I had proceeded but a short distance when I heard the sound of pursuit. I had no mind to stop and fight these men here when there was fighting aplenty elsewhere in the city of Kadabra—fighting that could be of much more avail to me and mine than useless life-taking far below the palace.

But the fellows were pressing me; and as I did not know the way at all, I soon saw that they would overtake me unless I found a place to conceal myself until they had passed, which would then give me an opportunity to return the way I had come and regain the tower, or possibly find a way to reach the city streets.

The passageway had risen rapidly since leaving the apartment of the switch, and now ran level and well lighted straight into the distance as far as I could see. The moment that my pursuers reached this straight stretch I would be in plain sight of them, with no chance to escape from the corridor undetected.

Presently I saw a series of doors opening from either side of the corridor, and as they all looked alike to me I tried the first one that I reached. It opened into a small chamber, luxuriously furnished, and was evidently an ante-chamber off some office or audience chamber of the palace.

On the far side was a heavily curtained doorway beyond which I heard the hum of voices. Instantly I crossed the small chamber, and, parting the curtains, looked within the larger apartment.

Before me were a party of perhaps fifty gorgeously clad nobles of the court, standing before a throne upon which sat Salensus Oll. The Jeddak of Jeddaks was addressing them.

"The allotted hour has come," he was saying as I entered the apartment; "and though the enemies of Okar be within her gates, naught may stay the will of Salensus Oll. The great ceremony must be omitted that no single man may be kept from his place in the defenses other than the fifty that custom demands shall witness the creation of a new queen in Okar.

"In a moment the thing shall have been done and we may return to the battle, while she who is now the Princess of Helium looks down from the queen's tower upon the annihilation of her former countrymen and witnesses the greatness which is her husband's."

Then, turning to a courtier, he issued some command in a low voice.

The addressed hastened to a small door at the far end of the chamber and, swinging it wide, cried: "Way for Dejah Thoris, future Queen of Okar!"

Immediately two guardsmen appeared dragging the unwilling bride toward the altar. Her hands were still manacled behind her, evidently to prevent suicide.

Her disheveled hair and panting bosom betokened that, chained though she was, still had she fought against the thing that they would do to her.

At sight of her Salensus Oll rose and drew his sword, and the sword of each of the fifty nobles was raised on high to form an arch, beneath which the poor, beautiful creature was dragged toward her doom.

A grim smile forced itself to my lips as I thought of the rude awakening that lay in store for the ruler of Okar, and my itching fingers fondled the hilt of my bloody sword.

As I watched the procession that moved slowly toward the throne—a procession which consisted of but a handful of priests, who followed Dejah Thoris and the two guardsmen—I caught a fleeting glimpse of a black face peering from behind the draperies that covered the wall back of the dais upon which stood Salensus Oll awaiting his bride.

Now the guardsmen were forcing the Princess of Helium up the few steps to the side of the tyrant of Okar, and I had no eyes and no thoughts for aught else. A priest opened a book and, raising his hand, commenced to drone out a sing-song ritual. Salensus Oll reached for the hand of his bride.

I had intended waiting until some circumstance should give me a reasonable hope of success; for, even though the entire ceremony should be completed, there could be no valid marriage while I lived. What I was most concerned in, of course, was the rescuing of Dejah Thoris—I wished to take her from the palace of Salensus Oll, if such a thing were possible; but whether it were accomplished before or after the mock marriage was a matter of secondary import.

When, however, I saw the vile hand of Salensus Oll reach out for the hand of my beloved princess I could restrain myself no longer, and before the nobles of Okar knew that aught had happened I had leaped through their thin line and was upon the dais beside Dejah Thoris and Salensus Oll.

With the flat of my sword I struck down his polluting hand; and grasping Dejah Thoris round the waist, I swung her behind me as, with my back against the draperies of the dais, I faced the tyrant of the north and his roomful of noble warriors.

The Jeddak of Jeddaks was a great mountain of a man—a coarse, brutal beast of a man—and as he towered above me there, his fierce black whiskers and mustache bristling in rage, I can well imagine that a less seasoned warrior might have trembled before him.

With a snarl he sprang toward me with naked sword, but whether Salensus Oll was a good swordsman or a poor I never learned; for with Dejah Thoris at my back I was no longer human—I was a superman, and no man could have withstood me then.

With a single, low: "For the Princess of Helium!" I ran my blade straight through the rotten heart of Okar's rotten ruler, and before the white, drawn faces of his nobles Salensus Oll rolled, grinning in horrible death, to the foot of the steps below his marriage throne.

For a moment tense silence reigned in the nuptial-room. Then the fifty nobles rushed upon me. Furiously we fought, but the advantage was mine, for I stood upon a raised platform above them, and I fought for the most glorious woman of a glorious race, and I fought for a great love and for the mother of my boy.

And from behind my shoulder, in the silvery cadence of that dear voice, rose the brave battle anthem of Helium which the nation's women sing as their men march out to victory.

That alone was enough to inspire me to victory over even greater odds, and I verily believe that I should have bested the entire roomful of yellow warriors that day in the nuptial chamber of the palace at Kadabra had not interruption come to my aid.

Fast and furious was the fighting as the nobles of Salensus Oll sprang, time and again, up the steps before the throne only to fall back before a

sword hand that seemed to have gained a new wizardry from its experience
with the cunning Solan.

Two were pressing me so closely that I could not turn when I heard a
movement behind me, and noted that the sound of the battle anthem had
ceased. Was Dejah Thoris preparing to take her place beside me?

Heroic daughter of a heroic world! It would not be unlike her to have
seized a sword and fought at my side, for, though the women of Mars are
not trained in the arts of war, the spirit is theirs, and they have been known
to do that very thing upon countless occasions.

But she did not come, and glad I was, for it would have doubled my
burden in protecting her before I should have been able to force her back
again out of harm's way. She must be contemplating some cunning strategy,
I thought, and so I fought on secure in the belief that my divine princess
stood close behind me.

For half an hour at least I must have fought there against the nobles of
Okar ere ever a one placed a foot upon the dais where I stood, and then
of a sudden all that remained of them formed below me for a last, mad,
desperate charge; but even as they advanced the door at the far end of the
chamber swung wide and a wild-eyed messenger sprang into the room.

"The Jeddak of Jeddaks!" he cried. "Where is the Jeddak of Jeddaks? The
city has fallen before the hordes from beyond the barrier, and but now the
great gate of the palace itself has been forced and the warriors of the south
are pouring into its sacred precincts.

"Where is Salensus Oll? He alone may revive the flagging courage of our
warriors. He alone may save the day for Okar. Where is Salensus Oll?"

The nobles stepped back from about the dead body of their ruler, and
one of them pointed to the grinning corpse.

The messenger staggered back in horror as though from a blow in the
face.

"Then fly, nobles of Okar!" he cried, "for naught can save you. Hark!
They come!"

As he spoke we heard the deep roar of angry men from the corridor
without, and the clank of metal and the clang of swords.

Without another glance toward me, who had stood a spectator of the
tragic scene, the nobles wheeled and fled from the apartment through
another exit.

Almost immediately a force of yellow warriors appeared in the doorway
through which the messenger had come. They were backing toward the
apartment, stubbornly resisting the advance of a handful of red men who
faced them and forced them slowly but inevitably back.

Above the heads of the contestants I could see from my elevated station upon the dais the face of my old friend Kantos Kan. He was leading the little party that had won its way into the very heart of the palace of Salensus Oll.

In an instant I saw that by attacking the Okarians from the rear I could so quickly disorganize them that their further resistance would be short-lived, and with this idea in mind I sprang from the dais, casting a word of explanation to Dejah Thoris over my shoulder, though I did not turn to look at her.

With myself ever between her enemies and herself, and with Kantos Kan and his warriors winning to the apartment, there could be no danger to Dejah Thoris standing there alone beside the throne.

I wanted the men of Helium to see me and to know that their beloved princess was here, too, for I knew that this knowledge would inspire them to even greater deeds of valor than they had performed in the past, though great indeed must have been those which won for them a way into the almost impregnable palace of the tyrant of the north.

As I crossed the chamber to attack the Kadabrans from the rear a small doorway at my left opened, and, to my surprise, revealed the figures of Matai Shang, Father of Therns and Phaidor, his daughter, peering into the room.

A quick glance about they took. Their eyes rested for a moment, wide in horror, upon the dead body of Salensus Oll, upon the blood that crimsoned the floor, upon the corpses of the nobles who had fallen thick before the throne, upon me, and upon the battling warriors at the other door.

They did not essay to enter the apartment, but scanned its every corner from where they stood, and then, when their eyes had sought its entire area, a look of fierce rage overspread the features of Matai Shang, and a cold and cunning smile touched the lips of Phaidor.

Then they were gone, but not before a taunting laugh was thrown directly in my face by the woman.

I did not understand then the meaning of Matai Shang's rage or Phaidor's pleasure, but I knew that neither boded good for me.

A moment later I was upon the backs of the yellow men, and as the red men of Helium saw me above the shoulders of their antagonists a great shout rang through the corridor, and for a moment drowned the noise of battle.

"For the Prince of Helium!" they cried. "For the Prince of Helium!" and, like hungry lions upon their prey, they fell once more upon the weakening warriors of the north.

The yellow men, cornered between two enemies, fought with the desperation that utter hopelessness often induces. Fought as I should have fought had I been in their stead, with the determination to take as many of my enemies with me when I died as lay within the power of my sword arm.

It was a glorious battle, but the end seemed inevitable, when presently from down the corridor behind the red men came a great body of reenforcing yellow warriors.

Now were the tables turned, and it was the men of Helium who seemed doomed to be ground between two millstones. All were compelled to turn to meet this new assault by a greatly superior force, so that to me was left the remnants of the yellow men within the throneroom.

They kept me busy, too; so busy that I began to wonder if indeed I should ever be done with them. Slowly they pressed me back into the room, and when they had all passed in after me, one of them closed and bolted the door, effectually barring the way against the men of Kantos Kan.

It was a clever move, for it put me at the mercy of a dozen men within a chamber from which assistance was locked out, and it gave the red men in the corridor beyond no avenue of escape should their new antagonists press them too closely.

But I have faced heavier odds myself than were pitted against me that day, and I knew that Kantos Kan had battled his way from a hundred more dangerous traps than that in which he now was. So it was with no feelings of despair that I turned my attention to the business of the moment.

Constantly my thoughts reverted to Dejah Thoris, and I longed for the moment when, the fighting done, I could fold her in my arms, and hear once more the words of love which had been denied me for so many years.

During the fighting in the chamber I had not even a single chance to so much as steal a glance at her where she stood behind me beside the throne of the dead ruler. I wondered why she no longer urged me on with the strains of the martial hymn of Helium; but I did not need more than the knowledge that I was battling for her to bring out the best that is in me.

It would be wearisome to narrate the details of that bloody struggle; of how we fought from the doorway, the full length of the room to the very foot of the throne before the last of my antagonists fell with my blade piercing his heart.

And then, with a glad cry, I turned with outstretched arms to seize my princess, and as my lips smothered hers to reap the reward that would be thrice ample payment for the bloody encounters through which I had passed for her dear sake from the south pole to the north.

The glad cry died, frozen upon my lips; my arms dropped limp and lifeless to my sides; as one who reels beneath the burden of a mortal wound I staggered up the steps before the throne.

Dejah Thoris was gone.

FIFTEEN

Rewards

With the realization that Dejah Thoris was no longer within the throne-room came the belated recollection of the dark face that I had glimpsed peering from behind the draperies that backed the throne of Salensus Oll at the moment that I had first come so unexpectedly upon the strange scene being enacted within the chamber.

Why had the sight of that evil countenance not warned me to greater caution? Why had I permitted the rapid development of new situations to efface the recollection of that menacing danger? But, alas, vain regret would not erase the calamity that had befallen.

Once again had Dejah Thoris fallen into the clutches of that archfiend, Thurid, the black dator of the First Born. Again was all my arduous labor gone for naught. Now I realized the cause of the rage that had been writ so large upon the features of Matai Shang and the cruel pleasure that I had seen upon the face of Phaidor.

They had known or guessed the truth, and the hekkador of the Holy Therns, who had evidently come to the chamber in the hope of thwarting Salensus Oll in his contemplated perfidy against the high priest who coveted Dejah Thoris for himself, realized that Thurid had stolen the prize from beneath his very nose.

Phaidor's pleasure had been due to her realization of what this last cruel blow would mean to me, as well as to a partial satisfaction of her jealous hatred for the Princess of Helium.

My first thought was to look beyond the draperies at the back of the throne, for there it was that I had seen Thurid. With a single jerk I tore the priceless stuff from its fastenings, and there before me was revealed a narrow doorway behind the throne.

No question entered my mind but that here lay the opening of the avenue of escape which Thurid had followed, and had there been it would have been dissipated by the sight of a tiny, jeweled ornament which lay a few steps within the corridor beyond.

As I snatched up the bauble I saw that it bore the device of the Princess of Helium, and then pressing it to my lips I dashed madly along the winding way that led gently downward toward the lower galleries of the palace.

I had followed but a short distance when I came upon the room in which Solan formerly had held sway. His dead body still lay where I had left it, nor was there any sign that another had passed through the room since I had been there; but I knew that two had done so—Thurid, the black dator, and Dejah Thoris.

For a moment I paused uncertain as to which of the several exits from the apartment would lead me upon the right path. I tried to recollect the directions which I had heard Thurid repeat to Solan, and at last, slowly, as though through a heavy fog, the memory of the words of the First Born came to me:

"Follow a corridor, passing three diverging corridors upon the right; then into the fourth right-hand corridor to where three corridors meet; here again follow to the right, hugging the left wall closely to avoid the pit. At the end of this corridor I shall come to a spiral runway which I must follow down instead of up; after that the way is along but a single branchless corridor."

And I recalled the exit at which he had pointed as he spoke.

It did not take me long to start upon that unknown way, nor did I go with caution, although I knew that there might be grave dangers before me.

Part of the way was black as sin, but for the most it was fairly well lighted. The stretch where I must hug the left wall to avoid the pits was darkest of them all, and I was nearly over the edge of the abyss before I knew that I was near the danger spot.

A narrow ledge, scarce a foot wide, was all that had been left to carry the initiated past that frightful cavity into which the unknowing must surely have toppled at the first step. But at last I had won safely beyond it, and then a feeble light made the balance of the way plain, until, at the end of the last corridor, I came suddenly out into the glare of day upon a field of snow and ice.

Clad for the warm atmosphere of the hothouse city of Kadabra, the sudden change to arctic frigidity was anything but pleasant; but the worst of it was that I knew I could not endure the bitter cold, almost naked as I was, and that I would perish before ever I could overtake Thurid and Dejah Thoris.

To be thus blocked by nature, who had had all the arts and wiles of cunning man pitted against him, seemed a cruel fate, and as I staggered back into the warmth of the tunnel's end I was as near hopelessness as I ever have been.

I had by no means given up my intention of continuing the pursuit, for if needs be I would go ahead though I perished ere ever I reached my goal, but if there were a safer way it were well worth the delay to attempt to discover it, that I might come again to the side of Dejah Thoris in fit condition to do battle for her.

Scarce had I returned to the tunnel than I stumbled over a portion of a fur garment that seemed fastened to the floor of the corridor close to the wall. In the darkness I could not see what held it, but by groping with my hands I discovered that it was wedged beneath the bottom of a closed door.

Pushing the portal aside, I found myself upon the threshold of a small chamber, the walls of which were lined with hooks from which depended suits of the complete outdoor apparel of the yellow men.

Situated as it was at the mouth of a tunnel leading from the palace, it was quite evident that this was the dressing-room used by the nobles leaving and entering the hothouse city, and that Thurid, having knowledge of it, had stopped here to outfit himself and Dejah Thoris before venturing into the bitter cold of the arctic world beyond.

In his haste he had dropped several garments upon the floor, and the telltale fur that had fallen partly within the corridor had proved the means of guiding me to the very spot he would least have wished me to have knowledge of.

It required but the matter of a few seconds to don the necessary orluk-skin clothing, with the heavy, fur-lined boots that are so essential a part of the garmenture of one who would successfully contend with the frozen trails and the icy winds of the bleak northland.

Once more I stepped beyond the tunnel's mouth to find the fresh tracks of Thurid and Dejah Thoris in the new-fallen snow. Now, at last, was my task an easy one, for though the going was rough in the extreme, I was no longer vexed by doubts as to the direction I should follow, or harassed by darkness or hidden dangers.

Through a snow-covered cañon the way led up toward the summit of low hills. Beyond these it dipped again into another cañon, only to rise a quarter-mile farther on toward a pass which skirted the flank of a rocky hill.

I could see by the signs of those who had gone before that when Dejah Thoris had walked she had been continually holding back, and that the

black man had been compelled to drag her. For other stretches only his
foot-prints were visible, deep and close together in the heavy snow, and
I knew from these signs that then he had been forced to carry her, and I
could well imagine that she had fought him fiercely every step of the way.

As I came round the jutting promontory of the hill's shoulder I saw that
which quickened my pulses and set my heart to beating high, for within
a tiny basin between the crest of this hill and the next stood four people
before the mouth of a great cave, and beside them upon the gleaming snow
rested a flier which had evidently but just been dragged from its hiding
place.

The four were Dejah Thoris, Phaidor, Thurid, and Matai Shang. The two
men were engaged in a heated argument—the Father of Therns threatening,
while the black scoffed at him as he went about the work at which he was
engaged.

As I crept toward them cautiously that I might come as near as possible
before being discovered, I saw that finally the men appeared to have reached
some sort of a compromise, for with Phaidor's assistance they both set about
dragging the resisting Dejah Thoris to the flier's deck.

Here they made her fast, and then both again descended to the ground
to complete the preparations for departure. Phaidor entered the small cabin
upon the vessel's deck.

I had come to within a quarter of a mile of them when Matai Shang
espied me. I saw him seize Thurid by the shoulder, wheeling him around
in my direction as he pointed to where I was now plainly visible, for the
moment that I knew I had been perceived I cast aside every attempt at
stealth and broke into a mad race for the flier.

The two redoubled their efforts at the propeller at which they were
working, and which very evidently was being replaced after having been
removed for some purpose of repair.

They had the thing completed before I had covered half the distance that
lay between me and them, and then both made a rush for the boarding-
ladder.

Thurid was the first to reach it, and with the agility of a monkey
clambered swiftly to the boat's deck, where a touch of the button controlling
the buoyancy tanks sent the craft slowly upward, though not with the speed
that marks the well-conditioned flier.

I was still some hundred yards away as I saw them rising from my grasp.

Back by the city of Kadabra lay a great fleet of mighty fliers—the ships of
Helium and Ptarth that I had saved from destruction earlier in the day; but
before ever I could reach them Thurid could easily make good his escape.

As I ran I saw Matai Shang clambering up the swaying, swinging ladder toward the deck, while above him leaned the evil face of the First Born. A trailing rope from the vessel's stern put new hope in me, for if I could but reach it before it whipped too high above my head there was yet a chance to gain the deck by its slender aid.

That there was something radically wrong with the flier was evident from its lack of buoyancy, and the further fact that though Thurid had turned twice to the starting lever the boat still hung motionless in the air, except for a slight drifting with a low breeze from the north.

Now Matai Shang was close to the gunwale. A long, claw-like hand was reaching up to grasp the metal rail.

Thurid leaned farther down toward his co-conspirator.

Suddenly a raised dagger gleamed in the upflung hand of the black. Down it drove toward the white face of the Father of Therns. With a loud shriek of fear the Holy Hekkador grasped frantically at that menacing arm.

I was almost to the trailing rope by now. The craft was still rising slowly, the while it drifted from me. Then I stumbled on the icy way, striking my head upon a rock as I fell sprawling but an arm's length from the rope, the end of which was now just leaving the ground.

With the blow upon my head came unconsciousness.

It could not have been more than a few seconds that I lay senseless there upon the northern ice, while all that was dearest to me drifted farther from my reach in the clutches of that black fiend, for when I opened my eyes Thurid and Matai Shang yet battled at the ladder's top, and the flier drifted but a hundred yards farther to the south—but the end of the trailing rope was now a good thirty feet above the ground.

Goaded to madness by the cruel misfortune that had tripped me when success was almost within my grasp, I tore frantically across the intervening space, and just beneath the rope's dangling end I put my earthly muscles to the supreme test.

With a mighty, catlike bound I sprang upward toward that slender strand—the only avenue which yet remained that could carry me to my vanishing love.

A foot above its lowest end my fingers closed. Tightly as I clung I felt the rope slipping, slipping through my grasp. I tried to raise my free hand to take a second hold above my first, but the change of position that resulted caused me to slip more rapidly toward the end of the rope.

Slowly I felt the tantalizing thing escaping me. In a moment all that I had gained would be lost—then my fingers reached a knot at the very end of the rope and slipped no more.

With a prayer of gratitude upon my lips I scrambled upward toward the boat's deck. I could not see Thurid and Matai Shang now, but I heard the sounds of conflict and thus knew that they still fought—the thern for his life and the black for the increased buoyancy that relief from the weight of even a single body would give the craft.

Should Matai Shang die before I reached the deck my chances of ever reaching it would be slender indeed, for the black dator need but cut the rope above me to be freed from me forever, for the vessel had drifted across the brink of a chasm into whose yawning depths my body would drop to be crushed to a shapeless pulp should Thurid reach the rope now.

At last my hand closed upon the ship's rail and that very instant a horrid shriek rang out below me that sent my blood cold and turned my horrified eyes downward to a shrieking, hurtling, twisting thing that shot downward into the awful chasm beneath me.

It was Matai Shang, Holy Hekkador, Father of Therns, gone to his last accounting.

Then my head came above the deck and I saw Thurid, dagger in hand, leaping toward me. He was opposite the forward end of the cabin, while I was attempting to clamber aboard near the vessel's stern. But a few paces lay between us. No power on earth could raise me to that deck before the infuriated black would be upon me.

My end had come. I knew it; but had there been a doubt in my mind the nasty leer of triumph upon that wicked face would have convinced me. Beyond Thurid I could see my Dejah Thoris, wide-eyed and horrified, struggling at her bonds. That she should be forced to witness my awful death made my bitter fate seem doubly cruel.

I ceased my efforts to climb across the gunwale. Instead I took a firm grasp upon the rail with my left hand and drew my dagger.

I should at least die as I had lived—fighting.

As Thurid came opposite the cabin's doorway a new element projected itself into the grim tragedy of the air that was being enacted upon the deck of Matai Shang's disabled flier.

It was Phaidor.

With flushed face and disheveled hair, and eyes that betrayed the recent presence of mortal tears—above which this proud goddess had always held herself—she leaped to the deck directly before me.

In her hand was a long, slim dagger. I cast a last look upon my beloved princess, smiling, as men should who are about to die. Then I turned my face up toward Phaidor—waiting for the blow.

Never have I seen that beautiful face more beautiful than it was at that moment. It seemed incredible that one so lovely could yet harbor within her fair bosom a heart so cruel and relentless, and today there was a new expression in her wondrous eyes that I never before had seen there—an unfamiliar softness, and a look of suffering.

Thurid was beside her now—pushing past to reach me first, and then what happened happened so quickly that it was all over before I could realize the truth of it.

Phaidor's slim hand shot out to close upon the black's dagger wrist. Her right hand went high with its gleaming blade.

"That for Matai Shang!" she cried, and she buried her blade deep in the dator's breast. "That for the wrong you would have done Dejah Thoris!" and again the sharp steel sank into the bloody flesh.

"And that, and that, and that!" she shrieked, "for John Carter, Prince of Helium," and with each word her sharp point pierced the vile heart of the great villain. Then, with a vindictive shove she cast the carcass of the First Born from the deck to fall in awful silence after the body of his victim.

I had been so paralyzed by surprise that I had made no move to reach the deck during the awe-inspiring scene which I had just witnessed, and now I was to be still further amazed by her next act, for Phaidor extended her hand to me and assisted me to the deck, where I stood gazing at her in unconcealed and stupefied wonderment.

A wan smile touched her lips—it was not the cruel and haughty smile of the goddess with which I was familiar. "You wonder, John Carter," she said, "what strange thing has wrought this change in me? I will tell you. It is love—love of you," and when I darkened my brows in disapproval of her words she raised an appealing hand.

"Wait," she said. "It is a different love from mine—it is the love of your princess, Dejah Thoris, for you that has taught me what true love may be— what it should be, and how far from real love was my selfish and jealous passion for you.

"Now I am different. Now could I love as Dejah Thoris loves, and so my only happiness can be to know that you and she are once more united, for in her alone can you find true happiness.

"But I am unhappy because of the wickedness that I have wrought. I have many sins to expiate, and though I be deathless, life is all too short for the atonement.

"But there is another way, and if Phaidor, daughter of the Holy Hekkador of the Holy Therns, has sinned she has this day already made partial reparation, and lest you doubt the sincerity of her protestations and her avowal of a new love that embraces Dejah Thoris also, she will prove her sincerity in the only way that lies open—having saved you for another, Phaidor leaves you to her embraces."

With her last word she turned and leaped from the vessel's deck into the abyss below.

With a cry of horror I sprang forward in a vain attempt to save the life that for two years I would so gladly have seen extinguished. I was too late.

With tear-dimmed eyes I turned away that I might not see the awful sight beneath.

A moment later I had struck the bonds from Dejah Thoris, and as her dear arms went about my neck and her perfect lips pressed to mine I forgot the horrors that I had witnessed and the suffering that I had endured in the rapture of my reward.

SIXTEEN

The New Ruler

The flier upon whose deck Dejah Thoris and I found ourselves after twelve long years of separation proved entirely useless. Her buoyancy tanks leaked badly. Her engine would not start. We were helpless there in mid air above the arctic ice.

The craft had drifted across the chasm which held the corpses of Matai Shang, Thurid, and Phaidor, and now hung above a low hill. Opening the buoyancy escape valves I permitted her to come slowly to the ground, and as she touched, Dejah Thoris and I stepped from her deck and, hand in hand, turned back across the frozen waste toward the city of Kadabra.

Through the tunnel that had led me in pursuit of them we passed, walking slowly, for we had much to say to each other.

She told me of that last terrible moment months before when the door of her prison cell within the Temple of the Sun was slowly closing between us. Of how Phaidor had sprung upon her with uplifted dagger, and of Thuvia's shriek as she had realized the foul intention of the thern goddess.

It had been that cry that had rung in my ears all the long, weary months that I had been left in cruel doubt as to my princess' fate; for I had not known that Thuvia had wrested the blade from the daughter of Matai Shang before it had touched either Dejah Thoris or herself.

She told me, too, of the awful eternity of her imprisonment. Of the cruel hatred of Phaidor, and the tender love of Thuvia, and of how even when despair was the darkest those two red girls had clung to the same hope and belief—that John Carter would find a way to release them.

Presently we came to the chamber of Solan. I had been proceeding without thought of caution, for I was sure that the city and the palace were both in the hands of my friends by this time.

And so it was that I bolted into the chamber full into the midst of a dozen nobles of the court of Salensus Oll. They were passing through on their way to the outside world along the corridors we had just traversed.

At sight of us they halted in their tracks, and then an ugly smile overspread the features of their leader.

"The author of all our misfortunes!" he cried, pointing at me. "We shall have the satisfaction of a partial vengeance at least when we leave behind us here the dead and mutilated corpses of the Prince and Princess of Helium.

"When they find them," he went on, jerking his thumb upward toward the palace above, "they will realize that the vengeance of the yellow man costs his enemies dear. Prepare to die, John Carter, but that your end may be the more bitter, know that I may change my intention as to meting a merciful death to your princess—possibly she shall be preserved as a plaything for my nobles."

I stood close to the instrument-covered wall—Dejah Thoris at my side. She looked up at me wonderingly as the warriors advanced upon us with drawn swords, for mine still hung within its scabbard at my side, and there was a smile upon my lips.

The yellow nobles, too, looked in surprise, and then as I made no move to draw they hesitated, fearing a ruse; but their leader urged them on. When they had come almost within sword's reach of me I raised my hand and laid it upon the polished surface of a great lever, and then, still smiling grimly, I looked my enemies full in the face.

As one they came to a sudden stop, casting affrighted glances at me and at one another.

"Stop!" shrieked their leader. "You dream not what you do!"

"Right you are," I replied. "John Carter does not dream. He knows—knows that should one of you take another step toward Dejah Thoris, Princess of Helium, I pull this lever wide, and she and I shall die together; but we shall not die alone."

The nobles shrank back, whispering together for a few moments. At last their leader turned to me.

"Go your way, John Carter," he said, "and we shall go ours."

"Prisoners do not go their own way," I answered, "and you are prisoners—prisoners of the Prince of Helium."

Before they could make answer a door upon the opposite side of the apartment opened and a score of yellow men poured into the apartment. For an instant the nobles looked relieved, and then as their eyes fell upon the leader of the new party their faces fell, for he was Talu, rebel Prince of Marentina, and they knew that they could look for neither aid nor mercy at his hands.

Talu took in the situation at a glance, smiling.

"Well done, John Carter," he cried. "You turn their own mighty power against them. Fortunate for Okar is it that you were here to prevent their escape, for these be the greatest villains north of the ice-barrier, and this one"—pointing to the leader of the party—"would have made himself Jeddak of Jeddaks in the place of the dead Salensus Oll. Then indeed would we have had a more villainous ruler than the hated tyrant who fell before your sword."

The Okarian nobles now submitted to arrest, since nothing but death faced them should they resist, and, escorted by the warriors of Talu, we made our way to the great audience chamber that had been Salensus Oll's. Here was a vast concourse of warriors.

Red men from Helium and Ptarth, yellow men of the north, rubbing elbows with the blacks of the First Born who had come under my friend Xodar to help in the search for me and my princess. There were savage, green warriors from the dead sea bottoms of the south, and a handful of white-skinned therns who had renounced their religion and sworn allegiance to Xodar.

There was Tardos Mors and Mors Kajak, and tall and mighty in his gorgeous warrior trappings, Carthoris, my son. These three fell upon Dejah Thoris as we entered the apartment, and though the lives and training of royal Martians tend not toward vulgar demonstration, I thought that they would suffocate her with their embraces.

And there were Tars Tarkas, Jeddak of Thark, and Kantos Kan, my old-time friends, and leaping and tearing at my harness in the exuberance of his great love was dear old Woola—frantic mad with happiness.

Long and loud was the cheering that burst forth at sight of us; deafening was the din of ringing metal as the veteran warriors of every Martian clime clashed their blades together on high in token of success and victory, but as I passed among the throng of saluting nobles and warriors, jeds and jeddaks, my heart still was heavy, for there were two faces missing that I would have given much to have seen there—Thuvan Dihn and Thuvia of Ptarth were not to be found in the great chamber.

I made inquiries concerning them among men of every nation, and at last from one of the yellow prisoners of war I learned that they had been apprehended by an officer of the palace as they sought to reach the Pit of Plenty while I lay imprisoned there.

I did not need to ask to know what had sent them thither—the courageous jeddak and his loyal daughter. My informer said that they lay now in one of the many buried dungeons of the palace where they had been placed pending a decision as to their fate by the tyrant of the north.

A moment later searching parties were scouring the ancient pile in search of them, and my cup of happiness was full when I saw them being escorted into the room by a cheering guard of honor.

Thuvia's first act was to rush to the side of Dejah Thoris, and I needed no better proof of the love these two bore for each other than the sincerity with which they embraced.

Looking down upon that crowded chamber stood the silent and empty throne of Okar.

Of all the strange scenes it must have witnessed since that long-dead age that had first seen a Jeddak of Jeddaks take his seat upon it, none might compare with that upon which it now looked down, and as I pondered the past and future of that long-buried race of black-bearded yellow men I thought that I saw a brighter and more useful existence for them among the great family of friendly nations that now stretched from the south pole almost to their very doors.

Twenty-two years before I had been cast, naked and a stranger, into this strange and savage world. The hand of every race and nation was raised in continual strife and warring against the men of every other land and color. Today, by the might of my sword and the loyalty of the friends my sword had made for me, black man and white, red man and green rubbed shoulders in peace and good-fellowship. All the nations of Barsoom were not yet as one, but a great stride forward toward that goal had been taken, and now if I could but cement the fierce yellow race into this sodality of nations I should feel that I had rounded out a great lifework, and repaid to Mars at least a portion of the immense debt of gratitude I owed her for having given me my Dejah Thoris.

And as I thought, I saw but one way, and a single man who could insure the success of my hopes. As is ever the way with me, I acted then as I always act—without deliberation and without consultation.

Those who do not like my plans and my ways of promoting them have always their swords at their sides wherewith to back up their disapproval; but now there seemed to be no dissenting voice, as, grasping Talu by the arm, I sprang to the throne that had once been Salensus Oll's.

"Warriors of Barsoom," I cried, "Kadabra has fallen, and with her the hateful tyrant of the north; but the integrity of Okar must be preserved. The red men are ruled by red jeddaks, the green warriors of the ancient seas acknowledge none but a green ruler, the First Born of the south pole take their law from black Xodar; nor would it be to the interests of either yellow or red man were a red jeddak to sit upon the throne of Okar.

"There be but one warrior best fitted for the ancient and mighty title of

Jeddak of Jeddaks of the North. Men of Okar, raise your swords to your new ruler—Talu, the rebel prince of Marentina!"

And then a great cry of rejoicing rose among the free men of Marentina and the Kadabran prisoners, for all had thought that the red men would retain that which they had taken by force of arms, for such had been the way upon Barsoom, and that they should be ruled henceforth by an alien Jeddak.

The victorious warriors who had followed Carthoris joined in the mad demonstration, and amidst the wild confusion and the tumult and the cheering, Dejah Thoris and I passed out into the gorgeous garden of the jeddaks that graces the inner courtyard of the palace of Kadabra.

At our heels walked Woola, and upon a carved seat of wondrous beauty beneath a bower of purple blooms we saw two who had preceded us— Thuvia of Ptarth and Carthoris of Helium.

The handsome head of the handsome youth was bent low above the beautiful face of his companion. I looked at Dejah Thoris, smiling, and as I drew her close to me I whispered: "Why not?"

Indeed, why not? What matter ages in this world of perpetual youth?

We remained at Kadabra, the guests of Talu, until after his formal induction into office, and then, upon the great fleet which I had been so fortunate to preserve from destruction, we sailed south across the ice-barrier; but not before we had witnessed the total demolition of the grim Guardian of the North under orders of the new Jeddak of Jeddaks.

"Henceforth," he said, as the work was completed, "the fleets of the red men and the black are free to come and go across the ice-barrier as over their own lands.

"The Carrion Caves shall be cleansed, that the green men may find an easy way to the land of the yellow, and the hunting of the sacred apt shall be the sport of my nobles until no single specimen of that hideous creature roams the frozen north."

We bade our yellow friends farewell with real regret, as we set sail for Ptarth. There we remained, the guest of Thuvan Dihn, for a month; and I could see that Carthoris would have remained forever had he not been a Prince of Helium.

Above the mighty forests of Kaol we hovered until word from Kulan Tith brought us to his single landing-tower, where all day and half a night the vessels disembarked their crews. At the city of Kaol we visited, cementing the new ties that had been formed between Kaol and Helium, and then one long-to-be-remembered day we sighted the tall, thin towers of the twin cities of Helium.

The people had long been preparing for our coming. The sky was gorgeous with gaily trimmed fliers. Every roof within both cities was spread with costly silks and tapestries.

Gold and jewels were scattered over roof and street and plaza, so that the two cities seemed ablaze with the fires of the hearts of the magnificent stones and burnished metal that reflected the brilliant sunlight, changing it into countless glorious hues.

At last, after twelve years, the royal family of Helium was reunited in their own mighty city, surrounded by joy-mad millions before the palace gates. Women and children and mighty warriors wept in gratitude for the fate that had restored their beloved Tardos Mors and the divine princess whom the whole nation idolized. Nor did any of us who had been upon that expedition of indescribable danger and glory lack for plaudits.

That night a messenger came to me as I sat with Dejah Thoris and Carthoris upon the roof of my city palace, where we had long since caused a lovely garden to be made that we three might find seclusion and quiet happiness among ourselves, far from the pomp and ceremony of court, to summon us to the Temple of Reward—"where one is to be judged this night," the summons concluded.

I racked my brain to try and determine what important case there might be pending which could call the royal family from their palaces on the eve of their return to Helium after years of absence; but when the jeddak summons no man delays.

As our flier touched the landing stage at the temple's top we saw countless other craft arriving and departing. In the streets below a great multitude surged toward the great gates of the temple.

Slowly there came to me the recollection of the deferred doom that awaited me since that time I had been tried here in the Temple by Zat Arras for the sin of returning from the Valley Dor and the Lost Sea of Korus.

Could it be possible that the strict sense of justice which dominates the men of Mars had caused them to overlook the great good that had come out of my heresy? Could they ignore the fact that to me, and me alone, was due the rescue of Carthoris, of Dejah Thoris, of Mors Kajak, of Tardos Mors?

I could not believe it, and yet for what other purpose could I have been summoned to the Temple of Reward immediately upon the return of Tardos Mors to his throne?

My first surprise as I entered the temple and approached the Throne of Righteousness was to note the men who sat there as judges. There was Kulan Tith, Jeddak of Kaol, whom we had but just left within his own palace a few days since; there was Thuvan Dihn, Jeddak of Ptarth—how came he to Helium as soon as we?

There was Tars Tarkas, Jeddak of Thark, and Xodar, Jeddak of the First Born; there was Talu, Jeddak of Jeddaks of the North, whom I could have sworn was still in his ice-bound hothouse city beyond the northern barrier, and among them sat Tardos Mors and Mors Kajak, with enough lesser jeds and jeddaks to make up the thirty-one who must sit in judgment upon their fellow-man.

A right royal tribunal indeed, and such a one, I warrant, as never before sat together during all the history of ancient Mars.

As I entered, silence fell upon the great concourse of people that packed the auditorium. Then Tardos Mors arose.

"John Carter," he said in his deep, martial voice, "take your place upon the Pedestal of Truth, for you are to be tried by a fair and impartial tribunal of your fellow-men."

With level eye and high-held head I did as he bade, and as I glanced about that circle of faces that a moment before I could have sworn contained the best friends I had upon Barsoom, I saw no single friendly glance—only stern, uncompromising judges, there to do their duty.

A clerk rose and from a great book read a long list of the more notable deeds that I had thought to my credit, covering a long period of twenty-two years since first I had stepped the ocher sea bottom beside the incubator of the Tharks. With the others he read of all that I had done within the circle of the Otz Mountains where the Holy Therns and the First Born had held sway.

It is the way upon Barsoom to recite a man's virtues with his sins when he is come to trial, and so I was not surprised that all that was to my credit should be read there to my judges—who knew it all by heart—even down to the present moment. When the reading had ceased Tardos Mors arose.

"Most righteous judges," he exclaimed, "you have heard recited all that is known of John Carter, Prince of Helium—the good with the bad. What is your judgment?"

Then Tars Tarkas came slowly to his feet, unfolding all his mighty, towering height until he loomed, a green-bronze statue, far above us all. He turned a baleful eye upon me—he, Tars Tarkas, with whom I had fought through countless battles; whom I loved as a brother.

I could have wept had I not been so mad with rage that I almost whipped my sword out and had at them all upon the spot.

"Judges," he said, "there can be but one verdict. No longer may John Carter be Prince of Helium"—he paused—"but instead let him be Jeddak of Jeddaks, Warlord of Barsoom!"

"Judges," he said, "there can be but one verdict. No longer may John Carter be Prince of Helium"—he paused—"but instead let him be Jeddak of Jeddaks. Warlord of Barsoom!"

As the thirty-one judges sprang to their feet with drawn and upraised swords in unanimous concurrence in the verdict, the storm broke throughout the length and breadth and height of that mighty building until I thought the roof would fall from the thunder of the mad shouting.

Now, at last, I saw the grim humor of the method they had adopted to do me this great honor, but that there was any hoax in the reality of the title they had conferred upon me was readily disproved by the sincerity of the congratulations that were heaped upon me by the judges first and then the nobles.

Presently fifty of the mightiest nobles of the greatest courts of Mars marched down the broad Aisle of Hope bearing a splendid car upon their shoulders, and as the people saw who sat within, the cheers that had rung out for me paled into insignificance beside those which thundered through the vast edifice now, for she whom the nobles carried was Dejah Thoris, beloved Princess of Helium.

Straight to the Throne of Righteousness they bore her, and there Tardos Mors assisted her from the car, leading her forward to my side.

"Let a world's most beautiful woman share the honor of her husband," he said.

Before them all I drew my wife close to me and kissed her upon the lips.

In the Bison Frontiers of Imagination series